WOLF'S EMPIRE
GLADIATOR

WOLF'S EMPIRE
GLADIATOR

CLAUDIA CHRISTIAN

and

MORGAN GRANT
BUCHANAN

TOR

A TOM DOHERTY ASSOCIATES BOOK ‣ NEW YORK

WOLF'S EMPIRE: GLADIATOR

Copyright © 2016 by Claudia Christian and Morgan Grant Buchanan

All rights reserved.

The quotation on page 13 is from *The Satires of Juvenal,* translated by Rolfe Humphries (Bloomington: Indiana University Press, 1958). The quotation on page 15 is from Virgil, *The Georgics,* translated by J. B. Greenough (1900). The quotations on pages 78, 169, 258, 317, 366, 393, 430, 451, and 481 are from Virgil, *The Aeneid,* translated by J. W. Mackail (1885).

Diagram of the Eight Noble Houses by Morgan Grant Buchanan

Map of the Galactic Roman Empire by Dr. Catherine Buchanan

Milky Way image courtesy of NASA / JPL-Caltech / ESO / R. Hurt

A Tor Book
Published by Tom Doherty Associates, LLC
175 Fifth Avenue
New York, NY 10010

www.tor-forge.com

Tor® is a registered trademark of Tom Doherty Associates, LLC.

The Library of Congress Cataloging-in-Publication Data is available upon request.

ISBN 978-0-7653-3774-0 (hardcover)
ISBN 978-1-4668-3573-3 (e-book)

Our books may be purchased in bulk for promotional, educational, or business use. Please contact your local bookseller or the Macmillan Corporate and Premium Sales Department at 1-800-221-7945, extension 5442, or by e-mail at MacmillanSpecialMarkets@macmillan.com.

First Edition: June 2016

Printed in the United States of America

10 9 8 7 6 5 4 3 2 1

To the legions of science fiction fans around the world
who have brought me so much love and support through the years.
—Claudia Christian

To Catherine, my bright swan.
—Morgan Grant Buchanan

ACKNOWLEDGMENTS

Thanks to our editor, Bob Gleason, for his love of ancient Rome and his willingness to invest in the idea of one that never fell. Elayne Becker and Paul Stevens for their assistance. Our agent, Frank Weimann, for all his hard work and the encouragement of his assistant, Elyse Tanzillo. Cover artist Daniel Dociu, and Michal Dutkiewicz and David G. Williams for their Accala artwork.

Morgan would like to thank Bill and Ann for their support and Calum, Liam, and Sean for being generally wonderful. Special thanks to the Reverend Dr. John Dupuche for his support and encouragement.

Claudia would like to thank Dr. David Sinclair, Dr. Roy Eskapa, and Jenny Williamson for being her real-life heroes and a very special thank-you to Morgan Grant Buchanan for traveling the road from *Babylon Confidential* to *Wolf's Empire* with grace and integrity—thank you, mate.

THE EIGHT NOBLE HOUSES OF THE GALACTIC IMPERIUM

with provincial territories and team emblems

I. HOUSE NUMERIAN

WARDENS OF TERRA FIRMA PROVINCE

(The Imperial family's emblem is the Golden Lion but they are not obliged to compete in Jupiter's Gladiatorial Games)

VIII. HOUSE OVIDIAN

WARDENS OF ILLYRICUM CARBUNCULUS PROVINCE
Team Emblem: The Amber Boars

II. HOUSE VIRIDIAN

WARDENS OF PONTUS LUPUS PROVINCE
Team Emblem: The Golden Wolves

VII. HOUSE TULLIAN

WARDENS OF SYTHIA LYCHNITES PROVINCE
Team Emblem: The Blue Bulls

III. HOUSE SERTORIAN

WARDENS OF AERIA SERTORIUS PROVINCE
Team Emblem: The Blood Hawks

VI. HOUSE FLAVIAN

WARDENS OF GALATIA SMARAGDUS PROVINCE
Team Emblem: The Silver Sparrows

IV. HOUSE ARRIAN

WARDENS OF QUATRUS LYCAONIA PROVINCE
Team Emblem: The White Rams

V. HOUSE CALPURNIAN

WARDENS OF MARE BYZANTIUM PROVINCE
Team Emblem: The Black Ravens

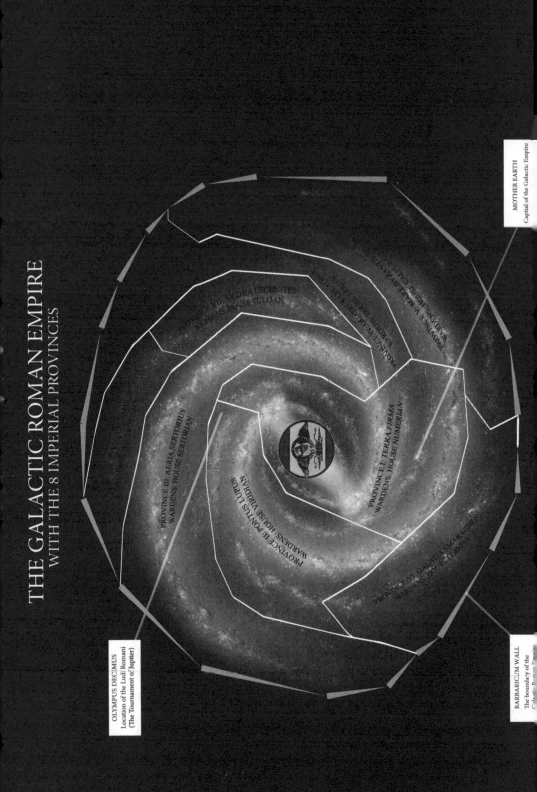

DRAMATIS PERSONAE

ROMANS

Accala Viridius Camilla—the heroine

SERTORIAN TEAM

    Licinus Sertorius Malleolus—tribune, the team leader and war chain fighter

    Gaius Sertorius Crassus—the team trainer, gentleman, and javelin fighter

    Gaia Sertorius Barbata—a trident-wielding gladiator

    Servius Tullius Lurco—a hammer-wielding beast fighter

    Castor Sertorius Corvinus—a one-armed charioteer

    Pollux Sertorius Corvinus—a one-armed charioteer

    Mania Sertorius Curia—a trapper of beasts and dreams

VIRIDIAN TEAM

    Vibius Viridius Carbo—tribune and team leader

    Gnaeus Viridius Metellus—the team trainer

    Darius Viridius Strabo—Accala's cousin, an archer and a gladiator

    Titus Viridius Nervo—a charioteer

    Trio Viridius Mercurius—a charioteer

    Scipio Viridius Caninus—a dart-throwing beast hunter

    Capitulus Viridius Pavo—a crossbow-wielding beast fighter

    Taticulus Viridius Leticus—a club-wielding gladiator

OTHER ROMANS

Julia Silana—a Vulcaneum immune

Marcus Calpurnius Regulus—Accala's lanista

Caesar Numerius Valentinius—imperator, emperor of the Galactic Roman Empire

Quintus Viridius Severus—Accala's uncle, the Viridian proconsul

Aquilinus Sertorius Macula—the Sertorian proconsul

Lucius Viridius Camillus—Accala's father, a war hero and senator

Alexandria Viridius Camilla—Accala's mother, a philosopher and scientist

Aulus Viridius Camillus—Accala's younger brother

BARBARIANS (ALIENS)

Lumen—a Hyperborean child

Concretus—a Hyperborean warrior, Lumen's guardian

Alba—an Iceni body slave

Bulla—Accala's Taurii body slave

TRIA NOMINA

Typical Roman names of the Galactic Empire have three parts (the "tria nomina"). For example, for *Accala Viridius Camilla:*

- *Accala* is the given name.
- *Viridius* is the *gens,* or house name (House Viridian).
- *Camilla* is the family name.

PROLOGUE

THE VIRIDIAD, PART I

The History of Accala, the Noble-born Gladiatrix,
from the Chronicle of the Seventh Empire, 7753–7901 A.U.C.

Justice—Goddess, sing of the retribution of Lucius' daughter, Accala. Driven by a thirst for vengeance, she cost House Sertorian countless lives. Like raindrops striking the ground, they died, black-hearted warriors, their souls cast down to Hades' boundless halls. What terrible price did she pay to see justice carried out? Tell us what Fate drove her to brave such hardship. To endure so many trials?

But wait. First, O Muse, sing of Galactic Rome, master of ten thousand worlds, the stage upon which her story is set.

Rome! It was the twins, Romulus and Remus, who laid her foundations eight thousand years ago. Abandoned at birth, they were found and suckled by a she-wolf until they grew in strength and power. From her they inherited resilience, loyalty, and ferocity—qualities they bestowed upon their city. Unconquerable Rome! The city that grew to rule over Mother Earth, crushing all efforts to bring about her fall. Eternal Rome! That expanded into space over five thousand years to become the heart of a galactic empire.

In Accala's time, seven noble houses ruled the empire's galactic provinces, each vying for the imperial throne, held by the eighth, the emperor's own house. Fighting between two houses—the virtuous and brave House Viridian and the corrupt and heartless House Sertorian—had driven the empire to the brink of a civil war.

The shining Viridians! Accala's own family, bearing the standard of the golden wolf. Steeped in military honors, placing service and duty above ambition. For two thousand years, they embodied and upheld the best of Roman virtues.

The black-hearted Sertorians! They bore the standard of the ruby hawk—a hawk with outstretched talons, seizing wealth and power at any price.

Begin, Muse, when the two first clashed, the boldest of each house—Crassus Sertorius, lord of corruption, and the brilliant Lady Accala Viridius. Both young and reckless, both gifted in the gladiatorial arts and filled with the spirit of ambition, desperate to triumph at any cost.

PART I
BURNT OFFERINGS

Let justice be done though the heavens fall.
—Lucius Calpurnius Piso Caesoninus

I intend to speak of forms changed into new entities.
—Ovid, Metamorphoses

Who has not seen the dummies of wood they slash at and batter
Whether with swords or with spears, going through all the
    maneuvers?
. . . Or, it may be, they have deeper designs, and are really preparing
For the arena itself. How can a woman be decent
Sticking her head in a helmet, denying the sex she was born
    with? . . .
What a great honor it is for a husband to see, at an auction,
Where his wife's effects are up for sale, belts, shinguards,
Arm-protectors and plumes!
. . . Hear her grunt and groan as she works at it, parrying and
    thrusting;
See her neck bent down under the weight of her helmet;
Look at the rolls of bandage and tape, so her legs look like tree
    trunks,
Ah, degenerate girls from the line of our praetors and consuls,
Tell us, whom have you seen got up in any such a fashion,
Panting and sweating like this? No gladiator's wench,
No tough strip-tease broad would ever so much as attempt it.
—Juvenal, Satires

ACT I

SHE-WOLF

Gods of my country, heroes of the soil,
And Romulus, and Mother Vesta . . .
Preservest, this new champion at the least
Our fallen generation to repair . . .
Here where the wrong is right, the right is wrong,
Where wars abound so many, and myriad-faced
. . . new strife
Is stirring; neighbouring cities are in arms,
The laws that bound them snapped; and godless war
Rages through all the universe.

—Virgil, *Georgics*

I

Rome, Mother Earth, 7798 A.U.C

EVERY NIGHT THE SAME dream—a blast wave of atomic fire raced across the surface of a distant ice world, an inferno that would envelop the planet's capital in a matter of minutes, transmuting sturdy buildings to slag, consuming three and a half million lives with the same dispassion as it liquidized steel and stone. But before that could happen, I had to bear witness.

Mother ran toward me as the bright firewall rose up behind her, rapidly gaining ground. Ever Stoic, her face registered no fear, only a dread urgency—there was something important she had to tell me before the fire claimed her—but I was trapped behind a wall of thick, dirty ice, entombed alive in it. In place of words, all that reached my ears was a dull, brassy drone.

Mother tore out her hairpin and used it to scratch two words into the ice, but they appeared back to front, and I couldn't read them in time because my little brother suddenly entered the scene. Aulus' small body was trapped in the press of stampeding citizens as they fled the city, his eyes wide with panic. Mother turned from me and rushed to aid my brother, hair flailing behind her, the tips of the tresses catching fire as the burning wind rushed over her. Arms outstretched like a dragnet, she made an instinctive but futile effort to catch Aulus and wrap him up before the thermal currents scorched them both to ash. The ice was the only thing protecting me from the unstoppable fire, yet I battered it with my fists, clawed at it until my fingernails splintered and snapped. I fought to stay, prayed to Minerva that I be consumed with Mother and Aulus, disintegrated by heat and light.

* * *

I WOKE IN A fevered state, burning up, heart racing, breathing rapid and shallow. The silk sheet was drenched in sweat, clinging to my body like a hungry ghost. The urge to sit up and grasp for a lungful of air was strong, but instead, I kicked the sheet off the end of the bed and lay there, tears stinging my eyes, forcing my lungs to take the slowest, deepest possible breaths.

A clear golden light bathed the high ceiling of my bedchamber, the kind that follows a summer dawn. The gilded cornices that skirted the ceiling's edges bore seventy-one cracks of varying lengths, and I slowly counted each one in turn until I could breathe normally and all that remained was a residual choleric anger—the outrage that any human being must experience at witnessing the murder of loved ones. The sharpest sword dulls with repeated use, but the dream never lost its cruel edge. My ears still rang with the sound of Mother's voice trying to penetrate the wall of ice between us. No instrument could replicate the unsettling drone that poured from her mouth. The closest analogy I could come up with (and in the aftermath of the dream each morning, I had plenty of time to turn things like this around in my mind) was the sound of a living beehive submerged in water.

I sat up on the hard edge of my bed, ignoring aching muscles and the patchwork of bruises that peppered my body, still tender from my last match. My cameo lay on the bedside table, projecting a holographic scene into the air on endless loop—the sky was blue, a field of golden wheat blew back and forth in the wind behind them. Mother was playing with Aulus out front of our country villa on the Amalfi Coast, throwing a ball for him to catch. Her hair was tossed gently this way and that by the summer wind. It was the same as mine, that hair. Jet-black and dead straight with one curvy bone-white shock that originated in the roots above the right forehead and ran all the way down like a skinny waterfall tumbling over a shiny onyx pillar. My brother was laughing. Some of his teeth were missing. He was nine years old. I'd taken the video myself the day before they left on what was supposed to be just another one of my mother's research trips. Aulus was on holidays and had bothered Mother for weeks to take him with her to Olympus Decimus until she finally caved in and agreed. I was seventeen years old, busy with my final year of studies at the Academy, and had no intention of tagging along as a glorified babysitter. So I was sleeping soundly in my apartment in Rome when, fifty thousand light-years away, the talon fighters of House Sertorian's attack fleet peppered the ice world with their bombs.

Seven hundred and fourteen days had passed since. For almost two years their deaths had gone unavenged, their spirits tossing and turning in Hades' dark caverns.

Slowly rising from the bed, I allowed gravity to ground me, feeling my weight sink to my feet, finding each sore muscle on its journey, letting the pain signals pass over me. On day seven hundred and fifteen, when dawn stretched out her rose-red fingers, I would journey down Via Appia with my team, cheered on by the city before boarding a carrier that would transport me to Olympus Decimus to join in the Ludi Romani, the emperor's great gladiatorial games. There, on the ice world where Mother and Aulus had been killed, I'd either suffer their fate and be killed or survive and triumph, with the men responsible for the bombing dead and bloody at my feet. Then Mother and Aulus would be at rest and the dream of fire would depart, leaving me to the embrace of a cool and silent sleep.

Peeling off my nightdress, I hurriedly threw on a loose-fitting training outfit and snapped my armilla over my forearm. My armilla—a long utility bracelet bordered with gold piping and inset with a small monitor, input pad, shield, and holographic projector eye—was thin and comfortable, like a second skin.

I strode from my bedchamber, down the hall toward the center of my apartment, past the shrine surrounded with holographic busts of my ancestors, until I reached the atrium, where the open-roofed courtyard provided the most available vertical space. Tapping the panel on my armilla, I projected research nodes into the air about me. A dozen screens presented notes and files, media streams from all corners of the empire, studies in history, tactics, law, ancient and modern arms and armor—my research. A sharp turn of the wrist unhitched the screens from the device, leaving them hanging in space. My hands swung through the air, managing my information like a conductor leading an orchestra. First I scanned the morning news on the vox populi forum. I had keyword alerts set up, but you couldn't anticipate every eventuality. My mother had taught me self-reliance and critical thinking—"Never trust technology to cover every base, Accala. Always make the extra effort to bring your brain into the equation."

I brought the day's arena schedule to the fore and read it again. The final trial rounds were being fought in the morning. There were two places out of fifty-six still undecided. Vacancies in the teams of House Calpurnian and Flavian. It would all be decided before noon, after which the final team complements would be announced in full. In the afternoon there'd be speeches (the galactic audience would be watching eagerly via the vox populi forum from the most distant corners of the empire) followed by the contestants' private dinner. The speeches would be the most unbearable part of the day. The game editor would release some clues about the obstacles and challenges in the coming events, then senators and committee officials would follow with dreary speeches designed to remind the empire of their value and importance. Finally, each gladiator would occupy the podium for a few seconds and state his or her hopes and reason for fighting. I loathed public speaking, but there was no way out of it; the audience demanded a predeparture speech from the gladiators. It added spice to the games, gave the audience a chance to decide whom to back, and aided a vast network of bookmakers in the sharpening of their odds. So I'd be brief. I'd speak of Viridian honor, of avenging the souls of our fighters and colonists who died at Sertorian hands. I'd thank Marcus for training me, be conciliatory to my fellow Golden Wolves who'd missed out on a place, and I'd bite my tongue no matter how much the Sertorian contestants or the withered chauvinists of the Galactic Committee for Combative Sports riled me. I wouldn't mention my personal goals and grievances, no ammunition to give anyone cause to disqualify me.

Switching back to the vox populi forum, I scrolled the latest news items. Locally the Festivities of Minerva on Mother Earth were already coming to a close in the southern hemisphere. There was coverage of our own dawn service at Nemorensis. A special report detailed a new Sauromatae revolt on their worlds near the galactic rim—rioting on the streets, a magistrate from House Arrian killed in an explosion, but the local legion already in the process of restoring order. Five thousand and one already dead. One Roman magistrate and five thousand blue-scaled Sauromatae, most of them extended family members of the rebels who were executed as both punishment and deterrent. No surprise. That was how barbarian uprisings usually played out.

The main news, as expected, was about the coming Festival of Jupiter, the most important and extravagant holiday of the year, and its games, the Ludi Romani, which were always the most eagerly awaited and most hotly contested. Long ago we'd learned that the key to sustaining a galactic empire lay in delivering a never-ending serving of bread and circuses. Emperors and politicians talked about honor and tradition, but all the masses wanted was to be fed, employed, and entertained in peace. Then the whole system ticked over. As one holiday festival ended, you had to wait only a week or two before the next one started up.

Scanning through the multiple streams of media coverage, I listened to brief snatches of discussion on strengths and weaknesses of the gladiators, the rules, and various contests that might be brought into play, but it was all speculation until the emperor's officials announced the nature of the course. And the prize. They couldn't stop talking about it, the greatest prize ever offered in the empire's long history.

Satisfied, I tapped the panel on my armilla to shut down the information nodes. Once the sun set, I'd be home free, on track to depart the galactic capital with nothing but the tournament to focus on. Until then though, my father still had the time and the means to try and derail me. He'd been suspiciously silent on the topic of the coming tournament, refusing to discuss the matter or acknowledge my part in it, and so I'd set aside the whole day to manage any potential disaster that might rear its head. I'd sacrificed everything to secure my place in the coming games, overcome every hurdle put in my path. Nothing was going to stop me from fighting in the Ludi Romani. That was my fate. It was set in stone.

I headed to my training area. My green steel trunk, packed with armor, auxiliary weapons, warm clothes, and cold-weather survival equipment, was waiting for me by the door, ready to be shipped. Written on the side in neon yellow was A. VIRIDI—an abbreviation of my name. Father gave me the trunk for my eighteenth birthday, two months after Mother and Aulus were killed. He hoped it would carry my belongings to the home of my future husband, but I had no mind to play the part of a broodmare and make noble babies with an influential senator. Happily, though much to my father's consternation, when the news of my first fight in the arena broke, the suitors who'd been lining up to pay me court dried up like a drought-plagued riverbed.

My training area had once been the triclinium, the living area where guests could recline on comfortable couches, but it contained no divans, couches, day-beds, or hand-carved crystal side tables bearing expensive, exotic fruits. Viridians are practical, functional people by nature. We do not seek comfort or decoration in our rooms, but even so, my large chambers were decidedly spartan compared to the others in the family compound. A plain wood table held two bowls—one containing olives, the other honeyed figs—a pitcher of watered-down wine, and the sling case that held my combat discus, sharp-edged Orbis—only the bare essentials required to sleep, eat, and train.

I ran through my calisthenics without arms or armor, visualizing my ene-mies. Sidestep the incoming javelin thrust, kick the opponent's knee, lock and disable the weapon arm. A finger strike to paralyze the trapezius and finish with a sharp folding elbow technique to the back of the neck to rupture the medulla oblongata and bring on heart and lung failure. Next, catch a steel whip on my forearm and counter with a high kick to the throat to crush the larynx, followed with a scissor-leg takedown.

* * *

AN HOUR PASSED BEFORE I was satisfied that I could move freely from my center of gravity without any residual tension to obstruct strength or speed. I bathed, dressed in my stola—white robes with a twin trim of gold and emer-ald green, a gold embroidered wolf on the breast marking me as a member of House Viridian—and went to my ancestral shrine to make offerings to Minerva so that she would pour her blessings and favor upon me.

Before I could start my initial libation, an incoming news alert flashed on my armilla's screen accompanied by a sinking feeling in my stomach. A newly posted story revealed that two Sertorian gladiators had died overnight, one from a sud-den illness, the other murdered by an obsessive fan, leaving the Blood Hawks with two vacant slots that had to be filled by the end of the day to make up the standard team of eight. Additional trials had been hastily arranged by the com-mittee as the rules stated that all the slots needed to be filled before the teams departed for the arena world. My hands shook, fingers fumbling to bring up the list of Sertorian competitors. Titus Malleus and Gorgona were the sudden fa-talities. I mouthed a quick thanks to Minerva that my targets had not been re-moved from the field. Just the same, it didn't add up. Those gladiators were at the top of their game, two of the best, their health and safety carefully managed by a team of physicians and attendants. The report went on to say that the Ser-torians were desperate to find suitable replacements and had even been consid-ering gladiators from allied houses. A quick check of the Golden Wolves team list showed my name still there, right after our team leader and trainer. The galactic betting pools confirmed that the Blood Hawks were substantially weakened. No longer considered the outright favorite, they were now rated third to last. No bad news at all! A weakened Sertorian team would make my job all the easier.

Kneeling, I looked up past my ancestors to the alabaster statue of Minerva that crowned the small shrine. Beside me, in a sapphire bowl that rested on a tripod, were dozens of small figurines, each the size of my thumb's tip and formed in the shape of a bull. For each figurine I deposited in the shrine's incinerator, an instantaneous signal would transmit to one of the empire's many temple worlds, ordering that a dozen live bulls be slaughtered on my behalf and burned as an offering in the name of my chosen deity. To ensure an auspicious day and a victorious tournament, I planned on dropping in every last one of them, but just as I gathered up the first handful, a soft chime sounded, giving me a second's notice before the doors of my chamber slid open and Bulla, my bronze-skinned Taurii body slave, came barreling in on large hoofed feet. She snorted and pulled herself up, stamping her right hoof on the ground. Her pierced cowlike ears pricked up with excitement. "Lady Accala! Domina! You awake? Domina, you awake?"

Gods, but Bulla could be intimidating when she moved at speed—an eight-foot mountain of muscle in a green tent dress, cinched at her broad waist by a thick belt with an iron buckle. Bulla's fine fawn-colored fur was combed over the jagged battle scars that covered her body in a futile attempt to mask them and soften her appearance, but there were so many cicatricial scores running against the natural line of fur, some like white worms, others purple and swollen with scar tissue, that it only made her look more formidable. She caught me by surprise; I thought she might have been my father come for a showdown over the tournament, and I accidentally dropped the handful of figurines, sending them scattering across the floor.

"No. As you can see, I fell asleep at the altar," I said in an irritated voice.

"Oh. Then you wake up. Wake up. You must." Taurii do sleep on their feet, and sarcasm and sharpness of thought are not a strong point of the species. Bulla had been my mother's slave and served first as a matron then as pedagogue to my brother, seeing him safely to and from school. After they died, Bulla shared her grief by lowing outside my room night after night. That didn't comfort me at all of course, but she was fiercely loyal to my mother and had nursed both my little brother and me. I could hardly allow Father to send her to the slave markets when she found herself without a position.

"I'm awake now," I said. "What is it?"

"A messenger come from the Colosseum. From the Colosseum. They turn him away at the gate but I hear him call out your name, domina. I push the guards away and ask him what he want. What do you want I say?"

"That's strange. Why would they bother to send someone in person?"

"The man says your lanista, Marcus, he try to send you message after message, but they all blocked."

My armilla still showed nothing out of the ordinary. I ran a quick diagnostic and discovered that some incoming frequencies were being weakened to the point that my armilla couldn't pick them up—a customized signal jam. A quick power boost to the armilla's receiver, and just like magic the screen flickered, and communicats and alerts came pouring in, accompanied by warning alarms. Seven messages from Marcus alone, and he'd never written me one before that day. They all said the same thing.

> Come quickly. The committee is moving to scratch you from the tournament. I'll do what I can.

I quickly flicked to the list of confirmed Ludi Romani contestants I'd checked only moments before. With the signal block removed, it contained one vital alteration. My name, Accala Viridius Camilla, had a line running right through it. I'd been scratched. The match to find my replacement had already been held that morning, and my second cousin on my father's side, Darius Viridius Strabo, had been confirmed.

My head felt light and dizzy, like someone had taken my feet and spun me upside down inside my own body, and I leaned back against the wall to stop from falling. This was impossible news. The Golden Wolves needed me. I had three more wins than Darius and seventeen unbroken victories in the galactic league. I was a crowd favorite and the Viridian team's best shot at victory.

It was Father's doing. It had to be. As an unmarried woman, I was still subject to his will. He was trying to sabotage all my hard work, still trying to force me into a mold of his making. How would he have done it? Call in a favor or two with the senators who served on the committee and order the security staff to jam certain incoming transmissions of my armilla. I was outraged, partly at his sneak attack—I'd always considered him too noble to do anything other than confront me directly—and partly at my own ineptitude—how could I not have seen it coming? So focused on a potential attack that it never occurred to me that the fight was already over and I'd lost.

My hands tightened into fists, so tight that my flat nails bit painfully into the flesh of my palms. The pain helped focus my thoughts. There were still trials under way at the Colosseum. The committee would be there. I could plead my case, try to get the judgment against me overturned. More important, Marcus would be there. He'd know how to turn things around. With his help I could fix this.

"Is Father still in the compound?" I demanded as I rushed to my dressing room.

"He left before the sun rise up," Bulla said, thumping along behind me. "Off to the Senate house to talk. To talk at the Senate."

"Then quick, fetch my fighting clothes, help me dress."

"You already dressed, domina."

I threw off my stola. "Fighting clothes first, then robes. You know what I mean."

"You going to fight, domina?" Bulla asked, gathering up the robes as she followed after me.

"You're damn right I am."

"That not going to make your father happy. Not happy at all."

"His happiness is just about the farthest thing from my mind right now."

"Domina, do not let your father know that Bulla was the one to tell you," she said as we entered the dressing room. "Not Bulla."

"You have nothing to fear from him."

"I fear he will send me to the slave markets. The slave markets or worse."

Bulla and I had something in common. We were both subject to my father's will. He could legally kill us both if he wished, though with me he'd have to show reasonable cause, not that that would be a problem. A noble-born woman entering the arena. In the eyes of any magistrate, I'd already given him more than enough. "Nonsense. He'd have me to deal with if he did that." I pulled back my thick black hair and wrapped it into a knot at the base of my neck while Bulla hurriedly laid out my garments.

A formfitting base layer of fine, flexible alloys over which I pulled cotton trousers and a short silk tunic. Next my armored running shoes. Last of all I rewrapped my stola. And then I was up, striding through the training area, grabbing my weapon case, slinging it over my shoulder as I headed for the balcony.

"Breakfast!" Bulla protested. "You must eat."

"Later."

Before I could get past her, three thick, blunt fingers closed about my arm in a stonelike grip.

"Humans tire and die easy," Bulla said, "and you are only a calf of nineteen summers. Don't tire and die. Eat."

Bulla was right. Food was fuel. Snatching up some honeyed figs from a bowl on the table, I stuffed them into my mouth.

"What you do when you see the enemy?" Bulla asked.

"I spear them on my horns. I pummel them with my hooves."

She nodded, satisfied that I remembered her Taurii maxims, and released me.

"Make sure you know who friend and who enemy before you charge," she called out after me. "Except with Sertorians. With them you kill first. Kill first, ask questions later."

II

OUT ONTO THE BALCONY, past my clusters of miniature fruit trees, I stepped right up to the railing and in between two parallel bars. The bars ran back toward my apartment for a length of four feet before curving down to terminate in the balcony floor. The hot summer wind buffeted me as I gripped the bars on either side, thumbing the small built-in disc controls. At once my aer chariot broke away from the structure of the balcony and glided out over the Wolf's Den, House Viridian's family compound on the Aventine.

The Den was home. I was born and raised there, schooled in Viridian history, fed lists of Viridian virtues, surrounded by Viridian cousins so that when I reached eleven years of age and entered junior school with the children of the other noble houses, there should be no doubt in my mind that the greatest gift Fortune could bestow upon a newborn was that it should come into the world from the womb of a woman who had married into House Viridian.

We had been taught that Viridians traced their genetic origins to the sons and daughters of Remus and Numa—honest and hardworking, rising from simple stock to achieve a nobility based on honor and tradition, renowned for our skills in strategy and our logistics expertise. As such, we had always occupied the Aventine. Our allies, House Calpurnian and House Flavian, held the Esquiline and Caelian Hills. The Calpurnians were skilled agriculturists with a long history of seeding barren planets with carpets of oxygen-rich greenery, while the Flavians were experts in the design of faster-than-light engine technology and communication platforms, connecting the citizens of the empire as she continued her eternal expansion. Together, we three houses were formally known as the Caninine Alliance.

Steering the chariot away from the plaza and parade ground (no point announcing my presence to the guards and soldiers), I shot low over the roofs of the stacked, terraced buildings that housed my extended family. Great flags bearing the emblem of the golden wolf flapped in the morning breeze atop the barracks hall. The compound's armored walls, decorated in faded gold and malachite green, wore cracks like old cowhide. Its ancient structures might be worn and crumbling, but the Den, like the hill fortresses of the neighboring houses, was considered a sacred beacon—a center from which a house's power radiated outward, managing its galactic province, territories, legions, assets, and possessions. Tradition dictated that each of the eight houses should possess one of the seven sacred hills upon which Rome was founded. The obvious problem of sharing seven hills among eight houses was pragmatically and symbolically solved by the emperor and his family—encompassing the other hills by classifying their "hill" as Mother Earth herself. The emperor's house, the current being House Numerian, took on the honorific *Sons of Romulus,* the hero who founded Rome city after slaying his brother Remus in a fight over whose village had bigger walls.

Activating the homemade frequency decoder on my armilla, I dropped below the sensors of the western guard tower and slipped over the boundary wall. The decoder flashed to indicate that it had completed its job a split second before I passed right through the yellow-tinged security dome, thankfully without suffering disintegration.

I shot past the small balconies of administrators and military officers who lived in the crowded apartment blocks below the fortress, opened up the throttle, and pulled clear of the Aventine, the wind whipping my robes about as I met with the aerway and vanished into the rush of morning traffic, dodging in and out of flying chariots, palanquins, and transport convoys.

Eternal Rome spread out before me, gleaming in the light of the morning sun. Perpetually pristine—white marble temples, majestic porphyry towers, and haughty civic buildings of shining granite, architecture infused with vertical light-filled channels that lent the city a celestial glow. She was breathtaking. The noise and bustle of the traffic dropped away when you beheld her magnificence. The capital of Mother Earth, which was in turn capital of the imperial province of Terra Firma. Jewel of the provinces, the wellspring of civilization, the axial city upon which the entire galaxy turned. Honor, justice, loyalty, imperium, the Pax Romana, the Senate and the people, the Twelve Tables of Roman Law—these were the virtues and institutions that made Rome great. That was the way we were taught to think of the city, the way her solemn beauty reflected those ideals, but the last two years had taught me to look past the surface of things. I'd learned that the real Rome, devoid of honor and justice, lay behind the scenes, where old wounds festered. Three hundred families governed the empire. Forty-nine families led by consuls ruled over the three hundred. Seven families led by proconsuls ruled over the forty-nine, and one emperor and his family ruled over all. Like unruly children in the class of a strict tutor, the representatives of the great houses of the city feigned amity and cooperation as they carried out the dirty business of running the empire. Feuds between families, some millennia old, played out in assassinations, espionage, and double-dealing, but none of it was ever publicly acknowledged; it all stayed hidden beneath the façade of civilization. On the surface everything was peacefully perfect. You'd never have known that a civil war was raging, threatening to tear the empire apart.

* * *

THE CIVIL WAR STARTED the moment House Sertorian launched their unprovoked attack on Olympus Decimus, but a potential conflict had been brewing for a long time before that. Two decades earlier the Sertorians began making a long play to take a step up in society and become one of the eight great ruling houses. They even bought up property in the Carinae, the fashionable district at the base of the Esquiline, to be near one of the sacred hills, but internal power disputes and factional fighting prevented them from rising very far; tolerance and cooperation were not natural Sertorian traits. Then the charismatic Aquilinus Sertorius Macula came to power. Aquilinus not only united his house, he gave them the essential ingredients they had lacked in their quest for upward mobility: roots and a connection to the ancient past.

He reminded his people that, as the Viridians looked to Remus and Numa, House Sertorian could trace their genetic lineage to the ancient emperor Caligula. Although it was commonly understood that Caligula was completely insane, as well as demonically creative when it came to indulging his sadism, the Sertorians weren't dissuaded in the slightest from adopting him as their ancestor and guiding influence. Aquilinus argued that what others called madness and cruel excess in ancient emperors could not be seen as sinful or blameworthy. He didn't believe in the gods but he was of the opinion that emperors were a close equivalent, the highest point of human achievement. So a superior man's passions could not be understood or contextualized by mere mortals. He argued that Caligula's excesses should be embraced as an essential component of Roman character and emulated by those of the Sertorian nobility. To concretize this, Aquilinus developed a manifesto of genetic superiority, a path that he promised would lead to a Sertorian-led empire, a shared vision all Sertorians found very appealing. His manifesto united the factions of his house like nothing before, and within a few years they were powerful, influential, and wealthy beyond belief, exploring every avenue for profit in the most ruthless and backhanded ways. They were just waiting for their chance to swoop on a weakness, and ironically it was my own house, which sought to deter them more than any other, that gave them the means to elevation.

It came about when the old emperor Julius Heliogabalus Caesar died, his mind and body crippled by millennia of inbreeding that even radical gene therapy couldn't correct. Heliogabalus' madness reached its zenith with the decision to memorialize himself and each prior Julian emperor going back to Julius Caesar by sculpting the planets of a distant solar system into a series of monumental busts—which turned out to be not so easy, as some of them were gas giants—leaving the imperial treasury's coffers nearly drained. My uncle, the Viridian proconsul Quintus Viridius Severus, led a contingent of houses seeking to reestablish a republic in which the elected representatives of the Senate ruled the empire in place of a single dictator. Unfortunately, House Numerian, famous for its powerful warriors and land barons, chose to reestablish the existing model, and our house was left in the lurch, having backed the wrong horse.

The Sertorian leader went out of his way to make a strong impression on the new emperor, promoting his house's mastery of finance and commerce, and donating vast sums of money to fill the empire's coffers. The result was their elevation to the Council of Great Houses, commonly known as the Eight, and possession of the Palatine Hill, right opposite us, on the other side of the Circus Maximus, a position of honor, traditionally owned by the wealthiest house after the emperor's. Aquilinus became a proconsul and was granted a province that they named Aeria Sertorius. He wasted no time introducing corruption into areas of commerce no one had previously thought to exploit and using the proceeds to shower the mob with festivals to increase House Sertorian's popularity.

Soaring high above the River Tiber, I passed the Palladium—the atmosphere-scraping statue of Minerva in full armor with her shield raised, lightning spear ready to cast, the great guardian of the city wreathed and decorated to celebrate her festival.

A niggling voice at the back of my mind told me to stop into the temple at the base of the statue and make a sacrifice. I'd missed my chance back at the apartment when Bulla surprised me. But no, Minerva would have to wait. I simply didn't have the time. Roman life was set to a strict calendar of festivals. The Festival of Minerva was drawing to a close, and tomorrow the teams for the Festival of Jupiter's games would depart. My life would be over if I couldn't get back on the team today. How could I live with myself if I stopped to honor Minerva and in doing so missed a vital window to turn things around?

The aerway I was on ran on a counterclockwise route around the outer edge of the city, a longer route but normally quicker unless it was a busy day, and now that the news of the new rounds at the Colosseum had been released, I could already see the traffic starting to bank up, so I prayed for Minerva's help and switched up two lanes to Via Cordia, which would take me right into the heart of the old city.

The downside of my new route, though, was that I had to double back a little, passing the eastern side of the Palatine. It took me right past the imposing ruby-and-onyx compound of House Sertorian. Great black flags whipped about in the wind—the emblem of the crimson hawk at their center, wings and claws outstretched in the moment before it snatched up its prey. The building had a circular base and interlocking layers of smooth, curving arcs that rose up and terminated in sharp points. It was supposed to symbolize the hawk's talons rising up from a drop of divine blood, but to me it best resembled a bruised and bleeding artichoke.

*   *   *

SHORTLY AFTER HOUSE SERTORIAN joined the Eight and had a powerful voice in the Senate, they started questioning the precise location of the traditional boundary between their new province and ours which neighbored it, insisting we were in possession of a couple of thousand light-years of space that was rightfully theirs, specifically the ice world Olympus Decimus. The world had only one major asset—its ionosphere was filled with supercharged particles that accelerated the speed of transmission signals passing through it. It was a valuable communication hub, but even so, not important enough to go to war over. Everyone was shocked when Aquilinus sent ships into Viridian space, bombed our settlement on Olympus Decimus, and laid claim to the world for House Sertorian.

Our side protested to the Senate immediately (my uncle Quintus had served in the legions with Aquilinus and hated the man with a passion) and began to mobilize to retaliate, but before a ruling could be made, Aquilinus ordered thirty-six simultaneous bombing strikes on key Viridian outposts spread across the border of the contested space. His ruthlessness impressed houses Tullian and Ovidian, and they allied themselves to the Sertorians. Turning their backs on their gods, sacrificing worship of Mithras and Diana in order to follow Proconsul Aquilinus, they joined what became known as the Talonite Axis, a coalition of self-serving greed and ambition that threatened all the ideals that made Rome great.

Aquilinus had judged his combined fleet powerful enough to eliminate our defenses in a single, coordinated assault, but in typical Sertorian fashion, he overestimated his strength and underestimated ours. Uncle Quintus commanded our legions with those of our three allied houses in a counterattack that repelled the Sertorians and secured most of our territory, though not Olympus Decimus. He showed them that Viridians are tough, resourceful. We fight to the end; we don't surrender.

By the end of the first year of fighting, we had the Sertorians on the back foot and were close to total victory, but then Proconsul Aquilinus, as if by some minor miracle, managed to convince one of our allies to abandon us and take up with his axis. The defection of House Arrian was a shock no one saw coming. Arms manufacturer and creator of the force field technology vital to the running of the empire, House Arrian was an ally we couldn't do without. The tide turned, from four houses to three in our favor to four to three against.

*   *   *

PASSING BY THE PALATINE brought me bad luck because when I was right over it, the traffic came to a standstill. The city was gripped with festival fever, and gladiator fans were out in force, clogging the aerway. The streets below were no better, bustling with Sertorians heading in on foot to see the final shake-up of the tournament teams before tomorrow's parade. The clusters of buildings that streamed down from the Palatine were painted with strikingly luminous Ichthyophagi vermilion, a color most people had the good taste to use sparingly, due to the vast numbers of sentient barbarians who had to be killed to produce it, but the Sertorians had laid it on thick, and the streets of the Palatine looked like running sores.

If only I had a bomb of my own that I could drop right now without any repercussions. I'd wipe out the Sertorians and their ugly architecture. It'd even be worth destroying the entire Palatine just to be rid of them once and for all, but that could never be anything more than a fantasy. No Roman could overtly attack another citizen in Rome without violating the ancient and sacred peace of the city and facing execution.

In the distance I could see the sacred hills occupied by our enemies. As our Caninine Alliance occupied three of Rome's seven hills, the Sertorians and their allies held the remaining four—the Tullians, shipbuilders who held the contract to engineer the imperial fleet, on the Quirinal Hill; the Ovidians, renowned for their hunting prowess, possessed the Capitoline Hill; and the Arrians, who occupied the Viminal.

*   *   *

UNDER THE ASSAULT OF superior numbers, the Viridian border worlds of Pontus Primus, Lupus Adamas, and Australis Valere all fell quickly and were occupied. The Sertorians even cleaned up the fallout from the bombing of Olympus Decimus and built a new city—Avis Accipitridae—setting up their own communication network in our province. After a year facing defeat after defeat, House Viridian was cash-strapped and underresourced, close to defeat. Just when it seemed there was no hope, the Sertorians made a strategic blunder, and everything changed.

The imperial province Terra Firma encompassed the tens of thousands of light-years of space around Mother Earth and the galactic center—a buffer zone to protect and preserve the cradle of civilization, the hub of the empire. On taking office, proconsuls had to swear to preserve the city of Rome and the sacred boundaries of Terra Firma province.

When the forty-second Sertorian fleet drove the sixteenth Viridian (a combined force formed with House Calpurnian) across the border into Terra Firma, Caesar Numerius Valentinius felt that both houses had overstepped the mark and needed to be reminded who was in charge. Reaching out through his personal Praetorian fleet comprising three hundred ultimare-class dreadnoughts, the emperor annihilated them all. Forty thousand Sertorian and Viridian troops and eight deceres-class war carriers wiped out in less than an hour. That slap on the wrist cost us more dearly than the Sertorians, but it ensured that the proconsuls of both houses paid attention when the emperor declared an armistice. Any house that broke the emperor's peace would face decimation and demotion—the execution of ten percent of their house's total population and exile to the galactic frontier. The emperor also decided upon an ingenious solution to resolve the war once and for all.

*   *   *

I SPAT OVER THE side of my chariot to try to ward off the bad luck, hit the throttle again, and started zigzagging in and out of the stationary vehicles to screams of abuse and blaring sirens until there was no room left to maneuver. Using my decoder, I broke through the force fields that demarcated the lanes and rushed into the open air. I'd be pursued and fined by the road safety authority, but I couldn't worry about that. With no traffic to obstruct my path, accompanied by blaring warning sirens the whole way, it was only a matter of minutes before the Colosseum complex came into view.

The ancient arena was surrounded by four circular towers that housed the great training schools of the empire, rising up like horns about the head of a massive beast. Mine was the biggest and the best, the northern tower where the best gladiators of the capital trained—the Ludus Magnus.

Swarms of people who were unable to get a seat were gathered out front watching huge holographic projections of the tryouts taking place inside. I came in over the crowd, passing through a giant hologram of fighting gladiators.

"There! Lupa She-Wolf! Accala!" The people below were calling out, pointing at me. "Take your place back, She-Wolf! Don't let them cheat you!"

Before I entered the arena for the first time, my trainer, Marcus, gave me the name Lupa She-Wolf—the noble Viridian lady turned savage fighter.

"I'd prefer Minerva—the bringer of justice," I told him.

"It'll be Lupa; it's more theatrical. Besides, you're named Accala for the she-wolf who suckled Romulus and Remus. It suits you."

This did not please me, but Marcus knew what he was doing—the name had made me a hit with gladiator fans.

The air was thick with black media spherae—floating cameras marked with each house's news station—and I had to navigate around them to land my chariot in a clear space behind the barricade to the athletes' entrance. The moment I hit the ground, it was like I'd kicked over an anthill. Swarms of fans pressed against the barricade, calling out for autographs, yelling support. Some Sertorians in the crowd hurled obscenities at me, but I'd heard much worse in my time in the arena. Buoyed up by the crowd's enthusiasm, I strode confidently into the Ludus Magnus. Having the audience on side meant everything to a gladiator.

An eight-foot Tullian barred my way. He'd undergone a treatment to make the skin cling to his bones, giving him the appearance of a human skeleton. I knew him by name—Charon Sextus. Underworld-themed names were popular. I stared up at him and growled, daring him to make the first move. When he didn't, I walked right at him, but he wasn't as stupid as he looked and stepped aside at the last moment. I was tempted to punish him for delaying me, but this man was a second-rater, not worthy of my anger.

I passed the statues of the Twelve that lined the athletes' entrance hall—the greatest gladiators of all time. Every competitor dreamed of approaching their score, the more delusional of actually winning enough matches and glory to find themselves included among that elite group. Caladus, Saturnilos, Scylax, Julius Ovidius, Orosius, Hermes, Toxaris, Varus, Cerberus, Gnaeus Arrius Diocles, Heracles, and Achillia—the only female grand champion. But immortal glory wasn't of interest to me. Justice, bloody and righteous, was my goal, and I would not be denied it.

III

A SEA OF COLOR and movement greeted me in the training hall—hundreds of costumed gladiators working out with every kind of traditional weapon—javelins, bows and arrows, spears, shields and gladii, daggers and clubs. Arms devised by conquered species that had, over millennia, been integrated into the Roman arsenal were also popular. Some of them were electrified, others radiating colored energy fields. Many purists used the arms in their ancient forms without any additional power enhancements. The only restriction was that they not fall into the category of advanced weapons—explosives or energy casters like ion pistols. The day board showed that more than six hundred gladiators had submitted their names for consideration in the trials, and the rounds had already been drawn by lot and scheduled. I had my work cut out for me.

I pushed my way through them, House Viridian's Golden Wolves, House Ovidian's Amber Boars, the Silver Sparrows of House Flavian, the Blue Bulls of the Tullians, the Black Ravens of the Calpurnians, the White Rams of the Arrians, and the Sertorians' Blood Hawks.

Even gladiators who didn't have a chance at being selected because they were part of a house who already had a full complement were in attendance, eager to see how the final rounds played out. They all looked impressive enough—feathers, jewels, precious metals, styled helmets and armor laid over the top of sweaty, oiled bodies. Some sported genetic modifications, a tactic used by gladiators of lesser standing to garner attention they couldn't get by way of skill in arms. Sharks' eyes, lions' manes, but gods, the smell. Even with the oil clogging their pores, there was no escaping the distasteful stink of too many male athletes in a confined space.

My first arena match had taken place without my father's permission or knowledge. I bribed a selector to pit me up against a respected Sertorian gladiator named Harpia. It was as close a match as any I'd fought since. The Sertorians were breaking arena records all over the place, but I managed to defeat her by crippling her right knee. As I stood over her, discus in hand, the crowd demanded that she be killed. The referee gave the thumbs-down but I couldn't do it. I hated the Sertorians, but that particular Sertorian hadn't wronged me. I turned and walked from the arena to a cavalcade of boos and jeers. My trainer, Marcus, was furious with me and whipped me with good cause—he'd risked a great deal in training a noble-born woman, and I'd assured him I had what it took to be the best. My father found out when the other senators started snickering during one of his orations. Shamed that his daughter had shunned her noble birth and submitted to the orders of a common lanista, he threatened to banish me from the family if I didn't quit at once. Calling his bluff, I told him that the only way I'd stop would be if he'd use his influence to have me conscripted to the legions so I could go and fight in the war. If he did try to banish me, I swore I'd get illegal gender reassignment surgery and join the legion anonymously. That bought me more time. I convinced my trainer to let me fight again and, once more, I stood over my defeated opponent and refused to deliver the deathblow. That brought more of a wave of confusion than outright hostility. The audience just didn't understand why I wouldn't go through with it, even though that's what they demanded. They were used to getting what they wanted. That should have been the end of my arena career, except word went around that I was a worshipper of Minerva and that I had shown the mercy of the goddess to my fallen opponents. I was not incapable of killing, but I chose not to, even though it broke with tradition and risked my advancement. I'd decided that I would save death for those that deserved it—the men responsible for the murder of my mother and brother—and to do that I had to work my way into the toughest league, the most challenging arena—the Ludi Romani, the emperor's great games. In the strange way popular opinion works, instead of ending my career, my display of mercy made me an overnight hit. After that Marcus didn't mind so much.

"You've found your own style and it works. You took a big risk and it paid off so I can't complain, at least for now. But watch out. There might come a time when you have to strike true and end a life. When that time comes, don't hesitate."

From my third match on, I loudly dedicated each victory to the memory of my murdered mother and brother, which fired up the Viridians in the audience and once even caused a riot. When my father objected a second time, this time to my riling up the mob, I argued that it was ludicrous that Romans could go to war and murder each other, send dozens of imperial worlds into starvation and poverty, but we were not allowed to be rude about it, or at least a woman wasn't. But father-daughter arguments seldom verge on the rational, and he seemed angry enough that he might really remove me from the arena, so I complied. It was a small sacrifice. After that, I simply raised my discus when I won a match, remaining silent. I instructed Bulla to sell my golden victory laurels and donate the money to wounded soldiers. This earned me a following, especially among the more influential women in my house, who argued that I boosted troop morale, and made it difficult for Father to remove me from the arena.

Marcus was at the other end of the hall, a sea of competitors between us. I waved my arm high in the air, and by some small miracle, he saw me. The crowd parted as he headed my way. A legion veteran and an ex-gladiator, Marcus owned a stake in the gym and was one of the most respected trainers in Rome.

"You're late," he said grimly.

"Father jammed my armilla. I came as soon as I could."

"Not soon enough. Darius has your place."

Darius was a sagittarius-style gladiator, a bow and arrow expert.

"I'm twice the long-range fighter Darius is. He can barely see a target at fifty yards, let alone hit it."

Marcus shrugged. "It is what it is. The tournament teams are complete bar four remaining vacancies."

"I count two. One on the Calpurnian team, one on the Flavian team."

"There are two Sertorian slots as well," he said. "One of those will be taken by Servius Tullius Lurco. He set a new record in the bestiarii matches by single-handedly killing ten Sauromatae."

His arena name was Lurco Giganticus and he was well known. Nine feet tall and all muscle, he wore a helmet with a death's-head faceplate. I'd seen him killing poison-spitting Equidae in the Ludus Silvaticus, one hoofed beast dead for every swing of his hammer. Lurco belonged to House Tullian, Sertorian allies. So the morning report I read was accurate, the Sertorians *were* drawing players from houses allied to them.

"That leaves one vacancy on the Talonite Axis," Marcus said. "You want to fight for the bad guys?"

"Don't even joke about it." Marcus had a dry sense of humor, and I wasn't in the mood for it. "Tell me how to fix this."

"I've already complained to the committee."

"What did they say?"

"That the rules are the rules. If your team leader scratches you, there's nothing they can do. They're making a big fuss over the fact that you haven't killed anyone in the arena."

"And you don't disagree. You know I'm up to this, Marcus. I can kill."

"You can't know a thing like that in advance. A moment's hesitation can cost you your life or that of your teammate. I told you not to show mercy in the ring and now look where it's got you."

"This is my father's doing, nothing more."

"Yes, but you've given him leverage by sparing your opponents. I could talk to Cossus Calpurnius Blaesus, but even if he agrees to let you join the Black Ravens, the committee would still vote against it. Your father has Spurius Viridius Silo in his pocket, and he's in charge of selection."

Silo Viridius had made an art out of creating difficulty where there was none. He was part of the old guard who saw the sport as theirs and theirs alone and constantly lectured the younger players. *Gladiators must be cautious, careful. You've never fought to the death, you don't know the meaning of this game.* The fact that I was young and a woman didn't work in my favor. "Silo hates me," I said.

"That he does."

How could Marcus give up this easily, after all the work he'd done to help me qualify? "If the committee won't listen, then I'm getting on the Calpurnian team," I said. "I'm better than three-quarters of their fighters as it stands. The Sertorians are fielding players from allied houses to fill their missing slots, so why not the Calpurnians? What's good for the goose is good for the gander."

"The rounds have already been drawn up," Marcus said.

"There must be something I can do," I said, forcing down the panic rising in my chest. "You sent a man to the compound, sent me all those messages. You wouldn't have risked Father's ire if there wasn't a chance."

Marcus shrugged again. "Perhaps Fate will weigh in on your side, perhaps not. Be calm, walk with me awhile, and let's see what unfolds."

Patience was the last thing I was interested in exercising, but Marcus had his way of doing things, and I'd learned from hard experience not to press him too soon. He led me down the underground tunnel that connected the gym to the most ancient and revered gladiatorial arena in the galaxy.

"Who's fighting now? Anyone interesting?" I asked.

"The emperor's cousin from Mars is in a bestiarii match. Only for show, of course, since the Numerians aren't fielding a team this year. He wants to go up against the barbarian Sauromatae, the same as his hero Lurco Giganticus."

The beast-hunting matches lacked the prestige of the gladiatorial arena—I never liked them.

"The emperor's cousin? Bucco Numerius?" I said.

"That's him. Authentic gear down to the last clasp."

"They'll eat him alive," I said.

"Ha, you're not wrong, except he's only going up against one lizard man and fully shielded at that. I'm sure the emperor will be squirming in his seat. His cousin's an embarrassment. Not worth his salt."

For Marcus, that was the worst insult he could give, reserved for undisciplined amateurs, the hopefuls who were not willing to make the sacrifices required to be the best.

We emerged into the bright lights of the arena. The stands were packed to bursting, the roar of the crowd deafening, like storm waves crashing against a seawall, matched only by the blaring musical accompaniment that lent a sound track to the arena drama—trumpets, horns powered by the strong lungs of row after row of Taurii trumpeters. There was even an organic pipe organ in a specially devised tank played by three water-breathing Aqua Marinians—green-and-blue-striped barbarians from Mare Byzantium. The old arena lacked the awe-inspiring immensity of the emperor's planet-circling Rota Fortuna or a

Sertorian city-hunter arena, but as I walked beside Marcus, I could feel a vibe, a palpable drama that saturated the air—an energy born of millennia of history mixed with blood and sand.

Marcus pointed to the royal balcony above us, draped in purple, with images of golden lions.

"The emperor," I whispered. Sitting behind a protective energy field up on his private balcony was Caesar Numerius Valentinius himself. Attendants rushed to and fro within the box, anticipating his every need. When Marcus spoke about the emperor being embarrassed by his cousin, I thought he meant that the emperor would be watching the match from some distant location, not be present in person, right here in Rome. This changed things. The emperor in the arena represented the last vestige of democracy in the empire. What the audience demanded, the emperor was likely to grant. Was this what Marcus wanted me to see? How could the emperor have any interest in helping me? I certainly wouldn't dare petition him. No one asked the emperor any favor lightly in case his judgment ran contrary to expectation. A man who crushed fleets of warships as easily as another might swat a bothersome fly wasn't someone to irritate needlessly.

Searching the various matches taking place in the center stage, I located the emperor's cousin by the glint of his gold armor, trident, and net swinging back and forth before his opponent.

"I feel bad that you have to watch this fool," Marcus said.

My trainer had something in mind but was clearly undecided on whether he was going to help me. I had to work out what was going on in his mind and tip the scales in my favor. What was he holding back?

* * *

I sought Marcus out a couple of months after the deaths of my loved ones, sitting on my own in the empty benches at dawn training, front row every morning, studying the fighters and taking notes, until after two weeks, Marcus' curiosity was piqued and he came over to speak to me.

"Can I help you, my lady?"

"Perhaps. I'm looking for someone that can show me how to use this," I said, opening my weapon case to reveal Orbis.

Marcus whistled in appreciation. "A homing discus. That's a lot of weapon for a little lady."

"It was good enough for Julius Ovidius. He won three Ludi Romani using one," I said.

"That was over four hundred years ago." Marcus reached forward to touch my weapon, but Orbis, sensing a stranger, began to rotate in his restraining gel. "It only likes your touch, hey?" He tried again and Orbis spun faster in anticipation. "This one doesn't like being constrained. He wants to cut me."

"I noticed that you don't have a discus player training here," I said.

"None have the patience to learn."

"Then you know how to use it?"

"I learned the fundamentals on Quatrus Negra. They duel to settle public disputes. Two people stand on opposing hills, each one wielding a discus. The first person to receive a mortal wound loses the dispute. It's a difficult weapon to master, but once you have a sense of it, it's the hardest to defend against."

"Then teach me. Let me join your team."

He smiled. "I don't have women fighting here. Do you see any women in my gym?"

"What have you got against women fighters?"

"You brought up Julius Ovidius, the last great discus fighter. He could throw his homing discus on a half-mile returning orbit. Those skinny arms of yours would be lucky to make a spirited throw of thirty yards."

"Most arena fighting is in close. Who cares how far the weapon can be thrown? Speed, flexibility, and agility make up for brute strength, and I've developed a new method of medium-range fighting focusing on spin and rebound."

"Really, I've got nothing against women in the arena. I've known some who could hold their own, one in particular who was astonishing, but everyone will compare you to Julius Ovidius, and you won't measure up. A discus fighter needs a strong arm, and powerful legs."

"I'm at the top of my class in military studies and close-quarter combat," I said. "I'll win many victories for your team."

Marcus closed the lid of the weapon case in a way that let me know the conversation was over. "Thank you for bringing this in. It's beautifully crafted and it's been a long time since I've seen one, but you should understand that it's not fit for a lady. It takes years of training to discipline both yourself and the discus, and trust me, no father wants to see his daughter cavorting in the arena. It's asking for trouble. You should find another way to upset him, one that doesn't put your life on the line. Or if it's self-defense you're after, then learn to fire a concealable ion pistol, or if you want take some combat courses, some of my students teach them after hours to make a little extra. There's even a class for high-born women."

He was already walking away, but I wasn't going to take no for an answer.

"Your spear fighter, Lenticulus. He drops his right elbow before he thrusts. It slows down his attack as well as telegraphing so his opponent can counter."

"You've got a good eye, I've been telling him about that," Marcus said. "But it doesn't mean you're cut out for the arena."

"You will train me. I command it."

He laughed out loud at that.

"When you become a gladiator, the moment you step into the arena, you are considered a slave. It is a public ritual. You must swear an oath to give up not only your titles but also your citizenship until you cease training under your lanista and leave fighting in the sacred arena for good. Do you understand? No matter who you were before you stepped in, in the arena there are only slaves. You make legal and potentially lethal submission to the games, the team, the trainer, the editor. It's the last even playing ground in the empire."

"There are plenty of nobles who fight in the arena and those rules are over-looked."

"None of them are women. Even the idea of ritual slavery would create a scandal. Go back to your fine chambers and pretty robes."

I flipped open my sling case, snatched up Orbis, and ran ahead to block his path. His face darkened. "You've got spirit, but it's the spirit of a spoiled princess who's used to getting her way. You had best move aside."

"The Sertorians killed my mother and my brother. A Viridian woman can't join the military, and I need to make them pay. Personally."

"I know you now," he said. "There was a news story all about you a few months back. You're Lucius Viridius' daughter. Your family was on Olympus Decimus when the bombs fell, and you've been hanging around the Senate bothering them in the hope they'll let you join the legion. Let me save you the trouble—petitioning the Senate is a lost cause. The Sertorians have more than half the Senate in their pockets."

"You think I haven't worked that out already? Why do you think I'm here? The men who killed my mother and brother fight in the Ludi Romani. I have to work my way to the top of the league if I'm to kill them."

"You want to fight in the Ludi Romani? You can't be serious."

"I need this. I was told you'd understand, that you'd lost someone unjustly and bore no love for House Sertorian."

His face hardened but didn't betray any emotion. "I don't teach beginners."

"I'm no beginner. Let me try out, you'll see."

"The Ludus Magnus is for serious athletes. If you're injured, you can't go running to papa and complain. When a gladiator swears the oath, it's with total commitment, there's no going back. How would that work? You an aristocrat and me a commoner? How could you take my orders? And even if you make the cut, the men won't make it easy for you."

"It doesn't matter. I won't stop."

"Won't stop until what?"

"Until I'm the best."

He didn't look impressed.

"I heard that you were the only trainer in the capital who heeded his own mind, that's why I came to you," I said. "Now I can see you're a coward, afraid of what the old men in the Senate will think of you."

He shrugged and turned to the gladiators running through their drills. "Lenticulus! There's a girl over here who says you're too slow with your spear."

"Come to my bed tonight," the man called to me, "and I'll show you a spear that will be more than enough to satisfy you."

"You'll have to suffer that kind of ill-mannered talk and much worse if you train here," Marcus said to me. "You see, this is hardly the place for a lady."

"If you can last a round against me, you can show me whatever you like," I yelled at the spearman. Striding past Marcus and stepping into the practice ring, I let Orbis fly. The spearman managed to deflect my first cast, but by then I'd closed the gap. I snatched my weapon out of the air and recast, and within twenty seconds, Lenticulus lay bleeding on the ground, both his hamstring and spear tip neatly severed.

"Not bad," Marcus said as the medic rushed to treat my injured opponent. "You're a left-hander; that will give you an advantage. Make it hard for your opponent to work out which way the discus will fly."

"You'll train me?"

"I've got to tell you, it will be a big pain in the ass having you on board, I'll never hear the end of it from the other owners, and these gladiators will complain about having a woman fighting, they're very superstitious. But you know what I like more than anything? Winning matches and earning the prize money. That means I can keep doing what I love. You worked over Lenticulus good and proper, and he's one of my best. You could be a winning horse. The odds in the gaming pool will be stacked against you from the outset, so I'll win some money betting on you when they put you up against second-raters, and if you survive long enough to get a few matches under your belt, the crowds will swarm to see a noble Viridian gladiatrix. Win and keep winning, and we'll get on just fine. You lose one match and you're out, even if the crowd spares your life. If you talk back to me or complain, you're out. If you're late for practice, you're out. Understand?"

I could barely contain my excitement. "I thank you."

"I'll have to teach you to control your weapon, teach it to retract its edge. We can't have you wounding my fighters in practice. The only question is, when the crowd makes their call, can you deliver the death sentence to a gladiator you've wounded?"

"I'm totally focused on my goal. Nothing will stand in my way."

"All right. Training starts at five A.M. tomorrow. And don't thank me—now is when we'll see who's the coward. Personally, I don't think you'll last a week."

"The art of the discus is all about anticipation and timing," Marcus said to me on my first training session. "Your weapon has a limited intelligence. It will always find the shortest path back to your hand, but you must help it. To use it effectively, you must know not where your opponent is but where he will be when the discus strikes. Remember, while you're waiting for the discus to return to your hand, you are unarmed. Sometimes your weapon will ricochet off an object or another opponent. Before you even cast the discus, you must have planned its course and anticipated your enemy's attack. To do that, you must know all of the other weapons, their strengths and weaknesses, you must study your opponent before each match, calculate all of the potential strategies and ranges, or your discus will make a laughingstock of you."

After the first week, Marcus permitted me to sign the gladiator's contract and swear the oath of the novice trio, solemnly promising that I would obey him and endure burning, flogging, and even death in order to learn his art. In turn, he officially accepted me into his school, becoming my lanista—my master and trainer.

I was placed on a diet of calcium-rich stalactite powders to strengthen my bones and prevent them breaking, and I practiced with the team every day, before and after school. My male cousins mocked me for playing a man's game, and my female relatives, whom I'd never bonded with due to their incessant prattling about fashion and matchmaking, made an extra effort to ostracize me, turning away to huddle and whisper if I passed them. They'd heard all sorts of gossip about me, most of it true.

Gladiators mixed with the undercurrents of society. I learned that very quickly. Thieves and criminals, disgraced soldiers, ex-prisoners—they were always hanging about the gyms. Instead of shunning them like any well-bred young lady should, I befriended the ones who supplemented their arena income by engaging in even less respectable activities. From those men, and even a few women, I learned the art of scaling walls and breaking codes, gaining access to sealed rooms, and combat techniques that were deadly to opponents in the arena and on the street.

During training time with Marcus, if I didn't get a move the first time, I'd keep at it until I'd mastered it or twisted an ankle, sprained a finger, burned or cut myself. If I fell from exhaustion, Marcus would push me onto my back with his boot. "Get up. You said you wanted to be the best, so get up. You don't get to be tired. No exhaustion, no giving up, no yielding. You want to fight because you're a natural, you like exercising your innate power, but I'm going to push you until you hate being here. Until each day you will wake up in pain and fear at the thought of coming here. Then, if you can stick it out, you'll come to a new place, beyond like and dislike, where you breathe battle, where the fighting mind saturates your every move. You must be the loosed arrow, no hesitation, a straight line between you and your target. Then, perhaps, one day you'll be counted a real gladiator."

No complaints, I never spoke back to him. He wasn't a cruel man, and I saw his gift for what it was—Marcus was the whetstone against which I sharpened myself until I could cut through anything that stood in my way.

The men would hit me with their wooden swords during practice, leaving egg-size bruises on my back, arms, legs, and breasts. They'd goad me, insult me, knock me unconscious, and I kept going until, one by one, they fell to my discus and I earned their respect. Except for Marcus. I could never beat him, nor could any of the others in the gym. I asked the other gladiators why he didn't give up being a lanista and enter the arena as a competitor. Even at his age he could have been a champion. They told me that although there was a rule that allowed the lanista of a gym automatic entry into any bout with any opponent (a rule originated to give impoverished trainers a chance to stave off bankruptcy and lure new students by displaying their skills), Marcus had refused every offer to fight for money since returning to Rome.

"Your suffering has given you divine fire," Marcus said at the end of my trial period. "You still don't have a firm grasp on your temper, but you're ready for the arena. Remember, let your tragedy fuel you, but be careful not to let the fire consume you. A thousand times more gladiators have died from overconfidence than have reached the Ludi Romani."

✳   ✳   ✳

I owed Marcus everything, and if he told me not to fight, I'd have to honor that, but turning our shared history over in my mind had done the trick. I'd worked out what he was holding back, and I knew I had to ask him for one last favor.

IV

The emperor's cousin issued a bloodcurdling scream as he unsuccessfully warded off the vicious attacks of a single scaled Sauromatae—six feet of teeth and claws, two legs and a balancing tail that allowed the barbarian to move in swift zigzag patterns. The warding field surrounding Bucco Numerius' armor took the brunt of the assault.

"Look at him carry on," Marcus said. "You think he'd lost an arm."

Just as it looked as if the emperor's cousin was going to be overwhelmed, referees with plasma brands accompanied by aides with attack dogs moved in to drive the lizard man back. The shining green transmission lights of the media spherae suddenly vanished; the Colosseum editor had ordered the match be brought to an end to spare the emperor embarrassment. Even though it was the editor's job not only to sculpt the events but also to protect the emperor's public reputation, I'd wager he never had a choice in Bucco Numerius' appearance. That would have been at the bold insistence of Bucco himself, the same man who filled the arena with his cries of fear and pain.

"A lot of noise for a handful of bruises, isn't that what you used to say to me when I started out? I've come a long way since then. I've earned my place in the team."

"You have."

"And as a lanista of one of the great schools, you have special privileges. You have the right to compete without waiting for the outcome of the draw. You have the right to insert yourself into any contest, even this one, and choose your opponent." I reached out and touched him on the arm. "Choose me, Marcus. Enter us in the next match."

He was old—I guessed he was in his forties. Fighting him would be the toughest match of my life, but I could take him. Arena teachers always keep some techniques back, and there was no way I'd learned everything Marcus had to teach. He was a walking encyclopedia of fighting methods, but I was young and I could ignore the bruises, aches, and pains from yesterday's match. My speed and flexibility would give me the edge.

He coughed and turned from me, pretending something in the stands had caught his attention, unwilling to meet my gaze.

"What?" I demanded.

"What if you do win and the crowd calls for my head? Could you even do it?"

"If I have to, but it won't come to that. I've got a reputation for sparing my opponent; they won't expect me to kill you."

"You've got away with that for a long time, but it won't wash today. If the emperor gives the thumbs-down, the deed has to be done. There's no refusing, no standing on pride or principles, not if you want to keep your head. Besides . . ."

"Besides what?"

"Nothing. Listen, it's not going to work."

"Besides what?"

"Besides, I would have to *let* you win, and even if the crowd decided to spare me, no man would come and train under me if I were publicly beaten by a woman. My career would be over."

His words were like a slap in the face. Marcus was probably right about his career and the stupidity of men, but that's not what hurt. It was that after years of training and camaraderie, he still saw me as a silly girl playing at war. It never occurred to him that I might beat him in the arena, let alone win the Ludi Romani itself. That's why he wouldn't back me.

"I hadn't thought of that," I said. "I'm sorry, please forget I said anything."

I owed Marcus everything. If he didn't want to do this thing for me, then I had to accept it. Not willing to disgrace myself with tears, I went to leave. The way back to the tunnel was blocked by a crush of people, and I couldn't pass. Some fans were mobbing one of the gladiators near the gate, creating a human roadblock. They were mostly pathetic young girls, fawning over some local hero. Pushing through them as I tried to pass, I caught sight of the object of their affection. It was Gaius Sertorius Crassus, champion gladiator when he wasn't serving as the Sertorian propaganda minister. He was one of the men I'd sworn to kill.

The sight of Crassus, surrounded by his followers, his place in the Ludi Romani secured thanks to his status and gender, stirred the fire inside. Once, when I was a girl, I'd overheard one of the house matriarchs at the Academy, a tutor of no small ability, discussing the rise of a lazy male teacher through the hierarchy. *He has a penis, Livia. What can you do? You know how it is—have a penis, get a promotion.* Anger boiled up inside of me. Two years of hard work and here I was, back at the beginning.

I quickly turned away before Crassus could see me and bumped right into Marcus, who was following behind me.

"You know him?" Marcus asked.

"By name only," I lied.

"So you should. He's the two-time champion of the Talonite arena. They say he's the best javelineer in the galaxy, a natural."

"I doubt that," I said, thinking back to the time when I had Crassus pinned up against the wall at the Academy, my discus at his throat.

"Look how he moves. He's a real gladiator, all right."

Marcus meant that Crassus was what I was not. Crassus had killed, fought to survive against the odds. Marcus respected him. When I tried to leave again, Crassus saw me and grinned. He offered a slight bow in my direction, and all the girls surrounding him looked my way to see who'd caught his eye. I pushed past Marcus, heading for a different exit. I'd never felt like such a fool, and I knew that if I didn't get out of there that second, I'd burst out in tears, or kill someone, or both.

"Hey, Accala. Where have you been? The early bird catches the worm, hey?"

My idiot cousin Darius walked toward me, the bow-and-arrow man who had been so quick and willing to snap up my spot. Marcus was his trainer as well, though he wasn't ranked nearly as highly as me. "Not another word," I warned.

"It's just as well," Darius said. "The Ludi Romani is no place for women. Gladi-atrix. Gladiatrices. Pfah!" He spat on the arena floor, right at my feet.

Gladiatrix. Darius, like most of the other male gladiators, used the feminine suffix to try to demean me. They didn't want to give me the respect that came with the title *gladiator.*

Marcus put a restraining hand on my shoulder just as I was about to take Darius' head off. "Don't be petty," Marcus said to Darius. "She's twice the fighter you are. Be grateful for the training I've given you and that you have a place in the coming tournament at all."

Darius didn't like that. "It's just common sense," he said to me. "Not only are women weaker than men, but it's a proven fact they have smaller brains and can't overcome their nurturing instinct when it comes to combat in . . ."

I tuned out. That was it. He was going down. But before I could strike, Mar-cus stepped in front of me and hit Darius square on the jaw, sending him flying back into the benches. He stayed there, knocked out cold.

"Why come to my defense?" I said, rounding on Marcus accusingly. "What he said is little different from what you said to me."

Before Marcus could reply, someone behind me said, "Accala. What a plea-sure it is to see you again. Still caught up in the thick of things, I see."

Crassus! I spun about and threw a punch, but the Sertorian easily caught it in midair.

"You should cultivate more of an air of dispassion," he said mildly. "You tele-graph your intentions when you're angry."

It was not only his speed that caught me by surprise. Crassus was bigger than when I'd last seen him. A chiseled jaw, strong blue eyes, sharp cheekbones; his features had matured to take on an aura of strength and beauty, the result, no doubt, of Sertorian genetic streamlining. Despite my irritation I had to admit that he was strikingly handsome.

"I've got nothing to say to you," I said, pulling my hand free.

"Come," Crassus said. "There's an armistice. We're not at war right now. We can agree to be civilized."

"Your idea of civilization is House Sertorian with its foot on the throat of the empire and the members of the other houses reduced to slaves. There's not a single thing we can agree on."

"Things are always so simple with you, black and white. I prefer to see the galaxy in shades of gray. It suits the complexity of the Sertorian mind. You know,

I admire you Viridians; in a way you're the house closest to our own. Viridians always talk of self-reliance, but you don't apply the principle to its ultimate end and eliminate the weak and the poor. You allow yourselves to be bridled by tradition and ethics."

"I won't be lectured on ethics by a member of a house that has none."

"You know that however distasteful you may claim to find our enlightened cultural perspective, Accala, we do not discriminate against women. Gaia Sertorius Barbata, the net fighter, is an equal member of the Blood Hawks, as is the trapper Mania Sertorius Curia. Look at your Caninine Alliance teams. Viridians, Calpurnians, and Flavians, and not one woman among them. If you want progressive thinking, you must look to the Talonite teams, especially my Blood Hawks."

"If there wasn't an armistice, I'd happily castrate you with my discus," I said. "Then you could stand proudly side by side with your sister fighters."

I went to move past him, but he grabbed my upper arm. "In fact, I have not come here simply to exchange pleasantries. There was something I wanted to say to you, in private if I may."

"There's not a thing in the universe I'd like to do with you in private."

Marcus stepped closer, locking eyes with Crassus. "You heard her now. Fly away, little bird."

Crassus looked at Marcus like he'd just stepped in something distasteful. "A little young for you, isn't she?" When Marcus didn't back away, Crassus smiled slightly and continued. "You're old enough to be her father and with plebeian dirt beneath your fingernails to boot." He made a little *tsk tsk* noise to reprimand Marcus and remind him of his place.

Now it was my turn to step in. I couldn't care less if Marcus struck my cousin Darius; Marcus was his lanista and able to punish him at will. But if Marcus struck a nobleman he wasn't training, especially during the armistice, then the Praetorian Guard that he'd once belonged to would execute him.

Crassus smiled and looked right past Marcus as if he didn't exist, returning his attentions to me. "It's a shame you're not competing. I'd have very much liked to be there when you had to finally finish an opponent. Losing your arena virginity, all caked in blood and guts. You'd have looked resplendent in red." He gave a slight bow and then briskly strode away. Crassus was the type of upper-class Sertorian who made a big deal out of manners and gentlemanly behavior, at least what passed for that on Sertorius Primus, right up until you got in the way of what he wanted.

"You said you didn't know him," Marcus said after Crassus was gone.

"We were in the same year at the Academy. I haven't seen him for a long time. Besides, you saw him. Who would want to admit knowing a creature like that?"

"He's one of the Sertorians you've sworn to kill," Marcus stated. It was an astute guess, as I'd never told anyone the names of any of the men on my list.

"You can tell?"

"I saw how you looked at him. It was either love or hate."

"How dare you make a joke of this," I snapped. "You think I couldn't take you in the arena? You think you'd have to roll over for me? I think you're old and frightened."

He looked me over. I'd seen that expression before. He was assessing me, considering my ability.

"I know what it's like to hate someone so much it burns like acid in your mouth, and it's not the way. Revenge will lend you wings, but they will carry you only so far before they fail. If you seek justice, then you might just survive. It's an important distinction, Accala."

"I do seek justice, I swear it in Minerva's name."

"Well, you can say it, but the doing is not always so easy. All right, then. Go and get changed. You'll get your shot."

I was stunned. Marcus was so decisive. He never changed his mind.

"Why?"

"What do you care?"

"It matters."

"You want to know why I changed my mind? It was that trumped-up Sertorian turkey. You know what? That pompous ass was right. It's not that they think you can't kill if you have to. They're not letting you fight because you're a woman, and the stakes for the coming games are too high for the Caninine teams to be risking victory over a penis or lack thereof. You say you've got what it takes, well now's your chance to put your money where your mouth is."

"I thank you, but what about the committee?"

The six stone-faced judges for the Galactic Committee for Combative Sports—withered and intractable ex-gladiators, soldiers, and senators—there wasn't an ounce of fondness for me among the lot of them.

"Leave them to me."

"And you'll list me as trying out for the Calpurnian team? What about the team leader? Will he take me on if I win?"

"Cossus Calpurnius Blaesus? I spoke with him this morning. You should have heard him cursing the Golden Wolves for being stupid enough to cut you. Don't worry, it won't take much to twist his arm. He'll take you on if you win and, more, he'll expect you to win the tournament for House Calpurnian."

"I'll win him the moon and the stars if he'll give me a shot at the Sertorians," I said.

"Don't get cocky. We've clashed in practice many times, and you've never bested me yet. I won't roll over for you out there. Stay focused. When we fight it'll be for real."

He said it so dismissively, like life and death were nothing to him.

And it was true precisely because of what Marcus had said—the stakes were indeed high. Faced with the problem of resolving a civil war without destroying the empire, Caesar Numerius Valentinius had conceived the idea of using the Games of Jupiter to decide the winner. Over fifteen days on the emperor's chosen arena world, the strongest fighters of the great houses would compete in

chariot races, beast hunts, and gladiatorial combat spread out over a lethal obstacle course set to test the mettle of the bravest Roman. The teams would be
arranged to represent, in small scale, the makeup of the two sides as they stood
in the civil conflict, the Sertorian Blood Hawks and their allied houses versus
the Viridian Golden Wolves and theirs. The team that won in the arena won the
whole ball of wax—victory in the war, ownership of the contested ice world, continued membership in the Council of Great Houses—everything. The losing
house would be outcast, decimated and banished to the galactic frontier, stripped
of influence and resources so as to never again disturb the Pax Romana, the
emperor's peace. There was, and never had been, a greater prize to be won in the
arena. For me it meant not only a chance to kill the Sertorians responsible for
the deaths of my loved ones, but the added bonus of bringing down their entire
house, cutting it out of Roman life root and branch.

* * *

THE CHANGE ROOMS STANK of blood and sweat. Nervously excited hopefuls
prepared for matches, while the defeated, including those wounded by my cousin
Darius and the Sertorian hammer fighter Lurco, were being treated by physicians.

When I first heard the emperor's announcement that the games would decide
the fate of the empire I was elated. It seemed like divine providence. I'd already
built up enough points in the arena to qualify for the Golden Wolves and turned
all my efforts to getting on the team. A one-off opportunity for me to right the
wrongs visited against me by right of arms.

I unslung my weapon case and removed my armilla and stola. My costume
went over the top of my base-layer fighting outfit, that of a provocator, a legionary
soldier's armor with the minimum of weight—golden breastplate, dark green
leather gloves and boots, a manica that ran from the wrist to the shoulder of my
discus-wielding arm, and a helmet capped with two feathers, one on either side,
to symbolize swiftness. As I was a woman and therefore forbidden to fight as a
soldier, I'd decided to dress as one in the arena. Less armor and more mobility
allowed me to focus on a strong offense, and in green and gold, there was no one
watching who could doubt that I was a fighting Viridian. Then came the band of
five short tassels tucked into my bracers.

More than fifty victories to my name, but I fell short of being awarded the sixth
tassel, indicating the highest grade of gladiator—primus paulus—because none
of my fellow gladiators had died at my hands in the arena. When there were
enough bloody victories to my name, the committee would be forced to grant
me a sixth. I tied my hair back tight. No hair in my face, nothing that might
give Marcus the edge.

My instructors at the Academy had taught me that if I knew the enemy and
knew myself, then I'd never be defeated. What did I really know about Marcus?
He was a plebeian member of House Calpurnian, an ally of my own house
and therefore an enemy of House Sertorian. What I knew about Marcus I had
pieced together from the stories other gladiators told and historical records I'd

accessed via the vox populi. He never spoke about his past to me or, as far as I knew, to anyone else.

Marcus had lied about his age and joined the legion at fifteen, fighting on a dozen barbarian worlds between Mother Earth and the imperial frontier. There was even a rumor he'd spent a year in a Sertorian hard labor camp on suspicion of espionage. By the time he was in his thirties, he had more medals than you could pin on his chest, had attained the rank of centurion, and was assigned to the Praetorian Guard, which would ordinarily be a high honor and an easy commission, except he found himself close to the emperor Julius Heliogabalus in his final years, when the old man was at his most unstable and unpredictable.

It so happened that the emperor had seen Amphiara Calpurnius Merga (reputedly the most beautiful woman in Mare Byzantium province and a skilled huntress to boot) display her skills in marksmanship, and he developed a hankering to add her to his collection of consorts in the imperial palace. The only problem—Amphiara was the favorite daughter of Mare Byzantium's proconsul Caius Calpurnius Oceanus, who had spoken out repeatedly against the emperor's excesses and was willing to set his whole province on a war footing if old Julius Heliogabalus tried to take her by force. Oceanus figured the emperor couldn't afford a war, not with the coffers of the treasury being plundered to create the largest series of memorial busts known to human history, and he was right. So the emperor decided to send in one man, Marcus, in place of a fleet. The emperor's thinking was that since Marcus was a fellow Calpurnian, he'd know how to convince Oceanus to part with his daughter with a minimum of fuss.

When he arrived in Mare Byzantium, Marcus explained his predicament to Oceanus. He understood the man would not part with his daughter, but if Marcus returned without her, he would have failed the emperor—he would lose all honor and be tortured and executed before his own men. At the same time, Marcus assured him that he would personally guarantee Amphiara's safety and that although she would have to serve the emperor at his whim, he would not permit her to be beaten or physically harmed.

When Oceanus was unmoved, Marcus added that the very next thing the emperor would do after ordering Marcus' death would be to put the terrasculpting project on hold, divert funds to the Praetorian fleet, and take Mare Byzantium by force, killing one in every ten members of the local nobility in a good old-fashioned decimation, ensuring Oceanus' name was at the top of the list. Oceanus had to agree, but he couldn't be seen to be backing down in front of his local court without a fight and so he made Marcus an offer.

No one had ever survived the obstacle course in Mare Byzantium's famous aquatic arena. If Marcus could make it through to the end, defeating every beast and gladiator, then he would be granted the rudis, the wooden sword of freedom, after which he could make a single request of Oceanus, anything he liked, including possession of Amphiara. Marcus turned out to be a natural gladiator; his years of combat experience, instinctive quick thinking, and a dose of good luck ensured his triumph. Oceanus, unsatisfied, made Marcus fight again and again until Amphiara, admiring Marcus' courage as well as wishing to spare her people, convinced her father to let him take her. On the return journey the pair fell in love, and although she obeyed the emperor, the old man saw how Marcus and Amphiara looked at one another and took to beating her to expose Marcus' feelings. A man of honor to the last, Marcus remembered the oath that he would protect Amphiara and reminded the emperor of the deal made in his name, warning him to stop. The emperor, displeased at being lectured, ordered Marcus killed, and the man had to slay his own commander and ten fellow Praetorians before leveling his sword at the emperor's throat in warning, though his own vow to protect the emperor prevented him from carrying out an execution.

The emperor had the pair of them thrown into the Ludi Romani—that year's being a re-creation of the slave uprising and subsequent massacre of Illyricum Novinus—with the intention that they should die terribly, hunted down and humiliated before the whole empire. Against near-impossible odds, Marcus and Amphiara succeeded in surviving the gladiatorial teams by mobilizing the six-legged Hexapoda, a highly intelligent insect species, each one the size of a ten-year-old human child, into an effective fighting force. Amphiara hit upon the idea of using smoke to disrupt the spread of a naturally produced fear pheromone that had caused the alien uprising to fail in the first place. The ploy worked, but only because Amphiara sacrificed her life to buy Marcus the time he needed to set a forest alight. The image of him, triumphant and howling with grief as he cradled her body, the untouchable winner of the tournament, was transmitted across the empire. Marcus' fate led to a mass outcry. The houses opposed to Julius Heliogabalus, including my own, used the tragedy of Marcus and Amphiara as a rallying point and led the charge to overthrow the Julians.

Refusing all honors and a generous commission to join up for another twenty years, Marcus completed the last few months of his military service under the Numerian emperor before being discharged with the rank of centurion, dozens of medals, and the standard retirement offering of an allotment of land on the galactic frontier. He traveled the many gladiatorial arenas of the galaxy, competing in some but mostly studying different fighting styles. On returning to Mother Earth, he sold his land and purchased a share in the Ludus Magnus. Why, after all of the grief he had experienced by way of the arena, he should choose it as a new career, no one could say.

He had a will of iron and was an experienced killer. When it came down to it, could I defeat him? If I hesitated for even an instant, he could turn the tables and steal my life.

My armilla slotted into the right bracer, becoming part of my armor. Finally, I snapped open my weapon case, revealing Orbis. My near-unbreakable discus, his razor-sharp edge rotated within a circular moat of black restraining gel—a mercurial silver eye, slowly turning, impatient for speed and action.

Orbis was a rare thing. A slender ring one and a half inches high near the center, tapering out to a thin edge. Forged from the semisentient mineral lapis negra, he was sharper and harder than steel and light as a feather. About the body of the circular blade were four thin grooves, evenly spaced to improve aerodynamics and also produce a frightening hum as he took flight.

After my father's legion had crushed an uprising of the barbarian Mandubii of Quatrus Negra, their chieftain had given him the homing discus as tribute. Orbis had been fashioned by the first Roman settlers there during the seventh republic, more than two thousand years prior. Father could have sold it to a museum or collector for a small fortune, but he wanted to save the discus for my brother, Aulus, a rare weapon to enjoy when he became a man. Mother convinced him to let me have it, though. "You never objected to me continuing my research and no bad luck has come of it. Trust me, I know how to help Accala find her path," she counseled, and he accepted her wisdom, as he always did, though not without complaint, and all through my childhood I had the memory of my father bemoaning his misfortune, how the boy in the family took after his mother while the girl was feisty, argumentative, always turning household objects into weapons. Mother was a pacifist and philosopher, but she knew that Aulus didn't have a fighting bone in his body, he was a natural scholar. On the other hand, she knew intuitively that Orbis was meant for me.

I picked up Orbis gently, and he blunted his edge to accommodate me as he always did, whether I was gripping him for close combat cutting and thrusting, or snatching him from the air as he returned to me after a cast. The homing discus was temperamental, difficult to wield, but after years of hard work my weapon and I had achieved a symbiosis of sorts, where Orbis could sense my position and work with my body, enhancing my combat strengths. He was eager to be free, created to cut through the air in deadly, sweeping arcs, not to be constrained in a box. "There, be still," I said in a soothing voice. "Soon you'll have your chance to fly."

*   *   *

I STARTED LIMBERING UP but soon found I was too impatient to work through all my exercises. Where was Marcus? The longer he took, the more chance there was that Father would receive word that I'd fled the Wolf's Den and seek me out, and he wouldn't be easy to deal with. The loss of Mother and Aulus changed him, and the war that followed had only made things worse. He had become overly cautious, paranoid, and easily angered. He drank too much and didn't sleep well. Most of his waking hours were spent at the Senate dealing with matters of war and the affairs of the empire, trying to keep House Viridian from collapsing like a house of cards under the strength of the Sertorian advance. He'd managed me at a distance through Bulla and the other household staff. Perhaps because I shared too many of my mother's features, I reminded him of what he'd lost. In his heart, I was certain, he wished I'd gone on the trip to Olympus Decimus in place of my brother. Then he would have a son to follow in his footsteps, a real warrior instead of a daughter who knew only how to shame him.

My thoughts were wandering into dark places. Already, I was ignoring Marcus' advice to focus on the present, but every moment my lanista failed to appear, I felt less self-assured, less capable, and then, just when I thought he would never come and that I was abandoned, he returned.

"We're on," he said with no more drama than if he were ordering some food off a street vendor.

Now I saw what had taken him so long. He'd stopped to get changed into his own costume.

Marcus was dressed as a murmillo. His helmet was crested with a stylized fish, and he also wore a manica and light armor, black streaked with patterns of silver designed as an abstract representation of a bird's wings. His weapons were those of a soldier, the tower shield (that would be projected from his armilla) and a short twenty-five-inch gladius. Marcus took the only traditional weapons that were part of a legionary's basic equipment and turned them into an artwork of attack and defense.

"The committee's on board?" I asked.

"I had to assure them a real blood match," he said.

"So whoever wins, if the crowd turns against the loser . . ."

"The Colosseum sand will soak up the blood," Marcus said, "as it has for millennia."

"I'm ready."

As we headed back into the arena, we passed the emperor's cousin being carried out on a stretcher, bruised and bleeding.

The crowd chattered loudly in anticipation of our match. The She-Wolf fighting to regain her place and against her own trainer.

V

WE STEPPED INTO THE bright light of center stage. A separate spotlight illuminated the announcer.

"Next up, Accala Viridius Camilla—Lupa She-Wolf—and Ludus Magnus' Marcus Calpurnius Regulus—The Regulator—who is making use of his trainer badge to enter the contest. Lupa is competing for a place on the Calpurnian team!"

The crowd howled with excitement, chanting Marcus' fighting nickname again and again. My reputation was solid, but Marcus' was solid gold. Here was a living legend reentering the arena after refusing to fight for so long.

The arena floor could be reconfigured in thousands of ways by the game editor to cater to the competitors' strengths and weaknesses. For Marcus and me, they'd arranged three floating platforms, each level higher than the other, with stairs running between them. On each platform were half-a-dozen translucent high-wall formations, each in the shape of an equal-armed cross, providing corners that would give Marcus the advantage if he could manage to maneuver me into them. There were also an equal number of metallic posts that I could use to ricochet my discus off of as well as position myself behind to keep Marcus at optimal range.

The media spherae swung in lazy arcs above us, green eyes glowing, capturing every moment, every word. How many citizens were watching? A surprise match like this could summon an empirewide flash audience, and when there was a buzz on the vox populi, who knew who many would tune in? The referee called us to take up our positions center stage. The crowd grew silent.

"Show me that I haven't wasted my time on you," Marcus said.

My heart raced. Everything rested on this. I offered a silent prayer to Minerva. We donned our helmets, saluted one another, and then turned to salute the emperor.

From down on the arena floor, the galaxy's most powerful man seemed a long way off, but the moment he stood, the glass enclosing his private balcony magnified his image imposingly. As he was in attendance, we were bound to follow tradition and make the ancient call. We raised our weapons and together called out, *We who are about to die salute you.*

Emperor Numerius raised his hand to return the salute. I'd heard that some people had a strong reaction to being in the presence of the emperor, but I was determined to keep a level head. Except the hand holding my discus was trembling and my heart rate was going through the roof. Deep breath, focus on the match. The slightest tremor could affect Orbis' path and give Marcus the advantage.

Marcus adopted his fighting stance and activated his shield. It was the energy projection of a full-length tower shield, tinted bronze and translucent, so he could see his opponent through it. It covered him head to toe; its shimmering surface featured a classical spiral styling that the Calpurnians favored to remind everyone of their ancient Gaulish origins. My armilla was just as capable of generating a shield as any other, but it generally didn't suit my style of play and got in the way of casting and retrieving my discus, so I tended not to use it.

The audience buzzed with excitement, eager for the no-holds-barred blood match to begin, and to have their say in its outcome.

We faced off, the referee between us, hand raised and ready to signal the start of the fight. Marcus' sword and my discus, deadly line and circle ready to clash. A tingling sensation passed across the skin of my palm as Orbis absorbed the sweat, improving my grip. This was just another opponent. Not my teacher, not a man I admired, not a fight for my life. Just another match. At the exact moment the referee cut down with his hand and stepped back, the image of my mother embracing Aulus as the flames burned them to cinders flashed into my mind. Then he yelled, "Fight!"

I took Marcus at his word, no quarter, and threw my discus right at him, forcing him to take cover behind his shield. Marcus had always taught me to simultaneously play to my strengths while denying the opponent the opportunity to bring his to bear.

Marcus surprised me by retreating, jumping up to the first platform and then heading up the stairs toward the second, challenging me to follow. He wanted to take the fight to the cross-shaped structures on the higher platform where there was less room to move. My best strategy would be to hold my ground, to wait him out, but I started after him at once. I couldn't just stand around. A good arena match had to burn from the first clash and build in intensity. If I wanted to keep the audience on side, I had to keep up the pressure on my opponent, and if Marcus reached the second level as I tried to climb to the first, he'd have the high ground and could pin me down with his shield.

As soon as my boots hit the second platform, he turned and charged. I cast Orbis to try to slow his advance, but he batted the discus aside at the last second, angling it away behind him so Orbis would take longer to return to my hand. I was exposed and unarmed. Marcus had closed the range between us to five feet by the time my weapon returned. I threw a new kind of cast I'd been practicing—a spin shot. As Marcus went to ward the discus away, Orbis nicked the edge of the tower shield and then spun about the shield's edge, hitting Marcus' shoulder guard. The force knocked my lanista off balance, sending him back onto one knee. Orbis returned, and I threw again at once, right past Marcus. Orbis struck a post and rebounded toward my opponent, forcing Marcus to turn away from me to defend. Rushing forward, I closed the gap and launched a high side kick at Marcus' head. He turned to block my foot with his shield just in time, but my kick had all my body weight behind it and the impact still sent him flying. He landed hard on his back, arms flying wide in a ready-to-be-beaten position.

I regathered Orbis as I fell onto him. Too late I saw it was a trap. As I landed on top of his shield, he turned and sent me falling down over the edge to the first platform. Now it was my turn to land on my back, except I wasn't pretending. It was a six-foot fall, and the impact knocked the wind out of me, leaving me gasping for air like a fish on dry land as Marcus leaped after me, the point of his sword aimed at my chest. I rolled aside at the last moment and jumped to my feet, only to find myself trapped right in the corner of one of the transparent cross-shaped walls. Marcus was fighting two steps ahead of me. He pressed me into the corner with his shield, and a blossom of pain erupted in my side as his gladius made rapid-fire thrusts at my torso. Somehow I managed to raise Orbis, using him to ward the short sword aside, buying me a vital second so I could turn my way out of the corner.

Marcus tracked me as I backed away, turning right into me with his shield, herding me toward the next nearest cross. The gladius wound wasn't deep, but as the blood trickled down the plates of my armor and ran over the platform edge to the arena floor below, the crowd went wild. My blood was the first to touch the ancient sands.

Quickly surveying the field, I could see only one chance to take down Marcus. The distance was perfect, the alignment of posts ideal, but to work, the technique required a successful return orbit of seventy-five yards, more than I'd ever thrown before. My shoulder charge hit Marcus square in the chest, forcing him back as I launched a follow-up kick to his shield and then cast Orbis wide and far. My discus hummed with power as it skimmed the curved edge of the ancient arena, drawing calls of surprise and fright from the audience as Orbis passed only inches away from them. Seeing I was weaponless, Marcus advanced. Nine seconds, that's how long I had to hold my own against him before Orbis returned. Would my risk pay off? From his menu of assaults, Marcus chose a series of lightning thrusts with his gladius close to the edge of his shield. Three more strikes hit home before I could get my body out of the way of his blade and seize the edges of his energy shield with both hands.

Throwing myself backward, I pulled his shield and him behind it down on top of me. Another short thrust into my belly, another shallow wound, before I could reach past his shield and loop my arms around his, locking them down, grabbing him to me in a tight clinch. His breathing was fast and short. Five seconds to go. He stopped pulling, tapped his armilla, and the energy shield vanished. He fell right on top of me, leading with a sharp and sudden head butt. My right cheekbone screamed in pain as he broke it, but I pulled him closer, squeezing him tight, as he tried to pull away. He was strong, but I had to hold him down. Three seconds. Two. There. I released him, and he pulled up and away sharply just as Orbis returned and struck him square between his armored shoulder blades, throwing him forward once more. Rolling with the momentum, I flipped him over the top of me. The technique was less graceful than I'd planned, and he went flying overhead, landing three feet behind me. By the time I found my feet and gathered up Orbis, Marcus was up and ready, shield reactivated, eyeing me warily.

There were eighty thousand people crammed into the Colosseum, but somehow, out of the corner of my eye, I managed to spot Gaius Sertorius Crassus. He was the only person in his section standing up. Arms crossed, he stood staring right at me. It was only a split-second distraction but one that I couldn't afford. Looking back at Marcus, I saw he'd followed my gaze and spotted Crassus too. He regarded me with disdain, utter contempt. He'd risked a great deal to give me the chance to fight for a place in the Ludi Romani, and I'd just insulted him, letting my attention wander like a rank amateur.

Marcus hit me with a quick thrust to the shoulder. My armor took the brunt of it, but it still hurt like Hades. I tried to back away, but he stuck to my every move, advancing aggressively. The way he held his body, his whole style of movement was suddenly different. This wasn't the cool, collected fighter I'd faced in training. I'd triggered some deep rage and unlocked a different man—the frontline veteran soldier, the gladiator of the old school who showed no mercy. He struck like lightning, an arcing cut that edged between the plates of my left arm, slashing my shoulder open, and then followed up with a thrust at my heart. I barely got Orbis up in time to ward it away.

Fear hit me unexpectedly. Marcus was out to kill me. The Colosseum's audience fell deathly silent. They saw it too, my death only seconds away. Another thrust at my face, but I managed to ward again.

Marcus was not helping me get on a team, he was doing his best to stop me. From deep inside, the fire flared up, my anger rising to match his, burning the fear away. The committee, my father, and now Marcus—all these men were determined to be rid of me. What better an example to other women not to ruffle the feathers of tradition than Accala Viridius Camilla, a senator's degenerate daughter, dead and bleeding like a stuck pig on the arena floor? And at her own lanista's hand, no less. If I was going to die, then it wouldn't be like this, humiliated and chastised before the empire. A liquid heat infused my limbs, my eyes burned like hot coals. Screaming, I charged Marcus' shield, raining down cut after cut in sweeping arcs, forcing him back.

He warded every blow without effort and then pushed up with his shield. I knew what would come next—a low thrust up between my ribs and into my heart— the killing blow. As the thrust came, I hooked the tip of his sword with the inner ring of my discus and turned, trapping the sword against my armored glove, locking it in place as I drove my right shoulder into his shield, stopping his advance in its tracks.

Before he could recover his footing, I released the sword and jumped high, coming down over the top of his shield, using Orbis to hit the top of his helmet with every ounce of strength, momentum, and body weight I could bring to bear. The blow cleaved the helmet, splitting it in half before continuing down, cutting his face.

Marcus stepped back, managing to raise his shield. He was bracing up, expecting me to launch a frontal assault. Instead I fell to the ground, dropping sideways and throwing my right leg under his shield, sweeping his out from under him. As he crashed to the ground, I rolled up and pounced on him, mounting his chest as I pressed the edge of my discus against his throat, all my body weight pressing down. A line of blood formed where Orbis touched his neck and trickled slowly down. Any movement on his part, even a strike that would render me unconscious, would see my weight drop onto the blade and steal his life.

"Is this what you seek?" I yelled at him. "The fate you intended for me?"

"It's the crowd's call now," he croaked. "Listen."

They were chanting, but it was so loud I couldn't make out what they were saying. Did they demand Marcus' death? Gods, they did. "Death" they chanted again and again.

"No hesitation," he ordered. "Don't disgrace our profession. Swear it," he said, staring hard into my eyes.

My throat was dry, my heart pounding, my reply barely audible. "Yes."

But there was only one man who could deliver the verdict. I looked to the emperor's box on high. He sat silently, listening to the will of the crowd, not just those in the Colosseum but the greater audience that looked on via the vox populi. The air above the arena was filled with the holographic projections of flying thumbs, some turned up, some turned down, each one representing the combined will of a billion viewers. And there were a lot of thumbs. We must have had five trillion watching us, more than I'd ever seen for a qualifying round.

Enough to rival the audience of the Ludi Romani itself! Marcus and I were a palpable hit.

A loud chime signaled the end of the voting period, and the tallies appeared above the emperor's box. The audience had voted that Marcus should die at my hand. Then the emperor extended his fist, the telescoping glass that shielded his box magnifying it so the whole arena could see the verdict.

Up. The thumb was up! "Marcus Calpurnius Regulus fought bravely. He deserves life." The emperor had ignored the crowd and spared Marcus as was his prerogative. A sigh of relief escaped my lips as I pulled Orbis away. The siren signaled the end of the match, and the referee used his shock stick to indicate that I should climb off Marcus and move away. "That's it. Lower your weapons and separate."

The thin cut I left as a souvenir on Marcus' throat ran perfectly straight. Normally I would have wounded only his Adam's apple, but lying on his back had pushed the flesh of his throat up to make a nice, even platform. Complementing it was a neat gash running from forehead to chin. Dark blood seeped from it and ran down either side of his nose.

"Good," he said matter-of-factly as he sat up. "A spirited bout. I expected nothing less."

Good? Blood ran down my arm and legs, wounds in my abdomen and side ached with each panting breath, my heart was still racing, and my shoulder was burning in pain. I'd thought I was going to die. Or kill Marcus. Or both. And here he was chatting like we were walking through the marketplace on a Sunday afternoon.

"When I fought before I always knew I'd come out on top but with you it was . . . terrifying, exhilarating all at once."

"That's because the arena is pure, a sacred space. The true empire is all dog eat dog, all the rest is a pretty lie designed to keep the status quo," he said. "In the arena though, you never forget the truth, you're never lulled into thinking for a second that things might be any other way. But not everyone's up to facing the truth.

"Your rage burns within your breast, but I had to know if that heat could be focused and transformed into a point of light. I wanted to see if you could shine. Better to die an honorable death here before the emperor than disgrace yourself and your house in the Ludi Romani."

"And?"

"Shine you did. Like a diamond. You've been tested for true."

What if the emperor's thumb had turned the other way? Could I have gone through with the verdict?

Marcus held out a hand, pulling me up to my knees as the medics rushed in and started applying their steroid poultices and antibiotic shots to seal our wounds, reknit our bones, and accelerate the healing factor of our bodies.

"Sorry about your face," I said, resisting the urge to reach out and touch his nose.

"I've had worse. You're a proper gladiator now. Remember that when you're fighting in the tournament."

"Truly?" It seemed so unreal that I could hardly believe that I'd actually done it.

"Truly," he said. "I don't think getting on the tournament's going to be a problem. Listen."

The audience were up on their feet, roaring their approval. In an excited frenzy, they chanted as one: *Daughter of Minerva! Handmaiden of justice!*

"They're calling for the goddess," I said. There was a sea of hands stretching out, trying to push through the protective barrier to touch me. There was a desperate, hungry quality to the sea of faces, like some mindless organism that wanted to eat me whole.

"They're calling to you," he said. "They're comparing you to her. You're a hit. Just let those old gasbags on the committee try to stop you now."

I needed to thank him, but the right words wouldn't come, just an overwhelming sense of gratitude. Before I knew it I was hugging him. He pulled away, slightly embarrassed (and I think, by accident, I managed to hit his nose after all because he winced in pain). I wasn't thinking of the emperor anymore or the crowd or the tournament. This was all about the art of the arena, about defeating the toughest opponent I'd ever faced.

"But you and the gym . . ." I said to Marcus.

"After that match, I don't think there's a man in the empire who would think me weak for losing to Minerva's warrior-maiden. You're ready, Accala. You're a force of nature."

Don't disgrace our profession. That's what Marcus had said. *Our profession.* For the first time I felt like a real gladiator. Not only a woman seeking justice, but someone who had earned her stripes and her place in the arena.

"I can't believe it," I said. "I need to see."

Anxiously, I checked the lists on my armilla to see if I'd been added to the Calpurnian team, but there was no change. The referee should have entered the result. I looked to the man and asked him for the result, but he was shaking his head. What was the problem?

"Accala." Marcus pointed to the committee table, where a flock of squabbling men in official robes had clustered. It took me a moment to recognize the largest of them, gesticulating angrily, yelling threats and curses at the committee men. Senator Lucius Viridius Camillus—tribune of the seventh legion, hero of the battle of Cynosura Vallis, and not least of all, my father—had come to the Colosseum in person. He turned and strode toward me.

"Stop!" he cried out, addressing the referee. "Accala Viridius cannot be legally permitted entry to the Ludi Romani."

"On what grounds?" the referee demanded. "The emperor has already ruled on the outcome of this bout."

"On the grounds that I, her father, forbid it!"

VI

FOUR DAYS AFTER THE war began, a Viridian soldier delivered an official handwritten letter with the news that my mother and brother had died. It was the first time I'd ever seen words written on parchment. He kept repeating in a monotone voice that he was sorry for my loss, and I just kept reading and re-reading the words on the textured paper and thinking how nice the handwriting was. One part of my mind was perfectly calm, processing the words, and another part, way at the back, was crumbling apart like the ancient mortar in the Colosseum walls.

That's how it felt as my father stepped into the light of center stage like a bulldozer demolishing a home, yelling at the committee members to keep my name from the board. I struggled to breathe, was unable to speak. He was in full flight—old but tall and muscular, making an impassioned oration about the rights of a father and the travesty of seeing his daughter participate in a public spectacle. His red bionic eye, the replacement for the real one he'd lost in battle, flashed angrily as he spoke. My right fist squeezed into a tight ball.

"If you strike your father before the emperor, it might cost you your life," Marcus murmured.

"I don't want to strike him. I want to kill him," I said.

"Gather your wits, Accala. Listen, the emperor is looking for something to take the crowd's mind off of his cousin's embarrassing performance, and we've just given it to him.

"Let's see how it plays out. Remember, one step at a time. You have to play the part of dutiful daughter now. Rush to your father and plead for him to see reason. Get the crowd on side and the emperor may follow. Hurry!"

"I won't beg my father for a crumb. He can go to Hades."

"See that bitter taste in your mouth? That's the flavor of grown-up choices. Now's when you really decide if you have what it takes to see this through."

I would rather have been skinned alive than run to him and play the contrite daughter, but Marcus was right. This was my only chance and I had to act. "Father! Do not do this!" I called out as I ran to intercept him. His bionic eye picked me up first, followed by his human eye, which widened in surprise. He didn't expect me to press him here, in the arena, to force him to air our dirty laundry before the galactic audience.

"You leave me no choice!" he bellowed. "What can I do with a daughter whose disobedience breaches all the standards of morality and good judgment?"

The crowd booed and became quickly hostile. They began pressing and battering the energy barrier that kept them separated from the arena. They'd followed my career, knew what I'd overcome to fight before them. I felt a rush of energy. They were behind me, they understood.

"Let me go! Let me fight!" I pleaded. "Look at these people. They call for justice."

"The mob's approval is fleeting and mindless. Look at them," he said, indicating the screaming crowd. "Look at you, you're no better," he snapped. "You can't master yourself or your emotions, you can't follow orders. You play in the arena, but you're not a real warrior."

"This is no game. I'm fighting for justice."

Suddenly, the energy barrier flickered and vanished and the crowd surged into the arena like water overflowing a dam. How could that happen? Had it been turned off intentionally?

Things were quickly getting out of hand. They rushed toward my father like a flock of greedy crows, eyes gleaming, screaming as one. They wanted to kill my father in order to avenge me, but there was a vacancy in their eyes, as if they'd all been possessed by a single chthonic spirit.

"Get behind me," I said to Father, putting myself between him and the crowd.

"I don't need you to protect me," Father objected, as spectators rushed at us. I gripped Orbis. How did things change so quickly? Was I really going to kill my supporters to protect my father? Judging from the faces on the crowd as they surged toward us, it seemed as if they'd be just as happy to kill me if I got in their way.

"And I think we'll stop this now."

The voice was loud and clear. Not booming like my father's, not angry, the almost-bored voice of a schoolmaster, laden with an unshakable authority. Everyone stopped and looked up to the emperor's box. The telescopic glass magnified his face to giant size.

"Will the audience please show some self-restraint? I think we'll save the fighting for the gladiators, hmm?"

Just like magic, they looked at one another like they had awoken from a spell, and then they returned to their seats like cowed schoolchildren.

"Senator, must we have this out in a public forum? Can this not be dealt with privately?"

My father marched toward the box and offered the emperor a salute.

"Imperator. I beg your forgiveness. I did not mean for the error that has occurred here today to inconvenience you. Please allow me to excuse both myself and my daughter and allow the trials to continue."

None could speak to the emperor unless he addressed that person first, and I knew it would not even occur to the master of the empire to ask me my mind, leaving me to choke on the words that sought to find their way out of my mouth. According to the most ancient rules of Roman law and custom, I was no more than my father's daughter and had no voice.

"Senator Viridius, did you see her fight?"

"No, Imperator. I came as soon as I heard she'd left home. Against my explicit instructions."

"She fought bravely, much more so than some others here today. She brought honor to your house, and I for one would like to see her fight in Jupiter's Great Games."

The audience roared their approval. Perhaps this madness would work out after all.

"And what do you have to say for yourself?" the emperor asked me.

He was riding right over the top of Father's rights, addressing me directly. I was dumbstruck. The words that were bursting to rush forward like a team of chariot horses only a moment ago had suddenly been spooked and run off. I took a deep breath to collect myself and gave a silent prayer to Minerva that I could keep my temper in check. "I believe that what we earn, we deserve," I said. "I have fought and won today to secure a place I had already earned. I've won it twice over now."

"If every man got what he deserved," the emperor said, "who would escape a whipping?"

The crowd burst out into laughter.

"Thank you, Imperator," Father said. "You are the father of the empire. If it is your wish that she go to the tournament, then I will yield, but as paterfamilias, the head of the household and her father, it is my fervent wish that she remain here in Rome and attend to the duties appropriate to a noblewoman of her station."

He was using his oratory skills, politely reminding the emperor that although he was the most powerful man in the galaxy, Rome as a civilization worked only if every individual man in the hierarchy was permitted to exercise the rights and power assigned him.

"A moment ago, I asked that the audience barrier be turned off," the emperor said. "I wanted to see how Accala would react. She was brave in the arena. To see a woman challenge and defeat Marcus Calpurnius Regulus is no small thing and now she has faced down her own supporters when they were about to tear you limb from limb. Is that not a fine example of filial loyalty?"

"Yes, Imperator. She is possessed of many good qualities, but her weaknesses overcome her from time to time. She is a horse that bites at the bit and pulls at the bridle."

The emperor sighed. "As you said, the bond between a father and his household is sacred, as is the bond between a proconsul and his province, an emperor and his empire. These relationships are set in place by the gods to give us order."

A murmur of displeasure arose from the crowd as they sensed where he was heading. Some even yelled out their disapproval. In response, the emperor's balcony detached from the wall, becoming a rectangular hovering transport, carrying him up above the audience and out over the arena. "Citizens, what the gods have set in place we cannot sully, no matter how bravely the lady has proved her mettle. This seems to be a day for family disappointments, so why not one more? I've made my decision in accordance with her father's wish and petitions received only moments ago, one from the Committee for Combative Sports, another from the Senate. Accala Viridius Camilla will not be permitted to join the Calpurnian team today."

The wave of despondency from the audience was palpable and, as for me, there was no fire left. Cold and limp, I couldn't hold back the tears of hopelessness and shame that ran down my face.

"Now, my fellow Romans," the emperor boomed, "enough gloom! Food and wine for everyone! And a comedy pantomime. I need to laugh."

The crowd cheered as the lighting changed and entertainers streamed onto the Colosseum stage, their interest in me diminishing with each passing second. However good the Sertorians were at propaganda, the emperors were always the masters of bread and circuses. The fate of Accala Viridus Camilla was already fading into an amusing footnote in the history of the tournament, a story told to feisty daughters by their fathers when they stepped out of line—the girl who tried to play at being a man.

Attendants escorted us off the stage. I went without a fight. My father strode ahead of me. He'd won his victory, what more was there to say? Well, I had plenty to say.

"How dare you do this," I called out after him. "You think I'm a mare to be bridled? Mother would never have let you get away with spouting such narrow-minded rubbish. You're devolving into some primeval ape without her."

The mention of my mother stopped him. His anger was gone, replaced by dismay. "I've let you play fight here long enough, despite the embarrassment it has caused our house. I thought this fighting would help to contain your violent tendencies, keep you from making even more foolish choices. That's what your mother would have had me do, and I tried to follow her way in her absence, but I was mistaken. You've forced me to publicly petition the emperor. Some of the Viridian senators want me to disown you, to banish you from our house! Hear me clearly. This is the last straw. Your life as a gladiatrix ends here."

"The arena is my life. I won't live outside of it."

"Are you threatening suicide over this? Pah! Don't be ridiculous. I'm trying to manage our house in the midst of war, I have important duties that must be carried out. You carry on like a drama queen, like the whole universe revolves around you."

His words stung deeply because there was a truth to them, but at the same time, I knew he was wrong.

"If I rail at your authority, it is because I am not permitted to exercise any of my own. I am an adult and the gods have given me intelligence and skills. How could I not use them to fashion my own destiny? Not doing so would be a sin to my own creation as well as the memory of my mother and brother. By cutting me from the Golden Wolves, you've doomed the Caninine Alliance to failure."

"There's no talking to you. I'll have your aunts find a suitable man immediately," he said, walking on impatiently. "Once you're married off and have some babies to care for, you'll see what life's really about. Children will ground you, and I'll be free of a daughter who uses words like 'authority' and 'destiny.'"

"Father! I won't stand for this. I won't—"

"Control your gods-be-damned tongue!" He seethed, turning on me suddenly, his anger barely contained. "Do you wish to force my hand? No house, no name, abandoned to the winds of fate. The life of a stateless exile. Is that what you seek? A status no better than that of a slave? One more word and I will do it, do not mistake me. Use what brains your mother gave you. See sense, or I will be forced to let you feel the consequences of your actions. I can shield you only up to a point. You're right that you are an adult, a citizen. Now you must learn to be responsible and behave like one."

"I do not seek your protection. If you wish to exile me, then do it."

His eyes widened with surprise that I should test him so. I expected him to disown me then and there, but he only shook his head in disappointment. "You speak as a child speaks, without thinking things through. Your words are tinged with hysteria. This is Rome. Family is everything. Without our protection, you have no idea how dangerous this empire would be for you. You would be devoured in an instant by the forces that are unleashed at this time. Learn your place. Serve your family and you will find, in time, a way to be content."

"Contentment? I want justice. I burn for it."

"There is no justice in this life. Your mother's death should have taught you that, as Aulus' death taught me. House Viridian is working in the Senate and behind the scenes to ensure victory in the coming tournament and in the war at large. You know nothing and yet you strut around, a hothead, a spoiled brat. You've had your run, Accala. You wanted to run off the rails and you've done it, but I won't allow you to tarnish the reputation of our house. Not now when there's so much at stake. You're done. That's my final word on the matter."

As he stormed away, I became aware that I was surrounded by dozens of my fellow gladiators. Standing quietly, staring at me, no doubt laughing to themselves now that the she-wolf had finally been muzzled. Back on my leash, no voice, no opinion, no justice. Just as I began to follow my father out of the Colosseum, I heard my full name called. Had the emperor changed his mind? No, it was that damned pest Gaius Sertorius Crassus.

"Lady Accala, you were magnificent. A thrilling performance. Allow me to congratulate you."

I looked at him, through him. What was he saying? Was he mocking me? What possible thing could he have to say to me that I would care to hear at this moment? He leaned in close and whispered, "Come to my town house on the Palatine. Come late, after the contestants' banquet." He pressed something into my hand. A card. My fingers numbly closed around it, and then he was gone. Did Crassus actually think now that I was humiliated there would be an opportunity to bed me? That I was so desperate I would come crawling to him for affection? My head held high, I resisted the urge to flee the arena floor and chose an even, steady pace. A roar of laughter started up behind me as I passed into the tunnel to the Ludus Magnus. The comedy play had started up. Or perhaps it was me they were laughing at, for I had certainly played the part of a fool that day.

The change rooms were empty, a small mercy. The sooner I was free of the arena the better, but first things first. I carefully oiled Orbis, properly returning him to his restraining gel. "You were perfect," I said, gently touching him before slowly closing the weapon case and storing him on the top shelf of my locker. As for the rest, I hastily threw my armor into a heap at the bottom of my locker. My armilla was beeping. Journalists were sending me communicats, trying to arrange interviews. As I shut off the device, I saw the alert at the top of the list—a dozen traffic infringement notices for violating aerway regulations. As if I needed any further proof that the gods were against me. Back into my clothes and stola, I shoved the card Crassus had given me into one of the inner pockets and fished out a light gray cloak with no house markings that I'd stored for just such an occasion. I threw it around my shoulders and pulled up the hood to conceal my face.

"Accala!" Marcus was searching for me. That day, my father, my team, my own house had let me know what they thought of me. I would have given them the chance to win not only the tournament but the war itself, but apparently it was a far better fate that all the best houses of the empire burn and fall than be aided by a woman. Right then I didn't want to speak to any man, not even Marcus. Exiting by way of a service door, I bypassed the arena crowds altogether, exchanging them for the anonymity that came with the crush and drive of Rome's bustling streets.

The sun was high in the sky; it was almost noon. Every muscle hurt. Raw and drained, I headed south along the Vicus Patricius. Sertorian ships were docked to the north above the Campus Martius, hovering like a flock of vultures over the city. They would depart the following morning, transporting the Blood Hawks to Olympus Decimus, but I wouldn't be around to see it. Father was set on marrying me off at once. He wouldn't budge now that I'd publicly quarreled with him, and life as a good Roman wife, ever obedient to her husband, was unimaginable. The future held nothing for me, and after the tournament, if the Caninine Alliance lost, what would become of my empire? What of House Viridian? Better to commit suicide, an honorable, private death, and join Mother and Aulus in the underworld as a shade before the whole empire went to hell.

After a few blocks, I spotted two men on my tail. Father again, sending agents to manage me. I ran. My injuries cried out as I sped down one street after another. The arena medics had been able to stanch bleeding and accelerate healing, but only with the proviso that we rest and give our bodies the chance for their medicines to take. I welcomed the pain; it stole away my thoughts. Running hard, I weaved my way through the city's ever present crowds, choosing the way without consideration. When I finally came to a stop, I found myself in the Subura, the city's ancient slum. Several emperors had tried to clean it out but all in vain. It was where the collegial guilds and organized crime gangs had their headquarters, the base from which they managed their empirewide interests, and they liked it just as it was, seedy and crime ridden. My mother used to say that every city needed a shadow place, even the great and shining Rome. In the Subura, the darkness of the soul could find expression so that its impact on the sanity and order that must prevail in the light of day was minimized.

The main strip was crowded, lined with bright holographic signs advertising exotic local clubs where every variety of drug and sexual fantasy, human or alien or both, was on offer. Distracted by the flashing signs, I ran right into a pack of Sertorian officers out front of the Baths of Venus. Six in total. They were off duty, there to partake of the gambling halls and brothels. "Watch where you're going," the lead soldier barked at me, but his expression softened when he saw that beneath the cloak I was a woman. "Forget I said anything, look at those cheek-bones. You've got to be a Viridian, don't you? And a pretty little thing you are." Some of the others started up with wolf whistles. "Come with us, darling, we'll show you a good time."

Iceni slaves followed behind their Sertorian masters, struggling to keep large chests of luggage from falling off overloaded hover carts. The Iceni were short, slight-bodied aliens with pale white skin and a large single red eye in the center of their foreheads. My appearance had caused their convoy to come to a sudden halt, resulting in the Iceni at the rear bumping into a trunk and sending it clat-tering to the marble-clad street. The officer at the rear began beating the Iceni immediately, cursing its clumsiness. House Sertorian, the master race at work. When the man realized I was watching him, he smiled and sank his boot into the alien one more time.

"You like this, pretty girl? Does this turn you on?"

"Wouldn't you like to know what it's like to have a Sertorian man?" another asked. "We are genetically enhanced, veritable stallions in the sack!" Then he put his hand on my shoulder. "My friends and I won't take no for an answer."

Placing my left hand across my body and over his so he couldn't pull it away, I twisted to the side and turned, locking his arm straight and then rolling my right elbow over his. The action twisted his wrist at a bad angle and caused him to hunch over with bent knees. I looked down at him, appreciating the fear in his eyes, before dropping my body weight into the lock, tearing all the tendons in his forearm. He screamed as he dropped to his knees, and I released the hold and sank a kick into his chest, sending him flying back into his comrades.

"I don't know what it's like to have a Sertorian man," I said, "but I'm betting none of you has had a Viridian woman. I'm going to make sure you all get a taste." They'd picked the wrong target on the wrong day. I was going to beat those buffoons senseless, really sink my teeth into them. But then the sound of armored boots followed by a warning siren signaled the arrival of a patrol of heavily-armed Praetorian peacekeepers. They were clearing the street of pedes-trians, coming for me, shock staves ready to enforce the armistice. It would be only a matter of moments before aerial reinforcements arrived, and there was no escaping their electrified nets. I'd be charged with breaking the armistice and sentenced to death, a fate that I was not ill-disposed to—only, before execution, I'd be paraded before the Senate and Father, and I'd be damned if I gave them the satisfaction. One quick kick to the abdomen of the closest Sertorian to clear a path and then I sprinted hard down the nearest side street, pushing through clusters of people. It started to rain, a sudden summer shower that drenched me as I wound my way through alleys, behind the main streets.

When I stopped to catch my breath, my pursuers were long gone. Soaked through, I wandered toward the oldest part of the Subura. Deadly at night but a ghost town during the day as the seedy elements of the city retired behind the high walls of their town houses. The rain hadn't let up, so there were only a handful of customers braving the weather, and as I drew close they scuttled away down side alleys like cockroaches, heading for the private entrances to their favorite haunts.

The largest billboard in the street was right above me, so large that I was half the size of the perfect Sertorian men and women depicted in it. The scene was a constantly shifting tableau. In a series of scenes the Sertorians traipsed about sporting the latest fashions, engaging in naked orgies, fighting heroically in wars, eating the finest foods and wines. All the scenes were framed by the caption THE NEW GODS—POWERFUL, VIRILE, ETERNAL. This was part of that bastard Gaius Sertorius Crassus' propaganda campaign.

The billboard had done its job, caught my attention. As I studied it, a new scene appeared, one created in honor of the coming tournament on Olympus Decimus. The caption read LUDI ROMANI: THE NEW GODS FIGHT FOR A NEW FUTURE. The Sertorians styled themselves as new gods, but they didn't believe in the old ones. The genetic streamlining they employed had led them to embrace the delusion that they were the highest point of human evolution, best suited to guide the empire into the future. An even greater folly was that some of their allied houses actually believed it. Next the billboard served up a scene featuring three majestic black-and-red-armored warriors riding a black war chariot ornamented with lines of shining ruby and gold. The driver was styled to resemble the god Apollo. Behind him stood a powerful, handsome man holding a javelin aloft, ready to cast it into the maw of a saw-toothed barbarian that rushed him on all fours. It took me a moment to realize it was Crassus. He'd inserted himself into his own propaganda campaign. Above him in golden letters a caption read MIGHTY CRASSUS SERTORIUS, SUPREME JAVELINEER, THIRTY VICTORIES AND THREE CROWNS, HEARTTHROB OF YOUNG GIRLS! Crassus the rising star. I, by comparison, had become a burning meteorite crashing to earth.

The third warrior was a woman of striking appearance, styled after the goddess Minerva but fused with the form of Hecate, the dark goddess of the underworld—dark hair, clad in tight-fitting black armor, with red stripes that reminded me of a spider's web. Her spear was ready to cast at a swarthy-looking Roman, unshaved, long hair tousled to resemble a mane. There was no doubt that the wild man she attacked was supposed to be an exaggeration of an archetypal Viridian—stout nose, strong jaw, wide forehead. This was how the Sertorians saw everyone who didn't share their house's bloodline—human barbarians, positioned higher on the ladder of civilization than the brightest alien but by only one rung.

In the background of the image was Proconsul Aquilinus, the leader of House Sertorian, with chiseled features and a noble, beaklike nose. Aquilinus stretched his arms wide like wings to encompass the scene, radiating a divine light that kept the encroaching barbarian darkness at bay.

Propaganda, lies, deceits that I'd hoped to lay to rest in the Ludi Romani. Lost hopes.

Eventually, I found shelter in the area's historic temple district. It existed to meet the needs of those exiting the vice dens of the Subura. Wandering through the network of narrow streets lined with crumbling ruins, I eventually found myself out front of an ancient shrine to the Furies, the chthonic goddesses of vengeance. It seemed like a small miracle that my wandering had taken me there. I had no thought in mind to visit that place, and yet there I was.

In my early teens I was attracted to quiet, abandoned places, a habit my mother encouraged. *You don't run with the pack, Accala. You like to work things out for yourself, and sometimes that means you're going to get hurt. You need to find places where you can be alone with your thoughts, where you can escape the noise of the city.* But not that place. She didn't like my going there. I suppose that's why I chose to frequent it. No one ever visited that particular temple, not even the poorest and most desperate of the Subura. They thought it was cursed, but for me it was a rare, quiet place in the hustle and bustle of the galaxy's busiest city and, to be honest, there was something exciting about going against my mother's wishes.

Most of the roof was intact, with the exception of a few holes through which the rain fell. The water trickled in, passing through dull light to hit the ancient flagstones. Judging by the shadows, it was late afternoon. How long had I been wandering the streets? Time must have slipped by somehow. Sitting there, soaked through, unmoving in the silence, the temple seemed smaller than I remembered, but the feeling of darkness and peace was the same as I'd experienced as a child. It felt as if I'd found a little pocket of reality cut off from everything, that outside the small stone boundaries of that place, the rest of the galaxy didn't exist at all.

Tapping a small pressure switch on my armilla, a paper-thin translucent dagger slid out. I drew it with my left hand, a floppy blade that I snapped with a flick of my wrist, activating the element that turned it hard. Then I just stared at it for a long time, at its sharp point and razor edge, repeating the names like a mantra—*Proconsul Aquilinus Sertorius Macula, Tribune Licinus Sertorius Malleolus, Consul Gaius Sertorius Crassus.* I'd become a gladiator in order to deliver justice to those three men, and now all hope that the shades of my mother and brother could rest in peace was lost. At some point I realized it was growing dark, and with that came the memory of Crassus' card crumpled in one of my stola's inner pockets. It was made of old-fashioned paper, like the note announcing the death of my loved ones, an expensive gesture now water-stained thanks to the rain. On the front was his name and the address of his town house on the Palatine. On the rear was a short note written in what would have been neat calligraphy if the rain hadn't added its own blots and streaks.

> *Your house can still be saved. The revenge you seek can still be realized.*
> *Come tonight. Tell no one.*

Was this some new torment? Now that I'd humiliated myself in the arena, Crassus thought he'd have some additional fun at my expense. Perhaps I was being invited to a Sertorian party where they'd ask me to dance on the stage for their amusement. There was no way I was going to go. The very thought was ridiculous.

* * *

GAIUS SERTORIUS CRASSUS AND I had met at the Academy for Strategic Studies. Before that, junior school tutors reported to my father that I was capable of thoughts and reason beyond my years but my emotions were unbridled, my will strong and defiant, and that unless something was done to curb my stubbornness, only trouble would ensue. To this end, Father, to my delight, enrolled me in *the* elite military school for my collegia juvenum years, where I learned the classics by rote and achieved a comprehensive understanding of the traditional arts and sciences required to be the member of one of the eight great houses. I dropped out of the classes Father enrolled me in, though—protocol, etiquette, and home economics (balancing accounts and managing servants and other tedious torments)—and forged his seal so I could shift all my subjects to warcraft—studying combat, tactics, and strategy; targeting the best military tutors with practical experience. No theoreticians. I received instruction in modern and classic arms and armor and, of course, the combat discus. Father never noticed my educational sleight of hand, or if he did, he was too busy to correct my subject choices or chastise me.

In combat classes, there was only one other as gifted as I, a handsome Sertorian boy. It was before the start of the war and, although our families had feuded for a long time, he was never objectionable in the way the other Sertorians were. He poured all his focus into his studies, and I reluctantly admired him for it, albeit from a distance.

The war began when I was in my last year at the Academy. I stopped attending school. Father went along with it at first; I think he hoped that some time to myself might help me get back on track. I waited for him to comfort me, to help me make sense of Mother and Aulus being ripped from my life so suddenly, but he never came to my chambers, and when I sought him out, he would put me off with talk of the war effort. The more I pushed him to talk, the more distant he became, until finally he even stopped coming to meals. That was until I started completing application forms to join the legion. Then he reappeared as if by magic, arguing about the choices I made in his absence. If I couldn't talk with him about how I felt, I could at least have someone to argue with. When I defied him and put in an application in person, refusing to leave the recruitment office until the legion accepted me, the result was wasted days filling out form after form, each application rejected until Father ran out of patience and dragged me home and demanded I go back to school and complete my studies.

The teachers at the Academy were the best; they made the strong stronger, but they didn't coddle the weak. Academy classes were competitive and demanding. With a month's absence, my ranking had fallen from first place to last. My teachers pushed me for two weeks, to see if I'd reclaim my former level of academic and martial performance, and then left me to fail. The strange thing was that I didn't *want* to give up, but it was as if an invisible barrier stood between me and success. I couldn't see the point to fighting drills or studying. No arrow would hit the bull's-eye, no essay was judged passable, no rhetoric I composed was deemed sufficiently moving. Everything I tried my hand at turned out stale and plain. Even the miniature fruit trees I cultivated on my balcony stopped flowering.

One day after javelin practice, when everyone else had gone, Crassus found me sitting against the wall of the Academy's gymnasium, staring out the window. Even though we'd been in the same classes together for three years, we'd never spoken before.

"Your discus is a magnificent weapon. It soars like a hawk. May I see it?"

"No. Go away."

"Although I am a Sertorian, I have the utmost respect for House Viridian. Yours is a noble and ancient family with a strong bloodline."

He moved to stand in front of me, blocking my view. His cologne had a musky, overpowering scent. "You want to see some lines of blood? Now, that I can help with," I said, turning Orbis this way and that so my discus caught the light.

"Very well, lady. I shall come to the point. You have a problem. The word is that you're about to be expelled. You will become a disgrace to your family, and your future marriage prospects will be severely marred. I also have a problem that needs solving. I think we can help one another."

"You're assuming I want to solve my problem," I said.

"Of course you do. You're not the type to throw down your arms and surrender."

"You don't know a thing about me, but I know everything I need to about you. You're a Sertorian, a vulture," I told him, staring unblinkingly into his dark eyes. "I despise all of your kind more than words can say. Go away now and take your javelin with you, or I'll shove it in the most unpleasant place you can imagine."

That made him laugh. "I've heard worse from your Viridian friends during my time here. They naturally despise my genetic superiority, but you, they think you're crazy, that you're on your way to the asylum if you don't kill yourself first."

"Maybe I'll kill you instead."

"I think we have more in common than you'd like to believe. You don't sleep, do you? You are plagued by nightmares. I suffer in the same way."

"What do you dream of? Little children escaping before you can kill them?"

He considered my flippant question more carefully than it deserved before deciding that he would provide a truthful answer.

"Sometimes I dream of spiders, of long needles inside my body that someone else uses to control me. I wake up screaming, my whole body aching."

His frank confession caught me off guard. I didn't know what to say.

"I sense a restless spirit in you that matches my own," he continued. "We are ambitious by nature, you and I, even if you can't see it right now. My father sent me here because the Roman Academy has the best economics course in the galaxy. He fosters the delusion that one day I will be a merchant and take over his slave business, but I only wish to indulge my passion for the arena. At home I'm a ranked bestiarii."

"That's the sport where you kill barbarians who can't fight back?"

"Ah, you do not understand. We fight monsters, barbarians, anything that provides sport, but they have a fair and equal chance to kill us as well and earn their freedom. The Sertorian gladiatorial circuit is one of the most ruthless in the empire, but it is through that conflict that we prove human superiority over other species."

"And Sertorian superiority over the other houses."

"Naturally. My people prize the exercise of superior strength and power. The arena gives us a pathway to rise up the ranks. In order to follow this path, I must kill and supplant everyone who stands between me and the position I seek in the public service. When my first opponent is dead, they will offer me his heart to eat and smear his blood across my face. We call it the Blooding of the Hawk. If I continue to triumph, I continue to rise. Even the proconsul's position is open to be challenged. Now here's my problem. In order to reach the upper echelons of society, I must master all three arena skills—chariot racing, beast fighting, and gladiator combat. My initiation match takes place on my homeworld next month, but my father has me stuck here in Rome studying, and my regular training routine has been disrupted. I've lost the edge in gladiator fighting. I need a training partner who can challenge me, and you're the only person at the Academy who fits the bill. Or at least you were. I need you to get back to your former standard and quick."

"Go to gladiator school," I said.

"I have. The professionals there practice only with their regular training partners, and I wouldn't pull a hair for the amateurs, but you, you have real potential."

"You don't need a training partner. Just shoot your opponent in the back or plant a bomb. That's the Sertorian way, isn't it? Win at all costs."

"You're not wrong," he agreed, "but when it comes to the initiation, such methods are frowned upon. We're not as ancient as House Viridian, but we do have our traditions, and since you've mentioned bombing, and remember that you brought it up, not I, let me just say that that is precisely the reason I think you will help me. You see, I can give you the name of the man responsible for the bombing of Olympus Decimus."

"His name is Proconsul Aquilinus Sertorius Macula, and one day I will take his head with my discus."

"You must not say such things. The proconsul is a man of peace, a visionary who seeks to create a bright future for all Romans. No, it was not he who launched the attack but rather a man with no respect for history or culture. An uneducated but ambitious centurion seeking to advance in the same circles as I. It was this man who not only devised and executed the plan, it was his hand that pushed the button, his ship that released the first bomb."

I was on my feet, the edge of my discus at his throat. "The name. Tell me."

Until that time the Sertorian proconsul had been the focus of my anger, but he'd always seemed too difficult a target. Proconsuls are distant, overarching figures, heavily guarded family heads only one step removed from the emperor. Since my own uncle Quintus had become a proconsul, I'd hardly seen him.

Frustrated, I'd been scanning the vox populi, seeking information on the squadron commander who dropped the bombs, but it, along with everything to do with the attack on Olympus Decimus, was classified, a tightly held Sertorian secret.

Crassus stepped back and warded Orbis away with his javelin, using the pointed tip to hook my weapon and flick it out of my hand. It flew across the gymnasium and ended up embedded in the stone wall, quivering in place. "I will tell you . . . if you can beat me."

Until that moment I hadn't realized just how far my standards had dropped. Before I could reengage, Crassus said, "Come, let's see some spirit," and pulled me close, kissing me on the mouth. I wrenched myself out of his grasp and hit him with a right cross.

"Not bad," he said, licking his bloody lip. "More."

The kiss burned on my lips like acid, like poison, and in response to it I felt the fire from my nightmares burning inside of me, fueling my action. This Sertorian would die for his impudence, and after him I'd kill the rest of them, every gods-be-damned Sertorian who stood between me and the man who killed my mother and brother.

The moment I recovered Orbis, Crassus' javelin thrust at me again, and I warded it away and attacked. Again and again we clashed, but each time he beat me until I lay exhausted on the floor. I was out of shape. Shamed, I watched him walk away.

"Again," I called out. I wanted that name. Burned for it.

"Tomorrow," he said. "And every day after that."

"You will tell no one of this," I said.

"Not a soul. It would be as bad for me as for you. Imagine, a Sertorian having to seek out a Viridian for assistance?"

"If I help you and you don't have a name for me, or if your story turns out to be false, then it will be you I come for."

"Lady, I am a Sertorian and I am a gentleman. My word is my bond."

As we fought, I absorbed his skills, becoming increasingly better with each session until the day I disarmed him and left him with something to remember me by—a long cut across his upper chest.

On my last session with Crassus, as he left for his match on Sertorius Primus, he said something in passing: "You fought well and learned quickly. You'd make an excellent gladiator. A shame you're not Sertorian. Our women fight at will wherever they wish."

It was like a door had been opened in my mind. Crassus was using the arena to get what he wanted, so why couldn't I?

For all the aid Marcus had given me, it was Gaius Sertorius Crassus who gave me direction and fire as well as the fighting edge to catch Marcus' attention in the first place. And when he left, he gave me the name—Licinus Sertorius Malleolus—a first-spear centurion recently promoted to the rank of tribune and personal adviser to the Sertorian proconsul. He had led the Black Peregrine squadron as they conducted the bombing run. That name became my watchword. It gave me focus. Licinus was a famous competitor in the Sertorian arena circuit and even continued to fight in death matches in his spare time for enjoyment. The video I was able to obtain showed a masterful and merciless opponent. I made it my goal to improve my fighting skills each day so that when the time came, I would be able to steal his life.

Crassus went on to easily win his first arena match. How could I have known that he'd rise through the Sertorian ranks so quickly? The power he held in House Sertorian as propaganda minister was partly thanks to my decision to help him train. If only I'd turned him down, he might have failed in his arena challenge and been killed. At the time, I wanted what he offered so badly, a means to focus myself, a lifeline, that I helped him. To my shame, I had colluded with the enemy. Crassus had gone on to become not only an arena legend but also one of House Sertorian's greatest assets.

His first order of business on attaining the rank of propaganda minister was to publish false reports bearing my mother's name, blaming House Viridian for trying to steal land on Olympus Decimus legally purchased by the Sertorians. He plastered her image everywhere, ran her name through the mud, accusing her of being a Viridian spy, of instigating the Sertorian attack in the first place. That's how he made my list, by slandering her good name, for adding insult to injury. He had to pay for that in blood.

Your revenge can still be realized. It was a cruel joke, another attempt to rub salt into my wounds. The justice I sought, the retribution I deserved, was surely lost, but how dare he insult me again?

I stared into the shadows of the ruined temple. The privacy of the place left me with a dark peace, a deep satisfaction. The more I thought about it, the more it seemed that it was the place where I'd been closest to happiness.

The dagger seemed to take on a weight far greater than its mass would suggest. Was that a sign? Wouldn't it be easier for everyone if I just ended things once and for all? My left palm weighed the dagger; the right, Crassus' card. A thin trickle of blood flowed down my left wrist. I must have cut myself as I handled the knife and not even realized. Turning my hand over I found the source of the blood—a thin wound in my palm. Red blood fell onto the flagstones beneath me like an offering. Small drops, liquid grains, one after another like sands falling into the bottom of an hourglass. The old stones received my blood, mixing with the dust and grime. My wounded hand closed about the dagger. One quick, fearless thrust and it would be over.

But I hesitated, thinking of the souls of my mother and brother, unavenged. Nothing mattered, only that before I die, I correct at least one injustice. Crassus was strong. I had no doubt that as I plunged my dagger into him, he'd strike back, taking me with him. Well, I would drag his soul, kicking and screaming in my wake, all the way down to Hades—a much nobler death than mere suicide. Although he was the least offensive of the men on my list, his death would still serve to offer some small consolation to the shades of the dead.

VII

Drenched by rain, my hair matted with sweat and blood from my arena fight, I stood at the armored front door of Crassus' town house and waited to be permitted entry. The street was inlaid with crystalline bands of light that cast the building in an eerie cyan tinge.

My plan was perfect. After the day I'd had, no blame would fall on my family for my breaking the armistice. Crassus' murder would be dismissed as the act of a woman driven mad with hysteria.

What was taking so long? My cloak, the night, and the rain helped conceal my identity, but the longer I stood there, the greater the risk I'd be identified, and I didn't want anything to interfere with my plan.

His house was a double-story villa with a sloped terra-cotta-tiled roof, in the most expensive part of the Palatine, and surprisingly, it hadn't been remodeled in ruby and onyx to suit the latest Sertorian fashion. The place reflected an owner with a commitment to Roman culture and history, a man of style and sophistication.

Finally the door was opened by a tall human servant, looking down at me like I was a lice-ridden mutt. "No beggars," he said and went to close the door, but I shoved Crassus' card at him and his demenor instantly transformed. "Come in, lady. Please accept my apology. Come in out of the rain. Let me take your cloak."

The servant led me through the entrance hall and along a corridor bordering the inner courtyard. A beautiful garden and well lay at the center of the courtyard, catching the falling rain. With the exception of the small Iceni slaves scurrying about performing their duties, walking through that house was like stepping back into Rome's past. Up the stone stairs to the second story and along another corridor, the servant led me to a formal dining room lit by beeswax candles. The air was thick with the scent of cologne. Crassus was waiting for me, seated at the head of the table and dressed in a hand-tailored evening toga with designer trim. Long-stemmed wine flute in hand, Crassus was drinking iridescent Opimium Moselle, the most rare and expensive of wines imported from Galatia Smaragdus province. Before him was a plate of larks' tongues surrounded by oysters.

"Lady Accala." He jumped to his feet. "Please come in and make yourself at home."

I was dripping, making a mess of his expensive carpet, but he didn't seem to notice. The utility blade had been returned to its sheath in my armilla, but it wouldn't take more than a second to draw it, snap it into form, and bury it in his heart.

"Well, don't just stand there. What's wrong? Would you like some dry clothes?"

My resolve deserted me. I was a gladiator, not an assassin. The fire that fueled me had gone missing at the crucial instant, and here Crassus was, carrying on like we were best friends. I needed more, needed to hear him speak of my mother, or taunt me. A harsh word, a spark from this man to start the fire and then I could go through with it.

Crassus tried to take my hands in his, but I pulled away. "Speak. Say what you've got to say. Be frank."

"Very well." He dismissed his slaves and servant with a wave and then resumed his seat. He took another sip of wine, put the glass down, and flashed me a confident smile. "I've called you here because I want you to help me end the war."

"It may have escaped your notice, but I'm not on a gladiatorial team anymore. I've been scratched."

"Of course. That's precisely what I'm talking about. How do you think the Viridians will do without you?"

"They have a fighting chance."

"Perhaps. My guess is that the entire Caninine Alliance will be eliminated before the final round. With you they had a chance. Don't get me wrong, I'm not attempting to flatter you, only stating the obvious. You tilted the odds in their favor. They were probably going to lose anyway, only now it's a sure thing."

Sertorians were cocky, overconfident. I didn't entirely agree with Crassus' assessment. There was no doubt the Caninines were going in weak, the reconstruction of the civil war pitched four houses against three, meaning the alliance was going in with eight fewer players than the Talonite Axis, not to mention that they didn't have me, but that didn't mean they weren't real contenders. The way the games were structured, the way Fortune swung on the day, any one of a dozen factors could give the underdog a chance to seize the advantage.

"Is that all? You called me here to state the obvious?"

"Of course not. I called you here to offer you the final place on the Sertorian team. I want you to fight for the Blood Hawks."

I burst out laughing. I couldn't help myself. After the day I'd had, I never expected to hear something so ridiculous. "Is this some Sertorian joke? Do you have the rest of your teammates hiding nearby?" I stepped closer to Crassus, discreetly tapping the blade release on my armilla, bracing my right hand on the table near him. It was time.

"No joke. I'm deadly serious. My interest lies in the preservation of the blood-lines that make Rome great. Powerful, ancient, noble families whose genetic contributions are interwoven into our character. Ferocity, loyalty, bravery—these are the traits that House Viridian embodies, traits that I would hate to see lost."

"I'm sure the thought of us dead and buried keeps you awake at night."

"You're not taking this seriously," he said. He took a moment to offer me a small plate of larks' tongues. I knocked them from his hand and he shrugged with indifference. "Tell me, what do you think will happen when the Caninine houses lose the Ludi Romani?"

"The terms of the contest are common knowledge. Demotion. A loss of status and wealth."

"It's a death sentence, Accala. The cry of a great house falling is seen as an opportunity for lesser houses to strike. The emperor will certainly not come to your aid, and the other houses will distance themselves from House Viridian to preserve their own standing. Already your allies regret teaming up with you. Better to keep half your power under a hostile ruler than lose all of it by backing the wrong horse. House Viridian's prospects of survival are dim at best, but with your help, the destruction of your people need not be an inevitability."

"Go on," I said. I let him keep talking. Every suggestion was an outrage, an added offense. The fire was building and soon it would explode.

"I have poured honeyed words into my proconsul's ear. I have told him of your brilliance, your bloodline, your abilities. Imagine how effective it would be if you publicly stood with us. Showed the Caninine Alliance and all their citizens that there was nothing to fear by cooperating? Fight with us. Preserve your house. Outside of the arena, not one more Viridian life need be lost."

"Why would you want me on your team? No one cares if I live or die," I said. "I'm just a woman who had some success in the arena."

"On the contrary. I've watched the footage of all your matches. When you dress in Viridian armor, when you raise your discus and proclaim that you're fighting for the green and gold, you cause quite a stir. The Viridian legionaries on the front lines of this war revere you. We've found graffiti of a female gladiator with a wolf's head drawn all over battle sites, not to mention cameos containing your official arena hologram. You've become more than a woman or a gladiator. You're a symbol."

"So you want me to aid you in one of your propaganda campaigns? To become a Sertorian collaborator?"

" 'Collaborator' is a strong word. You'd be an ally. Technically a slave."

"A slave?"

"My slave. Technically speaking. For your own protection."

"To submit to your commands?"

"It's no more than you offered Marcus when you accepted him as your lanista."

"I trust Marcus."

"It would be for only a short time, until you survive the trial period and pass the initiation. After that you'd be a fully blooded member of House Sertorian. You'll regain your freedom and be reborn into new life."

"The very notion is ridiculous," I said. "You're ridiculous for even suggesting it."

"Ridiculous? In fact Proconsul Aquilinus and I think that you are a vital ingredient in our future plans. A prominent Viridian gladiator, especially now that the audience feels you were robbed in the arena today. Your house and its allies will lose and you can help them adapt. All the poor, lost plebeians and nobles who don't know how to behave will look to you as a role model. So I beg you to think of your countrymen near the fringe of Viridian space who are beaten and starving, your military forces close to defeat. We both know that the emperor called the armistice just in the nick of time. Is saving them more suffering ridiculous?"

He paused, studying me, but I wasn't going to be led into any of Crassus' insanity. He was a trickster, a conniving con artist who'd talked me into working with him once before. Now that the stakes were so high, I wasn't going to be tricked again.

"Or is it that I'm not putting enough on the table to entice you?" he said. "Do you think I can sweeten the pot? Listen. Proconsul Aquilinus has two advisers in whom he places absolute faith. I am one, the other is my rival Licinus Sertorius Malleolus, a man you have given every indication of wanting dead. I delivered his name to you some time ago, and yet he still lives."

"The Ludi Romani was to have been my chance." No point in telling Crassus that he too was on my list. He was about to find out firsthand.

"It still can be. If you joined the Blood Hawks, you would have to serve under him, and me, but during the course of the match, at a discreet and appropriate moment, I plan to see Licinus dead."

"Good for you."

"On the back of his bombing of Olympus Decimus, it is Licinus' voice that has convinced Proconsul Aquilinus to seek the ascension of our house though the exercise of military power. As a result, House Sertorian has raped, burned, pillaged, and looted your worlds."

"Why don't you show those images in your propaganda campaigns?"

"Believe me, I find them as detestable as you do, especially when there are other more civilized ways to accomplish the same outcomes—reason, education, political persuasion. It need never have come to this. I am a member of the aristocracy. We understand that while House Sertorian will eventually reign supreme, we must still learn to live with the other houses. I prefer to dangle the carrot in front of the donkey. Licinus prefers to beat it half to death with a stick. By the end of the Ludi Romani, only one of us will be left alive to help Proconsul Aquilinus shape House Sertorian's destiny. If you join with me, the pleasure of ending his life will be yours. You'll be saving your people and, call it a fringe benefit, indulging in a satisfying personal revenge. What do you think?"

"I think that if you try to ride a wolf like a donkey, then she will turn and rip out your throat," I said.

"That sounded like a no."

"It was. It sounded like a joke at the beginning, and it still does. I wouldn't spit on if you were dying of thirst, and you want me to come fight for you as well as advertise how gods-be-damned glorious House Sertorian is?"

"Think logically, not emotionally. Did you understand the options presented to you? That you can save your house? And have your revenge? I can explain it again if you like, the way they do on the broadcast game shows—highlight the prizes you can win if you play. In fact, I've staked my reputation on my ability to convince you to join with us and smooth the way for House Sertorian.

Proconsul Aquilinus is quite taken with the idea now. I can't permit you to re-fuse. Please reconsider and speak again; we both know there's only one sensible choice available to you."

"Yes," I agreed. "You're absolutely correct."

The knife was out in an instant, but I lost time flicking the blade into its ac-tive state. He was able to get up from his seat. I spun and rammed him into the wall, the knife at his throat, but he managed to get a hand to my wrist, stopping me from plunging the weapon home. I struggled against him, but his fingers pressed the nerves in my wrist to the bone, causing me great pain.

"I have something you must see," he said. "Stay your hand."

He went to reach for something in the pocket of his robes and I used the op-portunity to try to force the blade into his body, but he squeezed my wrist tightly again, and this time I let out a small cry of pain. "Please. I must show you," he pleaded.

"One last thing to sweeten the pot?" I growled.

"Something like that. I'll take it out slowly, without making any move to defend myself. After you've seen it, you can do what you want with me."

"That's a crude pickup line from the likes of you, Gaius Crassus."

But he was so earnest and I was so surprised to hear the pleading tone in his voice that I indicated he should go ahead. From his pocket he drew a shiny me-tallic object and then reached out slowly to place it on the dining table beside him.

It gleamed in the candlelight. A pin, platinum, in the shape of an arrow with three golden apples forming the clasp. My mother's pin. The one she never let out of her sight. The same pin I'd dreamed of night after night as my mother used it to scratch out her urgent, unintelligible message.

"Where did you get it?"

"We found it in your brother's hand."

"Aulus?"

My grip must have weakened in that instant, for Crassus shot an uppercut with his free hand up under my ribs and then knocked the knife clear of my hand. It went skittering across the stone floor. He stepped back and held up his hands to indicate that he was done.

"He lives, Accala. Aulus Viridius Camillus lives, and we have him. If you join the Blood Hawks and carry out my instructions, when the tournament is over and House Sertorian stands victorious, I will release him to you."

The fire overwhelmed me in an instant. I slapped him in the face, hard and fast. "Liar," I shrieked, preparing to hit him again. This time he moved like light-ning, catching my hand in midair.

"I speak the truth," Crassus said, releasing me. "And if you attempt to strike me again, the deal is off. It's your choice."

It couldn't be true. I picked up the pin with trembling fingers and then almost dropped it as a shock ran right up my arm. It was the strangest feeling. Somehow, holding it, I could feel my mother's presence.

"I have never lied to you, and I never will." Crassus plucked his cameo from his robes and placed it on the table. A holographic image was projected into the air above the cameo, and for the first time in almost two years, I saw my brother. At first I thought it was a single static image, then I noticed the time code counting forward. He was frozen, unmoving. As I examined the hologram up close, I saw that Aulus was behind a transparent surface that was smoky and spotted—the same dirty ice that I found myself trapped behind in my nightmares. I leaned in close; there was something else strange about his appearance—three black streaks, burn marks, on the right side of his face. Two on the cheek, one running across his eye to his forehead.

"Radiation burns from the bomb blast," Crassus explained. "Your brother survives but is currently frozen in a state of suspended animation while his body heals."

A holographic watermark, the rolled-up scroll of the guild of archivists, attested to the video's authenticity.

The pin, Crassus' claims about my brother's survival, the correlation between my dreams and what I was seeing—it all threw me completely off guard. I felt as if I had woken up inside a dream, that the world had ceased operating in a way that was predictable.

"What of my mother?" I asked.

"We made a positive identification of her body during the cleanup of the planet, prior to colonization. There is video footage if you wish to see it. Her body was in some state of decay, but I believe you would still be able to recognize parts of her."

"No." My voice was shaky, my whole body trembling. I knew I'd burst into tears if I spoke, so I remained silent. Aulus. My legs were going to give out under me, so with as much dignity as I could muster, I lowered myself into the chair beside me, placed my hands on the table, and took a deep breath.

"If you truly have him, where is he now?" I said. "I want to see him."

Sitting down opposite me, he took a leisurely sip of wine. "Of course, I would like nothing more than to take you to him, I despise using children as leverage. What I can tell you is that he is held safely in one of our facilities on Olympus Decimus. Yes, that's right. Your brother is on the arena world. Are you sure you don't want to join the Ludi Romani yet?"

My brother's frozen face still floated above the table, right in front of me.

"You want me to fight for you? To stand by your side?" I asked. My body and the words it generated were numb, expressionless.

"To win the tournament together. To make a joint statement with our actions," Crassus said. "As soon as we have won the tournament, your brother will be released into your custody. You have my word of honor."

"You ask me to swallow a bitter pill. I'm no traitor."

"Traitor? What is a traitor? When the new era comes, all those who stood against us now will be called traitors, war criminals, terrorists. What matters are not labels but results. The billions of lives you spare, the culture you preserve will prove you to be a peacemaker. Let us help one another as we did last time."

"That was a mistake."

"Don't you see? Twice you've been denied your right to join the tournament and yet here you are, your place secured yet again. Olympus Decimus is calling to you. You have a destiny to fulfill, we both do. Our potential must be realized. House Viridian would remain untouched, unharmed, improved. You could make changes to how women are treated—expand the code of honor your people consider to be so important so that it applies to both sexes."

The words he wanted me to say were like small bones caught in my throat. I couldn't make them come out.

"Accala?"

Standing stiffly, I touched the cameo, terminating the image, and moved to leave, but he caught me by the wrist and pulled me to him. It took every ounce of willpower not to strike him. "Why do you ask for an answer at all?" I said. "You know I have no choice."

"We Sertorians understand business," he said. "A deal is a deal only when we both agree to the terms. You do have a choice. You can choose to walk away, to stay safely here in Rome, marry and bear children, watching your team fail in the games, your brother die, your house fall, its citizens turned to slaves. You don't want that, though, and I don't want that. Let us save your people together."

He waited for me to speak, but I still couldn't make any words come.

"I can't let you leave here without giving me an answer. I need to know. Right now."

He was keeping me off balance, making clear thinking difficult. What if the Caninines really did have a fighting chance, and by joining the Sertorians I'd steal that slim hope away? But if Aulus was alive, if there was even a chance . . . I had to get away from Crassus, to buy time to think things through. With time, I could find a way to turn things around.

"Yes," I said quietly.

"Then we have a deal?"

"You heard me the first time. Now I need to go home. To pack."

"As long as you return here before dawn—and please leave the pin. You can reclaim it in the morning."

The fire in my heart burned bright, and I wanted nothing more than to set it free, to allow my rage to engulf him. Instead, I obeyed him and placed the pin on the table.

"Remember, I am not your enemy. I am your ally. Licinus is our target, peace is our goal. We'll work together and this unpleasant business will be over before you know it."

Crassus stood aside, smiling as if we were the best of friends. He knew the lead he had me on was both invisible and long. "And you understand, as you did with our prior arrangement, that mutual circumstance binds us to silence and believe me that we will be watching you, everything you say and do. If you utter a word of anything we've discussed, I won't be able to help you or your brother. Aulus will be handed over to Licinus, who keeps two Crimson Inquisitors in permanent employment. You know what that means, don't you?"

He didn't have to spell it out. Sertorian inquisitors skinned their victims alive for starters, dragging out their dying for the longest possible time.

* * *

I FLED FROM THAT place as if dark floodwaters were about to rush over me. Crassus had made an offer that was impossible to refuse, but it didn't lessen the urge to run back into his fancy town house and beat him black and blue until he set Aulus free.

An empty, unmarked chariot was docked in front of Crassus' place, and I took it. The weather shield kept the rain at bay as I soared high above the city at night, right into the path of a storm. The wind and rain buffeted me, knocking the chariot this way and that as I tried to piece together what the Sertorian had told me. My mother must have given her pin to Aulus. The image of her calling out to me in the dream filled my mind, of her desperate attempts to communicate, scratching out her message before she and Aulus died. Except Aulus wasn't dead. Crassus had never lied to me, and he wasn't lying now, I was certain of that. Somewhere on Olympus Decimus, my brother was frozen, immobile and helpless in some Sertorian facility. It was worse than if he were a shade in the halls of Hades, because nothing could be done about that.

Thunder rumbled, lightning flashed about me, and I flew on, daring the gods to strike me down. Better that than to kneel before Crassus in submission. Better that than to fight against my own house or face my father and be unable to tell him that his only son, my brother, still lived.

About three hundred feet up, surrounded by black clouds, the chariot's weather shield inexplicably failed, exposing me to the elements. My robes billowed wildly, the wind and rain lashed me. I felt like an actor in some tragic opera. From out of the clouds ahead of me, a dark shape emerged. A ship. The conical nose of a sleek trireme split open into six steel parts like a black orchid, revealing a bright interior chamber. Hitting the throttle, I tried to swerve out of the way, but the storm and the speed of the vessel made escape impossible. My chariot was consumed by the larger ship, the control of the chariot's engines seized, my speed reduced to a snail's pace. With me securely inside, the nose closed back up. My engine cut out entirely without warning. The chariot fell to the deck below with a loud clatter. I tried to land gracefully but couldn't get my feet under me in time, falling awkwardly to the unyielding steel. Unarmed, no Orbis, no dagger, I scrambled to my feet and awaited the enemy who had captured me. The walls of the hangar bore Viridian insignia, a wolf's head surrounded by emerald laurels, signifying that this was the personal trireme of the Viridian proconsul himself.

"Hello, dear niece. I see that, as usual, you are having difficulty staying out of trouble."

My uncle, our leader, Proconsul Quintus Viridius Severus, looked down at me from the raised platform of the ship's hangar bay. Thin and wrinkled, his eyes flashed with a mixture of amusement and penetrating intent. There was only one reason my uncle would seek me out: He knew all about my visit to Crassus. That

I'd agreed to betray my house. His eyes said as much. Dragged before the Senate and my father, I would face a traitor's death—to be whipped, crucified, and then thrown from the Tarpein Rock while all the empire watched on.

"Come. We have much to discuss," my uncle said, dismissing the guards on either side of him.

Climbing the metal stairs like a prisoner going to the gallows, I followed him to his great cabin, a space that incorporated his office—a simple minimalist square workstation and large, bulky cube-shaped chairs with only a little padding—the workspace of an utterly focused, practical man, lacking any of the ornamentation I'd seen in Crassus' town house.

Uncle Quintus motioned for me to sit on a low divan opposite his desk.

"Accala, I know all about your brother," he said in a calming tone. "I know where you've been tonight, but you have nothing to fear. My agent inside Gaius Sertorius Crassus' house has told me everything that transpired. I know that you are loyal and true."

The human servant who answered the door. He must have been my uncle's inside man. Or perhaps one of the small white Iceni. Crassus had warned me not to speak, but if my uncle knew and was pressing me what choice did I have?

"I'm not sure what to say," I said.

"You're worried that Crassus is watching you? Don't worry, we scanned you when you came in. There were two spherae following you, but he'll assume they got caught up in the storm. We've got about ten minutes and then I have to send you back to the Wolf's Den so we don't raise too much suspicion. Go ahead. Ask what you want."

"It's true, then? He has Aulus?"

My uncle's words came as a great relief, but I had to be cautious. I sensed I was still on shaky ground.

"It is. My own agents have confirmed what Crassus told you. I'm going to use every resource at my disposal to find and liberate your brother." Uncle got up from his desk and came to sit beside me. "Don't worry, dear niece, I'm here to help."

"Thank the gods," I said, throwing my arms about him. "I didn't know what I was going to do."

"You can tell me anything," he said, placing a reassuring hand on my knee. My words came flooding out. Taking his hands in mine, I confessed everything to him—about the arena, why I went to see Crassus, the offer Crassus made. My hands were hot and sweaty; his, surprisingly cool. "Now you can help him," I said. "You have to help him, he's your nephew, he's family."

"Rest assured, I intend to do precisely that."

"I will make offerings to Minerva for your health. You bring a desperately needed hope, Uncle."

"Good, good. We're going to start with the offer Crassus made you," Uncle said, putting his heavy arm about my shoulders and pulling me close.

"I can't believe the things Crassus said to me."

"He's an unusual Sertorian, that's for certain," my uncle said. "He truly does seem to have some strange vision of preserving the noble houses, albeit as slaves to House Sertorian. What interests me, though, is his fascination with you. He's truly struck by Cupid."

"For who?" I asked, and then felt like an ass when I realized my uncle was referring to me.

"He's in love with me? I don't know about that."

But it made sense. All the talk about me joining their team for a propaganda campaign, it sounded so far-fetched. A creature like Crassus couldn't know actual love, but if my uncle was right, if he desired me, wanted to possess me, somehow it made more sense. Men were stupid when it came to sex, and I wouldn't put it past a Sertorian megalomaniac to come up with some bizarre scheme to satisfy his desires.

"Take it as a given. He's head over heels."

"He certainly had some strange ideas. I can't get over his asking me to join the Blood Hawks, to be his slave. Imagine that? It was like some bizarre school-boy fantasy."

"I can imagine it well. In fact, that's precisely what I want you to do."

"I don't understand," I said, pushing his arm away. "Don't joke, Uncle, I can't take it right now."

"This is no joke, Accala. Gaius Sertorius Crassus is cracked, there's no doubting that, but his madness is a gift from the gods that we can turn to our advantage. If he wants you by his side, then that's exactly what he shall have. I want you in the Ludi Romani, on the Sertorian team, hand in hand with the enemy. You're going to break House Sertorian apart for me, dear niece, from the inside out. By the time you're done, every last hawk in the empire will curse the day they tried to tame House Viridian."

ACT II

MOCK HAWK

Ah my sister, long ere now I knew thee, when first thine arts
    shattered the treaty, and thou didst mingle in the strife;
and now thy godhead conceals itself in vain.
But who hath bidden thee descend from heaven to bear this sore
    travail? Was it that thou mightest see thy hapless brother cruelly
    slain?

—Virgil, *Aeneid*

VIII

IT WAS PARADE DAY, and the gladiators of the Ludi Romani departed Rome with great fanfare. The processional float bearing the Blood Hawks slowly emerged from the darkness beneath the Colosseum and began to make its way down Via Appia. At the back of the float, I, Accala Viridius Camilla, sat beside my new master, Gaius Sertorius Crassus. The summer sun was bright, the clear blue sky hummed with hovering media spherae, and two hundred thousand people screamed and cursed my name.

At dawn I'd slipped out of the Wolf's Den. My uncle had arranged for my father to travel to Londinium on house business so I wouldn't be disturbed, and also arranged for Orbis to be brought to me at home. Strangely, the cameo from my bedside table was missing. Had Father taken it with him? A way of punishing me, forcing me to let go of the past? I returned to Crassus' town house with my trunk and belongings loaded onto the chariot. He presented me my mother's pin like a tutor bestowing an award to a clever schoolchild and showed me the press release he'd posted notifying every media outlet in the empire that I had switched sides. Then I was whisked away to the arena and shuffled onto the back of the float, away from the rest of the team. "It's Licinus' decision," he said. "You'll be introduced to everyone once the journey to the arena world is under way."

The vox populi's morning news bulletin ran my defection to the Sertorian team as its lead story, so every citizen in the city of Rome had time to be shocked, absorb the news, and then come to the parade stocked with an ample supply of outrage and rotten food.

They lined the streets, Viridians and their allies to the left, Sertorians and their cohorts to the right, Praetorian Guards in between using their shock staves to keep the street clear. The Viridians, my Viridians, hurled insults my way.

The six other house teams had already passed ahead of us, and the mob had showered them with cheers and blessings. Julius Numerius Gemminus, the tournament editor, had refused my request that the Blood Hawks come out on the first float and get the whole thing over and done with quickly. "I do not modify my presentation to accommodate the feelings of the competitors. Do you know how much work I have done to prepare every last detail of these games? I am a very important man. The Blood Hawks will come last and on the heels of the Golden Wolves. That is how I planned it and that is how it shall be." He was an obese old man with a cherubic face and, when he was done yelling at me, he reached out and tenderly touched my right cheek with a fat hand. "You have added some unexpected spice to the day. I suppose I have to thank you for that. Don't expect anything but suffering, sweet thing. You are a tender morsel, and the mob will want to chew you well before they spit you out."

Crassus insisted I wear the plain black robes of a novice Sertorian gladiator—the garb of a child yet to pass her blood initiation. A small red talon insignia marked my breast, symbolic of the blood I would shed for my new house. Orbis was clipped on my belt, but Crassus had warned me not to use my discus or even take it in my hand. I trembled with humiliation and dread, my stomach lurching from side to side in time with the movement of the hovering float, my ears ringing. My mother's pin was clutched like a talisman in my sweaty hand. I whispered my brother's name, again and again, squeezing the pin tight, welcoming the distracting pain as it bit into my palm.

Near the front of the float stood Servius Tullius Lurco—Lurco Giganticus—the hammer-fighting bestiarii, moving from one side of the float to the other, revving up both sides of the crowd. Behind him were four gladiators I knew only by reputation—competitors from the Sertorian arena circuit. Gaia Sertorius Barbata—a female retarius, expert with net and trident. Lustrous dark hair curled about her face, accenting her arched eyebrows. Beside her were identical twin brothers—the famous charioteers Castor and Pollux Sertorius Corvinus, generally referred to under the collective title Dioscurii. In the old stories, the beautiful Leda was mother to the Dioscurii, though only Castor was born to a mortal father. Pollux was the son of Jupiter, who had adopted the form of a swan to seduce and impregnate Leda. When Castor died, Pollux begged Jupiter to let his brother take a share of his immortality, and both were transported into the heavens to become the constellation Gemini. This pair were stars in their own way—lean, handsome, built for speed. As I observed them, the twins turned to regard me with an unblinking, reptilian coldness.

Next to the Dioscurii sat the bestiarii Mania Sertorius Curia, a skinny and pale young woman with white hair tied back in a tight ponytail. She carried a bow staff, a hunter's weapon, and at her sides two needle knives, but she was so small. She didn't look like she could fight off a cold, let alone an alien beast. The girl was animated, excited, chattering away at the Dioscurii, who ignored her completely.

Standing apart from the others, up front, was our team leader, Licinus Sertorius Malleolus. He was right there, the man I'd dreamed of killing, within my reach for the first time, only I was powerless, constrained. How would I survive the voyage? Forced to take orders from my sworn enemy, suffering under his command; it would be impossible. Only the thought of Aulus gave me strength. For Aulus I could endure this.

Rotten food—tomatoes, pomegranates, apples—hit the force shield that protected the float, sliding down the invisible barrier, creating the illusion of the air surrounding me being smeared with streaks of waste. My countrymen screamed and spat—*traitor, whore, Crassus' bitch, wolf slut*—the insults all ran together. I hadn't bothered to check my fan page on the vox populi that morning; I knew it would be filled with the same kind of vile insults and threats. And the hatred that surrounded me in Rome would not end when I departed Mother Earth. It would be waiting for me on the arena world. The jeers of the audience, their continuous calls for my death would stir my cousins and allies to spill my blood and win the mob's approval. I was now the number one target in the Ludi Romani.

"Accala?" Crassus held out his hand. "Take it," he said. "A public gesture so they know you're here of your own free will."

"I'm not here of my own free will."

"Of course not," he replied pleasantly, "but it's important that the people think you are."

* * *

THE NIGHT BEFORE, MY uncle had walked casually about his shipboard office, plucking fat purple grapes from a large cluster in his hand as he explained what he wanted of me.

"You're asking me to betray my house," I said. "I said yes to Crassus only to buy time. To work out a strategy for rescuing my brother."

"Then allow me to save you some time. I've already got one worked out for you."

"The Sertorians will put me to work killing my own family members for sport. I'll be despised, an outcast. There must be another way, or another person who can do this."

"No, it must be you, and not just because of Gaius Crassus' infatuation. Your mother was in possession of a great secret, a secret that can destroy House Sertorian once and for all, and she meant for you to uncover it. Destiny is calling to you, Accala, and it's speaking one name—Olympus Decimus."

He offered me some of his grapes, but I had no appetite.

* * *

QUINTUS VIRIDIUS SEVERUS WAS career military. He served alongside my father in the legion, and before being elected proconsul he served as the head of the curiosi—the emperor's secret police. When I was a child, he would sit me on his knee and ask me to try to figure out which of the servants in the compound were spies from enemy houses. He was fond of grapes back then too, and would give me one, along with a sesterce for each correct guess. "Children see clearly," he said to me, "but you have an especially good eye for uncovering secrets and to my mind that should be rewarded and encouraged. Secrets have value." The servants whom I pointed out would quietly disappear, one by one. Once, when I looked into their whereabouts, all I turned up were obituaries. The next time he asked for my help I turned him down.

"But withholding a talent that can aid your house is positively un-Roman. You must always be willing to sacrifice your own needs for those of your house—that's what real Romans do." And so I helped him one last time, a young kitchen maid who seemed to know how to reprogram a security panel. One last time, that was all he asked for. "A test, dear niece, to see if you have potential, to see if you have the stuff heroes are made of." Those were powerful words to an impressionable young girl, but it didn't change the fact that for months afterward I had nightmares, plagued by the thought that I might have been wrong and sent innocents to their deaths.

* * *

AND THERE HE WAS eating grapes again. The sound of them being crushed, seeds and all, by his back teeth was a reminder of how efficiently my uncle dealt with any enemies who threatened the billions of Viridian lives that were his to protect and command.

"Listen carefully, dear niece. What I tell you now is a state secret and of the utmost importance to the survival of our house."

He walked around his desk and tapped at the built-in console. A hologram of a familiar ice world filled the center of the room.

"Your mother traveled to Olympus Decimus on a highly classified mission for me."

"My mother was a philosopher, a scientist, not a spy," I said. "Her research was her life."

"What child can ever truly know her parents?" he said. "Now listen. I know this is the first time you've heard this news, but I beg your patience. Hold on to your questions until you're fully briefed."

How strange. I was prepared to kill Crassus for slandering my mother's name, for branding her a spy, and here was my uncle confirming it.

"The Sertorians stumbled upon something of great importance on Olympus Decimus—we first cottoned on to it when they started buying up unusable land in the mountains and tundra about Lupus Civitas, the capital city of the Viridian settlement. Before long they were sending out expeditions into the wilderness. Frozen wastes, barbarian-infested hills, useless land. I needed someone to investigate and tell me what they were up to. It wasn't the first time I'd asked your mother to serve our house in such a way. She arranged her research expedition so it would venture near the Sertorian properties, and after several weeks reported that they were searching for some kind of mineral. I've since learned that they call it *ambrosia*. The Sertorians considered this ambrosia to be so important that they were willing to attack and invade Olympus Decimus to stop the news of it getting out."

"Ambrosia? What's so important about it?"

"Why don't I let your mother answer you. This was her last transmission, just before the bombs fell."

The projection of the planet gave way to the scene of an icy cavern. Mother was in the foreground, looking right at me, dressed in a heavy jacket. It was surreal to see her after so long, wonderfully surreal. There was no sign of Aulus. Her black hair hung loose about her face, the white shock at the front as visible as ever. She didn't have her hairpin.

"Quintus, I don't have much time—the Sertorian invasion fleet has entered the atmosphere and started bombing the planet. I've uncovered much but dare not share it all now for fear that this communiqué will fall into enemy hands."

She spoke slowly and evenly, her usual unhurried pace, despite the looming danger. She always had a good sense of timing, how to communicate exactly what she wanted to say in the available time.

"What I can tell you is that the Sertorians are expending vast resources to covertly mine this world. They're digging deep underground, into the hives of the indigenous Hyperboreans, searching for a rare mineral that has unusual transformative properties. I managed to throw a wrench into the works, so to speak, but it doesn't look as if I'll be around to finish what I've started." She looked away for a moment as the cavern about her began to rumble. In the background stalactites crashed to the ground. "I'm afraid I'm out of time. Listen carefully! I know how stubborn my daughter can be so make sure you show her this next part of the message."

The entire cavern was caving in now. Mother continued talking with a Stoic resignation, making no effort to protect herself as the rocks fell about her.

"Accala. It's important that you come here to Olympus Decimus and find Aulus. I've taken steps to ensure that your brother will survive the attack. I've given him my pin, the one that's been in our family for generations. It's been modified so that the two of you will be able to use it to complete my work here and deny House Sertorian that which they seek. It will take both of you to finish what I have started. Aulus is the lock, but you are the key, Accala. The pin will ensure you work together. If you become parted, it will help you find each other, so guard it carefully. Know that I love you, dear daughter, even in the life after this."

Finally, she stood erect, removed her jacket, and straightened out the creases in her robes. A serene countenance, like a goddess.

"Quintus, I trust that you will act as you always have, to secure the interests of House Viridian. Hail and farewell," she said with a slight smile. "And now I pass into eternity." Then the rocks fell upon her, breaking her body apart like matchsticks. The projection cut out, leaving me standing there with tears streaming down my cheeks, my lips trembling. Her last words were a quote from Catullus, written as he mourned his brother's death.

"I'm sorry you had to see that, but now you know why your mother was really on Olympus Decimus," my uncle said.

It was difficult, reconciling what I'd just seen with the dream that plagued me each night. They had nothing in common and the discrepancy confused me, threw me out of myself so that I felt like I was standing outside of my body, watching myself act from a distance.

"What do you make of the message?" my uncle asked. "I'm interested in your analysis. Your first impressions."

"My mother didn't know how things would play out. Something must have gone wrong. She must have sent Aulus into hiding somewhere underground, somewhere where he could safely wait for me to come for him, but she didn't anticipate that the Sertorians would find and capture him."

"A good assessment. You said he was in a cryogenic system in the footage Crassus showed you. That might well have been her solution, the Sertorians simply haven't had the need to take him out of suspended animation."

"They must have taken him out at some point," I said. "In order for them to recover the pin."

"Yes, the pin. It's Fate, Accala, don't you think? Whatever measures your mother put in place to cripple the Sertorians, they required three elements— you, your brother, and the pin."

"Unless the Sertorians got their hand on Mother's message and this is some kind of trap."

"No, I can assure you that it came to me via secure channels. There is no way they could have intercepted it. Only I, and now you, know her last words. That's why I had to intervene the moment Gaius Sertorius Crassus offered the pin to you. Did you have the chance to study it? Was there anything written on it? Any markings or signs that could suggest a message?"

"No, it was as I remembered, though I did feel something when I picked it up. A shock. I thought it was just static, or maybe a physical reaction to the memories it stirred up."

He shrugged, suggesting that my experience shed no light on the problem. "The pin coming to you like this, it's a sign from the gods, an omen that you must be the one to find your brother and finish your mother's work."

"Tell me more. What of the mineral she refers to?"

"Yes, the Sertorians call it ambrosia."

"Is it a metallurgical agent? For ship building or forging weapons?"

"It could be, but in truth we've been able to learn very little. Whatever it is, my intelligence tells me the Sertorians believe it is powerful enough to ensure their victory over us. A demonstration of its potential sent the Arrians scuttling over to their side."

My uncle was pushing me to jump out of the frying pan and into the fire, but I needed to know more. His news was so sudden, and a million questions were running through my mind, competing with grief and exhaustion.

"Uncle, how long have you had this message?" I asked.

"Ah, you are naturally suspicious and I don't blame you. I'll be honest with you, I've had it since the war began."

"And you only shared it with me now?"

"You've only just come into possession of the pin, besides, how was I going to get you onto a Sertorian occupied world? They've had it locked down tight. But don't think I haven't been working behind the scenes for you. Who do you think suggested the Olympus Decimus solution to the emperor in the first place? Who ensured you be allowed to continue in the arena? Do you think your father would have let you run as long as he did unless you had my support?"

"Father knew of the message?"

"No, of course not. Lucius and I have never seen eye to eye. Everything is black and white to him. He never even knew your mother worked for me. One thing you learn as a proconsul is to give people only the information that moves your plans forward. He would never allow me to send you to Olympus Decimus. He's like a bulldozer, your father. Look at the mess he made scuttling all my behind-the-scenes work to secure your place with the Golden Wolves."

My uncle as my patron. It made sense.

"You see, you can trust me. I have only ever acted in your interests, dear niece."

"Where did Mother's transmission originate from?"

"You want to know where she died? You wouldn't be surprised to learn it was near the site of our old capital, the point where the bombing began. As best we can tell, it was beneath the mountains just to the north of Lupus Civitas. Near the tallest peak, Nova Olympus."

"Mother's message. It's urgent but it's light on detail," I said. "There are so many unanswered questions. That talk of keys and locks. I don't understand. Do you?"

He slowly shook his head.

"Listen, your mother was one of my best operatives, Accala, and one of the most intelligent women in the empire. I'm sure she said precisely what she was able to say, given the circumstances. There are secrets that need to be uncovered on Olympus Decimus, dear niece, and it's our job to do it. That's why I need you to accept Crassus' offer. Once you're on the ground, with the pin, I'm certain you'll pick up the scent and find your brother. You have your mother's sharp mind."

Just like when I used to spot spies in the household. He wanted to make use of me again.

"I . . . I don't know. This is all happening so fast and nothing has played out anything like Mother envisioned. How can I possibly search for Aulus in the middle of a gladiatorial contest? If I joined their team, the Sertorians would be watching me all the time."

"I have it on good authority that the course will start at Avis Accipitridae and finish near the ruins of Lupus Civitas, two and a half thousand miles to the east. We know that your brother is being held somewhere between those two points at one of the hidden Sertorian mining bases established before the war started. We have a rough idea of where the bases are, peppered around the range of mountains, but we can't give you a precise location, except to say the most significant bases are all around the middle of the continent. That's our guess as to where they're keeping him."

"So that means by the middle of the tournament I'll have to have established Aulus' location," I stated.

"Yes. You'll be using the games as cover, so where the tournament course goes, you go. It's the easiest way to get close to your brother without rousing the enemy's suspicion—or that of the emperor, for that matter. Now this next part is very important. The Sertorians are double-crossing bastards, each and every one, so don't believe a word they tell you about your brother from here on in. Follow your own instincts until you see Aulus with your own eyes, a solid visual confirmation, nothing less will do."

I walked over to the nearest portal and looked down on the city below. The thought of joining the Sertorian team, of being disciplined and beaten by the men who were responsible for all of the misfortune to befall my family, was almost too much to bear.

"Don't look at your proximity to the Sertorians as a disadvantage," Uncle continued, as if reading my thoughts. "The very people who imprison Aulus will be your teammates. You'll be in an unprecedented position to gather intelligence. And know that I'll be there, keeping an eye out for you the entire time. I have hidden resources on that world, and the moment you find Aulus, I can move heaven and earth to get him out of there, but nothing can happen unless you do your part."

I looked back down at Rome. It vanished suddenly as we passed into another black storm cloud. What was that Uncle said? About there being an advantage in being close to the Sertorians?

"Make no mistake," my uncle continued, "Crassus may have a tenderness for you, but Licinus will try to break you, and all the while you will have to endure his commands, the orders of the man who killed your mother and imprisoned your brother. Remember the hero Mucius Scaevola. His bravery in the face of adversity led to unexpected outcomes. Let them abuse you, let them visit every humiliation upon you, and all the while hide that you're burning away on the inside. Store it all away in your heart, hidden deep within your breast like a burning coal, allowing every indignity to stoke its heat until it is time to unleash the fire."

Mention of Mucius Scaevola did stir the fire inside. The Roman who went to kill the Clusian king, Scaevola was captured before he could do the deed, and when questioned under threat, he thrust his hand into the flames of a brazier to show that Romans had no fear of death. The Clusians were so intimidated by him that they let him go free and begged Rome to forge a peace treaty.

"There is no easy road ahead, but I ask you, can you live with yourself if you remain here in Rome now that I've told you? Now that your mother has petitioned you from beyond the grave?"

"I'll go. That's what a real Roman would do, isn't it?"

"Good girl."

"But there's one thing I must insist upon, Uncle. You know I will do everything in my power to find Aulus, but what then? What of the Sertorians? I set out seeking justice and I mean to have it. If I join with the Blood Hawks, can you promise me that the Sertorians will pay in full and at my own hand?"

He gently pulled me round to stand before him and placed both hands upon my shoulders.

"Oh, but you are my favorite relation. Make no mistake, you shall make them pay, in full and a thousand times over." He crunched another fat grape with his teeth.

"Ah, you know I've got a story for everything. Tell me, dear niece, have you heard the one about the Trojan horse?"

* * *

STANDING ON THE SERTORIAN parade float, I took the hand that Gaius Sertorius Crassus offered me and the damnation that went with it. The Viridian crowd screamed vitriol, hysterical with rage. To my irritation, the people in the Sertorian crowd who did not hurl abuse at me cheered for Crassus. His reputation was enhanced by my presence—I was a coup, a wolf tamed for their amusement.

The only consolation was that my father was nowhere to be seen.

Holographic billboards filled the sky above the parade, projecting live images of the contestants aboard the floats, posting their arena statistics interspersed with crowd shots and sponsored advertising.

The giant oaf Lurco seemed to be positively enjoying the abuse hurled at him by the Viridian crowd. He jumped up and down, swinging his hammer, returning insults.

The procession would come to an end at the Carmental Gate. Passing through it and out of the city's ancient walls, the Blood Hawks would be carried via shuttle to *Incitatus,* the Sertorian proconsul's flagship in stationary orbit above Mother Earth. The gate was so close, but the floats moved at an infuriatingly slow pace. Hades himself could not have devised a more drawn-out torment.

Through a gap in the stained bubble of our protective shield, a large work of graffiti came into view. Painted high on a wall in red was a crude depiction of a crucified woman with a hawk's head. At the foot of the cross was a bad drawing of a severed wolf's head. To remove any potential for confusion, beneath the drawing was written ACCALA MOCK HAWK and the caption A WOLF THAT WILL FLAP ITS ARMS AND SQUAWK FOR FOOD IS NO WOLF AT ALL. Suddenly, a man dressed in a Viridian toga pushed the crowd aside and leveled a supercharged ion pistol at me. He called out something. It might have been *Rome does not reward traitors.* Or perhaps *Rome has spoken.* I couldn't be sure because of the noise. Before he even had the chance to pull the trigger, a purple-cloaked Praetorian lowered his staff, releasing a blast that killed the man instantly. His scorched corpse fell to the ground, twitching and smoldering. Here was the first of my countrymen to die in the wake of my choice to join the Blood Hawks. How many more would follow once the tournament began?

The Viridian team sailed on twenty yards ahead of us, the crowd roaring their approval, trumpets blasting. Their float was showered with confetti and streamers, holographic fireworks and sparklers. The team leader, Vibius Viridius Carbo— friend of my father and champion nobleman athlete—saluted the crowd, lapping up their approval. Their team trainer, Gnaeus Viridius Metellus, swung his steel club to and fro. Behind him came the Viridian charioteers Titus Nervo and Trio Mercurius. Mercurius was my second cousin, a year younger than me, talented but relatively inexperienced. Next were Scipio Caninus, the one-eyed bestiarii, and his counterpart, Capitulus Pavo, shooting bolts of colored light into the sky from his crossbow, much to the crowd's delight. In the arena, the same weapon would fire bolts of black steel, barbed and deadly. Bringing up the rear was Taticulus Viridius Leticus, with his Sauromatae throwing swords—medium-size blades that started out straight before branching out into smaller curves in two places—the middle and hilt. They were similar in nature to my discus as a projectile weapon, though nowhere near as accurate, but they more than made up for that deficiency in close fighting where Leticus could wield them as swords to cut and thrust. Right up front beside Carbo, in the place that should have been mine, was my first cousin, the infuriating Darius Viridius Strabo, sporting his golden bow and arrows. I looked up at the aerial billboards, unable to stomach the regret I felt when I beheld the Viridian team. The Calpurnian float was finally passing through the gate, and the media spherae seemed to have captured the moment from every angle. Standing at the front of their float, heading up the procession, stood Marcus, fist raised high in the air, rallying the crowds. But it couldn't be. Marcus didn't want to fight in the tournament. But then I remembered that when he stuck his neck out to give me my chance, he'd also put himself in contention—and now it seemed he'd taken the last place on the Calpurnian team.

The roar of the crowd was deafening now, so Crassus couldn't hear a word of the oaths and accusations I fired at him. His smile only broadened and he continued waving graciously. Had he arranged Marcus' inclusion? At the very least, he could have told me my lanista would be part of the Ludi Romani. I'd been desperately holding it all together, but the sight of Marcus there nearly broke me. When we reached the arena world, could I kill my mentor? His very presence meant that he certainly felt no compunction about killing me—he was there to eliminate Talonite gladiators, and I was their newest recruit.

Finally, the other floats passed through the gate, and ahead of us I saw the Viridians boarding their team shuttle. Then it was our turn and the nightmare of the parade was over. The sleek black-and-red Sertorian shuttle was only a dozen feet away, waiting to carry me to a much worse torment, servitude to my enemies. What I had endured was only the beginning.

Licinus and the others were already off the float and moving toward the open shuttle door, ignoring the gaggle of news reporters and their insistent questions. Crassus and I weren't so lucky. The reporters formed a ring about us, to delay our departure until they'd secured a quote.

Accala, are you here of your own free will? Why have you betrayed your house? Are you and Crassus lovers?

No words would come and I was glad of it. If they did suddenly burst forth, who knew what I would say? I squeezed Crassus' hand. Better to let him do the talking.

"Of course she's here freely. She hasn't betrayed her house. On the contrary, she's serving it as a beacon of cooperation. By becoming an honorary Sertorian,

Accala Viridius is demonstrating to the Caninine houses the one sure way to ensure galactic peace. Are we lovers?" He smiled at me and then looked to a female reporter from his own house. "All I'll say now is that we have a special relationship." Crassus oozed charm while I tried to keep the contents of my stomach down. My father suddenly came into view, striding toward me in his senatorial robes. He was arguing loudly with a Praetorian officer who had unsuccessfully tried to detain him behind the crowd barriers and was now keeping pace by his side. Crassus saw him too and signaled a Sertorian legionary guarding the shuttle. The soldier went to grab my father, who backhanded the man with his robotic arm. There was the sound of crunching bone as the guard flew away into the crowd.

Lucius Viridius Camillus' face was red, his body trembling with anger. A man who prided himself on discipline, I'd never seen him so close to losing control. I tried to pull Crassus as discreetly as I could toward the shuttle, but there was no escape. My father barreled through the ring of journalists to confront me.

"You're going to walk out of here with me right now," he said. "No arguments." His words were not loud, but they spat and crackled like angry flames burning damp wood. While he spoke, the Praetorian who'd tagged along with him decided that the best course of action would be to leave my father be and clear the space of reporters.

"Please leave, Father. You shouldn't be here. It will only make things worse." My mouth was dry and my words sounded thin and desperate.

"Worse? You have no idea! The entire Senate is in chaos over this incident. You are noble born. What you do, the decisions you make, they impact the world around you, they change things. You're going to come home now. Right this instant."

"Father, I cannot." I fixed my eyes on my feet, refusing to meet his gaze.

"Why? Why have you done this? Tell me, it's not too late. We can still fix this. If they're pressuring you in some way, blackmailing you . . ."

I wanted to grab his robes and scream that that was exactly what they were doing, that I was working for Uncle Quintus, that Aulus was alive and I was going to save him, but Crassus was watching me like a hawk. I could say nothing that would expose our deal, so I looked back down at the ground and tried my best to keep the shame in my heart from my face.

"She's made her choice," Crassus said, putting his arm around me as if we were some eloping couple. His grin made my skin crawl.

"Get away from her before I kill you where you stand," Father growled at Crassus.

They were about to start up a fight over me right there. I placed a restraining hand on Crassus' chest. "He's my father. I'll make him understand."

Crassus shrugged and backed off a few feet but made sure to stay within earshot.

"Accala?" Father asked.

The Praetorian had succeeded in keeping the reporters at bay, but their media spherae still hovered above us, capturing every word.

"Horace says that a person who can be both useful and agreeable will win every point," I said. "I tried my best but since my own house considers me both disagreeable and useless, perhaps another house will see value in my skills."

"I can't believe that," Father said. "Change your mind, say what's really in your heart. Speak again."

"I must do what I must do," I replied. It was the closest I could come to the truth.

He pulled me to him in a strong embrace and whispered, "I'm sorry. I'm sorry I wasn't there for you after they died. Please, you are my child. I don't want to have to disown you. Come home, Accala. I don't want to lose you."

He'd never apologized to me before. Never. And he chose that moment? He sought to find a soft place inside me by using soft words, but I couldn't allow him to steal my momentum. Not now. All the secrets I'd so rapidly acquired were burning inside of me—hot embers I couldn't spit out. There was nothing I could say, no words that would bring him the least amount of comfort. Pulling away from him, I said, "I will swear allegiance to House Sertorian and fight for them in the Ludi Romani." There, that could not be clearer. I'd closed the door, stated my case in a public forum. Father glanced up at the hovering media spherae. I was a lost cause. He had to think about his reputation, and the best interests of House Viridian.

"You've chosen to renounce your family, to sour the noble blood that runs through your veins and become a common slave to this Sertorian man." His words were deliberate, his face heavy with disappointment. "We are done," he said to me. "Make your own choices and survive them if you can. You are no longer my daughter, you may no longer bear the name Viridius. You are out-cast."

And then Lucius Viridius Camillus, senator, hero, my father, whom I had now publicly betrayed in word as well as in deed, turned his back on me and walked away.

The spherae dispersed; the journalists had their juicy footage. The rest of the Sertorian team had already boarded. Crassus waited for me by the shuttle en-trance, tapping his foot like an impatient master waiting for his dog to come to heel. Playing my part, I obeyed.

IX

THE MOMENT THE SHUTTLE ramp closed behind us, I confronted Crassus. "What in the hell is going on? Why is Marcus there? This wasn't part of the deal."

The other members of the team had already moved along the corridor to the main cabin, the door sliding shut behind them.

"I am not Jupiter on high, controlling everything that transpires in the uni-verse," Crassus said. "I had nothing to do with it."

"Then who? Was he forced to join the contest? A way to punish him for sup-porting me?"

"Quite the contrary," Crassus said. "Marcus volunteered."

"He what? I don't believe it."

Crassus turned to a screen on the wall and brought up the morning news clips with a few deft touches of his fingers. My lanista appeared, standing before the altar at the feet of the Palladium, surrounded by a crowd of cheering admirers and journalists, all eager to hear his reaction to my betrayal. Although the patron god of the Calpurnians was Saturn, the Palladium Minerva was the guardian of Rome itself, linked to both the city and the empire's fate, and any citizen could pay to make an offering at her feet. But Marcus was never one to make a public spectacle of his religion. No, this was a statement, letting everyone know that he planned to act on behalf of the whole empire. A large white cow entered the scene, a rope attached to a ring through her nose allowing the beast to be pulled into position before the altar by a robed priest. Ready for the offering, the cow's body was adorned with ribbons and strips of scarlet wool. Three priests consecrated the animal, pouring wine upon her forehead, trailing the sacrificial knife across her back.

"As Accala Viridius Camilla has betrayed you, so has she betrayed me—the lanista whom she vowed to honor and obey," Marcus announced. "She has broken a sacred trust." His face was white, his jaw tense like granite.

The cow lowered her head, a sign that she was willing to be sacrificed, and Marcus cut her throat, quickly and efficiently. The animal's legs gave out and she fell forward to her knees, a river of blood flowing down the front of her white chest and onto the stained marble slab at the base of the altar. She bled out and died in less than a minute. A haruspex, the soothsayer of sacrificial animals, cut the cow's underside open and pulled at the animal's entrails like a greedy crow securing his share. A half dozen Iceni slaves hefted the body onto the hot coals of the ritual fire, the flesh mingling with the smoke, her spirit offered up to the heavens. Then Marcus spoke. "I have dedicated my life to the service of the empire, and so for this last public offering of Minerva's festival, I swear that I shall have justice. I will use all my skills to challenge Accala Viridius Camilla, to prevent her from giving aid to the Blood Hawks and, if Minerva blesses me with the opportunity, to return victorious with the traitorous bitch's head as my trophy."

A bad heat rushed to my head, and the nausea that had been threatening me all morning finally won. I fell to my hands and knees, and vomited onto the shuttle's cold steel floor. Marcus' haruspex must have completed his series of arcane gestures over the mess of organs, because as I retched on my hands and knees, unable to stand, I heard him deliver his prognosis. "The organs are healthy and without flaw. Minerva has accepted the sacrifice!" The crowd cheered and yelled out their approval.

I had meant to make an offering to Minerva that day, first at my altar and then at the Palladium temple, but everything had happened so quickly that I'd forgotten. So focused on solving my own problems, I had also forgotten my obligation to Marcus, and in breaking the bond between us, I had insulted and dishonored him. He had no choice but to act or be shamed and disgraced as my chief supporter. And what of the gods? The goddess knew my heart, but had Marcus' offering and my neglect been enough to make Minerva turn from me?

In four weeks, Marcus and I would meet on a distant world and he would single me out, my death his only goal, and if I wanted to complete my mission and save all that was dear to me, I would have to steal his life instead.

Rome was visible through a series of transparent panels set low into the shuttle wall. The city fell away, like a coin dropped from a great height, until it resembled a white barnacle on the curve of Mother Earth's back. The die was cast. There was no going back.

"Come," Crassus said, gently pulling me to my feet. "You were very brave. That was a great ordeal, but now it's over."

"I don't need your help or your false courtesy."

"Come now, lady. That's not how the game is played. You don't have to like this, but you do have to play along. You're not in a position to be discourteous, and although I am, I refrain from a display of bad taste. Isn't that how civilized people should conduct themselves?"

I was a loathsome being, covered with sweat and the acrid stink of vomit. "You forget, I've been disowned, I'm humiliores. I'm no longer a lady, not even a member of a noble house. I'm a plebeian with no aspiration to civilized manners."

"Breeding tells," he stated. "Your bloodline, your performance in the arena indicate that you have superior genetics, and that can't be taken away by removing a title. In the Sertorian utopia, your unique bloodline will be all the currency you need to prosper."

"I don't know a single Sertorian who is worth his salt. What does that say about your genes?"

One moment he stood before me, the next he was behind me so suddenly I didn't even see him move. He was fast, supernaturally fast. My arm had been seized and was being twisted up into the small of my back. "I've improved since we last sparred, Lady Accala," he said, his head beside mine, his hot breath on my cheek. "You're the one who's going to have to work hard to earn your salt on our team." And then he was in front of me again. Gods, how did he get so fast?

"Come. It's time to meet your teammates. I think you'll find them rather impressive."

Courage. I needed more than I had. Crassus stopped outside the door to the cabin.

"Remember, whatever happens in there, you must remain calm. Do not raise a hand to any of them."

My heart was beating like I was entering the arena. I tried to recall all I had read about these competitors in my research. When the door slid open, I found that there were only six in the cabin. Licinus was absent—a small mercy—he must have been in the partitioned cockpit at the front of the craft.

"Did you see them out there? They loved us!" Lurco crowed. He had his back to the door and hadn't realized Crassus and I had entered.

The sultry, dark-haired Barbata silenced him with a gesture and then smiled at me, a frighteningly warm smile. Her teeth were perfect, like shining pearls. "Welcome, sister. Come, join us." She was beautiful, confident, and flawless, dressed in a body-hugging red leather gladiatorial outfit. Black stripes down the sides and horizontal ring designs about the torso accentuated her curves, and lines of sharpened steel studs glinted in the shuttle's bright light. By contrast, I was a self-conscious mess, dressed in vomit-spattered novice's robes.

Crassus wanted me to play it humble and submissive, but I couldn't afford to show weakness so early on. A wolf understands pack dynamics. You never wanted to be the weakest member of the pack. They needed to know I wasn't an easy target.

Ignoring Barbata, I left her standing there expectantly, and scanned the room. The identical twin brothers, Castor and Pollux Sertorius Corvinus, stared at me with cold, expressionless faces. They were dressed in neatly pressed black robes with thin, angular scarlet lines running their length. The oddest thing was that they had only two arms between them and sat together, giving the appearance of one wide body with two heads. Each one had a long knife strapped to his belt. They would have looked a perfect mirror image, but for their hair—they were both blond, but Castor wore his short hair straight up like he'd just received an electric shock, while Pollux's was combed back to give the impression of a hawk's plumage.

"No arms, huh? Get caught on either side of a land mine?" I asked. They didn't bite, though, not even a hint of an expression.

"We know this must be hard for you, but there's no need to be unpleasant," Barbata said. When she spoke, I saw an unsettling, reptilian glimmer in her eyes. "Come, we mean you no harm."

"Unless you don't follow the rules," Castor Corvinus said matter-of-factly. "Then you will be punished."

"You won't need to punish her," Mania Sertorius Curia said. The skinny, pale little girl with white hair didn't seem any more imposing than when I observed her on the float. In fact, if anything, she looked smaller, like I could have snapped one of her arms in half like a twig. "We're going to be best friends, I just know it," she said to me in her childish voice. "We'll share everything. All our secrets. All our hopes and dreams."

The brothers made their disdain clear as day, but Mania had a kind of faux innocence that was genuinely frightening. She projected the essence of a child who mindlessly pulls the wings from flies. Another might have set upon her as an obvious target, but Mania wasn't weak; she was deadly, a bear trap waiting to snap shut, and I wasn't going to put my hand in to see what happened—not yet, anyway.

"Thank you, Mania," Crassus said, cutting her off. "You must learn not to go on and on."

Team Blood Hawk was like a circus act in an insane asylum. The ancient Julii were inbred, and it led to all sorts of problems. The Sertorians had not learned from this and continued to breed among themselves, eliminating the weakest and least aggressive from each generation and enhancing the tendencies of the cunning and violent with the science of genetic streamlining. It seemed to me likely that every Sertorian had a genetic predisposition toward psychopathic megalomania. That left Lurco, then, the only other non-Sertorian in the room. He was an outsider, like me, and the Sertorians wouldn't be as irritated if I took him down. At the same time, he was almost twice my size. Humbling him would make the others think twice about harassing me.

"I'm here, I'll do my part," I said, "but don't expect me to like it, or any of you, for that matter." I made certain to eyeball Lurco as I spoke, challenging him.

"Accala," Crassus said in a warning tone, "play nice."

"Can I take first shot at her?" Lurco pleaded, like a dog whining for its share of the carcass. "I've been wanting to humble this pretty little wolf for a long time."

"You know what they say?" I responded. "The bigger they are, the harder they try to form a coherent thought."

"You most certainly cannot," Barbata said to Lurco. "Accala's like a prize mare. We must look after her, train her to perform to the best of her ability."

"Come," Lurco protested, "she's not from a Talonite house. We can have a bit of fun with her on the voyage. Just like any wild beast, she'll warm to my touch with a little coaxing." As he spoke, the giant Tullian reached out to touch my breast, but before I could teach him the price of such discourtesy, Barbata stepped in between us and struck his left pectoral muscle with her fingertips, just above his heart. The big man's knees weakened, and he winced in pain. His left arm hung at his side like a cut vine, useless until the nerve Barbata had struck recovered. "Get out of my way, woman, or I swear by Dis Pater . . ."

Lurco went to push Barbata aside with his right hand, but she was up against him faster than I could blink, a claw hand seizing his groin. It was the same uncanny speed Crassus had displayed. Lurco groaned and stretched up onto his toes as she squeezed, his body trying to escape the pain. "You swear?" Barbata demanded. "Do you swear upon your testicles as men do when you testify in court?" She gave a quick, sharp squeeze, and the giant fell to his knees like a riverbank collapsing to mud in heavy rains, cradling his crotch.

The Dioscurii regarded the shamed Lurco with the same cold dispassion they directed at me. Lurco was one of the best fighters in the Roman arena, but Barbata had dropped him like a sack of potatoes. Clearly the Tullian didn't possess the speed of either Crassus or Barbata. So why did they pick him for their team? Did they have an alternate use for him as Crassus claimed he had for me, some kind of personality in a propaganda campaign I wasn't privy to?

"You are new here as well," Crassus said to Lurco. "And I suggest you don't underestimate Barbata because she is a woman. She may be a dark beauty, but she's able to manage all kinds of beasts with appropriate ferocity."

"And panache," Barbata added with a sly smile. "Because without style, what's the point of living?"

"I don't see why you had to do that," Lurco muttered in annoyance. "I was just asking a question."

"What this silly boy doesn't understand is that Sertorians are not cruel without good reason," Barbata said to me with a conspiratorial wink. "We are efficient, we eliminate divergence. Lurco Giganticus here was laboring under an antiquated notion about the combat effectiveness of women. I wished to highlight the erroneous thought so it would be easy for him to correct it." She held out her hand to help Lurco stand, but he refused it and struggled awkwardly up on his own. "Once we're all on the same page, all part of the one idea, then we're able to be of better use to one another."

"A single idea. Even a flower with eight petals has the same corolla at its center," Castor Corvinus added.

"That's a reference from Proconsul Aquilinus' manifesto," Crassus said. "You'll learn more about that later, Accala."

"The Seven Precepts of the Eagle," Castor added.

"Don't you speak?" I asked Pollux, but he didn't reply. I'd met clinical professionals before, fighters who were so focused on training and winning that they wouldn't give you the time of day, but the Corvinus brothers were different. They looked at me like a scientist contemplating a laboratory mouse.

Gaia Barbata put her hands on my shoulders. Long, sharpened nails protruded from the ends of long fingers like a bird's claws, pressing painfully into my skin. The nails were painted black with a molecular resin, making them near unbreakable and sharp as steel. I remembered reading that she'd killed more than a dozen opponents in the arena using them alone. "You shouldn't tease Pollux Corvinus. We are what our nature dictates," she said in a condescending tone. "You, for instance, are a mangy wolf that we must try to transform into a resplendent hawk. This will not be an easy undertaking for you or for us, but fear not, we'll all make the sacrifices necessary to help you fit in. As long as you cooperate and follow the rules." She walked over to Lurco and put an arm around him, causing him to flinch. "This large Tullian broke the rules of civility," she said, smiling. "He too has much to learn."

"Yes, the rules are all important," Mania chirped.

"How can I follow rules when they haven't been explained to me?" I asked.

"The rules are simple. Everyone here is your master," Crassus said. "Except for Lurco," he added, waving dismissively at the Tullian. "We all have something to teach you, and you'll be expected to learn willingly and fit in with the team as quickly as possible."

"You will submit, body and mind, to the proconsul's precepts," Castor Corvinus said.

"And can I add something?" Mania asked, bouncing up and down in her seat. "Honesty is very important to me. I want her to know that she has to be completely honest if she wants to be my friend. I can't stand liars."

"They will not use you poorly," Crassus said, "or I will see them punished. But you must do what they ask."

"I will use you poorly." Licinus Sertorius Malleolus, the man I'd imagined killing a thousand times over, strode into the bridge from the cockpit. Lean and hard, not tall but still imposing. Steel-gray eyes matched his close-cropped hair, giving him a ghostlike quality. Small white scars lined his face. This was no Sertorian cast from the same mold as Crassus, no aristocratic veneer of manners and culture. His eyes held none of Crassus' playfulness; they were devoid of mercy—Licinus was a vulture in human form. Orbis vibrated at my belt, sensing my need to attack, but my uncle's words were ever present in my mind.

Let them abuse you, let them visit every humiliation upon you, and all the while hide that you're burning away on the inside.

"I trust they've been making you feel welcome, Mock Hawk," Licinus said. It seemed he also had seen the graffiti during the procession. Picking up a black steel pitcher, he slowly poured water into a glass. "That's what the mob is calling you now: Mock Hawk. It makes sense. You're not really a wolf anymore, are you? A wolf is proud, fierce, loyal. A wolf is part of a pack, but I think your pack just showed you what they think of you. Even your father won't claim you as his own. As best I can make out, you are a dog. A mangy unblooded mongrel bitch." He smirked slightly, as if at some private joke, then slowly drank the water in the glass. "You are a slave and I am the team leader, which makes you *my* slave," he continued. "If you wish to earn your freedom as well as your brother's life, then you will comply with my every order. You will behave as a slave is expected to behave. Tell me you understand."

"I do," I said, clenching my teeth, letting the insults fan the embers in my heart.

"Good." Licinus moved in close to me. Dipping an index finger into his glass, he slowly trailed a wet finger across my cheek, over my closed lips. His eyes were filled with a dark excitement, an anticipation of what would follow if I dared resist him. When he saw that I would neither pull away nor fight back, a bored expression passed over his face. "Don't worry, Mock Hawk, you and I will have a grand time. I'll burn you as I burned your mother. Nice and crispy like a good side of bacon."

The fire flared at once, filling me with rage. All I could see was the new ear-to-ear smile I planned on giving Licinus with Orbis' edge. That'd wipe the smirk off his face. Before I consciously realized it, Orbis was in my hand. Crassus called out for me to stop, reaching out to me. The next thing I knew I was on the floor, screaming in pain. Intense, like electricity flowing through every nerve in my body, a whole-body agony like I'd never experienced before. Then, just as quickly, the shock ended.

"Are you getting her readings?" Licinus asked Castor Corvinus.

"Heart rate, adrenaline levels, brain hemispheres are mapped and lit. She's an open book," he said.

Lying there twitching as the last of the electricity left my body, I became aware of a unexpected jangling weight on my right wrist. A thin, delicate chain of blood red calcedonius had been fastened around it. Crassus must have slipped it on me when he tried to stop me attacking Licinus. Calcedonius was a mercurial substance, programmable by way of electric currents to alternate between fixed and fluid forms. The design of the clasp was of a small and intricate hawk with talons outstretched. The other end of the chain had Mother Earth represented in the shape of a ball that the hawk grasped in order to close the loop. There was no catch to open the clasp, so I started pulling on it. Gently at first and then more fervently as it did not yield. I forgot about the others on the shuttle. If I couldn't free myself of this one small thing, what hope did I have to stand against House Sertorian? What possible hope to even begin to search for Aulus? Like a spirited horse being fitted for a bridle, I wanted to buck, to scream, but I carefully kept panic out of my voice. "Take it off," I said to Crassus as I sat up. "Now."

"It stays. A dog needs a collar in order to be trained," Licinus said. "All the Sertorian team members have the code to activate your bracelet. It will help remind you of your place while we're en route to the tournament."

Gaia Barbata came over and helped me to my feet.

"We use a variation of it to train the barbarian slaves. Of course yours is more attractive so that it will go unnoticed while you're competing," she said. I pulled away from her, but she just smiled graciously. "Don't be upset. It's to help you listen and learn. We don't need to use it unless you're trying to fly in a different direction from the flock. No stragglers allowed."

Licinus grabbed my arm and demanded I tap in the code to remove my armilla. He handed it to Mania and then he pointed to Orbis. "Your weapon too."

Crassus saw my hesitation. "Give it to him," he urged, producing my weapon case from a corner of the room and holding it open. "You'll get it back when we train."

As I submitted to his command, I thought of Aulus. The gap in his smile. He was so young. He deserved a chance at life, and I was willing to endure anything to see he got it. The case snapped shut like an alligator's mouth. Licinus snatched it from Crassus and held it with the satisfaction of a pawnbroker facing down a customer with a lost ticket.

"When does training start?" I asked.

"Your obedience training has started already. You will become the Mock Hawk and learn to mimic Sertorian thought, culture, and action to perfection. If you attempt to strike me outside of our practice sessions or disrupt the functioning of my team, then the deal is off and you will be killed along with your brother. The journey to the arena world will take four weeks. In three weeks we will exit the Janus Cardo closest to Olympus Decimus. You have until then to impress me."

"That wasn't what we discussed," Crassus said angrily, rising to his feet. "She's paid the price of admittance."

"I have no interest in helping you achieve your outcomes," he said bluntly to Crassus, "and she might have paid your price, but she hasn't paid mine. She's not officially on the team until I say so, and for that privilege she's going to have to pay and keep on paying."

"I will personally speak to Proconsul Aquilinus about this—" Crassus started, but Licinus moved in close to him.

"Whatever delusions you have about your influence with the proconsul, you'd do well not to express them in my presence," Licinus growled. "I am the team leader and, even though the proconsul has spoken and we must see your ridiculous plan to its conclusion, you are still second in charge. Now get on with your job and keep your pet on a short leash, Crassus." For the first time I saw just how much they hated each other.

To the rest of the team, Licinus said, "We start drills tomorrow, get settled in and rest while you can." As he passed me on his way back to the cockpit, he made a kissing motion with his lips. "Good dog."

"Don't mind him," Barbata said. "The commander is only cruel to be kind. Win his approval and you will find him to be the best of allies. Yes, even to you. Get settled aboard *Incitatus*. Have a bath and then I'll see what we can do about your appearance."

I felt like a soiled dishrag. Barbata had a way of belittling those around her. As she went on about my appearance, I saw that Pollux Corvinus was leveling a finger at me, just sitting there silently pointing at me.

"He's upset," Castor said. "You shouldn't have laughed at his missing arm. My brother doesn't like being reminded of it."

"I can tell. He looks positively distraught," I said. Neither brother had registered anything resembling a human emotion since I'd entered the shuttle.

Castor Corvinus had an attachment that extended from the underside of his armilla to the base of his palm, permitting him to tap out commands with one hand alone. He mapped out a sequence with his middle finger, and suddenly the bracelet shocked me again, sharp and hard. It was short this time, not enough to send me to the floor, just enough to make me squirm for their amusement.

Training under Marcus had equipped me for this. Let them all burn and torture me, it wouldn't matter. I could endure.

Crassus led me from the room. I suppose he figured I'd be less danger to myself or the others if I were out of the way, back by the shuttle doors.

"I like you," Mania called after me. "You know, I trap more than just animals. I trap dreams and I'm pretty good at it too. I bet yours are filled with fire and pain, aren't they? I can see it in your eyes."

"You shouldn't play with fire unless you want to get burned," I replied as the door slid shut. Her astute guess about my nightmares unsettled me, and I hoped I hadn't given any sign that she'd hit the mark.

The second Crassus and I were alone, I demanded he remove the bracelet.

"You gave me no choice. Quid pro quo, Accala—I do for you and you do for me. We'd agreed that you would be obliging, and you decided to have your own bright ideas. You were going to attack Lurco and then Licinus, don't try to say you weren't. If I hadn't put that on your wrist, you'd be dead and your little brother not far behind. Is that what you want?"

"You know it isn't," I said, gritting my teeth.

"Once the tournament is under way, when the time is right, we will work together to strike at our mutual enemy. Until then, you must play along. So let me hear you say it. Do we have an understanding?"

"Yes. For now. I will obey."

X

OUR TRIREME WAS A speck against *Incitatus,* the vessel that would carry us to Olympus Decimus and the Emperor's Great Games. Ominous and foreboding, clad in black-and-red armor plate, it hung in dark space and resembled a giant bird in flight, outstretched wings and a narrow prow, the Sertorian standard of the crimson hawk emblazoned on its primary communication tower.

The pride of the Sertorian fleet, Proconsul Aquilinus' flagship was a deceres-class ten-deck war carrier, capable of transporting a squadron of attack triremes, quinqueremes, and single-pilot talon attack fighters. It had been stripped of most of its cannons and missile turrets to satisfy the tournament rules restricting heavy armaments within a light-year perimeter of the arena world.

Crassus explained to me that *Incitatus* was named for the favorite horse of Caligula, the mad emperor of ancient days whom the Sertorians glorified as their genetic ancestor.

Caligula had given his horse a fine house, slaves, a stable of marble, a trough of ivory, and a decorative harness dripping with rare jewels. In similar style, Proconsul Aquilinus had his flagship embossed in shining gold, platinum, and ruby—liquefied and cast in decorative channels along the ship's hull. My remembrance of the story was that Caligula was mad enough to make his horse a high priest and would have made him a consul if the Senate and Praetorian Guard, tired of his outrages, hadn't teamed up to assassinate him. I assumed they probably killed the horse as well, or maybe they set it free to roam in the countryside, far from the strange demands of human beings. Aquilinus, the Sertorians' proconsul, hadn't made any public display of madness to rival Caligula, but who knew what he would be capable of if he rose to take the emperor's throne? History had borne out again and again that dark desires and near-infinite power were never a good combination.

The shuttle entered the docking bay, and we exited to a vast hangar buzzing with Sertorians in red-and-black uniforms. The noise was tremendous—hundreds of soldiers and technicians moved purposefully, preparing for departure. It was like being dropped into a bird's gizzard. All of them worked together, like a hawk's body breaking down its food.

"You see?" Crassus said proudly. "This is the seventeenth legion Sertorian. Strength through discipline. Our greatness is built on more than just good genes."

A train of black steel cages with narrowly fitted bars was being transported across the docking bay floor. Sauromatae claws stuck out through the gaps of one cage as the creatures tried to escape. The serpentine tail of a Galatian chimera flicked briefly out between another set of bars, and something was shrieking. It was a cavalcade of imprisoned barbarians who were none too happy about the future that awaited them aboard a Sertorian ship. I didn't blame them. I felt a headache coming on as I watched the beast cages, a dull buzz at the back of my skull like tinnitus but with a pulse.

As Crassus led me through the vessel, the legionaries around us began sniggering and chattering. Their jeers grew increasingly louder; some were running ahead to tell others so they could join in the fun—the wolf that stumbled into the hawk's nest. I was the new inmate in the Sertorian madhouse. I tried to maintain an air of dignity, but every dozen steps or so, I'd realize I was holding my breath and be forced to take a big, gasping inhalation like a fish suddenly finding itself marooned on dry land.

The interior of the ship was sleek, antiseptic. Efficient, streamlined, like a well-run abattoir. Everywhere alien slaves polished, swept, scrubbed, and cleaned. We traveled to the officers' quarters on the mid-decks. Polished steel and black marble floors and walls were embedded with bands of illuminated ruby. It had no life, no art, none of the organic lived-in quality of Viridian ships, which had simple, utilitarian designs and were rough and scuffed with honest wear. The Sertorian deck was clean enough to eat off of.

"The accommodation aboard a military ship is primitive, but it will have to suffice until we reach our destination," Crassus said.

Gaius Crassus' rooms were the most lavish ship's quarters I'd ever seen. A wall-length portal, handmade rugs of deep crimson, plush divans, floor lamps made from the hides of exotic animals, the walls lined with hunting weapons and gladiatorial trophies—wreaths, banners, the helmets of worthy enemies. The room reeked of his musky cologne.

"Please refresh yourself here. I'll join you later after I've reported back to the proconsul."

"Proconsul Aquilinus is aboard the ship?" I asked.

"He's on Sertorius Primus for now but will arrive on Olympus Decimus in time for the games," Crassus said with a curt bow to excuse himself.

"Wait, these are your quarters. I will require my own rooms."

"You've made your bed and you might as well lie in it, and why not with me? I am the closest thing you have to an ally aboard this ship. Remember, as you reminded me earlier, you are humiliores now, a person without a house, a slave whose humanity is the only advantage you possess over a common alien."

"Go to hell. I'll take any other cabin."

"Are you certain? Humble quarters may not be suitable for a lady. Here with me you will have fine food, warmth, comfort at night to help you survive the difficult days ahead. Our bodies are merely vehicles for our will; there's nothing unnatural about taking pleasure in them." He reached out to touch my cheek, but I jerked away.

"As you've pointed out, I'm your slave, so here's where we find out how civilized a Sertorian can be. You can legally torture me or rape me. I'm less than a prostitute, you wouldn't even have to pay a sesterce to use me. I have suffered many indignities today in the interest of saving my brother's life. Will you add the offense of rape too?"

"Lady, I—"

"I told you, I'm not a lady anymore."

"Very well, it shall be as you wish," he said, somewhat taken aback. "We are not all animals, as you might think. Civility is important to me, and I can only hope that your attitude toward me softens over the course of our voyage. I desire you, I think you know that, but I will not take you unless you will it, unless you offer yourself to me."

"Not even if Hades were to freeze over."

"Perhaps, we'll see. Remember, I am your ally and guide. To treat me as the enemy is to miss the mark and endanger your mission."

Crassus snapped his fingers, and an Iceni stepped forward, head lowered and palms open, awaiting his orders. I hadn't even noticed it on entering.

"Alba here will be your body slave and help you prepare. I can't send you to the female legionaries' quarters. The fights would never end." Crassus covered his mouth with his hand, thumb pressing upon cheekbone as he pondered my situation. "I've got it. Alba, show Accala to the collegia's quarters."

"Any collegium in particular, dominus?" the Iceni squeaked. "There are not many vacant bunks."

" 'Not many' means that there are some. Send her wherever there's a spare bed. Must I think of everything for you?" He looked back at me as he left, as if to say, *Slaves! How much stupidity must a master endure?*

Alba led me to an elevator which took us down into the depths of the overcrowded lower decks. Here were to be found the cramped quarters of the collegia's auxiliaries.

I'd encountered collegia representatives many times at home and at the Senate. They came to negotiate terms with my father, to cut a better deal for their members. Nothing could be built, shipped, mined, healed, traded, or repaired without the collegia's manpower and in an eight-thousand-year-old galaxy-spanning empire, that made them the most powerful force after the noble houses. Even prostitution had its own collegial guild. The houses disliked the collegia intensely, regarding them in a slightly better light than organized criminal gangs (and vice versa—the collegia bore no love for the houses), but mutual need kept them on functional, if not friendly, terms.

The small alien led me to the women's wing, where I saw the symbols of collegia nurses, slave handlers, prostitutes. Just as in every aspect of Roman life, the men held the prestigious positions and the women were left with the dirty work.

The Iceni opened the door, revealing a room that was so small it could easily have been mistaken for a kitchen lardarium. It had a single portal, a thick, narrow bench top emerging from the wall, a tall storage locker, and a double bunk. If Crassus' quarters were classed as a cabin, I didn't know what to call these accommodations—a tin can?

"What's *she* doing here?" a voice asked.

A redheaded woman lay motionless on the bottom bunk. She certainly couldn't be a Sertorian—they'd eliminated redheads from their gene pool. A tool chest on the floor was marked with the symbol of the Vulcaneum immunes— trained auxiliaries, hired to build and repair machines, often in stressful environments. A female field engineer? That was admirable. She wore the orange-and-gold uniform of her collegium. They trained them tough; some members of the Vul-caneum saw more action than a legion soldier.

"Dominus, Crassus Sertorius says she is to sleep here," the Iceni slave said.

The woman looked me up and down. "You're that Mock Hawk everyone's talking about, aren't you?" Before I could answer, she said to Alba, "She's bad luck. Take her somewhere else."

"There are no other rooms for her," Alba said. "She is a contestant in the tour-nament."

"I know damn well who she is. She's the only Viridian on a ship full of Serto-rians. She's trouble on two legs. Send her back to Crassus."

"I am no longer a Viridian," I said.

"The master offered her his best rooms. She won't stay in them," the Iceni said.

The redhead snorted like she'd heard something funny. "Hmph. I don't blame you. Most of the women down here swoon as he walks by, but Crassus isn't my type either."

"Why not?" I asked. "He's handsome enough."

"He makes my skin crawl. Don't ask me why, he just does. Come to think of it, I have the same reaction around most Sertorians."

"This is a funny place to end up, then."

"It's a means to an end. The Sertorians have the most money and that means I can get my hands dirty working on the best engines."

I took an instant liking to her and her uninhibited expressiveness in discuss-ing Sertorians. The skills possessed by the collegia granted them a certain im-munity from the houses and the confines of polite society. It was not permitted to assault or torture collegia members without good legal cause, and even then, if their guild membership fees were paid up, they could expect their particular collegium to come to their aid if they were unduly harassed or injured.

Departure imminent. An announcement came through a speaker panel above the door.

"If you're going to stay, then lie down," the immune said.

"Pardon me?"

"Lie down. On the bunk."

"I shall stand," I declared. She might be an amusing character, but if we were going to be bunked together I had to teach her from the outset that I had no intention of jumping to every time a plebeian laborer wanted to show me who was boss.

As I walked over to the small portal, a faint vibration carried up through the deck. The ship's engines were firing up. Out the portal I could see Mother Earth. Within a few hours we would reach Jupiter, and from there enter into the first Janus Cardo—a gateway of folded space that would allow our ships to travel vast distances in relatively short time. It would be a four-week voyage to Olympus Decimus passing through four Janus Cardo—an equivalent journey of count-less generations without them, even with the empire's most powerful engines driving us through the darkness. The empire couldn't run without the Janus Cardo. If they collapsed in on themselves like a house of cards, the distances between the provinces would suddenly become impossible to navigate. Looking down at the blue and green sphere I'd called home my entire life, I wondered if it wouldn't be a bad thing—if the network did fail and every house just stayed in their own province, thousands of light-years apart—peace through the tyranny of distance.

All of a sudden, the ship's thrusters kicked in and I fell to my hands and knees, weighed down as if a mountain had been dropped on me.

"It's the acceleration required to escape Earth's gravity," the redhead said. "It's a killer, isn't it? They don't turn on the inertial dampeners until after the launch; it slows the initial thrust."

My muscles gave out and I fell flat to the floor, trapped by the invisible pressure until a pinging chime sounded, the dampeners kicked in, and I could sit up and move. My muscles ached from the sudden strain.

"That never gets tired," my cabinmate said with a chuckle. "Like a crab on its back. You should have seen yourself. Never been away from Mother Earth a day in your life, I'd wager. Next time, if someone offers you well-meant advice, you should take it."

"Come, domina. I'll help you clean yourself," the Iceni said, helping me to my feet.

"I don't need your help," I snapped, brushing her away. As I regained my feet, I saw that the redhead was still smiling at my predicament.

"Wipe that smirk off your face before I do it for you."

"You're very fiery for someone without a house or a guild to protect her," she said mildly. "You'd do well to remember that you're no princess anymore. I can talk to you any damn way I please."

"Domina, please," Alba pleaded, pulling me toward the door. "It will be quicker if I help you. I can take away your used clothes. Come now."

The servant didn't want me getting in a fight; it would make her job harder if I lost the room for fighting. And the redhead's matter-of-fact tone and lack of aggression helped me get control of myself. It would be all too easy to beat this woman to a pulp and release some of my mounting frustrations, but if I lost the bunk, I could end up being forced into Crassus' bed. Whatever ideas my uncle had, I wasn't going to throw my legs open for any Sertorian.

"Better hurry up, it's almost curfew time," the redhead said. "The Sertorians have a gods-be-damned list of rules as long as your arm, and they expect them to be followed."

"It's still too early for a night curfew," I said. "It's not even lunch yet."

"We're on arena world time now. Get our bodies adjusted so we arrive ready and raring to go."

Alba led me to a communal washroom on the other side of the corridor. Thankfully, as most of the passengers had gone to their cabins for the launch, it was empty.

"I didn't see you fall," I said to the Iceni as she helped me undress.

"We have been traveling through space for millions of years. My people fashion buildings and ships with our very bodies. This amount of force is easy for us to bear, domina."

Her account reminded me of an article I'd read on the Iceni body ships. It speculated that there was a vast hidden empire of them out there, far beyond the boundaries of Rome, and that we'd only scratched the surface of their civilization with the few planets we'd colonized near the Barbaricum Wall, the boundary marking the edge of the empire. I placed my mother's pin safely in sight on a shelf in the shower. "I can wash myself," I said to Alba, snatching the sponge from her hand. She blinked her red eye as if confused but then withdrew to stand facing the wall, affording me some privacy.

It took me a moment to work out how to operate the shower. I'd only ever used baths before, like a civilized person, but soon the soothing warm water ran over my body, putting an end to the trembling that had beset me. Holding the bracelet under the water, I tried to use the soap to slip it off, but it only seemed to tighten in response. I jerked at it again and again until it rubbed the skin around my wrist so raw it was about to bleed, then gave up, beating my fist against the wall, cursing Crassus' name.

Humiliores. A low-class citizen, adrift without a house. A house protected you, upheld your rights. Without a house, you had none. It wasn't until I spoke with my new cabinmate that it hit home: I wasn't just Crassus' slave, I was everyone's slave. Every citizen of Rome with a house or guild behind him or her was my better and could punish me with impunity. Silent tears mixed with the shower water. The sharp light in the showers lit up my pin, covering it with a golden sheen. I squinted; my eyes were sensitive to the light. It was that relentless buzzing headache, droning away in the background.

He therefore who does not view with equal unconcern pain or pleasure, death or life, fame or dishonor . . . clearly commits a sin. . . . Despise not death; smile rather at its coming. . . . I do that which it is my duty to do. Nothing else distracts me.

The quotes that surfaced from the pool of my memory while I showered were from Marcus Aurelius, drummed into me by my mother.

* * *

WHEN I WAS FOURTEEN, I saw two large Tullian boys thrashing a homeless boy for sport. I intervened and broke the arm of one, the leg of the other. The next day I was dragged before a magistrate and charged with assault with a weapon. The Tullians had contrived a story that I'd attacked them with a pipe, since they couldn't admit to being beaten by a girl. The injured boy was without a house to represent him and too frightened to testify. The magistrate found me guilty without hesitation—the testimony of two males, the perpetrators, outweighing that of a female. Due to my family connections, I was only fined and managed to avoid the whip and imprisonment.

My mother entered my bedroom that evening, not with a chastisement or to lecture me about violence begetting violence, but instead quoting philosophy.

"You can rise above pleasures and pains, you can resist the urge to clamber for adulation, you can keep your temper with the foolish and ungrateful, yes, and even care for them." She smiled and sat down on my bed. "That was Caesar Marcus Aurelius Antonius Augustus, the greatest leader of the empire's first Golden Age."

"I'd rather you tell me how I can get back at those Tullian thugs and the idiot magistrate who let them walk away unpunished."

"Philosophy will give you everything you seek," Mother said. "I know you only want to know about fighting and be like your father, but this is not something that weak, navel-gazing bookworms have made up to fill their spare time. Philosophy is about survival. It's about making sense of the chaos of existence before we succumb to its emptiness and destroy ourselves."

"I don't need philosophy, I need justice. If I were a man, I would never have been charged. I wish I'd killed those boys and saved myself all that trouble."

"They deserve death because they bullied a boy? What they did was wrong, but does it merit that severe a punishment? Is that justice?"

"What if it was me they thrashed? Or raped? What would your conclusion be then?"

"You are too smart for your own good, Accala Viridius. Try to grasp the point. It's how we perceive a situation that can mean the difference between life and death, satisfaction or misery, hope or despair.

"In this empire, a woman must be more intelligent, more perceptive than a man if she is to exercise power for the greater good. We are constrained by custom and history, but our minds and spirits give us the power to transcend any boundaries."

"A thousand barriers stand between a woman and real power," I exclaimed.

"The only true barrier is within yourself, and if you learn philosophy, you can learn to transcend it."

Even though she herself was a Platonist at heart—seeking to realize the perfect world of ideal forms in the muddy reality of the everyday—my temperament, she counseled, would be best managed by following the Stoic school, the path embraced by Marcus Aurelius when he was a young general.

"Stoicism is the philosophy of the practical, of the individual, so that no matter what storms life throws at you, you will be armed with a grim determination to tough it out and see things through to the end. You embrace the law, universal galactic citizenship, rationalism, the laws of nature, the benevolent workings of Providence, and the divine reason that permeates the universe as a designing fire. Moral ideals will become your shield and sword when you have no physical ones."

"Those are fine words. The kind Father bandies about in the Senate. Swords and shields are real. They make a difference."

"You remember when you started at the Academy? How difficult the initial training was."

"They said they had to weed the weakness out of our limbs."

"And to learn philosophy, you must weed the weakness out of your mind by not taking our beliefs and opinions for granted but by examining them. First, though, we begin with memorization."

I groaned and resisted every step of the way, but she read and then made me recite Marcus Aurelius' *Meditations* in its entirety until I hated it and would hear the words in my dreams. After that followed Epictetus and Seneca.

"Don't complain, Accala," Mother said. "If you know something by heart, then it is always with you. Your body can always be confined and tormented, but your mind is your own. No one can take away from you something you know by heart—it's there with you for comfort and counsel, yours for all time."

* * *

MOTHER WAS WISE. IT was her voice I heard when I recalled Marcus Aurelius' words. I reminded myself of my duty again and again. What I endured aboard this ship would be nothing compared to seeing my brother alive. Every indignity the Sertorians visited upon me would be accounted for in good time.

"Crassus had my trunk. Is it on board?" I asked Alba as she dried me off. Everything had been moving so quickly, I had forgotten about it. As it stood, the only possessions I could be certain of were the vomit-stained robes and Mother's precious pin.

"Master has seen to your clothing," Alba said. She left, only to return a moment later with a small, sheer black silk night gown. This was what he wanted me to wear in his cabin. It was little better than being naked. "Find something else," I instructed. "Something practical."

The alien nodded, bowed, and scuttled away, returning quickly with a full-length black sleeping robe, warm and modest. When I returned to the cabin, the small portal framed a field of bright and distant stars.

"You look much better," the redhead said from her bunk. "I thought I'd been bunked with a leper when you first came in."

Ignoring her, I studied my reflection in the portal. The woman who looked back at me had wide, frightened eyes. It wouldn't do to wear my heart on my sleeve. The Blood Hawks must see only strength when they looked at me. A woman able to withstand any battering like the walls of the Wolf's Den back in Rome. Thinking of home triggered the memory of my father hugging me at the end of the procession.

I'm sorry. I'm sorry I wasn't there for you after they died. Please, you are my child. I don't want to have to disown you. Come home.

Right now I wished for nothing more than just that. To hug Father as I did when I was a child, to curl up on my bed back home, but I was an adult now with my own share of family commitments. Father would forgive me everything when I returned Aulus to him. He must be home by now. And Bulla, I never had a chance to say good-bye to her. Was she outside the door to my chambers, lowing at my sudden absence as she had for my mother and brother?

"It's not much of a view," my cabinmate said, interrupting my thoughts.

"I'm imagining that I'm somewhere out there, anywhere but here," I said.

"You don't like the Hawks much, huh?" she asked.

There was no point replying to such a stupid question. How could anyone like the Sertorians?

"I try not to get involved in politics," she went on. "It's the collegia way. We just keep our heads low and do what we do. I work on machines. They're slow, I make them run faster; they're broken, I put them back together."

"Some things can't be put back together," I said, climbing up the ladder and onto my bunk. The bed had a hard, rectangular pillow and no sheets, only a radiant heat plate built into the mattress. While the Sertorians slept on plush mattresses, those who served them received only the bare essentials.

Alba was hovering about the foot of the bunks, a length of thin chain in her hands. One end of the chain was fixed to the bed's steel frame.

"What are you doing?"

"It is the rules. All slaves are to be chained at night. It is the same for me. I will go from here to the place my people are kept and be secured in my cot."

"For what purpose? There's nowhere to run to."

"It is to remind us that we are slaves," she said. "That we have no freedom other than that which our masters provide."

"Don't fight it," the redhead said. "Take my advice—pick your battles aboard this ship."

"I will return to free you in the morning, domina," Alba said.

The Iceni touched the calcedonius strip at the free end of the chain to the bracelet on my wrist and they melded together, joining as one unbreakable piece. I was secured, unable to move far from the bed. Would I have suffered this same humiliation if I'd stayed in Crassus' quarters?

A chime signaled curfew. The lights faded to darkness, and I curled up, clutched my pin, and tried to pretend I was back home in my room, surrounded by the comforting noise of the capital. But my constant buzzing head, agitated by the vibration and roar of the ship's engines—the sound of a wave always moving forward, never crashing or coming to rest, never pausing, eternally constant— stopped me from indulging in escapism.

I silently mouthed my prayer to Minerva: *Please, goddess, forgive me my neglect and any wrongs I have committed. I offer you my life. My life for my brother's, my life for justice, and if this is the trial I must endure, then so be it, but do not disappoint me. Stand with me. Bless the way ahead.*

Three weeks. Three weeks to prove myself to the man I hated more than any other. I buried my face in the hard pillow to muffle the great sobs that racked my body.

XI

THAT NIGHT I DREAMED of Aulus. I was sitting in the family compound's library studying an old book when he came rushing in. I didn't look up to acknowledge him. The Wolf's Den was an enormous labyrinth of buildings, and I'd made myself intentionally scarce so I could study. Aulus demanded attention and wasn't past irritating the hell out of me to get it. It was about a week before he was due to leave for Olympus Decimus with mother. I was seventeen, he almost nine.

"Hey, dog breath, what are you doing?"

I ignored him.

"Okay. Accala, I'm sorry, it was wrong for me to make fun of how you smell. What are you doing?"

"I'm studying. Go away."

"What are you doing?" he asked as he walked over to the desk.

"I just told you. Learn to listen."

"Want to see a new magic trick I've been working on?"

"Not particularly."

"I can turn a peach into a lemon with a wave of my hand."

"I can turn an irritating little brother into a stain on the wall with a wave of mine."

"Vegetius," he said, reading the cover. "You don't need a gardening book. Those prize peach trees in your apartment look pretty good to me. Perfect, in fact."

"Vegetius is the author's name," I said absentmindedly.

"*Epitoma rei militaris*," he said, reading the title. "It must be old if you have to read it as a physical book."

"I don't *have* to read it in book form, I choose to," I said wearily. "It's a military classic from the era of the first republic. Now go away."

"All right."

As he headed off, it occurred to me that he'd given up much more easily than usual. "Wait. What did you say about my peaches? Were you in my quarters?"

"That they were perfect. Perfectly delicious. In fact I think I might go and have another one right now."

He sprinted out of the library, laughing, and I dropped my book and chased after him.

"If there's even a tooth mark on one of my peaches, I'll cut out your tongue! Stay out of my chambers!"

I was in the dream but also watching it from a distance. It was a true dream, a recounting of a real event, and it struck a bittersweet chord. It had always been like that because of the age gap between us. Me distracted with training or study, him endlessly annoying. Chasing him around the Wolf's Den that time was the exception; mostly I ignored or dismissed him. The happy scene that followed—my mother separating us as I wrestled him to the ground and then taking us to make up over honey cakes—only made his sudden absence in my life a few months later all the more acute. On some level I resented that as a male he had every opportunity that I longed for offered to him, ready to pluck if he showed the slightest interest, only he never did. Magic tricks, mathematics, and exobiology (collecting crystal-encased samples of ugly insects from the distant corners of the empire to trade with his friends) seemed to be all he was interested in, that and irritating his older sister.

The happy scene suddenly fell away, and I slipped into my old dream of fire and pain, and the wall of dirty ice, except this time I found myself on the other side, looking through my mother's eyes at a screaming Accala. Confused, exhausted, I took the hairpin in my clenched fist and started scoring words on the surface of the ice wall.

MINERVA OLYMPUS

As my mother, I felt that these words were exactly the thing I needed to communicate. That if Accala could read them, then she'd understand and everything would be all right. Then Aulus appeared, the firewall behind him. I rushed to him, my arms wide, filled with a hope that this time I'd save him, but my arms passed right through his body as if he were a hologram. Again and again I tried to grasp him, but he was like a ghost. Aulus' mouth was moving, trying to speak, but all that came out was a hollow, insensible buzzing noise. He was reaching out for something. Too late, I realized it was the pin in my hand. It was gone, I'd dropped it somewhere as I'd run to him. It was important, the pin, though I suddenly couldn't remember why. I had to go and look for it, but then the light of nuclear fire erased the need for any further thoughts or actions.

* * *

I AWOKE TO BRIGHT light, not the summer sun falling into my bedchamber but a powerful cabin light flickering inches from my face. My hand was empty, my mother's pin gone. I was sitting in an instant, almost banging my head on the low ceiling as I searched frantically. Where was it? Maybe Crassus had stolen it. Maybe the small female barbarian. Then my fingers brushed against it under the pillow. The wave of anxiety subsided, and I crashed back down onto the bed, using my forearm to shield my eyes from the harsh light.

Two words: Minerva Olympus. Beneath the mountain Nova Olympus was the point of origin of my mother's last transmission, and the place where she died. Was the dream an omen? Was that where I should be looking for Aulus? Olympus was the home of the gods in ancient times, the peak of Greece's highest mountain. The ice world had been named Decimus for its being the tenth planet from the golden sun of its solar system and Olympus for its being possessed of the largest mountain range with the highest peak. That mountain had been named unimaginatively after the lesser mountain in Greece. I knew little about it other than it rose up behind the ruins of Lupus Civitas, the old Viridian capital, its peak so high it scraped the upper atmosphere. And what of Minerva? Was I supposed to make amends for not sacrificing to her back in Rome? Or was it all just useless dream stuff, fantasies tossed up by a troubled mind? The only thing I knew for certain was that I felt terrible, like I hadn't slept at all.

"The light burning your eyeballs out of their sockets right now is supposed to simulate a gentle sunrise," my redheaded cabinmate said. "It's supposed to gradually waken you and help reset your body clock."

"Turn it off," I groaned.

"Can't. It's hardwired into the controls for the whole deck. All the Sertorian cabins on the ship have custom fittings. *Their* lights work just fine, but us plebs only get a stock legion fit out. For dawn simulation, read shock and awe light explosion. Now you know why I didn't take the top bunk."

There was a divine aroma coming from below, a new smell but a good one. The field engineer was dressing in her overalls, and a tray with a pot of dark blue liquid—the source of the smell—lay on the narrow bench.

"You'd better get up or the deck officer will come and beat you. We don't let sleeping wolves lie here," she said. "Did you like that, by the way? That was a joke."

"It was not funny." I bundled my hair up and slid Mother's pin into place. Without thinking, I went to jump down, but the chain pulled tight, yanking me back. "Where is that damn Iceni?"

"Here, domina," the small white being said. "Sorry, domina." She gently took my wrist and touched a calcedonius keystone to the connection point between chain and bracelet, releasing me. Alba had a cup of the liquid ready to offer me as soon as my feet hit the ground.

"What is it?"

"Blue lotus tisane from Mare Byzantium province, domina. It will help sustain you today."

"You bet," the redheaded engineer said. "It keeps us plebs working harder for longer. The whole machine of the empire would grind to a halt without that stuff."

"I think you underestimate the value of the Senate and nobility," I replied automatically.

"The noble houses? And those old men in fancy robes? Are you joking? They're glorified managers enjoying the hereditary rewards of mass territorial ownership. They've built nothing, done nothing to earn their status other than to randomly fall out of a noble-born vagina, and they spend most of their useless lives prancing about in the Senate shoring up those rights at everyone else's expense."

"The noble houses embody the spirit of the empire," I said. "Without them, Rome would be a disorderly rabble, a misshapen monster trying to devour its own tail. Much like the collegia."

"You're kidding, right? You don't really believe that? It's what the noble houses want the lower classes to think, but the truth is that if the combined senators of the empire were struck dead by a freak epidemic tomorrow, the empire wouldn't miss a beat. But try to last one day without the collegial guilds? Life wouldn't be worth living." She took the cup from the Iceni and pushed it at me. "I can't believe you've never had a good, honest cup of blue lotus. Get it into you. It'll put hairs on your chest."

I'd heard of it, a popular mild stimulant. The blue was so dark that it was almost black, and the smell was potent and aromatic. I felt an instinctive reluctance to try it, but the redhead was looking at me expectantly, the smell was so good, and I needed something to help make me feel like a human being after such a terrible night. The first sip lit up my brain, washing away the worst of my tiredness—bitter but satisfying. Each subsequent sip unraveled a knot of fear in my stomach.

I indicated that Alba should pour me another cup.

"You might want to take it easy with that stuff if you're not used to it," the redhead said offhandedly. "It can pack a punch."

"And you might want to mind your own business," I replied, taking another sip.

"And you might want to keep in mind the lesson you learned yesterday on the cabin floor when gravity had its foot on your back," she said. "Besides, when we're stuck in a steel shoe box in space, your business is my business. You kept me up half the night with your crying."

"I wasn't crying."

"All right, call it weeping, then, if you like. You gladiators are supposed to be tough, aren't you?"

"Want to try me and find out?"

"I build things, you break them, to each her own." She smiled again and stuck her hand out in front of her. "I'm Julia Silana. Vulcaneum immune."

No house name. Just Julia Silana. As she turned to the light, I saw that she had freckles, small dots about her nose and cheeks. Somehow it softened her, took the edge off her determined, argumentative features.

"You've never seen any of my arena matches?" I asked.

"Sorry, I only watch the chariot races. Professional interest; they have supercharged engines. Now's the part where you tell me your name."

"You said you knew who I was," I said.

"And that I knew you'd be trouble."

"Accala," I said. "Just call me Accala."

Her open hand had been hovering there before me as we spoke, and now she impatiently pushed it forward. "Then let's have a pax between us, Accala," she said. "We don't have to be friends, but we do have to share this cabin."

Julia Silana was my better in the eyes of society and the law, she owed me nothing, and I certainly wasn't there to make friends. The Sertorians were probably paying her to spy on me, but she was right, we were going to be stuck together. My mother taught me to seek equanimity, never be hostile to one who bore me no hostility.

"Pax," I said, clasping her forearm. "I spoke to you too harshly when we met. I'm no princess, I never was. I believe all citizens of the empire should be treated with equal respect."

That made her laugh. "Don't get carried away and speak to anyone else like that. You Viridians style yourselves as the sons of Remus, born and bred on the Aventine, but at the end of the day you're no different from the other houses. Your origins are so far behind you that you've forgotten what it means to get your hands dirty. That kind of talk will get you a beating down here and worse up there with the Sertorian nobles, maybe even crucified."

"I'll keep that in mind," I said. "Have you been aboard *Incitatus* long?"

"Since the war started. Two years eating hawk shit, day in, day out."

"Then why serve them? Is it just about money and expensive gear?"

"Hey, don't knock money and tools. For me that's a lot of what makes life worth living. There's lots of reasons for me doing time here right now. After you work for a team in the Ludi Romani, you can walk into any job in the galaxy. They know you can fix anything, make anything, come up with workarounds at high speed, and all under enormous pressure."

"So where are you going to go afterward?"

"That's a secret. When I'm done here I'm leaving everything behind me. No one will know where I've gone, no one will be able to come after me. It'll be a new beginning, an entirely new life. Each day I'll wake up happy and relaxed."

"That's some fantasy."

"You wait and see. I've got it all worked out. You though, you'd better be careful if you want to survive the trip to the arena world, let alone the games themselves. The Sertorians don't tolerate poor performance. Luckily I'm your bunkmate, and despite the arrogant tilt to your head, I've always had a soft spot for the underdog, so I've decided that I'm gonna help you out."

"I don't need anyone's help."

"Now you're really talking stupid. This is Rome. Without an ally you'll be dead by the end of the week."

"Wait and see," I said.

I wasn't sure how to feel about Julia Silana, but no one in Rome, especially someone you hardly knew, did anything for nothing. She had an agenda; I just had to work out what it was.

"Please, domina. It's time to dress. We must hurry," Alba prompted. The Iceni had laid out a Sertorian novice's uniform for me—black leather pants and high-collared formfitting doublet. Vibrant crimson stripes ran up the sides of the pant legs and torso and down the arms, and seven grooved black rings surrounded the doublet. It was a striking outfit, and those who wore it reminded me of shiny, deadly spiders. The clothes represented the oppression, murder, torture, and rape of my brothers and sisters and their worlds.

"I'm not wearing that," I said. "A clean tunic will be fine."

"Master will be displeased," Alba said.

"Good."

"Maybe good for you, not so good for me. Please, or he will whip me, maybe kill me or my family."

Alba was helping me understand that we were all in this together, all under the Sertorian thumb—her, me, the beasts in their cages pushed across the floor of the docking bay. If I protested the oppression of my people by refusing to wear the uniform, I would in turn guarantee the oppression of the small Iceni slave and hers.

There was a tiny sip of blue lotus tisane left at the bottom of the mug. I tilted the cup up and waited for it to drizzle down onto my tongue. Every last drop for courage, and then I allowed Alba to help me into the formfitting uniform.

"You will please master," she said, as if that was the sole purpose of every being in the universe—to make Gaius Sertorius Crassus happy.

* * *

MY FIRST WEEK OF training aboard *Incitatus* began in the gymnasium—an entire cargo bay converted for gladiatorial practice. After the regulated heat of the ship, the freezing cold atmosphere of the bay was a surprise but not the physical shock I would have expected considering I was dressed in nothing more than a single layer of clothing. My skin prickled, but the cold didn't seem to penetrate the surface. It must have been the blue tisane drink. Perhaps it had medicinal properties because the buzzing in my head waned to a barely audible whisper. Breathing out through my mouth as a kind of experiment, I saw the air turn to foggy vapor at once. I ran my hand up and down the material of my sleeve quickly and then touched my nose with my bare finger. A strong static spark came as a surprise. It must have been at least fifteen below zero.

The other Blood Hawks had assembled and were in the process of donning thermal training armor over their uniforms. They looked like killers. Not athletes or sporting celebrities—killers in and out of the arena. Even skinny Mania, armed with her needle knives and bow staff, looked dangerous.

"It's because you haven't been blooded yet," Gaia Barbata explained when she noticed my eyes lingering on the red circle on the front of her doublet. Their uniforms had grooves also, though they were all red. "Once you've passed the initiation, you'll get a uniform just like mine."

"Each time you absorb one of Proconsul Aquilinus' precepts, a band of red will be added to your uniform. Once you've been blooded, you'll receive the circle," Castor Corvinus said.

"Crassus tells me that you've never even killed a barbarian, let alone a human," Barbata said. Her voice was breathy and excited, like a seductress anticipating the touch of a virgin lover.

"But don't worry, we'll help you," Mania said. "We want you to be one of us."

"Yes," Barbata purred, "one of us."

"Very good, Accala," Crassus said when he saw me. "You look very smart."

"I look like a bat with its wings cut off," I rebuffed.

He contemplated the comment, his finger hovering over his armilla, judging if it was worth shocking me, but then he simply shrugged. "You'll look better when Barbata's done with you," he said.

"Done with me how?" I asked.

Gaia Barbata placed her hands on my shoulders. She looked me over like she was appraising the merit of an unfinished painting. "I've been put in charge of managing your appearance. It's important to make the right impression when the whole empire will be watching your every move." She saw my look of apprehension and added, "Don't worry. I see some primitive potential in those features. We can make you beautiful yet. Just you wait."

I would show her my primitive potential in the Ludi Romani. We'd see how condescending she was then.

The gymnasium course was made of grid-covered terraform blocks—geometric shapes overlaid with holographic images that simulated the types of terrain we'd encounter on Olympus Decimus. At the far end of the gym were ten enclosed cages, the same ones I'd seen when we boarded. The creatures inside were making plenty of noise, but then Licinus appeared and signaled to the handlers, who walked along the cages, jabbing their shock staves in between the bars. The menagerie quickly grew silent. The farthest cage in the lineup was much larger than the rest, and I couldn't help but wonder what kind of a monster it held.

Licinus held his ten-foot-long steel war chain gathered up in loops. Three segments—a sharpened steel whip head for cutting, a middle with a spike caltrop to trap and entangle, and a steel ring on the end wrapped in leather to help him manipulate the weapon and draw it back after it was unleashed. On his belt, he also carried a standard military-issue vintus, the centurion's disciplinary shock stick.

Crassus handed me my armilla, which I eagerly snapped on to my wrist. A brief scan revealed that a series of sophisticated blocks had been placed on it, rendering its more complex functions useless. It could be used for basic shield functions and team and tournament communications, nothing more.

"I can't fight without my discus."

Crassus reached into a metal storage chest and pulled out my weapon case. "You'll have to return it to this chest after each training session," he said, passing it to me. "That's not negotiable."

Fighting the urge to thank him, I snapped open the clasps of the case, threw it open, and snatched up Orbis. I felt a surge of renewed confidence as he vibrated with pent-up energy. With Orbis in hand, I felt I could take them all at once.

"Patience," Crassus said in a warning tone. "You and Lurco will be pushed to meet the team standard. Endure and allow our form of training to give you the strength and speed you will need to withstand the challenges ahead."

"Into formation, you gallows birds! Line up!" Licinus barked, and we all obeyed, even Crassus, who hated him but still knew his place as second in command. "Listen up, you scabby vultures. The war's about to start up again in the emperor's arena. You think you're gladiators, charioteers, barbarian hunters? You're wrong. You're soldiers, and I'm your commander." He strode up and down our line, looking at each of us in turn. "Any time you've spent with me before, any relationship we've had in the arena or in governing House Sertorian means nothing now. All that counts are results. Each day you will jump to my command. No punishment will be spared for the weak." Licinus stopped in front of me. "Crassus and Barbata here will be concerned with managing your arena style," he continued. "In the Talonite arena we don't care for such nonsense, but in the Ludi Romani winning the crowd's approval is a vital ingredient in victory. At crucial moments, the game editor will freeze play and the mob will vote on life or death. That is why appearance is important and also why I will not tolerate a single mistake. No kill will be denied the Blood Hawks because we didn't bring down the enemy with enough flair to titillate the mob!"

Licinus resumed his pacing. "The emperor hasn't released the details of the course yet, but we know that all three arena disciplines will be brought into play.

Every day for the next four weeks, each of you will train your skill—essedarii, bestiarii, and gladiatorii—as well as the rudimentary skills of the other two arts. Should any one of us fall, any other should be in a position to take up the slack. For the first three weeks we'll focus on one skill at a time—chariot training—followed by bestiarii combat and then gladiatorial bouts. After that we'll mix them together in every conceivable combination until, by the end of our time together, I will have forged you into the fastest and most lethal gladiatorial meat grinder the Ludi Romani has ever seen!"

Bestiarii combat. We would be fighting the barbarians in the black cages, then. I'd have to kill them—if they didn't kill me first.

Licinus led us to the edge of the course where two gleaming black, high-powered war chariots awaited. "Behold! The Quadriga Essedarius—the four-horse war chariot—the deadliest arena combat vehicle ever created."

Pulsing illuminated streaks of ruby red coursed down the sides of the chariots in stylish sweeps. They'd been constructed from the best, most up-to-date materials, with no expenses spared. Money was an essential component in chariot racing. More sesterces meant better machines, engineers, mechanics, and racers.

"Each team is permitted one chariot equipped for fighting, with a second vehicle to carry the auxiliary immunes, survival equipment, and supplies. Treat them with care. These chariots are your lifelines—there'll be no alternate forms of transport in the field—and on an ice world like Olympus Decimus, that means the elements can kill you just as easily as an enemy swinging a gladius."

Licinus then had the Corvinus brothers demonstrate the parts of the vehicle.

"Chariots come in different sizes and shapes depending on a team's strategy and fighting style," Castor explained. "Ours are a balance of speed and strength—fourteen feet long, six feet wide in the middle, tapering to a point at both prow and stern. The antigravity discs on the hull will allow them to travel evenly at a height of one-and-a-quarter feet."

The central carriage, called the bigae, was designed to accommodate all eight team members with the charioteer riding up front. Beneath it were two square hoverplates that kept it elevated above the ground. Four cables ran ahead of it attached to powerful hovering engines that pulled the chariots forward. Halfway between the bigae and the engines, the cables interfaced with a central differential ring. The ring transferred precise control over the floating engines to four leather reins that the chariot driver wrapped around his forearms. Using subtle combinations of movement, the charioteer was able to steer the vehicle at high speed through a wide range of motion. Castor Corvinus explained that if the driver of the vehicle lost control and the engines stripped the control ring, then he would be pulled forward by the reins, right out of the carriage. For that reason, all charioteers carried a falx—a short, curved blade—that they could use to try to cut themselves free before they were dragged to their death.

The third major section of the quadriga chariot was the two desultore skirmishers—light and fast speeder bikes for attack and defense that were integrated ingeniously into the main body, barely adding to the width of the chariot.

The skirmishers could break away from and reconnect to the bigae as needed. Each skirmisher, long and thin, was intended to carry a single rider with greater speed and mobility than the bigae and was powered by an independent thruster cell at the rear.

The breakdown was very informative, but my main concern was how the twin brothers, with only one arm apiece, could hold their own against veteran charioteers with two. The Corvinus brothers raced in the hippodromes of Sertorius Primus, and no footage of them had ever got out of Sertorian space. All I'd been able to discover was that they used a kind of harness adapter, but that was hardly reassuring considering each gladiator had to trust the driver of the chariot with his or her life when engaging in high speed combat.

Licinus climbed into the nearest chariot and took position behind the driver's podium.

"Chariot drivers, take your positions, the rest of you get up here with me."

Castor Corvinus strapped himself into the harness in a matter of seconds. He picked up the reins and flicked them around his forearm in a smooth, effortless movement.

"The Dioscurii are the best," Licinus said. "The Viridian charioteers can't do half as well with two arms as our boys can with one."

Licinus went on to explain how the chariots had been modified for the Ludi Romani. Strategically placed spikes and blades emerged from the armored hull and sides, designed to gore or upturn enemy vehicles or any barbarian beasts that drew too close during a melee. A central pole emerged from midvessel like a ship's mast. From the base of the mast, reaching to either side of the chariot, were narrow standing platforms that could be extended or retracted as needed. "These war chariots are big and strong. The antigravity plates attached beneath the hull are suitable for the craft to accelerate over most types of terrain, but the bow of the hull means the chariot can also function at high speed in water. In mountainous terrain, auxiliaries can attach caterpillar tracks and grapple lines to permit climbing. They're big, all right, but don't let their size fool you—they're fast. If you're fighting on a quadriga, you'd better be strapped into a harness, holding on to a rail or the central pole, or you'll fly off and be minced or crushed. Remember, on average, five percent of gladiators in past Ludi Romani tournaments have died at the hands of their own team chariots."

Pollux Corvinus demonstrated how we could hang off the platform using a hand or connector strap to secure ourselves as we attacked with our weapons. We had to learn to move as a team—the chariots were fast and highly responsive, but the cost was stability. It was possible to tip a chariot if there was too sudden a weight change on one side and no one to act as ballast on the other.

"Charioteers, you must be swift and deadly," Licinus instructed. "Protect your human cargo, for they will surely protect you. Bestiarii, you will kill this world's indigenous barbarians and any other beasties they throw at us to preserve your life and that of your teammates and, make no mistake, they will be coming at you thick and fast. Gladiators," he said, turning to me, "you must protect your teammates and eliminate enemy competitors with merciless efficiency."

Licinus then demonstrated how the narrow run could be used to find the best position for casting long- to medium-range weapons and that the central pole had strips of lapis negra sealed into it, which would work like a magnet to help my discus find its way back to me if I made a cast as the chariot raced across the ice.

"Right. Let's go at it. For training, we will divide into two teams and compete against each other," Licinus ordered. "I will command Castor's chariot, Crassus will command Pollux's. In addition to leader and driver, each chariot will carry one bestiarii and one gladiator."

I was paired with Mania and put on Crassus' chariot, my long-range weapon set to complement Mania's knives. Barbata with her trident caster was paired with Lurco and his hammer on Licinus' vehicle.

"We'll be thick as thieves," Barbata said, smiling seductively at Lurco. The giant visibly flinched as she passed by him, angling his groin away from her.

Licinus signaled the technicians in the observation booth high above us. Holographic snow began to fall. The terraform blocks took shape, as the holo-gram overlaid them, transforming the deck into an approxmation of flat tundra surrounded at the edges by clustered outcroppings of layered ice and rock. Along with the freezing temperature, we had our own small-scale ice world and at its center a makeshift hippodrome—a classical oblong racing track. A razor-sharp spina—a metal spine that each chariot had to avoid and turn about—ran down the middle of the track.

"The winning team will be given additional recreation leave at the ship's baths, and the losing team will be punished," Licinus said. "Right!" he barked. "First round of chariot fights. Nonlethal force for starters. Go!"

Licinus' team shot away, leaving us to scramble to our chariot, fumbling to fasten harnesses and straps.

Licinus' chariot braked suddenly, allowing our quadriga to draw alongside before hitting us with a sideswipe. By pure luck I managed to get a hand to a rail and prevent being thrown over the side. Grasping the pole for balance, I threw Orbis, aiming to take out Barbata at the rear of the other chariot, at the exact moment that Castor Corvinus reversed and rammed us again. Instead of making a clean cast, I had to jump back to avoid losing a leg as a curved blade protrud-ing from their hull cut into our armored hide. Orbis' transit was way off, and Barbata unhurriedly deployed the energy net from her trident caster. It covered Orbis and sent him scuttling to the ground. Disarmed like an amateur, I lost my balance and fell, hitting the deck hard.

The Sertorians were all so fast. By comparison, I felt like I was drowning un-derwater, flailing my arms and legs about, instead of fighting. I scurried out of the way to avoid the enemy chariot's blades as they tried to run me down. Lurco went for our driver, but Crassus threw his javelin and caught the giant a glanc-ing blow on his shoulder, throwing his hammer swing off target. Lurco was having the same problem as me—he was too slow and lacked chariot combat experience. The two drivers were excellent though, turning in sharp, tight arcs, working to outposition each other. Pollux managed to angle our chariot and ram his brother's into the spina, but at the last moment Castor countered and tilted his craft, coming under our chariot and using one of his spikes that was bent like a horn to displace a hover disc. I watched on as our chariot skittered across the floor, creating a trail of sparks until it crashed at high speed into a terraform block. Castor's bold move cost his own team, though, sending Lurco and Barbata flying onto the deck. Lurco landed flat on his back and took a knock to the head, but Barbata spun in midair and landed gracefully on one knee on the deck beside me.

Licinus called time. "The fact that my team won matters little because right now none of you are worth a rat's ass! I thought you were supposed to be a discus fighter?" He snarled at me. "You throw your weapon like a retarded monkey." Before Lurco could recover his senses and rise, Licinus put his boot on his chest and pushed him back down to the ground. "It should come as no surprise to anyone here that the weak links in our chain are Accala and Lurco. I want to win that tournament decisively, and I won't have the team carry deadweight." He tapped each of us quickly with his vintus, delivering a sharp electrical shock that took my breath away.

"Immunes, get in and get to work. You've got sixty seconds to get the chariots up and running." Like ants on a carcass, the collegia immunes moved quickly and efficiently to tend to the team and the vehicles. Licinus explained that our crushed chariot was now classified as a naufragia—a shipwreck. To keep the pace of the games running hot, the rules stated that if the immunes couldn't get it up and running again in two minutes, then it was deemed unrecoverable and the team had to move on without it. Licinus gave them half that time.

At Licinus' order, medics tended to everyone on the team with the exception of Lurco and me, additional punishment for our poor performance. They received salves, poultice patches, and stimulant shots, and when the sixty seconds were up, both the chariots and the injured were in working order again. As I pulled Orbis free of Barbata's net, I spotted Julia finishing up work on my chariot. Was she also going to be there with the immunes on Olympus Decimus? Lending us support in the arena?

"I'll save you a poultice for the pain," she said quickly as she passed by, lugging her heavy toolbox. "Watch out for Licinus, he's the fastest."

"Right, mount up, you morons," Licinus said. "You're going to keep at it until you can complete a circuit without falling off your fucking vehicles."

We fought six more chariot rounds before Licinus called it quits for the day. At the end, he drew out his vintus once more and tapped Lurco and me on the chest. No shock this time though, he was registering his displeasure as a centurion would, signaling the team to deliver an administrative beating to the worst players of the day.

"Don't try to defend yourself," Crassus said as they moved in. "It'll only make things worse."

Lurco tried to stand his ground, but Barbata singled him out and dropped him at once.

"It's nothing personal," Mania said, driving the tip of her bow staff into my solar plexus. "It's for your own good." I doubled up and fell to the cold deck.

And then there was just pain as the blows rained down upon me quick and hard.

Afterward, the team wandered off and I lay there bleeding and bruised. How was it possible for the Sertorians to be so superior in strength and speed? Not to mention resilience; the hits they took during training washed right off them. The medics had virtually nothing to do in the aftermath, but the Hawks should have sported the same cuts, bruises, and breaks that I did. It wasn't just that they were good; they were beyond good. I'd studied countless hours of footage of Crassus and Licinus and I'd been pushing myself under Marcus' direction to get to a standard where I could hold my own against them, but these were not the same fighters. The Blood Hawks didn't need me at all, or Lurco, for that matter. The six Sertorians on their own were an unbeatable combination.

* * *

ALBA LED ME TO shower and change before returning me to the cabin. Julia Silana was there, staring out the portal.

"Good timing," she said, "we're about the leave the solar system."

I went to look, ignoring the aching muscles and stinging cuts.

"We're going through the Janus Cardo now."

From where our cabin was positioned, I couldn't see *Incitatus'* bow or the entrance to the shining energy gate that would transport us, but the ship lurched quickly forward and the view changed to amorphous gray clouds charged with crackling lightning that sent flashing light into the cabin as *Incitatus* was sucked into the gateway. A last bright flash, and the clouds gave way to a field of violet-streaked mercurial silver as we entered hyperspace.

"Not bad, huh?" Julia said.

She was dissatisfied with my lack of enthusiasm and nudged me with her elbow. "I don't think much about the gods, but you know what I do believe in?"

"I don't care," I said. "Where's that pain patch you promised me?"

"I believe in celestial mechanics," she continued, ignoring me. "That the entire universe is one great machine and we're all little parts of it. From the smallest atom to the largest nebula, all one great celestial city. Doesn't that make sense? That we've got little universes of bacteria within each one of us and maybe we're also part of a big body, something so big we can't see it, just as the bacteria aren't aware of us. Wheels within wheels. That's what I think of when I see something like this Janus Cardo. It's a beautiful thing."

"Nothing is beautiful," I said. Exhausted and injured, the intrusive buzzing headache returned.

"Those two quadrigas you're working out on are," Julia said, as I climbed up into my bunk and Alba secured my lead for the night. Forearm over my eyes to block the harsh overhead light until they called curfew and turned it off. I was so tired I couldn't move a muscle.

"Look after those chariots. The immunes have decked both out for combat so you can practice against each other, but before we reach the arena world, we'll be taking one and stripping it of arms for our own use."

"You're definitely on the auxiliary team, then?"

"You bet. Julia Silana, first-grade field engineer. When your chariot gets trashed, I'll be there to get it up and running again."

"That's hardly reassuring," I said. "You couldn't even fix the light in the ceiling."

"I guess you're screwed, then, right?" She laughed. Julia tossed a pain poultice, a small adhesive patch, onto my bunk and sat down at the cabin's bench, sorting through her toolbox. I tried to summon a word of thanks as I pressed it onto the back of my right hand, but I was running on an empty tank and could offer nothing of myself, even so small a gesture.

When I was a girl I'd daydream about leaving the familiar confines of the solar system and taking my first steps out into the greater empire, but as we passed through the hyperspace tunnel, I felt deflated, desolate. The violet light outside spilled through the portal and played across my hands so that if I held them over the side of the bunk, I couldn't see the bruises. When I drew them back under the overhead light, though, all the bruises were gone. Julia's poultice must have had healing properties too. Muscular pain slowly ebbed away too, although the headache lingered on, and I found I could think enough to turn the day's events over in my mind. Did the Sertorians' newfound abilities have limits? How hard would they have to be worked before their strength and speed waned? I resolved to find out.

"Julia?" I asked. She was still tinkering away on the bench. "Back in the gym you said to watch out for Licinus. I could barely see him move. It's . . ." I searched for the right word.

"It's gods-be-damned creepy is what it is, hey?"

"He wasn't always that fast, was he? I've seen old footage of him fighting. How long has he been like that?"

"Can't say," she said.

"Can't say because you don't know or because you've been told not to?"

"Pick any one, but I can't say."

"Another secret?"

She smiled and turned back to her work.

*　*　*

Every evening I would go to bed with a headache, and each morning the buzzing noise was there when I awoke, louder than ever, as if it had slowly increased in volume while I slept. The best part of the day was the morning in my cabin, sipping Alba's blue lotus tisane that stole away all pain, body and mind. I felt like a clock being reset, and by the time I reached the gym I was fresh and ready.

Prior to chariot practice, Castor Corvinus tutored us on the history of the art, the different styles of vehicle, and the traditional strategies preferred by each house. Analyzing the strengths and weaknesses of the great charioteers of history was the only time I ever saw him register something that resembled excitement. "All modern essedarii combat has its roots in the past," he repeated again and again, extolling the virtues of the great Blood Hawk charioteer of the previous century, Porphyrius Sertorius Scorpus, victor of two thousand races. "Study the races of Gnaeus Arrius Diocles of the fourteenth republic," he said. "A thousand years dead and still no one has been able to match him. In his twenty-seven-year career he amassed thirty-five billion sesterces in winnings, making him the highest-paid athlete in galactic history."

Next Licinus had us run track sprints and chariot battles. I mastered using the pole and center run of the chariot, casting Orbis as we raced the track. I worked harder and learned more than I thought possible, fighting on with pain and injuries that would have laid me up for a week back home. When Licinus was satisfied with our combat skills on the chariots, he had each of us run endless drills on the desultore skirmishers, breaking away on the speeders from the main body of the vehicle to fight and then rejoining. He seemed almost as tough on the immunes, and when I sympathized with Julia about her harsh repair schedule, she commended Licinus. "In the field, with the tournament railing about you, there isn't much time to get it right," she explained. "Anything and everything can go wrong. By making us train at double speed, he's preparing us. The quicker we can repair the chariots, the better the team's chances of survival. The longer you'll live."

Each day I endured a beating after training, but the pain became fuel, driving me to improve, so that by the end of the week I was gaining some degree of expertise on the desultore skirmisher and even managed to score some hits, mostly against Lurco. I just couldn't match the Sertorians' strength and speed, so I focused on defense, doing my best to suppress the opposition's assaults. Concentrating less on attacking put me in a frame of mind where details I'd have otherwise missed were revealed. After heavy fighting sessions, the Sertorians who'd expended the most energy had an exhausted, hollowed out quality. Their hands trembled and their skin took on a yellowish tinge, like they were suffering jaundice. I noted that any gladiator with those symptoms was immediately excused from the gymnasium after practice. Never Licinus though. He was always the most dangerous, the fastest and strongest. Now that I knew the Sertorians did have limits, I was curious to know what Licinus' were.

Each night the same dream replayed itself, only the roles were reversed and once more I was Accala, trapped behind the ice, unable to decipher the words Mother carved upon it. I wouldn't wake up at the end. After the nuclear fire there'd be new dreams, nightmares to be accurate, that would follow on, and costarring alongside me was little white-haired Mania.

I was in a dark cave running from Mania. She was like a ghost—in the darkness all I could see was her white hair, face, and two gleaming needle knives. Terrified, heart pounding, I tried to outpace her, but she was like a cheetah running down a lame antelope. "Sister? Don't run away. I have a game we can play," she called out as she tracked me. Then her thin blades sank into my back like two long teeth and she brought me down and flipped me over as I fell. Straddling me, she drove her knives into my eyes, stealing my sight, chattering away all the while about what good friends we were and how much she was enjoying my company, like we were two little girls playing with dolls. Then she rose and I found myself completely paralyzed, unable to move. My perspective shifted to outside my body and I continued to watch the scene unfold from above. Mania ran a line down the middle of my naked torso with her knife and then peeled the skin back to expose the ribs and organs. She kept on pulling at the skin, stretching it out further and further so it made a kind of large blanket around me. Then she cracked the ribs open and started pulling organs out, inspecting them, laying them out onto the skin like a temple priest trying to predict the future. As she did, the organs shifted and changed shape, becoming the elements of my recurring dream—I saw small scenes, my mother scratching her unintelligble message, me in the ice, Aulus being burned, all laid out before her. "Dream, dream, dream away," she hummed as she worked, a simple, nursery song that I was unfamiliar with.

Then I'd wake, sweating, the paralysis lingering for a few seconds until I could move freely again. As I continued to experience the same nightmare each night, the dreams that preceded it seemed to fade, losing fidelity, until, on waking, I couldn't recall them at all.

As the final chariot session of the week started up, I targeted Licinus to see if I could push him beyond his limits. Licinus' war chain snaked out toward me, and I raised Orbis to ward it away, but the chain folded around the point of contact, trapping my weapon. The team leader tried to jerk me from the chariot, but I locked Orbis to the central post of my chariot so that Licinus instead would be pulled to the deck. It was a sure thing, only it didn't work. With the power of Castor's chariot pulling at him, Licinus wound his whip around his arm, braced himself, and pulled with all his strength. Everyone was astonished to see the central pole of our chariot bend and then snap in two. It was an amazing feat of physical strength, and the result was that the whip pulled free and still caught me and knocked me to the ground. The end of the round found me flat on my back, struggling to breathe, Licinus' boot pressing on my throat, threatening to crush my larynx and kill me. He didn't, though, and even as I lay there, red-faced and struggling for air, I knew my risk had paid off. His hands were trembling, his face pallid, skin tinged yellow. I'd pushed him hard and learned the limits to his strength.

One week down, and although surviving was no small accomplishment, I still needed to know more. Challenging Licinus had been a great risk; if I pushed him too far, Aulus would be killed. Over the course of the week I'd grown closer to Julia, and that night I decided to try and ferret out what she knew about the Hawks that might be of use.

"The other day you said you couldn't talk about Licinus or the other Sertorian gladiators . . ." I started.

"Really. Can't say a thing."

She tapped a code into a locked panel on the end of her toolbox. She thought she was quick but I picked up the combination and stored it away for future reference. From the compartment Julia drew out a small, square device. Putting it on the floor, she tapped its surface, and it began to emit a soft blue glow.

"Yep, couldn't say a thing, that is, if I didn't happen to have one of these little beauties."

"A privacy cube?" I said.

"Yeah. It samples our voices and generates random conversation based on things we've already said. At the same time, it jams any listening devices in a ten-foot radius.

"The day after you came and bunked here, I had the deck officer say he'd force me into a new career as a lady of Venus if I talked about anything that went on aboard the ship before you arrived."

"Really?" That piqued my interest.

"Really that they said they'd force me into prostitution or really that they didn't want me to say anything?" she said with a smile.

"Why would you tell me anything if the Sertorians told you not to? They'll flog you if they catch you, to death most likely."

"Oh, I've done much worse and got away with it. I know how to cover my tracks. You don't have to worry about me, but you should definitely worry about you. Go on, we don't have much time. If the cube cycles around the same topic too many times, they might become suspicious. What do you want to know? They don't let me in on their secrets or anything, but I see what I see."

I was on dangerous ground but felt that if I wanted to learn something new from her I had to take a risk opening up and sharing some of my observations.

"I've been trying to improve, but they're just too strong. I can't help but think that they're taking some kind of supplement," I said.

"You noticed the yellow skin and shaky hands, huh?" she asked.

"Yes."

"They're on something, all right," she said. "Licinus wasn't much faster than you until a few months back. That's when he really started moving like lightning. The other Sertorians, too. All the immunes noticed, how could you not?"

"When they're tired they leave the arena right away. Do you know where they go? Maybe to rest at the baths or in their quarters?"

She shook her head. "They go to Licinus' quarters."

"Really? All of them?"

"All of them. They might leave at different times but that's where they all end up. Every time. It's a running joke among the immunes, wondering what goes on in there."

I certainly did.

"It's weird, right?" Julia went on.

I wondered if the substance they were taking was the ambrosia my uncle spoke of but discounted the thought. Ambrosia had been impressive enough to get the Arrians to switch sides, and it would take more than a performance supplement to do that, even one as impressive as this.

That night I lay in my bunk, overtired, turning things around in my mind.

"Tell me, do you know the story of the Trojan horse?" my uncle had asked that night aboard his trireme.

"Of course."

"Tell it to me."

"I'm not in the mood for stories," I said.

"Please, humor me."

"The Greeks left a huge, hollow wooden horse outside Troy's impregnable walls, claiming it was a peace offering. When the Trojans took it inside their city, the warriors hidden within sneaked out and slaughtered the sleeping Trojan soldiers."

"Precisely. I want you to become a double agent—my very own Trojan horse. Find out where they're keeping Aulus by midway through the contest, and I'll whisk him to safety. Then, dear niece, the remainder of the games will be your reward. Pick off the Sertorian team from within and kill them, each and every one. With the Blood Hawks dead, you can switch back to the Viridian team (don't worry, I've already cleared it with Vibius Viridius Carbo, the team leader, though he is the only one who knows you're working for me). You can reclaim your honor in the eyes of your house and the Roman people as you help the Golden Wolves win the tournament. No one's pulled off a successful double cross in decades—the audience will go crazy for it. After that, we'll be the chosen house of the emperor and everything will unravel for the Sertorians, they'll be finished. With no victory and no ambrosia, their allies will turn on them . . ."

"And their proconsul, Aquilinus, will be assassinated by his own men for failing," I finished.

"You understand the Sertorians well, dear niece. They can't abide weakness. We'll crush them from without and within, but it all relies on you, Accala."

My uncle's plan had seemed straightforward at the time, but the Sertorians' unexpected prowess now posed a massive stumbling block. If I couldn't find some way to weaken the Blood Hawks before the games started, there wouldn't be any Caninine teams to defect to after I found my brother; they'd all be dead within the first week.

XII

WEEK TWO HERALDED THE commencement of bestiarii training. Aside from my need to please Licinus and keep my place on the team, I started working on a strategy to break into his quarters. It wouldn't be easy, not by a long shot. I'd noticed Crassus' armilla chiming before the door to his quarters opened—the security codes for each cabin were stored on its occupant's armilla. If there were something valuable in there, it would most likely be hidden, so I'd need uninterrupted time to search. Since I was only ever taken from my cabin to the gym and back again, I would have to trick my Iceni body slave in such a way that she, or anyone else for that matter, never knew I had slipped out. Nothing was simple.

Mania lectured us each morning on the geography of Olympus Decimus and the indigenous species we were most likely to encounter as we traversed the tournament course. Her childlike tone dropped away as she got down to the business of sharing her expertise on barbarians and their habitats. A large topographic projection showed in detail the vast mountain range that ran the breadth of the arena world's lone continental landmass like the spine of a great animal. On either side of the mountains were forests of crystalline trees and, surrounding them, countless miles of tundra that alternated between ranges of low hills and dead flat land. Strong winds and icy snowstorms were the norm, with temperatures seldom rising above freezing due to the planet's distance from its golden sun.

The indigenous barbarians we'd most likely encounter were the Hyperboreans, the name the ancient Greeks gave to the people who lived beyond the North Wind. A new holographic projection was cast before us, a thin, crystalline humanoid with four arms—two ending in clawlike hands, and two ending in sharp ice-pick-like blades for cutting and shaping ice. The Hyperborean in the projection was about five feet tall and had chiseled, simple humanoid features, with clear, shining vertical slits for eyes, and a bridgelike nose with diagonal grooves carved on the sides. It had no mouth and could not speak. Mania explained that the horizontal slit vents where a human mouth would be aided nutrient absorption from the atmosphere and filtered impurities. Long, sharp white filaments that resembled hair extended from its scalp to serve as atmospheric sensors, reading weather, allowing it to pick up vibration and movement. Its body was pale blue and reflected light like diamonds or ice. Within its torso a vaporous fluid, almost a gas, swirled about. Mania said that this was like blood to them. The nutrients they absorbed from the atmosphere were processed in their torso before being allocated to their different bodily functions as required.

"The Hyperboreans have much in common with bees in terms of their traits and psychology," Mania said. "Their primitive society can be roughly divided into two castes—warriors and workers. They are sexless and have neither male nor female forms. It is unknown how they reproduce."

"That is a worker," Mania said, gesturing toward the projection. "They're thin and feeble. You can shatter their torso with a single strike; the liquid gas you see swirling around escapes and they die. They avoid conflict if they can, and focus on collecting nutrients and carrying them into their hives. Now, this is a warrior."

A new image formed. A creature similar to the one we'd just seen except three times the bulk and twice the height. It had retractable spines along its arms, chest, and back, which looked sharp and deadly. "Now, these are a bit more trouble. They're territorial and they protect the workers and the hive. Their crystalline shell acts as a natural armor that will repel most weapons. Some of the larger specimens can fire darts of crystal from the arms and torso." Mania told us how she had worked with the Vulcaneum immunes to install X-ray scanners in our helmets that would reveal weaknesses in the crystalline structures of the barbarians' bodies. "In general the weakest place, and that means the best place to strike, is the neck. A lancing attack, a fast in and out with a sharp point, will do the trick. Make a big enough hole and their life fluids and internal gases will escape, but don't let your guard drop; even after a fatal strike, they can still continue fighting for several minutes."

I studied the image of the warrior, and despite its fearsome countenance, it didn't frighten me at all. My morning cup of tisane had dispelled any fear and I felt bright and alert. I wasn't even bothered by Mania's presence, needle knives strapped at her waist. When she caught me looking at them, she flashed me a pretty smile. She'd mentioned dreams when we were in the shuttlecraft. Could she really pick through mine as a crow picked at a carcass?

Next came the beast-hunting practice with Licinus.

"The weakest man from each team will be the first to brave today's course," Licinus said when we were gathered in the gym. "Or should I say the weakest bitch. That's right, Mock Wolf. That means you. Again."

And it meant Lurco as well.

The terraform blocks had been reassembled, transforming the gymnasium into a new configuration—a maze was created, with dead ends and misdirecting paths. In place of rocky outcroppings, the projectors gave the blocks the appearance of continuous shining walls of crystal.

"What's in there?" Lurco asked.

"It's a surprise," Licinus replied. "Now get a move on, you blockheaded jackass."

"I'll give you a clue," Barbata said. "There are several paths out of the maze, but only one is safe."

I wasn't sure her advice would be helpful at all.

"Try not to die," Mania chimed cheerfully, her girlish voice returned.

Lurco and I took up our weapons and moved to the maze entrance. A corridor ran fifteen feet and then split into left and right paths. The rest of the team had gathered in the viewing gallery on the gantry above, enjoying the aerial perspective that we were denied on the ground. They could watch us blunder into whatever surprises Licinus had planned. Lurco and I looked at each other uneasily as we entered the maze. As much as he hated me, I had the sense that we were in this together, both apprehensive.

The first path to the left was a dead end occupied by one of the black steel cages I had seen when we first boarded. The cage door was open, and whatever barbarian had lain within it was gone.

From the shadow behind the cage a black, fast-moving humanoid came rushing at us, razor-sharp mandibles clacking open and shut—an insectile Mandubii. It shot stinging spines from holes in its thorax, two of them hitting Lurco in the chest before the giant could crush the alien's black-plated skull with his hammer, covering the shining wall with purple brain matter.

Lurco laughed as he ripped the needlelike spines from his chest and strode with confidence back to take the path leading to the right.

"We should form a temporary alliance to improve the odds," I said as we approached the next set of branching corridors. "At least until we're near the end."

"I'll kill anything else the same way I killed the bug, but you'll die before you find the way out," he said, heading to the left. "Unless you agree to come to my cabin after training and do whatever I want. Then I'll help you stay alive."

"Go to hell." I stormed off down the right path, his laughter following me as I took another right turn and came face-to-face with a Sauromatae. Its clawed talons swung at my throat, but I stepped back just in time, cutting off its hand, using the momentum of that swing to turn inside its arms, cutting the soft, un-armored area of its throat. Only the slightest resistance registered as my weapon severed the brain stem. Black blood rushed over my arm. The lizard man took one step back and fell dead to the floor. My first time. A barbarian, an alien savage. Just like that, without a thought, I'd ended the life of another sentient being. My heart was racing, exhaustion and pain forgotten as the adrenaline raced through my veins. How should I feel about the dead lizard man at my feet?

And then another Sauromatae was coming at me and there was no time to think, and within a few seconds I'd killed again. Doubling back, I followed the maze's twists and turns, looking out for alien aggressors around every corner. From somewhere to my right, I could hear Lurco's war cry at the roaring of what might have been a red-maned Leonii, a large feline that secured its prey with two wiry tentacles. I hugged the left wall, traced along it without taking any diverging path, hoping it would lead me out, but I clashed with another Mandubii and had my right thigh pierced with the barbarian's black spines before I claimed its head with a rebound shot. It seemed that there were no "safe" paths. Every turn took me into danger, and judging by the sound of Lurco's cries, he was faring no better. My trick of following the single wall worked in the end, though, and I stumbled out of the maze. I went to take my hair down, but as my hand touched my mother's pin, I experienced an unexpected burning heat and had to pull away at once. The pin was radiating intense heat. But why? The medical immunes—doctors, nurses, bonesetters, and chemists—treated me quickly and then rushed on to Lurco, who came stumbling out behind me, covered head to toe in black and green blood. He fell to his knees, using the long-handled shaft of his hammer to stop himself collapsing with exhaustion.

"What kept you?" I asked. Despite the pain in my leg, my blood was up. The whole experience had been exhilarating. I felt like I could go through the course again.

"Both of you were just terrible," Barbata criticized. "You came out the other side, all right, but you displayed no intelligence, no finesse, and you didn't find the safe way through."

Licinus tapped Lurco with his shock staff and the big man yelped in surprise.

"Lurco's the one to receive administrative punishment tonight," Licinus said. "Mock Hawk was right to offer to team up. When it's Roman against barbarian, there is no going it alone. We band together, wipe the mongrel bastards out, and then worry about what human throat to cut. Killing in the right order, that's the Roman way!"

Now Licinus and the other Sertorians moved through the maze, and there were howls and screams as the remaining beasts inside died swiftly and from the sound of it, horribly. In under a minute the Sertorians emerged covered in different colored bodily fluids—green, blue, red—none of which belonged to them. "Now that's the way to do it!" Licinus crowed, flicking his steel whip into the air, causing the flexible tip to crack again and again. This was what made him happy, wholesale slaughter.

Licinus studied us all, casting his experienced eye over his team. I did the same. Who was the weakest? They were covered in blood, so I couldn't judge by skin tone and had to guess which of them had expended the most energy. Certainly Licinus had been full of zest and after him . . . definitely Mania and Crassus if the amount of blood staining their armor was anything to go by.

"Barbata. You have the honor," Licinus said, leaving the dark-haired beauty to deal with Lurco. And sure enough Licinus summoned Mania and Crassus and left the room. I'd correctly guessed his picks for the day.

"I'll give you a choice," Barbata said to the big man. "You can take your beating here or you can come to my quarters and bed me. I'll warn you though, I'm very hands-on when it comes to lovemaking." She squeezed her hands open and closed a few times, the long nails biting into her palms so that blood flowed onto the deck.

As Alba led me away, I head Lurco screaming at the pummeling Barbata was giving him. He'd chosen to avoid having sex with her and she'd taken it as an insult, if the curses she hurled at him were anything to go by. All in all, he probably made the best choice, though. The beating seemed the more survivable of the two options.

XIII

CRASSUS ANNOUNCED A CHANGE to my routine and charged me to go with Alba; he would join me shortly. I complained that I was still battered and bruised from training and covered in alien blood, but he wouldn't permit me a moment's rest. Alba helped me remove my armor before leading me up three decks to the science and medical division, where I found myself waiting outside a large steel door. There was no sign of Crassus. An hour passed and I began to worry.

Perhaps I hadn't performed well enough. Was this where my life would end, strapped down to a bed in a Sertorian hospital, the recipient of a lethal injection? With time to kill, I experimented with the pin, trying to make it hot again, but it had reverted to its usual state and I wondered if I hadn't imagined the heat in the aftermath of the maze. There was no damage to my hair, no smell of burning that should have accompanied such a strong radiation.

"I want to go back to my cabin," I said when I ran out of patience. "I need to shower and change." Not to mention I was bone-tired and my vision was blurring.

"I'd prefer we get started right away," said Crassus as he rounded the corner.

He looked fresh and rested, in clean black robes, whereas I was still sweating, my body covered with bruises the size of eggs, and so tired I could barely lift my arms.

"Where were you?" I demanded.

"Administrative duties."

"What kind of administrative duties?"

He raised an inquisitive eyebrow, but nonetheless answered, "When we pull out of hyperspace, before we enter the next Janus Cardo, it is standard procedure for the team to meet and update the proconsul and senators on our preparations for the coming games. It's part of the responsibility that goes with being a fully blooded Sertorian."

"I was worried you'd gone to see Licinus. I feared he would cancel our deal and have me executed after my performance in the maze. I asked one of the immunes, and she said she thought you might be going to the officers' quarters."

"No, we meet in the conference room on the bridge, and don't worry, Licinus won't harm you, not yet at least. I'm here, I'll protect you as long as you play ball. Now come along."

We entered a large circular room with a domed ceiling. The only furniture was a black steel table and two chairs, one on either side.

"What is this place?" I asked.

"This is a schoolroom, and today I'm going to start teaching you. Then everything will become clear. Come in, please."

"Teaching me what?"

"Barbata is in charge of reforming your body, but Mania and I have the pleasure of educating your mind and your heart. You can't help convince your countrymen that they should lay down arms and come to our side unless you look and act the part. That starts with knowing something about what we stand for."

"Two years of war have told me everything I need to know about what House Sertorian stands for."

He indicated that I should sit opposite him, and I was glad to take the pressure off my aching legs, but when I sat in the chair opposite him, I felt a sharp stab of pain. The medics must have missed one of my cracked ribs when they healed me, because it was agonizingly painful to sit and breathe at the same time.

"Some tisane," I said. "If you want me to concentrate after this morning's fighting, then I'm going to need something."

"The peasant drink? How quaint. Why not?" Crassus clapped his hands and ordered Alba to bring a fresh pot.

Crassus pressed a button on the table display, and the Sertorian anthem started up. Trumpets, a choir, pounding drums. High drama, typical over-the-top drivel.

"First, I want to introduce you to the most important document ever written in Roman history." Crassus looked so pleased with himself, like a child showing off his Saturnalia presents.

"The Twelve Tables of Roman Law?" I said sarcastically. "Somehow they managed to bind an entire empire together."

"Fear binds the empire together. Fear of the chaos that would consume us if it were to fall," Crassus said. "This book is a way to overcome that fear of the unknown by learning to seize our own inner power."

He pointed to a small white book on the table before me. It was rare to see

printed matter, let alone a whole book, but that particular book had been distributed widely throughout the galaxy at great expense. The title—*The Seven
Precepts of the Eagle*—was printed on the front in shining golden letters. At
the bottom was the name of the author—Aquilinus.

"I've read it. I remember it being tedious in the extreme."

"This is a subtle document. It takes time to be realized, and a teacher is needed
to guide you in full comprehension. Luckily you have me."

At Crassus' command, images formed on the ceiling and circular walls,
triumphant images from Sertorian history along with series of despicable
acts associated with House Viridian and the other two houses of the Caninine
Alliance.

"You think that's going to work?" I asked. "Pointing out that we are imperfect? That we've made mistakes, committed crimes in times of war? Nothing that
compares with the Sertorian efforts—civilian bombings, gas attacks, mass executions. Where are those images?"

"You already know all that. I'm just reminding you that we Sertorians have
our heroic moments, and that our enemies are not without fault. It's a simple
starting premise." The images began to rotate like a children's carousel, cycling
about the room. "Stand when you read, please," Crassus instructed. "As a sign
of respect."

"Where's that tisane?" I demanded.

"Up, please."

I sighed and rose to my feet. I noticed that the images on the wall were
emitting a soft glow, filling the entire room with a constantly shifting spiral of
red and purple light that enveloped Crassus and me. I picked up the book and
read.

"One. The gods are dead."

"Read it again with more vigor, please. That was not satisfactory." Crassus
had fully become the schoolmaster now.

"I can't read with vigor that which I do not believe. The gods are an eternal
constant, the embodiment of the forces that shape the galaxy, the empire, and
the people within it," I said.

"It can be a challenging truth to contemplate, but once we have resigned ourselves to the fact that we are at the top of the genetic ladder, and that there is
nothing above us but infinite potential, does that not liberate us? Force us to
mature?" Crassus' tone was unbearably condescending.

"Are you talking about humans being above barbarians, or Sertorians being
above everyone else? You're committing hubris. It's the fatal error of the antique
plays. Those who think themselves above the gods are ultimately humbled not
only by the gods but also by their own conceit," I replied.

Alba appeared with a pot of tisane on a tray, the smell soothing me at once.

"Just a small cup please," Crassus said.

I wanted to countermand the order, grab the whole gods-be-damned pot and
down it at once, but I had my pride. The small cup the Iceni poured was sweet
going down but hardly enough.

"The gods are a fairy tale told to frighten children too afraid to embrace their own potential," Crassus continued patiently.

"The gods keep a check on how much damage we would do to ourselves and the galaxy if we were stripped of their influence," I retorted, glaring at him. "Without the gods, there is no humility. How terrible are we when we think we are accountable to no one?"

He pointed to the empty tisane cup. "Feeling better now?" he asked.

"A little . . ."

Before I could continue, the bracelet about my wrist sent a shock through my body like a sledgehammer breaking up concrete. I fell back onto the seat. The aching bruises on my back from that morning in the gymnasium began to throb. This wasn't my plan, to argue with Crassus over this. I had planned to pick my battles with greater care, but Crassus' smug pomposity made it impossible to keep the fire under control. Why didn't my goddess come to my aid? Was she so fickle that she would abandon me for not making an offering on her feast day? Why had she let me, her faithful daughter, endure this misfortune? My faith was vulnerable, and now Crassus was pressing on that weakness, and it made me react instinctively. I had to defend my gods, because without them, I'd be totally at sea. I needed Minerva now more than I'd ever needed her before.

Crassus took a deep breath and calmed himself.

"It pained me to have to do that," he said. "I recall reading in your file that your mother schooled you in philosophy. That makes you argumentative. Too much of the wrong kind of education can be as bad as too little. You are permitted to question; just remember that I am the teacher and you are the student."

"If you want some quid pro quo, you can start by taking this thing off my wrist," I demanded, pulling at the bracelet. "And giving me some more tisane."

"Refrain from indulging in your animal nature. We must prove Licinus wrong together. We must show him that you can learn to master your base instincts and cooperate fully."

"You'd feel differently about it if I was the one delivering the shocks."

"I've suffered to learn these precepts too. Their value far outweighs any physical pain you might receive in the learning of them."

I looked up from pulling at my bracelet to see that there was something different about Crassus. He had a quality of authority that I immediately responded to. My father, he reminded me of my father at that moment. More than that, it seemed like there was a transparency laid over the top of Crassus so that he actually took on Father's physical qualities, his age, his bulk, his robotic eye and arm. With that came a feeling of guilt and remorse, a need to atone for the sins I'd committed against him. I'd do whatever he wanted, if only he'd embrace me and tell me he understood, that things were going to be all right.

"Now listen, Accala," the being that was both Crassus and my father said. "I'll tell you something very important. Each of the precepts has been constituted not from some impractical theory but from Proconsul Aquilinus' direct experience."

*   *   *

WHEN AQUILINUS WAS A young man on Sertorius Primus, he raged about the sybaritic overindulgence of the ruling members of his house. He championed a theory that there were two predominant streams in House Sertorian—those who were genetically fierce and capable of grasping power with their bare hands, and those who were inherently weak. The latter had become fat and lazy, reliant upon their family's past prestige and the armies of slaves they commanded to carry out their orders. Aquilinus longed to cut these withered branches from his genetic tree, but there was nothing he could do without his father's permission. As the head of the household, his father held the power of life and death over him, and in a Sertorian household, it was not uncommon for a father to kill a disobedient son. Then a fateful day arrived.

Aquilinus' father became inflamed with lust for a priestess of Vesta—one of the sacred Vestal Virgins—and raped her, destroying her virginity. The priestesses of Vesta were thought to uphold the cohesive integrity of the empire but only as long as they retained their purity. The virgin herself was thrown into a cellar beneath Vesta's temple on Sertorius Primus and entombed alive so as not to bring misfortune on the empire, the ancient customs making this foul act unavoidable, and Aquilinus' father was castrated before his throat was cut by the priests of Vesta. Aquilinus saw his opportunity—he was now the head of the household, and although it would ruffle the feathers of his natural enemies within House Sertorian, it would not be considered unusual for a son to seek revenge for his murdered father. Therefore, in retaliation, Aquilinus marshaled together the members of his immediate family and convinced them to aid him in destroying and sacking not only the temple of Vesta but also the temple of every god on the planet that wasn't a patron of House Sertorian. Priests were castrated and killed, priestesses were raped before being slaughtered, the statues and shrines were crushed. Aquilinus spurned the gods and dared them to punish him. Afterward, he suffered retribution and loss as his enemies imprisoned him and stripped him of his power, his wealth, and his allies, and finally threatened to kill those closest to him if he didn't stand down.

*   *   *

IT WAS ABOUT HALFWAY through the story that I realized the machine was having a kind of hypnotic effect. I was totally engaged, on the edge of my seat waiting to hear how it ended, like a child listening to a bedtime story. I wasn't going to give in so easily, though. The overlay of my father vanished. Cheap tricks, just like the flashing red and purple lights.

"Let me guess, he let his friends and family be killed," I said to Crassus.

My resistance surprised Crassus, I could see it in his eyes.

"He did let them die," he said, "and with good cause. His mission was of greater value than any personal relationships. He demonstrated his strength."

"Or supreme selfishness."

"His destruction of the temples codified the first precept, the first link in a chain of personal revelations that Proconsul Aquilinus has used to shape the empire toward its ultimate purpose."

"If the gods are real, then it takes more than the delusion of one man to supplant them. The gods don't punish immediately," I said. "Hubris is paid back in kind when the gods judge the time to be right. Minerva will take her due, have no doubt."

"You are no follower of Minerva," he scoffed. "I saw dark potential in you the moment we first met. Why do you think I approached you? Admit it, you have already spurned your gods. You're adrift, looking for something to help you make sense of the universe, something more mature than childish beliefs. You're ready for these precepts, Accala. Now, please, read on," he said. "You are permitted negative thoughts for now, but please restrain yourself from expressing them out loud." He motioned for me to continue.

I wished I had my discus at hand so that I could express exactly what I was feeling.

"Two," I continued. "Man is the preeminent species in the universe. All other species are inferior and subject to man's will."

"This precept should be self-evident after your time in the maze fighting off monsters. Do you pity them?"

"How can you tell the difference between a monster and an angry barbarian? Maybe the barbarian has good cause to attack. It's sentience. A monster reacts violently without any ability to consider its actions," I said. "The Sauromatae, the Ichthyophagi, the Leonii, they're self-aware."

"So you think they're the equal of a Roman citizen?" he asked with an amused smile. "Or even an exiled human who lives on the galactic rim, beyond civilization?"

"No, of course not."

"Precisely so," he said.

"But we should be generous and liberal in our attitude to irrational creatures, for we have reason and they have none," I said.

"That is like asking us to be compassionate toward ants," he said. "Do you think about the feelings of an ant as you crush it underfoot?"

"What about people? Are they to be crushed without thought as well?"

"Some. The weakest, those who contribute the least, who have no economic or personal power drain the strength, like leeches, from those who drive a society forward, and if they're not burned off, they will eventually cause it to collapse."

"Some people think that helping the weak makes for a more robust and well-rounded society."

"I've never heard such poppycock," Crassus said, laughing. "It flies in the face of reason. I'll have an intelligent debate with you, but we must stay within the bounds of common sense. Read on."

"Three. Men can acquire divine power through the exercise of their will. Four. Inferior men who lack the will to seize what they want in the face of opposition are weak and can be recognized by their talk of mercy and compassion."

"So true, so true," Crassus said. "You see it is not much of a leap to realize that, as all barbarians are inferior to all humans, so some humans are inferior to other humans. You don't know it yet, but the precepts will shape you. They can seem obvious, but there is more to them. They are like a river that appears still and shallow, but once you start to cross, it reveals deep currents."

"Five," I continued. "The Virtus Optimus Magnus—the strongest and greatest of men—will lead us into a new golden age. Six. All men, even inferior men, can benefit from these precepts and find their place in the universe."

Finished, I put the book back on the table as if each page were dripping with plague, and gently sat, making an effort to maintain my composure. "Listen, Crassus, I'm not here to embrace your philosophy, only to endure it for the sake of my countrymen. We both know what this is, so why pretend any different? Do you know what I believe? Marcus Aurelius says that in death, Alexander the Great's end differed not a jot from his stable boy's. It will be no different for you and me. We are not gods, you are not fundamentally better than me, and I deserve no more or fewer rights than any other citizen."

"And what of the emperor? Is he not above others? And proconsuls, consuls, senators, nobles, and so on?"

"I'll admit we do not have the democracy of the ancient Greeks, but the current system sounds better to me than what you're suggesting. Hang on. It's supposed to be seven precepts, right? But there were only six listed in the book."

"The seventh is yet to be revealed," he replied. "It is a teaching for those of us who are chosen to usher in the golden age."

"So your Proconsul Aquilinus is your strongest and greatest of men, then? Isn't he a bit short and unattractive? You know, the big nose and beady eyes?"

I took another shock. It hurt as badly as the last one, except now my mouth tasted like glue.

"I advise you to take this process seriously," Crassus warned. "I have my conditions as well as Licinus. If you want to pass my test and ally yourself to me, you must be able to recite the proconsul's precepts by heart."

"My mother taught me the art of memorization. I could recite them for you again now, if you like."

"I would like to see more quality than quantity," he said. "A hundred stale recitals are not worth one heartfelt reading. I want to hear your voice filled with conviction. Take some tisane if you feel you need it to steel you," he said, indicating Alba should pour the same quantity as before.

My redhead bunkmate had advised me to choose my battles, and right then I couldn't see the point in denying him this one little thing. What was the point of digging my heels in? But the stunt he had pulled with the swirling lights, which were still spinning around the room, had irritated me, and I couldn't bring myself to please him or accept the steaming drink.

"I can't do it," I said. "Maybe my mother's had too much influence over me but I just can't get excited about a political system that prizes raw power above all else. It's not the basis for a philosophy; it's just schoolyard bullying on a galactic scale."

"I don't disagree but why is that a flawed concept? Is it not honest and true? The strong always defeat the weak. I noticed that you quoted Marcus Aurelius before. *Liberal in our attitude to irrational creatures.* I enjoy him also." He searched his memory before reciting, "'If anyone can show me, and prove to me, that I am wrong in thought or deed, I will gladly change. I seek the truth, which never yet hurt anybody. It is only persistence in ignorance and self-delusion which does harm.'"

"Ignorance and self-delusion. Funny, I've thought of that exact quote in relation to House Sertorian. It makes me think of those billboards back in Rome. The ones with you lit up as the savior of the universe, javelin in hand, fighting off the evil barbarians."

"You see it that way because in the arena back in Rome you were engaged in a propaganda fight. I, on the other hand, sought only to spread the truth," he said with the utmost sincerity.

"You're joking."

"I most certainly am not. This is not a game. I believe in the proconsul's vision with all my heart and mind, and all I ask is that I be permitted to state our case and that you give it due consideration. Nothing more," he said as he rose from his seat. "We'll try again tomorrow. Each day after you've recited the precepts, we will engage in debate. You're welcome to express your opinions as long as you refrain from insulting the proconsul or his precepts."

"Well, that was productive. Can we go back to the gymnasium now?" I asked. "All of a sudden I have a burning desire to punch a Sertorian."

I stood and was immediately struck by a powerful dizzy spell that caused me to stumble. Crassus' strong arms wrapped about me before I hit the floor. It must have been the effect of the room—the spiraling lights and spinning images of Sertorian glory.

"Come. You've had enough and it's late afternoon," he said.

I pushed him away at once. "Don't be ridiculous. It's been no more than an hour and a half since we finished in the gymnasium."

He showed me his armilla as proof and I checked my own and found it the same, though I still couldn't believe it. What had felt like thirty minutes at most had in fact been three hours.

"I warned you. The precepts are very powerful. They affect the deep mind."

"It was nothing, I just lost my balance," I said, keeping a hand on the table to stop myself falling over. I had to get out of that room.

"Isn't she perfect, Gaius? I want to snatch her up and play with her all day."

Mania. My slight jump was involuntary, and I hoped she didn't notice. The girl with bone-white hair sauntered up to the table and, with a little jump, sat on its edge. I forced myself not to pull away. Had she been watching the whole time? The door was directly in my line of sight. How could she have entered without me noticing?

"You're very patient with her, Gaius," Mania said. "I don't think I could be so patient. But it makes me happy that you're so nice. I want her to be our friend."

"Where did you come from?" I asked, as casually as I could manage.

"From the world of dreams," she said, smiling at me like we were best friends. "From the lands of hydras and gorgons."

"You're as mad as a cut snake," I said.

"Mind your manners," Crassus said. "Mania is a hunter and tracker, but she is also an auspex—she divines the future through signs and sacrifices."

Just like in my dreams.

"I thought you didn't believe in sacrifices to the gods."

"I sacrifice to the New Gods," she said.

"So in essence you worship yourselves?" I asked.

"Don't be silly. We acknowledge our own enlightenment and potential in public ritual. It's not the same thing at all."

"I'm sure it's not," I replied sarcastically.

"Speaking of divination, tell me, Accala, what have you been dreaming about?" she asked.

"None of your business."

"You know we can divine a great deal about ourselves and our destiny from dreams. For instance, I wonder if you dream of your mother? And your brother?" She peered at me like my skull was made of glass. "He was very precious to you, wasn't he? I think you must dream of them very strongly," she said sweetly. "Of the bombs falling, of the atomic fire."

"I told you it's none of your business!"

"Don't be upset," she said. "Crassus asked me to help him teach you. You should feel you can be completely candid with me."

"I don't dream of that at all," I said. "I dream of a flock of hawks being eaten by wolves, devoured by lions, their bones picked clean by ravens."

She giggled like a schoolgirl. "That's funny. You're funny, Accala. We're going to be great friends, I can see it. As clear as crystal."

"Then maybe you should get your eyes tested."

XIV

THAT NIGHT I CLIMBED onto my bunk and curled up, my whole body trembling. Despite the long and difficult day, sleep would not come. The carousel of images from Crassus' circular room kept flashing into my mind, round and round—powerful Sertorians in shining armor, the great heroes of their past. The anthem of the great song that drove them forward had Aquilinus' precepts as its lyrics. The gods were dead. Will and power. Mercy and compassion were weak. Power was civilization. All those notions were wrong. Intellectually I knew that, but Crassus' words lingered, needling my mind. *Filled with dark potential.* Were my actions selfish rather than noble? Putting my own need for revenge above the duty I owed my father? And if so, maybe I was more like the Sertorians than I thought. I did have a choice, I could have told my father everything, trusted him to act to save Aulus.

I'd made progress on one front though. Crassus had told me that he and the other Hawks regularly held a private meeting whenever we exited hyperspace. Partway through my third week, that was the next time we'd exit the Janus Cardo. That would be my first and only chance to break into Licinus' quarters.

Fitful sleep finally came, bringing dreams of my father and Aulus. No sign of my mother. As Father turned to me, he vanished and in his place was Gaius Sertorius Crassus. He was smiling at me, he approved of me, and that made me happy. He reached out to me and I took his hand in mine, our fingers interlocking. An electric charge of pure arousal rushed through my body. And then I remembered Aulus was there, and I was mortified with shame. My little brother wouldn't show me his face, wouldn't respond when I spoke to him. I pulled him around and found myself staring right into Mania's face. She smiled at me, a smile like a poisoned dart, driving terror into my heart. "Do you want to see a magic trick?" she asked.

My screams woke me, my body tense, covered in sweat.

"It's all right, Accala, calm down."

It was my cabinmate, Julia, shaking me like a rattle.

"It's okay, you're just having a bad dream."

"Don't touch me," I said.

"You're welcome. Next time you wake me up with your screaming, I'll just smother you and do us both a favor."

I took some deep breaths. Bad dream didn't begin to describe it. I felt like a dehydrated spider, but the smell of the morning tisane stimulated me and helped me to stir. My head was pounding, buzzing, my mouth parched. Alba placed a fresh pot down on the shelf.

"Gods, I need some of that," I said, crawling awkwardly down the bunk's ladder out of bed.

"Well, you're officially a pleb now if you've got a tisane addiction," Julia said.

"Don't say that."

"That you're a pleb?"

"No. I'm happy to be a plebeian, but don't say I need this." I sipped the drink, which began to calm me at once. It was saving my life, I couldn't face the arena without it. Julia's suggestion that I did need it, was becoming reliant upon it, rang a warning bell somewhere in my mind, but I didn't care. If I needed a crutch to keep me standing and fighting, then the tisane seemed harmless enough. It gave a lot and asked for nothing in return. "I don't need anything—not slaves, or this, or you," I spat at Julia. Except the first cup was gone already and I was reaching for a second.

"Domina!" Alba exclaimed. "Your friend is right. Not too much."

"I don't want an argument," I said forcefully. As soon as the hot liquid of the second cup passed my lips, relief flooded through me. My head cleared, my stomach settled. I sat on the bench and took a deep breath.

"Everybody needs something, but not everything we need is good for us," Julia said. "Take Crassus, for instance—"

"I don't know what you mean," I snapped.

"I do. You were calling his name out in your sleep. *Oh, Crassus. Take me, Crassus.*"

"Shut your mouth." I gave her a look that told her that she'd better pay attention, and she held her hands up in mock surrender and grinned.

"Pax. Pax. We don't need to bicker, I was just teasing. Besides, you should pay some respect to your elders."

"You can't be much older than me."

"Twenty-two," she said, "but I left my homeworld to start my apprenticeship when I was sixteen. It's been a busy six years. I've traveled through four Janus Cardos, seen nine planets and two wars."

"Which ones?"

I had to admit she had caught my interest.

"Planets or wars?"

"Wars."

"Sirius Terminus on the galactic frontier and a yearlong campaign against the Ichthyophagi in Mare Byzantium province. I volunteered for service with the forty-seventh legion. They have the best engineers in the galaxy."

"That last one was a nothing fight," I said dismissively. "But you were on the frontier at Sirius Terminus? That was a battle between the Viridians and Sertorians, the first land battle after the bombing of Olympus Decimus. You fought against my people. Aquilinus himself led that battle."

"I didn't kill anyone. I just did the same thing I do here—fix things that are broken. Don't hold it against me."

"I won't." I said, my regained sense of well-being making me magnanimous.

"Why don't you take the tisane pot away for today," Julia said to Alba. The Iceni hesitated, looking to me.

"Send her away with the pot and I'll tell you my secret," my cabinmate offered.

"Secret?"

"Where I'm going to go after the games."

"I don't care," I said, dismissing Alba just the same. A part of me did want to hear Julia's fantasy escape plan.

"All right," I said. "This had better be good."

"The cloud cities of Quatrus Lycaonia," Julia said with an impressive flourish. "The emperor has his equinox palace there. No war, no intrigue, it's a place of peace and beauty, an idyllic paradise." She sighed.

"You think there's really such a place as that?"

"Why not? I mean, there should be, shouldn't there? A place where there's no suffering. They have big air-recirculation systems there that need specialized servicing. Without them, everyone would die, so the engineers there are treated like royalty."

"There's no place where we can get away from ourselves," I said. It was one of my mother's sayings and it sprang to my lips without effort.

"Yeah? Well, when I get there, I'll let you know."

I stood up to begin dressing but stumbled and fell back against the bench. Julia pulled her privacy cube out and activated it.

"They had you in the machine, huh?" she asked in a quiet, conspiratorial tone. "I was servicing the hypnogogic projector a few months back. It messes with your head, unbalances your body and your mind. That's why you're having problems standing in one place without moving."

"More advice for the underdog? I'm fine. It's just made me a little dizzy, that's all," I said.

"Yeah, it won't last. You'll be back to normal soon enough," she said. "But they'll have you back in it again. Reckon they want to wipe the wolf out of you, huh? Worst thing you can do is try to fight it. You can't beat the machine. The Sertorians feed your genetic profile into their database. They've refined that thing over hundreds of years so it goes right into the deep mind."

"What would you recommend?" I asked. What was she up to? What did she want from me?

Her eyes narrowed, and for the first time her face lost the flippant, carefree attitude I'd come to expect.

"You want some well-meaning advice? If you want to survive the machine, then find a thought or idea that is strong—a fixed point that is part of who you are. Hold on to it and don't let go. No matter how stupid the idea seems, no matter how ridiculous they make it sound. You hang on to that and don't let go."

"Why would you want to help me? What do you want in return?"

"If I need anything, I'll let you know. I help you because I build things, I fix things. I don't like seeing things get pulled apart and broken. That's what they do with that machine."

"You mean me? Then how do you tell if something's broken? Don't you have to pull it apart first to see inside?"

"Well, there's always something wrong; there's no perfect machine. But as a general rule, we mechanics say—if it ain't broke, don't fix it."

"Crassus says he has to do that. That I *am* broken, inferior."

"Really? I think you're fine just as you are," she said with a grin. "And seriously, lay off the tisane. That variety they're feeding you, I think it's more potent than the usual brew. Much more potent."

*　*　*

DAY AFTER DAY, LURCO and I were sent into the maze. It was reconfigured each time but the results were the same—the pair of us emerging after a half-dozen or so bestiarii fights. The only difference was Lurco's willingness to cooperate with me and a gradual familiarity that made exiting slightly more efficient with each repetition. Despite our enmity, the giant would have piggybacked me through the maze if I'd asked, rather than face Barbata's tender mercies again.

Next the entire team lined up, and fifty feet opposite us were more black cages, stacked in a long row, brimming with deadly barbarians. Licinus signaled and the first four cells burst open, revealing blue-skinned Ichthyophagi with poisoned spines on their arms and back, red-maned Leonii with black tentacles, and more Sauromatae. There were a dozen, four of each.

"Right, any of you barbarian scum that can understand me," Licinus said. "Get past us and reach the other end of the training area, and you'll be granted your freedom. I give you my word of honor."

Some of the more sentient creatures registered signs of interest and excitement at the offer, but they didn't know that Licinus had no honor and certainly no intention of granting them freedom.

The Sertorians charged at top speed, and I was surprised to find that I was ahead of them, at the front of the pack. How had that happened? I wasn't as fast as they, but there I was. The momentary confusion allowed them to roar past me, leaving me to confront a wounded Ichthyophagi that had survived Crassus' first pass. They whittled away at the aliens, breaking them down and then killing by the most ruthless and painful means. All their moves were designed to incapacitate and then mortally wound, ensuring a prolonged death—arterial cuts, broken spines, stomach wounds. Even skinny little Mania, the white-haired slip of a thing, proved herself to be a killing machine, shooting with her bow staff, stabbing with her needle knife. Joining the fray, I was able to distract and wound, but their sudden brutality cooled my fire, and I found myself a spectator, watching on, even feeling pity for the beasts as they were slaughtered.

After bestiarii training, I'd return to Crassus' brainwashing room and recite his precepts, and he'd reward me with tisane. Why not? If he wanted me to put on a show, it wouldn't cost me to oblige him. It would be the least ridiculous of a long list of absurdities to be endured. I even embraced the absurdity, reciting his precepts like some revolutionary fanatic.

At night I'd ask Julia to tell me again and again the stories of Quatrus Lycaonia and its cloud cities (of billowing aerial landscapes peppered with floating platforms that housed the colonial towns, and at their heart, one enormous palace filled with carefully cultivated fruit trees from all eight provinces). Who knew if I'd survive the Ludi Romani and ever see those cities, but knowing they were out there, great towers and domes rising up through the billowing peach-colored clouds, gave me some small comfort. It suited me to stay friends with Julia. She felt comfortable around me, so much so that she left her toolbox on the bench without worrying about whether it was sensible or not to do so. In return for her stories, she asked me to tell her about the things that were most important to me. "You'll need to keep them in mind to survive the machine, fresh in your short term memory, so telling me about them will help you a lot."

I told her about my own fruit trees that I carefully pruned on my balcony, and some stories about Roman heroes I admired, Mucius Scaevola in particular, and finally I opened up to her about Aulus. I didn't tell her the Sertorians had him.

"He sounds like just the thing. I've got a younger sister. You should keep your brother in mind. Hold on to the thought of him when Crassus has you in the domed room."

One night, when Julia was sound asleep, I made a play for her toolbox. It was just close enough to get my hand to if I stretched out my lead to its limit. I drew the box slowly and quietly back to my bed and then tried the combination on the locked compartment. Damn. She'd changed it. But there were other things of use. A microscanner for recording data. I couldn't remove the blocks placed on my armilla, but I could still use its power to run the scanner. It was paper thin and transparent, fitting in neatly between the skin of my forearm and my armilla. The only other thing I took was some black foil tape that would help me with my little Iceni minder. I concealed the roll between an exterior rail of my bunk and the wall. Steadily, I was crossing things off my checklist, one item at a time. Everything was going to plan and then, when I woke for the second last day of bestiarii training, there was no tisane to be had.

"You must be joking," I said to Alba. "Where is it?"

"I was ordered not to bring it in this morning," she said.

My head was starting to ache; the dull buzzing headache I'd experienced during my first week aboard *Incitatus* was back. This was Licinus, trying to pull the rug out from under me.

"Well, go and get some," I yelled at the Iceni. "I'm not fucking kidding. I need to wake up if I'm going to fight. You tell our lord and master Gaius Sertorius Crassus that I'm not going to perform today if he's going to mess about with my diet."

"I don't think—" she started.

"I'm not asking you to think. I'm telling you to obey! Now go and don't come back without it!"

"Yes, domina." The small creature bowed and left.

"Hold your horses," Julia said. "It's not the Iceni's fault."

"Did you say anything to them?" I said, rounding on Julia. "You were the one pushing me to stop. Did you tell them I'd had too much? Are you here working for Crassus?"

I had her up against the wall, my forearm pressing against her throat. She was using all her strength to try and push it away, but to no avail.

"Well? I want the truth."

"And I want to know how you suddenly turned into just another gods-be-damned Sertorian," she hoarsely whispered. "Gonna kill me for something I didn't do?" I released her and walked off, hammering the wall with my fist. It was hard to clear my head and think straight. My vision was blurry, and the buzzing headache was only getting worse.

When I confronted Crassus, he assured me he had played no part in the decision.

"It came down from Licinus. He's probably received reports saying you're fond of it and is playing games with you. My advice—ride it out. Jump through the hoops until we get to the arena world and then get your own back. In the meantime have a cup of tea or some wine," he said.

I slapped him hard in the face. I was slowing down. He saw it coming but let it land anyway and then floored me with a right cross.

"Really, you have to do something to get rid of all that pent up tension, Accala. If you don't have tisane, there are always other options," he said suggestively.

I struggled through practice without it and Lurco regretted teaming up with me. I let him take the lead, setting up the kills while I did the easy job and finished the beasts off.

It was a hard day and it was only going to get more difficult. The next morning there was no tisane to be had either, and I could barely put a coherent thought together, thanks to a splitting headache. Like when a mosquito buzzes above your bed in the dark, I couldn't pinpoint the exact point inside my head that the buzzing noise originated from, but it was busily needling away like a dentist's drill.

The final day of the week arrived and Lurco and I were sent into the maze again. What a waste of time. I'd been forced to run the same maze each day with Lurco, and although I'd progressed as a killer of barbarians, I hadn't improved my maze navigation skills or found Barbata's safe way through. That day, though, something was different. Struggling without the tisane, I followed behind Lurco and noticed that the buzzing ache had shifted to a point that felt, strangely, outside my body. Somewhere just away from me. As I moved through the maze, the buzzing oscillated, growing stronger when I moved to my left and weaker when I moved to the right. Experimenting, I found that it was definitely directional, as if the sound were originating from a specific location. When the noise seemed the loudest, I came to a full stop alongside a length of maze wall. Lurco was engaging some beast ahead, but I let him take care of it. The source of the sound was directly opposite me, on the other side of the wall. I reached out to touch the surface, and my hand passed right through it. There was no wall; it was a projection. Stepping through, I found a long corridor on the other side, a straight path to an exit, right out of the maze and back to the hangar.

But between me and escape stood a cluster of five Hyperboreans. Right there before me, the indigenous beings of the arena world. Finally I'd found Barbata's path. Only I had to kill the barbarians to exit the maze. There were none of the workers Mania had taught us about, they were all warriors, seven to eight feet tall, each one twice my width. And the sharp spines, so many points to kill an opponent upon. They looked dull, weakened compared to the ones I'd seen on the holovids, but what Mania's instructional holograms had not reproduced well were the beautiful swirling liquids and gases that moved within the crystal forms. Like an opal or shining mother of pearl, the dance of subtle, shifting color was captured and reflected by the crystal prisms that formed the shell of their bodies.

As I walked toward them, instead of turning to confront me as the other beasts had, these parted like water to either side, opening a way to the exit. They were completely nonhostile. It seemed so strange when every other barbarian that week had been set on ending my life. I walked past them, wary but not sensing any threat, and cleared the long corridor.

To my surprise, they followed along behind me in a neat line. The Sertorians cheered when the Hyperboreans trailed out, whooping and jeering.

"Would you look at that! The mother wolf has lost her cubs and found ducklings instead!" Licinus roared.

"You magnificent bitch!" Barbata yelled, but it didn't sound like her at all. Her voice sounded completely different. "You found them and tamed them!"

"Go back," I hissed, trying to wave them back into the maze with my discus. "Go away." But they kept coming until they all stood in the gymnasium, surrounding me.

"Right, get on and kill them," Licinus called from the gantry above.

"But there's no fight in them," I argued.

"So what? This is a beast hunt, not a petting zoo. You found the hidden way out, and the only thing standing between you and victory for the day is killing those ice monkeys."

"Get on with it!" Crassus yelled.

"I'm bored already," I heard Barbata say, and then an electrified net fell over one of the Hyperboreans and the dark-haired retarius had leaped down from the gantry and was sprinting toward it. Just then, Lurco emerged from the maze and charged the barbarians as well.

"Defend yourself," I hissed at the creatures, but they just stood there, facing toward me, oblivious to any danger.

Suddenly the alien warriors sprang into action. They were surprisingly fast and dangerous, slicing at Barbata and Lurco with their ice-pick arms and grabbing with their sharp claws.

"That's more like it!" Mania yelled.

Strangely, they seemed to avoid me altogether. I had an easy opening to take the fourth, but it just stood there before me as if waiting to be cut down.

Barbata pushed past me, trident raised and ready to strike. Without thinking Orbis flew from my hand, ricocheted off some terraform rocks and, just before Barbata's weapon could arc down, Orbis struck the forked end and knocked it right out of her hand. The trident clattered to the ground and at the same time spun Barbata aside. She missed the stationary barbarian and fell awkwardly.

"You dare, you filthy little bitch?" Gaia Barbata screamed at me. Vicious abuse and insults streamed from her mouth, and her usually beautiful features were twisted with rage.

"Hold!" Licinus commanded. "Barbata and Lurco, back off. Retreat from combat."

The two of them stepped away, leaving me to face the Hyperboreans, but instead of attacking together, they reverted to their previous state, standing and staring dumbly at me.

"Mock Hawk, you called the kill when you stole it from Barbata."

"Quickly, Accala," Crassus called out. "Kill! You've got no future here unless you kill!" There was an edge of desperation in his voice.

I had to keep my little brother in mind; nothing mattered but saving Aulus. I spun two, three times and let Orbis fly. He went out on a line before the spin kicked in and he arced back. It was more like stationary target practice than a fight. Orbis cut into them, one, two, three heads were severed and fell to the hard floor. The bodies remained standing upright, the swirling opalescent gases inside their bodies leaking out into the air around us, creating a rainbow cloud that hung above the gymnasium. The fourth was already down, struggling out of Barbata's net, and the moment Orbis returned to my hand, I fell upon it.

The net's charge had faded away and the barbarian reached out through the holes to grip my hand. Sharp claws held me tightly, cutting into the meat of my palm, as the creature pulled me close. My buzzing headache vanished; I'd forgotten it was there at all in the rush of action, but suddenly I felt like a perfectly clear pool. An image flashed sharply into my mind, like someone had activated a holographic projector only inside my head. It was a mountain, immense and majestic, and I knew it at once—from my dreams and from my research—the arena world's largest peak, Nova Olympus.

It was only there for an instant and then my hair was grabbed and I was dragged off the alien, kicked in the back, and tossed aside. Barbata pushed past, burying her trident in the creature's neck. A kill shot. The gases floated up from the puncture holes, joining the cloud above before the vapors were sucked into the air vents set into the ceiling.

I was so tired I could barely get to my feet. My mouth was dry, my vision swimming.

"A magnificent display from both gladiators," Crassus announced, trying to keep the peace. I expected Barbata to come at me, to spew more invectives, but her face was strangely calm.

"Good practice," she said to me. "Keep it up."

I couldn't believe the sudden change in her. A second ago she wanted me dead, there was no doubt about it, and now it was like nothing had happened at all. Crassus took me aside and congratulated me on my performance.

"You came out ahead of Lurco for finding the right path and I was able to convince Licinus to let you have a reward. It'll be waiting for you back in your quarters."

Back in my cabin I lay on the bunk and wept for the dead barbarians. I'd executed beings that meant me no harm, had stood by while a being that was trying to bond with me was executed, for I had no doubt that the mountain image was some effort at communication. The pot of tisane, my special treat, lay on the bench. I waited for Julia to come back. She'd advised cutting down on the amount I consumed, but the last few days without it had been a living hell. The second she came in, I could talk to her, ask her to help me. It bothered me that I felt compelled to drink it; every nerve, every muscle longed for the relief the tisane would give. Where the hell was she? But she didn't come. Maybe she was sore about being slammed up against the wall and screamed at. I couldn't take it another second. I tore the top off the pot and drank the whole thing in one go, steaming hot, burning my throat and stomach, but I didn't stop. It spilled over, ran like rivers down the sides of my mouth. I didn't care, I just wanted to stop all feeling. When it came to insulating my heart from fear and sorrow, the tisane had done the trick before, and just like magic, it did the trick again.

XV

THE THIRD WEEK BEGAN, my final week to prove myself to Licinus. My dreams were no longer of fire or ice but solely of water. Drowning in a red-and-purple sea, I heard my mother call out my name, but I couldn't see her or keep my head above the water long enough to find her.

Each morning, when Alba brought her offering of tisane, I swallowed it greedily. The strong dreams gave me no rest, no chance to recharge as I slept, but the tisane made up for it. Crassus had started feeding me more and more of the stuff in our sessions in the domed room, and if I had to be honest, I had never felt better. This was where I had to shine and show my real value or, by the end of the week, when we exited the last Janus Cardo, I'd be out of time and so would Aulus.

But I wasn't concerned. This was my area of expertise—gladiator fighting! Both one-on-one and team-versus-team timed matches. I worked hard to make an impression.

Suddenly I was no longer the weakest. I defeated Mania in one round by disarming her and then beat Barbata on points. I couldn't harm her, but she couldn't harm me either. Within two days I progressed to being among the strongest. I was on a roll. Maybe my luck had changed, so I decided to test Fate and see what would happen.

"Come on," I goaded Licinus after practice. "I'm holding my own against the others, but you and I haven't fought a one-on-one match yet."

"You're calling me out?" he asked in disbelief. "Are you really that deranged?"

"The way to get to be the best is to challenge the best."

"You don't remember what happened last time? You're taking a great risk that I won't just out-and-out kill you for your impudence," he said, stepping out onto the gymnasium floor, steel whip in hand, "but come, I could use a laugh and it'll keep morale high among the others."

It was all over in twenty seconds. I warded the biting tip of his weapon and sprinted in to close the gap, but his whip curled back, and before I could strike, it wrapped about my chest and pulled me off balance. Instead of pulling up, though, I let myself go with it and pretended to fall, running right into him and sending us both flying over. I got lucky; he wasn't expecting me to lose my balance (or pretend to) and I landed on top of him. He rolled me off, drove the hard butt of his whip into the side of my skull, and before I could regain my feet, set about launching hard kicks into my lower back and kidneys.

"Don't break her spine," Crassus suggested. "She might not heal up in time for the tournament."

"You'd better not fuck up like that again if you want to live, Mock Wolf." Licinus spat on me and stormed out of the gym.

Twenty seconds, but that was all the time I needed. When I fell on him, I'd pressed my armilla against his. Returning to my cabin that night, bruised and sore, I checked and confirmed that I had, in fact, scanned a bundle of security access codes from Licinus' armilla.

Despite my humbling at Licinus' hands, Crassus was pleased with my performance and laid off on his demands for recitations of the precepts. He was supportive, encouraging, bringing me tisane when I asked for it. I still despised him, that had never changed, but there was no denying he was handsome, noble, ruthless, just like a hawk. Despite his delusions and planet-size ego, there was a certain magnificence to him, an enviable confidence.

Instead of discussing ideology, we discussed arena tactics, and our sessions became a welcome distraction. My eyes returned again and again to his hands, big hands with strong, thick fingers. I'd catch myself daydreaming about those hands, of his running those fingers through my hair and pulling me forcefully to him. Other times I'd find myself caught up in dark fantasies where I was dismembering the Blood Hawks one by one, using Orbis to cut them to pieces for their offenses.

One afternoon as Crassus was walking me back to my cabin, Barbata met up with him. She kissed him passionately on the mouth and they went off together, her arm around his shoulder. A wave of jealousy hit me. I wanted to be in there with him. Not her.

"I saw how you looked at Crassus," she said to me the next day. "Don't let me stop you if you wish to pursue him. I'm certain he has feelings for you. There is no love in our lovemaking. We simply take pleasure in each other's forms like two eagles with locked claws, falling through the empyrean. He's quite magnificent."

"You're wrong. I have no interest in him."

"And you're right." She smiled. "He's probably not for you."

I turned away from her to hide my confusion. Right then, I'd never wanted any man as much as I wanted Crassus. If we'd been alone right then, I'd have dragged him onto the nearest bed and ridden him until I screamed. How could I have such strong feelings? If I bedded him, that would make me every bit the traitor and whore the Viridians at the parade had accused me of being. Besides, I was no gladiator's moll. I had become a gladiator myself. I did not fawn and lust after other fighters from the sidelines. Juvenal wrote about the kind of woman who would sacrifice everything for a gladiator (the curse of having memorized the classics was that they were always with you, reminding you how inadequate you were). I allowed the urges to wash over me. The fantasies about Crassus were a wholly unwelcome distraction, no doubt a result of the extreme stress I'd been forced to endure.

*   *   *

IT WAS THE SECOND to last day of the week, and I was making headway, moving toward a final round where I'd face either Licinus or Castor Corvinus. After practice Crassus bid me follow him. "Today you spend time with Gaia Barbata," he said. "She still has to share a gift with you. Something that will prepare you for the tournament."

I was anxious. We'd exited the Janus Cardo the day before and entered normal space. I'd been expecting the Sertorians to hold their meeting and give me a chance to break into Licinus' quarters, but there'd been no announcement and Crassus was frustratingly punctual. Had they found out? Had Licinus discovered his code had been stolen? It might have been changed already. I might risk everything only to find myself locked out once I reached his cabin.

"Silly wolf cub," Barbata said when I was in her charge. "Your problem is that you take things too seriously." She seemed to have forgiven me for attacking her during bestiarii training, but I wouldn't make the mistake of trusting her.

"You don't think the tournament is a serious business?" I asked.

"Of course, but if you take it seriously, then it's all too much to bear, isn't it?"

"Maybe you should take the next after-practice beating for me, then," I said wryly. "Then I'd feel much more relaxed about the whole thing."

"You're all set to take pain like a good pleb, but you've got to learn to appreciate pleasure from time to time. You're going to come to the baths with me."

"I'd rather have every hair in my body pulled out at once."

"Funny you should say that. We're going to visit the ornatrix."

"An ornatrix? I don't need to have a painted face and coiffed hair to fight in the emperor's arena."

"I'm afraid I'm not going to give you any choice," she said with a pout. "Now wipe that sour look from your face. You look as if you've eaten a raw olive."

We took an elevator down to the recreation deck. The doors opened to another world. Gone was the clinical design that lined the rest of the ship. These were not the pleasant and functional washrooms of modern-day Rome; the Sertorians had re-created the indulgences of the past—a library, gardens, galleries filled with sculptures and carvings, ivories and treasures, no doubt plundered and looted from their victims. The entire complex seemed to stretch on forever. However much I hated the Sertorians, I had to admit they did opulence well. They were disciplined and efficient in their duties and self-indulgent sybarites in their leisure time.

"Shall we bathe, sister? Once you're all clean, you won't feel so much the mangy dog."

"I'm fine as I am. I can shower later."

"They make you shower? Now, that is punishment. All that water beating you. It makes the skin blotchy, ruins its luster," she said with a horrified expression. "Please, just look at you, covered in sweat and blood and grime. I can barely stand next to you without wanting to run away. Bathe."

We moved on past restaurants and a large natatorium where people swam. We passed bordellos where the ship's prostitutes called out to us to come and join them. Vaulted, light-filled spaces of shining steel and black marble softened by greenery—small fruit trees and flowering plants. It was an exorbitant waste of resources in space, an ostentatious display of wealth.

My body felt a pang for the baths as we passed them. Viridians are Stoic by nature. We don't indulge in sensuality on that scale, but baths are the birthright of every Roman.

"A short bath," I conceded. "Just to clean off the dirt."

"That's the spirit, Accala. You know what they say—cleanliness is second only to godliness."

Barbata and I disrobed and bathed, surrounded by naked Sertorians. They were graceful specimens, like portraits painted by a generously paid artist. Steam and perfume filled the air, creating a miasma, a hedonistic fantasy world. While they reveled in their own sensual beauty, slaves rushed to serve them, delivering food and drink, carrying towels, massaging bodies, grooming them. I blinked and shook my head, reminding myself of what they really were—all perfectly formed thanks to genetic streamlining, all the same, like children's dolls rolling off a production line. They left it to styling to give them their uniqueness—fashion, hairstyles, painted nails. They were beautiful. They were grotesque.

Barbata had a perfect body, even by Sertorian standards, richly endowed with sensual curves. The Sertorian men and women admired her greatly, commenting on her beauty before their eyes trailed over me and their faces soured. Some even laughed at my appearance. Baths are public places, and I'd never before felt vulnerable bathing or been ashamed of my body, but I did there. Grabbing a sponge from a passing Iceni, I began scrubbing at my skin. I'd never felt so unclean.

"This was a mistake. I shouldn't be here," I said. The bath should have been a luxury, but I was feeling the sting that accompanies every Sertorian gift.

"Be patient, Mock Hawk," Barbata soothed. "It's important to learn to use what assets you have. A woman's body can be a weapon to sway the audience, to confound a male opponent. Every advantage must be seized." She reached out to touch my hair with her fingertips, but then hesitated and pulled away like she'd spotted a nest of lice. "You are not unattractive in a homely way. Do you think that your current popularity is solely due to your skill in arms? Men and women like watching an attractive, athletic body in action. It's part of a whole package to thrill the senses and stimulate the eye." She could tell I wasn't convinced. "Wait, then, until after the ornatrix has given you a little polish. Then see how you'll shine. And don't wash yourself," she chided, plucking the sponge from my hand. "We bathe, the slaves massage us and then scrape the oil from our bodies. How do you Wolves get by at all?"

I didn't give a fig for Barbata and her expectations of what an ideal Sertorian female should look like. I hated feeling vulnerable, and if it weren't for the potential threat the bracelet about my wrist represented, I'd have been out of the water in a flash.

After the bath we dressed in clean robes, and she led me into a salon where dozens of Sertorian women reclined in padded chairs while slaves and stylists preened and prodded them. Their chatter stopped at once when we walked in the door. They looked at me with disgust and started whispering among themselves.

"This will be grand," Barbata exclaimed. "A chance for us to really bond," she said to me in a quieter voice, "like two sisters, so mind your manners and don't make me use the bracelet. Agreed?"

"I'll do my best," I replied curtly.

A thin, elegant woman with alabaster skin and long fingers sailed toward us.

"Accala, this is Publia Sertorius Regilla," Barbata said. "Publia is one of the most famous stylists in Aeria Sertorius province."

"Gaia Barbata, what have you dragged in?" the woman asked as she flapped about me.

"Come now, don't pretend you don't know who this is."

"The Mock Wolf," the woman said sourly.

"Yes, and we need to turn our prickly wolf here into a resplendent hawk."

Publia Regilla laughed like it was the most ridiculous thing she'd ever heard. "My dear, you're asking for a miracle. It would be easier to make a silk purse from a sow's ear!" Publia turned to me. "Perhaps you've heard of me? For several months I was the personal ornatrix to Proconsul Aquilinus himself."

"Did he sack you when he realized that nothing you could do could make him look good?" I asked plainly.

The women in the salon started chattering in outraged whispers. If Publia's shocked expression was anything to go by (at least I think it was shock—the skin was pulled so tightly over her face that I couldn't say for certain), you'd think I'd just killed her favorite aunt. "A barbarian! You've brought me a savage barbarian from the provinces. You tell her to keep a civil tongue in her head if she wants to stay in here."

"Accala . . ." Barbata warned, her hand beside mine, nails tracing the inside line of my bracelet.

"Sorry," I apologized to the ornatrix. I was starting to get a sense of just how crazy the Sertorians were over their beloved proconsul. They insisted they'd gotten rid of their gods, but all they'd done was to bundle them up and pack them into the small frame of that horrid little man they worshiped instead.

"Leave her with me," Publia said to Barbata. "Get your own treatment, there's no rush. This creature is going to take a great deal of craft and more than a little art."

Publia shooed me over to a reclining divan next to a cabinet with dozens of tiny drawers and trays containing all the tools of her trade. I went to lie down, but she put out a hand to stop me and clapped. Iceni slaves rushed in from the sides and began to undress me.

"No, I don't want to disrobe," I said, pushing them away. The Sertorians in the pool had made me self-conscious, and I wasn't keen to repeat the process.

"Don't be such a diva. Didn't you just bathe in public? I have to see what I'm working with."

I took a deep breath and let them get on with it. I steeled myself, thinking of the moment when I would claim Barbata's life, but right then she seemed the least objectionable of the team, and the thought of her without a head didn't really bring much consolation. The other Sertorian women who lingered in the salon sat up and stared, enjoying the show, commenting to each other on my appearance, giggling and snickering.

"Now the hair, put it down." I pulled out my mother's pin. The black locks fell to the middle of my back. Publia reached out and briefly ran it back and forth between her fingers. "It's like a dishrag, oily and dirty. The body isn't bad, but too tight and muscular, like some starving animal."

"I'm an athlete," I said.

"You're forgetting that an athlete in the Ludi Romani is a performer, and the audience is the emperor and the galactic mob," she said dismissively. "Yes, some softening, rounding, and smoothing required on the surface. We'll leave the muscles below, of course. The main focus will be above the neck." Publia turned my head this way and that like a sculptor appraising a rough-hewn statue.

Her comment stung, but when she turned me round so I could see my body in a full-length mirror, I realized just how run-down I was. The tisane had been bolstering me in place of sleep, but I hadn't realized that I looked so haggard, so worn.

"I want a robe," I insisted. "Now."

Publia sighed and clapped her hands. A slave brought a sheer robe and fastened it to my body, then guided me onto the divan. The ornatrix opened a large casket like a high priest opening some sacred repository. Inside were dozens of tiny little bottles, each one holding a different-color liquid.

"True beauty stored in a hundred phials," Publia said, brandishing a silver comblike wand. For a second I thought it was a weapon, but she turned it on and it hummed quietly. "Don't fret. This is a calamistrum, the baton with which I shall conduct the transformation of your body."

"What does it do?"

"Why, it reshapes you. Just subtle alterations."

"How?" I wanted to know if what she was about to do could be undone.

"A conjurer never reveals her secrets," she said with a mischievous smile.

"I'm only nineteen."

"Yes. If you'd started treatment when you were nine or ten, you would look much better now."

"What I meant was that they're making me do this. Let me tell you right now that if you make any permanent change to me, anything that can't be undone, I will tear this place apart before Barbata can stop me."

"For a first treatment, the effects are only cosmetic," she said disdainfully. "You'll need to receive regular treatments for months for the change to be anything resembling permanent. You should be grateful. There are women in here who would give their firstborn child to be on the receiving end of my special treatment."

Publia ran her hand across the glass of the mirror, and it turned matte black, offering no reflection.

"Just wait," she said.

She massaged the substances from the phials into my skin, and then she passed the wand over the muscles of my face. It vibrated with heat.

"You see," she said, "it is not unpleasant."

The wand felt like it was turning my muscles to jelly, but the experience was warm and, indeed, not unpleasant. I felt small hands on me and looked down to see Iceni slaves applying lotions to the rest of my body.

"Close your eyes," Publia said. "I'll need to soften the area around them."

I welcomed the darkness, pretending I was floating in light-filled water. The humming of the baton was melodic now, almost soothing.

"No silk purse, but certainly not a sow's ear," she said when she was done.

Publia's voice woke me with a start, and my eyes snapped open. I'd drifted off. How long had it been? What had she done to me while I slept?

"Come, let's have a proper look at you," she said, calling Gaia Barbata to my side.

Publia waved her hand over the mirror, and for a second, I thought the glass had turned transparent and I was looking at someone standing on the other side, but no, it was my own reflection. My hair had been braided into thin strands and pulled back tight to resemble the plumage of a bird. The shock of white hair I'd always known was replaced by a vivid vermilion streak. My eyes had been subtly widened, lips made more full and luscious, cheekbones sharpened, my strong Viridian jawline softened. My skin was naturally buoyant and elastic, but Publia had pulled and stretched it so that instead of natural curves and soft rises and hollows, my face was now like a porcelain bowl, perfectly smooth and flawless. Beneath the robe, the hard lines of my fighting body had been rounded out and my skin had taken on a shining, plastic hue. She'd turned me into one of the Sertorian dolls I saw swanning about the baths.

"It was too much to hope for, but look!" Publia exclaimed. "A masterpiece!"

"Put me back the way I was. Right now!" Even my mouth and the muscles of my face moved differently.

"Are you completely mad? I have given you a great gift. You'll be a hit! A palpable hit!"

"You look just splendid." Barbata was also pleased. "A vast transformation. You can express your gratitude to Publia now," she said to me, her fingers tugging at the bracelet on my wrist.

I forced myself to smile, but it wasn't easy. Just like Publia's, the muscles of my face were trapped beneath tight-stretched skin. "Thank you."

"Good. It's the shock of sudden improvement, I expect. Look again," she said. "I thought of changing your eye color, but your natural green has been eliminated from the Sertorian gene pool. It actually provides a perfect contrast to your new look. We don't want to do too good a job. Leaving that one aesthetic imperfection is a masterstroke. I shall be the talk of Aeria Sertorius, the ornatrix who made a mangy Viridian shine! Who would have thought it possible?"

I gazed in disbelief at my new appearance, amazed at the speed of the transformation. They'd dressed me in a crimson undergarment and the black, body-
hugging Sertorian uniform. The only thing worth appreciating was my mother's
gold and platinum pin, which shone brilliantly in contrast to the black leather.
There was both a shocking newness and all at once a familiarity, as if I'd seen
this version of myself somewhere before. Then it hit home: the billboard back in
Rome. The fighter who had stood in the chariot beside Crassus. The New Gods.
That's what the billboard had read. I looked just like her, I *was* her. The realization was horrifying. How far in advance had Crassus planned on having me
here? Undergoing this procedure? Knowing how I'd appear? His propaganda
campaign was much more advanced than I'd suspected. I had already been
packaged and presold to the empire as a Sertorian. As I was led out of the salon,
the Sertorian harpies were whispering again, but I didn't see any smiles now. Was
I so hideous that I wasn't even worth a joke? A true mock hawk now, a wolf
dressed as a bird.

"They are jealous of you," Gaia Barbata whispered reassuringly.

I glared at her, not appreciating the joke at my expense. I looked farcical, ob-
scene. Passing men and women stopped and stared at me. No smiles, no whispered jokes. I was offensive to the eye.

"You could at least show some gratitude!" Publia cried out as Barbata led me
away.

The truth was, despite my displeasure with the changes to my appearance,
overall I felt great. Somehow the ornatrix's treatment had reenergized me, and
washed away that unclean and vulnerable feeling.

"You might not thank me now, but you will," Barbata said. "Remember, use
every weapon at your disposal."

"Some of us prefer to fight fair," I said. I was thinking of that billboard again,
of Crassus and his machinations.

"This is a blood match, a death race. There is no fair, only life and death, and
make no mistake, your Viridian friends will be gunning for you. If you're as
smart as you pretend to be, you'll work that out."

When Crassus saw me, he was at a loss for words.

"You look . . ."

"Like something from a ridiculous pantomime," I said.

"No. You look most appropriate," he said, recovering himself. "Most appropriate. Your external transformation is remarkable. But for your green
eyes, I'd have sworn you were a pure-blood Sertorian. I knew you had potential."

"The stylist kept them this color. She said they were an aesthetic imperfection that enhanced my beauty, if you can believe such claptrap."

"Oh, but she was right," Crassus said, reaching out to touch my face. I didn't
pull away. His skin on mine was electric, his hand warm. Gods, but I needed a
night of comfort and rest. In Crassus' room with the animal skins on a comfortable bed. No harsh lights to awaken me. And what other pleasures could we
seek together? *Like two eagles with locked claws, falling through the empyrean.*

The image of me mounted atop him, our fingers intertwined, sprang into my mind with such powerful intensity it took all my willpower to pull away from him.

"Accala?"

"Are we done? I need to rest," I said flatly, looking away. My face was flushed, my heart palpitating. Crassus was red-faced, maybe even aroused, and definitely puzzled. Good. For a change he was the one off balance. Perhaps my new appearance could be put to some use after all.

"You need to be careful," Crassus said. "You've been making great progress in the gladiatorial rounds, but Licinus has his eye on you and I'm sure he's got something up his sleeve to make things difficult." I didn't care. I was beyond fearing any of them. The only thing that frightened me was the face looking back at me in the mirror, and the thought that I was running out of time to steal the secret of the Sertorians' super-powered performance.

XVI

IN THE FINAL ROUND on the last day of the week, it turned out Crassus was right—I faced Licinus in the gymnasium's arena.

"You want on the team, now's your chance, Mock Wolf. Lose and you die."

"That's ridiculous," Crassus argued.

"That's the deal. Let's see what she's got."

His war chain was like a winged serpent, chasing me about the arena, but whichever way it turned, I countered with Orbis. He could not score a hit on me, but the chain came at me so fast that I couldn't make a cast with my discus. It came down to the last minute and, unable to decisively score, Licinus tapped the controls on his armilla, and his armor began to generate a powerful electrical field. The energy ran out through his chain. The air around it crackled with the intensity of the charges. I tried to advance, but each time, the chain licked my armor and sent a shock into my body. The closer I drew to him, the more intense the shocks became. I could win only by moving into close range and striking with Orbis but then I'd expose myself to the fatal amount of electricity generated by his armor. He would not let me win and join the team. He'd see me dead first. I spotted a gap and raised my arm to throw. He repeated his last move, but I was ready. The chain snaked around my casting arm, the electricity flowing painfully into me. As he went to pull me to the deck, I ran forward suddenly, stealing his momentum. He pulled up in surprise and was forced to take two steps backward. Shaking Licinus' weapon from my arm, I stopped in front of him, as close to the electric field as I could bear, Orbis raised.

"Strike! Strike!" he yelled furiously, but I held my ground and refused to advance any closer to the crackling field that was already damaging me with each passing second. The alarm signaling the end of the match chimed. Stepping away from the Sertorian, I couldn't believe I had done it, and that Licinus' charged armor hadn't killed me. What was happening to me?

"You failed!" Licinus yelled at me.

"I did not. You said that if I lost, I would be out," I said. "I have not struck you down, so I cannot claim victory. But at the same time, you have not struck me down, and so I have not lost. Ergo I cannot be thrown off the team and must be included in the tournament."

He leaped to his feet, furious, ready to strike me, but Crassus intervened. "It is not a Sertorian solution, but it is a solution, and is that not why we value Accala? Her fresh perspective, her will to attain power that brings about innovation."

"We shall see," said Licinus. He backed off, but he was still seething with anger when he gathered us together. "The trial period is over."

"So that's it, then? I'm officially part of the team?"

"Not quite, Mock Hawk. There's one more hoop to jump through." Licinus raised his voice, addressing the entire team. "Tomorrow, in accordance with Sertorian tradition, the two weakest members of our team will face each other in our time-honored initiation. Lurco Giganticus and Mock Hawk will fight in a battle to the death. The strong shall live, the weak shall perish."

I looked to Crassus, thinking he would come to my defense, that this was another of Licinus' excesses, but he didn't offer any support. Lurco didn't look impressed either. He strode past me, bumping me with his shoulder as he passed. "You're easy meat, and after the bout, I'm going to have them bring your corpse to my cabin so your spirit can feel me in the afterlife."

"This is madness," I said to Crassus when we were in private. "Whichever of us dies, you'll be a person short for the team."

"Cutting the weak link is the Sertorian way," Crassus explained. "We're stronger without the weakest among us. Besides, we're so far ahead of the Caninine teams they couldn't beat us even if we were down to five."

Now I saw what was going on. This whole time a contest had been under way. Licinus building Lurco up, Crassus focusing on my survival, until they faced us off, the two outsiders against one another. I expected my session with Crassus in the domed room, but this time he put me off. "I've got a meeting to attend, and besides, we're finished with our sessions. You need to rest for tomorrow's match."

"You're reporting to Proconsul Aquilinus?" I asked.

"Yes, why?"

"No reason. I . . . miss our sessions, that's all. I thought you might bring tisane."

"I'm sure something can be arranged," he said, putting an arm around my shoulders.

"We'll see," I said, pushing it away.

"You're always running hot and cold, Accala. It doesn't serve you well."

He clapped his hands to summon my body slave. "Alba will take you back to your quarters," Crassus said curtly, and then strode off to carry out his official business.

Finally, this was my chance. My battle to the death with Lurco was something to worry about later. It was time to put my plan into action.

* * *

As usual, Alba took me back to my quarters. Since our altercation, Julia had been giving me a wide birth, which suited me, and thankfully she was absent again, conducting weapon repairs with the other immunes. The Iceni went to lock me to the lead, but as she brought it up to the bracelet, I offered my wrist, black foil wrapped tight about the chain to prevent a connection, and touched it to her lead. I gave the lead a pretend jerk to let her think I was secured. Satisfied, she bowed and left.

Discarding my clothes, I dressed in one of Julia's Vulcaneum uniforms stored in her locker and snatched up her spare toolbox.

The journey to the officers' quarters was much easier than I had expected. The Sertorians looked disdainfully upon Vulcaneum members—people of no house deserved no consideration in their eyes—and so I was, for all intents and purposes, invisible. There were no guards, only the locked door. A quick swipe of my armilla over the code panel and I was in. So far, so good.

The apartment was lavish, like Crassus', but with floor and walls decorated in black and gray slate, the space demarcated by pillars of solid ruby. The moment the door slid shut behind me, I gave the room a quick once-over, making sure to put everything I touched back in its proper place. Nothing. Not a thing that matched the theory I'd devised. Nothing that would account for the enhanced abilities of the Blood Hawks. My heart was racing, I was risking my brother's life for nothing. I had to get back to my cabin before I was missed.

Licinus must have forbidden Iceni cleaners from entering his quarters, because everything had a thin veil of dust covering it. The dining table was made of solid onyx, and as I passed it on the way out, I saw a thin line that would normally have been imperceptible but for the gathered dust.

I ran my armilla over the surface of the table, and a rectangular section of stone slid back smoothly, revealing a cavity containing a small casket about two feet long and one foot high. It also had a code key panel set into the front of it and I swiped again. There was a click and the lid opened. An internal light came on, and rows of small phials were raised up from the casket. They contained a black-green liquid. Written on a small copper plaque inside the casket was a string of numerical latitudinal and longitudinal coordinates and an identifying line of text—AMBROSIA BATCH DLXIX.

Ambrosia. The mineral the Sertorians had started the war to obtain.

"Get out. Quick." The hissed words interrupted my racing thoughts.

Licinus? No. "Julia?"

My bunkmate stood just inside the door.

"What are you doing here? How did you get the codes to Crassus' room?"

"You stole my tools, so I stole your codes off of your armilla while you slept. Now, get out. He'll be here any second."

Licinus was coming? That wasn't good, but I wasn't going anywhere without the ambrosia. I reached for one of the phials, but Julia grabbed my hand and told me to leave it be. "You are a stubborn pain in the ass. Put that phial back and get out! If he finds one missing, he'll kill your brother."

It seemed the redhead immune knew a lot more about me than she'd let on. She took a phial from the chest, and swapped it with another that looked almost identical.

"Look familiar?" She said, holding it up.

Now that she called my attention to it, I knew the liquid at once. It was the tisane.

"They've been feeding it to you all along, diluted ambrosia. This stuff in the box is condensed ambrosia, the strong stuff reserved for the Sertorians."

"You knew all along?"

"No. I couldn't say for sure until now," she said. She used her armilla to close the casket and table.

"You shouldn't have those codes," I said. "Who are you working for?"

"Meet me back in the cabin after this. We'll talk then."

"Why should I trust you?"

She cast a quick glance at her armilla. "Because I'm about to save your life. Hide behind the pillar over there. When he's distracted, make a run for it."

She took out a small device and pointed it at the ceiling. The gentle glowing overhead light fizzled and then suddenly burst forth with bright intensity.

"Who's in here?"

I ducked behind the pillar just as Licinus stormed into the room. Julia snatched up the toolbox I'd left by the bench and quickly pointed up at the ceiling.

"Sir, we had a circuit malfunction in your quarters. The regulator on your lighting panel blew out. This is the same setting the plebs on the lower decks have to suffer."

"These are my personal quarters. How did you get in?"

Julia held up her armilla.

"Maintenance pass gives me access to most parts of the ship. The job came up on the system, and I came up to fix it. My pass worked fine."

"It shouldn't give you access to my private quarters. No one should have that code."

Julia shrugged. "Just one of those things, I guess. My pass does open just about everything aboard."

"Shut your mouth. Do you want to be whipped to death?"

"Um, no."

"I'm going to order that you receive ten lashes from your supervisor with the electro cat."

"Sorry, sir, I didn't know, sir. I'll leave the light as it is, then, and report to my superiors," she said and made to go.

"Wait. I know you. You're one of my immunes."

"Yes, sir."

"If I had the choice, there would be none but Sertorian legionaries, but others have the idea that the Vulcaneum produce the best field engineers money can buy."

"I heard the same thing, sir. I'm sure my replacement will be just as good."

"Replacement?"

"After ten lashes, I'll lose my finger dexterity. They'll have to swap me out for the tournament."

"Hmm. You've been drilling well enough, meeting my requirements. I don't like to tamper with a winning lineup. Fix the light and then return to the lower decks. It'll be three lashes of the electro cat, and you can count yourself lucky I don't have time to administer them myself. Three will teach you a lesson without leaving permanent damage."

"Yes, sir, thank you, sir. It's gonna take me five minutes or so. I have to repair the unit. It might get a bit bright in here."

"You have two," Licinus announced as he marched off to an adjoining room.

Julia gestured to me and I slipped out, calming my breath. No sense hurrying and drawing attention to myself. Julia had kept the ambrosia sample, but I planned on taking that from her the very next time I saw her. Just let her try to hold on to it.

Back in the cabin, I changed, jumped onto my bunk, and tried to make sense of what I had just learned. What was going on with Julia? Was she a collegia agent? I knew she had an agenda and that I'd been used, but at the same time she'd risked her life to save me, was at that very moment enduring administrative punishment on my behalf.

I was alone again, trembling from the risk I'd just taken, barely escaping and with Aulus' life and my whole mission at stake if I got it wrong. At that moment I didn't know how I could keep going. I felt helpless, totally abandoned. So much pressure was being brought to bear upon me that I never realized how much Julia's friendship had been buoying me up.

And now I was a victim, a test subject, dosed up to the eyeballs with ambrosia. I'd thought I was so smart, but everyone aboard the ship was making use of me and I hadn't seen it at all.

Julia's locker was open. When she found me gone, she must have been in too much of a rush to shut it. Inside I found what I needed: a lightblade—a laser cutter. I climbed onto my bunk and made thin diagonal cuts along my right forearm with the red-hot lightblade. My heart raced. I broke out in a sweat, but I wasn't getting what I wanted. It wasn't helping me wake up, it wasn't making me feel like myself. Was I too far gone to even shock myself back into feeling? The wounds cauterized instantly, leaving swollen black-and-red scars. Sertorian colors. Even my body was betraying me. I should have been the one caught by Licinus. I was trapped in a nightmare and the feeling of the cat striking my back might have woken me up. Then I'd be back in my bed in the Wolf's Den. Constrained by safety, the empire's problems were something I could do nothing about. But instead I was alone in the depths of space, preparing to fight for my life in the arena to please the insane whims of the Sertorians.

I wasn't scared, not an ounce of fear. The ambrosia had stolen it. No nerves, no anger. Only a deep sorrow, an encompassing darkness that swallowed my fire. As I sat and watched the result of my handiwork, the four black scars became increasingly thinner and fainter until they vanished entirely. I tapped my arm lightly, seeking sensation, then harder when I felt no pain. Curious, I repeated the experiment and slowly carved two new cuts into my arm. It took longer to heal the second time, but within a few minutes, my skin was clear and unblemished. I turned my arm this way and that, looking for any trace of a scar, but there was nothing. At first I thought it was the poor lighting in the cabin, but on closer inspection there was no doubt—my skin was yellow.

"It's the ambrosia. You've got enough of it inside you to float a trireme." Julia shuffled awkwardly into the cabin. "When you're starting to run low, it causes a skin discoloration. One of the less debilitating side effects of withdrawal and easy to spot."

"Did he whip you?" I asked.

"Not him personally, but yeah. Three lashes. Hurt like a bitch."

"We need to talk," I said.

She took the privacy cube from her toolbox and activated it.

"Now we can talk."

"What the hell is going on? Tell me now. Why were you watching me?"

There was some condensation on the surface of our shared portal, and she used it to write a word:

TROIA

The ancient word for Troy. "Your uncle sent me," she said.

I rubbed my hand over the word, erasing it at once.

"Is that so?"

"Of course. He came to you the night after the match in the Colosseum. He asked you to go along with Gaius Crassus' offer in order to spare your brother's life. He has promised to rescue Aulus once you find him, freeing you to sabotage the Sertorian team from within. You didn't think he'd throw you in the deep end without any support, did you?"

"I didn't know House Viridian was in the habit of hiring collegia agents to do its dirty work or that the collegia had any interest in helping the houses."

"There's a lot you don't know."

"Then you'd better explain yourself and quickly," I demanded.

"I really am a field engineer," Julia explained. "I like hardware, but I'm just as adept at mercurial engineering. I specialize in digital architecture design and system programming. I'm considered a rising star within the collegia; I've even taken on an honorary role as the voice for workers' rights. Your uncle has formed an alliance between your house and the collegia, and I'm here to make sure he keeps his end of the deal."

"What deal is that exactly?" I asked suspiciously. "The collegia have wealth and power independent of the houses. Their best strategy is to avoid this conflict altogether, to sit on the sidelines and then support whichever house emerges victorious. What could possibly motivate you to support House Viridian when we're on our back foot?"

"The only thing that is of any interest to us," she said. "Legitimacy."

"I don't know what you mean."

"We've been trodden on for so many years by the nobles, the only thing that could interest us . . ."

"Is your own house," I finished.

"Exactly. A noble house with our own compound on one of the seven sacred hills—we don't really care which one. If the Sertorians come to power, nothing will change. We'll be little better than slaves. What we want is a future, a house that encompasses every member of the trade colleges, a seat in the Senate, a right to vote on our future, to influence what jobs we will take or won't take. We want the say we deserve."

"Gods, are things that bad?"

"What?" she asked sharply.

"I'm sorry. I don't mean any offense. Only, plebs in the Senate, it's never happened before. My uncle would never go for it unless we were truly close to defeat."

"You know how hard it was for me to rise up through the ranks of the Vulcaneum as a woman? You know what it's like to be held back because of your sex, but you don't hesitate to look down on those from a different class."

"You're right. I'm sorry. It's just habit. I didn't think."

"No problem. Just think before you speak. And you're right, your house is desperate. Why do you think they sent you?" She smiled. "Here we are, two women, with the job of pulling all those proud male peacocks out of the fire. You know, I volunteered for this assignment. I lied before when I said I never saw you fight. I saw. You were told to keep your mouth shut and be a good girl, and instead you lit the arena on fire. I respect that, so I stepped up. I volunteered to keep you alive, to make sure you finish your mission so your uncle can make the empire fair for all citizens."

"It's a noble ideal," I said.

"I plan on making it a reality."

"We have a lot in common," I said. "We're stuck in a terrible situation with big ambitions."

"We're in exactly the right place," Julia said. "I was at the battle of Sirius Terminus. They consider that battle sacred, it was Aquilinus' first victory over the Viridians after the bombing of Olympus Decimus, and because I was there at their beloved proconsul's rise to power, supporting them, my loyalty is never questioned. It made me the perfect person for this mission, and now you and I are going to become sharp splinters in the Sertorians' side."

Could it be true? I felt like I could breathe for the first time in weeks. I wasn't alone.

"So, ambrosia," I said. "Tell me what you know."

"Your uncle instructed me to gather intelligence while the Sertorians were focused on you. All the team members are taking it, you've probably noticed. It enhances the senses, brain function, nervous system, and muscle twitch response. It makes you stronger, faster, and smarter. It's amazing stuff, but it has addictive properties. You may have noticed that too."

"Addictive properties?"

"Yes, shaking, mood swings, yellow skin, withdrawal, and craving for more. All in all, you've been performing amazingly well considering you're on about half the dose the Sertorians are receiving. You really are a natural in the arena."

"A natural guinea pig," I said angrily. "Did my uncle know about this? He sent me onto this ship knowing they'd do this to me. He's turned me into an addict to find out his enemy's secrets."

"Whoa, slow down," Julia counseled. "I don't know if it's the machine Crassus has been working you over with or the ambrosia, but you're getting a bit paranoid."

"You're right," I admitted. "I'm overreacting. I hardly know myself anymore. My head's been spinning, it's hard to think straight. I have dark dreams. When you told me I was calling out Crassus' name in my sleep . . ."

"The ambrosia makes both your mind and body more plastic," she said. "It's what's making Crassus' machine so effective. They're reshaping you inside and out, but I've been diluting your pot of tisane where I can, trying to help you keep your head, or you'd have been all over Crassus like a rash by now."

No wonder Crassus was getting so frustrated with me during our sessions. I shouldn't have been able to resist. I should have been completely compliant to him. He'd expected me to be in his bed in the first week, to be his slave, body and soul. He was every bit as dangerous as Licinus.

"The stuff they were giving you wasn't good enough for your uncle's scientists. They needed a better quality sample, high-grade stuff." From a compartment in her tool belt she took out the small tube. "That's why I nudged you in the direction of Licinus' cabin."

"You used me."

"I might have kept quiet about certain things, but I'm here to help you," Julia said. "The Sertorians are trying to mess with you, trying to blur the lines between friend and enemy; that's why I couldn't let you in on my mission earlier. I had orders to wait and see if you could bear up under the pressure, but you've got to believe that your uncle's on your side. That's why he sent me: Family looks out for family. What's more Roman than that?"

"Getting what you want at all costs? And you're not my family."

"No, the Vulcaneum is my family, and as long as I'm looking out for them it means I'm looking out for you. That's the nature of the deal."

"And the sample?"

"I'll pass it off to a courier the moment we exit the next Janus Cardo. It'll go to Viridian scientists for analysis, and once they've read my report I'd say it's a good bet they'll try to synthesize their own version of ambrosia for use in the tournament. They're gonna have to do something to keep up with the Hawks."

"That's all I wanted, for the Wolves to have a chance in the games," I said. "And now I'm done with the stuff. I won't touch another drop."

"Uh-uh, no. We've all got to keep up appearances, Accala. The Sertorians will get suspicious if you suddenly quit cold turkey. Besides, it'll play hell with your health and you can't afford that right now. You need to be at your best in the arena."

"But you said yourself, it's helping them break me."

"It removes inhibitions, helps you cope with stress, gives you an accelerated healing factor. I'm not saying it's a good thing, and I'm not saying it hasn't come at a great cost, but in a way the Sertorians have made you a much more dangerous competitor and that means you just might survive long enough to find your brother. You have to keep taking it, at least for now."

Yes. The Sertorians had unintentionally turned me into a weapon capable of destroying them. Without the speed and strength the ambrosia bestowed, I wouldn't be able to take them on.

I sat down on Julia's bunk, cradling my head in my hands.

"You're cooperating with the enemy, but it's for the greater good. It's a worthy sacrifice and I'm your backup, here to help you get through this."

She sat down on the bunk, putting a comforting arm around me. I wanted to push it away but I needed her, needed someone to help me before I sank under the waves.

"You had orders to observe me. To see if I broke under the pressure. What if I did? What then?"

"Best not to ask about what might have been," she said. "Besides, it didn't work out that way. You're doing very well. They've been throwing everything at you—brainwashing, pumping you full of ambrosia, and now these physical alterations—but you're surviving."

"I need to speak to my uncle."

"The second we reach Olympus Decimus, we'll contact him together. I swear it."

"I don't know what kind of a backup Uncle thinks you'll be," I grumbled. "You said you couldn't fight."

"You'd be surprised how much damage a field engineer can do."

She stroked my hair as she comforted me.

"Hang in there, Accala. You'll find your brother."

I turned to say something, but when I looked into her pale green eyes the words fell away. Dark red hair, hands marked with grease, dirt beneath her fingernails. Those fingers were short, slightly fat, not at all like Crassus' perfect digits. I couldn't remember seeing anything so beautiful.

"No going back," she said.

"Like Caesar crossing the Rubicon."

"Huh? What does that mean?"

She was smart, but I forgot that she was a pleb, no classical education drummed into her.

"In the early days of the empire, Julius Caesar led his army across a stream named Rubicon, and in doing so broke the law forbidding a tribune from leading an army out of his province. It put him on a course of conflict with the Senate and Pompey. It was the start of the first civil war for the control of the empire between the noble families."

"Yeah? How'd that play out?"

"Three years of Roman blood spilled on Roman soil before Caesar was declared victor."

"Nothing changes, huh? Seven thousand years and the nobles are still at each other's throats. Things will be better once the collegia have some power, just wait and see."

Julia was kidding herself, but who was I to question the hopes of the collegia if they were willing to back our house?

"Can you help me?" she asked. "I've got a poultice that will heal up the scars, but I can't apply them to my back." She took her tunic off and the cloth blouse beneath. Her small breasts were round and smooth. She turned and in contrast to the clean curves of her chest were three jagged gashes running diagonally across her back.

"Gods, that must hurt," I said.

She lay on her bunk and I applied the poultice to the wounds as gently as I could. When I was done I reached out and brushed her hair away from her neck, trailed my fingers along the small freckles that decorated her skin. She sat up on the edge of the bunk, smiling at me, kindly and with compassion, and then gently kissed my lips. Her lips were soft. Amazingly soft. The feeling of human contact, the touch of someone who had my well-being at heart, was overwhelming, and I returned the kiss with force.

"Gently," she said. "You don't know your own strength."

She reached over to turn off the privacy cube, then pushed me down onto her bed, and I willingly lost myself in her soft embrace.

* * *

SEX ON THE BUNK was awkward. Julia winced and cried out on occasion when my hands accidentally brushed the long red welts that marked her back; I apologized and kissed away her tears.

After, I ran my fingers through her red ringlets. Dark red, almost black, like blood from a deep wound.

"You really volunteered for this?" I asked.

"I did."

"Why?"

"I was seven years old when I started clawing my way up the Vulcaneum ladder, salvaging parts from wrecked ships, and trust me, it's not like the noble houses. The collegia are more like a gang—you have to be good and have street smarts to boot to get to the top, no one cares who your mommy or daddy is. Know what my skill was?"

"Fixing things?"

"Nope. Everyone's good at fixing things in the Vulcaneum. You want to survive you have to specialize. I'm good at streamlining. I can identify any system's essential components, bring out the best in it, and cut away the crap. That kind of skill gives you a good eye. I can spot potential not just in machines, but in people as well."

"What part am I, then?"

"Easy. You're the differential. You transform and convert the power from one part and direct it to another. You're the hub around which things turn, and I'm here to make sure you don't break down. You've got potential, and right now the empire's dying from lack of it. You can serve a function that the system needs and just maybe we can set the whole thing back on track."

It seemed that Julia had been hiding many things from me, including grand ambitions.

"Your views are not so different from my own," I said. "But what of your cloud city? Was any of that true?"

"Every word," she insisted. "I've been as honest with you as I could. As soon as I've sorted things out for the collegia, that's where I'm heading. I don't care for fame or fortune; my kick will come when the big machine of the empire is running smoothly again and the collegia have their due. Then I'll be gone. Get through this in one piece and you can come with me. You'd have to undo whatever the hell it is they've done to your face, though, and gods, that hair—it's pulled back so tight I reckon your scalp could double as a harp."

I laughed, flooded with relief. Just the thought of coming out of this alive, of there being someplace to go with my brother, created an immediate euphoria, and when the laughter ended, a flood of emotion that I'd kept locked up came pouring out. Maybe it was only a fantasy but it was a welcome one. I wept and Julia held me, stroking my hair the way my mother used to when I was a girl.

"You can do this," she said. "I'm sure you can take Lurco tomorrow."

"I'm not so sure," I said.

"It's good to be cautious. The Sertorians are like bandits on a dark road, just waiting to rob and kill you when you least expect it, but you will survive. Keep focused on your brother, the real goal, and don't let them twist you to see things through Sertorian eyes."

XVII

JULIA WAS GONE WHEN I awoke. Alba was there, though, like clockwork, waiting for me with her pot of poisoned tisane, hot and ready.

She stared at me with her single, unblinking red eye as I took my first sips. The small alien wasn't to blame. She didn't want to die by disobeying Crassus, but it was hard not to resent the owner of the hands that served you poison.

"Master says he wants you to go to the arena. You must do your very best. Please do your best," she said.

Before I could stop myself, I took another gulp of the tea right from the pot, and Alba rushed forward to pull it away. "No, domina, not too much!"

Crassus, Mania, and Castor Corvinus met me outside the gymnasium. The muffled sound of wild screaming and chanting rose in a crescendo as they opened the door and led me inside. The gym had been transformed. The terra-form blocks were arranged in a stacked circle, and the projector cast the appearance of ancient, weathered sandstone upon them. All was darkness except for the makeshift arena, its center illuminated by a single spotlight. My team helped me on with my armor and then guided me through a gap in the circle, into an ancient stadium configuration—there were stands filled to bursting with the Sertorian crew, a sandy floor and posts set around the perimeter, peppered with long spikes and ready to skewer any gladiator who fell or stumbled in combat. The crowd was chanting Lurco's name. I used to ride on the crowd's approval back in Rome, but no one there was cheering for me. Upon a low balcony sat Licinus as if he were the emperor himself; on either side of him stood Pollux Corvinus and Gaia Barbata.

Lurco stood at the opposite end of the arena, nine feet of muscle, hammer in hand. He wore the masked helmet that made him famous in Rome—the skeletal face of Dis Pater, the underworld king. His long-handled hammer had changed; there was a short spike on the butt and two long spikes protruding from either side of the head. Lurco's body was glistening. He'd received one of Publia's treatments as well, by the look of it.

I didn't feel any anxiety. The ambrosia had bestowed its gift of stillness, of calm. No fire, only dark, still waters moving beneath the surface.

"Go," Crassus said. "Show no mercy."

Licinus stood and raised his hands, silencing the crowd. He'd dressed in long ceremonial robes—playing the part of high priest.

"And now, in time-honored tradition," he boomed, "it's time to see who will keep pace with the flock and who will fall short."

"Only the strong!" the crowd chanted together, as a deep drumbeat began.

"Let the match begin, and may the true hawk be blooded!"

The drumbeat came to a sudden, sharp finish, signaling the start of the match. Lurco ran right at me, spiked hammer raised, issuing a raw, aggressive scream. He was incredibly fast, closing the gap before I could make a throw, and owning the range between us.

The first blow came in unnaturally fast for the weight of the weapon he was carrying. The right-to-left arc took me on the upper arm, sending me flying sideways, compressing my ribs and knocking the wind out of me. My arm ignited in a blossom of pain. My ability to heal might have improved with the ambrosia and I might not feel fear, but I could still feel pain.

Lurco came at me again with an overhead swing meant to crush me. No time to roll. I thrust up with Orbis and blocked the blow in midswing. The pain in my left arm was intense and my block collapsed under the force, but not before stealing his momentum, rendering his blow ineffectual. But now he had those spikes, he was pressing down, pushing on the haft and angling the hammerhead to catch me in the face. I rolled to the side, slicing at his knee with Orbis and forcing him to draw his leg out of the way. Rising and running back to give myself space, I made my first cast, and my opponent was forced to stop and deflect.

Three seconds until Orbis returned, four until Lurco reached me. I stood my ground and waited, analyzing his form. Marcus had taught me patience, and how to use each second to its full advantage. Lurco had changed. He was bulging at the seams, he looked like he'd been packed full of air. Not air, ambrosia. I had suspected that Licinus took more than the others, and now he'd done the same with Lurco. Licinus had dosed him up to the gunnels, determined that I should be the one to die.

Lurco's hammer swung in at me just as Orbis returned to my hand, allowing me to deflect the blow and step under and inside his swinging arc. If Lurco was set to deny me my long-range advantage, I was going to get in close and deny him the middle ground. But he brought the hammer's haft down fast on my head, and I fell to one knee in pain, my skull cracked. I was still alive, though, and his knee was right before me, exposed. He screamed as Orbis cut into the meat and bone below the joint. I rolled to the side and sprang up, delivering a backhand swing to the underside of his helmet that sent it flying. Lurco managed to keep his feet under him, but he had all his weight resting on his left leg. He was injured, slow. Before he could counter, I retreated. His face and neck were exposed. My plan was to put some distance between us and pick him off with Orbis, but Lurco had other ideas. He spun on his good leg and made a hammer throw. It took me by surprise and struck me square in the sternum with a loud crack, knocking me backward to the arena floor. For a second I couldn't breathe. Then a rasping cough sprayed the floor around me red. The pain told me there was a loose rib, but Lurco had given me another present—a punctured lung. As he retrieved his deadly weapon, I spluttered and gasped for air, like I was drowning in my own blood. But I would not give in. This was not going to be the end. Assuming a low crouch, I thrust at his exposed midriff as he rushed in, his arms raised for an overhead swing. Lurco blocked it easily and thrust into my sternum again. The pain hit me like a black wave, but I rolled with the force of the blow back over myself and to my feet, breathing fast and shallow. My move put Lurco off balance and he lost a second as he struggled to regain his footing. I was barely conscious, but I'd bought four feet of distance.

There was no choice but to risk a close-range cast. I'd studied Lurco these last three weeks, his body, how he moved. Putting an angle on Orbis, I threw hard in as tight an orbit as I could manage. My weapon whipped through the air, right at Lurco's midsection. Lurco had been studying me too. He raised the long haft of his hammer to block the discus, and his next move would be to step in and sweep with the hammerhead, crushing in the side of my skull, but he didn't realize that his wounded knee was causing him to drop his guard slightly. Orbis ricocheted off the top of the haft of Lurco's hammer and sliced into the side of his neck, biting deep, practically severing his head. Moving backward, I kept out of range as Orbis returned to my hand. For a split second my opponent could see in my eyes that he was finished before he felt what had happened. I wasn't fighting anymore, just waiting for the inevitable. Lurco dropped his hammer and fell to his knees, his eyes filled with fear. A moment later he toppled forward, crashing face first into the deck, dead.

"How do you feel?" Crassus asked, coming to my side in the arena as the crowd screamed with the excitement and satisfaction. Iceni slaves dragged Lurco's body away ignominiously.

"I feel nothing," I lied.

"I can see it in your eyes," Crassus said. "Your heart is racing, the blood coursing through your veins. This is the joy of stealing life, the joy of survival over the enemy. It's how the hawk feels when it snatches its prey." He took my hand and looked at me proudly, expectantly, like he was the groom at the altar waiting for my vows. And he was right. I could feel it coursing through me. A primal, almost sexual electricity. I hated myself all the more because I liked it. I had never felt so alive.

The crowd became silent as Licinus stood and raised his hand. "And now," he announced, "the event you've all been waiting for: the Blooding of the Hawk."

"I thought that was it," I said. "Lurco's dead now. Isn't that what you wanted?"

"No, the true blooding only takes place when something dear to us is cut away," Licinus said. "Then we are set free to fly."

A black steel cage was pushed out into the arena by the menagerie handlers. The last and largest of the animal cages that had remained unopened. Crassus was moving away like everything was going according to plan.

Licinus clapped and the door to the cell was drawn up. I couldn't see what creatures they had waiting in the darkness, but with Orbis in hand, I was ready to face whatever he had in store for me.

"Go ahead," Licinus prompted. "Sever the ties to your old life. The sacrifice awaits. Prove your loyalty, and I will not question you again. Not once you are truly blooded."

I took another few steps, peering into the darkness. A form was beginning to emerge now, moving into the light. It was large, a well-built barbarian. Gods. It was no beast at all but rather the wounded and bleeding form of a bronze-skinned Taurii.

"Domina?"

"Bulla!"

How could this be? How could Bulla be there?

"Your father sent her to the slave market," Licinus called down from the balcony, unable to resist crowing over his little victory. "I think he was a little disappointed with how she performed the duties of managing his daughter. We had just enough time to snap her up, and at a good price too, I might add." He turned to address the audience. "The barbarian was the family nursemaid, if you can believe such a thing. These Viridians have an unnatural affection for animals. Would a Sertorian hesitate to sacrifice such a beast?"

"No!" the crowd roared.

"So now we shall find out if what we have here is a hawk or a wolf."

"Domina, why are you with them?" Bulla said. "This is a bad thing."

"Bulla, you must listen to me. Go back into the cage, let me try to work something out."

"Kill it quickly," Crassus said to me. "Don't hesitate, or it will be the worse for you, for your brother, and for this beast."

I took another step toward Bulla, who turned her head, regarding me with confusion. "Domina, your poor father, he was heartbroken." She still had nothing bad to say about him, even after he'd sold her.

Crassus was right—I had to do it. One foot in front of the other. But I couldn't. I'd never thought about it before, I'd always taken her for granted, but in my own way, I loved Bulla. She was like a member of the family, always there in the background, always willing to help and give of herself.

"Do it now or I will," Crassus urged. "It cannot leave this arena alive. Quickly now. Decide if it all ends here or if you will keep moving forward."

I closed in on Bulla, Orbis in hand.

"Domina?" Bulla asked. "Why do you do this? Why stand with our enemies?"

"They're forcing my hand," I said quietly. "If I don't kill you now, then they will kill you and then me and then my brother."

"Little Aulus is alive?" Bulla said, her head rising with renewed energy. "And your mother?"

"No. Not her."

Her head dipped. "I understand," she said. "Better you kill me than they. The Sertorians took all my calves from me. You and Aulus are the last ones I have raised. I don't want them to take you too."

She lowered her head as the sacrificial cow had done for Marcus back in Rome, waiting for the deathblow.

"I'm sorry," I said. I tried to make the blow fast and clean, through the back of her neck in one stroke. But the Taurii neck is thick and I had to hack at it three times to get through. Bulla never cried out once. Finally, her head hit the ground and rolled back into the cage behind her.

"Magnificent!" a voice called out from behind me, but I couldn't tell if it was Crassus or Licinus.

Crassus came forward and knelt down next to Bulla. He placed his hands into her blue blood, washing them until they were completely covered. Then he took my hands and bid me stand. He held up his blood-covered hands to the crowd and they screamed out their approval.

"Blood the hawk! Blood the hawk!"

"Now you have truly been blooded," Crassus explained quietly. With an air of reverence, Crassus ritualistically drew lines of blood under my eyes and down the sides of my cheeks, the thick blue liquid mingling with my tears. "The marks of the hawk!" he called out. He used two fingers to close my eyelids and smeared the lids. "The eyes of the hawk!" A line down the bridge of my nose. "The beak of the hawk!" Then three lines with his fingers on my forehead. "The feathers of the hawk!" He pulled my armor from my body and traced the blood over my arms. "The wings of the hawk!" And last he turned my hands upward and stained my palms with blood. "The hawk's claws!"

"The hawk is blooded," they all called as one.

My Sertorian teammates then stood around me, each one stepping forward to streak Bulla's blood over my body.

Barbata reached behind her, where a waiting Iceni was holding clean black robes with long red stripes running down the sides.

"Don't hide it, embrace it, own the kill," Barbata said as she placed the robes over my shoulders. "It's the finest of wines, a pleasure that surpasses all others. We're all part of the one nest now, Accala. Well done."

Licinus raised his hand again for silence.

"Congratulations. To all intents and purposes you are as one of us and therefore will be treated as one of us. You are bound to us now by blood in more ways than you know."

I'd survived Licinus' test, but what had I become in order to do it? The Sertorians were mad, each and every one of them, but when you're surrounded by the madness, it is they who become normal, your sanity becomes insanity, the abnormal thing, by default. I watched dispassionately as Mania knelt down to cut Bulla's stomach open with a sacrificial knife. She pulled out the entrails and began to inspect them.

"The omens are good!" she exclaimed, holding up the organs. They looked like a Gorgon's head, intestines like snakes, blue blood running down her arms. "Accala shall help us win the tournament!"

Bulla dead, her blood smeared over me. I cared nothing for Mania and her prognostications, but the death of my nursemaid was indeed an omen. It signaled to me, in no uncertain terms, that justice had departed, Minerva no longer watched over me. Dark waters had swallowed me up just as I was finding my way back to the surface, and now I was so deep under I couldn't feel a thing. A thick suit of insulation kept me cut off from the world. No more struggling. It had been a mistake trying to resurface, trying to find the self I'd lost. The moment I accepted my uncle's mission, I'd started a metamorphosis into a new Accala.

"You watch now," Crassus said to me. "The word will spread. The audience will love you."

I stepped in close to Crassus, grabbed a handful of his hair, and pulled him to me, pressing my lips against his, forcing his teeth apart, and plunging my tongue into his mouth. He pulled away and staggered back, eyes wide.

"Accala!"

Crassus was so self-assured, but he wasn't expecting the prey to turn and become the predator. The crowd broke out into excited cheering.

I walked over to where Lurco's helmet lay. The image of the skull-faced god of death on the faceplate looked up at me. Minerva's neglect of me was not her wrongdoing. Crassus was right, as was my uncle; everyone saw it except me, but my eyes were open now. I had never truly wanted justice. Revenge was what I sought—cold and sharp. For what they made me do to Bulla, for my brother, for the war, for everything. I needed darker gods to serve my needs. If I were to serve any divine power, then from that moment, it would be the Furies, the triple goddesses in whose temple I spilled blood back in Rome. No even accounting, no balanced scales. Servius Tullius Lurco was dead by my hand and, to be honest, I was pleased. A wave of satisfaction passed over me. I wanted blood, rivers of it. More blood than had been taken from me. A hundred, a thousand times more. I would pack the underworld fit to bursting with bodies, see Acheron, the river of sorrow, black and deep, its banks overflowing, brimming with Sertorian blood.

ACT III

DEATH RACE

But let him fall before his day and without burial on a waste of
   sand. This I pray; this and my blood with it I pour for the last
   utterance . . .
Let no kindness nor truce be between the nations . . .
I invoke the enmity of shore to shore, wave to water, sword to
   sword; let their battles go down to their children's children.

—Virgil, *Aeneid*

XVIII

FOUR WEEKS AFTER LEAVING Mother Earth, I joined Crassus in his chambers to watch through his wall-length portal as we came in on approach to Olympus Decimus. I had to keep reminding myself that it wasn't a dream. No longer a Sertorian novice, I was dressed in a new uniform, bearing the red circle of the blooded initiate. Six of the seven grooves around my torso were streaked with red.

In the distance, picked out against black space was a perfect shining band encircling a white pearl—the emperor's orbital stadium, the ring-shaped Rota Fortuna (named for the goddess Fortuna's spinning wheel that could grant either favor or destruction), so big that it completely surrounded the ice world Olympus Decimus.

The orbital stadium's ring structure was a symbol of the emperor's unbreakable power, and each year the Rota Fortuna traveled to the chosen arena world and, for the duration of the games, transformed it to suit the editor's vision. At a distance it would be easy to mistake the emperor's planet-encompassing stadium for a natural equatorial ring, like those that encircled Saturn or Jupiter, but as we drew nearer, its breathtaking artificiality became apparent—the gold plate covering the massive ship shone like a calm sea at sunset and the windows sparkled with the same golden light that the distant sun transmitted to the icy planet below.

While the rest of the empire watched via vox populi telecasts, thousands of Rome's wealthiest and most powerful citizens witnessed the contest live from the box seats that lined the station's interior like stacked rows of fish eggs. Each box featured windows of telescopic glass that allowed the games to be observed at any distance.

"Darling, just look at it. Have you ever seen anything more magnificent?" Crassus asked me. He put his arm about my waist and pulled me close.

I tried to make my heart like a lead sinker, falling to the bottom of the ocean, and yet a tingle of pleasure passed through my body when he touched me, when I heard his voice, even when he was standing close. It was the conditioning from his machine combined with the ambrosia. He'd been pushing for me to come to his bed for the last week. *After the tournament,* I told him. *I can't think of anything like that right now. I need to keep focused.* He always seemed astonished that I could resist him, and it only made him more determined, but so far, by allowing him these small moments of intimacy, I'd been able to hold more explicit relations at bay. More important, I'd ensured freedom from the chain that secured me to my bunk at night as well as a continual supply of the ambrosia-laden tisane, and I needed it now more than ever. During the final week, I'd been bothered by the thought that Aulus was already dead at the hands of the Sertorians. Something Mania had said during the second week—*He was very precious to you, wasn't he*—she'd used the past tense. When I quizzed him, Crassus was insistent that Aulus was alive, and I had to believe him. Just the same, to settle my nerves and put any errant thoughts to rest, that morning (and against Julia's advice) I'd consumed a whole pot of tisane. The ambrosia had thrown me into a state where my emotions were only just tangible, like a barely audible voice arising from the cacophony of a busy crowd. My body and mind, on the other hand, were sharp, wired, ready for action.

A steady flow of ships headed into the stadium's external docking bays, carrying the empire's wealthy and noble elite. Their tickets were incredibly expensive and went partway to subsidize the emperor's costs of staging the event. There were even locarii—scalpers who sold a scarce few tickets for exorbitant amounts to privileged sycophants who wished to be seen with the famous and powerful of the empire. Despite the cost of admission, just like at the Colosseum back in Rome, five percent of the seats were kept open for commoners who were selected by way of a galactic lottery. All spectators would have access to the world below to witness the opening ceremony of the Festival of Jupiter, followed by the commencement of the gladiatorial games, though they would spend most of their time enjoying our tribulations from the comfort of their private boxes and making wagers for personal fortunes, lives, planets, slave species, some deals so epic that they would get coverage along with the tournament itself. It only added to the excitement if the fate of a planet, its settlers, and barbarians depended upon the performance of the teams. The orbital spectators had one privilege that set them apart from those who watched via telecast: When the question was asked by the editor, each one of their votes to see a contestant survive or be condemned to death was worth fifty million votes of the viewing audience at large.

Incitatus docked at the Rota Fortuna. The emperor's ultimare-class carrier, *Horatius,* was already there, having brought the supreme ruler of the galaxy with it. Twice the size of *Incitatus,* it was stocky up front, symbolizing the lion's mane of House Numerian, streaked with emerald and Syrian purple, its cabins arranged behind, lean by comparison. Seven deceres-class carriers in total were docked about the stadium—one carrying the team for each house. Three berths down was the Viridian carrier *Scipio Africanus*. The sight of the bulky warship, streaked with green and gold, filled me with dire resolve. The Viridian team was here. Marcus also. I'd rather face the worst the Ludi Romani had to offer than what would come next—having to stand on a stage beside my lanista and my countrymen dressed in Sertorian armor with a Sertorian face, spouting Sertorian propaganda while the entire empire watched on.

Crassus leaned in close and smelled my tightly braided hair. I turned, my lips near his. I wanted to kiss him, to feel his mouth on my body. I looked at his reflection in the portal glass and imagined him with his throat cut open by Orbis' razor edge. That made me feel better. I marked every indignity he inflicted on me upon the board of reckoning I kept in my head. All I lived for now was the moment I would liberate Aulus. Then I would gather up these birds and clip their wings.

We headed off to join the rest of the team in the shuttle that would carry us to the planet below. In order to ensure that external, unofficial forces could not affect the tournament's outcome, once the Festival of Jupiter's games began the stadium's shields would be activated, enclosing the world in an impenetrable bubble. No one would be permitted to come or go from the planet's surface.

"Numerius Valentinius is a scum bucket! A filthy public toilet! No emperor at all! I shit on him! I will piss on his grave!" Crassus and I had entered the shuttle, and Mania must not have noticed us because she was jumping up and down on the spot, throwing a tantrum. Her pupils were dilated, and the muscles of her face had subtly changed, the jaw hardened. Her eyes were different too. Penetrating with a frightening intensity. But then Barbata gave her a warning nudge and the perplexing outburst ceased at once. Mania was back to her old self, like a switch had been thrown.

"Hello, Accala," the white-haired girl said sweetly. "I'm so excited we're going on this adventure together."

Strange. Barbata had behaved the same way when I'd stopped her killing the Hyperborean in the gym. Violently angry one moment, perfectly normal the next. None of the other Sertorians seemed to care.

The Sertorians were unhappy because they'd just got news that the emperor had forced the tournament editor, Julius Numerius Gemminus, to divert the course of the games, so that instead of running along the coast, it now followed the spine of the mountain range that ran west to east. Perhaps the new course was veering too close to the mining operations my uncle had referred to, the Sertorian search for the mother lode of ambrosia.

On the other hand, they didn't seem at all upset about the emperor's refusal to allow them to field a replacement for Lurco, and I didn't blame them. The final week of training had been the most challenging, but the end result was a team that moved in perfect unison, each athlete picking up the lead of another, each able to compensate for any sign of weakness. I prayed my efforts aboard *Incitatus* hadn't been in vain and that Uncle Quintus had received the sample Julia sent him and turned it to some advantage, because our team were like hawks soaring beneath the sun—sharp, fast, all-seeing. And I was one of them. I'd allowed them to transform me into the perfect Sertorian. I'd followed Crassus and his machine, obeyed Licinus, received my treatments from Barbata, let them shape me as they wished. I could see how they thought having me kill Bulla would be a good idea—to sever the ties to my old life—but it had had the opposite effect. It had given me something to hang on to, a fresh death of a loved one that highlighted the loss of my mother, the torment of my brother. It would never occur to them that I could love a barbarian, have feelings for my nursemaid. The coals of rage still burned brightly within my breast. Bulla wasn't the only casualty, either. The small Iceni slave Alba went missing at the end of the voyage. When I asked after her, Crassus informed me that he'd checked the records on the stone Alba used to tether me to the bed and found that on one occasion I hadn't been properly secured. "But it wasn't your fault," he explained. "It was hers, and she took her punishment gladly, rather than have her family be wiped out." I asked him what punishment had been administered, and he casually reported that she'd been thrown into the Sauromatae pens to double as sport and food for the lizard men.

We boarded the shuttle and commenced our descent to Olympus Decimus. Eight thousand miles in diameter and possessed of a single continent, rising out of the turbulent blue and green ocean, the same oxygen-rich waters that made the planet habitable to humans.

It seemed less like a shining pearl and more like a blind man's eye, blank and indifferent—its bright albedo reflecting away the golden sunlight that would otherwise end the small planet's eternal ice age.

The land contained inland lakes, sweeping tundra covered in a thick layer of permafrost, fissures, ravines, glaciers, and ice canals. Intricate patterns of lines, some running a thousand miles long and ten miles wide, crisscrossed segments of its surface like a cracked eggshell—the great ice canals formed by fractures in the planet's crust. Foothills gave way to clusters of mountains like jagged white teeth. The range of peaks formed a curved spine that ran for almost the entire breadth of the continent—two and a half thousand miles. The environment, combined with whatever surprises the emperor had up his sleeve, would be as much of an enemy as any of the other contestants. Frostbite and hypothermia, avalanches and crevasses would be constant dangers.

On the eastern coast lay the mountain from my dreams—Nova Olympus—towering above all other peaks. In its shadow lay the ruins of Lupus Civitas, the old Viridian capital, a black spot against fields of white snow. After the city was destroyed and the planet seized by the Sertorians, they built their own capital on the west coast, our destination, Avis Accipitridae. Seen from a distance, the new capital, all ruby and diamond, was like a shining red scab on the planet's surface.

The shuttle fired its engines as we entered the planet's atmosphere. Avis Accipitridae was a prefabricated construct dropped in on a four-square-mile hexagonal slab; the city was crammed with gaudy onyx and ruby Sertorian architecture. All the standard colonial city features were in place: a forum, a regional senate, temples, baths, a local arena and circus track, classically styled administrative buildings, lavish city houses, farming ovals, slave townships, factories, warehouses, and relay stations with massive antennas. What wasn't standard in a colonial outpost was the excessive scale of the city's ornamental features—statues, triumphal arches, and monumental columns all garishly large and overwrought in detail, loudly proclaiming the history and glory of House Sertorian. The best of everything in the wrong proportions, opulence crammed together to show off rather than reflect beauty or noble ideals. That's what you got when a no-class culture suddenly had a surplus of money to indulge bad taste.

By comparison, Lupus Civitas, before the Sertorians bombed it, was a thriving capital of simple architecture and classical beauty. Real quality and refinement didn't need to be rammed down one's throat. Avis Accipitridae would have been a real eyesore if it weren't for the transformation the emperor had visited upon it in time for the games—sparing no expense to convert the city into a winter spectacular capable of capturing the empire's attention for the fifteen days of the festival. Imperial banners lined the streets, the vibrant purple cloaks of the armed Praetorian peacekeepers made splashes of color in the snow. There was an abundance of festival wreaths, standards, and emblems emblazoned with the letters SPQR—the Senate and the people of Rome—and the tundra outside the city was lined with eight towering decorative totems carved from diamond and ice, brought from the distant corners of the eight provinces. Thirty-seven bull elephants had been transported from Mother Earth to participate in a reenactment of ancient Hannibal's crossing of the Alps. A squadron of imperial triremes and fighter craft flew impressive maneuvers over the city. These were a reminder to the Sertorians that, until the winner of the tournament had been decided, this world was under the emperor's direct control. As such, not one Sertorian flag could be flown above the city. The Sertorians had made up for this with projection billboards that filled the sky and streets of the city. The majority of them featured Crassus, arm in arm with me, Accala, the new Sertorian discus fighter, in postures that had been created from images taken of me while I trained aboard *Incitatus* and then altered to suit the purposes of Crassus and his propaganda team. Action was intercut with my recitations of Proconsul Aquilinus' precepts. Everything had been recorded and was now played back to the viewing empire. Beneath the billboards were catchphrases like DESTINY and STRENGTH THROUGH UNITY.

"You look magnificent, don't you think?" Crassus asked.

"I look dangerous."

"It suits you well. The crowd likes dangerous."

"They're going to hate me," I said. "They know me as a defender of Viridian values who willingly represents all she once hated."

"You have to project a new image to the audience," Crassus said, "and that starts here, today, right now. Remember what Tertullian said about the tournament mob: *The perversity of it! They love whom they lower; they despise whom they approve.*

The audience doesn't give a fig for virtue; people will like you because you are dynamic and interesting, and if you win, if you kill, then they will love you, they will adore you for shedding blood for them. If you do that, regardless of what side you're on, or what you personally believe, then they'll stand with you through thick and thin. Or at least until someone more interesting comes along."

Yes, there were no morals in the arena, only spectacle. I was certain he didn't intend it, but his words gave me a thread of hope. If I could keep the audience's interest through my arena display, then perhaps I could build a following, a loyalty, as I had once before with my countrymen. Any kind of following, as long as it wasn't Sertorian, might be there to support me when I made my switch back to the Viridian team.

Our shuttle landed near the forum, where crowds of spectators, tourists, and reporters had gathered to greet us. They were a droplet against the ocean of the empire-spanning audience that watched via the vox populi forum, but still there must have been at least two hundred thousand choking the streets of the city, more than enough to intimidate me after the farewell I'd been given by the howling mob of Rome.

The shuttle doors opened and a gust of air rushed over us. Even with the cold weather training aboard *Incitatus,* the air of Olympus Decimus came as a shock. So cold and sharp after the highly regulated atmosphere of the ship, it hurt my lungs to breathe. Crisp and clear, static electricity sparked against my lips like kissing a pane of shattered glass. Despite the amount of tisane I'd consumed, I felt my buzzing headache starting up again. The crowd below cheered with excitement.

"I don't know what you expect me to say," I said to Crassus as he led me up onto a vast stage they'd prepared for the contestants. This was a media assembly, a chance for the public to see the competitors answer questions before the big event, every word and action transmitted throughout the eight provinces for the empire's degustation.

"You know the precepts now," Crassus replied. "Keep them in mind when you speak, and everything will be fine."

The two factions of contestants were separated to either side of the stage. Built into the floor beneath us were two large wheels, each with twenty-eight colored segments, all embossed with a competitor's name so we knew where to stand. The first wheel belonged to the four teams of the Talonite Axis—the Sertorian Blood Hawks, the Ovidian Boars, the Blue Bulls of House Tullian, and the White Rams of traitorous House Arrian. I thought I might feel an instinctive pull toward the second wheel where House Viridian's Golden Wolves stood with the Calpurnian Black Ravens and the Flavian Silver Sparrows—making up the Caninine Alliance—but my feet stayed rooted beside Crassus without the slightest inclination to stray.

My uncle, Proconsul Quintus Viridius Severus, stood beside the Golden Wolves, talking up the merits of his team before a crowd of admirers and reporters. The Caninine teams contained so many eminent heroes, so many gladiators whom I'd admired over the years. Their skill at arms demanded respect, even from their enemies. Tribune Vibius Viridius Carbo, leader of the Golden Wolves, caught me looking at my uncle and scowled. Gnaeus Viridius Metellus, an old friend of our family, stared at me, his dark eyes transmitting my father's disapproval across forty-eight thousand light-years. My cousin Darius gave me a disdainful smirk. He thought me a fool, a desperate woman who had tricked her way into the games, an easy target. There were the charioteers Titus Nervo and another cousin of mine, Trio Mercurius, young and noble of spirit. Scipio Caninus, the one-eyed bestiarii, and his counterpart, Capitulus Pavo. Then the other Viridian gladiatorii—Taticulus Leticus and his sharp swords.

Next to the Viridians were the Calpurnians. I knew their leader, the gladiator prince from the rim, Cossus Calpurnius Blaesus, who had, for a brief moment back in the Colosseum, thought I was going to fight for his team. Only a simple purple rope barrier separated the competing factions. The Praetorians who stood upon the stage, shock staves in hand, were there to manage the crowd. No gladiator would dare to cross a border marked with the emperor's sacred color. Besides, this was an opportunity for the teams to show off what they had to offer, their last chance to win audience support before the fighting began.

The Talonite teams also contained great warriors. The charioteer Publius Calida, Arrian team leader. The stuttering gladiator Labeo Tullius, who found that the arena was the only place where his ever-present condition vanished. The Ovidian leader Bibaculus, famous for finishing his opponents with the goring tusks that covered his armor.

Standing between the two factions, facing the crowd, presided Magistrate Julius Numerius Gemminus, senior editor, now conducting his fourth Ludi Romani. His jolly face belied his true nature. Cunning, ingenious in sculpting courses that punished his contestants, driven by a need to please the audience and, at the same time, stave off the circling pool of junior editors who sought to steal his position.

"Citizens! Welcome to Olympus Decimus!"

Gemminus raised his right arm, weighty deposits of fat hanging from it in great sheaves, signaling he was ready to make an announcement. His voice and body were filled with conviction, every action designed to heighten anticipation. The crowd responded accordingly—the locals roared their approval and the trillions watching from around the galaxy signaled theirs by filling the sky with holographic projections of upturned thumbs, gold and silver digits, constellations in their own right, accompanied by sparkling multi-colored fireworks.

"I don't think I've ever sensed such excitement," the editor boomed. "We've got the largest audience in galactic history tuning in. Over seventeen trillion, evenly distributed across the provinces. I'm so glad you could all join me here today. With the aid of our glorious emperor, all hail his name, and despite last-minute alterations, I've bent, twisted, and cajoled this icy landscape in order to meet my artistic needs and can now assure you, that with galactic peace riding on the outcome, with so many star gladiators, with so much controversy, I've made this course my greatest creation."

A projection appeared above him, filling the sky and teasing the audience with footage of the course construction. The massive ion cannon mounted to the stratospheric stadium was being used to terraform the planet. Glowing red, it carved channels, leveled hills, and formed canyons. The cannon set the rocks alight, and they burned with phosphorescent green and blue flame.

"The teams will race from Avis Accipitridae to the ruins of Lupus Civitas, a two-and-a-half-thousand-mile journey across the emperor's arena world!" Julius Gemminus said. "Each day they will face one round of fighting. Some rounds will be long with the intensity paced out, others will be short with life and death packed closely together! Each night, energy shields will enclose the team camps to provide safety and security so they can emerge fresh and ready to fight on the following day. Over mountains and valleys, rivers and tundra, caverns and hills, they will endure chariot races, beast hunts, and an arena fighting spectacular! Each day and at the end of each of the three main segments, prizes will be awarded to the winning teams. The first player to survive the course and seize the laurel crown in the ruins of the town square of Lupus Civitas will win the tournament for their team and be selected as Jupiter's chosen champion. Are you ready, Romans? Are you prepared to witness the greatest, bloodiest, and most thrilling contest in the history of the empire?"

Applause, thumbs, cries of approval. Reporters crammed into the designated media area pressed closer to the stage. The sky was buzzing with media spherae, small and large. Some even projected celebrity journalists from the eight provinces who couldn't be there in person, yelling their questions over the top of their physically present counterparts.

"And now, would you like to meet the contestants?" he cried.

We took up our position on the segments of the wheels that bore our names and the large discs began to rotate slowly, stopping on Julius Gemminus' command so that enemy would stop next to enemy, building tension as the editor introduced the teams, shouting the competitors' names gleefully, giving each their moment in the spotlight as the leaders, trainers, and champion athletes answered short questions, while the cameras recorded snippets that would be intercut with games footage over the coming weeks.

I started in the segment on the side next to the editor but facing his back, so that as the wheel turned clockwise I would be the very last Talonite to be debuted. The wheels stopped again and again, putting bitter rivals within a few feet of each other (the Calpurnians hated the Arrians almost as much as Viridians hated the Sertorians), drawing in more and more members of the galactic audience to witness the emperor's spectacle.

By the time the wheel ticked around and there were only three ahead of me, I was at the closest point to the Caninine players, and found myself stuck right opposite Marcus, only a thin purple rope separating us.

Marcus didn't regard me with the anger or hatred I expected based on his declaration before Minerva's statue in Rome. My old trainer didn't have a single word to spare for me, not even a glance. He looked haughty, his eyes hollow and distant. Any feeling he had had for me had vanished; now I was merely an obstacle to overcome, one of many, nothing more. In his mind my death was an inevitability, and he would remove me clinically and dispassionately, as a surgeon would a tumor. Whatever clash the audience had hoped to see between teacher and pupil, they were not going to see it yet.

Next I found myself opposite my younger cousin Mercurius the charioteer. I had no grievance with him. At first I thought the editor had made a mistake, that there'd be no trouble between us, but then Mercurius came rushing at me. Carbo, the Viridian team leader, seized him by the collar at the last moment, stopping him from crossing the purple cord.

"Accala, how could you turn traitor? How could you turn on us? We're family!"

"Leave me be," I hissed.

"They'll disqualify you if you cross the rope," Carbo barked at him. Mercurius listened to his team leader and stopped struggling. "I won't miss out and I won't allow you to steal my life, Accala," he said. "It shall be I that kills you, not Marcus Calpurnius. For the shame you've visited upon our house."

Mercurius was the youngest member of the team, and the most innocent, honorable, and well regarded. He had never had a bad word to say about my exploits in the arena, and now he seemed genuinely upset, which was more than the other stone-faced Viridians were willing to concede.

"I'll watch out for you," I said. I felt I had to pay him some respect. During the last week of training, when Licinus went over the profiles of the Viridian team, I was asked to nominate which member I though the weakest, the most likely to fall to a concentrated group attack, and I nominated Mercurius. He would be the easiest mark of all the opposing gladiators in the field, the life easiest for me to steal, the one I least wanted to end.

Crassus pushed past me and shoved Mercurius back before the Praetorians could stop him. "Back to your pack, puppy."

Mercurius moved to strike Crassus, but to my relief Carbo pulled him away once more.

"Save it for tomorrow, boy," Carbo said. "Let your chariot and weapon speak for you in the arena."

The editor seemed genuinely pleased with the outbursts. The wheel turned, carrying me to the front of the stage. Julius Gemminus ignored me, finished up with Viridian trainer Metellus, the last Caninine, and then dismissed them from the wheel, beaming at me as he draped a fat arm about my shoulders and pulled me close.

"And at last, here's the girl you've all been waiting to meet," he announced. "A favorite champion of the Magnus Ludus back in Rome, praised by the emperor himself for her courage—Accala! Disowned by her father, betrayer of her house, newly minted member of House Sertorian. There are a million questions flooding the vox populi message boards and I've primed the media below with a range of . . ." I glared at him with a look Barbata would be proud of and he saw in my eyes the change I'd undergone on the voyage over. Gemminus' arm vanished from about my shoulders with surprising speed and he cleared his throat.

"Ahem. Isn't she a charmer? Like a beautiful snake, pretty to look at but deadly to touch. Now. Any questions?" he asked the press corps down in front.

I steeled myself, expecting them to hurl abuse again despite everything Crassus had just told me about the mob mentality, sure the sky would be filled with thousands of downturned holographic thumbs as the audience transmitted their hatred from all over the empire. But instead they cheered, and upturned golden thumbs showered me with approval. A spotlight lit me up as the reporters yelled excitedly at me, each trying to be the one to catch my attention.

Accala! You look spectacular! Over here, Accala, we love your hair! Your features! You're gorgeous, Accala!

The ruby-filled grooves of my uniform accentuated my natural curves. Publia and her team had spent the whole morning working on me. Judging from the reception, she'd be overjoyed.

"Accala! Why did you come here?" one of the reporters asked me. "What do you hope to achieve?"

"I came to win," I said.

"Accala! Tell us what you think of your new appearance!"

"Magnificent," I said, borrowing a word from Crassus.

They roared with delight.

I thought I'd have to ward off questions about why I'd changed sides, about the difficult decisions I'd made, but no one seemed to care. Barbata had said it well: I was no longer the mangy wolf, the woman who betrayed her kin. Now I was the new poster girl for House Sertorian, a carnival attraction, a shiny new doll, and they all wanted to be the first to have a play. I looked down at them with disdain. They were like fish at feeding time, mouths opening and closing while House Viridian was left standing there, no one interested in talking to them or cheering them on.

"What happened to Lurco?" one journalist asked me.

"He died en route as a result of a training accident," Licinus interjected.

"Is that true, Accala? Was it you who killed him?"

"Yes," I replied plainly. "It was during training. Like Licinus says, an accident."

"Are you disappointed by the emperor's ruling that you can't field a replacement?" another reporter asked. "Don't you feel yourselves to be at a disadvantage being one man short?"

"Not at all. I don't want to show disrespect to our opponents," Crassus said as he looked across at the Viridians with a sneer, "but we are quite confident. The tournament is less of a challenge and more of an opportunity to demonstrate what the superior man is capable of."

"Tell us what it's like to be one of the New Gods," I was asked. "Is Crassus as sexy in real life as he is in the arena?"

I felt Crassus press in beside me. He smiled and waved to the crowd, giving the cameras a couples shot, and I followed in turn, doing my best to appear happy as I swallowed the bile in my throat. "He's dazzling," I said.

More cheers of approval. Crassus had insisted that some humans were intrinsically better than others. These human gossip vultures certainly lent weight to an argument I otherwise found unpalatable. As I was bombarded with questions about my hair and Crassus' sexual prowess, my attention wandered and I caught sight of a small man who walked up onto the platform and stood quietly front and center stage, right behind Julius Gemminus. He placed his hands behind his back, waiting patiently. He didn't have to wait long.

Excited whispers passed through the crowd as their attention began to wander, away from me, refocusing on the small man.

"Who is he?" I asked Crassus in a low voice.

"Why, it's Proconsul Aquilinus, of course," Crassus said in surprise, as if to say, *Who else could it possibly be?* There was no way I could equate the small man before me with the almighty figure, arms outstretched, in the billboards and other Sertorian propaganda. "He has a very important announcement to make, and you're going to be part of it."

My hands started to tremble, the skin on my arms prickled, my mind was foggy as if I were in Crassus' brainwashing room back on the ship. Proconsul Aquilinus. I could kill him here and now. No one had weapons on the stage, but I could do it with my bare hands, even though it would cost me my life—if the Sertorians didn't kill me, the Praetorians surrounding the stage with their ion shock staves certainly would. What would all these Sertorian zealots do without their supreme leader? And then Proconsul Aquilinus turned to look at me, his face like the sun, radiating power. Dido's words when she first caught sight of Aeneas sprang to mind.

What guest unknown is this who hath entered our dwelling? I believe it well, with no vain assurance, his blood is divine. Were I not sick to the heart of bridal torch and chamber, to this temptation alone I might haply yield.

He was shining brighter even than his depiction in the billboards. I had to snap out of this. The proconsul was thin and narrow eyed, the least attractive Sertorian I'd ever seen, and all I wanted to do was throw myself at his feet and pledge my undying allegiance. Gods, what was happening? I couldn't fall to pieces over this comical little man. This wasn't me. This was Crassus' conditioning at work. I'd thought Licinus was oversaturated with ambrosia, but Proconsul Aquilinus was radiating so much energy that I thought it must be seeping out of his pores. Julius Gemminus must have sensed it too, because he yielded the stage to Aquilinus without a word.

"Come, daughter, come stand here beside me," he said, and although my mind wanted nothing more than to run in the opposite direction as fast as I could, my body was drawn irresistibly toward him. I couldn't kill this man even if I had Orbis in my hand and no witnesses, not while he was exuding this kind of magnificence, more even, an imperial magisterium. He drew me close and the crowd became silent.

"Behold Accala, who was once a wolf and has now become one of the New Gods."

The crowd screamed with delight.

"She has come to House Sertorian not out of anger or hatred but because of the love she bears for her countrymen. She wishes to see all Viridians unified with their enemies. Her transformation into this magnificent specimen demonstrates that a fragmented empire can be united. That all Romans can overcome their differences to see the way forward to universal brotherhood and enlightenment. Whichever house wins the Ludi Romani, I want to commend Accala on having taken the first step toward peace."

Before the crowd could erupt again, Proconsul Aquilinus continued.

"I know you want to ask these mighty warriors about the tournament, but before I depart the stage I have an announcement to make that I think will be worth stealing a moment of your time—perhaps the greatest announcement of the millennium. There has been intense interest in my New Gods campaign across the empire, and I'm beset by billions of citizens begging to share in the genetic inheritance of House Sertorian. Moved by their petitions, I have performed a mighty act of creation."

He raised his arms, and the air around the stage was suddenly filled with holographic billboards. In the distance, other billboards around the city flickered and changed as well. I had no doubt the same was happening all over the empire. These billboards showed not just majestically proportioned Sertorians in action, but also members of the other houses, arm in arm with Sertorians, fighting off barbarian invaders. Tullians and Ovidians, Flavians and Calpurnians, even Viridians. As allies. As genetic equals. The slogan beneath them revealed Proconsul Aquilinus' newest sales pitch: AMBROSIA BY AQUILINUS. THE ELIXIR OF THE GODS FOR EVERY ROMAN.

XIX

GODS, HE WAS REVEALING his own secrets. What kind of a game was he playing?

The audience went wild. News tickers on the billboard screens showed that the odds at the betting houses for the Blood Hawks dramatically fell and the payout for a Viridian win skyrocketed. He was winning the empire over right here and now, before the tournament had even begun. Aquilinus had just won the audience, bribed the galactic mob with the sweetest of promises. They'd side with him, with the Sertorians, the favors and decisions would all swing our way. And worst of all, I was the walking advertisement, the proof that he'd share what he had. I felt sick.

"As you can see from the treatment Accala has undergone in such a short space of time, House Sertorian is no longer the sole possessor of genetic superiority. I'm pleased to announce that I have bottled the substance that gives us our unique strengths so that it can be made available to all Romans."

An Iceni slave stepped forward holding a red cushion upon which lay an elegant phial, the same as the one I saw in the casket in Licinus' cabin. The proconsul held it up before the bedazzled audience, which hung on his every word in grotesque adoration.

"This is ambrosia—the elixir of youth, of strength, of beauty. For the first time in human history, the ladder that ascends from dull mortality to the realm of the gods can be ascended by mere mortals. I offer it as a gift to be made available to every single Roman regardless of house or station!"

The crowd was delirious; a hundred hands clambered for the phial of ambrosia. The cheers were mixed with cries of astonishment. Questions flowed from the crowd below, but the proconsul only smiled and waved, refusing to answer them.

The cost! What is the cost?

Aquilinus was about to turn away from the podium when he made a deliberate pause, deciding to field one question after all.

"Cost? Do you charge for a gift? Ambrosia will be free, even to our Viridian friends here," he said, motioning to the Golden Wolves. "All that is required in exchange is that you profess your belief in the precepts laid out in my book."

The crowd was nearly stunned into silence. There was no precedent for generosity on this scale. But there were dissenting voices. The general gist of which was, *But I am loyal to my house! I cannot swear allegiance to House Sertorian.*

"Nor would I ask you to," Aquilinus said. "An affirmation of the precepts is an affirmation of Romanness, of the exercise of strength and power that makes us the great empire we are. I ask no man or woman to dishonor his or her house." He put his arm around me again. I felt that I should have said something, but what was there to say? That the Sertorians would make use of me was to be expected, but I was naive as to the extent to which they would go at it. Standing beside him, I realized that like a good butcher, Aquilinus would use every part of me, let nothing go to waste.

"If you have any doubts, watch my warriors perform," he continued. "Watch them dominate in the arena, and ask yourself, wouldn't you like to be just like them? Stronger, faster, more intelligent. Study Accala and know that if we are prepared to transform our enemies, you can be certain we will do the same for you."

He finished to rapturous applause. However much of a threat Licinus and Crassus were, this man, their master, was without a doubt the most dangerous man in the galaxy, and I was a pawn in his game. I risked a quick glance at my uncle, seeking some reassurance that he had expected Aquilinus' revelation and knew what to do next, but he was already delivering a speech to the Caninine teams.

Proconsul Aquilinus spread out his arms and drew Licinus, Crassus, and me aside, speaking quietly but deliberately to us so we could hear his voice over the noise of the crowd.

"Tribune Licinus, it seems that Gaius Crassus' approach has merit after all."

"Yes, Proconsul," the sour-faced tribune replied, head lowered, abashed. I'd never seen him like this before, cowed like a contrite son before a strict father.

"If she can survive your tests, has she not proved she has enough power to keep her place on the team?"

"As you say, Proconsul."

"I am well pleased with you, Accala. You will help many of your people. I look forward to seeing what you are capable of in the arena," he said. The thought that I might win his approval sent a tingle of excitement coursing through my body.

"Thank you, Proconsul," I replied. The words galloped out of my mouth like wild horses fleeing before I could bring them to rein.

"You've made a bold move today, Proconsul," Crassus said. Did the announcement come as a surprise to him as well? It seemed so.

"Those who wish to embrace greatness must never fear to exercise their strength," he said, and, as Aquilinus made to leave, Crassus and Licinus each took one of his hands and kissed them reverently.

Handlers led the Talonite teams to a transport that carried us through the streets to the contestants' complex.

It seemed that this tournament, much like the war, was as much a battle of perception and politics as it was an exercise of force and power. Licinus said that the war hadn't stopped, that it had merely relocated to Olympus Decimus for the duration of the games. He was right. Now I must pretend I hadn't known about the ambrosia they'd been slipping into my tisane.

"What have you done to me?" I demanded of Crassus. "That's what you've been giving me, isn't it? Ambrosia."

"I thought you'd be pleased," he said. "Why do you think your transformation has been so rapid? You must have suspected the change was more than just cosmetic. You are what I said you would be: a symbol of a new future. Be honored, you are the first non-Sertorian ever to receive it. Right now there's an empire's worth of citizens who long to obtain even a taste of what you've had in plentiful supply. Don't worry, you saw the proconsul. He is pleased with you. That is everything. For both of us." He put his arm around my shoulder, and a warmth spread through my body.

Cheering people lined the streets as we passed. Some priests in purple robes led a parade of fifteen enormous white bulls through the snow on the way to the city's local arena, where the opening ceremonies would be held the following morning. One would be sacrificed to Jupiter for each day of the event.

The purpose-built athletes' village was part of the emperor's upgrade of the planet—a round dome, separated into eight sections like a cut-up pie, permitting accommodation for each house team. It was an imposing classically designed complex fronted by a traditional portico with Doric columns and wide steps. Banners of imperial purple had been unfurled along the columns.

Inside it was luxuriously warm, with tropical palms and ferns transported from Mother Earth's equator along with a humidity to house them.

"Thank Mars for this heat," Barbata said. "I'm tired of that biting cold already! It's playing all hell with my skin."

"You'd do well to watch your tongue," Licinus snapped at her. "We don't let the old gods slip into our thoughts or speech!"

Barbata turned pale. "I'm sorry, I . . . it was a slip of the tongue. Don't tell the proconsul," she pleaded.

Licinus smiled and said nothing, but I had the sense that later, in private, she'd pay some penalty.

Before we were permitted to retire to our quarters, the games editor, Magistrate Julius Gemminus, summoned all the athletes into the welcoming hall, a round room at the center of the building.

"Welcome, welcome. I know you're all going to put on a splendid performance. You know, I've never put so much thought into a course before. I think you'll all find it quite stimulating."

Out of the media spotlight, groans and complaints were thrown freely, mostly to do with wasting valuable recreation time.

"Be patient, athletes. I've summoned you here with important news! You should know before we reveal it to the media outside." His voice boomed around the vast dome and instantly grabbed everyone's attention.

"Yesterday, several of the course technician stations were overrun by indigenous barbarians."

"Those Hyperboreans?" Vibius Viridius Carbo called out.

"Yes."

"How many?"

"Quite a lot," Gemminus said evasively. "It turns out there's a lot more of them than we initially anticipated, and it would be fair to say that the natives are restless. There's been something of an uprising among the beasties. They're led by a bull, a large warrior who seems to act as their chief."

The news caused some squabbling and outrage, and several team leaders and trainers started objecting that they hadn't had enough prior warning, that they weren't prepared to have the spirit of the games violated or their athletes' energies spoiled by putting down a local wild animal problem when they should be reserving their killing powers for the games.

"Yes, I understand, I understand," Gemminus soothed. "Fear not, the emperor has approved that we include them in the fun, but they will not be permitted to interfere in any way with the running of the games. They'll be included for sport, nothing more."

"And if there are too many?" Publius Ovidius Bibaculus, the gruff Ovidian leader, called out. "If they swarm?"

"Trust me, you have nothing to worry about, I will not allow the spirit of the games to be violated. The ice monkeys will have as much chance of killing you as you do of them, but no more. The majority of audience members polled believe it will add spice to the games."

Mass swarms of Hyperboreans were not on anyone's schedule of daily drills, and the level of complaint and swearing when Julius Gemminus withdrew was intense.

Praetorian attendants separated the teams, ushering them to the segregated house quarters.

"This is the emperor's doing, he's playing with us," Licinus grumbled.

"All of you have been assigned private rooms," Licinus said. "Enjoy your last night of comfort and rest and forget everything you just heard. Don't give the barbarians of this world a second thought, let the other teams worry about that. If you see a Caninine fighting a barbarian, take the opportunity to stick him in the back. The Blood Hawks will claim a minimum of two dead enemy contestants per day, preferably Viridians. After that, all I care about is that one of you stays alive long enough to cross the finish line and seize the laurel crown for House Sertorian." Once we were in Sertorian quarters, the Praetorians seperated us again.

"Sweet dreams." Mania smiled at me as we split up.

I hadn't felt her presence in my dreams since the night Bulla died, but then I hadn't been having any dreams to speak of. The small woman used to unsettle me, but now I had the sense that the tables had turned and she was slightly unnerved in my prescence. Out of all of them, she sensed most keenly my desire, my need, to make the Blood Hawks suffer and bleed.

I signaled to Julia that I needed to see her at once, but as I left, Gaia Barbata sauntered up to me and spoke in a conspiratorial tone. "Don't think I don't see what's going on between you and the redheaded grease monkey."

"Nothing's going on," I said carefully. "Except that she knows how to make herself useful. We were bunked together on *Incitatus*."

"Useful?" she asked with a smirk. "Don't worry, I understand. Sertorians take what they want, and we all have needs, don't we? It's the ambrosia, you know. One of the side effects is that it makes me want to fornicate and execute all day long in equal measure. It makes life sharper and the taking of it all the more sweet. We were all wondering, taking bets on how long you'd be able to divert Crassus' advances, but now I see you're seeking satisfaction in other areas. You could have come to me, you know. I don't know what you see in that low-born mismatch of genes. Redheads are unlucky; we culled them from our gene pool centuries ago."

"It's like you say," I replied. "She serves a need . . . and doesn't have the code to shock me."

"Well, you'd best not let Gaius Crassus find out if you want to keep your little pet."

It suited me for Barbata to think I was using Julia for sexual release. It would help explain if Julia was caught in my room on other business. I did feel the urges Barbata talked about, but I channeled them, turned them into fuel that kept me focused and accelerating toward my goal. I hadn't revisited my night with Julia or engaged her in conversation much since Bulla's death. I'd been too busy with preparatory training drills, and if my redheaded immune had been disappointed by my lack of attentions, she hadn't made mention of it.

My private chambers were large and comfortable, the bed big enough to house an elephant, but I couldn't afford to relax. I waited for Julia to come, and when my frustration reached its limit, I took Orbis and started throwing him, tearing the fine curtains to shreds. As I reduced the chairs and tables to splinters, I noted that they were made from actual wood. They must have cost a fortune.

"Gods, what happened in here?" Julia asked when she entered.

"Where in the name of Hades have you been? I've been waiting for hours."

She held a cautionary finger to her lips, placed her privacy cube on the table and activated it.

"There, now you can speak freely, and by the way, it's only been one hour."

"I want to know what in the name of Pluto is going on. Why did Aquilinus reveal the existence of the ambrosia? Where is my uncle? I need to speak to him now. "

"He can't just waltz in here," she said. "Not with the whole empire watching. What do you think I've been doing the last hour? I've set up an encrypted signal."

Then my uncle was there, projected into the room from Julia's armilla. She unhitched his image from the device and Uncle Quintus walked right over to me.

"First, tell me how you are, dear niece. How does the consumption of ambrosia sit with you? Have they given you any today? Based on Julia's report, it seems it might have some addictive properties. Do you cope well when you're denied it?"

"I'm fine," I said irritably. "It gives more than it takes."

"And overall you're well? Ready for the games tomorrow?"

"All my priorities are fine," I snapped. "I'm in this for my brother, but you, I don't know about you. I've been turning it over and over in my mind this last week, and I think you gave me up to the Sertorians as a guinea pig, to see what they'd do to me. Well, what do you think?" I demanded, performing a pirouette. "I'm a living commercial! I'm selling the empire on everything that's great about glorious fucking House Sertorian!" I slammed my fist down on the table beside the screen. The table splintered at once and groaned at the power of my strike. "What's more, I don't think you give a shit about Aulus. You care only about finding the ambrosia before Aquilinus."

"You're all over the place—calm down, Accala. Stop talking now," he said sternly. "I can't believe you would say such things. This is the effect of the drug on you. Remember, whatever they do to you, I'm family, you must trust me."

I took a deep breath. He was right. I'd lost control, but it was the first time in a month that I could afford any kind of emotional outburst and I supposed I was overdue.

"I do trust you, Uncle," I said, "and I'm sorry, it's been a long four weeks."

"I'm sure. Our preliminary analysis suggests that the effects of the ambrosia abate with use. The more you use it, the more you need each time to get the same performance enhancement."

Now that he mentioned it, I did feel tired. Had the presentation on the stage taken all my energy? I wondered if that meant the amount of ambrosia in a person's body was exhausted by emotional as well as physical exertion? If that was the case, I had to guard my emotions carefully, become more calculating in how I managed my relationships.

"You're too close to see things clearly, dear niece. Listen. I believe I have some news that will refire your engines and remind you that I'm on your side; but first, tell me, what did you think of the proconsul's news—revealing his secret weapon so publicly. An astonishing, bold move, yes?"

"It makes me feel like I've sacrificed much for little in return."

"Oh no, no. That's not it at all. We weren't able to synthesize and make an exact copy of the ambrosia, but our analysis of the sample you supplied to Julia Silana gave us a starting point to create new stimulants more powerful than anything we've ever had before. It's only three-quarters as strong as the ambrosia, but it'll give our boys a fighting chance."

I was pleased to hear it. Machinarii (robot enhancements) and advanced arms were forbidden in the Ludi Romani, but everything else, including stimulants and genetic streamlining, was permitted.

"Aquilinus might have made a bold move, but also a desperate one. We're certain that he never planned to reveal the existence of the ambrosia until after the tournament. He was so certain the Blood Hawks would win, but now the word is out that the Caninines have their own product to rival the ambrosia. Suddenly the Sertorian proconsul isn't so confident. He's had to move early to start promoting the ambrosia, to stake his claim so to speak. Aquilinus is terrified the emperor will discover that the ambrosia isn't some product made in a Sertorian laboratory, that he will look down from the Rota Fortuna and see that the bulk of the ambrosia is still undiscovered and on this world."

"The emperor knows?" I asked.

"No, but he suspects much. All this talk of redirecting the course—throwing the teams into the areas Aquilinus is least keen on us visiting, into the heart of the Hyperborean uprising, where the Sertorian mining interests lie. The emperor is no fool—he's stirring the hornets' nest and waiting to see what happens."

"What I don't understand is how Aquilinus is going to supply everyone with ambrosia. Even if he had every drop on this world it still wouldn't be enough to satisfy the empire."

"You're very astute, dear niece. It's a confidence trick. He doesn't need to supply the ambrosia, he just needs everyone to think he can. How do you increase the value of a thing? You create a demand and then you release it in limited supply. Aquilinus is playing a long game. First he gets the right people addicted to the ambrosia, and aboard the Rota Fortuna there's plenty of prime candidates. Combined with a victory in the Ludi Romani, having demonstrated what his Hawks can do, the plebs will clamber en masse to Aquilinus' service while they await their promised share. Ideally, he seeks a nonviolent rebellion, ascension to power without lifting a finger."

He gave me a moment to let the news sink in.

"You're talking about Aquilinus overthrowing the emperor," I said. "Making a play for the imperial throne."

"And once he's got it he won't stop at simply ruling, he'll destroy the whole imperial system, remake it from the top down. That's why we can't fail."

Aquilinus and his offer, all that crap about the precepts and abolishing the gods, was part of a strategy designed to abolish the system of noble houses, clearing the boards to make way for a new simple regime—Proconsul Aquilinus and the Sertorians at the top and all other Romans beneath him. Every citizen of the empire knew that nothing was free. Everything had a price, and Aquilinus had made his perfectly clear: submission to his precepts, his vision.

"This ups the stakes," I said. "A game not just for the civil war but for the empire itself."

"Yes. Aquilinus is a shrewd opponent, but his weakness is that he's a gambler. He plays for high stakes and takes big risks. His plan has many weaknesses. Even with the promise of ambrosia, he must decisively win the Ludi Romani if he wants to get the empire on side. The games aren't just an opportunity for him to show off the Blood Hawks' new power: The mob will see victory in the arena as a sign to run with Aquilinus; it will grant the Sertorians legitimacy. If they lose the tournament, they lose the mob, and everything becomes more difficult. The very next problem he'll face is delivering on the promises he's made to his allied houses. After today's public announcement, they'll be pressuring him, demanding their share in exchange for continued support."

"And the process my mother talked of? Her spanner in the works?"

"I don't have any new information except that whatever she did to disrupt the ambrosia mining process seems to be working. My agents report a sharp decline in ambrosia shipments leaving this world prior to the Rota Fortuna's arrival. And now we have this alien uprising—all the major hives are located near the Sertorian mining bases. Nothing's going right for Aquilinus. He needs an ocean of ambrosia and he can't get a drop out of this world. He's running short on supply. So what do you make of that, Accala? What's your analysis?"

"That he's vulnerable," I said.

"Right. He's got his back foot against the edge of the cliff and you, dear niece, are the one who is going to help me push him and his whole gods-be-damned house over the edge. You must stay focused, Accala, now more than ever. Keep going. The moment you find Aulus, you need only speak the code word *troia* to Tribune Carbo and he will rally the Golden Wolves to your aid. You and Aulus together will finish what your mother started and cut Aquilinus off from the ambrosia for good. Then you shall rip those Sertorian bastards to shreds."

"I think about little else, believe me Uncle, but I don't even know where to start. This pin she left doesn't do a thing that makes me believe I can use it to find Aulus. Maybe it was only meant for my brother to use."

"You're just now at the start of the journey and there's plenty of ground yet to cover," he said. "Trust in your mother as I do. If experience has taught me anything, it's that when we start in earnest to uncover a mystery, the gods come the other half of the way to help. Remember, this isn't just for the tournament, not even for your brother. Accala, the fate of the empire is in your hands." His image faded out as the transmission ended.

"The whole empire," I said to Julia.

"The whole empire," she repeated.

"Atlas carries the weight of the galactic disc upon his back," I said. "How can I bear such a responsibility?"

"I'll be there for you," Julia said. "We'll carry it together. And more, I've got a decoder built into my armilla. The tournament course will be demarcated with energy shields, but we'll be able to bypass them and escape at least once, maybe twice as long as the editor and the Sertorians don't catch on. The emperor's new course plan will take us near where your mother died, near where the Sertorians purchased land. Aulus has to be near there. As soon as you have some clues about your brother's location, I can help you track him down."

"I just wish I knew what to do with this pin," I said, turning the platinum rod around in my fingers. "Mother said it had been modified. That it would bring Aulus and me together and help me finish what she started."

"I've been thinking about your pin," Julia said. "What if it's a kind of antenna? A means of picking up a transmission maybe. You told me you've been having strange headaches and that the pin sometimes gets extremely hot. Maybe the heat is the result of the signal not being able to successfully transmit, a buildup of energy that has nowhere else to go."

"I don't know," I said. "Mother always believed in simplicity. If the pin had a message of some kind for me, I should have received it by now."

"I'd tell you to keep faith and that things will work out, but I'm a pragmatist. We'll keep anaylizing the data as we go and build a complete picture. You'll see, everything will fit together in the end."

"Ha. Hands-on pragmatism sounds good. I've got to tell you that my regular gods haven't been doing too much for me lately."

"They will," Julia said consolingly. "Your mission couldn't be any more important. That's when Winged Victory comes, right when you need her, but only if you're sincere and trying your damnedest."

"You worship the Greek gods?"

"Not formally. I don't believe in literal gods."

"Ah, your celestial machine. I remember now."

"But I like the idea of swift-footed Nike. I've got a thing for speed and winning."

"You know, Julia, I spent a lot of time in school daydreaming about being the one the empire depends on, like the heroes in the old stories. I've got to tell you right now that in real life, it feels like shit."

She laughed at that. "You look hungry. You should order some food, they'll prepare anything you want."

The only thing I really felt like was my pot of tisane. I hadn't had any since the morning and I was starting to feel it, but the last thing I wanted to do was go and beg Crassus for some.

"I've got what I want right here," I said, pulling her to me. "Stay with me tonight."

"I don't think that's a good idea," she said. "It's the night before the tournament. Gather your strength, get some sleep. For once, Licinus was right."

I grabbed her more roughly by the arms and pulled her to me, crushing my lips to hers.

"Accala!" She pushed me away. I grabbed her again. She wasn't strong enough to resist me.

"Stay with me," I insisted. "I won't take no for an answer."

She reached over with her free hand and tapped her armilla. All of a sudden I was on the ground, pain exploding through my body.

"Get control of yourself, Accala."

"The bracelet," I said through gritted teeth. "You know the code."

She tapped at her armilla again and the shock stopped. "I stole it from the shared network the Sertorian armillae use. I was working on disabling it, but now it looks like it might be better to leave it as is."

"Please," I said. "I'm sorry, I don't know what came over me. Please take it off."

"You do know that we're supposed to be working together, right? We're on the same side," Julia said. "I thought we were friends."

"We are, and you're supposed to support me. My uncle said as much. Now do as I say and take this thing off."

"I can't yet. I only have the activation code, not the release code." She smoothed her rumpled clothing.

"I'm so sorry. I don't know what I was thinking . . ." My tone was appeasing.

"You were thinking you'd take what you want, like a good Sertorian. I'd like to say I'm flattered, but I think you should be concentrating on hanging on to a semblance of that vaunted Viridian honor if you want to make it through this thing in one piece. You're not the only one with something riding on the outcome of this mission. You think I'm only in this for the glory of the Vulcaneum?"

"You're in it for a holiday, you told me as much. You want to spend your days staring at cloud sunsets. It would indeed be a great tragedy if that didn't come to pass. Unimaginable sorrow on an epic scale."

"That's a dream I shared with you in private, Accala, not to be brought up lightly, and no, that's not why I serve. I serve because I believe in an empire where everyone has the right to life and equality," she said.

"A real republican, that's what you are. What about all those different collegia? How many of those will intervene to secure their freedom? How many of those will stand with me in the arena to secure their rights? What about your Vulcaneum? How many other volunteers did you have to compete against to be here with me?"

"I was the only one," she said quietly.

"Because you are the sole shining light atop a mountain of cowards. Do you sometimes think that you're fighting a losing battle? That you're the only one who really cares about making a difference? I hope you do, because it's true. You and I, we're alone."

"I have a sister named Angelia. She has a rare genetic disease, a mutation. It makes her skin bulge, and the areas around her neck and back are scaled and purple. People think she's a half-breed, crossed with a barbarian, but she's not. It's just bad luck, and it's slowly killing her. Her bruises sometimes bleed, and the bleeding won't stop. Most medicine won't work, but there is a treatment on the cloud city that your uncle can secure for her. That's why I want to go there. It's not about the view. It's about how I'll feel when she's well again. I have a sister, you have a brother—we're not alone, as long as we can help them."

"I'm sorry, again," I said, more sincerely than before.

"It's a place where she can get the care she needs, a place that's private and beautiful. You have no idea, Accala. The temple world is like hell on earth. Aesclepius Novenus, where all those who suffer from genetic abnormalities are herded like animals. People assume that, because we've almost eradicated disease, anyone who suffers from disease should be erased from the gene pool. She's a beautiful soul, and I'll do anything to make sure she gets the help she needs."

"I didn't know."

"We've both got people to live for. And trust me, there's plenty about me you don't know, but right now my job is to keep you on track. I suggest you take tonight to refocus. Keep your mission in mind, don't be swung left and right by your feelings."

She left me alone.

I tried to sleep, but the bed was too soft and Julia's words and the sting that went with them lingered on in my thoughts.

Fuck her and her feelings. There would be time for sympathy after the tournament. And I wasn't happy about her having the code to my bracelet, not one little bit. Could I really trust Julia? Or even my uncle, for that matter? I couldn't decide whether the lack of ambrosia was making me edgy and paranoid, or if I was being wisely cautious. Everyone was out for himself or herself, and the only person I could truly rely on was me.

Tossing and turning in the dark, I drifted in and out of sleep. I came fully awake to the sound of the buzzing noise, so loud I could barely think. The pin, held securely in my hand while I slept, was transmitting a tingling sensation up my arm like a jolt of electricity. I jumped out of bed and resisted the urge to drop it like a burning ember. The sensation subsided, and I tried to settle my breath, still my heart. I walked over to the large plate windows and watched the snow fall. It was cold outside; I could hear the wind whipping to and fro. Suddenly, I realized there was someone standing on the other side of the glass, staring at me. A Hyperborean. I looked around for something to use as a weapon if it breached the window and attacked. I didn't know what had happened to Orbis and there was nothing else at hand. The beast was just standing there, staring into the room. It was big, twice the size of the largest Hyperborean I'd seen aboard *Incitatus*, though of a similar morphology. The spines that protruded from its body were long and sharp. I was still holding Mother's pin, and it was growing increasingly hot in my hand, but I ignored the discomfort now. The creature demanded my attention. I'd learned how fast they could move if they were provoked, so a slow, even retreat out into the corridor to call for reinforcements would be the best move. I couldn't take a monster like that unarmed. But my experience with the Hyperboreans on the ship made me think that perhaps this one was trying to communicate. I'd watched one of his kind die without demonstrating the slightest violence toward me, and I felt I owed it to that one to give this barbarian the benefit of the doubt. Every trained instinct said to flee, but I kept walking forward, one step after another, until I was right up against the glass.

Its crystalline body gleamed in the moonlight, and beneath the shining facets of its torso ran a quicksilver fluid. The source of the buzzing headache shifted so that now it seemed to be coming from the barbarian's body. It held out a clawed hand, pressing it against the glass. I reciprocated, reached out to touch the glass in turn, but suddenly the surface between us vanished like an energy field that had been switched off and I was falling through the window. The giant alien's arms were surrounding me, pulling me toward the long spines that rose up from its chest. I was surprised, off balance, and I couldn't muster the strength to escape. The spines impaled me and his wiry hair wrapped around my face like tendrils. He just held me there in a strange embrace. I felt no pain and no matter how I tried to pull away, I couldn't escape. The buzzing noise was intensely loud, a harsh, attacking sound. The pin in my hand was burning hot, scorching my palm, while the rest of me froze.

Beyond the spines, the swirling blue fluids and gases in the alien's body formed abstract shapes, which terrified me. Why those shapes should elicit such a response I didn't know, only that I felt with absolute certainty that the beast wanted to rend me in two, tear flesh from bone, devour me whole. It burned with hatred for me, not just humanity but me in particular.

The light from my room shone out behind me, enough to see that something strange was going on with my own body. It was as if every pore of my skin was opening and excreting something; I was sweating ambrosia. The alien was leaching it out of me. I couldn't allow this; I needed it. My fists battered its hard chest, but its spines pierced my hands, drawing ambrosia out of them too. Shifting about, I struggled to free myself. It was *my* ambrosia, every damn drop, and I'd die before I'd let this barbarian steal it.

I sat up in bed, covered in sweat, my heart pounding. A dream. Thank the gods, only a dream. I walked over to the window. Nothing but falling snow. As I went to go back to bed, the light gleamed on the surface of the glass, and I saw five point marks in a cluster. Were they Hyperborean claw marks? I couldn't be sure, but it looked like the exact place where the Hyperborean had touched the glass with its claw. No, I was fooling myself, the trick of a tired mind. Gods. What a dream. That's all it was—my mind's reaction to finally arriving on Olympus Decimus after so long. Sitting on the edge of the bed, the biggest gladiatorial event in the empire commencing early in the morning, I knew I'd never get back to sleep.

XX

We stood in the city's circus, fifty-five contestants—what should have been fifty-six but for Lurco's absence—champing at the bit, ready to race, awaiting the start of Jupiter's great tournament. The air was freezing, the wind swirled and impatiently whipped hundreds of flags. I was dressed in Sertorian light-weight cold-weather armor styled to fit over my black and red team uniform, my hair tied back securely with my mother's pin. The noise of the crowd filled the air completely, as half a million tourists, spectators, and the media waited excitedly with us for the opening ceremony to commence. As the gold sun rose above the mountains, the first of the great white bulls was tied down by ropes and sacrificed by the priests, long knives quickly stealing its life to honor Jupiter. Simultaneously, out on the tundra that would soon bear our chariots, ten thousand white bulls, twice the normal size, genetically perfect and purpose bred, were released. A moment later, a beam shot out from the Rota Fortuna, the ion cannon stealing the lives of the cattle. Their slaughter, blood and fire, consecrated the ground, preparing it for the tournament, and then a sweeping ray cremated the carcasses, transforming them into black dust, scattered by the winds as if their hooves had never stamped upon the surface of the world at all.

The excited screams of the crowd rose like a wave, carrying us, as the two factions were led out in our slow procession of chariots before the altar and the emperor's balcony. Points of stillness and silence in the chaos, we waited for the sun to travel high enough so that its long-fingered rays, the hand of Jupiter Light-Bringer, would reach out and touch the sacred brazier before us, triggering a photosensitive fuse. When the fire erupted, the games would begin. Priests blessed us with water flicked from sprigs of the sacred oak that grows in Rome's Capitoline Hill. By the time the water droplets traveled through a half dozen feet of freezing atmosphere, they struck like small beads of ice, making a light din as they bounced off the gladiators' armor plates.

Above all others in his private balcony sat the emperor in full regal glory. He was surrounded by banners and the imperial emblem—the golden eagle of Rome, its wing tips and claws reaching out to touch the borders of an eight-pointed star, symbolic of the provinces united under one house, one leader. On either side of him, positioned at a lower height, were the two proconsuls—my uncle and Aquilinus—sitting quietly like two muzzled attack dogs. No shining magisterium from the Sertorian proconsul today. He looked normal, unexceptional. He must remain humble in the presence of the emperor.

Seven war chariots. Our craft that had looked so large to me in *Incitatus'* training hall now seemed sleek and aerodynamic compared to some of the other vehicles in the field. The Tullian chariot was the largest by far, black and blue with sapphire accents like an electrified blowfly, bulked up with thick plates of armor for ramming like the bull that was their house emblem, ready to trample enemies underfoot. The Ovidians were mounted aboard a medium-size chariot that sported more blades and tusks than any other craft. They specialized in overturning enemy chariots.

Black was the prevailing color of the Talonite Axis, the four teams differentiated by house colors that swept the chariots in stripes and themed designs embossed into the armored hulls—the ruby red stripes of hawk talons, the jagged amber tusks of the Ovidians, the brilliant sapphire horn designs of House Tullian, and the curling white horn patterns of House Arrian. Flags in house colors flew from the chariots' central poles. The contestants were dressed in a variety of armor that started with base function—less armor plate but more padding for a chariot driver, more armor for the gladiators, less for the more maneuverable bestiarii—and then developed according to the gladiator's personal style, so that their fans could easily recognize them in the arena, accentuated by their traditional team colors. Helmets with polarized eyeshades and communications equipment protected our heads, shielded our eyes from the glare of the light from the ice, and enabled communication with our teammates and the editor.

The lineup of the Caninine Alliance chariots was a more colorful affair: the bright golden chariot of House Viridian's Golden Wolves—the long face of a wolf with teeth bared streaked along the sides with emerald green; the argent chariot of House Flavian's Silver Sparrows marked with wings in honor of their patron god Mercury and double bars of maroon and diamond; the bright bronze-layered chariot of House Calpurnian's Ravens, with a yellow eye depicted on each side of the prow, streaked with ebony inlay that reminded one of sleek plumage. Gold, silver, and bronze—a shining symbol of unity against darkness, the great wealth of the ancient world. The Caninines had chosen their colors well. The Talonites were the harbingers of the death of the old ways, the old gods, whereas the Caninines stood for tradition and continuance. Both sides were undeniably striking.

The Viridian chariot struck the middle ground—not too much, not too little—an all-rounder designed to cope with a variety of assaults. It was a smart strategy. As they were outnumbered, they couldn't afford to indulge too much in chariot specialization. The Calpurnian chariot was similar, with one difference to suit their predilection for hand-to-hand fighting—it was lined with more side blades for cutting into and trapping an opponent's craft. In fact, the only Caninine chariot that had any drastic modification was that of House Flavian. Their silver craft was the lightest of all, stripped back for pure speed. Risky—their team would have highly coordinated to maintain balance and control at such speeds. But their strategy was obvious. They were limited in resources, so the Calpurnians and Viridians would play the part of blockers to allow the Flavians to race ahead to win any bouts that depended on speed to determine the winner.

Each chariot was stocked with weapons and basic survival equipment. Most of the space was needed for easy movement during fighting and for the two detachable desultore skirmishers on the sides of each vehicle. Julia nodded in my direction as she boarded her support chariot with the other collegia immunes. She was focused, all business. The immunes' larger chariots could not be targeted and had their own force shields. They would travel behind us, avoiding danger as they carried shelters, food, medical supplies, and tools. The tournament would be fierce, and they wanted to keep us alive for as long as possible when we weren't fighting. One tournament under the mad emperor had lasted only four hours, before the contestants were wiped out by hordes of armored Mandubii barbarians, and it nearly led to a galaxywide riot. Romans took their games seriously, as a sacred right, so the committee made sure that our odds of survival were low but not suicidal.

Trumpets blared. Horns and water organs filled the air with triumphant anthems. Hovering black spherae waited to trail in our wake, capturing the day's action. The hysplex, or starting gate, was a force shield with the emperor's holographic seal turning at its center. Until that seal vanished, none dared start for fear of their chariot's vibrating engines at the fore hitting the shield wall and being disabled. Beyond the gate lay a vast tundra that formed the stage for the first day's course.

Until the challenge was upon us, we wouldn't know whether we were in for a short melee or a prolonged challenge. The audience would know, though. It was their pleasure to watch us from on high, to fantasize about how they might play a part in directing our fate.

No barren plain, the tundra before us had been modified for the Ludi Romani. Purple-tinged force shields marked out the course we must travel. Set wide for this event, they doubled as advertising billboards, displaying the most expensive brands and companies: armilla manufacturers, the super wine merchants and sellers of garum—the empire's most addictive delicacy (bar one, now that Aquilinus had ambrosia). But these were in the minority. By far the most prominent advertisements were for Ambrosia by Aquilinus. And there I was. Deadly, beautiful, a living advertisement.

The course would take us past the towering diamond-and-ice totems I'd admired from the air on approach to the planet. Four on our left—hawk, bull, boar, and ram—and three to the right—wolf, raven, sparrow—with the emperor's house represented by the lion totem positioned in the distance, where the tundra met hills and terminated. Beyond them, the great mountains loomed. My revenge was at hand. I tried to picture Aulus running and laughing, the way he was in the cameo beside my bed back in Rome, but all my memory could conjure was some weak and ashen version.

I thought of Licinus' instructions that morning. "Keep the focus on the young chariot driver, Mercurius. He's our target today."

Sleepless and with a dry mouth and trembling hands, I had waited impatiently for my tisane to arrive this morning, and when I could stand it no longer, I'd gone in search of Crassus. "Orders from Licinus," he had explained, holding up a small phial of the drink, barely the size of a little finger. "You're on performance ration for the duration of the tournament. If you want more, you have to perform."

"How am I supposed to deal with a death race on a thimble's worth of the stuff? I can't cast Orbis with a shaking hand. Can't you speak up for me?" I'd said to Crassus. "I thought I'd passed your tests. I thought you trusted me."

"I do, darling, but Licinus is ever suspicious. He wants you on a tight leash for the race. Don't worry, our time is near, and a minor withdrawal will help give you a competitive edge. It won't feel nice, but it'll make you sharp. Trust me, I'm your team trainer. Then tonight I'll make sure you get what you deserve." He kissed me on the forehead as you would a petulant child. I had two choices in terms of who to target. Licinus wanted Mercurius dead, but Julia had delivered some news that morning about Marcus.

"Your uncle thought that Marcus would be an unnecessary distraction—he was never meant to be in the tournament, and all attempts to get him to see sense failed. He's really out for your blood."

"I know."

"So they've arranged for his armilla to develop a problem early on. A well-cast discus might penetrate right through his shield. It's something he'll pick up and correct eventually, so your uncle says you have to take advantage of it right away."

"I see." They'd sabotaged the modulation of his shield. I thought the Sertorians had driven pity from my heart, but the thought of my uncle setting Marcus up, cheating to remove him from the tournament, despite his willingness to end my life, made me uncomfortable.

"I'd rather he didn't do that. If Marcus dies, it should be an honorable death."

"I'm just the messenger," Julia said. "What's done is done."

Julius Gemminus demanded silence and then proclaimed, "Welcome, quirites—blessed citizens of Rome—to this year's Ludi Romani, Jupiter's Great Games! Listen carefully to the words of Caesar Numerius Valentinius, Son of Venus and Jupiter, Ruler of the Eight Galactic Provinces of Rome, Divine Imperator."

The emperor stood to receive the cheers of the crowd and then raised his hand for silence. An enlargement of his face was projected into the air above the center of the circus.

Every citizen got a vote in the outcome of critical tournament events, but it was the emperor who had the final say. The vox populi forum was the means by which the audience cast their votes and communicated to the emperor their desires. Its integrity and security were fiercely guarded by the collegia to prevent any form of tampering so that the emperor knew that what was posted was, without doubt, the collective will of the Roman people.

There had been three previous instances in Roman history where the mob, displeased with the emperor's choices in the games, had joined together to overthrow him and his house. On one occasion they were carried with the spirit of such displeasure when their favorite contestant, whom the emperor saw as a direct threat to his throne, was executed that they had nearly burned the city of Rome to the ground. So even though he had the final say, the emperor had to deal skillfully with the citizens, subtly lead them so that his decisions were seen as just and right.

"This year's Tournament of Jupiter presents us with the opportunity to unite warring houses, to settle scores in a way that does not unbalance the humors of the empire's greater body. Although today's teams are made up of members from each of the seven competing houses, they are grouped into factions according to their alliances in the recent war."

Now Julius Gemminus chimed in. It seemed the two had rehearsed this presentation.

"Hawks versus Wolves, Sparrows and Ravens versus Bulls, ancient enemies along with the Rams and Boars, who were once rivals but are now united under House Sertorian's Talonite Axis. The greatest champions of the houses, you will compete, fighting to overcome each other and the obstacles placed in your path in order to reach the final arena, two and a half thousand miles from here, on this continent's east coast. You will overcome obstacles designed to test each combat style: first the essedarii round—the bold chariot racers; then the bestiarii round—the daring animal fighters and hunters; and finally the gladiatorii—the round for courageous arena fighters. The first and last rounds shall last five days, and the bestiarii round will run for four. The winning team in each of the first two rounds shall receive a reward that will give it an advantage over the other teams."

The emperor continued, "As this war began with the bombing of the city of Lupus Civitas, it seems that the ruins of that city are an appropriate place to locate the final gladiatorial arena where the tournament winner shall be decided.

"House Sertorian or House Viridian. Only one will win full possession of this world, be declared victor of the war, and be elevated to my right hand in the Council of Great Houses. Most important, the winner will receive the love of the people and my blessing.

"The losing house shall be banished to the galactic frontier, stripped of their territories and noble status. Here, before their emperor and the peoples of the empire, do the proconsuls of both warring houses agree to the terms?"

"I do, Imperator," Quintus said, nodding his head in acknowledgment.

"Yes, Imperator," affirmed Aquilinus.

"Then let's get down to brass tacks. What shall be our theme, this tournament's beating heart, so to speak?" The emperor walked over to stand behind Proconsul Aquilinus, placing his hands on the small man's shoulders. "House Sertorian and Proconsul Aquilinus have been most helpful in this regard. Their New Gods campaign, which has been so very widely distributed across the face of the empire, and so quickly and efficiently, has inspired me. This year's theme shall be one of transformation—from high to low, from old to new, from humans to gods and gods to humans."

"All presented with an icy twist," Julius Gemminus said.

This pronouncement pleased the crowd to no end, and they started talking among themselves, trying to anticipate what dangers had been drawn from the collection of ancient tales to test us.

"The old tales of transformation teach us how we ought to behave in relation to the gods and to one another, as well as the punishments meted out to those who think themselves above such universal laws. The ancient stories tell us what to do and, more important, what not to do." The emperor paused, turning his gaze on the Sertorian proconsul.

"Imperator," Proconsul Aquilinus said, "let me take this opportunity to assure you of House Sertorian's—"

"Absolute loyalty and obedience," the emperor finished for him, holding out his hand. Proconsul Aquilinus took it and kissed it in submission. The projection was so large and detailed that I could actually see his red face and the pulsing veins in his temples as the Sertorian proconsul restrained his anger.

"Aquilinus, I look forward to seeing how your New Gods face the challenges overcome by the heroes of old."

"I'm sure they will perform to your satisfaction, Imperator," he replied coolly.

The emperor stepped back up to his throne. All fifty-five contestants raised our weapons and cried as one: *We who are about to die salute you.*

We took up our positions.

The Flavian chariot was closest to our starboard side. Winner of countless equestrian league circuses, it was driven by Titus Flavius Cursor near the prow, behind him Tremelius Ralla in the fore with a mechanical crossbow that could load heads with a variety of lethal functions onto the bolts before they were loosed.

The Calpurnian chariot, a heavy quadriga, pulled up beside it, captained by Cossus Calpurnius Blaesus. He wielded a long mace with a spiked head, which he threw back and forth from hand to hand impatiently. Marcus stood on the port-side platform, waiting to come at me.

To our port side was the cruel-mouthed champion racer Cynisca, driving the Arrian chariot, the only female on that team. She wore a helmet that revealed only her large eyes, enhanced with makeup so that they positively glowed. Cynisca wielded a flail to whip the enemy chariots that tried to overtake her. A veteran of the games, the Arrian charioteer had ridden to victory in the last big Ludi Romani four years earlier on Quatrus Lycaonia, one of the cloud cities that Julia was so determined to reach.

The audience would be wagering heavily on the outcomes of the race. Lesser houses would be broken by bad wagers; others would rise. It was serious business. Fans kept detailed statistics of each chariot, its pedigree, technical makeup, and victories, along with as much information as they could get on the drivers, athletes, and their likely strategies.

On the far side of the Caninine lineup were the Golden Wolves themselves. Lean-limbed Pavo with his array of darts and slings, then team leader Tribune Carbo with his steel lasso and curved sword—a setup for trapping and severing limbs—and positioned at the outer aft was my cousin Darius, golden arrows ready to fly. Mercurius was at the helm, and Nervo, their other charioteer, stood with his spear poised. Their chariot was farthest away from us, which meant we'd have to go through a horde of contestants to get at Mercurius, but I could see that Licinus was not to be deterred. I had other ideas, though. For this first stage of the game, losing a chariot driver would be a great blow, and I had to keep the Viridian team in good shape—they would become my team when I switched sides later in the tournament. Somehow I would drive the course of action to see that the greatest threat to my mission was eliminated first: Marcus. This was no time for sentimentality. The mission was everything. My body vibrated with the chariot's engines as they waited to be unleashed. The reduction in my regular intake of ambrosia was having a powerful effect on me. I felt like a racehorse before a big meet. Adrenaline high, nerves and muscles wired for action.

They released the summa rudis—the flying robotic referee—into the field. He shot ahead of us, under the editor's direction. The staff he wielded was capable of paralyzing or punishing a contestant who violated the three rules of the contest—don't try to flee the course, obey the editor's directions, and accept the emperor's decree of life or death.

Suddenly, I caught sight of someone in the stands. My father. He looked so different that I'd skimmed over him at first, but there was no doubt it was him. He'd come to Olympus Decimus. Did he think he could press the emperor to disqualify me at this late stage? He was deluding himself. It seemed as if, in four weeks, he'd lost a third of his body weight. He looked old and tired, his vitality gone.

There was no more time to think it over. The emperor from on high lifted the mappa, the sacred purple starting cloth. It fluttered in the wind, whipping to and fro, waiting to be set free.

The high priest raised his arms as the first rays of the sun struck the brazier, igniting it, sending plumes of fire into the sky. Would this be my last sunrise? There was a grim feeling in my heart that I would never leave Olympus Decimus. That the falling snow would serve as my shroud, the only kind a traitor deserved.

"Contestants, you will fight well and die well. Bring honor to Rome, the Senate, her emperor, and your houses. In the name of Jupiter on high and the emperor, I declare that the games have begun!"

The emperor dropped the mappa, and we were away.

XXI

THE EMPEROR'S HOLOGRAPHIC SEAL vanished, and instantly the one-armed Corvinus brothers worked together to pilot our chariot, the black reins wrapped about their forearms, keeping our course straight and steady.

The tundra opened out before us. A sudden burst of speed threw us into the cold wind's biting maw.

The Rota Fortuna had atmospheric stabilizers to help regulate the planet's weather, but they were intended to ensure the view stayed clear for the spectators, not make things too easy for the contestants. The seven teams spread out, gathering into two clumps—my Blood Hawks headed up the chariots of the Talonite Axis, and the chariots of the Caninine Alliance were headed by the Golden Wolves. The auxiliary chariots followed behind, keeping pace but maintaining a safe distance from the action.

Julius Gemminus reappeared now in his holographic form—hovering above us like a giant cupid head—chubby face with little fluttering wings sticking out from behind his cars.

"Seven fast chariots, fifty-five contestants," Julius Gemminus announced. "Today's winners will receive an engine upgrade. As soon as you pass the boundary markers, fighting may begin. Fly, chariots! May Mercury and Apollo speed you on your way!"

There were still a hundred yards to go. The billboards flashed by to the left and right. Above us, the swarms of camera spherae swung this way and that, capturing the most dramatic angles. The chariots gleamed and weapons glittered in the bright light from the rising sun, reflected by the white ice, and I was grateful for the polarizing lenses built into my helmet.

Our first match was a race to the second set of flashing green markers mounted on high posts embedded into the icy ground. The tactical data streaming to my armilla indicated the course end was more than one hundred miles away.

Julius Gemminus' winged head zoomed ahead of us, continuing his monologue. "Champions! Noble Chiron the Centaur was struck by an arrow poisoned with the Lernaean Hydra's blood and, unable to face an eternity of burning pain, sacrificed his immortality. Because of his great deeds and noble spirit, the gods raised him up and transformed him into the constellation Centaurus. Now we will judge whether our champions are worthy to ascend to the heavens!"

Licinus had ordered the Ovidians and Arrians to act as blockers, clearing a way through for us to strike at the Caninine teams. The Tullians would sweep in behind to finish off the wounded.

I gripped Orbis tightly, waiting for the first pass. Marcus was closest to me, sword and shield ready, strapped to the center pole of his chariot by a wire belt.

The line of red flashing posts set into the ice ahead suddenly turned green as we passed them, and the first corner, a sharp right, was on us. The chariots all turned together into a crushing pack, taking care not to collide with the electrified purple energy shields that marked the course boundaries.

The Arrians and Calpurnians hated one another as much as the Viridians hated the Sertorians. I had to help fuel that fire, if I wanted to avoid killing Mercurius.

As we turned into the crush, our chariot was pushed ahead and the Arrians came up on our starboard, closest to the Calpurnian craft. I made a cast at Marcus, with no intention of striking home, but as Orbis sailed across the Arrian bow on his voyage he nearly hit Cynisca, who was forced to pull away to avoid injury. The action caused her to pull wide, clashing instantly with the Calpurnian chariot, which attacked them in response. Now their blood was up. Licinus called at them to hold, but instead of following the plan, the Arrian leader, Calida, true to his name, ordered his chariot to drive forward across our bow, blocking us so he could take a shot at killing Marcus. Before the two chariots could clash, Calida fell backward to the deck, Marcus' javelin through his shoulder. Excellent. Sensing a free-for-all, the Tullian charioteer, Salcus Tullius Coruntus, famous for his ramming skills, drove the Arrian craft aside and collided with Marcus' chariot, toppling the dark-skinned dart thrower Vibius Calpurnius Habitus from his perch. He fell beneath the heavy Tullian craft, his skull crushed like a corn husk beneath an ox's hooves, death finding him in an instant.

One dead already and things had worked out exactly as I planned. Instead of being clear to attack Mercurius, I found my chariot swinging alongside Marcus.

The chariots were forced to turn as the course veered left. Then the Caninine team managed to pull off the move we were trying for. The Viridians pulled their chariot longways, blocking off the Tullians, and the mercurial Flavians followed suit, racing across the bows of the Arrians and Ovidians. They'd opened the way for the Calpurnian chariot to charge right at us. Right at *me*. I saw it in Marcus' eyes. The Talonites had planned to target Mercurius, but the Caninine plan was to kill me.

I didn't even get a chance to throw before Marcus was on me, his chariot coming up on our port side, shield in my face, gladius thrusting quickly at my torso. Gods, he was faster than I expected. It must have been the new stimulant the Caninines had developed. Much faster. I swung away on the pole and, just like we'd practiced, Crassus stepped in with a javelin thrust over the top of Marcus' shield. Marcus threw himself back off the platform and to his chariot's deck rather than take a javelin through the eye, but then the Ravens team leader, Cossus Calpurnius Blaesus, charged forward. Marcus meant to be driven back; he was luring me in, sacrificing the pleasure of killing me himself to entice me into a trap. Blaesus' ax was falling toward my neck, Crassus was right behind me, blocking my escape. I was dead.

Suddenly, the ground dropped out from under us and the chariots plummeted. I had to grab at the center pole to keep from flying off. Blaesus was jerked off balance, unable to deliver the fatal blow. Gods, we were racing downhill on steep ramps cut right into the ice. They'd been carved out in such a way that they were impossible to see as we approached. Then, a second before we hit

it, I saw that the end of the ice ramp curved upward and managed to brace myself in time as all seven chariots ran off the end of the ramp and went flying high
up into the air.

Alongside us about fifteen feet on our port side was the Viridian team. Licinus
screamed out one of our plays and Barbata responded, shooting her trident
caster across our bow. She was casting a wide net, trying to entrap any one of
them, and she succeeded, entangling Caninus and giving me my chance to
throw. It was a hard throw—my body wasn't in the right position and the wind
was unpredictable. At best I'd wound him, which was an acceptable outcome. I
threw, but Carbo stepped in front of his man and pushed forward with his shield,
warding my discus away at the last second.

We must have looked like flying fish to the audience, suddenly vanishing as
we plummeted down the ramp and now suddenly reappearing, soaring through
the air high above ground level. We came crashing down again.

"There's more ramps!" Castor called out. "Brace yourselves."

We flew downward and then we were up again. This time, though, we found
ourselves soaring through the air alongside the house totems.

As the first volley of arrows flew, we learned that the totems were not merely
decorative—they were archer towers. At the top of each stood a four-legged Centaurii barbarian. Armed with bows, they resembled classical centaurs except for
their red skin, scales, and lizardlike tails.

"Testudo!" Licinus barked, and we moved into defensive mode, clustering
together near our drivers, our armillae projecting tower shields that we inter-
locked to the sides to form a makeshift "turtle" shell that covered us all. The
missiles struck from both sides as we flew through the zenith of the arc, presenting
as plum targets. An arrow clipped Pavo's shoulder, and he screamed; they must
have chosen a poison that would appropriately simulate the legendary agony
affected by the touch of Hydra's blood. As we hit the ice, Carbo threw his lasso
right over and past Marcus' craft, which had appeared alongside us, until it
found one of the upright spikes on our chariot's side. He pulled the loops closed
and wrapped it about the mast beside him, binding all three vessels together.

Marcus came at me again, his gladius seeking me just as a net attachment
from Caninus' crossbow entangled me. I took a cut to the arm, turning away
from my lanista's weapon just in time to meet Cossus' iron mace. I managed to
roll with the blow, but it still caught me on the back of the skull with a mighty
thump. Stars swam across my vision and I stumbled to one knee.

And then we were up in the air again, a cloud of black arrows coming at us.
I got my shield up just in time before the black shafts struck home. We cleared
the towers, and while we were airborne, the Dioscurii pulled starboard, and the
steel rope of Carbo's lasso was stretched taut. I switched Orbis out to my right
hand and swung with all the strength I could muster. Orbis severed the connection, which suddenly threw our craft to the right and Marcus' chariot to the left
where it collided midair with the Viridian craft. We started to drift apart, sailing through open space, and I saw that the end of Carbo's lasso, rather than
collapsing, sprouted tendrils and tried to grab at the chariot again, but Mania

stepped past me with her needle knife and stabbed it fast. The lasso reared back like a wounded snake—it was a living thing, made of lapis negra like my discus.

Still in the air and six feet off the ice, and Marcus' chariot had moved three feet ahead of ours. There was my shot. Marcus was at forty-five degrees to me, his shield covering him from the last of the arrows.

"Accala! Strike!" Licinus commanded.

He meant my cousin. Mercurius was open too, coming up fast behind the Calpurnian chariot. But I cast at Marcus. It was him or me, and he was certainly not holding back. And then the chariots landed hard.

The midair collision between the Calpurnian and Viridian chariots sent the latter spinning the moment it touched the ice, and just before Orbis reached my target, the Calpurnian chariot swung about, aft becoming fore. The angle changed and instead of Marcus, my discus struck the Black Ravens' central mast, ricocheted, and shot across the way. It took all my willpower to stifle a warning scream as Orbis severed the wrist and tender neck of my good cousin Mercurius in a single stroke, sending his body spinning off the chariot. But wait, his forearms were still bound with the thick leather reins. The weight of his body thrashing about between the ground and the chariot caused their craft to swing roughly, its engines turning in spirals. But the fine driver Nervo swiftly moved up from his position behind Mercurius, drew his falx, and with a stroke cut the reins free from my cousin's body. Nervo caught the loose ends in his hands and expertly gained control of the wayward Viridian chariot.

There was no time to stop and think. Ahead of us, the tundra dropped down and flattened out. There! The finish line. The lion totem and beside it a triumphal arch a half-mile ahead perched atop an icy hill. The first to pass through it would win the day. Orbis returned, clacking flat against our chariot's magnetic post. Mercurius' blood dripped onto my hands as I recovered my weapon.

The Dioscurii started to pick up pace, but we'd been so focused on the Viridians and Calpurnians, playing out our private grudge match, that no one had noticed the Arrians. Their chariot came bursting through, ramming wedges pushing the Viridians aside as they powered toward the arch. The Ovidians tried to keep up with them and then the Flavians tried to pass on the Arrian port. Their lightweight craft could outpace the midrange Arrian chariot, but then Cynisca was screaming, her whip lashing out at both the Ovidian and Flavian drivers, keeping them at bay until, at last, she drove forward and won the race. The Flavians and Ovidians came in second and third respectively. We placed fourth, the Calpurnians fifth, the Viridians sixth. The Tullians brought up the rear in their heavy rammer.

Julius Gemminus' cherubic face appeared before the lion totem at the end of the course.

"Well done, House Arrian! Felicitations! Noble winners of the first leg of the chariot races—your chariot's engine upgrades will be delivered to you at the first night's campground. All teams, there is no rest until you reach the designated campsite, so be swift lest you don't make it by nightfall!"

The course split to the left and right, demarcated with shield walls to separate the factions. I was glad for it. I didn't want to look at the Viridians, to be reminded of what I'd just done. The race was over for the day, the highlights already playing along the shield walls; I saw my throw that had stolen Mercurius' life from a hundred different angles.

I had survived the first day of the first round. Four more days of the chariot race to go. How many more family members would I kill? Assuming I even survived, that is. We were prepared for the ferocity of the other teams, but the kind of lethal traps we faced today made everything unpredictable. And I was trembling. I needed ambrosia. The incident with Mercurius had pulled the rug out from under me. My own kin dead and by my own hand. When it came to serving the Furies, was this my new path—an all-encompassing death to any who stood before me?

We cruised for the rest of the day, swiftly covering the vast tundra. The wind was growing in strength, spraying us with sharp showers of ice, which made visibility difficult. Julius Gemminus must have decided to expose us to the elements and turn off the Rota Fortuna's weather-stabilization technology. Or perhaps the audience had taken a poll and decided it would be amusing to see us freeze. It was bad enough to have killed a Golden Wolf, but I'd done it with my father watching. He was probably even now in some small room aboard the Rota Fortuna watching my every move, watching replays of Mercurius' death. Why hadn't Uncle Quintus mentioned that Father was here? My uncle knew everything. Was it to spare me distraction? The thought that Uncle Quintus might kill my father to prevent him causing trouble, because all my father ever did was cause me trouble, lurked in the back of my mind and wasn't easily dismissed.

The ground crested upward until we were high enough to catch a preview of the following day's course. Julius Gemminus had sculpted the terrain ahead, using the ship's ion cannon like a scalpel to carve long canals into the solid ice. The course took the shape of two continuous intersecting figure eights, like the intertwining snakes that ran the length of Mercury's caduceus, long, separate paths for the separate teams to gather speed, with intersecting points where we'd be driven together in order to clash and fight.

How deadly the Caninine teams were, especially the Wolves. Grim, determined, they went at it like they had a deathwish, seemingly happy to endanger their own lives to try and steal ours.

A sudden exhaustion overwhelmed me and the buzzing headache returned. It wasn't strong, just an irritant, a wandering mosquito, and I tried to tune it out and focus on the view as we passed. I found my attention wandering to a hill in the distance and for just a second I could have sworn that a figure stood upon it, a Hyperborean, judging by the shape. Then a wall of fog passed over the hill, and when it had gone upon its way, the figure, if it had really been there at all, had vanished.

The auxiliaries sped ahead to set up camp for us. The gold sun was hanging low in the sky by the time we caught sight of our sanctioned campsite—a cluster of thermal tents bordered by chains of icy boulders. The starting gate for tomorrow's leg lay beyond the camp—a canal with high ice-blue walls that traveled straight for a half mile before curving off toward the Cadeuceus-shaped course.

The Talonite camp's boundaries were demarcated with signal beacons and surrounded by protective shields. The Caninines would be camped some miles away. No killing after dark unless the editor scheduled a night round. This gave us a chance to rest and heal, but was also so that high-paying spectators could rest, take part in the entertainments, and not miss any crucial action. They were paying a premium for a live show.

We pulled in and the immunes rushed around us to offer medical treatment and repair damage to our chariot. Julia's red hair stuck out the sides of her helmet, making her easily identifiable, but there would be no opportunity to speak until later on, when the preparations for the following day were done.

The moment we dismounted, Cynisca was mobbed with congratulations. The emperor's representatives placed the day's victory wreath, a large band of white and black flowers, over the Arrian chariot, and a second wreath for Cynisca and the team leader, Calida.

The Sertorians gathered about me, congratulating me. Licinus seemed unusually jovial.

"None of ours dead to two Caninines. The Blood Hawks are intact but the Golden Wolves, they've taken it right up the ass!" he said, looking at me. "You didn't follow my plan to the letter, Mock Wolf, but it all worked out as expected, and I can't very well punish you for killing the enemy, can I? Wouldn't be good for morale, might confuse the other Talonite gladiators."

We gathered together—Sertorians with our allied Ovidians, Tullians, and Arrians—working on game plans for whatever the editor was going to throw at us tomorrow. Licinus wasted no time in chastising the Arrians for being too headstrong and sabotaging his plans with their eagerness to punish the Calpurnians.

"They shouldn't have been so strong!" Calida said to Licinus. "You assured us that the ambrosia would give us the edge. Well, it looks like the Caninines have something too, and we're going to need more. You hear me? We need more than the piddling little capsules you've given us. I know you're keeping the best stuff for yourselves."

Licinus backhanded the man, hard and fast, knocking him to the ground.

"You'll get what you get when we say you get it and you'll be grateful for it. Whatever the Wolves and their dogs are taking, it won't hold up like our ambrosia, you can bet on that."

That was the extent of his displeasure, though. Licinus couldn't afford to be too harsh with his allies this early on; he needed to keep the alliance together and he needed them all in fighting shape. We prepared for the coming day, the immunes tending to our wounds and massaging our bruised and aching bodies. We changed into robes and furs to keep warm and ate a hot meal. I felt physically and emotionally raw.

While we recovered, the immunes worked hard, spurred on by the fading daylight and rapidly dropping temperature. I noticed Julia from time to time. She did her work with the other Vulcaneum engineers who tended to the weapons and vehicles, installing the Arrians' engine upgrade that had been brought down with great fanfare in a shuttle from the stadium, but she kept her distance from them when the work was done.

But the day wasn't over yet. Mercurius had died a gladiator's death, and now we watched as the Libertine couch came to collect him. Robed attendants played the part of Viridian house spirits, picked up his parts and placed them on the white couch. The hovering couch would transport him through the Porta Libitnensis, the sacred docking bay aboard the Rota Fortuna above, and his body would be transported with honor, the proper libations made. It didn't make me feel any better. My whole body was cold, covered in a blanket of pain. I needed the ambrosia, but it was much more than that; the need was brought on by stress, and Mercurius' death had affected me more than I'd anticipated. It reminded me that I wasn't in control, that any power I had to accomplish anything was fleeting at best. What did that mean for my brother? For any hope of saving him?

Next came the pantomime that took place on the grand stage in the Rota Fortuna. From on high, it was projected upon the dome of the sky. Two comic characters entered the scene, Ursus and Pullus, the flute-playing bear and the horn-playing chicken. They acted out amusing moments from the day's matches, and the audience had to guess which scenes were depicted. At first, Ursus pretended to throw his flute off to the right, and Pullus reached down and as if by magic produced the flute from his rear end before Ursus moved in and took the chicken's hands, dragging the flute he was holding across his throat. They were making fun of me, reenacting how I meant to kill Marcus and then killed Mercurius instead, a move that apparently I pulled out of my ass. There were lots of flying thumbs projected by the audience. It was a popular comedy skit, but from where I stood it was hard to see the joke.

Waiting for nightfall was hell. My mind, like those of the Arrians, kept wandering back to ambrosia. When would the Sertorians take theirs? When would I have mine?

As night crept up on us, we moved to our separate house camping zones. Our immunes had set up a basic camp, but Sertorians being Sertorians, they had a red-domed tent each, laced with luxury items to ensure the best possible night's rest. Thick fur flooring from the hides of barbarian Ursurii warmed our feet, and soft divans and beds were laid for our comfort. After such a terrible day, I welcomed whatever small comfort such luxury could bring.

The Sertorian team gathered in Licinus' command tent, and Mania distributed small phials of ambrosia from a casket she carried carefully from the chariot, two for each teammate, three for Licinus. As predicted, he consumed more than the others.

Licinus dispatched Barbata to deliver ambrosia to the Talonite axis. The allied teams were sent much smaller portions of the precious liquid, capsules the size of a thumbnail. Despite Proconsul Aquilinus' big claim that he would share ambrosia with the masses, my uncle's intelligence seemed to be accurate. There was a shortage. There wasn't enough to go around, even here in the tournament, not even enough for the Sertorians themselves to indulge in anything but conservative quantities.

But where was my share?

"She performed well," Crassus said to Licinus. "She should be rewarded."

"We should have taken the victory wreath today," Licinus grumbled.

"But she did kill Mercurius."

"Perhaps she did and perhaps it was dumb luck. She gets a small dose," Licinus said. "Nothing more."

"It's all yours," Mania said, gently stroking a phial half the size of the ones the Sertorions had taken that lay on the table in front of her. "But first let's talk about today, and be mindful of your answers." She glanced at the bracelet. "Remember, I'll know if you're speaking truthfully."

I was surprised when, instead of quizzing me about the logic of my moves in the race, she asked me to recount in excruciating detail the moments when I wasn't fighting. She narrowed in on my description of the period after the fight, as we cruised toward the campsite.

"There's something you're not telling me. I observed you, you seemed distracted."

"I don't know what you mean," I said, my eyes fixed on the phial before her. "This is ridiculous, just give me my ambrosia," I said, reaching for it.

The shock hit me hard; Mania was hiding her armilla under the line of the table so I couldn't see her activate the bracelet.

"I hope that focused you and reminded you of your place. You've been blooded, but you're still a chattel of House Sertorian until the game is won." She touched my arm, helping me regain my feet. "You kept looking away to the horizon as if expecting to see something," she said.

I considered lying to her, but I couldn't see what difference it made, so I told her about the Hyperborean and admitted that I thought it was an illusion, that the stress of the day and the lack of ambrosia made it hard to think clearly.

She nodded, seemingly contented, and tossed the ambrosia to Crassus to administer as he saw fit.

Gods, I couldn't be more confused. It was hardly enough ambrosia, only just enough to keep me from clawing my eyes out. I wanted to complain, but I couldn't bring myself to argue that I deserved more for killing my cousin Mercurius.

"Well done," Barbata said, putting her arm about me and leading me from the tent. "First wolf blood to you, sister. You're truly one of us now. Don't listen to Licinus—it was a magnificently timed throw. Tomorrow you'll make another just as good."

And kill Carbo, or maybe I'd really murder Marcus. I was cursed. Why did the Furies not come to my aid? Mercurius' death did nothing to aid my revenge; it only created more of a deficit.

Before I exited the tent, they had me place Orbis in a secure container. I was permitted to possess him only during the daytime events. I retreated to the tent that I had to share with Crassus. Once we were alone, I immediately pressed him for what I needed most—more ambrosia.

"I feel like I'm going to throw up. If you want me at my best, you have to get me more than this. You saw the Viridians out there. They've taken something as well."

"You're right," he said. "Licinus is certain its not ambrosia, but whatever else they're using is a mystery. You don't have any ideas, do you?" he asked, gently holding my chin, forcing me to look into his inquiring eyes.

His physical proximity suddenly made it hard to find words. He reached behind me and pulled out my mother's pin. My hair tumbled down about my shoulders and I inhaled sharply. Gods, but I wanted him. I grabbed his hand and went to reclaim the pin. He let me have it. A tingling sensation ran so powerfully through my fingers that I nearly dropped it, but I made sure not to register any reaction that Crassus could pick up on. The sensation gave me a gap in which I could fight the desire and wrestle it back down. He wouldn't have me so easily.

"I have no idea how the Caninine teams are doing so well," I replied as calmly as I could manage. "But they're keeping up with us and I can't afford to be the only one who has to do without! Not if you want me in shape to take care of our mutual enemy!" I moved away, but he grabbed my hand and pulled me back to him.

"You want it, don't deny it," he seethed. I didn't know if he meant I wanted him or the ambrosia. Either way he was right.

"You want so much from me," I said, "and yet you keep so much from me. What's going on, Gaius? What was Mania playing at with her interrogation?"

"I don't know," he said. "She and Licinus have their own agenda and aren't exactly friends of mine."

"If you can't tell me that, then me something else. Where is Aulus?"

"Don't worry, I'll tell you everything when the time is right."

"Then when do we kill Licinus?"

He looked around anxiously and then gestured for me to lower my voice.

"Don't press me. You know better than to talk about such things out loud."

"It's blowing a gale out there," I said. "No one can hear us."

He paused, listening. I couldn't hear a thing apart from my headache and the wind outside. "There's always someone listening," he said. "But yes, I can speak now. We need Licinus' strength for now, especially as the Caninines have improved their chances with their own supplement. The tail end of the bestiarii rounds will be the time. That's when we'll strike."

"That sounds fine," I said. "When we head into the gladiatorial round, you will be new leader of the Blood Hawks."

"With you by my side," he said, touching my face tenderly. He tried leading me toward the bed, but I pulled away.

"Why so cold? Tell me, what would you do for this?" He held up the phial of ambrosia. A full phial.

"You want to play games?" I demanded, pushing his chest violently. "You want to keep me in the dark, and then whore myself for your drug? Go to hell." I hit him in the face. He hardly flinched.

He didn't hit me back. "You will be careful not to lecture me," he said condescendingly. "I do all that I can for you within the bounds of our agreement, and beyond, but now I'm running out of patience with you, Accala. You will learn what it is to live without my protection in a nest of Hawks."

I'd overreacted, mainly because I wanted both him and the ambrosia, and given a weaker moment, I knew in myself that I might well have yielded and danced to his tune.

"Wait!" I called as he turned to leave. "The ambrosia."

He looked at me with disdain, and I thought he was going to make me beg for it, but then he threw the phial casually on the ground and left. It took all my self-control not to rush at it, to take even steps, to pick it up slowly so that I knew I was the one in control. Not the ambrosia. Not the Sertorians. I deliberately removed the stopper and, unable to restrain myself, downed its contents in one quick gulp. A flood of relief washed over me. My head cleared, my vision was sharp, my hand steady once more, but for how long? My uncle told me that ambrosia was a drug of diminishing returns. You needed more to effect the same results. How long would it be before I started suffering the lack of it again?

I peeked out the opening of the tent just in time to see Crassus stride into Barbata's tent on the other side of the camp. My first instinct was jealousy. I wanted to to rush over there and pull him back to our tent, rip his clothes off and take him. Make him mine. Ashamed, I sat down on the edge of the bed. The pin was still in my hand and I flattened out my palm and stared at it. My mother's instructions hadn't been very specific. How could it be the key to lead me to Aulus? I tried visualizing my brother, stood and turned around with the pin in my hand to different compass points, waiting for some kind of sign, but there was nothing, not even the heat or tingling I'd felt earlier.

When Julia came to visit, I was still staring at it, trying to elicit some kind of response from the thing, getting more and more frustrated at my lack of progress.

"I don't have long," she said. "I'm supposed to see if all your armor and weapons are okay for tomorrow's round."

"They're fine."

"And what about you?"

"Terrible but thank you for asking."

"You have to play your part. What happened with Mercurius was Fate."

She looked at the pin in my hand. "No luck yet?"

"No. Just the same as before, some heat and a buzzing at the back of my head, but that was earlier today, when I thought I spotted a Hyperborean on the field. It was the same experience with the Hyperboreans on the ship."

"Perhaps there's a connection between the pin and the barbarians, but I can't see how that connects with what your mother said about how it would draw you and your brother together."

"Me either. I thought it would work like a compass needle and pull me to Aulus, but so far there's been nothing, and now Crassus has scheduled his attack on Licinus."

I filled her in on everything that had transpired.

"And you agreed?"

"I brought up the issue in the first place. It was stupid of me, but he was withholding the ambrosia and I wasn't thinking too clearly."

"Don't worry, we might manage to find Aulus before the end of the bestiarii, but you might have made a mistake pushing him away. You need to mend your bridges with Crassus."

"You mean you want me to whore myself out to him?" I snapped defensively. "The day I killed my cousin? A good man. You want me to let that Sertorian fuck me to celebrate?"

"Not so loud," she warned. "Dampen your fire. You use strong words to fuel strong feelings."

"I think *whore* is just the right word. That is what you meant, isn't it?"

"Now is not the time for fire. We need to be cool, like this world, to contain our emotions. I'm sure we'll work out how to use your pin, but have you thought about what we'll do if you can't figure it out in time? Or if it's faulty? All we'll have left then is someone who can reveal Aulus' location, and Crassus is the only Sertorian around here who happens to be smitten with you."

"My father is here, on this world. Did you know that?"

I threw the question at her suddenly, seeing if surprise would register, but she didn't try to hide the fact that she knew.

"Your uncle told me."

"And you didn't think to tell me?"

"He advised me not to. He didn't want you to be distracted."

"I am nothing but distracted right now."

She was right, though. Everything was harder knowing he was here, watching me, close by.

"And he hasn't caused any trouble? Tried to have me disqualified again?"

"No. Proconsul Severus said he would take care of that."

"Take care of it? What the hell does that mean?"

"Not what you think. Your uncle wouldn't hurt your father. He'll just make sure he keeps out of the way." '

"Father's like a bull elephant. Once he gets an idea into his head there's no stopping him."

"I promise you, it'll be fine. Focus on the mission."

"You mean sleep with Crassus?"

"Gods, Accala, *you're* the bull elephant. If it comes down to it, will you let your brother die to preserve your maidenly virtue?"

"Get out."

"What, now you're going to make the same mistake with me?"

"No, but I need to be alone. Leave me be."

She glared at me but complied. She wasn't happy and she wasn't confident that I could see the mission through, I could see it in her eyes, but she complied and left me alone. Julia had to understand that the Sertorians might have me on a leash, but *she* didn't. My redheaded Vulcaneum was there to support me, not order me around. Julia would learn to follow *my* lead.

It passed midnight and I tossed and turned without any hope of sleep. Despite the comfort of the tent, I started to shiver as the temperature plummeted. Even in thermal robes it was freezing. Had my ambrosia worn off so quickly? Then the buzzing headache started up again, loud and strong, and my pin was burning hot so that I could barely stand to hold it. What in Hade's name did it all mean? I hadn't moved an inch, was no closer to my brother than when I had sat on the bed and stared at the pin before. The buzzing was reminiscent of a blowfly slowly cruising around inside my skull.

Agitated, I nearly threw the pin away but decided that since I couldn't possibly be any colder, I might as well go for a walk to clear my head before I started tearing the tent to shreds. I was wrong. The cold outside the tent was much worse. Pollux was up too. He cast a cursory glance at me but didn't seem concerned by my presence.

As I walked around, I noticed that the buzzing noise once more shifted outside of my body and modulated in pitch, rising and then lowering depending on whether I moved forward or backward, left or right. Could this be it? Did the pin work only late at night? Was it just a matter of following the sound? If so, should I follow the higher pitch or the lower? I'd had a similar experience aboard *Incitatus* when I'd found the Hyperboreans in the maze. I ventured around the back of the tent, seeking the higher register, and found myself up against the dome-shaped shield wall that enclosed the camp. It glowed faintly purple in the night, warning against contact with its electrified surface. The shield wasn't the only source of light. A few feet away, some small clusters of native rock thrust up through the ice, emitting a pale light. I took two steps toward the rocks, until I was as close to the shield wall as I dared. The buzzing headache had lost its edge. Higher in tone and louder, it had become more songlike, and within the static of noise I was used to experiencing, some kind of rhythm could be discerned. I stood there for some time, despite the cold, staring out into the night at those rocks. The humming was almost like a chant, growing louder, surrounding me like an embrace.

Out of the corner of my eye, I caught a glint and turned to see a crystalline body walk right past me. I thought my time had come, that the giant warrior from my dream in the athletes' village had found me, but it was a Hyperborean of the worker caste. No long spines on their arms, these were small, thin versions of the warriors. There was more than one; before and behind it were many more, an endless row walking past the shield wall off into the darkness.

And they glowed. A line of faintly illuminated barbarians, each with an apple-size ball of light contained in the lower part of the belly. They looked like they were pregnant with light, and considering the way they filed by without giving me a second glance, totally harmless. As each one passed, the buzzing song wavered in pitch and the pin heated up, then the volume dropped and the pin cooled again until the next one came by and the pattern repeated. A decent cast of Orbis could have shattered a half dozen in one go. There was more. I peered closely and saw that in addition to the pool of light in their bellies there were dark cracks running through their bodies, black tendrils slowly spreading through the swirling light.

The buzzing and heat in the pin vanished as the last of the line passed. What the hell was going on? As I was about to head back to the tent, I saw there was something different about the rocks. Their glow was fading. I crouched down and watched as the last of the light seeped away like the final moments of twilight. Interesting. There seemed to be a connection between the light in the landscape and the Hyperboreans, almost as if they were carrying the energy from the rocks away in their bellies. But how did that relate to the buzzing song and Mother's pin or the means to locate Aulus? Why couldn't my mother have been blessed with only a few more minutes to explain things properly?

Back in the tent, shivering like a small, hairless dog, I crawled under the covers. Although I hadn't seen him that night, I dreamed of the giant Hyperborean standing behind the workers as they walked their trail. I joined the line and when I passed the monster, he saw right away that I didn't fit in and grabbed me. I struggled as the spines in his arms slowly sank into my heart. After that I lay awake, my headache humming away in the background, unable to get back to sleep. It was more than a dream. I knew that somewhere in the darkness lay the Hyperborean warrior, waiting for me. It was like a crocodile sitting by the riverside, still as stone, until the prey wandered too close.

When Crassus returned a few hours from sunrise and climbed in next to me, I pretended I was asleep. I could smell sex on him, but him being there, anyone being there, was better than lying alone. The giant Hyperborean was out there waiting for me, and it was more terrifying to me than any of these Sertorians.

XXII

"ACCALA, I NEED TO speak with you." Julia walked toward me when I exited my tent in the morning. Again, I'd been denied any fresh ambrosia until day's end and was irritable, on edge, and about to give the immune a piece of my mind when Barbata emerged from her tent and cut right across Julia's path.

"Sometimes a Sertorian man needs the kind of release that only a Sertorian woman can give," she said to me with a wicked grin.

I ignored her. Why should I be jealous of Barbata? The whole idea was preposterous. Whatever Julia had to say must have been private because she'd moved on the second she saw Barbata and had joined up with the rest of the immunes.

The Talonite teams packed up camp. There was an air of confidence as we headed out.

Julius Gemminus appeared over us, promising a shield generator to whoever won the day, an exciting incentive to victory. Licinus made it clear that he wanted such an advantage for our team, and also to deny it to the enemy teams. I was going to give my all for the Sertorians today. What difference did it make? Perhaps if I tried my best for the Blood Hawks, I'd accidentally kill a Talonite or save a Viridian. That was how my luck seemed to be running.

We raced along the curved channel for about ten minutes, no sign of our competitors. The high walls of the canals were coated with force shield barriers, tinged purple to remind us we were at the mercy of the emperor. The same signs built into the force field walls that advertised ridiculous frivolities—Achilles' Foot Spray, guaranteed to heal all fungus and bacteria, or Bibaculus' Finest Vintage Falernian, aged twenty years with genuine elms—were electrified to shock and would kill me if I collided with them. And then our path intersected the Caninines'. The first to clash were the Ovidian and Flavian chariots. The bald scythe fighter Lucius Ovidius Calvus tried to board the Flavian chariot but slipped and slid off, slamming the back of his helmeted head on the edge of his own chariot, his scythe flying to the ice as his body fell into the jagged crop of spinning blades between the racing craft. The Ovidian slipping on his chariot had died by the hand of Nemesis, death by misfortune. The image of Fortuna Mala appeared in the sky— a bearded woman— the personification of bad luck. There was no shame in misfortune and he would be carried away with honor.

In the melee, the fighter Sextus Arrius Salinator was knocked from his chariot. His team didn't know they'd lost him, and we were bearing down on the Arrian, Barbata with her trident raised ready to finish him. Salinator looked to his chariot, in the hope they'd come about, but he knew there was no chance. Then, to my utter amazement, he turned and ran from Barbata. But ran to where? The shields were impenetrable, he could only run back along the channel. He wasn't thinking. He was panicking, running blind in the face of certain death. Damn weak-willed Arrians, there was not a backbone among the lot of them. Before the coward could flee too far, the summa rudis swung in, and his staff shocked the fighter as in ancient times arena hands would use red-hot irons to drive gladiators into the fray, but Salinator didn't get the message. The shocks only frightened him more, and he tried to rush past the flying robot referee.

The next shock was more severe. The muscles in his body painfully contracted and locked as one, and he fell to the ground, paralyzed. Barbata caught up to him, and the referee projected a force field bubble about the pair. A siren signaled that all fighting should come to a halt. The judgment would be swift, and while it was being carried out, the condemned man and the contestant with the right to execute him were immune from interference from other contestants. The sky above us filled with downturned thumbs. I couldn't see all of them, due to the walls of the channel, but it was clear the audience had no truck with cowards. The emperor's judgment followed, and Julius Gemminus appeared to deliver it, his chubby face smiling as he spoke a single word that echoed throughout the dome of the sky—*DEATH!*

Salinator lay there like a newly caught fish flapping on the ground as Barbata speared him through, ending his life with a single thrust.

Lucius Ovidius Calvus had been carried away with honor. Not so Arrius Salinator, the coward.

A tall black-robed figure, powerfully built—depicting Pluto—appeared as if from nowhere and sank a large hook with a length of rope attached to it into the Arrian's body, dragging it away and onto his sled, where it would be carried off and dumped as carrion and fed to the barbarian Sauromatae so that his shame might continue in the afterlife. It gave all of us pause. It was the paradox of the arena that the gladiator must fight in contempt of life and glory if he wished to achieve them.

Then the referee directed us onto our separate paths again. Another ten minutes and we hit the next intersection point and clashed for the second time.

The heavy Tullian chariot positioned itself ahead of the Flavian craft and slowed, trying to drop its rear on the opponent's engines and crush them, but the Silver Sparrows were too quick. So the Tullian driver Salcus Tullius Coruntus swung about suddenly, turning his chariot into a bludgeon, smashing the Viridians into the electrified shield wall. But the bestiarii net fighter Gurges Tullius lost his balance, and flew out, touching the shield wall. He screamed as the high-voltage wall electrocuted him. The air was suddenly filled with the stench of burned flesh and, worse, burned hair. He crumpled to the floor of the chariot, death claiming him, and Potitus Tullius Silo stepped in and pushed the body with his boot into the central hull, out of the way so it couldn't trip any of his men on the next turn.

The Caninines headed down one of the two paths that led away Licinus ordered that we pursue them, and all the teams headed down a single curving path, creating an overcrowded death zone with electrified walls on either side.

The turning point of the curve was known from the intersection and, instead of us taking the other, the meta. If we kept going along the same channel, we'd have one more pass before the course finished, which meant each side would have the chance to be on the inside curve. The closer to the wall, the more speed we'd retain, but the more chance a member of our team would be fried, or of damaging our chariot's electrical system.

The bronze and ebony Calpurnians tried to ram the Arrians, who in turn used part of their engine boost to shoot out of the way, exposing the Calpurnians to our weapons. Licinus ordered us to target Marcus.

Marcus was ready, though. His teammates shielded him, allowing my lanista to bring his gladius to bear, thrusting quickly—not at me, as expected, but targeting the person beside me—Barbata. The thurst was like lightning and Barbata took a shot to the side, but quickly responded with a kick to the left side of Marcus' shield, creating an opening on the right for me to take advantage of. There! I cut in with Orbis, but Marcus countered and caught me on the shoulder before the chariots drew us apart coming into the next turn. I was bleeding and my shoulder felt like it had been stuck with a white hot poker.

Then the final turn was on us. The chariots clustered. We crashed into the Viridians, the intercepting blades protruding from each chariot clashing and

grinding, sparks flying. There was a rasping scream of metal on metal as the vehicles tore at each other, speed and gravity prescribing our course, the Viridians
on the inside, the Tullians on the outside. I didn't want to cut the Golden Wolves'
numbers down any more, but I had to be seen to be attacking. I made a swing at
the gladiator Taticulus Viridius Leticus. He warded it easily, and I followed up,
grabbing the central post of our chariot and sending a kick into his midriff,
hoping to knock him back out of range. The corner was a long arc, and we were
still locked in the curve.

Taticulus' stumble caused him to lose his footing and fall back against the
post of his chariot. I was supposed to step in and follow him up, but suddenly,
in the canal wall behind Taticulus, I saw the Hyperborean bull chief, right there
moving through the solid ice. I froze. Would he come at me? Encircle me in his
arms as he did in my dreams? I heard a yell and turned to see the Dioscurii
leap from the helm of our chariot, Mania stepping up to temporarily seize the
reins. The alien was gone when I looked back.

Castor boarded the Viridian chariot from the starboard side and Pollux
threw himself to the ground, rolling under the Wolves' craft, slipping under
the blades and all with lightning speed, and came up on the other side. Their
long blades flashed on either side of the post, and Taticulus Viridius Leticus was
dead. His throat cut, a half dozen swift puncture wounds to his abdomen. The
brothers were gone, like ghosts, vanishing and then reappearing as they boarded
our chariot and retook the reins, just as we pulled out of the corner. I'd never
seen anything like it—we'd certainly never practiced it aboard *Incitatus*—but I'd
read about it. It was a technique used by the ancient Greeks at their games. *Apoba-
tai*, the feat of leaping off of the chariot and then back on.

Then we were out into the straight, and the finishing archway was ahead at the
end of the canal. Gods, I just couldn't win. Was this the Furies' idea of a joke?
To have me kill everyone except the most deserving? And what was with that
damned ice barbarian? I wished he'd just come at me and be done with it. The
wind howled down the canal and over us. Again, combat had slowed us, and the
final race was now between the White Rams of House Arrian with their upgraded
engines and the light Silver Sparrows of House Flavian.

Then the Flavians proved their worth. Not worth their salt in clashes and
combat, but they had nerves of steel when it came to racing. Titus Flavius Cursor drove his silver chariot forward, matching Cynisca's pace. And then, when
her whip lashed out, the silver ship made a surprising move, ramming the larger
Arrian vessel. The piercing blades of the Arrian chariot drove into the Flavian
craft's side, locking them together. Cynisca whipped in fury, but Septimus
Flavius Stolo, the team leader, urged his men to lock shields and cover the driver.
Genius. He'd cut his power and was building up his energy while cruising on
the Arrians' engine upgrades. They were hurtling ahead of the rest of us, but the
Arrian ship was now burning through its power boost in order to maintain its
speed while pulling the Flavians along with it. And then, a quarter mile from
the finish, we could see the channel's end, opening out into a hilly terrain of

snow and ice. The Flavians pulled starboard, freeing themselves from the White Rams, and released the pent-up energy stored in their engines, rocketing forward. The Arrians charged on, but their upgrades wore thin just out from the finish line, and the Flavians sped through the triumphal arch, winning the day. Winners of the day, the Silver Sparrows were gifted with a shield generator that would protect them from harm for the next leg, giving them a significant advantage.

We camped on a plain of rolling ground, like the undulating waves of a frozen sea with rocks jutting up in clusters like little islands. Like the rocks around last night's camp, these seemed to contain their own light source, glowing softly as the daylight bled away. It was breathtakingly beautiful—even, rolling mounds of blue and white like a perfect sea. It reminded me of the beach on the northeast coast of Nova Australis where I'd been for holidays as a child. The water was always so smooth, so gentle. I wished I could relax like that here and now, but I had to be alert and that wasn't made easy by the onset of ambrosia withdrawal. I was certain now that the buzzing in my head wasn't a side effect of ambrosia or lack of it, it was related to the pin and this world. I felt if I could just get some distance from the pace of the games, I could figure out its secret and use it to find Aulus.

While we prepared for the following day, Ursus and Pullus performed their skit, recapping the crowd's favorite moment of the day in their aerial hologram show. They ran around in a circle and Ursus ran his hands over his body seductively before wielding his flute like a spear. Pullus shrieked and threw his hands in the air, running around and around in circles until he fell over from exhaustion and lay there while Ursus stabbed him with the flute. This was meant to represent Barbata killing Salinator.

*　*　*

PART OF THE PROBLEM with Crassus was that whenever I saw him, I experienced a building sensual arousal, and with it, a justifiable shame. The blood in the arena didn't horrify me or repel me as I had thought it would. I liked it. Despite mourning the death of my countrymen, something about the whole atmosphere was thrilling. Life, sex, death—it was all bound up together here. This was what Marcus was trying to tell me back in Rome after our match. In the artificial confines of the game, we were closer to nature than we ever were in the cities. We hunted each other and were hunted in turn. Survival was based on skills. Death was only a moment away. Everything was hyperreal, sharp, and in focus like an ice sculpture. As well, my sense of smell had taken on a new life. I hated it, loved it. It was pure, and that experience was bound up with my feelings for Gaius Sertorius Crassus.

Inside the Sertorian tent, I was once again put through the interrogation, and Mania asked if I had spotted any more Hyperboreans, or anything else, for that matter, that was not part of the day's scheduled events. I confessed to my momentary sighting of the creature in the ice walls, but that it was more than likely a figment of my imagination, and she made no objection to Crassus taking possession of my share of ambrosia. Tension was building, the air was thick with it, and it was more than the race. The Blood Hawks were also under immense pressure from Aquilinus—they had to perform, had to win him his empire, as much as I had to save those things that mattered most to me. Crassus withheld the phial, though, and walked out, clearly uninterested in my fate. Was he playing games, or had I really burned my bridges? What of the deal to save Aulus and kill Licinus? Was that also in jeopardy?

I chased after him. Julia's words had been on my mind throughout the day. Barbata couldn't be allowed to exert so much influence over Crassus—I had to recapture his attention.

Our shared tent was occupied when I entered. Crassus was talking animatedly with Mania, and I just caught the tail end of a conversation about scanners and deposits. I overheard a word I'd never heard them mention before—"ichor"— before Mania signaled that they were not alone.

"Crassus, I want to apologize for last night. I want to tell you how I feel." I reached out to touch his shoulder, but he turned on me, his face flushed red, swollen like a plum, his eyes bulging.

"You bitch slut. You mangy whore. Do you think I'd touch you with a ten-foot pole?"

He was screaming madly, raging at me, his eyes wild. Crassus always showed such self-control. Taken aback, I didn't even try to stand up to him, just withdrew cautiously from the tent.

I didn't know what had just happened then. It couldn't be ambrosia withdrawal because he'd just had a dose. Crassus seemed to have been struck with the same fit I'd seen pass over Barbata and Mania. Imagine them all like this and running the empire? It was too much to contemplate.

Whatever had happened with Crassus, I knew that I'd messed up. Again he marched across the campsite to Barbata's tent. They screamed as they copulated, like wild animals. Unrestrained, no-holds-barred, just like the tournament itself, and I couldn't help but wonder what it must be like to join with that enraged monster who stormed from my tent. How could she bear it? Could I?

I woke to a gentle prodding, right in the middle of a nightmare about the Hyperborean warrior coming for me, and nearly jumped out of my skin.

"Settle down, it's just me."

Julia. I looked at the bed. No Crassus. He was still with Barbata.

"What are you doing here?" I whispered.

"Come quick. I tried telling you this morning. Last night Licinus and Mania went outside the shield."

"What for?"

"I don't know, but they took with them canisters from a secure locker on the war chariot. When they returned, the canisters were gone, and they carried caskets in their place."

"Caskets? Like we saw in Licinus' quarters?"

"The very same. I think they're smuggling in ambrosia."

"Which means they're running short on supply," I said. "Tell me, have you heard the Sertorians use the word 'ichor'? I walked in on Crassus and Mania and overheard them talking about it. Crassus went crazy when he realized I was there."

"Ichor? No. It sounds familiar, though," she said.

"It's the blood of the gods, in the ancient stories. It is said that ambrosia is the food of the gods; ichor is the stuff that runs through their veins. But what they mean by it I don't know."

"Come on. Let's see what they're up to." She pulled up a peg at the back of the tent and went to sneak out, but I hesitated.

"Come on. I think this is worth the risk," Julia said.

But I couldn't go. What if they caught me? What if they stopped the ambrosia as punishment? What if I ran into my nightmare barbarian out there?

"Is that a real leash they've got on you?" she asked.

"They can track me with the bracelet," I said. "I can't go out there."

"I've already taken care of that," Julia said. "As far as their systems are concerned you're in your tent."

"It's not them," I admitted.

"Not frightened of the ice monsters, are you?" she asked with an edge of scorn to her voice. "I saw you stand up to them just fine on the ship."

"This one's different."

"Sure. All right, then. Let's stay in our nice warm tent and play with dollies."

"Shut up," I said, moving past her under the tent. Julia was pushing my buttons on purpose, but it did the trick and reminded me of how unreasonable my fear was.

She led me out to the edge of the camp behind the tent. The border of the shield dome lay ahead of us in the darkness, glowing a soft purple.

Julia tapped me on the shoulder and pointed to a position on the other side of the shield wall. As we crept forward, the surrounding rocks gave off their eerie glow, casting faint shadows in the night. There were two shapes in the distance. It had to be Licinus and Mania, about twenty feet ahead. They were crouched down, huddled over something.

I didn't see the small hole in the shield wall where Licinus and Mania had escaped the confines of the games, but I heard the wind rushing in through it. Julia pointed to a small box on the ice beside the wall, which generated the field that kept the gap open.

"Serve them right if I kicked the generator over and left them out there," I said.

"Probably not a good idea. The other Hawks probably know they're out there and will come for them if they don't return. Now listen up, I can come with you, but my shield decoder is only strong enough to open the shield wall from this side; it takes more power than I've got to penetrate it from the outside in. If we're both out there and the Sertorians get back first and close the shield, we'll be the ones stuck outside."

"What were you saying before about being a coward?"

"It's not cowardice, it's pragmatism. Which of us will go? One must stay behind to ensure the other's return."

I wanted to show Julia that I was running the show, still in charge, but the idea of going out into the darkness, not only risking being caught by Licinus but also facing the Hyperborean alone, was enough to make me hesitate. I took a deep breath and let the night swallow me. The moment I passed through the shield, the wind hit, whipping to and fro, cutting into my body and all but deafening me. But I had to overcome my fear because out in the darkness, there might well be a hidden storehouse of ambrosia. Ambrosia enough to take on Licinus and the rest of the Sertorians all on my own.

I followed after Licinus and Mania, some crystalline clusters providing cover as I crept around behind them. The rocks seemed dead, devoid of energy; they weren't glowing the way they had the night before. My body started to feel the ambrosia hunger and at the same time, the buzzing was filling up all the space around me, making the air vibrate like a stringed instrument.

As I watched, the Sertorian pair knelt over a cavity in the ground, a sinkhole about five feet across. Mania picked up a small canister and poured some substance out of the barrel into the hole. When she was done, she discarded the canister down the hole and they moved on. Licinus held another one, so I guessed they had more of the same kind of work to do. They were talking, but the howling wind and buzzing song prevented me from catching a word.

They walked off to the south, and as they went, the crystalline outcroppings around them that had glowed with energy began to fade, their light vanishing. I followed on until I reached the spot they'd just abandoned.

Before I had time to investigate, there was movement in the distance and a half dozen Hyperborean warriors emerged from the night like dark rushing waters, heading to strike down the Sertorians. Licinus, in the middle of emptying his canister into what looked like another sinkhole. looked up, completely unconcerned, and then returned to his work. A sudden electrical charge lit the scene for a split second. A black-and-red-armored form with the upper body of a man and spidery metallic legs in place of lower limbs drove a long pitchfork-style weapon into a crystalline barbarian. It was an arachnoraptor. I'd only heard rumors of them from the front lines of the war. They were elite Sertorian soldiers who'd been spared execution after falling in battle and genetically transformed to carry out military espionage and assassination programs. House Sertorian had established its eugenics program to cull those they considered genetically weak from their gene pool, but they didn't eliminate them. They were Sertorian, after all, and the crumbs from their table were still of value—and so they repurposed them. Unable to show them publicly, they genetically modified the men and women, wiped and reprogrammed them to serve behind the scenes, putting their natural cunning, ruthlessness, and fighting ability to covert use. Their upper bodies were recognizably human, but they wore masks with cyborg implants—a telescopic right eye and cone-shaped aural enhancers over their ears. Their lower bodies were set into a black steel cradle, which they shared with an alien life-form that fused to their spinal column. It contained dozens of thin, powerful legs that allowed the hybrid to scuttle along at a rapid pace on any surface at any angle. The aliens lived off the pheromones produced by fear, and so they aided their host in tracking prey, tuning to their human host's nervous system for detection. If the emperor found out that Aquilinus was sending them into his arena, violating the sacred rules of Jupiter's tournament, he'd have him beheaded and thrown off the Tarpein Rock.

If only the threat to Aulus weren't hanging over me. I could end the Blood Hawks' run right here and now.

The crystal body of the Hyperborean warrior vibrated with the electrical charge from the arachnoraptor and then shattered. I could feel it die. Somehow it was connected to the buzzing song I could hear. There was a sudden break or, rather, it was as if a subtle line of music from a symphony, one I hadn't even been aware of, had suddenly vanished, and that I noticed it in its absence.

The Hyperborean warriors were throwing themselves at Mania and Licinus as they poured the substance from the barrel into the sinkhole, dozens of crystal spikes glinting in the faint light of the rocks, and just as many Sertorian shadow warriors rose to drive them back. They had to have at least a contubernium—eight arachnoraptors working together as part of a larger team.

While Mania and Licinus were distracted, I looked down into the sinkhole at my feet. There was a strong, radiant light emitting from the octagonal cells that lined the walls of the small cavern below. A white-and-blue fluid moved through the cells and over the walls. It looked identical to the combination of fluids contained within Hyperborean bodies. Could this be ichor? The blood of the gods? It seemed it might well be, and I decided to consider it as such until I had evidence that led me to formulate another theory. It was like looking at a glittering crown from the top down, only as I watched, the black fluid that the Sertorians had poured down into the hole was moving quickly to smother the light like tendrils of ivy spreading across a wall.

I touched the black liquid with my glove and sniffed it. It was acidic and it wasn't ambrosia, at least not the substance I'd been taking. I scanned it with my armilla, and it registered as being highly toxic and radioactive. I wiped it off in the snow and backed up a few feet.

Whatever Licinus and Mania were up to, the Hyperboreans clearly didn't like them poisoning their land. Julius Gemminus had called it a barbarian uprising, but judging by what I'd seen, they were fighting to protect their lives and their land and the thing that connected both—the ichor.

I turned over the idea that the white-and-blue substance might be a kind of ambrosia, but that didn't make sense. The Sertorians would never intentionally destroy ambrosia; they were in desperate need of it. As the black substance spread over the interior of the sinkhole, the light faded and looked set to vanish entirely.

There was a faint glimmer of light down in the depths of the hole. I picked up a small pebble and dropped it down the well. It fell for some time before it came near the glow, and I didn't hear it strike bottom. The cavern must have been bigger than it looked. Was the canister of black fluid enough to contaminate and swallow all of the shining ichor below?

As the last of the light in the sinkhole faded, the buzzing song diminished too, becoming a peripheral noise, coming from somewhere distant, over where the Hyperboreans were battling. From the bottom of the sinkhole a familiar smell now rose up—ambrosia. In between the flashes of light generated by the arachnoraptors' weapons, I could just make out the the walls of the sinkhole. In place of the substantial amounts of white-and-blue ichor, thin trickles of ambrosia lined the walls, dripping down to the cavern below. I scooped up as much as I could with my glove but didn't have time to climb down and get more or even eat what I had, because more figures emerged from out of the darkness, moving in on my position, forcing me to retreat. Arachnoraptors, but they weren't looking for a fight. Their spidery legs helped them navigate easily down into the hole. They weren't down there for more than a minute before the first surfaced with a casket in hand, the same kind I'd seen in Licinus' quarters aboard *Incitatus*. They were mining ambrosia.

I was about to take them, even though I was unarmed. I had to injure only one and steal a casket, more ambrosia than I could dream of, but Mania and Licinus had driven off the Hyperboreans and were now walking back to camp. There was no time to return through the gap in the shield wall ahead of them, not without being seen. I backed away into the darkness until they passed by my hiding place where I crouched, concealed behind a snowbank. Mania paused, scanning her surroundings, and then both she and Licinus passed through the gap and sealed it behind them. After their efforts at poisoning the surrounding environment, there was plenty of darkness to go around, and scanning the landscape I couldn't see any trace of the arachnoraptors. They worked fast and had already cleared out.

Julia had taken cover, and I knew she must be nearby, but until it was all clear and she could call me, I was on my own. Crouched in the darkness, I had a moment to think over what I'd seen.

The Sertorians weren't poisoning the wells, destroying the ichor; they were transforming it. I'd been witness to a dark alchemy. This was how ambrosia was made, by poisoning the blue-and-white fluid that the Hyperboreans and the land they inhabited had in common. That's what I had seen—the Sertorians desperately creating ambrosia and their arachnoraptors stealing it away, while the Hyperboreans tried to flee with the essential ingredient—the ichor. While Romans played blood sport for empire during the day, the Hyperboreans were fighting their own small-scale war at night. Now it became clear how the uprising was affecting the flow of ambrosia and what a precarious situation Proconsul Aquilinus was in!

I was desperate for ambrosia and about to lick at the residue on my glove when the buzzing song that had been running in the background grew suddenly louder, reminding me that I was outside the shield wall with no light source, alone with Hyperboreans. Angry Hyperboreans. I couldn't see them, but if the sound was any indication, they were moving in on my position. The noise grew to a skull-shattering pinnacle, a deep chord and at the same time the sharpest treble tone. Looking around, I saw a dark silhouette emerging from the rocks. The largest of the barbarian warriors; the Hyperborean from my nightmare. The bull chief was coming for me.

"Accala! Quick!"

I sprinted for the shield wall and Julia waited until the last possible moment before activating her armilla. The purple field flickered, and I threw myself through it. There was a crashing sound behind me, more light and sparks, and I spun about to see the Hyperboreans retreating into the night, the giant warrior already gone.

Julia ran to rejoin the immunes' tent and I climbed back into my tent just as the sound of my teammates' boots came crunching past. The Sertorians chatted for a little and then dispersed. From the snippets of conversation I could pick up, they dismissed the noise for what it was—a final disturbance from the Hyperboreans who'd tried to breach the shield wall. I sat on my bed licking at my glove like a cat lapping up milk, cleaning it of every drop of ambrosia. Then I collapsed back on the bed, enjoying the relief that came as the withdrawal symptoms were washed away. The Hyperboreans were the ones pulling the rug out from under the Sertorians, jeopardizing the supply of ambrosia. That gave me ideas for helping the crystal barbarians in their efforts against the Sertorians. For whatever damage I had to do to my Caninine allies in the daytime, however much my deal to save Aulus bound me to follow the Blood Hawks like an obedient dog, in the darkness, I could fight in this secret war for ambrosia. I could strike back from behind the scenes, and if I managed to secure some of the dark liquid for myself, then all the better. If it weren't for the small quantity I'd scooped out of the sinkhole wall, I'd have been broken, desperate, and willing to do anything Crassus wanted for my next hit. I couldn't allow that to happen; I had to secure my own supply of the drug at the first opportunity. There was one nagging problem that wouldn't go away, though—it seemed irrefutable that my pin was a detector, an antenna as Julia had posited, albeit an intermittent one. A device that located not my missing brother, as my mother had suggested, but rather the alien Hyperboreans and their ichor.

The pin was putting me on a collision course with the bull chief of the Hyperboreans who was out there in the dark, waiting to kill me. And worse, it meant I was reliant upon Gaius Sertorius Crassus because without the pin to point me in the right direction I couldn't think of any other way to find Aulus.

XXIII

EARLY THE NEXT morning, Julia came to me on the pretense of helping me prepare and we tried to make sense of the events of the night before. I explained to her all I'd seen and my conclusion. "So I'm certain that the ichor is the substance that infuses this world, the substance the Sertorians are mining, not ambrosia. Ambrosia is the product the Sertorians create using the ichor," I said. "Ambrosia is contaminated ichor."

"Contaminated is right. The residue you scanned is radioactive as hell. I can't believe it would be part of making anything. If you'd ingested the amount you had on your glove, it might have been enough to kill you."

"What I do know is that if the Hyperboreans are hurting the Sertorians, then I want to help them."

"Stay focused," Julia said. "We need to work out why we're not getting a result from your mother's pin."

"Maybe the problem is the very nature of the pin. Marcus Aurelius says that we must ask of anything what it is in and of itself. Those are the first principles for understanding."

"You say it seems to activate sometimes and not others? And that it seemed to have something to do with being near the Hyperboreans?" Julia asked.

"Yes, but not because of the aliens themselves per se. It's the ichor they carry within their bodies—it's also present in the rocks and ground. The Hyperboreans are leaching it out of the earth and trying to transport it away from the Sertorians. The Blood Hawks are poisoning the earth to transform the ichor into ambrosia and take it for themselves. The problem is that I'm starting to believe that the pin doesn't detect Aulus, despite my mother's claim. The pin, in and of itself, is set to detect the ichor."

"Unless . . ."

"Unless what?" I asked.

"Unless Aulus *is* the ichor the Hyperboreans are carrying."

"That's an erroneous observation. Some might even say a ridiculous thought unworthy of expression."

"I'm just saying . . ."

"Marcus Aurelius doesn't ask us to consider the impossible. He's a pragmatist, whereas you are simply unhelpful."

"All I'm saying it that just maybe," Julia said, "when you've eliminated the possible, if your mother is telling the truth, the impossible might be the answer, huh?"

She was a plebeian; she didn't understand philosophy.

After Julia left I sought out Crassus and calmly requested my share from the night before and he gave it up to me at once without any protest. About the camp the Talonites also seemed less perturbed, and I guessed that the ambrosia Licinus and Mania had collected had boosted their stores and allowed them to be more liberal in dispensing the drug. In terms of his temperament, Crassus seemed to be back to normal. No red face or sudden screaming fit. He was intrigued, though. He'd meant to teach me a lesson, to break me by withholding ambrosia, and there I was calmly requesting my share, as if I could take it or leave it. In private I devoured the ambrosia at once and right away felt a spring in my step.

* * *

AS WE HEADED out on the third day of the chariot rounds, the track took us in a curving arc out along the eastern coast. The ground below us was fragile, layers of glacial ice that had frozen over time until they were hard and brittle, and brilliant like a vast, shining mirror. The forms of our gleaming chariots were reflected back up at us as we sped along. About a mile ahead, the ground suddenly sank into a series of deep valleys that almost looked as if they'd been cut into the ground, like a man-made mine, except they were full of indigenous flora—trees and bushes with leaves of emerald hugged the walls here and there. The largest of the valleys lay right in our path, about fifty feet deep and extending for about a mile. An artificial platform had been set up in the middle of the valley, about the height of the ground we were currently racing over. A ramp sat upon the platform looking out of place. I didn't understand. Even with some kind of launching device, no chariot could cover the half-mile to the pedestal; any to attempt it would plummet into the valley below. Nor there was an obvious place for the track to continue on. The road we were on simply petered out at the edge of the crevasse. To our right, level with us, the choppy white waves of the ocean crashed, sending fingers of foam up onto the frozen beach, droplets of white and green water flying through the air as if to touch us.

As we drove forward, the Caninine Alliance teams rocketed toward us from the northwest. The whole scene was lit from above by a flash of bright red light accompanied by an intense whining sound as the stadium's ion cannon fired from on high. It was so close, the beam struck the ice and a wall of steam rose up before us. In that instant I thought the emperor was done with the games and had decided to wipe us all from the face of the planet, but then the steam began to clear and we were surrounded by the sound of rushing water.

"Watch out, racers! You might get a little wet!" Julius Gemminus squealed with delight, like an overexcited hog, his little wings fluttering excitedly.

Water. Icy water. A wall of it was rushing toward us. As one, the chariots pulled port and moved away from the coast as quickly as we could.

The stadium's ion cannon wasn't targeting us but rather the landscape itself. Some in-play resculpting to keep us on our toes. The editor had destroyed a natural ice barrier, a seawall between the waves and the land, and churning white and blue waves were rushing over the land like a stampede of wild horses set to trample us underfoot. I watched from the rear of the chariot as the wall of water surged toward us.

Our chariot pulled north and started racing around the edge of the valley. The Dioscurii were the most experienced drivers on one of the fastest vehicles and they'd decided our best chance for survival lay in outpacing the water long enough for it to fill the valley and lose its deadly forward impetus.

The chariots of both factions followed suit and managed to stay ahead of the deadly torrent except for the Tullians, who straggled behind. Their chariot was so heavy they couldn't escape the water wall in time. It passed over them, and I was hopeful that the entire chariot would be lost, but then the water diverted suddenly; it had found the valley. A moment later, the Tullians burst clear, though they almost lost the steel-gloved Potitus Tullius Silo, his heavy spiked gloves grasping the central pole of the chariot to prevent the waves from sending him to his death far below. The valley was transformed into a great waterfall as the white waters rushed to fill it. The summa rudis, our robotic referee, sped back and forth before us signaling that we must hold, no fighting until it gave the green light. Within minutes the valley was filled, forming a choppy lake, and the rushing waters threatened to spill over its brim and flood the level land. Trees and large bushes ripped from the valley walls by the force of the waterfall bobbed about in the waves. Then the signal came and the referee withdrew. Before anyone could contemplate violence, a long shield wall began to move toward us on our flank, so fast that we were forced to head for the lake itself.

Again, the Dioscurii took the lead and the others followed. We hit the lake hard and fast, waves crashing over the bow, sending a spray of icy water into the air. The chariots worked as boats, the skirmishers acting as floats to help stabilize them in the water. Gods, but it was cold, each droplet like a little dagger of ice when it hit uncovered skin. Based on the depth of the valley and the volume charging in from the bay, the water must have been at least thirty feet deep, more than enough to drown in, and the cold guaranteed death to anyone who fell beneath the churning waves. The purple-hued screen of shield walls surrounded the lake—generated by strings of joined pontoons—with the exception of one gap at the opposite end. That was the continuation of the track westward toward the foothills of the great Olympian peaks. An archway on land near the edge of the lake marked the finish of today's round. Julius Gemminus had turned this leg of the chariot race into a naumachia, an artificial naval battle, with the chariots playing the parts of ancient triremes.

The artificial platform in the middle of the valley was now an island, with only one launching ramp leading off it. The chariots rammed one another as we vied to be the first to launch right over the lake and win the round.

I used Orbis to hack and slash as we crashed into the Flavians and Viridians. The Silver Sparrows pulled away, unconcerned. Their temporary shield module warded off blows from all sides, and they zipped ahead over the water, taking the lead.

Great sluglike creatures with long white horns atop their heads suddenly appeared, breaking through the surface of the water. I recognized them as being native to Olympus Decimus—the first settlers had named them *spectrum monoceros* due to their single horns and ability to change color to communicate. The writhing motion of their bodies propelled them through the water like eels. Their horns were near unbreakable, and they were dangerous territorial pack hunters.

They'd been dragged here from their ocean environment, disturbed, seconded for our amusement, and they were not happy about it.

The creatures came in fast, attacking the Flavians first, slowing them, before the remaining chariots caught up. Barely visible under the water until they were right before us, the creatures reared up into the air like snakes and attacked with sharp horns before disappearing again. All the teams became focused on defending against the monster water slugs, distracted from their goal of reaching the platform. The creatures were fast, but their great white backs, splotched with gray, breached the surface for a split second before they reared up and attacked. Once I saw the pattern, predicting their strikes was easy—the next was going to appear about ten feet off the Ovidian bow. I said nothing, offered no warning. I caught Marcus' eye in passing, though, and, without thinking, flashed mine quickly toward the spot where the monster would come. It was only for a split second, and I was certain no Sertorian saw, but it was enough. He caught on. We were used to passing fast signals, Marcus and I, and although he was suspicious of me, he was never one to pass up an opportunity. He had a split second to choose to trust me or not, and he chose right. That meant something, didn't it? It had to.

He signaled his driver to push starboard, nudging the Amber Boars' craft right over the top of the monster as it reared up. The creature pierced the base of the Ovidian chariot with its horn, sending it rocking violently to one side. Publius Ovidius Bibaculus, the team leader, was lost. With his heavy armor and goring tusks built into his helmet, he staggered and tumbled into the waters below. He squealed and grunted, trying to free himself as his heavy armor dragged him under the clashing waves, and the horned slug creatures moved to pierce his body before he vanished beneath the white water. Now the Fates struck again. The collision of the Ravens with the Boars saw the Ravens cripple their enemy but sent the Calpurnian chariot careening about and colliding with the Flavians as they made their dash forward. A slight nudge, but it was enough to send them into the long ramp at a slight angle, and they flew off the edge and landed on their side in the water. Their charioteer managed to right the craft, but they were going to have to make a big arc to come about again for another shot at the ramp.

Now was our chance. The Calpurnians and Ovidians aside, we could take the island.

I yelled out, but the Dioscurii were already on it. They drove up onto land for only a second before we reached the launching ramp. Our chariot was catapulted along its length and into the air, and we were flying. The other chariots fell away beneath us. Another twenty seconds and we hit the ice on the other side of the lake, powering ahead as we passed through the victory arch and won the day.

I felt a shameful satisfaction, but it was hard not to respond to the sky filled with thumbs and symbols of approval. The face of Julius Gemminus beamed, as he promised us an electromagnetic pulse generator that would fire once only and cause an enemy engine to seize up.

That night in the camp, spirits were high among the Sertorians. We'd won a leg at last, and the talk was of using the weapon's one charge on the Calpurnians, to disable their entire chariot at a crucial moment so as to ensure the destruction of every gladiator aboard. I wasn't sure how I felt about Marcus. He'd certainly made every effort to kill me, and even though he'd instinctively followed my lead, I couldn't allow myself to be distracted by old loyalties in this new world where all the rules were turned upside down.

Crassus might have returned to normal, but he still seemed uninterested in me. That suited me for tonight—I had other fish to fry—but I still needed my ambrosia. He went to leave the tent for the night and stopped only when he heard me moan at the thought of the ambrosia leaving with him. My skin had turned a yellow hue after the day's hard fighting and I needed the ambrosia more than ever. He threw it casually on the ground and then left me to scrabble forward on my hands and knees, gathering it up, desperately pulling the stopper from the phial, draining the tiny container, sopping up the remaining drips with the tip of my yellow-skinned pinkie.

My plan was to alert Julia and escape again, to try to secure some of the ambrosia and aid the Hyperboreans. I'd borrow Julia's armilla to escape the shield wall, but when night fell, Castor and Pollux Corvinus were keeping a close eye on me. The activity of the night before hadn't gone unnoticed, and the Sertorians were suspicious and doubly cautious. I wouldn't get another chance to leave the camp while Mania and Licinus carried out their ambrosia mining expedition. Even Julia was unable to attend me, having been set extra maintenance duties on the chariots. I watched her from the front of my tent having a long conversation with Crassus. What did they have to talk about? And for so long? I went to bed frustrated and alone.

* * *

THE SECOND TO LAST day of the chariot races began with our faction funneled into a narrow canyon. The terrain here had clearly been sculpted by Julius Gemminus' ion cannon, the edges of the canyon now shiny and regular. We fell into single file, the Sertorian chariot in the lead, and rode fast. There was no sign of the Caninines. We were being kept apart to avoid clashes while we transited between the official rounds, and they were presumably traveling along a similar course. At midmorning the canyon arced down to a low plateau with small lakes spread out across it and distant walls of green, glassy rock bordering its edges. We fanned out and headed for the other side of the plateau, where it narrowed again into a channel with high rock walls. When the Caninines did appear, it was to our port side at a distance of about a mile.

Before we could meet and clash, Julius Gemminus appeared above us.

"This shall be the last challenge of the chariot round based on the ancient stories. Tomorrow's final race will be an uninterrupted contest of pure speed. Welcome to The Passage of Scylla and Charybdis. The sea god Glaucus fell in love with the beautiful Scylla, but she was repulsed by his fishy tail and fled to land where he could not follow. When he went to Circe to ask for a love potion, the sorceress herself fell in love with him and instead prepared a vial of poison, pouring it into a pool where her rival bathed, transforming Scylla into a thing of terror. Charybdis, a daughter of Poseidon and Gaia, was extremely gluttonous. To satisfy her appetites, she stole cattle from the hero Hercules, and an enraged Jupiter transformed her into a monster. The two monsters, immortal and irresistible, beset a narrow channel of water traversed by ancient heroes, destroying their ships and devouring the crews."

The emperor seemed to be selecting stories from Ovid that he could use to remind Proconsul Aquilinus of his place. He was mounting his own propaganda campaign to counter that of the so-called New Gods. Scylla was supposed to represent Aquilinus and his genetic supremacy. In finding all others repulsive, he had become the monster, in which case Charybdis represented that monster's greed in seeking to devour the empire. Perhaps, though, the emperor meant me. I was Scylla and Crassus was Glaucus, and his quest to make me love him had ultimately transformed me into something so terrible that no other would love me, a monster with an appetite for blood and ambrosia.

Julius Gemminus offered another great prize. The winner would receive an engine boost that would allow a single chariot to run at maximum capacity for twice as long as usual without the engines suffering harm—a huge boon for tomorrow's final race.

Instantly, we picked up the pace, and the Caninines also sped forward, anxious to take the lead before there was no opportunity to pass. Their chariots showed signs of wear and the contestants themselves looked tired and grim but the announcement of the prize spurred us on, and the seven chariots all surged ahead even before the editor had finished his spiel. As the plateau narrowed into the channel, a lake at the left side transformed into a spinning whirlpool of white water, clouds of vapor rising up from its surface, a stout granite island twenty yards across, unmoving at its center. The fumes that it emitted burned my eyes and nostrils—not a place for a leisurely swim. The channel was partly blocked, but thankfully there was still plenty of unobstructed space between the pool and the opposite wall, allowing safe passage. Assuming, that is, that the enemy teams didn't butt and ram us into the deadly water. We had the advantage in that department, though. We were hugging the channel wall, so the Caninines were going to have to push in front of us to pass or be driven into the deadly waters. I was less worried about the encroaching Viridians, the team closest to us, and more concerned by the lack of a threat. If the whirlpool was meant to be Charybdis, where then was Scylla?

In answer, the ice on the other side of the channel, opposite the pool, cracked and suddenly burst open. Six great eyeless heads on tall stalk necks reared up high from below the ice near the channel wall, and we had to swerve to the middle to avoid going under.

The White Rams nearly lost their chariot. Four team members managed to escape by piling onto their two desultore skirmishers, the weighed-down speeders escaping just in the nick of time. The vehicle teetered briefly, then the skilled charioteers pulled the chariot away from the monster. Their best fighter went down, though: the plebeian league gladiator Faustus Arrius Cornicen, who fought with Phrygian rams' horns and used to crown every triumph by sounding his regimental bugle. Into the acid waters he went, screaming until the last.

All the monsters' heads split open like Venus fly-traps, revealing dozens of rows of thin, sharp teeth. The teeth were numerous and short, better suited to gripping than piercing armor and killing gladiators; but that didn't stop them from menacing us as the heads roamed everywhere, attacking both teams. There was no way past without risking the monsters' teeth on one side or the acid whirlpool on the other.

The Corvinus brothers tried to drive forward, and the Ovidian chariot came up alongside us, but three of the heads dropped to form a barrier, barring the way ahead, while the remaining three continued attacking the teams from above. Before the chariots could turn away, one of the heads shot out and ripped an arm off the Ovidian trainer Spurius Ovidius Ahala, devouring the limb and the net with it.

The Flavians were darting around, looking for a chance to run, when Licinus ordered Castor to use the single charge of the electromagnetic pulse generator we'd won the day before. It hit the Flavians and their chariot's engine temporarily cut out, leaving them unable to maneuver before the beast. Their gladiator, Achilius, wasn't fast enough to escape the attacking heads, and his screams filled the air as the gripping teeth sunk in and then flung his body into the acid whirlpool.

Marcus broke away on a skirmisher, lightening his chariot while he sped along the front of the three heads, ramming them side on as he passed. His distraction worked, allowing the main body of his chariot to speed past and out of the channel. Marcus didn't get clear, though—tendrils broke free from the stem neck belonging to the final head and ripped him from his speeder.

Our team wasn't faring much better. Each time we used our weapons to ward away the snapping teeth, the heads closed in and butted our chariot, pushing us into enemy craft and driving us all toward the acid whirlpool.

"Accala!" Licinus barked. "Engage! Throw your discus."

I hung back, though. I needed to think things through; there was something missing. I didn't know this kind of alien creature, but its six heads had no eyes. First principles led to deep understanding. So how did it see us? Did it possess sensory organs that might be vulnerable to attack? What was it, in and of itself? As I studied its form, it occurred to me that the stalks the heads rested on were more like extensions of a greater body than a body in and of itself. Was the body protected beneath the ice, or somewhere else? Perhaps camouflaged to protect a weakness? The rock at the center of the whirlpool. There were no igneous rocks on this world. This was a creature imported especially for the tournament, like the Centaurii.

"Accala! Engage!" Licinus yelled.

I cast Orbis back toward the whirlpool, away from the threat before us. He hit the rock and ricocheted off the channel wall on his return path. Hundreds of small eyes suddenly burst open like flowers all over the surface of the rock and the tendrils reared up as if in pain, dropping Marcus to the ice. The noise was tremendous, a shriek of pain and rage. The opportunistic Flavians, their engine recovered, darted through the gap and escaped. Marcus remounted his skirmisher.

"The rock!" I yelled. "All teams, all Romans must attack the rock if we want to escape!"

Licinus didn't seem happy about that, but he ordered Castor to pull the chariot around, and we drove toward the pool. The one-armed charioteer responded at once, his expression one of total concentration, his spiked hair laced with sweat. Now all six heads came at us, trying to drive us into the deadly waters. I threw Orbis again, and this time he was joined by Darius' arrows, Pavo's darts, and needle arrows from Mania's bow staff. The combined effort created another gap, and the Ovidian chariot was able to escape. We were too close to the whirlpool, though, and the remaining heads butted our craft into the water. The current took us quickly, spinning us about. The chariot could float, but not for long. The acid fumes were burning my eyes, and I could only imagine they were eating away at our vehicle. Castor was trying to pull us out of it, but that was a mistake. We needed to keep up our assault. If the stalked heads were tentacles and the rock was the head, then this whirlpool must be some kind of digestive system for trapping and breaking down the prey it captured.

"More speed!" I yelled at Castor. "Ride the current as fast as you can!"

"I give the orders on this chariot!" Licinus flashed me a furious look but then nodded to Castor to proceed.

We needed to get closer to the center to strike before the current pulled us under.

"The rock!" I screamed. "Give it all you've got!"

As we drew close, Crassus' javelin struck out at the eyes again and again, and I used Orbis as a blade weapon, cutting in rapid arcs, and then the stalked heads were over us, knocking us away, sending us flying out of the pool and skittering across the ice until we were clear.

We did it! We were through and out into the hilly ground ahead.

Behind us, the creature withdrew into the water to lick its wounds, leaving only the swirling pool.

I was without energy, and as before, that brought on the buzzing headache. I could confirm without doubt my uncle's theory about ambrosia use's diminishing returns. The small amount the Sertorians were rationing me was having less and less effect, and I was so tired I could have keeled over and gone to sleep right there on the ice. The buzzing in my head was no longer an irritation, it sounded more like the morning traffic rush in Rome. At the back of my neck I could feel the pin starting to generate heat. What was going on?

Ahead of us came a sudden cry, and I snapped my eyes open, forcing myself to wake up. What was wrong now?

The chariots that had already made it through the passage were pulling up, which was surprising. I thought they'd be surging ahead toward the end. And then I realized that we were surrounded. On the high ground to our left and right were crystalline Hyperboreans. Tall warriors, spines shining, long war staves made of crystal spikes in their hands. Vacant alien expressions stared down at us. There was silence but for the buzzing song. It was so loud I couldn't believe no one else could hear it. From all around, they swarmed out of the ice, the rocks—they came from everywhere until there must have been a thousand.

This was the alien uprising, right here and now, and there was my boy, right up in front standing ten feet tall. My nightmare. Their barbarian Spartacus fighting for his people and their ichor.

They'd brought the fight to us, shining liquid ichor flowing through their bodies, like quicksilver in the sunlight. Their ability to create their own tunnels must have made it easy for them to slip in beneath the energy fields that demarcated the arena zone.

We were exhausted after surviving Julius Gemminus' monster. Hands shaking, eyes stinging as they struggled to focus. The backs of my hands took on a yellowish hue. Ambrosia withdrawal. The barbarians had chosen their moment perfectly.

XXIV

THE CHARIOTS WERE PULLING up, no one volunteering to charge into the small army of Hyperboreans. This was not part of the games, and there was no point risking losses without gaining any advantage in the tournament. I looked up to the sky, searching for Julius Gemminus. No sign. They were deliberating on what to do. The emperor needed only to wave his hand, and the massive ion cannon beneath the orbital stadium would rain down hell on the Hyperboreans. They'd be melted back into the ice they came from in a matter of seconds. Ah, now Julius Gemminus came. "Well, isn't this exciting? We've asked the audience if they want to go with this and start the bestiarii round a little early, before the essedarii round has officially finished—what fun! Hold tight for the answer!"

There were now thousands of them, swarming toward us. All warriors, none of the pencil-thin workers I'd seen transporting ichor. These monsters were here to keep us from taking their precious elixir. Crystal spears and ice-pick arms sliced through the air. We couldn't take them all. Was Julius Gemminus really going to let the barbarians end the games here? But then the ion cannon from the Rota Fortuna arced down and carved a canyon between us and the majority of the Hyperborean forces. A loud screech sounded as ice and energy beam met, throwing up walls of water and mist. Segregated to either side of the newly created canyon, the ion cannon proceeded to vaporize the Hyperborean forces, leaving the odds at approximately three to one against. Romans, being innately superior, were expected to rise to the challenge and overcome adversity.

"The audience gave the thumbs-up," Julius Gemminus announced. "The people want to see how this turns out. Survivors will return to the normal schedule to complete the chariot races, but for now we're going to count this as the first round of the beast hunt." A trumpet blared. The armilla on each person's wrist chimed and would log the number of kills made while we put down the uprising. As the barbarians charged toward us, Gemminus explained that a worker Hyperborean was worth ten points; a warrior, twenty; the bull chief himself, the alien from my dreams and the leader of this uprising, had been allotted five hundred points. Whichever team brought him down was almost guaranteed to win the bestiarius.

"And here's the added incentive. Since we're fighting a war in miniature, there must be some real-world stakes. The side with the winning count will receive a thousand times that number of barbarian slaves from the losers."

Gods. If the winners killed a hundred Hyperboreans, the losing faction would have to cough up a hundred thousand slaves.

"Bag as many as you can in the first few minutes," Licinus barked.

Our chariots surged forward to meet the barbarians.

"The emperor has blessed you with his intervention, but now you're on your own down there. Good luck!" Julius Gemminus cheerfully exclaimed.

I'd have loved nothing more than to switch sides and help the Viridians, leaving the Sertorians to be massacred at the hands of the barbarians they'd wronged. How poetic that would be. But I couldn't blow my mission. For now, the Sertorians must live until I had my brother. And that meant that these aliens, however righteous their cause in defending their world, must die.

The Hyperboreans moved in, undeterred by the ion cannon attack. The lines between arena game and all-out warfare were about to be blurred for the entertainment of the mob. Furthermore, with the disorder among the different teams and factions as contradictory orders from different leaders were screamed, we were about to throw ourselves at our enemy like a pack of wild barbarians, disorderly and without strategy, while the Hyperboreans, not Romans by any stretch, came at us at a disciplined pace in orderly lines. They were calculating, not driven by passions and fears like creatures with blood and organs. Their nightmare chief ran up front, leading the advance. We needed to mobilize in an orderly fashion, or the games would end, every contestant dead at alien hands.

But I had momentum. It was I who led the fight against Scylla and Charybdis. It was up to me to make them remember that they were something more than contestants, more than warring houses; they were, above all else, Romans, and seven millennia of cooperative warfare, more than any spurious claims of genetic superiority, really were in our blood and bones. They just had to be reminded of that fact.

Licinus barked orders at me as I mounted a desultore skirmisher, but I ignored him and broke away, pulling across the chariots of my fellow Romans, allies and enemies alike. Adrenaline overrode the withdrawal symptoms that had debilitated me only moments before.

"To me!" I cried, swinging the skirmisher around and charging forward. Ambrosia or not, we were outnumbered and we had to attack as a unified, disciplined force or we were doomed. Gods, let this work.

Then the Hyperboreans charged. Like a swarm of killer ants, a fast, silent wave of shining spikes moved toward us. I launched Orbis in a wide arc. Even Piso the Arrian pila caster couldn't hit a target at this distance, but I could. A dark pride filled my chest as the head of one of the warriors racing at the front of the barbarian line hit the icy ground. My armilla chimed happily. Twenty points. The first kill of the day was mine. "Damn you! Come together. Unite. Flying wedge formation! Flavians! Arrian skirmishers! You have the speed. Move around behind them. Attack from the rear while we drive ahead."

The teams looked to their leaders, then (perhaps because I was my father's daughter and leadership was in my blood) began to move into formation, with my skirmisher taking point. I was riding a wave of energy that carried us forward as one. Each chariot sounded its hunting horn in anticipation.

"Javelins!" I commanded, and in a second, the long throwing spears flew through the air, a rain of dozens of electrified spears that struck without mercy. The advancing enemy line began to break apart. Another ten yards and the mid-range weapons flew: the crossbow bolts from Pavo, Mania's darts, Darius' arrows.

There were gaps between the chariots for the enemy to fall into, the blades emerging from the underside of each vehicle would be there to catch them and break them to shards. We were literally going to mow them down.

The barbarians were already losing cohesion by the time they reached us. We pushed back against their advance, the curved noses of the crafts driving the aliens to either side to be cut down by the chariot blades. Other Hyperboreans passed over the tops of the bonnets to challenge gladiators and bestiarii one-on-one.

The retarius Murena Arrius fell first, icy spikes piercing his belly and spilling his guts as the Arrian driver Piso swung his chariot about to avoid his own death. Next was Bestia Ovidius, whose crossbow bolts ricocheted off the thick crystal bodies without effect. He was about to try to jump clear of his chariot when great Hyperborean arms encircled him and pulled him into their chest spines, impaling him like some ancient torture device before sending his sprawling body to the hard ground.

Through the X-ray scanners in my helmet, I saw faint blue lines across many of the barbarians' bodies, the weaknesses in the crystal structure that Mania prepared us for, and I struck accordingly, my armilla chiming as I advanced. No holding back, no pity. I was like a bird of prey, delivering death in wheeling arcs. Whatever white-blue ichor ran through their veins painted the icy ground, mixing with human blood, colored gases rising from their bodies to form clouds above the battlefield. Crassus worked the opposite side of the chariot, riding the other Sertorian skirmisher. I caught a glimpse of him as he backed up—elated, a broad grin upon his face as he put his javelin to work, showing off his skills to his adoring public. One summer I visited my aunt on her farm in Toscana. They had a harvester—great blades of light and energy that cut the wheat neatly so that it fell and could be gathered and bundled into sheaves. That was what this was like. Our blades swung and bodies fell just as easily, though not nearly as neatly. The Blood Hawks moved in unison, the perfection of Licinus' vision—an alien meat grinder.

Crassus moved beside me, his face determined, his armilla chiming loudly. He was going for it: He wanted to break the record for the largest number of kills on a single day.

Then the Flavians and Arrians attacked from the rear, just as I ordered, and the wedge split into an arc so that the alien force was caught between our advance and the chariots blocking off their retreat. Then the cooperation ended. It was clear Rome was the dominant force, survival was assured, now it was all about points. The Caninine and Talonite teams were like two packs of dogs fighting over a carcass, like sharks circling and tearing at shipwreck victims. There was also nothing stopping us from killing one another. Two brave Calpurnians fell in the frenzy—Licinus' war chain squeezed the life from Cincinnatus, the chariot driver, crushing his ribs and racing heart like a hungry snake, and then Catullus, the lasso-wielding hunter, fell to Mania's needle daggers, extensions of her small fingers, plunging into his body again and again, sending him down to the bloody snow. Marcus cried out in rage over the fast deaths and slaughtered the nearest Talonite—the Ovidian beast master Ocella—with a parry and fast thrust to the throat near the collarbone. The man fell, his hands scrabbling to his neck, futilely trying to stanch the spurting blood.

My luck was holding out; Fortune finally seemed to smile upon me. The aliens seemed to be avoiding me, making my attacks seem all the more spectacular. My armilla was chiming. Chiming with each kill, allotting me points for my team's tally. At the rate I was going, I was certain I'd top even Crassus' score.

My blood was pounding in my ears, my heartbeat and the killing chime provided the tempo of my dance. I wanted to hear that chime sound again and again. I couldn't even feel the cold anymore, only the staccato rhythm—pulse-kill, chime-kill, pulse-kill. I saw Marcus, his body drenched in blue blood as he killed with machine-like efficiency. Crassus rode beside me. The grin on his face was wide and strong, his armilla chiming loudly. He was going for it; he wanted to try and beat my count. We became like hawks competing for prey. I lost sense of time and place, as if I were outside myself, watching events unfold.

The others had circled the remaining fifty or so Hyperboreans and moved in.

"Carry on," I heard Julius Gemminus squeal above the fighting. "You're going so well!"

His shrill voice reminded me that this was no beautiful symphony, no graceful dance. This was a massacre.

Suddenly the bull chief was before me, reaching out to try to rip me from the skirmisher. But then Crassus' lance was sticking out of his chest. The alien swung backward and caught Crassus with a powerful blow, knocking him to the ground. Then the giant Hyperborean warrior broke and ran away. Crassus was still struggling to reclaim his vehicle and the rest of the contestants were finishing the remaining barbarians. I was the only one with a clear line of pursuit and immediately gave chase.

He'd abandoned his people. Did these barbarians even understand concepts like honor and cowardice? In the light of day, as he fled the melee, I felt no fear of this alien. Nor did I care an iota for Sertorian glory or points in the bestiarius round, but my blood was up, Orbis was singing, and the buzzing song was irritating me. I was filled with red rage and cutting strength. I hit the throttle and drove toward him, full speed ahead. This was the time to bury my nightmares, all of them, human and alien.

The barbarian sped across the foothills at incredible speed on his long legs, but he couldn't outpace a skirmisher. Just as I was closing the gap, a sudden icy gale came out of nowhere and threatened to tear me off the vehicle. The blast of wind was so powerful it knocked me off course, and by the time I'd got back on, the bull chief was vanishing behind a low rise.

The snow whipped about me as I sped after my prey—shining, crystalline specks that gave everything a dreamlike quality.

As I came over the rise I realized the chief and I weren't alone. Below, in a bowl-shaped valley were thousands of Hyperborean workers, trailing like ants up steep paths in the direction of the mountain range beyond. Their abdomens, filled with pure liquid ichor, glowed in the low light. Upon a ridge on my side of the valley stood what appeared to be a barbarian child, similar to the workers but smaller and missing the two ice-pick-style appendages the others bore. Like a conductor leading an orchestra, the child moved his arms back and forth, directing the Hyperboreans, moving them to join this or that trail. There was a song the workers were following, similar to the buzzing headaches I'd endured, only it was clearer, made more sense, almost like I could make out the words and melody if I listened carefully.

The child suddenly pointed right at me. The bull chief turned at once and started toward me. The child was the leader, their Spartacus, not the bull chief. We had it all wrong. The warriors we were caught up fighting weren't there to take revenge or rise up against us. This little Spartacus had sent some of his troops as a distraction so we wouldn't stumble across the important thing—his production to shift ichor out of this part of the continent. They were smuggling it out right under our noses. The pair of them were coming at me now, but the bull chief was much closer. They couldn't allow me to survive and let my people know what was going on here. The bull chief was closing ground fast; if I tried to turn the skirmisher, he'd be on my back before I'd have the chance to pull away, so I did the unexpected, I drove the vehicle right into him and ran him over. Then the entire skirmisher was being upturned and I was flying through the air. I hit the snowy ground and rolled to blunt the jarring impact of the rock below, coming up into a low crouch, discus in hand.

"Gods . . ." A whisper was all I could manage as the bull chief towered over me, the spines extending from his arm leveled at my head. Behind him, the planet's distant golden sun surrounded the alien with an intense halo. The light hurt my eyes; they wanted to blink, to turn from it, but I was mesmerized by the crystal surface of its torso. The sunlight lit up the swirling ichor within him, beautiful and at the same time a terrible, monstrous violence saturated every facet of his form. I was determined to be brave, the other barbarians scared me not at all, but this one was like a Sword of Damocles hanging over my head, always there in the background, seeking me out, relentless in his pursuit until I was dead and drained of ambrosia. I skittered backward, trying to get my feet under me, coming up into a defensive stance just as his claws flashed forward like lightning. I pushed up with Orbis warding the blow, but the counterforce of discus and claw propelled me back awkwardly. I hit the ground ass first, legs splayed out before me. I rolled to the side, avoiding another thrust, and came up to one knee. The bull chief was fast, and his arms just kept on coming. There was no time to get to my feet; he was reaching for me again. Just like in the dream, he wanted to draw the ambrosia from my body, weaken me and then slaughter me. I threw my head back to avoid having my throat slit by the serrated edge of an ice-pick arm. The edge caught my cheek instead, opening a thin cut. It wasn't deep, but the cold made it sting like hell.

He drove me back toward a low ridge of upthrust rocks. Here was a more cunning opponent than expected—the only other way out was past him or the cliff edge to my right that ran down to the valley below. He was going to use the terrain to help finish me off.

Before the chieftain could press the attack, I pushed forward with Orbis, driving along the ice-pick arm that tried to catch me, and then shot up at the last moment, aiming for his throat. Crystal shards exploded into the air around me. Orbis impacted as if against solid ice, and a shock ran up my arm, numbing it. I had been certain I'd delivered a killing blow, but the crystalline surface was far more resilient than I'd expected, and now I was in close with nowhere to go as his four arms wrapped about me, pulling me in to the spines on his chest. Unlike the nightmare, there would be no escape. The spines entered my body, pushing right through the armor plate. Those arms were like stone, unyielding and powerful. I writhed in agony every which way, trying to escape, but without success. Then the ambrosia started flowing from my body, sapped out of my pores, running to those spines that pierced and held me.

Without the ambrosia, I'd be as good as dead in the games. In a last-ditch effort, I swung Orbis up with my remaining strength, striking at the undersides of the spines on his torso. I felt the points torn from my body as they splintered, and although it made no noise, I felt the buzzing song in my skull turn into something like a static-filled scream.

I fell to the ground and started to scuttle backward. I was frightened and disoriented, and needed to find my way to the skirmisher, but I didn't realize I was on the edge of a crevasse, not until I was free-falling through space. There was a dull, whole-body thud and then only darkness.

I came to with a blinding headache. A circle of dim sky above. My first thought was that I'd fallen into a crevasse but it contained no familiar icy formations. The walls were formed by large octagonal cells stacked together, shining ichor swimming within their transparent structure. This was a Hyperborean well similar to the one I'd seen when I crept out to spy on Licinus and Mania, though much bigger, a domed interior on a scale to match the larger ancient temples in Rome. Rising slowly and painfully, I examined my body. No bruises or breaks, no wounds from the battle with the bull chief. He'd stolen some ambrosia, but there must have been enough left to heal me. My surroundings were shrouded in shadow, so I activated the torch on my armilla to help push back the darkness. I'd only been down there for an hour or so, no time at all. I could still catch up to the gladiators if I acted quickly. There was what appeared to be a tunnel entrance at the far side of the cavern, but I didn't want to take unnecessary chances. There might be more barbarians down there, and if they didn't know I was here in their hives then I'd just as soon keep it that way. The best way to the surface was up. Some veins of granite with rocky protrusions might have served as handholds but it seemed my best bet was to use the hexagonal hive cells as a kind of ladder. Orbis had fallen only a few feet away and I picked him up and used him to tap and then strike at the ichor cells to see if I could gather samples of the substance, but the surface was hard, impenetrable, the fluid trapped securely within. I scanned a shining ichor cell with my armilla and it told me it was a crystalline-diamond composite material more than three million years old.

There was a repetitive dripping sound, multiple droplets hitting hard ground. Using the torch to scan my body, I saw black liquid running in rivulets down my arms and onto the icy ground of the well. Checking my reflection in the shiny cells of the hive I saw the substance running from the corners of my eyes, from my nose and mouth. However much ambrosia was left was now being leached from my body. But how? There wasn't time to hypothesize—with a sudden shortage of ambrosia, the withdrawal symptoms hit hard. A dizzy spell struck and I found myself on the ground, looking up at the round entrance to the cavern, out at the sky above. Then the pain started: tendons pulled tight, muscles locked, a needle lancing each pore in my skin. It was like a band of musicians had transformed my body into an instrument and were proceeding to pull and pluck, pound and stretch it to make their music. Then came the feeling of something clawing away inside my skull, through the middle of my bones. The body could do a lot with ambrosia, but it didn't deal well with the substance's sudden absence.

Somehow my mother's pin found its way into my hand and it grew hotter and hotter. I'd have dropped it in an instant if I could only make my fingers work and open my hand. The heat built, spreading to my body, burning me from the outside in. The buzzing sound increased in volume to the pin's heat, vibrating through my body until it felt like I was the queen at the heart of a beehive. If there was any ambrosia left in me, it was gone after that.

The pain gradually abated, and by the time it faded to a tolerable level, it was late afternoon, the light above fading to a brilliant gold and violet sunset. All I could do was lie there, shaking and numb, watching the golden light. Then, for the first time, without any distractions, completely exhausted and hollowed out, I could properly hear the buzzing sound that had bothered me since my departure from Rome. No buzz at all really, more like a song, a signal so densely packed with data that I'd been unable to receive and unpack it before now. I'd headed down the wrong track thinking the pin was actually leading me to the ichor. It was more like the ichor was powering the connection. At the other end of the line, like two children talking into tin cans connected by string, was Aulus. It was just a sense of him, a feeling of his presence, but it was so strong, and more, it was directional. Gods! The pin wasn't a compass; it was meant to turn me into a compass, and all the ambrosia I'd been consuming had been disrupting the relationship between antenna and signal, blocking it, numbing me so I couldn't hear the message. Julia was spot on. The heat generated by the pin was a sign the signal was blocked; unable to connect with me due to my consumption of ambrosia, the energy had to be released somewhere. Still, that didn't explain why the ichor had such a strong effect on the signal, causing a localized buzzing when I was near it. In the end I decided it was a kind of static, a powerful energy disrupting the signal, only in a different way than the ambrosia. The ichor disrupted and the ambrosia dampened and insulated. No wonder I'd been having so many problems—but no more.

I sat up slowly, scanned the ground around me with my torch. The ambrosia that had fallen from my body was gone. Despite the painful process I'd just endured, I felt surprisingly good, better than I had in a long while. My head was clear, my thoughts sharp. Not quite back to my old self, but a good way along the road.

So, what to do next? I was out here alone and if the tournament officials had sent anyone or anything to find me, so far they hadn't had much luck. Was I truly free of the games? All I'd have to do was climb out of the well and follow the pull of the pin right to my brother. I felt like a caged bird suddenly released. This was like a gift from the gods, all my petitions answered at once.

My body ached from the muscle seizures and, needing to conserve my energy, I judged it better to find a path back up to the surface rather than climb. Shining my armilla's torch, I found the tunnel entrance I'd spied before and decided to explore. It ran for a few hundred yards and led into another cavernous well. The moment I stepped into it, the feeling of connection to Aulus vanished. Even the buzzing song was gone. This space was identical to the last, with one difference.

Instead of the uniform, smooth surfaces I'd seen on the other cavern, these cells looked deformed, with strange growths protruding from the walls. Instead of the bright blue-and-white liquid crystal, these had a black-green oil slick substance pulsing inside them. Ambrosia. Having just been through the withdrawal process, I grew nauseous and nearly vomited at the sight of it. It wasn't even slightly appealing to me and yet, there it was, more than I'd ever need to kill the Blood Hawks. My own private supply. Without it I couldn't stand against the Hawks, but now that I was free, did I need it at all? Did I really need to take on Licinus and his team? I could fly under the radar, stay out of sight as the games surged on. Aulus was the goal, he'd always been the goal, and now I had a direct, uninterrupted path to him. The cavern piqued my interest though. Had the Sertorians already polluted it with their toxic canisters? No. This cavern was vast compared to the smaller wells I'd seen during the chariot rounds. A thousand canisters would have been needed to poison it. I gave the ambrosia cells a hit with Orbis, expecting them to be weaker than their ichor equivalent, but they were equally well protected. An ocean of ambrosia and no way of getting to it.

It seemed the gods were sending me a message—go to Aulus, rescue your brother. The thought of him out there, alive and well, waiting for me, was nothing short of electrifying. Yes, back to the first cavern and climb free. The future was my own to make, free of all the forces that sought to pull me this way and that for their own purposes. To my relief, as I started back along the tunnel, I felt the buzzing song start up. I was moving away from the ambrosia so the signal became strong. This was the right thing, moving toward Aulus. Finally on track with my mother's plan. To my right I caught sight of movement and brought my torch and weapon up, expecting an attack, but instead I was confronted by a horrific tableau—dozens of Hyperboreans were trapped behind the crystal wall of the tunnel, frozen in place as the black poison swirled about them, coating their forms. At certain points, alien body parts broke through the smooth tunnel wall, misshapen arms, heads, legs, sticking out at awkward angles. I stood there for a long time before I realized that they were still moving in tiny, almost imperceptible increments. It seemed to me that, with their hive polluted by the black fluid, these Hyperboreans were trying to flee, perhaps to join the little Spartacus and the others I'd seen leaving, only they weren't having much luck. Slow-motion agony—they'd never escape before the black fluid killed them off. It was like a classical description of a scene of Hades.

So if the Sertorians hadn't poisoned the place (if Licinus had known of that cavern, he'd have had the arachnoraptors scour it for every drop of ambrosia top to bottom), how had the poison come to be there in the first place? What was it that I was seeing?

I was able to use my first scan of the ichor to determine how much time had passed since the chemical makeup of the cells in that cavern had been altered by the ambrosia. The result: two years, give or take. The analysis also showed the same low levels of radiation present in the fluid from Licinus and Mania's canisters. Gods. It hit me like a thunderbolt. The black poison that turned ichor into ambrosia was the radioactive waste, the fruits of nuclear fallout—the result of the Sertorian bombing of Olympus Decimus. The substance in the canisters was residue from the bomb site. Shocked, I moved to the middle of the cavern and sat down on the cold ice to think things through.

I was still hundreds of miles from the blast site. Could the disaster I was witnessing really have happened as a result of the bombing that killed my mother? The data from the scans was conclusive, anything else would be too much of a coincidence.

As I went to get up, the torchlight brushed over a shining fluid on the cavern floor and I went to investigate. It was ambrosia, not trapped behind the hard cells but running free in the faintest, most miserly of trickles. The source was the tunnel wall. Set low into it, a few feet above the floor, I discovered that a Hyperborean worker had managed to partly breach the tunnel wall with the top half of his head, pointing face down. I knew he was dead because his skull was filled with ambrosia. The poison had mixed with the ichor in the barbarian's body to create the black fluid. It ran out of his skull from the finest of cracks, leaking out to drip to the floor below. All that ambrosia, right there if only the thin crack could be widened. I struck at the skull again and again with Orbis, but it had fused with the crystalline wall and absorbed its strength. What was I doing anyway? The plan was to leave, to climb out of the other cavern and find Aulus. It was a good plan, but as I walked along the tunnel, it occurred to me that all of my petitions had not been truly answered. I'd taken an oath to the triple goddesses of vengeance; they'd taken Lurco and Bulla as my offering. A deal had been struck and the more I thought about it, the more the fire burned within. As I went, I inspected Orbis and saw a small stain of ambrosia on his edge. I cleaned it off with my gloved finger and, before I could stop myself, put the tip of my glove in my mouth and licked it clean.

On the way back to the poisoned cavern, I formulated a new plan. I'd go back to the Sertorians after all. There was no need to choose between rescuing my brother and claiming my due revenge. I could have my cake and eat it. I'd hold off on consuming large amounts of the ambrosia for as long as possible so I could receive enough signal to find Aulus. It would be a delicate balancing act, but I was certain I could do it. Then, when I found my brother I'd signal my uncle, start up using the ambrosia again, and reclaim my fighting edge in order to eliminate the Sertorian team. Mania was the key to the whole thing. My revenge wouldn't be possible without taking possession of the treasure she guarded. My appointment with each of the Blood Hawks was written into the book of destiny. I couldn't let them off the hook. First though, I'd need enough ambrosia to brave the weather aboveground as I raced to catch up to the games.

I got down on my hands and knees and licked at the thin trickle running out from the split in the creature's skull. In the old stories Minerva was born when a rock struck Jupiter's skull, creating a hole, and she popped right out. The ambrosia drizzle was miserly, so slow that it would have taken me a whole day to acquire a phial of it, but after a short time it lit up my brain, infused my muscles with flexibility and strength. With each lap of my tongue, I grew stronger, sharper. I wasn't the same Accala; the ambrosia didn't allow the privilege of simple humanity—it turned you into something dark and powerful—but that's precisely what I needed. Just the same, it was only a small taste and the effects would wear off quickly. I had to hurry.

I scaled the cliff wall and back on the surface found the skirmisher. There was only an hour of light left. Navigation would become problematic and then the Hyperboreans might return, and the bull chief would have an advantage in the dark.

The Ludi Romani was a fast, forward-moving show, and it had gone on without me, but with ambrosia everything was possible and I was driven. I knew I could catch up if I reached the camp before morning and the next stage of the tournament. Exhaustion came on fast as I sped along. Having reintroduced ambrosia to my system, my body remembered that it wanted, needed, more or everything would go to hell. I'd been hoping that after being cleaned out I'd be able to start again, back at the beginning, where I'd enjoy the benefits for a whole day before feeling any side effects, but that wasn't the case. The addiction and its symptoms picked up right where it had left off.

I found my way back to the great scar in the landscape formed by the emperor's ion cannon. As I raced along the canyon edge, the ambrosia started to wear off and I cursed the onset of the withdrawal symptoms. I could see the remains of the dead Hyperborean hordes littered all over the ice. I followed the spine of the mountains and came across the camp just as night was falling. Two domed force shields enclosed the factions on a high plateau in the distance.

I crested a bank of snow and suddenly all the Blood Hawks were there, all out looking for me. I was dizzy with need for ambrosia and fell from the desultore skirmisher onto the snow. I clung to consciousness just long enough to feel my body being lifted up as they carried me back to hell. I'd had the chance to take the easy road, to possess the freedom I'd whined and pleaded with the goddess for, but now I saw that right there with the Blood Hawks was exactly where I was meant to be. I'd find Aulus and then I'd unleash a tide of Sertorian blood that would shock even the most hard-bitten and cynical viewers of the Ludi Romani.

* * *

I AWOKE IN MY tent, covered in warm blankets and steroid poultices. Barbata was watching over me.

"How long?" I asked.

"How long were you unconscious? It's a few hours to dawn. The last day of the chariot rounds is still ahead. We've returned to our normal scheduling."

"I can fight," I said.

"Of course you can, and you will," she said, tenderly stroking my face. "It's all been cleared with the game editor, he's embarrassed that you somehow got left behind, and has written the whole incident off as a genuine mistake. Licinus, on the other hand, wanted to beat you when you woke up, but I told him that it wasn't your fault and that you'd been a good dog and come home to your master. That seemed to satisfy him. Besides, we're well ahead in the contest."

"We are?"

"Not the Blood Hawks per se but the Talonite Axis teams as a whole. We're still twenty-four to the Caninines' twenty-one survivors, not to mention that there are no Sertorian casualties. We are still best positioned to win the games."

"And the day's match? Who won?"

"The race result was declared null and void due to the Hyperborean intrusion, so it came down to the largest number of kills in the fight. Crassus tipped us over the edge and we won with ninety-seven kills."

The Caninines would have to produce almost a hundred thousand slaves as an offering to the Sertorians and their allies. After weeks in bondage to the Sertorians, swallowing their precepts, watching Bulla die, I didn't want to ever have a barbarian wait on me again, and I'd rather have taken every slave in the empire right into the Wolf's Den than have them suffer life under the Sertorians.

"We got an engine booster as prize," Barbata continued. "It'll allow us to match the Flavians' speed for a short time."

"Then we might win the final round," I said.

"I'm certain of it," she said.

"Now tell me, and spare no detail, what happened to you? We lost track of you when you went to fight the bull chief."

"I chased after him and fell down a crevasse. He left me for dead as far as I can tell, and I had to climb my way back out."

She looked at me with her seductive, searching eyes. "You're holding something back," she said, a dangerous edge to her voice. "Don't think we didn't notice that your bracelet's locater didn't function."

"Maybe it got damaged in the battle or when I fell."

"Maybe."

"Aren't you going to take it away and repair it?" I asked, holding it up.

"The immunes have already taken care of that. What else? Tell me of this bull chief. Be honest."

"I was frightened of him," I said. "I didn't want to admit it before, but it's true."

"Really? How frightened? More frightened than you are of Licinus?"

"Yes."

"More frightened than you are of me?"

"Yes."

She put a chill hand on my cheek in a show of tenderness, and I worked hard not to pull away. "You should be more frightened of me than any of them. You know what I do to those who get in my way? I'm like the female spider. I mate with them, then I eat them. Do you believe that?"

"Yes." I could see she was telling the truth.

"And you're still more frightened of the ice ape?"

"Yes."

"Poor darling. I believe you," she said, pulling up a holographic reflector from her armilla. She held it out before me so I could see my face. "You see, that inelegant shock of white hair has come back. You must have had the fright of your life."

She had a fresh phial of ambrosia in her hands. I reached out for it, but she pulled it away and smiled. "I wish I could give you some. I know what it feels like to go without."

Barbata dangled the precious substance before her.

"I don't know what you see in her, you know, that redheaded grease monkey. Aside from being bad luck, fiery, and irrational, redheads are genetic abnormalities. When the precepts are more widely accepted, the proconsul's going to eliminate the gene. We'll be rid of the cursed things once and for all."

"She's a person," I reminded Barbata. "And a citizen of the empire."

"She's a manual laborer. All sweaty like a house slave and fat in the arms. You should have come to me," she said, as she unstoppered the ambrosia and took a small, seductive sip. "Am I not beautiful? And look at you—I gave you the gift of beauty. There's no point having a magnificent façade unless you rebuild the inside as well. You must be willing to upgrade your tastes, indulge in true pleasure. That immune like an old pair of work shoes."

She traced her fingers along my forearm, tripping the thin hairs. Gods. Really? She was jealous of Julia. Her hand trailed down my neck, between my breasts, but I pushed it away as inoffensively as I could manage.

"Really? You think you're in a position to deny me? Your name in the Roman arena was Lupa, wasn't it? The she-wolf? You know they also call prostitutes that, the brothel is the lupanar—the den of she-wolves."

She dangled the phial of ambrosia before me. Her words sank in and—at this point in the game, when I thought nothing could shock me—I was genuinely taken aback. She wanted to buy me with this. She really thought of me in this way, like a common whore who had overstepped her station. Still, that ambrosia. A whole phial could mean the difference between victory or defeat.

Before I could decide, Barbata held up the phial and swallowed the rest of the ambrosia. She smiled when she saw the longing in my eyes.

"Mmm. So bitter and sweet all at once. You can have a taste if you want, there's still some on my lips, on my tongue."

I surprised myself by sitting up and pressing my lips to hers. The smell and taste of the ambrosia triggered the pleasure centers of my brain. I opened my mouth, begging her to let me taste more. I hated myself, hated this indignity, but every drop of ambrosia was priceless.

"Why?" I asked her when she finally pulled away.

"Because it pleased me to take what I wanted and it pleased me to remind you and your collegia slut of your place in the scheme of things. I have power over you and I exercise it. If you are truly on the Sertorian path, you will learn to take pleasure beneath me until such a time as you can supplant me through your own exercise of power. That is our way. Consider it a lesson. Now, you rest and let the medicine do its work."

"The ambrosia, it wasn't enough."

"Try Crassus. He's your master," she said.

"I thought I didn't have a master now I've been blooded."

"We all have masters. That's how life is. Freedom is an illusion."

"All hawks without wings?" I asked.

"What was that?"

"Nothing. Where is Crassus, then?"

"Ah, now that isn't the interesting question. You should be asking where your Vulcaneum immune is."

"Where is she, then?"

"Why, with Crassus of course. He should be between her legs right now. He's very vigorous. I hope she can walk well enough to carry out her duties in the morning."

She walked off laughing, confident she'd rattled me, but I knew she was lying. Julia would never give herself to someone like Crassus. I slumped back on the bed to rest. I needed to conserve my energy for tomorrow's games. There was no buzzing song—with the ambrosia in my system, I was in the dark again when it came to Aulus' location. My hastily made plans in the ambrosia cavern were already crumbling to pieces. I'd been kidding myself. I couldn't hold out on the ambrosia. I'd have to do things the other way round. Take Mania's ambrosia, use it to kill the Blood Hawks, hard and fast, then try to wean myself off the substance so that I could find my brother. It could be done. As long as I struck quietly, not giving the Hawks a chance to send any messages or alerts to their agents who guarded Aulus. Yes, that was the best way.

I was just drifting off to sleep when I heard a familiar laugh. I crawled over to the entrance and peeked out. It was Julia. She and Crassus were emerging from his tent. He had his arm about her, kissing her neck playfully, and she was not resisting. She was enjoying it. Did Julia even know I was alive? Was this his way of getting back at me for not giving in to his desires? Her way of getting back at me for not performing to her satisfaction? I didn't want Crassus, I despised Crassus, and yet the thought of Julia having him, of them being together, made me sick. While I was out there risking my life to hamper the Sertorian efforts, was she cavorting with the enemy? I hated them with a burning intensity. She was not to be trusted. No one could be trusted. I was on my own and always had been. From now on I'd do only what was best for myself and my brother, and if Julia got in my way, it'd be all the worse for her.

XXV

THE NEXT MORNING, I intercepted Julia as she emerged from her tent. The entire night I'd tossed and turned, unable to get the thought of them together out of my head.

"Done with you now, is he?" I said to her.

"I'm glad you're alive," she said. "Everyone thought you'd had it."

"So the first thing you do is bed Crassus?"

"I'm an agent, Accala. I gather information. The first thing I did was tap the best resource we had to locate your brother."

"Is that supposed to be funny? Tap the best resource? I think you've wanted him all along. It's not the first time you bedded him, is it? That's why he's been so uninterested in me. That's where you got the code for my bracelet."

"I've been scanning his armilla without his knowledge. It's been a useful exercise."

"Is that how it works? I tell you everything, but you tell me nothing?"

"No, that's not how it works, but I also have a responsibility to look out for you. I didn't want to trouble you unnecessarily. You're under enough stress as it is."

"And what valuable information did you find out while Crassus was between your legs?"

"I got a look at some of their internal communications. They're planning to break away, Accala. Where the course runs past the alien tunnels, the Blood Hawks are going to head right into them. The uprising's got them spooked. They've got a hidden base down there, the center of their ambrosia-mining operation, and it's been overrun by the barbarians. Certain of their assets have been threatened. They sound desperate to protect them."

"Assets? Does that mean Aulus?"

"It wasn't specific, but I wouldn't discount it. They're going to direct all or part of the team into the tunnels to reclaim the base. They wouldn't do that if it wasn't critically important."

"That's something. That's useful," I said.

"You're welcome."

I mulled over Julia's words. "I want you to contact my uncle. Crassus is going to make his move on Licinus in the next round and that's going to be my time to strike at them from within. Tell him I'm ready."

"No, you're not. You're not ready at all."

"I didn't ask you for your opinion."

"Your uncle wanted you to sight your brother first, to have absolute confirmation of his location. Saving your brother is the number one goal. Remember, your mother said that both of you would be needed to deprive the Sertorians of the ambrosia. If you act too soon and fail, they'll kill Aulus."

"You just said the Sertorians might not even be in possession of the base where they're holding him."

"Exactly, 'might' being the operative word. You can't stake everything on tidbits of information. You need solid proof."

"I'm going to get Aulus, don't worry—I can find him, but it'll be after I've eliminated the Sertorians."

"How do you know he's near? Have you had some luck with the pin?"

"I've made some inroads. While you were cavorting with Crassus, I engaged in a fact-finding mission of my own. I've got a plan, I know what I'm doing."

A chime commanding the players to gather sounded.

"Just make sure you contact him," I said. "I'm making my move and after, when I have Aulus, I expect his full support."

"Accala . . ."

I walked off to the sounds of her quietly cursing.

The domes surrounding the different camps were lowered and the teams came together, summoned to neutral ground—flat terrain with no cover. The referee hovered, reminding us that fighting was not permitted until the day's race had commenced. The overall energy was low. Every team had suffered injuries from the fight with the Hyperboreans; everyone had had to rework their strategies to compensate for the unexpected losses. We were also drained from the constant wind, which seemed to be stronger and colder every day.

The emperor appeared before the assembled athletes, his head a massive projection, his figure sharply defined. Julius Gemminus' head was there too, one-tenth the size of the emperor's, little holographic wings still fluttering from beneath his ears.

"Well, well," said Julius Gemminus. "It appears that there's been quite a kerfuffle overnight. We'll be finishing the chariot rounds today as planned, but I'm obliged to notify you of some changes that will take place in tomorrow's bestiarii rounds. I do this at the behest of the emperor, as we'll be making considerable modifications to the course on the fly, yet again. I had planned to run through the barbarians' territory aboveground," he stated, "where everything could be easily observed from the Rota Fortuna. But now we're going to take a different route. Rather than going over the mountain's spine, we're going to go under it. The audience was quite animated by yesterday's battle, and they want more. The emperor, always pleased to accommodate the will of his people, has agreed to the request. Might I add, against the initial protestations of myself and the editor's guild. Unexpected things can happen when we divert from plans. The games are carefully structured. It takes me months to cater to every eventuality. To just discard those carefully wrought plans . . . it's a tragedy, a sacrilege to arena sport—"

"Julius . . ." the emperor chided.

"Yes, of course, Imperator," he said, collecting himself. "But we have seen the light of wisdom. We will deviate from the planned course and embark upon this new, unexplored course. As the contestants represent all the houses, the attack of the barbarians is being seen as an attack upon the spirit of Rome itself, and so now, for the bestiarii round, you will all retaliate in kind and take the fight to the Hyperboreans, cut them down root and branch for daring to resist Rome.

"Media spherae will of course follow you into the mountain. It's been no small feat reworking the spherae to operate in subterranean conditions and running hundreds of topographic surveys, but we've concluded that the tunnels have multiple entry and exit points on either side of the mountain range, so we should be able to pick up the contest on the other side. I've been a games editor for over three decades, and I can tell you right now that no good can come from wandering off the grid, from changing the rules." The emperor scowled, and the editor backed down at once. "But we serve at the pleasure of the emperor . . . and the people of Rome and so gladly modify our carefully thought-out course. The Ludi Romani is, after all, a sacred contest to allow the cheers of the people to reach the gods in adoration."

"I must object," Licinus called out. "We have rules, a system. What is Rome without order? We must stay with the path."

"Your proconsul said the same," Julius Gemminus replied. "But the emperor is intrigued by these creatures, and the people insist these barbarians are punished for daring to challenge Rome's authority."

It seemed as if the emperor also had an abiding interest in House Sertorian's business and what it was up to on Olympus Decimus. Julia told me the Blood Hawks were going to leave the course and visit the Hyperborean tunnels, and now the emperor was diverting the entire contest to the exact same area. That meant the Golden Wolves would be right at hand if I spoke the code word and requested their assistance. The emperor was turning out to be an unexpected ally.

"Now mount up," Julia said. "We've still got the final day of the chariot rounds ahead."

We returned to our camps and mobilized.

As we headed out, Julius Gemminus announced that today's round would be all about speed and maneuverability—and, as it was the last leg of the essedarius, the winner would be granted a great prize—a precious immunity amulet that would shield one contestant from all physical attack for the length of the bestiarii round.

Both sides raced toward low ground with small lakes spread out across it and high-walled cliffs of dark green rock bordering its edges. As with the first day, we could not commence combat until after we passed the green boundary markers.

As we arced around with the course, we saw a long object hovering off the ice ahead of us.

At first I didn't understand and, judging by the faces of the others, neither did anyone else. A spina, just like you'd find at a chariot race in the circus back in Rome. But they couldn't mean for us to go around it, could they? This was a post-to-post race, not lap based.

"The spina is an essential ingredient in any Roman chariot race," Julius Gemminus said. "But instead of circling it, all you have to do is be the first to race past it."

That sounded far too easy. It was a mile long, sitting in the middle of the tundra. There was no sign of a triumphant arch marking the finish of the race; it must have been miles off in the distance.

Then we were past the start markers and it was on.

We raced, angling for position, until the pack of chariots was halfway along the spina, and then suddenly it moved. A side to side motion, small at first but increasing as we raced along until it reached the point where it would move right away from the chariots before pushing back in, threatening to crush us against the electrified shield wall. On the inward swings, the chariots quickly fell into a single line in the narrow space left between spina and shield wall to avoid destruction. On the outward swings, the charioteers vied to overtake and be the first in line. As we approached the end of the spina, it moved faster. The Dioscurii used our engine boost and we surged clear, but those behind us weren't so lucky. The Viridians were driven into the Flavians and they in turn piled up against the Ovidians, driving them into the purple energy field. They managed to pull free in time, suffering some circuit problems to their chariot, judging by the sparks and sudden erratic path, but no deaths. The Tullians and Calpurnians weren't so lucky. They were caught trying to slip around the other side of the spina as the course drastically narrowed. The spina crushed them against the wall, and they each lost a contestant to electrocution—Salcus Tullius Coruntus, the charioteer famous for his ramming skills, and brave Sempronius Calpurnius Galeo, the well-proportioned hoplite from Marcus' arena team— their burned bodies falling to the cold ice, their hands reflexively clawing at the snow.

But the spina had finished its work. It moved away and the chariots were able to race past it. Perhaps Julius Gemminus had dictated that there had been enough deaths at its hands. We were charging ahead toward the finish, our attention on getting ahead of the other teams, when Licinus called out, "Brace yourselves!"

The victory arch constructed especially for the occasion was in view now, another mile ahead, and we came hurtling toward it. The Flavians and Calpurnians had made good ground, but we caught up, all three chariots racing neck and neck. Triumphant anthems played, spurring us onward as our chariots rushed at breakneck speed. The stadium pods had been permitted to descend to observe the final push firsthand. They lined the track, behind the barriers. I couldn't help wondering if my father was among them.

The Calpurnians couldn't match the Flavians or our chariot for raw speed, and it was a game of speed now. The Silver Sparrows, the flighty Flavians, were far and away the quickest and nimblest chariot racers, their war chariot stripped down for speed and lightness. I didn't see how we could outpace them with the finish line less than a mile out. We pulled away, leaving the Calpurnians' black chariot in our ice particle wake.

My armilla chimed and flashed, and I quickly glanced down to see the signal. Gods! The Dioscurii were going to unleash their secret weapon. I let go of the central pole and grabbed on to the starboard rail. And then we were separated. Split down the middle and sailing apart, slowing a little to allow the Flavians to pull ahead. The adamas-edged discs, the hardest substance in the galaxy, began to spin. The spikes shone and gleamed in the sunlight. Our opponents were going so fast that their driver, Titus Flavius Cursor, so intent on the finish line, didn't stop to think about what move we might make. Then the jaws closed. Before they could clear past us, the two halves moved above the line of the enemy chariot then reunited, drawn by powerful magnetic fields.

The Flavians were trapped; Septimus Flavius Stolo, their leader, trying to strike out at Licinus, was cut clean in half at the waist. Licinus, Crassus, Barbata, and Mania cut into them with efficient, mechanical precision. I reluctantly raised Orbis and put the Flavian bestiarii Tremelius Ralla out of his misery, his legs already severed by the cutting discs, his body skewered on the spikes.

It was all set to be a complete disaster for the sparrows until their backup driver—Macro Flavius Cato—who had ducked down to avoid our spinning blades, threw himself forward to the chariot's reins. He yanked them port side and down, and suddenly their vehicle pulled away. They were down to five contestants now. What was more, they were out of the race. With no more enemies to crush, we accelerated toward the finish line. But wait! We had slowed to employ our secret attack, and the Calpurnians had somehow managed to catch up. There was less than a half-mile to go to the arch. The Dioscurii tried to block them and stop them passing, but to our surprise, the Calpurnian driver Trio Calpurnius Trigeminus suddenly reared up, his chariot's prow pushing into the air, and then it was sailing right up on us.

"Down!" Licinus yelled. "Testudo!"

We crouched and activated our shields, locking them together above our heads in the tortoise formation, an impenetrable wall. We were beneath the rim of our vehicle, and its frame took the brunt of the weight as the Calpurnians ran roughshod right over the top of us. I was crushed to the deck along with the Sertorians until the Calpurnian chariot had passed and hit down on the ice right in front of us. They had the lead. We took up our posts once more, and the Dioscurii drove forward with everything they had, but it was too late. The Calpurnians pushed over the line, passing through the arch a second ahead of us—the undisputed winners of the chariot round.

We rode through the arch but had to veer off, denied entry by a crackling force shield to the winner's circle that was for the Ravens alone. For them there would be applause, cheering, garlands and wreaths placed about them, warm spiced wine thrust into their hands. They were victorious, the pride of their house and their faction. The Calpurnians would be granted privileges and an easy transfer to the start of the next round. For us there would be only recriminations and the pain of losing. Our team was silent with shock and anger. Along with the other remaining houses, we were funneled down various paths to transit to the camp location.

"Order or chaos. Peace or war. Harmonious music or a cacophony to make your head split!" Julius Gemminus zipped above us as we cruised. "We have a winner, but now it's time to pick the least popular house. Which team will you choose to punish before the next round begins?"

For a fee, wealthy audience members could direct that curse amulets studded with sharp nails should fall on their chosen team. Most times the amulets didn't actually injure the team members, but occasionally a gladiator was wounded or killed.

Each team was directed to take a different route—the Blood Hawks were to follow the course of a slender stream. After a few miles a sign flashed above us reading CACOPHONIA. I didn't understand it. Crassus the hero was with us. My own support had been strong, I'd kept track of the audience ratings on my armilla. And with Aquilinus' promise of ambrosia for the masses, why on earth would they choose us to punish?

"It's the emperor," Licinus grumbled. "He's strong-armed enough of the nobles and senators aboard the orbital stadium to throw their money behind registering his displeasure."

"It won't make him popular with the people," Barbata said.

"That doesn't do shit for us now," Licinus said.

The tunnel led us away from the other contestants. The moment we exited it onto hilly ground, the curses came. They fell from the stadium on high, small silver balls stamped with an array of customized curses chosen by the audience members who paid for the privilege. As they fell, they gathered speed and spikes emerged from them. They clustered, ensuring they fell close enough to have an actual chance of killing us.

"Testudo!" Licinus ordered, and we all used our armillae to generate shields, interlocking them to form a barrier to stop the curses from striking home. We had to hold tight to prevent the wind lifting our shields.

At first only a few fell, range finders to ensure accuracy. Then the rest arrived. The resultant noise of the spikes striking the shield barrier provided a deafening cacophony, just as Julius Gemminus' sign had promised. After ten minutes, my arms hurt, and my ears ached from the loud drumming. While we endured the lethal rain, the spectators would be watching us on giant screens, while others showed slow-motion replays of the highlights of the chariot round, especially the deaths and the killing blows in glorious detail.

Already I was feeing weak, hypersensitive, delirious with the need for more ambrosia.

We survived without injury, but the humiliation had clearly served to anger Pollux. "It's not fucking good enough! I'll take the eyes of the next one of you to fail!"

Unable to recall ever hearing Pollux Corvinus speak before, I was stunned; even more shocking was that the other Sertorians didn't challenge his sudden outburst. They only looked cowed and put up no argument, even Licinus.

The team meeting was unpleasant but mercifully brief. I didn't dare ask Licinus or Mania for ambrosia, but afterward I followed Crassus to our tent. Julia made sense, I couldn't take drastic action without enough information. She also said that if I couldn't detect Aulus with the pin, my next best bet would be to get the information directly from Crassus. Regardless of whether the Sertorians still had my brother or not, I'd still need a precise location. Then I wouldn't have to worry about doing without the ambrosia. Yes, that was the way. Only, if I wanted Crassus' secrets, I'd have to give him some signal that I could be trusted, a reason to let down his guard and embrace me as an ally. Julia had great success with him in the bedroom, and she was nothing to Crassus. If I decided to make the effort to win him over, to give him what he'd sought for so long, then, I was certain, there was nothing he would deny me.

XXVI

CRASSUS WAS WAITING FOR me when I entered our tent. His seat was cup shaped with a cross-piece base and padded with plump cushions. He was dressed in thick, white fur robes. Crassus indicated for me to sit in the one opposite him, but I stood looking down at him.

"You've come for your ambrosia?" he asked.

"You know I have."

"Then come and sit with me and I shall give it to you."

"What do you want with me? Call Julia if you want a companion."

"I don't want Julia, I want you."

"You made your choice, now live with it."

My body wanted him, to mount him or kill him in equal measure. Perhaps both at the same time.

"Ah, I must admit I did hope to fan the flames of jealousy just a little," Crassus said.

"To what possible end?"

"I think you know," he said. "I've made no effort to hide my interest in you, and I think it's fair to say that I've been patient beyond measure."

"The last time I expressed an interest, you cursed at me like a drunken sailor."

He looked at me, perplexed, his head cocked. He didn't remember.

"Come, Accala. Let's talk honestly," he said. "There's something I've been wanting to tell you, something you've earned the right to know."

"Tell me."

Was this the moment? Was he actually going to tell me about Aulus, serve it up to me free of charge?

"I want reveal the proconsul's seventh precept."

Gods, I felt like drowning myself. Was he serious?

"The seventh precept? Because you know I've been staying awake at night desperately anticipating the moment you'd tell me."

"This is serious."

"I thought you were going to tell me something useful. Like why Licinus and Mania have been interrogating me. They think I can be of use to them, above and beyond my role as a gladiator, and I want to know more."

"I don't know all their plans. You know Licinus is no ally of mine. And don't jest. The seventh precept masks a great secret. Now sit," he said forcefully.

I sat with a sigh, trying to appear nonchalant while hiding the pain of lowering myself into the chair. Crassus took a dramatic pause to ensure he had my full attention.

"The seventh precept of the eagle is the secret of the new order, the key to the coming golden age. It is an extension of the first precept: The gods are dead . . . but you shall now worship the New Gods as you did the old."

"I'm stunned," I retorted. "You could knock me over with a feather. You mean you Sertorians really are in it for your own glorification after all?"

"Don't make me use the bracelet," he warned. "Try to clear your mind. Let go of your prejudices. I don't want to think you're trying to undo all the good work we did aboard *Incitatus* on the way over. We don't want to have to go through that again, do we?"

"No," I whispered.

He leaned forward in his chair and took my hands in his.

"It sounds ridiculous, I know, except you're missing the key. It's all about the right perspective. You see, what you don't understand is that we actually are gods. Or at least the seeds of gods. It's the ambrosia—it changes whoever takes it."

"First you said the gods are dead, now you think you're next in line to replace them? Like when the Olympians took the place of their parents?"

"Exactly like that."

"Someone else already tried that," I said reasonably. "His name was Tantalus. He stole nectar and ambrosia, the food of the gods, and gave them to men. The gods stuck him in the underworld and punished him with eternal thirst and hunger. A river ran up to his chin and whenever he went to drink, the water level dropped. Fruit was always dangling above his head, but when he craned his neck to reach for it, the wind would blow it away."

"Hear what I'm saying, Accala. The proconsul named ambrosia quite deliberately. It won't really be made available to all, at least not in any significant quantity, not the way we consume it. It's more than it seems, so is this world." He turned my hands over, exposing my inner arms. "You've tried cutting yourself here, haven't you?" His fingertips brushed gently across the skin, making it prickle with desire. "And the cuts closed up by themselves, didn't they? Not even a scar remains."

I pulled my hands away from him. "Did Julia tell you that?" I asked. Gods, be careful. His touch fazed me. I must not give away too much, I'd have to watch every word I said!

"The mechanic isn't important," he said. "The secret of the ambrosia is. Haven't you found your injuries healing by themselves during the games?"

"It accelerates the body's healing factor," I said.

"No, it's much more than a stimulant, much more than something that improves performance. Listen to me carefully. I mean this literally. The ambrosia is the raw stuff of creation. It's not just the food of the gods, it's the food that makes you a god. And we found it here. On this world."

I tried to look surprised. Seriously, Crassus was just as cracked as the rest of his people.

"It's the Hyperboreans, isn't it?" I asked. "They make it somehow."

He hesitated, his eyes searching mine, his fingers trailing over my bracelet as he decided what he was going to tell me. Finally, he smiled and said, "Not make, collect. They're like bees. Their bodies absorb a substance called ichor as they travel through their tunnels and deposit it in their hives, but that's not really relevant."

"Right. Becoming a god is the important thing."

"Yes. Believe me, Accala, this world is the home of the gods—Olympus, hidden in plain sight," he said.

My dream. I saw the words—*Minerva Olympus*—scratched into the glass in my mother's hand.

"And that's why you bombed it," I said. "That's why you killed my mother. For some petty delusion of godhood?"

"Not me," he said. "Licinus was behind that, you must remember that, but you're partly right. This is what your mother discovered, it was the secret she was going to ferry back to House Viridian and your Proconsul Severus, and we couldn't allow that.

"And although you may find it hard to see it that way, the bombing was a blessing. We knew ichor was valuable, but every test and experiment to turn it to our uses failed. The radiation fallout from the bombing transformed ichor into the ambrosia you know and enjoy. Ichor, and now ambrosia, saturate this world, and the Hyperboreans are the universe's greatest joke. The most stupid of creatures carrying about the most valuable substance in the galaxy, and not a brain cell between their ears to know what to do with it. Happily, their loss is our gain.

"We haven't reached the zenith of our abilities using the ambrosia, Accala. We're only just beginning, and who knows what we will be when we finish. No false godhood like the emperor, claiming to be the son of Venus and Mars." His large hands enfolded my own, kissing them. Whatever he believed about the ambrosia, I was certainly feeling the absence of it. The clawing internal sensation of withdrawal immunized me a little from my feelings for him. I stood and tried to get my legs to move without throwing up from the pain.

"Don't go." Crassus reached out and touched my cheek. Gods, but I hated that. His permissiveness, his unwanted intimacy. "I've told you a great secret tonight. I hoped it would bring us closer together."

"Your secret wasn't that great," I said. "Besides, I've got a headache and just about every other kind of ache."

"I have something that will help with that," he said. "A present." He held up a phial of ambrosia. A whole phial. My whole body quivered in anticipation.

"I was saving it for you, for a special occasion. Now you've learned all seven precepts. Tomorrow you'll receive a uniform with seven red bands."

"You want to give me a phial of ambrosia for that? Is there an eighth precept I can learn?"

Never in my life had I wanted anything so badly. I wouldn't be able to take the Sertorians down if they kept me weak and desperate. I needed to be strong for the next round. But he wasn't where I needed him to be yet. Crassus had to be willing to tell me anything I wanted. One more step away from him, toward the entrance to the tent, and he jumped up from his chair to head me off.

"If you want me to stay, then tell me about my brother. Tell me where he is," I said.

"It's funny you should press the issue tonight. I had planned to talk to you about just that, especially based on the game editor's announcement this morning."

"That the next leg will be fought in the Hyperborean hive network?"

"Precisely."

"And what did you want to tell me about that, then?" I asked, pushing my body seductively into his.

"Your brother Aulus. He's near, Accala."

I was stunned at his honesty. He wanted me tonight, and it seemed he'd tell me just about anything I wanted to know.

"How near?"

"He's held on a facility of ours located beneath the alien tunnels. We'll be closest when we enter the new bestiarius course."

"You're sharing information very generously all of a sudden," I said.

"And with good cause. I suppose it's time to put my cards on the table. I have every intention of following through on our deal. I will reunite you with your brother if you help me kill Licinus and win the games, but a few complications have arisen since we arrived on this world, and I need your help."

"Complications?"

"We don't actually have possession of your brother at this moment in time."

So there it was. Julia's report was true.

"You don't have him? Is he dead?"

"He's alive," Crassus said. "We placed sensors on him. They're still in operation. He hasn't moved, his vital signs haven't changed. He's alive, I swear it." Crassus spoke quickly, trying to reassure me.

"We're heading into the tunnels in the next round, and once we've killed Licinus, we'll go and save your brother. I want to present him to you as a wedding gift. It'll be perfect, we'll do everything together, in perfect union."

"Wedding?"

"Of course, but we'll wait until after the tournament. Now listen. Licinus has a plan to trap the Caninine contestants. He won't tell me the details now, but the moment he makes his move, all attention will turn to the death of the Wolves and their allies. That's when we'll strike him down. Then we blame his death on the Hyperboreans."

"And the others?"

"They'll follow the strongest. That's how it works with us. After Licinus is dead, you and I will free your brother from the barbarians and then emerge from the other side of the tunnel network as the new leaders of the Talonite Axis. We'll win the tournament together, take the empire's breath away."

I had him hooked, I could feel it, he was hungry. Crassus was breathing fast. Just when he thought he was finally going to bed me, I was going to kill him.

"And the ambrosia that's on this world?" I asked.

"An offering to the proconsul. A gift to cement our position. This is a small step, but in the long run it'll be just you and me, Accala. Running the entire empire. One day, I'll make you my empress."

He placed the phial in my palm, tenderly folding my fingers about it. I pushed it back at him with the last of my willpower, uttering a feral groan, baring my teeth at him like a wild animal.

"Get away from me," I growled. Crassus pulled me close, his eyes burning with expectation. My body betrayed me and pressed seductively into his. His eyes widened in surprise; he'd been expecting resistance. But I couldn't do it. How could I give myself to him? How could I shame myself so? It was impossible.

They'd taken Orbis from me, and I wouldn't have him back until morning, but resting against the tent wall, just behind Crassus, was his javelin. I angled my body slightly backward, the fingers of my right hand brushing the weapon. Crassus was breathing fast.

"You are strong willed," he said. "A worthy choice, a perfect partner, a perfect vessel. Our children will rule the empire one day."

Before I knew it, I had the javelin in my hand, threatening him with it. Crassus wasn't surprised or alarmed.

He reached out slowly, his hands wrapping about the javelin's shaft, but he didn't take it from me. Instead he placed the point into the soft place at the base of his throat.

"Do you truly wish to kill me? Is that why you're keeping your distance, or is it really that you have feelings for me that you're afraid to admit?"

Any logical thought had fled; all that remained was the burning fire that couldn't be contained a moment longer. I despised Crassus, hated what he'd turned me into. He had to pay. Blood for blood, pain for pain.

Crassus slowly moved his hands away and held them at his side, palms raised, making himself an offering.

"I won't force you, Accala. I want you to give yourself to me freely or kill me. It's up to you."

He moved toward me, desire in his eyes, the javelin's point pressing against the tight skin of his throat so that I'd be forced to pull the shaft back to prevent his death. All of the conditioning aboard the ship, the hours in the machine, the countless touches and embraces—they weighed down my arm, made it heavy as lead. I wanted to yield to him, I wanted him to take me. Most of all, I wanted the ambrosia.

"Accala, you can't fight forever," he said.

I thrust suddenly, pushing the javelin up and into him. The sharp point pierced his throat, glancing off the vertebrae of his neck before emerging through the back right side of his neck. I couldn't believe it, but I had done it. I had killed him. Gods, what had I done? Crassus was my only Sertorian ally, the only one who knew where Aulus was. What would happen to me once the other Blood Hawks found out?

He didn't fall, though. He just stood there, looking at me. To my horror, he carefully reached up and pulled the javelin right out. Blood began to pump out of the wound, spilling all over the white furs he was wearing. I was stunned, frozen in place, my body in shock.

"You know, I didn't think you were actually going to do that," he said, the gurgle of blood in his throat making him sound like a nightmarish ghoul. "You're a constant surprise. Like a force of nature. I never know what you're going to do next. There's something Sertorian about you, an inherent ruthlessness. I suspect I overplayed my hand—telling you about the last precept at the same time as giving you the news that your brother was no longer in our custody. You were too distracted. You weren't able to make the conceptual leap I'd hoped for regarding the ambrosia. But sometimes words aren't enough. So I suppose I'll just have to show you."

He reached out, took my hand, and placed the phial of ambrosia in it again.

"Drink," he said. "You're going to need it."

I didn't argue. I needed it now or I'd pass out. Shock was setting in. I felt the cold cutting into me like a knife, passing right through me as if I weren't wearing any furs at all. I broke the top off the phial and downed the contents in a single gulp. The combination of pleasure and relief from pain was overwhelming and exquisite. As the ambrosia had its way with me, I noticed that the bleeding from Crassus' throat had stopped and the wound was beginning to close over.

Crassus spun the javelin about deftly, and fast as lightning, he thrust it into my belly. I felt it move through my skin, layers of muscle, all the way past my spine, and then just as quickly, he drew it out. The shock of it made me gasp. It paralyzed my whole body, but then I felt something unexpected, like a thousand little ants inside me. I couldn't tell if they were very hot or very cold, but they were rushing about. It felt like they were knitting, reweaving threads that had become unraveled. I looked down, pulling my furs aside, pulling up my jerkin. I touched the hole in the middle of my flat belly in disbelief as it began to close around my fingers. I didn't feel any pain. No pain at all.

"You see," he said. "We're gods already."

His lips pressed against mine, he slid my furs off, pushed my jerkin farther up, exposing my breasts. The wave of pleasure that hit me was tidal; it swept away any resistance before it. He was pulling at the pin that held my hair in place. I didn't stop him. It had been pulled back too tight for too long. I wanted it to be free, to feel him run his hands through it. I kissed him back, fiercely, biting his lip, drawing blood. When he stepped back, I snatched his javelin from him and swung it in an arc, slicing open his cheek. He snatched it back and thrust forward, piercing my breast, the weapon pushing through my beating heart. The hot ants swarmed about it instantly, healing me, knitting bone, muscle, skin back together even as he began to withdraw the weapon from my body.

"The stuff of creation," Crassus whispered. I reached up along the length of the javelin and pulled him into me, pressing the weapon through my heart, drawing him close so I could kiss him again. Hovering on the edge of life and death like that, I'd never experienced such pleasure—like an orgasm that never ended.

"Now, come to bed," he said, drawing out the javelin tenderly. I couldn't fight him anymore. If the other Blood Hawks were all this powerful, this unkillable, I didn't know how I was going to complete my mission. I fell into his arms, blood pumping from my body, and embraced him while I waited for the ambrosia to go to work. I needed Crassus. Now more than ever and in more ways than I cared to admit.

* * *

I WOKE IN THE middle of the night to find him stroking my hair, winding strands of it about his fingers and then pulling his hand away to see the curls cling to his fingers. Why had I held him at bay for so long? Crassus would do his best to feed me now as he did on the ship when I made an effort to please him. Barbata was right—he was magnificent, driven, anxious, even.

"You hair isn't straight," he said. "It has waves in it, minor imperfections. I didn't see that before. They're beautifully imperfect. And now you have this white streak back. I must admit, I always found it attractive."

"I thought I was one of your gods now," I said. "Immortals don't have imperfections."

"I'm sorry, I didn't mean it as an insult. It makes you more beautiful. Like the color of your eyes. Just a few abnormalities highlight the greater unity of your features and form."

"That's what Publia the ornatrix said." I stared up at the ceiling, trying to find the right way to say it, but in the end decided to be direct. "I'm sorry about trying to kill you before."

"You struck prematurely. I understand. You were addled by the desire for ambrosia and the sudden news about your brother, but I hope you're thinking clearly now."

One of us was. Could my uncle have been right when he said that Crassus had been struck by Cupid's arrows? It didn't seem possible that he could love me enough to discard all semblance of common sense, but all that talk of weddings and engagement presents—gods, what rot.

"More than ever," I said. "I need you, I see that now. What we need to talk about next is how we're going to kill Licinus."

"Yes. Think of that. His body at your feet, his head held aloft in your hand, the look of surprise on his face. You want it, I know you do."

"I do."

"I will give you all that you seek: your enemy dead at your feet, your brother free from harm. We will take this tournament by storm and the empire after it. Don't you see? The audience will fall in love with us."

"But how?" I whispered. "Licinus takes more ambrosia than any of us."

"Ah, now there's the rub," he said. "He seeks early ascension to godhood. He tries to walk the proconsul's path, but he's not ready. He's not worthy."

It was no surprise to me to hear that Aquilinus was the big imbiber. It was obvious from the way he shone when I first saw him on the podium.

"But how do we kill Licinus if he is taking large doses of the stuff? Gods, we had a fraction of that and couldn't kill each other last night."

If he could tell me how to kill Licinus, then I'd have the key to killing the lot of them.

Crassus' eyes studied me, searching for any sign of mistrust or betrayal. I pressed my breasts against his chest and he stretched up to kiss me. His hatred for Licinus was palpable and far outweighed any lingering doubts he had of me.

"Then let us sculpt our revenge," Crassus said with a grin. "What I tell you next, I tell you as a dowry, a promise of our future together," he said, brushing my cheek. "When all this is over, when I stand upon the victor's podium with you beside me, with the entire galaxy chanting our names, then we shall be bound together as man and wife."

I smiled at him, grateful for Publia's work on my face. It was still stretched back, making it more difficult to register some of the more subtle signs of shock and displeasure.

"I can't wait, darling," I said, imagining the very instant Orbis would steal his life.

"As I said, we're not yet gods; we're gods in the making, germinating seeds, if you like. If we stop consuming the ambrosia, well, you've seen what happens, terrible withdrawal symptoms. It's then that we're vulnerable, within hours of the effect wearing off. We're all on rations during the tournament. Mania gives us one dose first thing in the morning and another each night."

"But what you gave me last night. You have more?"

"That was my only backup," he said, stroking my face, "but I'd have paid five times as much if it meant winning you."

"I should have held out for more," I joked, and he laughed.

"Now, the key is that by sundown we start to feel the lack of ambrosia," Crassus continued. "You've seen the yellow skin, right? And the following morning we're desperate for our next dose. It's these periods when the ambrosia is at our lowest level and our craving at the highest that we're most vulnerable. We will choose one of these periods in the next stage. When we're underground and the media spherae find it harder to keep track of us all, we must escape the watchful eyes of the audience and emperor. I want no one to know that I have killed him."

"You don't want complications with Proconsul Aquilinus," I stated.

He looked pained. "Let's not think about such things. Let's focus on Licinus. The strategy I suggest can be summed up in three words: 'isolate,' 'decapitate,' 'incinerate.' Or an alternative for the last word might be 'incarcerate.' Separate Licinus from the team and then take his head from his shoulders with your discus. This will not kill him, but it will incapacitate him long enough that we can burn his body or bury his head in enough rubble that it can't be reunited with his body. When the ambrosia effect wears off, without a backup dose, he will die."

"Agreed. And what about the rest of the Blood Hawks?"

"I'll need you to help create a distraction when the moment is right. Something that will send Licinus in my direction, away from the others. Then come back around and launch a surprise attack from the rear while I tackle him head on. We can take him together."

"Yes. With Licinus dead, there's nothing to stop us," I said.

I kissed him on the mouth and felt his acquiescence. I'd help him right up to the point the Blood Hawks were dead and my brother safe. Then I'd help Gaius Sertorius Crassus to an early grave.

"The code word shall be 'Rubicon,'" he said. "When I say it to you, be ready to act."

Like Julius Caesar crossing the Rubicon, there was no going back.

"Yes. Rubicon."

We made love again, and I stared at him adoringly, smiling with approval. A smile was the best weapon I had right now. It bought me the time I needed to think while my mind was still clear, until the craving for the ambrosia returned, and I needed to do a lot of thinking. It turned out Julia was right—bedding Crassus was an informative activity.

ACT IV

BESTIARIUS

Each as he hath begun shall work out his destiny. Jupiter is one
   and king over all; the fates will find their way.
By his brother's infernal streams, by the banks of the pitchy
   black-boiling chasm he signed assent, and made all Olympus
   quiver at his nod.
Here speaking ended: thereon Jupiter rises from his golden throne,
   and the heavenly people surround and escort him to the
   doorway.

—Virgil, *Aeneid*

XXVII

I SOUGHT OUT JULIA in the early morning before the others arose. The red tents of the Blood Hawks looked like bloodstains on the morning snow. Overnight there had been only minor snowfall and the cutting wind seemed to have vanished. It was as still and perfect a day as one could get on this frozen hell—as if this entire world was holding its breath to see what would happen next. The frozen wastes looked majestic, like waves on a great sea interspersed with serrated peaks. My heart was racing with dark excitement. No fear. It was perfect. This was how it was always meant to be. Fortuna's hand was urging me onward. The Furies filled me with a fire that obliterated all hesitation. Things were coming into alignment.

The redhead was at the edge of the immunes' camp on her own, cursing as she tried to get her gloved fingers to hold on to a wrench that she'd buried deep inside one of the desultore skirmisher engines.

"Have a good night with Crassus?" she asked as I approached.

"I think you'd be the last person to criticize me," I said. She turned on the noisy generator she was using to charge the skirmisher's engine. "Besides, it doesn't matter—he'll be dead soon enough."

Looking at Julia, I became aware that with my body's transformation had come a shift in mental perspective. Knowing I couldn't be killed, that I was filled with a life force that buffered me from the effects of mortal decay, it changed things. When I left Crassus in our bed, he looked like a tower of strength and vitality, energy bursting from his body. Julia, young as she was, was dying. I could smell death on her. The strands of her red hair looked like thousands of tiny, brittle bones. I sensed her fragility and how easily her life might be stolen away.

"I'm worried about you, Accala." She reached out and touched my breastplate. "It's cold, you don't have your armor's internal heating turned on. Can't you feel the cold?"

"What's to feel? There's no wind this morning."

"It's still minus twenty. The sun's not up yet, and you're walking around without a heat source."

"I'm fine. I've never felt better," I said.

"I noticed. Crassus must have given you ambrosia last night. You looked terrible yesterday, and this morning you're shining like you've just come back from a holiday spa."

"What does that matter? All that matters is the mission. Have you contacted my uncle yet?"

"Yes," Julia said cautiously. "I've done as you asked and contacted your uncle. He's forbidden you to act. He says you must do things in the correct order to minimize risk. If you act too soon and it doesn't work out, the Sertorians will execute Aulus."

"They won't," I said.

"And you know this how? Did Crassus tell you that? You can't trust him."

"And I can trust you? Off to bed Crassus to celebrate the second you think I'm dead."

"That's not how it is and you know it. I'm your friend."

"You serve yourself and your collegia masters, you're no friend of mine."

"No?"

She looked around quickly to make sure no one was watching us and then moved to stand between me and the camp, shielding me from view.

"Quickly, give me your arm."

I did as she asked and she ran her armilla over my bracelet.

"What was that?"

"Another useful thing I picked up sleeping with Crassus. The code to your bracelet. It will register a mild tingle whenever they go to shock you instead of the real thing. How far did you think you were going to get with this thing still on?"

"I . . . I thank you."

"Really, remember who your friends are," she said. "And if you want to thank me, then fill me in on what you've learned."

I gave her a quick summary of my experiences in the hive and what I'd learned from Crassus.

"Gods, that's a lot to take in," she said.

"So you see," I said. "There is no risk to Aulus, at least not from the Sertorians. They don't have him anymore. You were right, their bases have been overrun by Hyperboreans."

"Did Crassus tell you that?"

"He did."

"And if he's lying?"

"He's not. I can tell."

"Because your skills in the bedroom are so mind-blowingly spectacular?" She paused. "I'm sorry, let me take that back. I shouldn't have insulted you, it's just that you're risking everything on unreliable information. What if Licinus leaked that information to Crassus, knowing he'd tell you? You can't trust the Sertorians, especially Crassus. They're expert liars. The goal has always been to keep you alive long enough for you to find your brother. If you can locate him, then surely playing along with the Sertorians while lowering your ambrosia intake is the key."

"I can't do that."

"Why not?"

"I've made a deal with Crassus. He'll lead me to my brother the moment Licinus is dead."

"I see now," Julia said. "You could have gone in search of Aulus back in the cavern, but you chose to return. You came back here to have your revenge on the Hawks. You put that ahead of finding Aulus."

"Don't you dare say that," I warned.

"Why not? It's the truth."

"How dare you talk to me this way? I who risk all. You sit on the sidelines and dare to lecture me?"

"Can you even hear yourself?" she asked. "You sound like a villain in an amateur theater production. The ambrosia has affected you more than you realize. We're a team and I have orders to support you, but I also have your uncle's permission to supersede you if, in my consideration, you might jeopardize the mission."

"Supersede me? Is that a threat?" I said quietly, my voice filled with danger. I was seething. How dare she? I was sick and tired of bowing and scraping. I wouldn't yield to the Sertorians, and I certainly wasn't going to bow down to a trumped-up grease monkey. She didn't care about me or the Viridians. This was all about the collegia and their agenda.

"It's no threat. You've raised the stakes and danger level, your uncle has to take measures to make sure that the mission isn't ruined if you go batshit crazy on us. Now tell me you're going to be able to keep it all together and I'll tell you the rest of your uncle's orders."

"I'm listening," I said.

"Your uncle wants me to leave a trail so the Viridians can find us if the Sertorians take you and I off course. I've put some radioactive discharge and a pinprick of a hole in the skirmisher's fuel line. Caninus is a gifted tracker; he could follow a trail like that blindfolded. The Golden Wolves will be right behind us, Accala. Ready for when we need them, but they won't lift a finger to help us unless Aulus is secured. So I'm going to ask you one last time. Will you hold off on attacking the Hawks? At least for now? Work with me, we'll cut your ambrosia, and as soon as you've got a fix on your brother we'll alert your uncle. How's that sound?"

"Better," I replied.

"So we have an understanding?"

I gave her a slight smile. "Understood. It's the ambrosia. I don't know what I was thinking. I came on too strong again, didn't I?"

"You sure did."

Julia returned to working on the chariot. She had made the same mistake as Crassus and forgotten that you should never try to saddle and ride a wolf unless you're prepared to get bitten. She might have weakened the control the Sertorians had over me via the bracelet, but I had no doubt she could still make it deliver a full strength charge with the codes in her possession. Julia wasn't offering freedom. She was just switching control of the lead from the Sertorians to herself. I headed over to where the Blood Hawks were gathering. Licinus would be dispensing ambrosia, and I needed to secure my share. The more I got, the stronger I'd be when the time came to strike. Barbata slipped her arm about my waist as I approached.

"I do hope you and your grease monkey aren't letting your personal relationship interfere with your professional duties."

"Don't be ridiculous," I replied, but I pulled away, pretending to be embarrassed.

She pulled me to her and kissed me on the mouth. Only when I stopped resisting did she release me. "You belong to Crassus, but he belongs to me. Always remember, I helped shape that body of yours. I know how to give it pleasure, how to take away its pains."

I checked my anger for the second time that morning, but this time it was because I became absorbed in watching Mania remove her casket from the lockbox aboard the chariot. She brought it to the team, removing one small, thin phial at a time from within.

Each team member was given a phial except me. As Mania closed the casket, I moved toward her to demand my share, but Licinus stepped into my path, cutting me off.

"You're on a tight leash for now," he explained. "Continue performing to my satisfaction, and you'll get a dose when we camp tonight. Fail me, and I'll let you spend the night without a drop. You haven't felt anything yet when it comes to withdrawal, trust me. It'll twist your bones and muscles, you'll be curled up in excruciating pain like an old crone." He gazed at me with sadistic pleasure. I took a step back and bowed my head in submission. He planned to dangle the ambrosia in front of me like a carrot. There was a slight tremble in my hands, but it wouldn't affect my performance. Thanks to Crassus, I had more ambrosia in me than Licinus thought. I could wait. It would be worth it to see the look on his face when I took his head.

Julia's words came back to me: that I should save Aulus, deny the Sertorians the ambrosia before anything else. All of it made sense per se, but Uncle's orders were issued from a distance—he couldn't see how things played out in the field— and Julia was clouded by a fog of uncertainty. She couldn't see that it needn't be one or the other. She didn't have the clarity and perspective that the ambrosia granted. I could see it all play out, clear as day. Kill my enemies *and* save my brother. Mania, little Mania, guardian of the ambrosia. Even before I lifted a finger to help Crassus, I'd need to claim her treasure as my own. I would grow strong while the Sertorians were weakened. Even if I killed all the others, what wouldn't Crassus do for his share? He'd lead me to Aulus no problem at all. My revenge would be a meal I had to taste, to savor, to relish. Nothing would quench my appetite except Sertorian blood. We were heading into the underworld, like Orpheus into the halls of Hades, and the Sertorians wouldn't be coming out.

*   *   *

JULIUS GEMMINUS GATHERED TOGETHER all the teams. Everyone's eyes were on Marcus, who was sporting the immunity amulet the Calpurnians had won. I'd have to watch out for him. The ambrosia might make me hard to kill, but while the amulet was in play no arena weapon could break its field and harm him. The games editor's winged head announced that there had been a few minor rule revisions to accommodate the sudden change of course—rules that had been approved by the emperor and the proconsuls of each house. One was that our immunes would not be following us into the cavern network, but every team was permitted to take as many collegia immunes on the chariot with us as there were vacant slots created by deceased contestants. I looked to Julia at once. I needed her, and we'd fared better than every other team—our complement was as it had been at the start of the tournament. We had only one slot vacant. She couldn't be left behind. But I didn't have to worry. Licinus summoned her to climb up and take a place in the middle of the chariot, before the pole. I sought out Julia, trying to find out what she made of this, but her face was impassive. It could be a boon, putting her on the chariot—she was the best immune, after all—but I couldn't shake the feeling that Licinus had something in mind, that he had chosen her in the hope of controlling me. If so, he'd guessed wrong. Julia loaded up her additional supplies and camp equipment, as the other important change was that we would make our own camp in the alien tunnels, no secure energy bubble to protect us. We'd have to be on guard night and day from attack both human and barbarian.

As we started off, the rest of the team was bursting with energy, positively glowing—the same quality Julia noticed in me earlier—but I had to put on a brave face. I was starting to feel the effects of last night's ambrosia wearing off. Even through my helmet's visor I could feel the glare of the sun on the ice clawing at my optic nerves. Even when it was beautiful, there was nothing soft on this world—not the terrain, the weather, the wildlife, and certainly not the light. I would welcome the darkness of the caves.

The tundra gave way to closely packed crystalline outcroppings and we had to wind our way through them to reach the hills. The wind had sculpted them over time to look like spiky waves, curling clusters of frozen lizard backs. As Castor and Pollux expertly navigated our path through them, I let my eyes wander over the approaching hilltops. No sign of my silent Hyperborean observer, but I couldn't shake the feeling that he was out there, watching me. As I sought to stalk and kill the Sertorians, did the giant Hyperborean bull chief wait ahead to do the same to me?

Julius Gemminus had performed some on-the-fly modifications while we slept. There were twice as many roving spherae, decked out with high-powered lights and new equipment to enable them to record for protracted periods in subterranean environments. He'd also moved a barrier of force field generators above and around the foothills—there had to be five hundred if there was one—forcing us to dive into the hives.

The foothills of the mountains rose up on either side of us, and the last of the tundra's flat terrain vanished away to rougher, less navigable landscape. The hills spilled out from the crest of the mountains for a dozen miles like billowing robes. The ice that formed them had a milky, waxy look to it, as if they might melt if a big enough flame could be brought to bear on them. We drove in from the northwest, enough of an angle to see that running down the back of the largest peaks of the mountain range before us was a wide glacier, angled toward the valley beyond. As we drew closer, it became apparent that the problem was not going to be how to enter the home of the Hyperboreans but rather which one of the hundreds of circular entrances we would choose as a starting point.

The Viridian team rushed ahead, and a cluster of camera orbs came flying into position to transmit the next stage of the tournament as we hurtled toward the alien hives. The flying referee traveled between the two teams, reminding them to hold from combat until the signal was given, then Julius Gemminus appeared again.

"Minos prayed to Poseidon to send him a snow-white bull," he boomed. "To show the world that he was chosen of the gods."

The Minotaur and labyrinth. The thought of my fleeing the Hyperborean who sought to kill me sprang instantly to mind. They were all out to get me, the Sertorians, Marcus, Julia, but the Hyperborean was the only one I was really afraid of.

"When it was granted," Gemminus continued, "duty demanded that he sacrifice the bull to honor Poseidon, but he could not give up such a potent symbol of power and sacrificed another bull in its stead. To punish Minos for breaking the pact between men and the gods, Venus made Minos' wife fall deeply in love with the bull. Their offspring was the monstrous Minotaur—wild and ferocious, a symbol of disgrace in place of one of honor. Minos had a gigantic labyrinth built to hide the creature, sending men into it each year as a sacrifice to try to atone for his crime against Poseidon.

"We've mapped out the tunnels and the routes out of them, so you won't have too much trouble navigating to the exits on the other side of the mountains. Your main obstacle will be the Hyperboreans, who seek to guard their homes as you charge through them. That and the Hyperborean bull chief, the largest and most powerful warrior who lives within the tunnels of this mountain. It is he who dared raise his hand against the might of Rome! He shall be our minotaur. Escape him and his warriors if you wish to survive the deadly ice maze. What sport! The emperor has personally requested the tunnel hunt format for this round, so the team to kill the bull chief and bring his head out the other side as a trophy will receive a special gift from the emperor himself."

The chariots sounded their traditional hunting horns.

A projection of a hawk and a wolf appeared beside Julius Gemminus and then raced towards the tunnel entrances each faction was meant to take.

"Before you turn on each other, make sure you teach these arrogant beasts a lesson!"

XXVIII

IT WAS ONLY WHEN we were right upon them that we realized that the entrances were not lateral pathways, not straight roads, but suddenly dipped down, cascading into darkness deep below. A quick side glance showed me the Caninines were streaming into another tunnel about a hundred yards to the northeast, and I managed to cling to the central pole of the chariot just in time before we fell into the darkness. We plummeted down, the lights from our vehicle arcing ahead, revealing shining walls of ice. There was a water flow beneath us, running in from rivulet streams that seeped through the walls themselves. A sphera that came too close, wanting to record the action, nearly knocked me off the standing platform of the chariot.

As the ground leveled, we sped along a high-ceilinged ice tube. At intervals, other tunnels branched off to either side. Silvery and shining, the walls cast a warped reflection of my black-armored body. The way ahead was just wide enough to accommodate one chariot. So we traveled in a train, one Talonite chariot behind the other with ours taking the lead.

"Accala! Barbata! Scout ahead!" Licinus ordered, giving the signal to mount the desultore skirmishers. I jumped into the saddle, pulled the lever on the dash, and disconnected from the main body of the chariot.

"I'm your babysitter," I heard Barbata say into my helmet's speaker as she pulled up beside me. "Stay close."

The long tunnel we were speeding down opened into a large cavern. The walls were of polished smooth crystal, fashioned somehow by the Hyperboreans, maybe with their ice-pick arms. Deposits of limestone and agate formed a natural basin in the center, which was filled with another smooth crystal formation, this one in the shape of a vast shining bowl about fifty feet in diameter. It looked like a reservoir, but it was drained of any water it might once have held. Leading off from the cavern were at least a dozen new tunnel entrances I could take. There were larger tunnels cut into the position of compass points, eight in total, and then smaller ones fitted in between them. My guess was the smaller ones were for the Hyperboreans to travel through; the large ones had concave bases and looked like water conduits.

Could they be a means of transporting ichor?

The humming song had made its appearance as the want for ambrosia started up. No directional pull, just the sound at the back of my skull. Before it was time to strike at the Blood Hawks, I needed to get my hands on some more ambrosia, no matter the cost, or I'd be left debilitated by withdrawal pain and unable to put my plan into action.

At the speed we were traveling, I didn't have time for a considered choice, and clear thinking was becoming increasingly difficult, so I just chose tunnels intuitively. Barbata followed my lead without complaint. The destination felt a long way off, and I was thankful for it. So much to do before freeing Aulus.

We entered another tunnel, which led to the next cavernous node and another choice. I took one tunnel after another, passing through miles of the network. Like Ariadne dancing her way through the labyrinth. That was the old version of the story. That the labyrinth was her ritual dancing space before it was converted into the maze for the monster. That was how she knew to give Theseus the ball of string to take along with him, that was how she performed her dance. Except my string was a song, a series of humming notes, and right then it was all but useless to me.

Some of the tunnels seemed to slope upward, but all of my choices took us on a downward path. I wasn't sure why he was letting me run ahead, but I supposed I must be heading in the right direction, toward their mining operations, because Licinus never corrected my choice of route. Although every cavern had the same massive empty bowl formation at its center, the rock formations were growing in size as we descended, stalagmites and stalactites of milky crystal growing from floor and ceiling giving the spaces an ominous feeling, like we were riding through the mouths of giants that might snap their jaws shut at any moment and devour us.

I hadn't seen any sign of the Caninines. Just when I was sure we'd lost them in the near infinite combinations of the labyrinth, Barbata's voice breathed into the speaker in my helmet.

"I've spotted them. They're traveling one node to the right on a parallel course with us."

I checked the side mirror and, just as we entered the next tunnel, spotted Marcus' chariot coming up fast behind the Ovidians at the rear of our convoy. Instead of engaging, he broke off to the left. But why?

"Keep up your pace!" Licinus barked in my helmet's speaker. "Don't slow for anything."

"I think the Caninines are traveling on parallel tunnels on either side," I said. "They're setting a trap."

We were trying to avoid combat, but the Caninines seemed to have no compunctions about targeting us.

"Keep moving!" Licinus insisted. "Drive ahead, no stopping and no response unless they engage. We want dead beasts—Romans can come later. We want to win the round. We're coming up on your rear to lend support. Make as much ground as you can before we're forced to stop."

He wanted me driving forward, gaining as much ground as possible before the Hyperboreans could form a coordinated response to our sudden invasion of their home.

We passed through another two tunnels before the Caninines made their move. As we approached a crossroads, Marcus' and Carbo's chariots suddenly pulled ahead of us from either side, riding the high curve of the walls. Darius' golden bow and Pavo's crossbow rained down fire upon us. Barbata got her shield up at once, but I took an arrow in the arm before I managed to do the same. The pain was sharp, it felt much worse than Crassus' javelin thrust into my belly the previous night, but there was still enough ambrosia in me that it was only a flicker of what it should have been. I swung out with Orbis before I could think, severing Darius' hand at the wrist, his bow falling to the ground as we continued to speed through the tunnels. I ripped the arrow out of my shoulder, feeling the hot ants inside my body start to patch me up, but they were slower than last night. The ambrosia was wearing off.

"Rejoin the chariot," Licinus commanded. "But do not dismount." I complied with relief, falling back from the firing line. Barbata and I locked our skirmishers back into the chariot's body as it sped forward to meet us.

The Viridian and Calpurnian chariots suddenly slowed, allowing us to hurtle past them. They were targeting the Arrians behind us. Pavo kept up his stream of crossbow bolts, now joined by Caninus with his long steel throwing darts. Piso the Arrian driver took a bolt to his helmet that pushed it up above his armored shoulders, just an inch. A split second later one of Caninus' darts hit home in the exposed spot, stealing his life, and their primary charioteer, Cynisca, pushed her predecessor aside, rushing to seize the reins before the craft crashed, and in the process knocked their bestiarii, Ancus, into the line of a javelin cast by Marcus, taking him in the shoulder. Before the others could fall prey to the trap, a side tunnel appeared and Cynisca pulled them out of the convoy and clear of the attack.

Now the Wolves and Ravens drove forward up the tunnel sides, gladiators hanging out from their chariot's pole. Marcus came up on my right, mighty Metellus, the Viridian trainer, to the left with his club. They were going to isolate and trap us, one chariot at a time, and attack from either side. A clever tactic but risky.

"Accala! Barbata! Break and full thrust forward!"

We obeyed, though I couldn't see the strategic value of the move. We broke away and shot ahead again, pulling out of harm's way, leaving the rest of our team behind, exposed on both sides.

In the side mirror I saw Marcus swing and cut Pollux in the side of the neck, sending blood spraying out. Metellus clubbed Crassus, who dodged but still took a hit to his left arm. I heard the bone crack, the strike was so powerful. The Calpurnian chariot fell behind the Viridians. And then I saw the Dioscurii perform another amazing maneuver. Without warning they hit the brakes and dropped back, then the central part of the black chariot split. With the weight of the chariots greatly reduced without the desultore skirmishers, they swung up the sides of the tunnels in an arc, so that for a split second they were directly above the Wolves and Ravens. They were swapping positions with our enemies, coming down on either side of them with the same trick they tried to use on us.

I had to do something. House Viridian was about to be eliminated entirely from the tournament. Carbo and the others were sitting ducks. As the two halves of the Sertorian chariot came crashing in, spikes in their interior edge struck the gold and green armor of the Wolves, piercing it and tearing great holes in the sides of their craft. The hoverplate from under the Viridian chariot was dislodged as the Dioscurii pulled away, sending it skittering out of control and smashing into the Calpurnians behind them.

Licinus ordered us to re-form the chariot. The two halves reconnected and the two skirmishers rejoined, then we pulled away at once, heading down a tunnel that would take us south and away from our rivals.

I couldn't believe that just happened. Every Sertorian instinct that they'd drummed into me told me that we should go back and finish them off.

We carried on downward for more than an hour before we came to a stop. Mania placed her palm against one of the internal storage lockers on the chariot. An illuminated outline of her hand appeared on the surface, and a second later the lid slowly opened. She reached inside and drew out her black casket and removed a phial of ambrosia. Mania guarded it carefully, her small body encircling it like a mother hen protecting her chicks. Once again, everyone was given a taste but me.

"I performed back there," I complained to Licinus. "You've got me running point. I can't concentrate on finding a way through unless you give me ambrosia." And I wasn't lying. As Licinus had predicted, my muscles and tendons were stiffening, pulling so tight it felt like they would warp and snap my bones. The pain that started as we entered the tunnels had been increasing with each passing minute. I wasn't sure how much longer I could bear it.

Licinus looked me over and, seemingly satisfied that I was telling the truth, told Mania to give me a taste but no more. I studied the small woman intently. As if from nowhere, she produced something that looked like an eyedropper, sucked a small quantity of the fluid from the phial, perhaps an eighth of an ounce, no more, and gave it to me. I raised the glass receptacle and squeezed the bulb at the top, releasing the miserly quantity onto my tongue. The relief was instant; it took the edge off, stopped the pins and needles, the consuming numbness, the tightening muscles, but it would be short-lived. Within an hour the suffering would begin again, but I wouldn't beg and moan. I only needed to buy time in hours; their time was nigh.

We continued on, Barbata and I again leading the way. Now maps from the Dioscurii's central navigation computer were sent to our skirmishers, showing a definite path. The end point was still a long way down. We were heading to their mining operation, I was sure of it. As we progressed downward, the size of the caverns increased. Some ran up into shadowed ceilings, so high that I imagined that beyond, in the darkness, they must go on and on, encompassing the entire interior of the mountain. Hours passed, and the bull chief and the other Hyperboreans who were the supposed guardians of these hives were noticeably absent. Whatever purpose these caverns served, they'd been evacuated now, and the Hyperboreans who dwelled in them were somewhere else. Watching out for them in each new tunnel and cavern wore on my nerves, already frayed by the increasing desire for ambrosia. Another hour, and it was almost with relief that we finally found our Hyperboreans. But no warriors, only workers. At first we saw only a few at the other end of the cavern, glowing in the darkness. As the light of our chariots added to theirs, another fifty or so before us were revealed. The glowing ones took off into the tunnels while the others moved toward us.

"Strike quickly!" Mania screeched. "Before they can alert the others."

We crashed into them, weapons working like scythes in a wheat field. They fell by the dozen with each pass, their bodies like glass cabinets, hollow and fragile. These were like scarecrows in a farmer's field, but made of glass instead of straw. I almost felt sorry for them as they made their futile stand, but it would be foolish to pity that which has no mind. They were drones, obstacles, nothing more.

We cut them down left and right, our armillae chiming points awarded with each death. They offered no resistance other than to keep marching toward us. They were buying time for the others to escape, the glowing Hyperboreans.

"What now?" Barbata asked, when we were surrounded by dead crystal bodies.

"Now we get the hell out of here," Crassus said. "We'll have only a few minutes before any warriors in the area come. They come when you attack the ichor, like stepping on a line of ants, except here it sends out a signal to summon the warriors to protect the substance. Just like soldier ants protecting their nest."

We cruised through the tunnels for several more hours without encountering any other conflict, from the aliens or our fellow contestants. The mazelike quality of the place made it as much of a challenge to navigate through the interlacing network of tunnels as it was to survive the inhabitants. Julius Gemminus appeared in miniature, projected from a custom-made small media sphera—calling an end to the day's match. The new rules stated that there were no fixed camps like in the essedarii round. Here we camped with our own provisions and established a watch roster to ensure no enemy took us by surprise. Here we had to survive whatever the environment threw at us.

Some of the spherae that traveled with us acted as relay stations, keeping us in touch with the stadium and transmitting the score to us from on high.

Julius Gemminus announced that the Blood Hawks had a score of three hundred seventy-one alien kills to date and the Caninine one hundred eighty-two, but most of the other teams' kills were warriors, whereas the cruel Talonites were massacring mostly helpless workers, worth only half as many points. The result was an almost even score. It would have been very different if Licinus hadn't adopted his strange new strategy.

There was no telling day from night, but we made our camp with the other Talonite teams according to the clock, and I was grateful for both the lack of privacy and Crassus' veneer of gentlemanly manners that prevented him from making any advances on me. I was ordered to take my shift at the watch with the silent Pollux.

We were taking our turn in the last hours of the night when noises of battle—the clashing of arms, the cries of pain—came echoing into the cavern via the tunnels.

"It seems as if the Hyperboreans have found the wolf pack," Licinus said, waking.

We rapidly packed up camp and followed the sounds. The noise led us to discover the Caninines fighting for their lives against a half dozen barbarian warriors in a light-filled cavern. Five led by the bull chief himself—the crystal spines rising up from his forehead like the Minotaur's horns. He smashed a crystal fist the size of a war hammer down into the nose of the Viridian chariot, crushing it like tin foil and throwing Nervo, Carbo, and Pavo out onto the ice, causing the two chariots behind them to crash and stall.

New Hyperborean warriors swarmed into the cavern, overrunning the Flavian chariot from the side while the chief assaulted it from the front.

The Flavian spearman Fimbria died in a flash, overrun by alien warriors whose spiny arms rent his flesh again and again like a flock of squabbling vultures. Then Garamantus the Calpurnian was down too—ambushed by an alien who appeared from the shadows of the wall beside him—his head wounded before he could raise his black-bladed gladius to defend himself. Marcus was up from the ground, warding the claws of the Hyperborean warriors before they could steal Pavo's life.

"Drive the barbarians back," Licinus ordered. "The wolf pack won't die today."

The Ovidians and Arrians obeyed, but the Tullians couldn't bring themselves to follow the order. "We need to get our beast count up, I'll grant that," Potitus Tullius Silo said, "but let's wait for the barbarians to wear them down before we get our hands dirty."

Licinus sent out his whip so that it licked the cheek of the Tullian leader. "I don't give a damn about slaves. What I want is for you to fucking listen to me when I give an order. Now get in there, you bone-headed ox!" Licinus yelled and they reluctantly complied.

I couldn't believe he was ignoring the chance to score points and let the enemy die. There was no charity in his orders though. Whatever plan he had in mind, it involved keeping the enemy team alive, at least for now, and that suited me fine.

The Blue Bulls were right to hesitate. With a swipe of its claws, the Hyperborean chief stole the life of Ancus Arrius, and just as the Tullians came up on his rear the crystal giant spun about, avoiding the thrust of their chariot. The monster plucked the stocky gladiator Labeo Tullius from his post. Before Labeo could free himself, the giant hoisted him up, pushing him right into the crystal wall that lay behind. Not against it but actually into it, like it was made of water. Labeo struggled, his mouth opened as if to scream, but no sound penetrated the crystal wall. The bull chief withdrew his hands and a crystalline cell formed about the big gladiator, a body-size transparent gem that enclosed his entire body like an indestructible capsule. His movement slowed as the wall resolidified, locking him in place. The inner structure of the crystal cell began to grow into his body. His face wore an expression of agony as thin crystal veins extended into his body from a hundred directions, and from out of those invasive points a shining green light emerged, running back along his veins, out of his body, and into the crystalline cell that surrounded him. The ambrosia. The Hyperboreans didn't want to kill us just for entering their hive. They wanted the ambrosia from our bodies.

"Accala, Crassus, take the bull," Licinus ordered. I was wired, trembling with fear. I was going to kill this nightmare monster. Down here, aside from my Viridian teammates, the bull chief was the biggest obstacle between me and my brother.

We rushed into the fray. The Hyperborean towered over me. The strike came at me like lightning and I warded the blow, but the counterforce as the weapons clashed forced me back onto one knee. He was strong. Keep moving. I rolled to the side and cut into his leg. A chunk of crystal flew off, but if he felt pain he didn't show it. As I came back up to my feet, my cousin Darius was there, aiming a throwing knife at me with his one remaining hand. Here I was coming to his rescue and he thought this was the time to finish me off? I swung Orbis in a protective arc before me and heard the sound of his arrow splintering as my discus hit it out of the air. Spinning about, I cut with my discus. I wasn't holding back, I was angry. He thought I was an easy target? I'd show him. Orbis took the top off his bow and sliced his throat open in a single move. Darius just stood there, shock registering on his face. I hadn't expected to take him so easily, but then I saw the crystal spines in his chest. The bull chief had shot him with sharp spines. I turned back just as the crystal monster's spiny arm hit me in the torso, forcing me backward toward the wall. Gods, the alien chief wasn't trying to kill me. He was going to stick me in deep freeze beside Labeo and collect my ambrosia. As the chief reached out to grab me, I pushed forward again with Orbis, driving his arm down with the flat of the blade and then cutting up with the discus edge hard and fast into the spot between his eyes.

The impact jarred my arm but delivered enough of a shock to cause the bull chief to reel backward. He'd lost some motor control and was struggling to stay on his feet. I moved to press the advantage. Another blow in the same spot might finish him, but he suddenly regained his balance and attacked, and now I was the one caught off guard. He knocked Orbis from my grasp and grabbed me by the throat, slamming me against the icy wall.

The buzzing noise in my head was so powerful now that I couldn't even think; it was overwhelming, filling up my senses. My body wouldn't work; I felt limp in his grasp. But no blow came. Then an image—the mountain, Nova Olympus—the same vision I'd received from the Hyperborean aboard *Incitatus*. There was more but the song was like the strands of a rug, woven together with such complexity that you had to get some distance from it for a clear image to be seen.

The bull chief let me go and I slid down the wall. The glow from the cavern walls faded as the last of the Hyperboreans withdrew, moving back into the shadow-covered walls, then vanishing. I turned around and looked into the ice, but Labeo Tullius had vanished as well. They'd taken him. The bull chief had me dead to rights. I had been certain that my nightmare was a premonition. It was the ambrosia—it tipped the whole game upside down and inside out. Killer aliens didn't want to kill. Licinus wanted to save Viridians.

In the silence left by the departing Hyperboreans, Carbo and Licinus eyed each other, wondering if either would make the first move, but then Licinus ordered a retreat again and the Viridians made no move to press the attack. We kept on our guard as we withdrew and assessed each other's wounds. Pavo had a gash across his face. Marcus was unscathed, thanks to his immunity amulet, but mercifully he seemed not to be in a hurry to take advantage of my weakened state.

"Let the Wolves go and lick their wounds," Licinus growled quietly.

As the hours passed, my insides twisted and screamed as we descended into the depths below the mountains, Barbata and I out front, the Dioscurii analyzing our course against the data they possessed of the tunnel system. Their map was so well detailed it had to be based on existing surveys.

I was given another minuscule portion of ambrosia as reward for attacking the Hyperborean chief. Then Licinus ordered the Talonites to split up. The Tullians would come with us, and the remaining Talonites would head back up toward the surface to continue fighting the tournament. We concealed ourselves while the Ovidians and Arrians waited until they were spotted by the Caninine Alliance and then fled, ensuring hot pursuit by the Calpurnians and Flavians. The wandering spherae attached to us picked up the action of the chase and headed off, leaving us free from observation. I wondered if anyone else noticed that the departing Calpurnians were short one man—Marcus. He had the immunity amulet, and the Viridians were keeping him down here, an ace up the sleeve in case the Sertorians pulled something.

The tournament would continue above, as the Arrians and Ovidians raced to exit the hives ahead of the Flavians and Calpurnians, killing barbarians for points as the opportunity arose. The Blood Hawks and Blue Bulls would play things out down here with the Golden Wolves of House Viridian.

We would fight the secret war far below the surface of Olympus Decimus, shrouded in a cloak of darkness. Whatever we did from now on would be hidden from the eyes of the empire.

XXIX

DOWN INTO THE DARKNESS, ever deeper, until after many hours we reached a spectacular cavern. As many as a hundred tunnels peppered it, like a wasps' nest, and its ceiling was so high it was lost in shadows. Only the milky points of dripping stalactites emerged from the darkness into the pools of light cast by our chariots. The stalagmites rising up from the floor were thick and had more milky liquid secreting from them than those in any other cavern we'd transected, and I wondered if that fluid was related to the ichor. Licinus led us right into the center of the cavern's bowl-shaped crystalline depression and then up the bank to the high ground on the opposite side so that we had a good view of the whole cavern basin below and a wide array of mouths to unexplored tunnels above us. Licinus declared that this was where we would set up camp. This came as a surprise, as it was our second day underground and still early.

"Set up a shelter and rest, but don't unpack any supplies. I want to be ready to move at a moment's notice. The rest of you, take up positions behind the chariots." He pointed to a tunnel on high ground fifteen yards behind us. "Crassus, Barbata, make sure the pathway to that tunnel stays clear at all times."

He ordered the Blue Bulls to hold the front line on the lip of the basin with their chariot. They didn't seem too pleased about that, but they, like the other Sertorian allies, were in no position to argue if they wanted a share of the drug.

"This is an exposed position," I said to Licinus. "We'll be vulnerable to attack from any direction."

"Our line of retreat is secured," he said dismissively.

He was expecting the Caninines. So unless he'd been helping them follow us, he must have known someone else had been leaving a trail for them to follow. Julia's cover might have been blown, her life in jeopardy.

"I don't understand," I said. "Aren't we better off moving up toward the surface?"

"We're waiting for our wolf friends," Licinus said.

"Why would they follow us down here?" I asked. "There are no bestiarii kills. This place is quiet as the grave."

"They will come," Licinus said confidently.

Gods, I wished I knew what game he was playing. What was he up to?

"You're going to trap them?" I asked.

"So many questions, Mock Hawk. You look like you're about to piss your pants. Worried we're going to cut up your friends?"

"I'm worried I won't be able to support the team unless I get some ambrosia."

"Ah, that's what I like to hear. The spirit of self-interest lets us all know where we stand. And no, you can't have any more." He spoke to me as if I was a spoiled child. "You won't need it for the fight, trust me."

From out of the chariot locker, Mania drew the black casket and dropped down into the center of the smooth basin. She placed the casket on the ground and kneeled before it, facing us. Mania looked very dramatic, like a performer on a stage, positioned at the edge of the pool of light cast by our chariots. The shadows deformed her perfect little face, making her appear like a grotesque dwarf.

Moving slowly and carefully, as if performing an offering to the gods, she opened the lid to reveal what must have been at least fifty phials of ambrosia.

The box was designed in such a way that as she raised the lid, all the stoppers were pulled up with it, opening the phials. It took only a few seconds before I could smell it. Subtle, overpowering, bitter and spicy all at once, just like the drink. Ambrosia. Just the smell of it lit up my brain, sharpened my senses. Mania turned and climbed out of the basin, leaving it there. It was all I could do not to rush down there and grab it. The Tullians' faces were full of greed. They wanted it, they'd seen what advantage it gave the Sertorians.

"Is that all our ambrosia?" I asked. I had to know.

"Yes," Mania said. "The Hyperboreans are attracted to ambrosia like buzzing little bees to pollen. They'll come now, you see."

"Our goal is to hold the Viridians on the low ground, in the center of the basin," Licinus said, addressing us all, "and at the same time keep our escape route open."

"Then we will move in and crush them," Potitus Tullius said.

"No. When they come, we'll retreat into the caverns above and leave them to fight the ice apes," Licinus said patiently.

Time. He was buying time.

Licinus planned to trap the Viridians in the basin. That was why he needed them alive. When the Hyperboreans arrived here, drawn by the scent of ambrosia, the Viridians would have to repel them to keep from being overrun. The way the terrain lay, with a sloping hill running up toward the tunnels behind us, the Viridians would be able to hold the barbarians at bay for as long as their supplies held out. But if they tried to run for the tunnels, they'd be overwhelmed. It was a clever plan. Licinus would keep our competition tied up here while he took care of his barbarian problem in their ambrosia mines. Aulus was close, I could sense it, I knew it. The buzzing wasn't strong, but it was constant. Not the same as the static caused by the ichor, rather a slight directional tug, though nothing powerful enough to lead in a specific direction.

"The Blue Bulls do not retreat," Potitus objected.

"Of course, you're right," Licinus replied. "The Blue Bulls will hold the ground and kill the Viridians when they come for the ambrosia. After the Hyperboreans have successfully engaged the Wolves, you may effect a strategic withdrawal."

"Yes. Strategic withdrawal. We do not retreat. And then you will give us a proper share of the ambrosia," the leader demanded.

"Agreed."

Licinus held little regard for the Tullians. They were allies but occupied a lesser sphere of existence in the Sertorian mind. The Bulls were there to play the same role Lurco played aboard *Incitatus*—sacrificial offerings, pawns to be moved as Licinus saw fit in order to guarantee his plans came to fruition.

This was the arena where I must make my play, and Marcus was the key. He had the immunity amulet. They couldn't kill him, so they'd have to contain him in the basin. I could only hope he'd come rolling in here with the Golden Wolves.

"It's time," I said quietly to Julia. "I'm going to take on the Blood Hawks."

She was in the midst of unfolding a shelter from the chariot and checked to make certain no one could overhear us.

"No you are fucking not," she hissed under her breath.

"I need you to disable their chariot. Make sure it can't go anywhere for now."

"You can't take them on alone. It's suicide. You're guaranteeing your brother's death."

"I won't take them all at once. First I'm going to split them up. Which is why I want that chariot grounded. Make it happen and then retreat to the tunnels above until I need you."

"Accala."

I walked away. She'd better do as she was told.

With the ambrosia in the casket in my possession I could accomplish anything, but without it I was a slave. True freedom comes only with power.

As I walked past Crassus, I squeezed his shoulder.

"Rubicon," I murmured.

"Rubicon," he replied with a nod. It was all set.

Julia required a ten-minute debate and a review of her orders before she could make a decision, but Crassus and I were gladiators—we knew how and when to act. Gods, I could taste it. I wanted to cut these Hawks so badly, to see them suffer as they'd made me suffer. The Rubicon was a trickle, a piddling stream. When I took my vengeance, I would create a tide of blood to equal the Nile in flood, and then, once I had my brother and the ambrosia, who knew what path the Furies would lay before me?

Hours passed as we waited for the Viridians. I avoided looking at Julia, except to ensure that she was where she should be, tinkering with the engines of the chariot. Aboveground, Olympus Decimus' golden sun would be rising. Anything resembling sleep eluded me. I needed rest desperately, but there was no winding down, not until the deed was done.

The Viridians snuck into the cavern with their lights off and tried to surprise us, but the sensors Mania and Barbata put in place on the path up to the basin had already triggered and we were ready.

Mania rushed down in the poor light, took one phial and smashed it into the center of the basin, spilling ambrosia everywhere, before resealing her casket and ferrying it back to our chariot. A second later, the Viridian chariot blasted the cavern with light and drove forward into the basin. We formed a defensive line along the upper lip. The Tullians were first, and behind them were the Sertorians. Castor and Pollux, Crassus, and Barbata to the front, and Mania, Licinus, and I, with our range weapons, behind them on higher ground.

"Hold the line!" Licinus ordered.

Marcus was there. Thank the Furies. He and Carbo charged along the outer rim of the bowl in desultore skirmishers while the rest drove up the middle in the chariot. They were trying to break our line with a three-pronged attack.

They clashed with the line of five Tullians. Six of them to our twelve, and we had the high ground. "Drive them down," Licinus yelled. "Keep them in the basin!" The Tullians held the chariot at bay while the Blood Hawks defended the side advances of Marcus and Carbo. Discus, bow staff, and war chain defended against gladius and darts, crossbow bolts and snaking lasso, throwing spears and steel club. Our line was like an unbreakable shield, stopping the Wolves' advance dead in its tracks.

Surprisingly, though, the Viridians with Marcus and his invulnerability amulet made a powerful team. The Tullian charioteer Galleo fell, Marcus' gladius ripping his life away as he passed. He virtually flew his skirmisher around the basin, using the bowl's arc to gather momentum for an assault that would breach our line.

"Mania!" Licinus yelled.

"Soon," she called out.

Then Nervo's chariot breached the lip, pushing up between the Tullians. They were going to get through.

"Not soon enough," Licinus replied. "Push!"

I was confused by the order until the Blood Hawks drove forward, shoving their Tullian allies in the back, forcing them down into the basin, onto the Viridian chariot. Arvinus Tullius fell on Nervo, and the chariot slipped back.

It had the desired effect. The Viridians were trapped in the bowl, forced to waste valuable time cutting down the Tullians. it took to cut down the Tullians while they struggled to preserve their lives.

"Now the driver!" Licinus ordered, keeping the pressure on.

His war chain lashed out, aiming for Nervo. I couldn't let him die, though; I needed the Viridians alive. I threw Orbis, aiming at Nervo, making certain that my hand was steady. There would be no more accidents, no more dead Viridians. The discus traveled on a wide arc, just enough time for Nervo to see and hear it coming and throw himself backward to avoid being struck in the head. The move had the added effect of dodging Licinus' war chain as well as forcing Nervo's hand to pull his reins sharply to the right, causing his chariot to flip onto its side and skid to a stop at the bottom of the lip, creating a barrier between the Viridians and us. This was perfect. It looked like I was working to keep the Viridians trapped down in the bowl, but in reality I'd created a ramp that Marcus could drive up with his skirmisher. Now all I needed was to be on the right side of the fight to make use of it, and judging by the speed with which Marcus was coming at me, I didn't think that was going to be a problem.

Then the Hyperboreans spilled out from the tunnels and swarmed into the cavern, hundreds of them drawn by the scent of Mania's ambrosia, and to get at it they were going to have to come right up through the Viridians in the basin.

"Forward, drive through the Hawks!" Carbo ordered when he realized that he was about to be trapped between a rock and a hard place. His strategy made sense, but in another few seconds we'd be in the chariot and away, and the Caninines would never cover the ground to the tunnels above before the Hyperboreans brought them down.

"Retreat!" Licinus ordered. "Leave the dogs to their fate."

Licinus and Barbata retreated to the chariot, and I turned, pretending to go along and praying that Julia had come through. Sure enough, the chariot, instead of moving forward, just started spinning in a circle in place. Julia had done well, and removed the port stabilizer.

I had to make my move now. Marcus was heading for the makeshift ramp in his skirmisher, coming right at me. It was easy to take on a fast-moving attack craft as long as you didn't mind breaking your back or neck. As the nose of the skirmisher sailed up over the lip of the basin and struck me in the chest, I borrowed a move the bull chief had used on me earlier and dropped under the craft, using the basin lip as a fulcrum. Using all my strength, I tipped it up and over, sending Marcus falling back onto Carbo's craft. The upturned skirmisher came down on top of both of them, driving them down into the center of the bowl, and I rode with them, on the upturned belly of the craft.

I hit the center of the basin right behind where Caninus, Pavo, and Metellus were holding back the advancing barbarians. Caninus' darts seemed to strike home; each one saw a crystalline body fall back. Pavo's crossbow alternated between black bolts and energy nets that filled the air, entangling the Hyperboreans as the Viridians fought to keep aliens from breaching the lower lip, while Nervo struggled with the upturned chariot's controls, trying to right it. The bull chief appeared. He clashed with Metellus, steel club against icy fists, but I'd swear he'd looked right at me. I leaped down from the desultore skirmisher as Carbo and Marcus pushed their way clear of their craft, and got ready for the fight of my life.

Marcus came at me, and Carbo left him to it, turning to help mighty Metellus against the bull chief. It was too late. Metellus and the alien warrior clashed again, but it was over in a few fast blows. The chieftain sent a spiny fist into Metellus' chest, the crystal spine emerging through his back. He was impaled again through the eye and out the back of his skull, rearing in agony before his lifeless body fell like a tall mast in a shipwreck, splintered and broken.

"Crassus, Barbata, Castor. Get in there and get her!" I heard Licinus yell above the cacophony.

It seemed Licinus wasn't so eager to see me leave the flock.

I needed to scatter the Sertorians, send them separately into the tunnels so I could pick them off one by one, and the key to that was Marcus. His immunity amulet made him the perfect candidate. I'd throw him into the midst of the Hawks, a raven with a sharp beak that couldn't be harmed. That'd stir up the nest. But I needed to make my actions look natural right up until the last moment. The Sertorians couldn't suspect I was setting them up—having them regroup and attack all at once was a no-win scenario.

I faced up to Marcus, but before I could say a word my former lanista bashed me with his shield.

I attacked with Orbis, swinging it around his shield, batting toward his head. Orbis bounced off the force field generated by his amulet, but the move surprised him, allowing me the second I needed to step to the side so that I was right behind his unmanned and now upright skirmisher. I hit him again. A buffet to the side of the head. I couldn't do him any damage, but the blow pushed him aside. It was an insult, a way of letting him know that I regarded him so poorly that I could afford to waste time and energy playing with him as I would a child. I needed to keep his energies focused on me and no other. His face was flushed red, his eyes wild. Now I just had to suffer the results and pray that my plan would work. My lanista drove forward with his shield, crashing into me. I left myself open and glanced up to see that three of my Blood Hawks had entered the basin. Marcus hesitated a split second when he could see I wasn't defending, but Marcus had something in common with Licinus. If he saw something he didn't understand, he didn't ask questions. He struck to kill. His shield hand grabbed my wrist to stop me bringing Orbis back into play, and then my old trainer delivered a fast thrust, plunging the point of his gladius into my breast, piercing my heart. The pain was quick and fast, it took my breath away. But, thank the gods, I could feel the ambrosia doing its work keeping me alive. I threw my arms around Marcus. I couldn't defeat him, but the shield formed close about his body and there was nothing stopping me from pulling him down on top of me. The action drove his sword through my torso, up to its hilt, and we fell back together onto his skirmisher.

I could see the surprise in his eyes as he thought he'd just killed me. Shock, even.

"The ambrosia in us keeps death at bay," I said quickly. "Rally the Wolves to take the high ground and I'll help scatter the Hawks into the tunnels. Let me finish them. Carbo knows I'm on your side. Tell him: *troia.*"

Marcus' sword hand was still trapped between his body and mine, wrapped around his sword. I hooked my foot into the metal stirrup of the skirmisher and threw my elbow back, driving the thrust control to maximum. We were away.

We shot up the makeshift ramp that was Nervo's upturned chariot, knocking over Barbata and Castor, who were coming to get me, and then sailed through the air, right up over the lip, crashing into the still-circling Sertorian chariot. Marcus was flung from the skirmisher. The Sertorian chariot slid across the icy floor into a curved outcropping, riding up on its side until it flipped over and rolled upside down, throwing Pollux, Licinus, and Mania out onto the ground. Crassus was hanging back near the tunnels, waiting to see which path Licinus would choose so he could follow and kill him. I ripped Marcus' sword from my chest, dropped it, and retreated to Crassus' position, leaving the weapon for Marcus to recover. He snatched up his sword, surveyed the scene, then turned from me, heading back to the basin to attack Barbata and Castor from the rear. I mouthed thanks to the Furies; everything was going like clockwork.

Licinus' trap was designed so that the Golden Wolves would hold the aliens at bay for some time before being overwhelmed, but now that I'd given them the chance at taking the high ground, they could retreat and live. Just the same, it'd take them some time to hold the Hyperboreans at bay while they got the whole team up the rise. Time enough. The Blood Hawks must die at my hand, not at Marcus' or Carbo's or some alien's spear. Plenty of time for me to take care of business. I'd come in search of them when I was done.

Pollux hadn't escaped the chariot in time. The flipped vehicle trapped him underneath, forming a perfect barrier that divided the Hawks. When they fell out of the vehicle, Mania had landed on my side of the craft and Licinus on the other, on the same side as Crassus. Crassus nodded at me and then called a retreat. Licinus yelled at him, outraged that he'd assumed command, but there was no countermanding order. If the Hawks didn't retreat now, they'd have to fight the Viridians, and then both sides would be overwhelmed by the aliens. Crassus moved into the shadows of the tunnel, waiting for Licinus to follow. Barbata and Castor retreated as Marcus harried them, creating a way through for his team. The Viridians had righted their chariot, and Nervo now shot up over the lip of the basin to take the high ground.

Mania pulled her precious casket of ambrosia phials out of the upturned chariot, stuffing it into a pack that she clutched possessively as she ran for the nearest tunnel entrance. The Hawks were scattered about the cavern, so each fled to the tunnel nearest to them, ensuring that only Crassus and Licinus shared the same exit.

Crassus expected me to follow after and help him finish Licinus, but he'd have to wait or hold his own because I didn't plan to lift a finger until my position was firmed up with Mania's treasure chest.

I strode after the small, white-haired woman as she fled down a long tunnel, running Orbis' edge against the shining wall, creating a dramatic trail of sparks.

"Mania!" I called out. "Come back, little sister. I've got such a fun game we can play."

XXX

LITTLE MANIA FLED INTO the darkness ahead.

"You're making a big mistake, Accala!" She was tapping at her armilla, wondering why the bracelet wasn't shocking me. Using the torch on my armilla to track her, I caught her white hair and gleaming knives in the light. The spirit of the Furies infused me. I threw Orbis on a zigzag arc and he made a satisfying gong each time he ricocheted off the tunnel walls, my own terrific drumroll.

"Mania? Can you hear me? I'm conducting a review of team performance. The word is that some heads are going to roll!"

A swift death was not enough. There had to be suffering to balance the ledger. Rifling through and polluting my dreams, controlling my intake of ambrosia, weakening me from without and within, shocking me with the bracelet. And she'd enjoyed it so. The twinkle in her eyes when she saw me suffering. She'd treated me like a doll, a toy for a pretty little girl to play with. Suffering, yes, but how much suffering? Ah, there was my training in philosophy rearing its head. Exactitude can be measured only by feeling, not logic. When it felt right, I'd stop cutting and take her head. Crassus' idea was to keep the head and body apart long enough for the ambrosia to wear off. That was going to take some inspired, and more than likely pleasurable, innovation. Perhaps I'd tear her flesh from the bone, hack at her, and eat it raw.

I paced along behind her like a wolf, closing the gap. As the tunnel exited into the next cavern, she put the pack with the ambrosia casket down on the floor and fired arrows from her bow staff. One missed, another took me in the shoulder. I let it hit. The pain was blinding. The ambrosia must be wearing off, but I didn't mind. Soon I'd have plenty to repair whatever damage I suffered. Orbis soared down the tunnel and severed her right arm below the elbow. She cursed, and having to choose between the ambrosia casket and lost limb, abandoned her arm and scuttled off into the darkness, awkwardly grasping her treasure.

I gathered up her arm as I passed. Did the dark blood that dripped from it contain ambrosia? Holding it upright, I allowed the drops to fall onto my tongue. Salty and sour to the taste but sweet all the way down. Ambrosia saturated. One hundred percent. At some point she must have looked back and seen me, because she howled with outrage. What must I have looked like to Mania? Licking at her severed limb? Some terrifying demon from the underworld, no doubt.

That struck me as such a strange observation, because on the inside I was flying, elated beyond measure. I was experiencing catharsis, a great unloading of negative emotion, and the more Sertorians I killed, the better I'd feel. This was my time.

I lost sight of Mania in the darkness ahead. She wouldn't make the mistake of trying to match me with long-range weapons again. She'd be positioning herself for an ambush.

My torch revealed a half-circle archway ahead of me, leading into a cavern. The moment I passed into it, Mania was on me, jumping down from a high rock, needle knife in hand. Even though I expected the attack, she came at me with such speed that there was no escape. I was forced back onto the ground, a crazed expression on her face. She stabbed at me repeatedly with the knife like she was hacking at ice. My shoulder, heart, lung were all hit. I beat her with her own arm. It must have looked farcical, absurd to anyone watching, but it worked. Mania flew off me after I started on her head, landing awkwardly on her side.

She was up in a heartbeat, a thrust aimed at my throat. I dropped her arm and put my left hand up and let the thin weapon pierce my palm. I pushed down, until I could close my hand about her small fist, the spike of her weapon sticking up obscenely from the back of my hand. She abandoned the knife and started to claw at me with her nails like a feral animal.

So much for sweet little Mania. She was strong, surprisingly so. Her nails tore across my face, tried to gouge out my eyes. I gripped Orbis and punched Mania in the side of the face with the weapon, cutting open her cheek. The impact was enough to dislodge her, and I quickly got my feet under me and delivered a kick to face, sending her flat on her back. As she tried to stand, I grabbed a fistful of her white hair, using her ponytail as a handhold. Digging my knuckles into her scalp to make sure she felt it, I walked toward the basin at the center of the cavern, dragging her screaming and flailing along behind me, and then, with one almighty heave, I tossed her small body over the edge. The beastiarii slid all the way down the incline, coming to rest at the bottom. She was up at once, trying to climb out, but with only one arm, she didn't have much success.

Mania hadn't had any time to hide the casket, and I found it tucked behind some rocks by the archway we'd passed through. It was still open, she'd no doubt grabbed some for herself and hadn't had time to close it up again. I picked up the ambrosia store and returned just in time to find that she had almost made it out of the basin on pure strength of will, and with no small amount of enjoyment, I landed a kick into her shoulder, sending her sprawling all the way back to the bottom.

"Now we can talk," I said.

"You're going to get what's coming to you, Accala, believe it," Mania screamed.

In reply, I sent Orbis sailing down into the basin, his hum echoing in the emptiness. He ricocheted off the walls of the bowl, eliciting howls of outrage from the small woman as she ducked and jumped, trying to avoid the razor edge.

"Do you know what these caverns and tunnels are?" I asked. "I've finally worked it out. It's a system for reclaiming ichor from the surrounding earth and channeling it deep into the mountains. The basins are like flowers—the ichor accumulates here and then the workers come to collect it. I think the Hyperboreans might be a tad smarter than we give them credit for."

"Mindless barbarians," Mania spat.

I threw Orbis again, cutting through Mania's right leg just below the knee. She crashed to the ground, screaming in pain as my discus arced back, returning to my hand.

"Well, I for one would be interested to see how all this works," I said. "We know there are Hyperboreans about. Your big batch drew the warriors, but I wonder if we could draw out some workers with a smaller dose?"

I took two phials from the casket and threw them at Mania. The glass tubes smashed, their precious fluid spilling over her.

"Are you mad?" she yelled. She started rubbing at her clothing, sucking at her fingers, trying to absorb as much of the thick black liquid as she could. She thought that the more she had, the longer she'd be able to survive me, but she hadn't cottoned on to what I was up to.

"If I am, then it is you who have made me so," I replied. "Now I'm going to ask you a question, and if you don't give an answer that satisfies me, I'm going to cut your head from your body and set it up here beside me, and then we're going to watch as the Hyperboreans come and feed on what's left of you."

"You wouldn't dare."

"Do you know where my brother is being held?" It was my intention that Crassus would lead me to Aulus, that I'd kill him at Aulus' feet, but it occurred to me that if he and Licinus had already clashed, then Crassus might be dead, and if that was the case it didn't hurt a bit to conduct an impromptu interrogation.

"You think you can frighten me?" she shrieked. "Look at you. You're exactly where we want you to be. A slave, a dog. You think you can go back now? You're blooded. Your body and mind know the pleasure of stealing life, of exercising power over others. You're the newest of the New Gods."

"I'm not a god, I'm the scourge of gods. I'm fury, jealousy, and revenge—all three Dirae wrapped up in one neat package. I'm your worst nightmare, you horrible little bitch."

Orbis was about to fly from my hand again, but I stopped, suddenly aware of movement in the cavern.

Mania followed my gaze to see a dozen or so worker Hyperboreans emerging from the tunnels about us, drawn by the scent of the ambrosia that covered Mania.

"Wait! Wait!" she cried as I raised my hand to cast Orbis. "I'll tell you where he is. I'll even give you the coordinates. Just let me out of here. Let me put my body back together."

"Why don't you give me the coordinates first. I swear to my gods that I'll take you with me."

"How can I trust you?"

"What choice do you have? Look, here come our worker bees to collect their pollen. I don't think you'll have much of a body left by the time they're done with you."

She disconnected her armilla with a flick of her wrist and with her one hand tapped desperately on it.

"Here's the location on my armilla, take it, see for yourself."

Mania awkwardly threw the device up over the lip of the bowl. It showed a sublevel, less than an hour's walk from my current location. I transferred the information to my own device. It was a lie, of course. I'd resisted taking any ambrosia from the casket, letting the damage Mania inflicted run me down, and sure enough, I felt Aulus. The directional pull was strong and accurate. He was far from here, many, many miles away to the northwest.

"You're lying," I said.

"I'm not! I swear it. You promised to take me out of here." She sounded very convincing. Maybe she didn't know where Aulus was.

"You're right," I said. "First, though, I'm going to have to cut you down to size, little sister."

Now I had no need to hold off on consuming ambrosia and I hungrily delved into the chest and downed two phials in quick succession.

"But we had a deal."

"I said I'd take you out of there and I will. In pieces. We'll go together and see if you're telling the truth, and then we'll pay a visit to the rest of the Blood Hawks."

I saw the terror in her eyes then, the realization that I was much more than the killer she participated in creating. I had given myself up to the dark fire that I'd nursed in my heart for so long, a fire that could not be resisted.

Orbis sailed down into the bowl on a leisurely, aesthetically pleasing path. A sailboat cutting through water. Mania started a desperate crawl, but I'd anticipated her movement. Her head rolled from her shoulders, cut right below the larynx, and hit the floor of the icy basin with a muffled thud.

Her body fell back and ended up sitting upright, legs splayed, like a rag doll. When the head came to rest, looking up at me, the mouth was still moving, still hurling abuse, still filled with outrage, though there were no lungs attached to lend breath to them. All that came was an amusing rasping whisper.

I slid down into the bowl. As with the bull chief, the workers observed, but directed no violence toward me. Grabbing Mania by the ponytail again, I dragged her head behind me as I climbed out.

Hoisting her head up before me, I considered her pained, angry expression. "Finally, we're seeing eye to eye," I said.

As promised, I set her down next to me on the lip of the bowl and watched the Hyperboreans go to work. They coordinated their efforts—three raised her body up out of the bowl to waiting hands and then carefully cleaned the floor, delicately touching any droplets that remained, their fingers glowing as they absorbed the substance into their bodies. The others took the headless body and pressed it into the far wall of the cavern. The cavern wall softened, as it had for Labeo, as Mania's small frame was accepted into it.

The horror on Mania's face as the ambrosia extraction began was palpable.

Here was one final nightmare for her to savor, though I guessed it was much less pleasurable to be the victim instead of the observer. I wondered if the ambrosia allowed her to feel the sensation of her disconnected body, or if it was just the sight of it that was causing her pain.

As we watched, I was surprised that I felt only a slight spark of satisfaction, not the elation I was expecting. This small portion of Sertorian suffering was not nearly enough to satisfy my craving.

The Hyperboreans seemed occupied with their role. There were about four or five sucking up the remains in the basin, and as before they paid no attention to me.

She screamed and screamed, and surprisingly, whether it was just vibration or the last vestige of air in her severed windpipe, I could hear her. I was expecting curses, but she was talking about something else. I held her head up to my ear and tried to make out the words.

"Dead. Your brother's dead! We played you for a fool!"

I dropped the head, her words stealing my fire. The soundless harrassment continued from the ground, but her words echoed on in memory. But she was wrong. I had to trust in the pin and its directions, not Sertorian lies.

I delved into the casket once more. There they were. So sweet. I downed another phial at once, transforming the underworld into paradise. I quickly closed the box back up. I didn't want the scent to attract any Hyperboreans to me. I was all dark fire and confidence. One was plenty for now, and I had work to do.

I put the casket in Mania's pack and shouldered it, picking up the small woman's head as I passed by. She was still alive, lapsing in and out of consciousness.

"I don't believe you," I said to her as I strolled along. "Not for a minute. Let's go and see who else we can find. I'll ask the same question to the next Hawk we meet. Sooner or later we'll get to the bottom of this."

I walked out of the cavern until I found a branching corridor and then started down it, heading toward the same tunnel I saw Crassus vanish into. Less than ten feet along, I ran right into Barbata as she came around a corner. She stumbled back, and I threw her Mania's head. She automatically caught it, and in the second her expression registered surprise, I stepped forward and cut her face from lower right jaw to upper left temple, a long deep cut. She screamed, more in outrage than pain, and dropped Mania's head on the floor. I delivered a kick to Barbata's torso and sent her reeling backward.

"Didn't see that coming, did you?" I asked.

"What have you done?" Barbata yelled as she cradled her face, blood seeping out between her fingers.

"I've made the first stroke in a new work of art," I explained. "I'm set to make you as disfigured on the outside as you are on the inside. Truth is the only real beauty, you know."

She struck out with her trident, an amateurish thrust that I warded easily. I had her rattled. I was starting to feel the pulse of the dark tide now. This is what it took to make things right. To humiliate each of them in turn. To drive each one of them into the place they feared the most. They had to know the fear and humiliation I'd endured. They had to know that it was at my hand that they'd been defeated. And only then could they be permitted to die.

Barbata cast her net at me and then, to my surprise, turned and ran. I cut through the net with Orbis, the electrical field not slowing me at all, picked up Mania's head, and paced after her. The dark-haired gladiator made good speed, but I was riding on fresh ambrosia. She was heading down in the direction of the coordinates Mania had given me, which suited me perfectly. I let her wear herself out. If that was the location of their mining base, then Barbata must have figured she'd find support there. Maybe the Sertorians were leading me into a trap, and if they were, that was fine. I had the ambrosia and they had none. I was ready for anything.

When we were halfway to Mania's marker, I got bored and cast Orbis off the wall so that he cut into Barbata's leg. She stumbled and fell to one knee.

I knew I had to ask her the question about my brother, but it was hard. I didn't want to hear the answer. What if she said the same thing as Mania?

"Where are they keeping my brother?" I asked her. "I won't ask again."

Barbata's answer was a trident thrust with better aim this time, but I was functioning at super speed. I dodged and put a neat slice right down the middle of her face. She seethed with anger and tried the trident again. I was on fire, unstoppable.

"Answer me, or I'll cut you up so badly that all the ambrosia in the world won't be able to fix your face."

Her lip curled with disdain, but I knew I'd hit a chord.

"Answer me!" I made a new, horizontal cut that sliced her nose.

"Your brother's dead," she spat.

"Liar," I said softly.

"Dead. Dead. Dead."

She relished saying the word, repeating it with each thrust she made at me with her trident. I blocked the outer fork and then ran Orbis down the long shaft of the weapon before checking him with my other hand and giving her a third cut from lower left jaw up to her nose, making a short line to match the three intersecting long ones.

"There you go," I said. "There's one cut for each of your precious precepts. You're not going to die today, Barbata. You wanted me to be the poster girl for House Sertorian? Well, you're going to balance things out. You're going to be the most repulsive Sertorian in the empire. You're going to be the living reminder of what happens when you treat a wolf with disdain." I hated that by embracing the ambrosia, I couldn't feel the connection to my brother that would let me know for certain whether the two Hawks really had lied to me.

She reeled back, then ran away once more down the corridor toward the crossroads. I let her go, laughing and swinging Mania's head as I went, enjoying the game. The Sertorians were more fun than I expected. I could hunt them all day. They must have contrived the lie about my brother in advance, agreed that's what they'd say to me if I broke free, to try to weaken me, to break me down. But they were wrong. I wouldn't hear any more poison.

Barbata scuttled off down the tunnel to the right, and as I went to follow her, movement flashed to my left.

"Accala!"

Julia stepped out in front of me, blocking the way.

"You couldn't help yourself, could you?" she said.

"Get out of my way. Barbata's escaping, and I'm not done with her."

"Where is your brother? You've totally lost it. You're placing the mission in jeopardy."

"Mania here tells me that I'm heading right to my brother," I said enthusiastically, holding up the small woman's head. "I know what I'm doing. Now get out of the way."

"Where are you going? I don't believe you're trying to find Aulus."

"No. He's in another direction. Father down and to the northwest."

"Then where?"

"As far as I can tell, right into a trap the Blood Hawks have set up for me."

"You did exactly what I warned you not to do. You put revenge ahead of duty," Julia said, indicating Mania's head.

"It was my call to make, and I made it."

"Is the ambrosia in that bag on your shoulder? Put it down and don't take any more. You can't see yourself. If you keep going down this track, you'll play right into their hands. You need to start listening to me and right now. It's not too late to put things right. We'll hole up until the ambrosia level decreases and then find the path to your brother."

"Get the hell out of my way. I really am losing patience with you."

"Or what? You'll do to me what you did to Mania? I counted you a friend, an ally, at least."

"And I'll count you a friend if you get out of my way. Now."

"Put the ambrosia down."

"Or you're going to supersede me? I'd suggest you don't try it."

Julia held up a small item. I anticipated a weapon, but instead she showed me something I didn't expect to see on this world. It was the cameo from my bedroom back in Rome. The scene of my mother and little brother running in the wheat fields.

It startled me and in that instant I saw through the projection to the shining tunnel wall behind. My focus changed and in the wall's shining reflection I saw myself. My hair was disheveled, my skin the palest white, eyes wide, unblinking and bright. My body was so wired that all I could think of when I saw myself was a spider, like the arachnoraptors, all edges and nightmare sharpness. I didn't look human. Then I was looking at my mother and brother again, laughing and carefree. Them at their best, before the bombs fell. I turned away, unable to watch.

"Turn it off."

"Remember what you're fighting for," Julia said. "It's not just your brother. It's every Viridian on every ruined world struggling for survival. You're fighting for the freedom of the empire."

"I told you to turn it off. I won't say it again."

She obeyed. "You're right. I'm sorry, Julia. It's been so hard to think clearly. The noise in my head . . ." I held out a hand to her and looked in her eyes pleadingly. "Please, help me."

She reached out, and I grasped her hand and pulled her forward sharply, head-butting her forehead, sending her flying backward to the ground. I walked past and she called out my name. I had hoped the hit would knock her out cold, but Julia was tougher than she looked. Glancing back, I saw she'd managed to struggle to her feet. She tapped her armilla. She must have hit me with the maximum setting because I felt it even with the ambrosia's insulating effect. Julia had disabled the Sertorian bracelet codes, but kept her own in place as insurance. The shock dropped me to my knees. It would have killed me outright if not for the ambrosia.

Enough. Orbis flew from my hand, and a moment later Julia lost part of hers, the little finger of her right hand. I turned and walked away, leaving Julia scrambling about after her digit as she cursed my name.

A part of me wanted to tell her I was sorry and give her some ambrosia to help her heal, but Julia had brought this on herself, and I couldn't let anything slow me down. The taste of Mania's ambrosia-infused blood lingered on my lips and I had a taste for more.

XXXI

AS I HEADED DOWN toward the marker on my armilla, the structure of the tunnel network began to change. There were additions to the wall, black-and-red machinery belonging to House Sertorian. The farther I went, the more prominent they became—pipes and cables, transmitters and bolsters, structural equipment, all integrated with the alien environment. I knew I was on the right track. After some time I came to a vast cavern, the entrance to which was a reinforced arch.

Sertorian mining equipment filled the cavern entrance—drills, laser cutters, pneumatic blasters, and other large machines I didn't recognize. They had their own light sources that filled the cavern with a sickly cyan glow. A large clear vat with a pumping device atop it filled the space, a central pipe ran down from it into the ice below, but the vat was dry of the ambrosia it was designed to steal.

Moving past the large machines, I got my first proper look at what was the largest cavern I'd yet encountered on this world. Hyperborean bodies were everywhere, most in the upper reaches of the arching cavernous vault where the Sertorians had excavated. The scaffolding and mining equipment lay abandoned. Dozens of steel taps hammered into each Hyperborean body connected them to thin hoses, which ran across the cavern to a large central pump.

These Hyperboreans were the same as the ones I'd seen in the tunnel wall days ago when I fought the barbarian uprising. The Sertorians had discovered them, trapped, dying at the hands of the black poison, and were milking them for the precious substance that had formed inside their bodies. As quietly as I could, I walked slowly through the vast cavern. A glint of movement in the rocks above caught my eye. My heart skipped a beat. For a second I thought my enemies had the drop on me, but it was only more of the worker barbarians. They were silently following me. It was the ambrosia. I'd fed them Mania's body, and now they wanted more. That could be arranged.

I continued moving quietly around a giant drill head mounted on a hover engine. There. Fifty yards ahead, beside a shallow basin much wider than all the ones that had come before, Licinus waited for me. And he didn't look too disheveled, either. Either he'd killed Crassus with a minimal amount of effort, or Crassus hadn't yet struck. Licinus stood in the center of the cavern, the place farthest from cover. Was he planning to draw me out into the open, where I'd have no objects to ricochet Orbis off of? He hadn't seen me yet, which gave me the advantage. Ducking behind the head of one of the large drills, I swallowed another phial of ambrosia. Mania's ponytail was held in place with a thick leather band. I took it and slid it over my right palm, tucking three more phials between the band and my palm so that they were fixed in place and out of sight.

"Come, Mock Wolf," Licinus called out. "I can hear you over there. Come. Stop cowering behind shadows. Step out into the light, and let's play this round out to its conclusion."

I tucked the bag with the casket in one of the compartments built into the side of the machine and then stepped out from behind the drill, holding up Mania's head.

"Poor Mania," he said without emotion.

"Save some pity for Barbata," I said. "You should see what I did to her face. It's a work of art."

I put Mania on the ground beside me so she could enjoy the show. Her disembodied head looked older somehow, her white hair disheveled, her skin pale and lackluster.

"No pity. Only shame that any Sertorian should fall to the likes of you."

"Don't worry," I said. "You're about to find out what it feels like firsthand. I'm going to eat your beating heart, and after we've won the tournament, I'm going stick your living head on a pike in front of the Wolf's Den."

"I expected you to rebel, but I didn't anticipate the level of vindictiveness and originality your rebellion would take. I expected something much more low key, not this glorious panorama of betrayal and violence. You certainly played Gaius Crassus for a fool."

"I played you all for fools," I said.

"I think not. You are a stunning example of what can be accomplished with a combination of ambrosia and Sertorian know-how. You're our little prototype, nothing more. When this is done, Crassus won't have any claim over you. You'll be turned to your true purpose, heading up my pet project. I've been aching to break you. Wait till you see what we've got planned, I can't wait to see the look on your face."

"I'll remind you of what you said when I add you to my collection of heads," I said.

Licinus advanced at a leisurely pace along the cavern, around the smooth central basin, his steel eyes gazing at me with confidence. His war chain snaked lazily out toward me, and I warded the tip away with Orbis and started to advance, matching his pace. The chain rippled, sending waves of steel at me, each crest of the whip topped with a sharp spike or hook. For each one that I knocked aside, another came behind it to try to catch or spear me. To and fro, war chain and discus engaged in deadly conversation. I kept advancing slowly, no rush, heedless of his weapon as it cut my face, my neck, my shoulders. The fresh phial of ambrosia was working wonders, the hot ants doing their clever trick, knitting me back together as Licinus was pulling me apart. Licinus was too good at defending against distance weapons. I had to close the gap in order to do some damage. Deliberately catching one of the long barbs on Orbis' inner ring, I folded the disc over, drawing in the chain. Now I reeled in the chain as I moved forward, shortening the length with each turn, winding it about my arms. Licinus lost his veneer of calm and yelled in frustration as he pulled, unable to free his weapon. The spikes pierced my forearms, but now only three feet separated us. He wrapped the last loose length of chain about his right fist and punched the spikes toward my face. I sidestepped and, thinking he had me on the back foot, he threw the last loop about my shoulders and pulled tight, drawing me in close. He thought he had me all nicely tied up, like a spider spinning thread about its prey, but I had enough mobility to raise my left hand at the elbow and smash the concealed phials against his middle back. He didn't look to see what I'd done, instead taking the opportunity to try to head-butt me in the face.

With the war chain wrapped about me, I threw myself backward and to the side. My falling body weight unbalanced Licinus, forcing him to step up against the lip of the basin, now behind him. All through our encounter I'd been edging him toward the shining bowl in the center of the cavern. He smiled. He thought I'd miscalculated. He knew I didn't have the strength to push him into the basin, but if I'd guessed right, I wouldn't need it.

The hands of the Hyperborean workers grabbed at his ankles. Just like with Mania, the fresh ambrosia on Licinus' back was irresistible. Licinus' eyes widened with surprise as he was unbalanced and pulled down into the basin. I was pulled along after him by the war chain, but I desperately unrolled myself, untangling my body, heedless of the chunks of flesh the chain took as its toll and then, before the last of it vanished over the edge, I grasped it and jerked with all my strength, ripping the chain free of Licinus' grasp.

I was bleeding black blood from dozens of wounds. I regained my feet and came to stand at the edge of the basin. The Hyperborean workers hesitated as if they were going to come for me as well, but they decided against it and refocused on Licinus. He was back on his feet, kicking and punching, shattering the fragile barbarians with powerful blows.

"Get your claws off me! Damned vultures," he spat.

He lacked Crassus' air of magnificence, but watching him at work, I had no doubt that he was the most proficient fighter I'd ever seen. If we had stood toe to toe with no ambrosia, I doubt I could have bested him. But the last thing I cared about right now was a fair fight. I had left honor behind long ago. Now all that mattered was blood for blood. The workers decided there was no easy food here and retreated from the basin, scuttling back up to the shadows of the walls behind us.

If I had any sense I'd have done it quickly. I should have sent Orbis down into the basin and taken Licinus' head in one fell swoop. But I'd wanted this for so long, I'd dreamed of this moment. I had to savor it. I wanted to wring satisfaction from him body and soul.

I picked up his heavy war chain and walked back twenty feet or so, dropping it to the cavern floor. Then I turned and waited for my enemy. Julia had used my cameo to project the scene of Aulus and my mother, and instead of settling the fire, it had stoked it to a new intensity. All I could think about was the bombs falling on this world. Of my mother burning. Missiles plummeting from the heavens. The hubris, the arrogance of the Sertorians. They thought no one would ever call them to account for their misdeeds.

"Tell you what," I called out to Licinus as he cleared the lip of the basin and headed toward me on level ground. "I'll give you the same deal as the barbarians on *Incitatus*. If you can make it past me, you can go free."

"Foolish wolf," he said as he started to advance. He was expecting me to cut him down with Orbis. Instead, I sent my discus sailing up toward the high roof of the cavern. The stalactites were set low enough for me to see them and I was hoping they were as fragile as they looked. I was expecting one or two to fall and was delighted when Orbis nearly brought down the house. Perhaps it was the effect of the nuclear fallout. The structures were much weaker than they appeared. A shower of deadly ice spines began to rain down, some as thin as javelins, others the width of the war chariot. Licinus ran a desperate zigzag maze, trying to avoid bring speared by the crashing spires. I didn't want the fun to be over too quickly, so I sent Orbis out again. He ricocheted off an icicle and took off Licinus' right foot at the ankle. The Sertorian fell to the ground and a stalactite pierced his back and spine, driving him face-first into the ground, impaled.

"That one was for my mother," I said.

I threw Orbis and split the stalactite right down the middle, weakening it and helping Licinus so that he could struggle out from under it. He managed to break it off by twisting from side to side—gods, that must have hurt—and then pressed into the ground with his arms, arching his back and head to look at me.

"Did it feel good?" I asked. "To play at being a god when you unleashed your fire on this world?"

Licinus remained silent and started lumbering toward me on his knees. He was determined, I'd give him that.

"Come on, another five feet and you'll have your war chain," I said. "You can do it."

As his right hand stretched forward toward the weapon, I sent Orbis out and knocked it away. I'd inflicted some serious damage, but he hadn't screamed once. Suddenly, it was very important to me that he scream, that he acknowledge the power I exerted over him.

"Feeling a little lopsided?" I asked. "This isn't a fight. This is an operating table and I'm the surgeon. How many pieces do you think I could cut you into before I eventually take your head? I'm guessing that I can make at least twenty-four, one for each month that's passed since you took my mother and brother from me."

"You've put a lot of thought into this," he said.

I severed his left knee, and he fell forward. His fingers stretched out, just inches from his weapon now.

"Scream for me and I'll let you have the chain," I said.

"You'll be the one doing the screaming, trust me," he said, looking up at me, blood dripping from his wounds, a feral grin on his face. Licinus seemed intent on denying me my satisfaction but I wasn't in a rush. Like a fine meal, this had to be taken slowly; I had to savor each course. I'd break him and when he was at my feet, weeping and begging for mercy, only then would I take his head.

"You're boring me, Mock Hawk."

I stepped forward, kicked him onto his back, and mounted him astride his waist. Orbis rained down cuts, slicing his face, his shoulder, splitting open his armor, slicing his chest. Someone was screaming. It was me.

"You bastard! How big will you talk when you don't have any balls?"

Licinus started to laugh. "Cut! Cut! That's the way to do it!"

I'd reduced him to a torso with stumps above the knee where legs should have been. In my mind I'd supposed that if Licinus took more ambrosia than the others, then he would feel the withdrawal come on more quickly, but based on how quickly his body was trying to heal itself, there must have been a saturation point where you were so full of ambrosia that the withdrawals were delayed or maybe even overcome for good. I took his advice and cut and cut, but no matter how much damage I did, Licinus wouldn't stop smiling.

Why wouldn't he break? He had nothing left. How could he possibly hope to recover from the mess I'd made of him?

"Now look at this. I knew you had it in you!"

I jumped off Licinus and spun about, ready to cast Orbis. It was Crassus. I hadn't even heard him coming.

"Well done. This is the Sertorian way," Crassus said, beaming. "Look at you, you are magnificent."

"There's no nobility in her," Licinus said through broken teeth. "She still looks like a rabid dog. All teeth and foaming at the mouth. No cool precision, no surgical detachment."

"She detached you well enough," Crassus said to him.

I didn't know what to say. I had betrayed him, stolen the ambrosia and left him to fight Licinus on his own, but things weren't all bad. I could lull him along until Licinus was finished. I didn't trust Mania's coordinates, which meant I'd still need Gaius Crassus.

"Darling, I tried to find you but ran into the others instead," I said. "They tried to stop me, but I defeated them and then rushed here to take Licinus. Let's finish him together."

"That sounds plausible," Crassus said. "But you go ahead, finish what you've started. I know you've savored this moment."

"He's lying," Licinus barked. "The moment you turn your back on him, he'll take you down. Just wait and see!"

Crassus scowled and responded by spearing his javelin down through his team leader's eye with enough force that I heard the crunch of the tip piercing the skull as it passed through the other side. Licinus fell limp as the javelin retracted.

"He's not dead," I said.

"No. We'll have to separate body and head and keep them apart, but in the meantime we won't have to tolerate his incessant prattling."

Was he telling the truth? This could still work. I'd finish Licinus here and now, and then let Crassus lead me to my brother. The best of both worlds.

"What I want is my brother," I said. "Take me to him."

"But he is here," Crassus said with a puzzled expression. "Right here in this cavern. Look."

I checked the location on my armilla and sure enough, I was right near the point Mania had indicated. But it had to be a trick. My brother wasn't here. And yet Crassus seemed so certain. I turned hesitantly, following the line he indicated with his javelin.

There was a glow coming from an alcove in the cavern wall, near all the rubble I'd created when I brought the stalactites down on Licinus.

Cautiously, I walked over to it, skirting my way around the basin, keeping an eye on Crassus and the ruin that was Licinus until I could get a better look. I maneuvered into a position where, if I turned to look, I could still catch any unexpected attack out of the corner of my eye.

Then I quickly turned and what I saw took my breath away. Perfectly preserved like a fly in amber, five feet into a wall of solid ice, wires running into his body through narrowly drilled holes into the crystalline rock face, transmitting data out to dozens of monitors on a central console, was my brother, Aulus Viridius Camillus.

* * *

AULUS WAS SURROUNDED BY a half dozen Hyperborean bodies, his own body huddled like a curled-up fetus. The monitors beeped and jumped faintly; his heart and brain were active, if only dimly so. He was alive. He truly was alive. It was a faint signal, but there was hope.

Gods, I was so certain I'd felt Aulus, that he was at the other end of the signal generated by the pin, but I'd been dead wrong. The pin must lead to deposits of ichor after all. Even now there was heat coming from the pin, an intense radiation that led me to reach back and pluck it out. I had no fear of it. It burned my fingers, but they instantly healed.

"We call it diamond ichor," Crassus said as he walked toward me. "It took them two years just to drill a hole to extract the pin from his hand. We can't get him out of there. It's up to you, Accala. Hurry now. Try to take him out. My armilla shows Barbata and the Dioscurii moving in on our location. We have only a few minutes."

"You said they'd follow you once Licinus was dead."

"Licinus isn't dead and it might take us some time to accomplish that. In the meantime he's still leader and, besides, I think Barbata might not be so well disposed toward you. I suggest we load up Licinus and your brother onto a transport and keep moving until we can solidify our position."

With my brother before me, all other demands faded away. His safety was all-important. Crassus' idea was solid, keep moving. I couldn't risk the Hawks getting their hands on Aulus and with time I'd have more of a chance to find the Golden Wolves, or have them find us. Carbo and Marcus would protect my little brother. Besides, I still had the ambrosia. I was strong and even though my brother's life signs were weak, I had fifty phials that I was certain could revive him. Addiction was a small price to pay if the ambrosia could save Aulus' life.

First things first, though. Pin in hand, I thought about the dream that had plagued me for so long. Stuck behind a wall of dirty ice, my mother hacking at the ice with her pin, and then the roles reversed, me scratching at it, her inside. Now Aulus was trapped and I had the pin and only one idea of how to free him.

I held the pin like an ice pick and slowly struck down at the surface of what Crassus called diamond ichor. The crystal rippled beneath the pin's touch. The Hyperboreans could warp the ice, and now the pin allowed me to do the same. I took a deep breath and moved forward slowly, extending the pin before me. There was no resistance as I tentatively reached into the diamond ichor. It parted before me like water. I stretched out as far as I could, keeping a foot on the cavern floor, ensuring I could get back out, but it wasn't far enough. I'd have to venture even farther into the crystal. I prayed for the Furies to protect me. This couldn't end with me trapped like a fly in amber. My fingertips touched Aulus' forearm and then I grasped his wrist and pulled. It was like pulling him through water and I kept at it until I was embracing him, slowly pushing through the substance until we were both clear of it, back in the cavern.

I held his limp form across my body, carrying him to the center of the cavern. Then I lowered my little brother to the ground, cradling his body. I felt for his pulse. Gods, thank you. Aulus alive in my arms. I had never dared hope. I could see his eyes moving beneath the closed lids. He was dreaming.

"We need to go," I said to Crassus.

"She ended up pulling your strings, didn't she?" It was Licinus. He must have partly healed back up. He sounded scornful. "It's classic. It's just too much. You can't even see that you've already lost our little contest with the proconsul."

I glanced up to see Crassus standing over him, javelin leveled at his throat. I couldn't be distracted. I had to get some ambrosia into Aulus to make certain he lived without the sustenance he'd been receiving from the ambrosia grotto. Then I'd take Licinus' head so I didn't have to hear one more damned word pass his lips.

"She's accepted the precepts," Crassus replied. "She's chosen to become one of the elect. She is the future and I love her. You, you're very soon to become the past, so I honestly can't see how you think you've beaten me."

"Love? Don't be ridiculous. You felt what you were permitted to feel in order to carry out your role. That role has now reached its logical conclusion. You've wandered too far from the precepts, Gaius. You need to come home."

"You're hardly in a position to lecture me on the precepts," Crassus said. "The strongest shall prevail. The weak deserve their own fate."

"Precisely. Now I think would be a good time for you to do your part. Look at her over there. So uppity and full of herself. She thinks she's got you dazzled, doesn't she? All kinds of plans for wrapping you around her finger, but I've told you a million times to watch out—wolf pussies have sharp teeth, they'll bite your cock right off just when you least expect it!"

I was just about to head over to where I'd stored the ambrosia when Aulus' eyes flickered open for a split second and he whispered, so quietly I could only just make out the words, "Look for me."

"You're the fool, Gaius. And I can't bear to see her waste one more drop of ambrosia. I think it's time you stick that wolf bitch in the knee with your javelin and make sure to twist it about a bit so she feels it."

I looked up to see Crassus standing over me, his face twisted with anger, purple with rage. It was too late, I couldn't defend myself. The steel spike plunged into the back of my left knee joint, driving me forward to the ground. With his boot, he crushed my wrist and then kicked Orbis out of my hand, sending my discus scuttling across the floor.

"Crassus?" I asked.

"How do you like that, you shit-eating whore?"

It was Crassus' voice, but there was nothing left of him in the face. The same face he had shown me in the camp when he rejected my advances, and that I'd seen in Mania and Barbata. I didn't know what was going on, only that I had to protect Aulus, get him out of there somehow. I couldn't stand up. My knee buckled, so I threw myself over Aulus' body. Crassus pulled me off and kicked me so that I found myself opposite Licinus, who was sitting himself up, reaching for his severed body parts. "And the other one, Crassus, get it in there," Licinus suggested, and the javelin drove home again. Despite the ambrosia, I felt it; the point grinding against bone was agonizing.

"How do you like that, you tease?" Crassus asked. "Nothing else seemed to satisfy you. A big fat lance, does that do the trick?"

"The good thing about your weapon is that it's easy to stick back pieces that it slices off," Licinus said casually, pushing his right ankle back in place. "Got to make sure to put the right foot back on the right leg.

"Crassus, would you please put the point of your javelin through the back of her neck? Right through the voice box. I'm so tired of listening to her bark on and on."

My mind was flailing to understand what had gone wrong. As I struggled to rise, the javelin withdrew and then reentered my body. The pain was like a white light, intense and blinding, and then there was only darkness.

XXXII

WHEN CONSCIOUSNESS RETURNED, I was pinned to the ground. For a second I couldn't see a thing. It was Crassus' javelin; he never removed it. I couldn't turn my head, was locked down with a quarter of my face pressed against the cold floor. Then my vision cleared. I could see Licinus with my left eye. I didn't understand what was happening. I'd had it all under control.

"She's awake," Licinus said. "Are you enjoying finally giving that wolf bitch what she deserves?"

"She's had it coming so long," Crassus spat. "Had it fucking coming."

This wasn't Crassus, not the man I knew. It was like he'd devolved to something little better than an animal, worse than an animal.

"What do you have to say about this relationship you've had going with Accala, Crassus?"

"Love. Gods, what a lot of rot," Crassus barked. "It would be laughable if it weren't so tragic."

Crassus wrenched his javelin out of my neck, grabbed my hair, and pulled my head back.

"I am well pleased with you, Accala. You will help many of your people. I look forward to seeing what you are capable of in the arena," he said, and then burst out laughing.

It was the same words, the exact same words spoken to me by Proconsul Aquilinus on our one meeting, the day I arrived on this world.

"Except what you are capable of is what any dog is capable of. You'll hunt out what I want and then I'll breed you. Crassus had the right idea there, at least."

He was mad, talking about himself in the third person. No, it wasn't Crassus. However it had come about, someone had managed to take possession of him, seize control of his body and mind.

"Aquilinus," I spluttered. "Proconsul."

"That's right, little wolf. You didn't think I'd miss out on all the fun, did you? Sit up there in a box while all the excitement was going on down here?"

"It's our little secret," Licinus said. "Proconsul Aquilinus can visit us. Like the eagle swooping down for its prey, he can catch us up, see through our eyes, touch with our hands. We're all talons of the same claw."

What was he saying? That Aquilinus could move in and out of their bodies? It made sense of the occasional crazy outbursts I'd witnessed.

"My ascension to godhood is at hand," Aquilinus said, "but I couldn't miss this moment. Missing the look on your face when you realized just how fucking dumb you've been all along would have been like missing out on one of the tournament highlights. It's right here at the top of my list—the delicious center of the dessert. And how sweet you've been so far. A tasty, well-deserved custard tart. I was there when Crassus rode you, when his hands touched you. Oh my, that was a sweet surrender, and your little friend as well, the lesbian grease monkey.

I've got to tell you, she was passionate. I'm going to keep her too, after all this is finished. It's true what they say about redheads—they might be a genetic abnormality, but they are on fire in the sack."

"Which was better?" Licinus barked out loudly, his voice tinged with amusement. He was up and moving now, almost finished putting his body back together.

"It was a close call," Aquilinus mused. "I couldn't decide which I enjoyed more. When this is all over, I'll send both bitches to your bedchamber and you can let me know what you think," he said to Licinus.

While they ranted on, I let the ambrosia go to work. I could feel strength returning to my knees, the wound in my throat repairing itself. I managed to get up, ignoring the pain, but before I could attack, Licinus' war chain sailed out and wrapped about my legs, binding them. As I toppled over like a rickety tower, he flicked his chain again and another loop passed over me, trapping my arms, and then I hit the ground hard, struggling against the spikes that lodged in my body.

"Look at you," Licinus said. "Thought you were a real Sertorian, didn't you? Dealing out suffering, torturing your enemy? This is nothing," he said, hitting his chest with his fist. "This is just a body, a shell. But don't worry. We're going to teach you a lesson. A sweet, sweet lesson in how to administer punishment to the soul."

I could see Crassus' boots as he walked toward me. No, not Crassus—Aquilinus. I had to keep that straight. If I could just get Crassus back behind the wheel of his own body, there might be a chance.

"Make yourself comfortable. We're waiting for the rest of the team to find its way here. There's a thing about ambrosia. The more you take, the more quickly you crave the next dose. You've taken enough to feed an emperor, far more than you were ever due or advanced enough to absorb. Now we've got to run you down, burn through that ambrosia in your body and the easiest way is to hurt you, make your body heal itself. That'll help you get tuned in to the right frequency."

He crouched down beside me, poking the tip of his razor-sharp javelin into my face—poke, poke, poke, drawing blood each time.

"You're a little brat, barely an adult. Did you think you could outsmart us? Outmaneuver me? But it's served my purposes to let you run, to let you indulge in your hubris."

His gaze wandered as Licinus carried Mania's head over. Licinus passed it to Aquilinus, who placed it down at eye level with me.

"Poor Mania. Don't worry, I have arachnoraptors down here. Right now they're gathering up her parts, putting the rest of her back together. It was Licinus who devised the strategy of bringing you into this game, but Mania studied you and assessed the best way to break the wolf's back, to put you in a position where you'd truly serve without question. Make no mistake, she'll see to it that you pay tenfold for what you did to her."

I had to keep them focused on me. Perhaps they'd leave Aulus here, and Julia or the Golden Wolves could find him. Think! Ignore the fear, ignore the pain. Licinus had started talking to Crassus, agitating him, putting him into an emotional state that allowed Aquilinus to enter. There must be a way to draw Crassus to the fore, to dispel the proconsul.

"Where is Crassus?" I asked. "I loved him. I had no thought of betraying him. He's the one I want. Not Aquilinus. Where has he gone?"

Aquilinus raised Crassus' javelin, and I felt its point pierce my voice box once again. But this time he didn't withdraw the weapon. He drove it into the icy ground, locking my head and with it my body in place.

"Gaius isn't here right now," Aquilinus said. "But don't worry, he'll be coming back soon."

Crassus hadn't lied to me, I was certain of it. Right on the other side of Aquilinus was Crassus, and he hated Licinus. I had to believe that.

Aquilinus smiled. "You're desperate now, aren't you? Sniffing about for some hope of salvation. Let me tell you, there is no move you can make from this position that I haven't anticipated. You are completely at my mercy. And as for Crassus, you should pray he doesn't return. I had Mania take away part of his memory, help him forget some parts of his life so that he could play his part and fool you convincingly, and when he comes back, my goodness, you never really knew the real Gaius Crassus. What he did to climb the ladder on Sertorius Primus these last two years. He makes Licinus here seem like a schoolboy by comparison."

"I'm not ashamed to admit it," Licinus said. "He is a bloody reaper, a calculating and ruthless savage. We are rivals, but I respected him and will again when he's restored to normal."

"Gaius Crassus volunteered to lure you, to pull you in one direction while Licinus pulled you in another. They've stretched you thin. You understand nothing about what has been done to you. You're too young to understand the punishments of the body, how they alter the mind on the deeper level and rise to the surface only later. You're so focused on survival that you don't see that you've already fallen over the precipice and are hanging on by the slenderest of threads. The final stroke has yet to come. Then you'll go plummeting down into the abyss. The hollow defeat in your eyes, the tears of helplessness, that's what I want to see. That will be worth its weight in gold, oh yes."

Forcing my tired and panicked mind to think, strategize, all I could think of was Tacitus' description of the mad emperor Caligula in his *Annals*:

> He was a man who masked a savage temper under an artful guise of self-restraint.

The savage anger, the cursing, the vile, twisted expression, the face purple and swollen with rage—this was the true Aquilinus. He couldn't hide what was inside him when he was possessing one of the Blood Hawks. I had indeed been a fool.

"Look what I found." It was Barbata. I had just enough of an angle that I could see her as she walked toward me. Julia was covered in one of her nets, her arms bound in front of her, Barbata's trident at her back. Over her shoulder Barbata bore the pack containing the ambrosia that I had tried to hide.

"Ah, this is truly sweet," Licinus said. "Bring her over here so our rabid wolf can see her. They say that if a dog makes a mess, you should rub its nose in it so it learns its lesson."

Gods. Now Julia. This couldn't be happening. I couldn't meet her gaze, couldn't bear to look at her. What had possessed me to hurt her? To dismiss her well-meant advice? None of this was just, it wasn't right. I was filled with the power of the Furies. How could they let this happen?

Barbata kicked the backs of Julia's legs, forcing her down to her knees.

"I'm going to cut this one up," Barbata said, "before I start on the wolf."

"That's fine," Licinus said dismissively, as he reattached his last body part.

"Now, now, don't waste a resource too quickly," Aquilinus intervened. "Castor and Pollux have been given the task of recovering our chariot, but we'll wait for Mania to be recombined before we conclude this move and begin the next. I want her to enjoy the show."

Barbata fished the ambrosia from my pack, preparing to apply some to the scarred mess that was her face.

"No," Aquilinus ordered. "Wait until we find the storehouse, then you can bathe in ambrosia if you wish, but now you'll not waste it."

"It's hardly a waste," Barbata complained. "Look at me."

"I think you look spectacular," Licinus commented. "I'd still bed you in a heartbeat."

"But there's still the other casket on the chariot," Barbata whined.

"Be patient. Remember, it's not ambrosia we want, it's ichor. Once we have the raw ingredient, we can make our own ambrosia."

"It's her fault," Barbata continued, walking over to me. The scarred beauty stuck her trident into my chest and then dragged the sharp forks over my face as she pulled away, scarring me.

"How does that feel?" she asked. "Don't worry, there's plenty more where that came from. Going to make me into a freak, were you? After all I did for you?" She leaned in close. "You know why you can't beat us?" Barbata asked. "Because you don't know what you are. You're not a hawk, you're not even a wolf anymore. Your mother made you into a dog that can sniff out ichor. That's right. The pin she left with your brother leads right to the storehouse, the place where the barbarians are stockpiling all their ichor, but we couldn't make use of it."

"It's tuned to your brother's genetic signature," Aquilinus said. "And you share that signature. That's why we've tolerated you for so very long. All this time we've been training you, observing how you interact with ambrosia."

"Ah, here are the arachnoraptors with the rest of Mania's body," Licinus said.

The multiple black metallic legs of the arachnoraptors skittered across the icy floor. At least a half dozen of them. On the back of one was Mania's headless body, still twitching.

"Barbata, give Licinus that phial of ambrosia in your hand," Aquilinus said, then asked Licinus, "Do the honors, would you?"

Licinus picked up Mania's head with uncommon gentleness, collected the phial, and then, with an almost reverential tenderness, placed it upon her neck and poured the contents of the phial down her throat. He made it into a performance for my benefit.

The first thing Mania did when her body was reunited was stare straight at me with an untempered ferocity. She climbed down off the arachnoraptor and put her hand out to Licinus.

"My bow staff," she said, and he handed it to her. "I demand to be the one to drive this wolf bitch."

"The honor is yours," Aquilinus granted.

The point of Crassus' javelin was withdrawn and Licinus' chain was roughly uncoiled, then the steel loop at the end of Mania's staff was placed around my neck and pulled tight so that I struggled for breath. Mania pushed on the staff, forcing me to flip over so I was trapped on my back. She put a boot on my chest and smiled down at me.

"Now, that's where you belong, dog. I can't tell you how happy it makes me to see you down there."

I coughed up blood and gasped for air. The ambrosia was doing its work, but it was slowing down—there was more damage to my body than the liquid could repair. I needed more.

"Strip her," Aquilinus ordered. "A dog doesn't need armor."

They moved in while Mania held me down and Aquilinus watched—Barbata and Licinus pulling at my armor, ripping it away until I was left in my thin undergarments, exposed to the cold ice.

"Now we can get this show on the road," Aquilinus said. "Get her on her knees and let's get moving."

Mania used the stick to pull me to my knees and then pressed me forward. I had to keep crawling along to stop from going face-first into the ice. I'd paid over and over, sacrificed everything in exchange for nothing—a Pyrrhic victory. All I'd earned was the chance to dance on the galactic stage like a fool. All of it was for nothing. But at least we were heading in the right direction. Away from Aulus. I'd do anything they wanted as long as my brother lived. That would be consolation enough.

"Oh, wait a moment," Aquilinus said, as if reading my thoughts. "I almost forgot . . ."

No. He turned back to Aulus. I tried to look back, but Mania kept my head pressed forward.

Aquilinus moved past me, over to where an assortment of mining equipment stood. He took his time, looking over each item—a pick, an ice cutter, a long steel driving pin. He gave each one due consideration, hefting it, swinging it, imagining how it might be used to end a life, and then he shook his head.

"No. None of these are right."

He opened the casket, took a phial of ambrosia, and swallowed it thoughtfully. None of the other Sertorians said a word. He was the master who dictated how the spoils were shared. I tried to struggle, but Mania kept me fixed in place, pressing my head down when I tried to move so I couldn't get enough leverage under me to stand.

Aquilinus searched the floor until he found Orbis. He picked my discus up. Orbis' edge wouldn't retract for him, it was razor sharp to touch, but the Sertorian didn't seem to mind. The fresh ambrosia would heal the cuts my weapon gave him as they were made. He motioned for Mania to drive me about now, so I could see Aulus as the proconsul stepped over him.

"We warned you that your brother would be killed if you betrayed us, and yet you couldn't help yourself. How fitting, that it should be your weapon that kills him now." Aquilinus said.

My throat was still wounded, but I had to make the words come. I had to plead for my brother's life.

"Don't," I said, my words accompanied by a spray of blood from my mouth, blood still pumping from my throat. "I'll take you to the ichor, but only if you spare him."

"His purpose was to lure you here and then to play the final part in breaking your spirit. Mania has profiled you well. While your brother lives, you have hope. That's what we reignited in you at the start of all this—hope that would lead you to endure all the glorious humiliations we heaped upon you, and having done this, it is this blow, the coup de grâce, that will truly put you on the path that you've always been destined to walk. Or in this case crawl," he said as he crouched down over Aulus' body like a great fleshy spider.

"Please . . ."

"You're our hound, you'll sniff out what we need. This one we don't need, except to shape you," he said, and in one smooth movement, he swung down with Orbis and sliced through the right jugular of Aulus' neck.

I screamed and railed against the leash but couldn't break free. My brother's body shook in spasms as the blood pumped from him. Aquilinus threw Orbis into the darkness and walked past me.

"Give her some lead so she can see," Aquilinus said. "She won't go anywhere."

The collar pressure and lead slackened and I half crawled to my brother's body as fast as I could, pressed my hand over the wound in his throat, trying to seal it up, to stop the vital blood from pumping out. Suddenly, his eyes flickered and opened, staring blankly up at me. I looked into the dark pools of his irises and pressed as hard as I could on his neck, but each heartbeat drove the blood flow through the gaps of my tightly pressed fingers and out over my arm in a torrent. I screamed, begging for him not to die, to live, for it not to end like this. And they let me be, let me sit, hunched over him until the light faded from his eyes, shrinking to pinpoints and then vanishing until only blank darkness remained. I fell into it, plummeting down into the abyss of darkness in his eyes until I was lost and didn't know which way was up. I couldn't see, only feel. There was a sharp rock beneath my hand. My fingers closed about it. I was going to do what I should have done in the temple of the Furies back in Rome. They'd abused me to the point where my body was bleeding and broken, crying out for ambrosia. One swift strike might be enough to kill me, to make a sacrifice of myself. To ease Aulus' path into the underworld. I drove up with it, but before the edge could hit home, Licinus' chain bound about my wrist, the spikes digging into tendons, forcing my hand open so that the rock fell to the ground.

"None of that, none of that," Aquilinus tut-tutted like a disappointed schoolmaster. "Your most important work is still ahead of you.

"Calculate the best point at which to intersect with the Dioscurii and our chariot," Aquilinus ordered Licinus. "In the meantime, let's give Accala some exercise and see what she can do."

The lack of ambrosia hit me like a tidal wave. The cold ran over my body like a thousand tiny needles, burning the skin that touched the icy floor. A thunderbolt struck inside my skull. I fell to the ground, clawing at my face, my nails digging into the three canyons Barbata had carved into it, because that pain was so much more welcome than the deep pain as the ambrosia craving returned. My eyes were burning. I should claw them out.

Mania forced me forward to the first intersection of tunnels. One led to the left, one to the right.

"Which way, bitch?" Mania snapped. "We'll give you a drop or two if you show us the right way."

The song was a distant buzzing, but I couldn't discern a clear direction. The pain was too great, it was turning me inside out.

A boot shoved me onto my back, limbs flailing out of control.

"Here you are, Mock Hawk." Aquilinus stood over me, shaking a shining phial of black liquid between his thumb and forefinger. There was only a quarter dose in it, but every fiber of my being wanted it. Needed it.

"This will make you feel better, won't it?" he said, dangling it close to my face. I wanted to curse at him, to tell him to go to hell, but my hand reached out for it just the same. He pulled it away.

"You must learn to use manners. Ask nicely and it's yours. It'll take all the pain away, let you focus on the task at hand. You can forget about everything if I let you have enough. Now tell me, what's the magic word?"

"Please . . ." The word crawled out of my mouth, desperate and shaking.

"Which way?" he asked. "Try hard."

"Left," I said. "The way is left."

"There, that wasn't so hard now, was it? Good dog." He smiled and poured a few drops of ambrosia onto the ground and I hurriedly lapped it up.

"Just enough to keep you going, not enough to disrupt your abilities. Lead on!"

They'd known all along. All along. Despite my sudden realization, the thought that I'd pleased the Proconsul Aquilinus sent an involuntary tingle of excitement through my body. He was in Crassus' body, but when I looked at him he appeared surrounded by a halo of light. He was so bright, so grand. I'd met him only once, but now I saw that all the training aboard the ship wasn't meant to make me respond to Licinus or the others; it was to recognize the importance of this man, to respond to his presence, his voice, his commands. I was weak. Defeated. I had nothing left with which to resist him. Nothing.

"Now, then," Licinus said, "take us to the ichor, or your little friend will be next."

My head was pushed to the side so I could see Julia, who was being pulled along by Barbata, still caught up in the gladiator's net.

"Licinus, can you help motivate our hound?" Aquilinus asked.

Licinus drew a knife from his belt and reached in through Barbata's net to take Julia's mutilated hand.

"Now, here's a new game," Licinus said to me. "I suggest we run with your idea of dismemberment. You've made a good start, so here's what we're going to do with your redheaded lover. For each hour that goes by that we don't find the Hyperborean ichor store, I'm going to ask Barbata to cut off one more of her fingers. Sadly, she won't be receiving any ambrosia to repair the damage. We'll know we're on the right track when we find the workers who are running away with our precious substance."

Julia said nothing. I didn't think I would care what they did to her, but I could see the accusation in her eyes. This was my fault, my failure. I tried to speak, but it was like I had shards of glass in my trachea.

"What's that, dog?" Licinus asked. Mania kicked me in the ribs, taking out her frustration on me. My humiliation hadn't yet satisfied her.

"Don't hurt her," I managed to say. "The Vulcaneum will come for you. All of the collegia will turn against you. They have guild assassins."

"Fuck the Vulcaneum," Aquilinus boasted. "I'll break the union of collegia as I've broken the noble houses. Those who follow will live, those who resist will have their bones thrown into the mix when the monuments to my greatness are being built. Now let's get a move on, dog. If you want to spare your friend's life, you'll lead me to the one thing that will secure my ascension to the imperial throne."

I crawled to the left, taking them where they wanted to go. The pain was vanishing already, the ambrosia doing its work. The humming song was far away but clear. I felt drawn like the needle of a compass, like iron drawn to a magnet. There was nothing left of me but the desire to avoid pain and embrace the numbness ambrosia offered. I couldn't kill myself, they wouldn't allow it, and so I embraced movement. I couldn't stop, because then I'd have to think, face my shame. I let Mania drive me down into the tunnels, taking turn after turn. I welcomed the increasing pain of my knees and wrists scraping along the hard, frozen ground. The humming song was growing ever louder, like a drumroll before an amphitheater finale.

XXXIII

TIME PASSED AND JULIA lost three more fingers on her right hand. Each time a digit was cut away, I saw the pain register on her face, but she did not scream out. She was braver than I ever gave her credit for. The ambrosia withdrawal began to overwhelm me. The cold gripped my legs and arms. Tired, I breathed out through my mouth and the air formed small icicles on my lips that cut me when I closed my mouth. I looked longingly up at Aquilinus. I couldn't hate myself any more than I already did, so I embraced desperation. Aulus was dead. Pride, humiliation—none of it mattered a damn now. Let the empire crumble. Everything was in vain. Aquilinus smiled at my submission. He took another quarter dose and poured a tiny drizzle onto the toe of his boot.

"A dog has no shame," I heard Barbata say as I leaned forward and started licking it up. The Sertorian laughter burned me more than any wound. I deserved this. A Sertorian's lapdog. The lowliest slave of the enemies I hated the most. This was where my choices had led me, and I couldn't see any way out. No strategy to turn things around, no way to protect Julia but to obey.

I guided them as quickly as I could, but it still cost Julia her thumb.

The Dioscurii eventually met up with us riding the chariot. One of the desultore skirmishers had been rejoined, but it was one taken from the Viridian chariot, the one I rode up over the lip with Marcus. I was grateful for the chariot because speed might spare Julia more suffering.

"What news of the Viridians?" Aquilinus asked.

Castor told him that when they left, the Wolves were still trapped in the bowl down to their last five, including Marcus, holding off the barbarians. Marcus. I promised I'd return and help them. Now we were so far away, so deep in the hive that they could never find us.

Julia was taken to the rear of the craft with Barbata and I was pressed to the front behind Castor and Pollux so I could continue to serve my role as guide.

As the Sertorians drove me through the tunnels, I communicated directions as quickly as I could to Castor, who checked them against the navigation algorithms he'd been plotting since we entered the hives, and then transmitted them to his brother.

The way started heading up again, and Aquilinus was displeased, believing the right course must be deeper still into the earth. He threatened me, first to disfigure Julia more and then to withhold ambrosia until I begged and swore to all the gods that I was leading them the right way. He seemed satisfied only when the next cavern we entered contained a small glowing pool of ichor in the central basin. And the next one after that slightly more, and so on. Streams of Hyperborean workers filed in and out of the basins, collecting ichor, storing it in the compartments of their bodies, then moved on. They ignored us. Perhaps they were drawn by the same buzzing song.

The light-radiating tunnels were fragile and there were signs of cave-ins. Dust fell on us from the places the natural rock blended with the alien pathways. I knew at once that the removal of the ichor was weakening the entire hive structure. As we drew closer to the mother lode of ichor Aquilinus sought, the tunnels became rich with it, giving off their own glow, some of them so bright that the chariot's beams became unnecessary, as the shining white liquid flowed in channels along the tunnel walls.

"I think we're very close, aren't we?" Licinus said. "But it's that time again, and we're not there yet. Off at the wrist please."

I assured him that we were close, begged him to hold off, but my suffering was his delight. Julia lost what was left of her right hand to Barbata's long knife, and Licinus used a burning element on the chariot to cauterize the stump. Unable to deny them their pleasure any longer, she cried out. Even in the half-light I could see her skin, blanched and bloodless with shock. They were going to kill her, but not before they stole away her hope. She was an immune first, a fixer, a builder. How could she do that without her hands?

"Next we start on the left hand. Better get a move on," Licinus barked at me with satisfaction.

And I did. That was my only thought now. To save Julia's one good hand, to spare her any more suffering. I should have listened to her. Gods, if only I had listened to her.

After a mile or so of following an upward curve, the tunnel merged into a fifty-foot-wide walkway filled with hundreds of worker Hyperboreans marching along silently in an orderly queue, five deep, their ichor-laden bodies glowing even more strongly than the light contained within the walls that surrounded them. They seemed unaware of us, and Licinus ordered Pollux to cruise slowly alongside the line. No more questions were put to me or torments delivered unto Julia. Licinus was pleased to have found the nonviolent workers, mindlessly carrying their small bundles of ichor in their bellies deep into the mountain.

"Move on," Aquilinus said. "This is it, I can feel it."

Before long, we approached a massive archway leading to a powerful radiant light source. Aquilinus seemed happy now to leave the operations of the team to Licinus. He was here as an observer, stepping into the scene only to pursue his interest in the ichor. If these Hyperboreans turned on us, we'd be dead in moments, though they didn't seem to have the slightest violent inclination, entirely focused on their mission, and it seemed Licinus was also troubled.

"If this is the Hyperborean storehouse, I can't believe they'd leave it undefended," Licinus said grimly.

The orderly march of the Hyperboreans was almost reverential, and the surrounding structure of the hives was changing too. The perfect symmetry we'd encountered, the smooth walls of the tunnels, the design of the ichor wells in the caverns, could all be the result of some primitive organism—a beehive, as Mania said—but the walkway now before us had clearly been created by a higher order of intelligence. Circular beams lined the walkway. Thick and round like the bones of giants or dragons, the simple beams were impossibly large, the width of the chariot and hundreds of feet long, elegantly curved, and connected together by oversized joints. They were covered in thin engraved designs that stretched along in pleasing geometric arcs. Along the grooves ran a substance of sparkling liquid diamond. Perhaps there was such a sheer volume of ichor in that place that it generated heat, because the cold had vanished. The air was a little warm, heavy with water, and there was a faint, sweet smell that reminded me of fresh-cut grass. The curves on the giant beams intersected, creating small circular wells where the substance gathered before streaming on its way. The entire effect was beautiful, like a great Saturnalia decoration or some deep undersea jellyfish with flickering lights.

We were only a few feet beyond the great archway when the chariot came to a halt. No one said a word. The scale of the spectacle before us was so vast that it was impossible to absorb immediately. We beheld a hollowed-out mountain, hundreds of feet from one side to the other, an immensely large space that ran to great heights and depths, and within it lay a city of crystal.

The ice walkway ran out onto a long crystal platform, perfectly smooth, incredibly thin, and nearly transparent. In the distance that walkway joined a large central platform, also see-through, that seemed to float in midair. From the distant walls, great torrents of liquid ichor flowed out of large channels, cascading waterfalls of shining white fluid that fell down to a great reservoirs below.

The others looked up first, I down, but we all discovered that there were at least five, maybe six of the same kind of walkways and platforms above and below us, all of them carrying tens of thousands of ichor-laden Hyperborean workers. They were all heading to a shining structure at the heart of the mountain. Running right through the center of each platform, from the shadowy heights to the depths of the waters below, was one giant unbroken crystal hub radiating a powerful light that was reflected in all the other surfaces of the city. Other, lesser crystals—some the size of the tallest trees on Mother Earth—grew out from it at every angle, forming an irregular starburst nexus. It was this central crystal that emitted all the light that filled the cavern, so strong and clear that it eradicated all shadow and gave the hidden city a celestial quality.

"It's a machine," Julia said. I looked up and saw her mouth hanging open, eyes filled with wonder, her plight and suffering forgotten. This was her celestial machine, or at least the greatest physical expression of it she was ever likely to see.

"Yes," Aquilinus agreed.

Their crude assessment was irritating at first, but when I looked out on it again, the functional pattern of the structure became obvious. It was like a complex, multilayered circuit board.

Some of the Hyperboreans traveled through the air, flying between the waterfalls and the shining heart on wafers of flexible crystal, like large manta rays, seemingly held aloft by the ichor mists rising up from below. The Hyperboreans riding these discs were different again from the others. Whereas the workers were slim and transparent and the warriors were solid with spines, these Hyperboreans had curved, vibrating filaments that protruded from their bodies, giving them the appearance of being surrounded by a field of light. They also created an incredible cacophony of humming noise, vibrating out loud the song I'd heard since commencing my voyage.

We were surrounded by a rarefied aesthetic that made Rome's magnificence look contrived, outworn like a veteran's old uniform. But something so beautiful was also delicate. The fragility I noticed earlier was represented here as well. Stalactites fell from the ceiling into the ichor mists below. The occasional rumbling of shifting rock echoed throughout the vast space, rising momentarily above the roar of the falls. The whole thing had the feeling of a stacked house of crystal cards that might collapse in a heap at the slightest disturbance.

At the same time if Julia and Crassus were correct and it was a great machine, then what kind of a machine might it be? Every machine had a purpose.

Aquilinus reached out and ruffled my hair like I was a well-loved pet. "Look at what you've done, you beautiful little bitch. You've given me the whole empire lock, stock, and barrel."

But I was looking down, through the many layers of transparent crystal platform to the reservoirs below the city. The mists had cleared enough that I could see black churning waters. Mania followed my gaze down and then grabbed Licinus' arm, pointing excitedly. "Look! Look! It's ambrosia."

"No, not ambrosia," he said. "It's radioactive waste. See, the crystal from the mountain takes the ambrosia from the workers, strips it of impurities and then expels the waste below."

There. This was a purification plant, or at least if that wasn't its sole purpose in the past, that was what circumstances dictated that it would become. The city, like the Hyperboreans themselves, was sacrificing everything in order to purify its ichor.

"It's like a big chandelier. I wonder how they managed to keep it from us for so long?" Barbata pondered.

"Because they are better than us," Julia said weakly. "We could never build something like this."

I had to agree with her, as hard as it was for me, for any Roman, to admit. Even non-Sertorians were raised to believe in humanity's inherent superiority, in Rome's divine supremacy.

"Nonsense," snapped Aquilinus. "This is nothing more than an oversized food storage and purification system, a giant fridge, unappreciated by these mindless barbarians and here for the taking by a higher species that appreciates its true value. We are the rightful inheritors. Humanity is the pinnacle of creation, as the Sertorians are the pinnacle of humanity."

I'd been fed all sorts of lies, had it burned into the depths of my being, to regard this man as something akin to a god, and yet he couldn't see it, couldn't appreciate the wonder before him. Seeing through Crassus' eyes didn't make a difference. All Aquilinus saw was the opportunity to take something, to appease his appetites. The gods themselves could suddenly appear and sing songs before him, and he'd still argue against their existence. The realization that behind the public figure, the proconsul was in fact a foul-mouthed, red-faced pig who could not recognize beauty of a higher order served to weaken the invisible chains that bound me.

"We'll advance and we will be silent," Aquilinus advised. "All the ichor's running toward the center of the mountain, to the shining crystal. I want to see it up close."

So much ichor. The air was thick with it. If that crystal was a storage unit, then all Aquilinus had to do was secure it and airlift it out of here. The whole empire would indeed be his—lock, stock, and barrel.

As we slowly cruised along the procession toward the center, I noticed that each platform, including the one stretching out before us, had large crystal towers rising from it, like temples set by the side of Via Appia leading into Rome, and sitting in a small alcove near the top of each tower was one of the singing Hyperboreans. The other singers were flying toward the circuit board alignments to integrate themselves. They were taking up positions in between the towers. Even though they were a great distance away, I could sense that these singers were emitting the most powerful vibratory chords to the humming chorus, as if the towers were enhancing their song. They were not the source of the song, though. The song that had drawn me to this place lay at the heart of the mountain. The great shining jewel was the place that I was called to go, the place where all of this world's ichor was pouring. The singers picked up the vibration and accelerated it, speeding up the purification process in the central gem. Every Hyperborean was lending its life force to feed that central gem, and we were joining their sacred pilgrimage.

The slow-moving workers we passed, shuffling toward the light, had shattered facets, cracks that seemed to be lengthening even as I watched. They carried black-green veins and bellies filled with our ambrosia. The pristine bodies I saw aboveground were here chipped, broken, caked in dirt. They were dying. Looking ahead, I observed that occasionally the radiant light of the central gem weakened momentarily but then returned, and I wondered if that was the moment a worker with ambrosia inside him entered the light.

We traveled for another half mile parallel to the alien queue, occasionally passing long connective ramps set at an angle to run between the different layers. The alien song had led me to this place, and the closer I drew to the center of the mountain, it grew not only louder but also deeper. It was like a ball of string that was slowly unraveling to reveal tonal levels of connection between the Hyperboreans and their environment. This city wasn't some dwelling separate from them; it was part of their body.

Eventually, we neared the tall towers that stretched up to the next platform high above us. The towers seem to be infected too, exhausted of light in places, filled with dark clouds of black ambrosia in others. The peaks of the towers from the platform below crackled with energy. The ground about us was increasingly littered with workers who had not survived the journey. Their bodies were blackened with poison, the course of the living Hyperboreans diverted around them before re-forming their perfect line. Up close, the clouds of darkness in the towers were revealed to be clusters of poison-filled veins, creeping through the interior of the clear structures like dark ivy.

Tower after tower went by until we were about halfway from the arch we'd passed through on entering the cavern, and our goal. The nexus point at the center of the crystal began to loom large, a geometric intersection of the eight great beams that were laden with shining white ichor. The crystal tips of the beams were facing inward, marking points about a circle, and at the heart of it all, like a sunburst, was a figure that seemed to be absorbing the energy from all the sources about it. The facets of the great crystal magnified the form, making it appear like a giant, but I recognized it at once. Short limbs, a smaller body than the Hyperboreans that were also magnified as they walked into it, and only two arms. This was the shining child I had seen earlier, commanding the uprising on the surface. Their little Spartacus. He was shimmering like a star as he absorbed all that world's ichor into him, into one compact package. But for what purpose? I turned back to see Aquilinus' face burning red and twisted with desire. This was all the power he'd been searching for and more, contained in one being, a being he would want to own and control, as I was controlled.

Once we passed the halfway point on our journey to the center, an ache started up all over my body and then became more acute. I saw a change in Licinus too, red lines appearing on his face and arms in places I wounded him. Wounds that had cleared up and vanished thanks to the miracle of the ambrosia. The same was happening to me—arms, face, hands—cuts and gashes reappearing.

Barbata looked around, slightly bewildered as her facial wounds began to weep a black, oily pus. She reached up to touch them and then lowered her hand to find it covered with blood and sticky black ambrosia.

"It's this place!" Mania said. "It's undoing the effect of the ambrosia."

"We have to leave," Barbata said. "It's killing us, leaching the ambrosia out of our bodies."

Hah! It was just as I'd experienced in the ichor well when I pursued the bull chief. Black bands of ambrosia started to drip from Licinus' wrists. He looked worried. I would bet he was feeling the same along every line I cut him. Nothing was more precious to a Sertorian than his own life. These aliens and we shared the same fate now. Our poison was killing them, and their response was to draw all the ichor into one shining heart, the same power that was now leaching the ambrosia from us. This had the ring of justice. That we die here, all of us, right before the prize we'd been squabbling over like a pack of seagulls.

"We're not going anywhere," Aquilinus snapped. "Get to the heart of the mountain and get me that child."

He could afford to take risks. I guessed he could leave Crassus' body anytime he liked. Go back to his comfortable private box in the Rota Fortuna high above this world.

And then eagle-eyed Castor raised the alarm. "The Viridians!"

They appeared on their war chariot, racing on the platform directly above us. Of course. Julia had rigged our chariot to leave a trail, and there was Caninus the tracker. They'd been following us all this time.

As they overtook us, Marcus looked over the side of his chariot, through the transparent floor and right at me. Did he tell Carbo the code word? Looking at the state of me, near-naked and wounded, the thong of Mania's weapon looped about my neck, he had to see that I wasn't here of my own free will. The Viridians were powering forward at top speed, heading straight for the heart of the mountain. They'd seen what was most important and weren't constrained by the leaching of the ambrosia that hampered the Blood Hawks.

"Go! Beat them to the prize!" Aquilinus screamed.

He had to have the alien child now. And more, at all costs he had to ensure the Viridians didn't possess it.

The Dioscurii raced forward, holding nothing back. No more tournament, no games, this was the battle for possession of the substance that would control the empire. Mania needed both hands to fight, so she pulled the loop of her bow staff about my throat tight and bound me close to the central post of the chariot—so that if I pulled away even a little, I'd start to strangle—and then used another strand of leather to bind my wrists together. She had to hurry. There was a little slackness, but she knew what she was doing. It would take some effort to free myself from her bonds, and I had to contort myself to see what was going on around us.

As I worked to free my neck, we sped along curved rows of streets formed by the circuit board layout of the crystal towers. Running parallel to us in the distance were more arches with more ramps leading toward our level. Thirty yards ahead of us, the Wolves took a downward path, appearing to fly as they raced down the transparent ramp. When they hit our level, a barrage of darts and bolts flew our way, and the Hawks were forced to take shelter behind their shields. The race was on. We had to pass them, except that the way ahead on either side of the Wolves was blocked by slow-marching Hyperboreans on their pilgrimage.

"Form a dire wedge! Cut through anything that gets in our way," Licinus ordered. "Charge!"

He began to swing his war chain, Barbata moved to the front of the chariot with her trident, and Aquilinus took his position with Crassus' javelin in hand.

There was little hope for me now. Weak and bound, I did not expect to survive, but I could make a sacrifice of myself. For Aulus, and for my mother. A last offering that would quell the ambitions of the Sertorians once and for all, here and now. Goddess, O Minerva, forgive me for turning from you. Please give me the chance to set this right. Take my life in exchange. Please.

"Barbarian warriors!" Castor called out.

A new threat entered the scene, far ahead of us, on the platforms that extended behind the gem. There was no mistaking the mass of the large bull chief and the other warrior Hyperboreans. And he'd brought friends. There had to be a hundred more behind him and that number again pouring through the archways to the east. So the Wolves didn't stand to fight the Hyperboreans. They must have held them off just long enough to right their chariot and then run, following the trail we left, leading the Hyperborean warriors right along after them.

The pointed steel grille on the front of the Sertorian chariot struck and shattered the weakened Hyperboreans in our path, plowing them like a mower cutting grass. The next ones in line were standing off center and were pushed to the side, maimed by the spikes and blades that protruded from the chariot's side. In addition, Licinus' spinning war chain, Crassus' piercing javelin, and Barbata's trident forked and tossed alien bodies like a pitchfork tossing bales of hay. Mania was sending arrows flying at the Viridians. We cut a path through the Hyperboreans with our speed and skill.

The seeping red lines on my body suddenly blossomed open into full wounds, wrapping me in a net of pain. The same happened to the others. The closer we got to the light at the center of the city, the more wounds appeared, the more black ambrosia spilled from our bodies like miniature tributaries of the Styx, the river of the underworld that the dead travel along.

We drew up alongside the Viridians, trying to pass. They rammed us port side, long blades targeting our stabilizers and antigravity plates. We sped along the flat crystal platform, heedless of danger, focused only on winning the prize. They pulled away and swung in to hit us again. Weapons clashed, and I had to position myself behind the pole to seek cover from the blades and spikes on the Viridian chariot as much as from the danger of the weapons they wielded.

Another clash, and this time Pollux angled our craft to strike theirs in such a way that it sent them flying into one of the towers on the right side of the path. We were already racing on, passing them, but I looked back and saw the entire tower begin to topple in response and then dramatically fall forward, crashing into the hundred-foot-high tower in front of it. That one fell too, and then another, creating a deadly domino effect as the tall buildings shattered, sending waves of crystal shards projecting through the air behind us.

"The buildings are weak. Use them against the enemy!" Licinus ordered. The Dioscurii charged ahead and then suddenly swerved intentionally into one of the massive towers, plowing through its delicately balanced foundations and bringing it down behind us. Although the Viridians weren't suffering from lack of ambrosia, they were earning new wounds now as the crystal shards showered down upon them.

The Viridians remained alongside but wide of us. Both sides had the idea now, and we started alternate snaking patterns through the city, surging ahead, intentionally sideswiping the towers, using them as weapons, sending them careening down at each other, forcing the race to ever-greater speed as we pulled ahead of the shattering chains of destruction.

The worker Hyperboreans finally began to scatter, running like ants that had just had their hill kicked over.

I was the only person not caught up in the fight, the only one who could see what was going on around us. Overtaken with desire and bloodlust, driven by the fear of the other side winning the prize, neither side gave a thought to what they were doing here. Listening to the song, I was suddenly aware that I could hear the damage that was being done. As each tower fell, the delicate interweaving of the song was greatly diminished, a level of depth lost forever. The destruction of this monumental crystal architecture and the glorious harmony holding it together was a crime against creation.

The source of the song was the child at the center of the mountain, and the damage we were doing was weakening him, weakening the entire mountain. The torrents of ichor had ceased flowing.

The entire place truly was a house of cards, ready to collapse. I was certain it was the lack of ichor. The more that was drawn from the ice and into that child in the gem, the weaker the entire mountain and the crystal city within became. That child was the key. They all wanted him, but no house could be permitted to have him.

Although the Sertorians were responsible for the destruction of Lupus Civitas, this particular catastrophe was all my doing. In seeking my revenge, in throwing myself into the Ludi Romani at any price, I had brought about the very thing I sought to set right—the destruction of a city on this world and the massacre of its people. But the alternative was to do nothing and risk Aquilinus seizing the alien child. I had to remove him from the equation. I wagered that the child's death would provide a shock powerful enough to bring the entire mountain crashing down about us. Bury us all deep, along with the ichor, one giant funerary mount that would mark the end of the threat to the empire. If Aquilinus was still in Crassus' body when he died, then maybe he'd perish here too, though that might be too much to hope for.

As we closed in on the bright nexus, the pain from the wounds was overwhelming, but I forced myself to focus. Now cracks about the great gem that encompassed the child appeared. Fragile, everything here was thin, weak, ready to break apart. The first team to reach that child could crack the crystal about him like an egg and seize him. I could just see the Viridians behind us. We had too much of a lead on them, and unless I did something, Aquilinus, fueled by desire and sheer obstinacy, might actually be able to reach the prize before the Golden Wolves and the alien warriors. He could claim it in time before we died from lack of ambrosia. Aquilinus cared nothing for the Blood Hawks, they were pawns whose sole purpose was to ensure that none other took possession of the barbarian child. Once all other obstacles were eliminated and the prize secure, it would be nothing for him to flee back to his own body and move to recover all he saw as his.

I remembered our training aboard *Incitatus,* that a chariot moving at such great speed could be disrupted by the slightest unbalancing movement. I tried to spot Julia at the rear of the chariot, to try to warn her what I was about to do, but couldn't turn my head around far enough.

I waited until the Viridians had come close enough, counting the seconds between the numerous walkways that ran back out to the hive tunnels. When I judged that Carbo's craft had enough speed to suit my plan, I threw as much of my body as I could manage over the port side of the chariot, the one minus the desultore skirmisher. Gods, please let there be enough ambrosia in my system to allow me to survive long enough to finish this. My weight pulled the port side of the Sertorian chariot down at once, tilting the starboard side up. Castor bumped into Pollux, and the sensitive controls were knocked sharply. The chariot capsized onto its side, careening across the platform and into the Viridian craft. All Hawks except the chariot drivers and me were cast out and onto the platform—the two brothers strapped to the vehicle and me still bound by the neck.

We all slid horizontally. I was caught between the two chariots as they turned on their axes, my wrists broken, my hip crushed beneath the weight of the Blood Hawks' chariot, but the momentum and the vehicle's sudden jerk were enough of a pull to loosen the thong about my neck. We slid for what seemed an eternity, and when we spun and came about, I was satisfied to see that my plan had worked. The Viridians were still going, their craft redirected down a walkway to the east. They'd lost valuable time, at least two hundred yards they would have to cover again to catch up. Struggling, I rose—I had to keep moving. Aquilinus in Crassus' body looked like he was out cold. Licinus was already up and charging at me. The others were struggling to their feet as I freed my hands and pulled the loop from my neck, letting the bow staff drop. There was a javelin attached to the side of the skirmisher, but no weapon was necessary; with the skirmisher I would become a living weapon. Stretching up awkwardly, I detached the starboard skirmisher, mounted it and had just managed to pull away as Licinus' hand grasped for my hair. He got a thick handful, and he was going to pull me right off the saddle, but his hand closed over my mother's pin. I could feel it vibrating beneath his hand, and he screamed in pain but didn't let go. No ambrosia to insulate him now. The foul odor of burning flesh filled the air as I struggled to seize the controls, but they were just beyond my reach. He jerked my head back, and just as I was about to fall from the saddle, I saw Julia behind him. She threw herself forward, sinking her teeth into his neck, biting into one of his opening wounds for all she was worth. Licinus roared and let me go, struggling to beat Julia off.

"Go! Don't let them get it!" Julia screeched, her mouth dripping ghoulishly with Licinus' black ambrosial blood.

I drove forward, casting a quick glance in the side mirror. Licinus was beating Julia across the face, knocking her to the ground. Barbata and the Dioscurii were righting the chariot. Ignoring the searing pain in my hands, I worked the throttle, the tendons pulling over the top of broken wrists. My hair was flailing about me. The buzzing alien song was suddenly absent; Licinus grabbing at my mother's pin must have loosened it. It had fallen away somewhere behind me. I had to keep moving.

The alien warriors reached the platform. They swarmed toward us, moving to protect the child and the procession of workers transporting ichor. I glanced back and saw the Viridians hesitating, a half-mile behind us now, by the ramp. Things were already starting to fall apart. Far below, the crystal platforms began to shatter and fall away into the polluted reservoirs below.

Go, Marcus. Go. Trust me to see this through to the end. Tell Carbo the code word and go. I could do this. Look what I have done to the Sertorians. Know that I am true and get the hell out of there. The wave of Hyperboreans were nearing their position, and thank the gods, Carbo signaled a retreat and their chariot turned on a sharp arc and rocketed back toward the cover of the hive tunnels.

Now it was just the Sertorians and me. They'd abandoned Crassus. Aquilinus had probably exited the scene when his host blacked out. I could take them on and try to throw their chariot again, but if the four of them made a break for the child, I couldn't stop them all. Instead I drove the desultore skirmisher into the last of the towers, the broadest one yet, crashing right through plate after thin crystal plate of its foundations. I surged forward and brought the skirmisher about just in time to see the crystal spire come crashing down across the path, blocking it, forcing the Hawks' chariot to pull away. They were all bleeding, all coming apart at the seams from the wounds they'd suffered at my hands. They couldn't afford to take any more damage if they wanted to survive. Licinus howled abuse. I'd cost them valuable time. The attacking Hyperborean warriors were only twenty feet away. Licinus was going to die. They all would, at the hands of the aliens or from ambrosia loss. I drove forward again. I had the lead. I'd be the only one to reach the prize. This was the final move. I threw the auxiliary thruster switches on the desultore skirmisher and started gathering speed. I was going to ram the gem, going to turn myself into what I was always meant to be—an unwavering arrow striking home.

Licinus ordered the retreat, and the chariot turned about just as the Hyperborean swarm was about to overrun them. Off he went, saving his skin. Then, without warning, a massive stalactite crashed down from the roof and smashed through the platform, taking the Sertorians with it. A cascade of rocks and falling Hyperboreans followed them down. The sheer scale of the stalactite meant that there was no possibility of survival. All that power and darkness, they'd seemed so invincible and now they were crushed, dead. Just like that.

I was at maximum speed, the child in my sights. He looked small now, helpless within his crystal shell, the magnification effect gone now that I was up close. I didn't want to kill him. I had to kill him. One more sin, one more wrong action for the greater good, and then I would be done. The light was near blinding now as I entered the corona. O Minerva, guide me now!

There was a flash of light, and I was thrown from the desultore skirmisher. When I came to, I was lying on my back looking up at the mountain collapsing in on itself. Great stalactites fell, piercing the crystal platforms, sending them cascading down. I turned my head toward the light and discovered that I'd failed. The child was there before me. The crystal shell was falling to pieces, slowly shattering, but the child inside still lived, unharmed. Reaching back along the side of the skirmisher, my hand found the javelin. I'd die with a weapon in my hand. I'd die a warrior.

He stood within the shell, arms upraised.

The internal destruction of the mountain stopped suddenly. No more shaking or rumbling. There was sudden silence, just like that. The little Spartacus was doing it. Though I couldn't hear it anymore, I was certain that he was the source of the song as well as the power that was keeping the mountain upright. He was so bright, like the sun, I could barely look at him. I started forward and his eyes flicked open. Not vacant slits like the other Hyperboreans, but small orbs that resembled eyeballs lay within.

His expression was inhuman but somehow conveyed the feeling that he was judging me, looking right into my soul, and that made what I had to do next even more difficult. I was bleeding in so many places, my skin was burning, peeling away in sheaves, I knew I couldn't keep going for long. The alien child's radiance was powerful, blinding, but I didn't need to see to complete my mission. I struck with the javelin, a wound into his side that pierced the crystal shell of his body more like it was made of flesh than mineral. Rocks tumbled from above, the rumbling and crashing started up again. My strike weakened him, but he didn't lower his arms. I risked looking right at him now, I'd only get one more chance to finish him. His eyes never wavered. They should have been expressionless, heartless, alien, but I felt only compassion radiating from him, pity for the state I was in. Tears rolled down my eyes. There was no evil here. This being was good. A child. I raised for a second strike, the deathblow that would end both our lives and bring down the entire city.

A flash of movement out of the corner of my eye, but before I could react, I was hit and fell backward to the ground. It was the bull chief, my old friend. The spine on the back of his fist was raised, and I looked down to see a large wound in my chest. He'd stabbed me in the heart. Somehow I'd managed to keep hold of the javelin, though. The child was only five feet beyond me, on the other side of the bull chief. The child's diamond body was bright, reflecting my face, capturing the image of a hundred Accalas in its facets, but the Accala they reflected was one I barely recognized—body broken, without armor, hair billowing about me like black ghosts. The radiation from the child had burned away my nerves. I couldn't feel a thing. I was gnarled like a root, eyes darting forward, red skin peeling away, hands tense like claws. Haggard, raw, wired. Ready to kill, ready to die. If this was the price of absolution, if this was how the empire would be saved, then so be it. I got to my knees and started crawling forward. A great blow struck me in the back, throwing me forward to the ground, face-first. I got up again. Only a few more feet. The bull chief grabbed my hair and yanked, and a second later I was hanging in space, blood and black ambrosia leaking from my wounds like a fountain.

I stuck the javelin into what passed for his face, and he dropped me. I threw myself forward. The bull chief grabbed my hand and ripped the javelin from it, then lifted me up again, holding me out from his body with one hand while the sharp spine on the other sailed in toward me—a swift swallow soaring through the air. Then, just like the bird, I felt light and free. I was falling, and at the same time it was like a great weight had been lifted from me. I hit the ground. There was something beside me. I could only turn my eyes, and it took me a moment to realize what I was looking at. My charred body, still smoking, black ambrosia seeping from countless wounds only to be licked away by the intense, radiant heat. He'd cut off my head.

My head had come to rest on its back and slightly to the right side, angled so I was looking up. I could see stars. How strange. And above that a shining band tracing the bowl of the sky—the Rota Fortuna. Black spherae were swarming into the collapsing mountain, recording everything. I felt like laughing. I'd meant to bury this place once and for all, and instead the mountain had partially collapsed in on itself, exposing everything. I'd revealed the ichor store and the ruined alien city to the entire empire. Now the emperor would know; he'd see what the Sertorians had been keeping hidden down here and move to stop them. And what of my father? He was up there. Would this be the last thing he saw of me? Beheaded and alone? The fate of his rogue daughter whom he'd tried to reason with.

I lay there, staring up at the stars, thinking about my brother, my mother,

Julia, Bulla, all the beings in my life who meant anything to me. All the people I'd disappointed or betrayed. I thought about them until an irresistible darkness began to move over me. The experience reminded me of when I was a little girl. I'd lie in bed and Mother would create a wavelike action with my blanket. One moment everything would be dark and then light as she rolled the blanket up. That's when I'd see her smile at me before the sheet fell and it was dark again. A good last memory. As I lay dying, the sky was suddenly aflame. Fire and explosions erupted on the orbital stadium. I couldn't see anything in detail, couldn't even focus my eyes, but I knew it was Aquilinus. He was back in his body. He couldn't have this, couldn't permit the emperor to stop him, to take away his ambrosia source, not now. He'd ordered *Incitatus* to fire on the stadium. He was staging a coup, making his move for the throne while the emperor and the empire's elite were all in one place. And I could do no more. Now for the last journey—to join my mother and brother in the halls of Hades to suffer eternal torment, eternal shame. There was no redemption, no good that would come from any of my deeds. Perhaps they'd turn my story into a tragedy play. The tale of a woman who betrayed her house and her father so she could fight and die in the arena. More likely it would be written as a comedy—the story of Accala, greatest of fools.

PART II
OLYMPUS FALLING

He could not control his natural cruelty and viciousness, but he was a most eager witness of the tortures and executions of those who suffered punishment, reveling at night in gluttony and adultery.

—Suetonius, *Lives of the Caesars*

All the previous fighting had been merciful by comparison. Now finesse is set aside, and we have pure unadulterated murder. The combatants have no protective covering; their entire bodies are exposed to the blows. No blow falls in vain. This is what lots of people prefer to the regular contests, and even to those that are put on by popular request. And it is obvious why. There is no helmet, no shield to repel the blade. Why have armor? Why bother with skill? All that just delays death.

In the morning, men are thrown to lions and bears. At mid-day they are thrown to the spectators themselves. No sooner has a man killed, than they shout for him to kill another, or to be killed. The final victor is kept for some other slaughter. In the end, every fighter dies. And all this goes on while the arena is half empty.

You may object that the victims committed robbery or were murderers. So what? Even if they deserved to suffer, what's your compulsion to watch their sufferings? "Kill him," they shout, "beat him, burn him." Why is he too timid to fight? Why is he so frightened to kill? Why so reluctant to die? They have to whip him to make him accept his wounds.

—Seneca

ACT V

LUMEN

O sprung of gods' blood . . .
Easy is the descent into hell; all night and day the gate of dark Dis
  stands open;
but to recall thy steps and issue to upper air, this is the task and
  burden . . .
Yet if thy soul is so passionate and so desirous twice to float across
  the Stygian lake, twice to see dark Tartarus, and thy pleasure is to
  plunge into the mad task, learn what must first be accomplished.
                                                    —Virgil, *Aeneid*

XXXIV

DEAD IN HADES' HALLS, I was flotsam, the splintered remains of a wrecked
ship adrift in a vast black sea. Hunger for ambrosia infused my being. I longed
to die. I prayed that the crashing waves would swallow me and send me down
into peaceful oblivion. A great figure towered above heavy storm clouds. It was
Jupiter, but at the same time it was Proconsul Aquilinus. He scowled at me as I
sank, and cast a lightning bolt. The sharp shock charged the sea around me,
electrocuting my entire body, refiring the hunger, throwing me back up to the
surface, denying me peace. Each bolt carried an additional barb, a momentary
reliving of my sins. *Flash.* My brother's eyes flicked open and his throat was cut,
but the hand did not belong to Aquilinus or Crassus—it was my own. His blood
pooled out over the ice floor unceasingly, gushing like a fountain. Aulus looked
at me, confused, the hope draining from his eyes. *Flash.* There I was, tiny, the size
of an insect, looking up at Aulus, who was now a giant, his torrent of blood a
rising flood. His body, transparent and made of ice, held within it the great Hyperborean city as it was destroyed. I saw that the city was a living thing, a great
organism—the Hyperboreans like blood cells, transporting ichor back to the
heart, where it could be cleansed of the pollution of ambrosia and stored, a hidden celestial machine, a magnificent temple. I watched while what should have
been regarded as one of the Seven Galactic Wonders was destroyed. Again and
again I watched myself lead the Sertorians into it, transforming their sacred
space into my private battleground. All taking place within Aulus' body. The
towers and bridges were his bones; the vapor that rose from the ichor waters,

his energy; and the collection chambers above the city, his lungs. A city inside a body, and as it fell, he died. Then the darkness and floating again for so long that I thought I was finally going to be allowed to die before the lightning strikes started up once again.

This was the punishment of traitors, of those who betrayed all that was dear to them. Like Sisyphus who eternally pushed a giant boulder up a mountain, only to have it roll down again, or Tantalus, who must starve with the food and drink always just beyond his reach, this was my eternal torment. I prayed for the end; I welcomed my torture; I deserved it. I wondered if the shades of my mother and little brother watched me. Was Aulus laughing or crying at my fate?

Time passed. The same cycle repeated itself again and again, so many times that I began to notice that there was one change, one small difference each time. Every time a bolt struck, it affected the water that buoyed me up. The dark sea was gradually lightening, and the storm clouds parted until, after an eternity, after countless repetitions, the sea was now clear and bright, so brilliant it hurt my eyes, and then I was finally falling below the waves, not into darkness and peace but instead to an agonizing awareness.

I grew used to the light—my eyes adjusted. I was in a cell carved into solid crystal, eight feet square without any visible entrance. The perfectly smooth walls generated their own penetrating brightness.

I had a sense of my body, but it was completely sapped of strength, unwilling to move, like a spoiled child refusing to obey her parents. My nerves were on fire, my bones like frozen pipes, every muscle and tendon taut with cold. The ice vapor burned my bare skin, but I was alive. I was awake and alive, I was absolutely sure of that, if nothing else. And I needed ambrosia. Gods, but I needed it. Ambrosia would take away the pain of reality.

There were no tools, no means of escape, no sign of Orbis or my armor or armilla. There was something in the ice just beyond the cell wall, though, right opposite me. It was a strange form, like a piece of abstract art, and I stared at it for some time through watery eyes trying to discern its nature. Looking beyond the object, I realized that there were no landmarks on the other side of the clear cell wall, just a solid sea of crystal that went on and on in every direction.

A wave of pain hit me. Gods, what was happening? It wasn't just the cold. I felt like I was being turned inside out. I tried to ride out the pain, but after withdrawing for a few seconds, it returned with a vengeance. I needed to move, to dig my nails into my thighs—a sharp, localized pain would help distract me.

When I finally worked out what the object opposite me was, I just stared at it, numb with shock. It was my body. Like Mania, my head lived on apart from the rest of me. My body hung in the ice like an old toga, just as Labeo's had. It was yellow, a sickly cyan color. Hundreds of clear, needle-thin fibers entered it horizontally, pushing through the suit of flesh before exiting the opposite side. My naked carcass looked like a bass viol strung the wrong way. Ambrosia was slowly being drawn out through the needles. And I could feel them. Despite the disconnection, I could feel everything that was going on in my body.

This was an eerie fusion of biological technologies. I had never thought of it before, but the human body could be seen as a vehicle for storing and transport-ing water in the same way that these aliens stored and transported ichor. In the process of leaching the substance that was most precious to them from my body, they would deliver me a second death, the darkness I so desired. The ambrosia sustained me. It kept me alive even though I was apart from myself. Perhaps this head of mine would be left there as some kind of totem, a trophy to display as I had done with Mania's head.

A day passed, maybe more, it was impossible to say, as the light that illumi-nated the cube never altered in any way. The ambrosia was drawn from me with agonizing slowness. My body was starving for that alien drug, wracked with the pain of withdrawal. I fantasized about being whole—clawing my way through the solid rock, excavating it in an instant, and drinking so much ambrosia that, like the Lotus Eaters in Homer's *Odyssey*, I would forget everything—my name, my past, my hopes and dreams, my nightmares. No memory, only an oblivion of pleasure.

As each drop was pulled from my body by the needles, I inched closer toward true death. Or perhaps I was already dead and this was some underworld torment.

It was all too much to get my head around. Too much to get my head around—that made me laugh, and once I'd started I couldn't seem to stop laughing even though no sound escaped my lips. I was literally off my head, and what did it matter? What else was there to do in hell to pass the time but to go mad?

Trojan horse. Hero. I told myself that I hadn't paid any heed to the thick, sticky flattery my uncle laid on back in Rome, but stick it did. Those words had weight. They lingered. I'd actually believed it, especially when the ambrosia was driving my every thought and action. Destined for greatness, prepared to achieve it at any price. I wasn't sure that I ever wanted victory for my house or justice for my family more than I wanted to be renowned for bringing it about. It wasn't about defeating the Sertorians for the good of the empire; it was about crushing them beneath my heel and about them knowing that I was the one doing it. That sentiment felt like a distant dream. Like looking at a snake through the force shield of a zoo enclosure.

Some distant figures moved toward me. It was like spotting some tiny specks of habitation on a desert horizon. They grew in size as they drew near. How strange—they must have been moving right through the crystal rock itself. It was the alien child from the heart of the city, and behind him was the bull chief. The solid mineral around the child seemed to liquefy and part as they walked, not daring to restrict his passage. As far as I knew, the Hyperboreans didn't have sexes, but I found myself unable to think of the child as being anything other than male, an alien boy. I could hear his wordless song again. *Buzz, buzz.* By the time they came to a stop outside my cell, it was like having a beehive lodged between my ears. That damn alien song had plagued me since I left Rome and for what? What was the point of it all? Unintelligible gobbledygook.

Standing on either side of my headless body, they looked in at my head. I wondered if this was alien theater and I was a comedy and a tragedy all rolled up in one. I didn't blame the boy for wanting to watch as the last ounces of ambrosia were siphoned from my body. I knew what it was to burn for revenge.

The boy started to emit an intense glow, which I'd have turned from if I could have. Closing my eyes didn't help a bit. I could still see him, as if my eyelids were slices of transparent film. His presence orchestrated the last of the ambrosia being drawn out through the needles, a muddy brown sludge. Surprisingly, the pain that plagued my body decreased. Although I was still immobile, a gradual sense of well-being spread through my body. My muscles didn't ache at all, and the biting of the cold had vanished.

Now the needles slowly withdrew from my flesh. Then a wavelike ripple passed through the crystal around me, washing my body out into the cell before me like a cow expelling a calf from her womb. The bull chief entered the cell and picked it up from the ground, holding it up firmly by the shoulders. His icy claws dug into the flesh like sharp forceps, but I couldn't feel the body now. No pain but also no sensation. I wondered how long it would be before true death came. Certainly no more than one minute, perhaps two, before my brain would cease to function.

The child came from behind the bull chief to stand before me, placing a small crystal hand on either side of my head. I was raised up so that I was looking right at him. Now he carried me over to the center of the cell. I couldn't see it, but I felt that my head was being lowered onto my body, slowly and reverently like a priest placing an offering upon an altar.

The boy's song stopped, and suddenly I was a burning shuttle on reentry, plummeting down into my body. I was thrown back into myself, and my arms flew up of their own accord, my body thrown on the ground, my mouth wrenched open in an endless scream. The spasmodic movement subsided in decreasing waves.

There was movement in my fingers and toes. Gods. This wasn't an execution. It was a healing. They were curing me, putting me back together minus the ambrosia. It didn't make sense. Perhaps it was a kind of torture—healing me so they could have the pleasure of taking me to the edge of death all over again.

With mind and body reunited, my feelings returned. The images of the massacre, the nightmares, my guilt and fear, my anger and self-loathing all washed into my organs like polluted floodwaters. My stomach clenched and my kidneys ached. Shame, horror, regret. I began to weep and wail, curling up in a ball on the floor of the cell as my stomach cramped. Emotions tumbled out of me like clothing from a dropped case.

I tried to stand up, to say I was sorry, but my vocal cords had frozen, and when I tried to speak I ended up in a coughing fit. I fell to my knees, and a fine sprinkle of blood fell from my mouth onto the clear, crystal floor.

"Gods, I didn't know," I said when the words finally came. "That you were what you are. The massacre, your city . . . I was half mad. Gods, I'm so sorry."

The bull chief lifted me and set me down with my back leaning against the wall. I was like a newborn, a helpless baby. The warmth of circulation coursed through my body. I had to take slow, shallow breaths. Deep breaths left me gulping for air and sent a pain through my lungs. I had to relearn the art of breathing that I'd taken for granted.

I was so certain I was dead, that this was my place of punishment. How did you know in hell if you really were dead or alive? If anything that happened next was real?

The child touched the surface of the wall directly in front of me, and it transformed, becoming a mirror.

I crawled up to it and searched for any mark around my neck where my head had been severed, but it was perfect, the same as it ever was. I looked normal again, all of the Sertorian modifications gone. It was a relief to see that Accala, like running into an old friend I hadn't seen in a long time. And at the same time as I recognized my old self, I realized that I was no longer starving for ambrosia. The hunger was gone. My mind felt like there was a cool breeze running through it. My thoughts were clear for the first time since I'd left Rome. And despite my nakedness, I couldn't feel the cold. I should have been freezing in there, suffering frostbite and hypothermia, but I was pain-free.

The humming song, ever present, was different now, somehow deeper and wider. I had a sense of it coming from behind the boy, through the boy. He was not its source. Rather, he was a conduit of the song, a great river running back to an ocean. His expression of that ocean, his song, took on the rhythmic drone of a beehive on a hot day, a meandering tone that filled me up and vibrated off the walls. It resonated in that chamber, increasing in volume until I was drowning in sound. The inside of my head felt like it expanded to encompass a vast interior space, like that of the hollowed-out mountain that enclosed the hidden city. A thousand hatches had been thrown open in my skull, and the song spread out to fill every part of that space—mixing every thought of mine with the thoughts that were woven into the song that filled the air, the cavern, the mountain.

The sound filled me with . . . with what? Not words as such, but whole ideas, like sudden inspiration stitching together tumbling cascades of rich, dense images that passed on too quickly to be grasped. There were images of this world, but I sensed that beneath their forms they had a great meaning that I was unable to interpret. Water dropped onto a boulder, one drip at a time, drilling a hole through it over hundreds of years to join the stream below. An icicle slowly melted, not yet water, not fully frozen but hovering in an in-between state. This communication was heart-to-heart, mind-to-mind, like two tributaries running into the same river. This was real seeing, real talking. This was what communication should be, without room for subterfuge, double meaning or mistakes, except I was missing most of it. I couldn't make out the message. I was a dunce, a simpleton with a limited vocabulary.

The child raised an empty hand and reached past my left ear. Like a magician performing a trick, when he drew it back he held my mother's pin in his hand. They found it! He let the pin fall into the center of his palm and offered it back to me.

I snatched it up. It felt hot in my hand, subtly vibrating like the point of friction as fire sticks are rubbed together. All at once, the parcel of images and meanings that I couldn't decipher came into focus. I could feel the child plucking forms from my mind like an angler hooking fish from a river—images, sounds, concepts he needed to communicate. He sampled words from my lexicon like a butterfly tongue uncurling into a pool of nectar. Gradually forms clarified into thoughts, and the buzzing song gave way to intelligible words that passed from mind to mind.

Hello, Accala.

The voice. It was Aulus. My brother.

XXXV

"AULUS?"

It couldn't be. It couldn't. It was some kind of trick.

No trick.

A rippling wave moved over him, and his body of ice and cold was suddenly gone, replaced by the image of Aulus as he was. Small and thin with brown hair the color of mouse fur. Two big front teeth and gaps on either side as he waited for his grown-up teeth to come in. A mischievous smile and bright eyes. He was perfect. I reached out to touch him, but there was no flesh, no warmth. Only coldness, hardness. It was a projection.

"Stop it," I warned. Tears flowed, I could barely speak without wanting to vomit. I couldn't bear to see this. Aulus was dead. "Stop it now."

The image vanished, and once again I was looking at the small crystal child.

I am Aulus. And at the same time I'm not Aulus. A little of this and a little of that. It's not easy to explain. It's like clusters of oil on top of water. I'm the collected droplet of Aulus floating in a new form.

"This doesn't feel right."

It was Mother's idea, he said. *Come. She can explain.*

"My mother? She's alive?"

No. I'm sorry. Communicating like this makes it hard to differentiate between the past and the future. Come, I'll show you.

He held out a small crystal claw toward me. His other hand reached out to touch the solid cell wall. It rippled and yielded to his touch.

But I couldn't follow.

"She's not your mother. You're not my brother," I stated. That feeling of being adrift had not abated. I was clinging to reality. After Crassus and his machine, after all the Blood Hawks put me through, I wouldn't let someone warp and dictate my perceptions.

I told you. I'm a mixture. Aulus is in here. This body has a great deal of work to do. It encompasses many things, many beings. And I won't hurt you. I'm here to make things clear. That's my role.

I saw Aulus die, saw the life run out of his eyes. This wasn't my brother.

You're partly right. There was only a little of me left in that body. I tried to tell you that. Remember.

Aulus' last words—*Look for me.*

I can see you're having some trouble with this. I don't blame you. Romans place so much importance on appearances. It tells you how to treat people, how to categorize them.

He studied me a moment and then continued. *Names. I think you're stuck on my name. I'll tell you what the Hyperboreans call me. Actually, I can't really work out how to say it. It's easier if I just show you.*

From the center of his chest came a powerful glow, a light from his heart that was so strong it forced me to shield my eyes. And yet with it came a message of light—strong, a powerful flood of clarity that illuminated, that made things transparent. I could barely stand to look at it.

"Lumen," I said suddenly. The word seemed to fly out of my mouth.

Lumen, he agreed. *That's a good fit. I think it might be easier for you if you call me that instead of Aulus.*

"Lumen." He was right. It did help to not call him by my brother's name.

Lumen had been responding to my thoughts as if I were talking out loud. He didn't have a mouth, and hadn't actually said a thing. How could I trust anything he said?

Because we're hearing each other's thoughts, communicating mind-to-mind, at the stage before things come into conscious realization, when they're still packages filled with potential. It takes careful listening to catch our thoughts. The process you've been through here helps, but as time passes you'll slip back into your old way of listening and it'll become harder to hear me. So you should practice. Try to find the way to respond to me in a similar way. Try to communicate without moving your lips.

How long have I been here? I formed the words in my mind.

Try again. You've started with a difficult question. Anything involving time and the self is difficult.

I knew then why I couldn't hear the buzzing song anymore. That light, that direct communication, was the song, only now I could understand it. No more unintelligible alien static—I'd been pulled apart, cleaned out, and put back together. Inside me was the space that had allowed the muddy waters of my heart and mind to settle and dissolve.

He asked me questions, and we went back and forth while I tried to copy him. It involved catching the thought before it became fully realized—that was the ignition point, the wind, and then stopping short of speaking it so that the wind had something to catch, like a sail.

You're getting it, he said. *Words on the edge of thoughts.*

"You're being kind." I said aloud. "I'm hardly getting it at all. It's very difficult. A very subtle thing. I might get the hang of this if we had a few years to practice with no distractions, but time is something I don't have to spare. I don't have a problem hearing you in my mind, but do you mind if I talk to you with words?"

Go ahead, only speak quietly while in these caves. I can hear you through the filaments on my head, which are tuned to pick up vibrations in the air, among other things.

"Please, how long have I been here?"

Listen.

When my question caught the right impetus, the sense of myself in a place was conveyed and the answer was already there, bound up in the package of the question. I saw the sun rising and setting and my body deep below the mountain to the west of where the city came tumbling down—two cycles of the rise and fall of the golden sun.

Two days? Gods, anything could have happened in that time! Did Aquilinus' attempt to take over the stadium succeed? Was the tournament already over? Did Marcus and the Viridian team survive?

If you come with me, I'll show you what's been going on, but you have to come now. There's great danger if we stay.

A ripple passed over the wall, and I saw an image of dark shadows scuttling through the shining Hyperborean tunnels.

"Arachnoraptors," I said in as low as whisper as I could manage.

I wagered that these were the very same ones I saw that night collecting ambrosia from Mania and Licinus' poisoned ichor wells. Dozens of alien legs emerged from the steel cradles that held their human upper bodies. The skittering legs along with the black uniforms and hoods, with listening devices and shock staves, gave them a frightening insectile appearance.

They're about a mile away from here. Your body creates heat, and our movement, any word you speak, sends a vibration through the rock, Lumen explained. *They can detect it, but the rock is thick and the transmission is slow. It takes many minutes, sometimes hours, for those signals to reach them.*

The sight of them snapped me back into action. I was still at sea over this situation, but I knew one thing—I didn't want to be captured by the Sertorians again.

"All right, let's go," I whispered. Survival first. Somehow Minerva had heard my plea for forgiveness. I'd managed to regain my life and my freedom, but not without cost. The process of being imprisoned in the ice was hard, perhaps more painful than the worst humiliations the Sertorians had inflicted. But here was hope, a chance to make up for the part I played in visiting destruction and suffering upon them and their world.

Hold my hand. The walls won't close on you.

I put my hand in Lumen's small claw. I expected it to be cold, but a warmth flooded from his hand to my body. It was as if the insides of my bones were filling up with liquid heat.

Lumen's gentle, insistent pull reassured me as I followed him into the crystal wall, and instead of meeting the solid resistance I had encountered before, I felt the wall yield like water. It moved aside, forming a narrow, rippling tunnel as we passed.

I stumbled as I went. My body was still getting its coordination back. If I'd had to fight right then, I'd have been dead meat. The overbearing form of the bull chief followed us.

If you want to call him something, try Concretus, Lumen said. *Bull chief sounds so . . . colonial.*

"Concretus? You named him?"

Just now. You did so well with Lumen, I thought I'd give it a try. He has a strong, sturdy quality, so it seemed to fit. Don't worry, his function is to guard me and ensure the work proceeds, that's all. He won't hurt you.

"He doesn't speak either," I said.

All the time. We all do, this whole world does. You just have to learn to listen. Keep listening, and the heart of this world will open to you like a flower. The song of the pin was meant to draw you to me and at the same time help Concretus to find you. Only whenever he came near you, you attacked him. You weren't supposed to have the ambrosia inside you. It's poison to the Hyperboreans, so it stopped you from understanding him, or me, for that matter.

"I needed it to stay alive."

Fate has not led you on a kind path to me, but I'm glad you're here.

"And what of you? What would my brother think of the cards dealt him?"

That we can work only with what's in front of us. Feeling sore for not getting our way would be childish.

He sounded like Marcus, not my brother Aulus.

When a child is forced to take on the burden of an adult, a part of him ceases to be a child, Lumen continued, reading my thoughts. *Concretus tried to clear the ambrosia from your system, so he could help you understand that he only wanted to help and teach you this mind-to-mind communication.*

That was how it was supposed to be for you and me. The song of the pin was meant to draw us together, and at the same time help Concretus to find you. Only whenever he came near you, you attacked him.

"He tried to kill me. He's been hunting me. Terrorizing me."

The problem is that the Hyperboreans are reflective by nature. You don't ever really see them. . . .

"You see yourself," I finished.

I saw now what he meant. The thing that terrified me, it was what I had become. My own hatred, anger, need for revenge, all reflected back at me, and it was truly horrible.

"I didn't make that easy, I know." I conceded. "Gods, what a fool I've been. But how could I know? I still don't entirely believe it. This whole business is so . . ."

Un-Roman?

"Yes. Exactly."

"And during the uprising? He pulled me onto his spines, tried to steal my ambrosia."

Concretus lured you to me. I tried to communicate but you weren't supposed to have the ambrosia inside you. Mother never anticipated that. It caused a communication breakdown. Concretus tried to take it out of you. He wasn't stealing your ambrosia, he was trying to cleanse you so that I could speak to you as I do now.

"But I attacked him before he could finish. I see now. I didn't know . . ."

After that, I've had to keep orchestrating the removal of ambrosia from this world. That is my primary mission.

"I needed to hold on to the ambrosia," I said. "To stay alive and save Aulus. I couldn't do without it, but it was for a good reason."

But that wasn't the whole truth.

You should say it, speak that thought you're holding back, or it will linger, like rubbish clogging up a stream, and then other thoughts will cluster to it and pollute your mind.

"And I wanted to kill the Hawks," I finished. "I wanted to hurt them because they hurt me."

There, the stream flows once more. You feel it?

"Yes."

As we walked through the body of the mountain, the surface of the tunnel walls liquefied and rippled. Images began to form.

These memories are of what has been, Lumen said.

I found myself surrounded by Lupus Civitas, the Viridian outpost as it was before the bombing. It was just like walking through a holoprojection. There were gold-and-green-armored Viridians going about their day's business, leaving trails in the snow. I saw clean, shining buildings laid out in orderly rows. Members of the other houses roamed the streets—Tullians, Numerians, Atilians, even Sertorians.

When the Romans arrived and built their cities, the Hyperboreans kept themselves hidden.

The cavern that appeared now was larger, the architecture similar, but there was no cluster of six great crystals, no Lumen at its heart. The focus was on a vast central reservoir of ichor and massive crystalline stalactites dripping with Hyperborean bodies. Some lay within the transparent ceiling, others were partly ejected, in the process of being born, arms and legs sticking out of the tapered deposits like spare parts in a sculptor's workshop. Crystals bursting with Hyperborean bodies grew out of every wall, at crisscrossing angles. A powerful, clear light, like a small sun, was floating above the lake of ichor. At its heart was a continual energetic motion, like thousands of flowers opening at the same time only to be replaced by the next batch an instant later.

"Is this where the Hyperboreans are born?" I asked.

It is. The voice in my mind changed, became older and wiser as Lumen explained. *This place is the interior of the Hyperborean queen's body, as it was before the bombs struck. She is the place where all ichor is pooled, as well as the vehicle that will carry us to the celestial realm. We come from one source and we go back to one source.*

"Death? You're talking about dying?"

There is no death. Only a return to the source—a remembering. While the droplet is cast from the crest of a wave, for the instant that it flies through the air it forgets that it is part of the sea. When it returns, it remembers.

There was a pause, then the voice resumed in the tone of Aulus. *The only difference is that the Hyperboreans don't forget. They're still connected to the before and after. Life or death doesn't matter to them, only completing their great work.*

"And that is . . . ?"

Mother will explain.

As I looked up at the ceiling, I noticed something out of place: thick pipes, definitely Roman plumbing, that looked like the kind they used to stream hot water into the public baths.

"This place you're showing me, the queen's body. If this scene is set before the bombing, then she must be right under the old settlement of Lupus Civitas," I said.

Not under it but near enough. The hiding place worked well for a time, but the Hyperboreans never anticipated that we would seek to destroy our own kind. Romans killing Romans. It's not how their minds work. They thought they would be safe if they stayed hidden near the city.

A new scene appeared.

I saw my mother approaching the entrances to the hives in the mountainside. Thick strands of black and white hair escaped the confines of her hood and flickered about her face in the freezing wind. The image was so real that I had to resist the urge to run toward her.

Mother took samples from an ichor stream that ran out from a large hexagonal hive entrance, and behind her my little brother rode on the shoulders of Concretus. It was like a weird family snapshot, the ice world equivalent of the scene I had of them in front of our country estate. I felt a pang of jealousy. That I wasn't there for those last, happy moments. That they bonded so quickly with alien beings instead of being at home, with me.

The Hyperboreans could sense she was here to learn, Lumen explained, *to seek wisdom and understanding. They were close to the source in spirit, they shared a like mind, an open heart that transcends appearances or even interspecies difference. For the source, there is always only one unity. Mother offered an understanding of the Romans and how to deal with them to ensure the survival of the queen and her people. An alliance would have been forged for the betterment of the entire empire, but then the Sertorians came.*

The scene changed, and now we walked through a dark laboratory lit by red lights. Hyperborean workers were strapped to operating tables by metallic bands. Sertorian scientists experimented upon them. Large drill bits cut into their bodies, extracting each Hyperborean's precious cargo of ichor.

Mother didn't realize she was being spied on, Lumen said. *The Sertorians ventured into the hives. They wanted to know if the ichor Mother was taking samples of had any strategic value. They started rounding up Hyperboreans for experimentation.*

The images around us vanished, and we were surrounded by darkness, illuminated only by a faint trail of light surrounding Lumen's small body. He ran his hand over the surface of the wall next to him and it became transparent.

Two feet away were a half dozen arachnoraptors. Some of them were upside down, some at right angles to the tunnel floor. Their predatory, frightening sensor staffs slowly swept the walls.

Do not fear. They can't hear or see us. At least they won't for a few minutes. Let them pass, and then we can continue.

Don't fear. Easy to say. My heart rate was accelerating, my mouth felt dry. One of them paused and looked right in our direction. The small suction pads on the ends of long black fingers touched the surface of the tunnel wall. Fine, sticky bristled hairs on their tips listened for vibration.

They could not detect our noise or heat, but somehow they could sense my fear, I was sure of it.

No sudden noises, Lumen said. *They have suction bombs they can use to blast their own rough passages between our tunnels.*

I could hear the sound of my heart pounding in my ears. I was sure the one before us was about to blow the wall away, when he unexpectedly turned and scuttled away with the others.

The tunnel was suddenly illuminated, and I nearly yelped when I found myself confronted by my own reflection. It was me but not me. I had wrinkles and looked old, determined, and urgent. No, not me. It was my mother. She was in the hive beneath Lupus Civitas. Suddenly she started talking, looking directly at me.

"Accala. If you are hearing this, then it means you have arrived on Olympus Decimus and have found Aulus. I wish I could have told you my plan, but the Sertorians are monitoring every signal I try to send out, and that would have jeopardized our best chance of defeating them."

Then the whole shining cave she was in began to rumble. Stalactites laden with alien bodies fell from the ceiling to crash to the floor behind her.

"Please listen carefully. There is much to explain and not much time. It begins with the gods." She took a deep breath before continuing. "I know you've never heard me speak much of the gods. That's because I didn't understand them until I came to this place. They're not as most Romans see them—giants sitting on high, above the clouds in a place with pillars and temples, or in some distant realm in outer space. The gods are great Platonic forms, vortexes of pure thought and feeling. From them radiate millions of lesser expressions of life, including human beings. Listen. During the period of foundation, when these primeval forces shaped the universe, they left in their wake a reserve of pure creative power. The remnants of this energy congealed into a perfect sphere, and the sphere attracted passing matter over time. It acquired an atmosphere and became a world—this world. The ichor is the key to everything on this world—it sustains the atmosphere, it holds the elements in check. The Hyperboreans are born of it, and their great work, their sacred charge, is to gather up the ichor from this world, refine it, and transport it to the celestial sphere where the energy vortexes that we'll call gods dwell. The ichor is fuel to the gods. They require it to sustain creation. For millennia the Hyperboreans have carried out their duty. They're celestial agents, servants of the gods. Only now, as their work draws to a close, we have interfered."

Gods? Aliens serving gods. Our gods. If it weren't my own mother telling me this in her final moments, I'd have dismissed it as nonsense. She was always a rationalist, a scientist and philosopher, always so focused on her research. She'd be charged with heresy if she said such things out loud on the streets of Rome. And yet, after seeing the city hive, the forces at play in there, I knew I must keep an open mind.

"I'd hoped that the ichor would help bring about a golden age, but now that I know the secret of the Hyperboreans, I know that can never be. No house can be permitted to possess it. Not the Sertorians, the Viridians, the emperor's house, none of them. It is pure power, and great power laid upon weak shoulders will warp and deform the noblest frame. If the Sertorians can work out how to integrate it with their genetic program, the ichor will grant them great power but also magnify all the impurities of the human spirit—fear, desire, bitterness, self-pity, anger, pride. Men embodying those energies will rule the empire as demons rule the halls of the underworld. Imagine the wars among houses magnified tenfold in cruelty and obsession. No reasoning voice, no compassion or common sense, only Aquilinus leading the empire to his tune—evil fueled by idealism—sustained by holding every spirit in the empire in dark bondage. It would be an era where the human spirit is enslaved as never before. It must be avoided at all costs."

Now the rocks began to fall. My mother looked around quickly and then addressed me with more urgency.

"I could not allow that to transpire, and so I made a deal with the queen of the Hyperboreans," she continued. "We are both mothers, and so she understood what I would do to protect both my children and my civilization from House Sertorian's aspirations. The Sertorians have unleashed nuclear fire aboveground. I will be dead any moment. But the queen has protected Aulus, taken him into her body. He is charged with interfering with the Sertorians' efforts to acquire the ichor, but he's only a child, he can't do it alone. The Hyperborean queen can see much that I cannot. Her vision is not limited by the constraints of time and place. I have asked that she draw you to this place, and she has said that it will come to pass. Aulus will need you. I need you, Accala. There's too much at stake for me to trust anyone but my own children. I have raised you to understand the difference between right and wrong, to put duty and honor before glory and self-interest. The queen has taken my pin and infused it with the purest ichor from her body. I've left it with Aulus. The pin will draw you to the ichor like a compass as well as create a bridge to permit communication with the Hyperboreans. Aid them in their mission. Help them escape this world with their cargo, help them take the ichor back to the realm of the gods, far from human hands. This is a sacred charge, a celestial quest that I entrust to you, my daughter. It is no exaggeration to state that the fate of the empire rests in your hands."

The image faded, and now I saw only my face reflected in the tunnel wall.

I'd failed my mother, but I'd only ever had half the information. I didn't know what to make of this talk about the gods, but one thing was overwhelmingly clear: My mother made a deal with an alien power and the deal was a bad one. She couldn't have known the Sertorians would come to possess her pin, that the Hyperboreans would turn Aulus into whatever this thing beside me was. She acted out of desperation; she put the empire before the needs of her children. I understood why she did it, but it didn't stop the anger from rising up to cover me like funerary robes. How dare she make offerings of us. Move us about like pieces on a chessboard. I willingly suffered every humiliation to avenge her death, and now it turned out that she was the architect of my suffering. Aulus and I were the only ones who could use the pin to find the ichor, making us a priceless commodity ripe for exploitation.

Quick. Let go of that idea, Lumen said. *It's like a poison dart that will worm its way toward your heart. Pluck it out. Drop it like a hot coal before it burns you. You must not blame her. She made a difficult decision in a difficult situation. Would you have done any different?*

"She's not your mother," I snapped. "You don't get to speak for her. A mother is supposed to protect her children. She should never have left home, never have come to this world."

Weren't you desperate to leave Rome and play your part in the game of empire? Lumen asked. *Hadn't you already made a sacrifice of yourself to try to right a wrong? Why would you deny her the same right? With so much at stake?*

"So much at stake for your people," I said. "Your concern is for the Hyperboreans, don't pretend any different."

My concern is for all beings, for the fate of the galaxy. Yours should be too. Don't be too hard on the Hyperboreans. The queen reached out from her mountain and cast me into the place where you found my mortal body, deep into a deposit of pure ichor. She thought I'd be safe, but she didn't understand the damage a nuclear strike would bring to this world. We were both trapped. She inside her mountain, I inside mine. The radiation was slowly killing my physical body, so she made me another, this body. What you saw when you held Aulus was the last breath of organic life in my old body, but my soul had already moved on to this form you see here. The queen honored the deal with our mother as best she could—to preserve my life so that I could help the Hyperboreans complete their mission. So that together you and I could finish Mother's work.

I stumbled, suddenly dizzy, and he lightly touched my arm to right me. A cool breeze flowed through my mind, clearing my thoughts, calming me.

No one is forcing you, Accala. I've made my choice, but you must decide for yourself if you want to be here.

"Aulus was too young to choose anything." I turned from him. "I can't do this. I can't treat you like him. You're not him."

I am what I am. Are you the same Accala who left Rome? This world has remade you too. How you see me is up to you, as is your decision. I must go on, but I can make a place here in the mountain for you to hide, or show you to a tunnel that will lead back to Avis Accipitridae. You might be able to stow away on a transport and escape to some distant part of the empire.

Were these the choices my nine-year-old brother rejected when he had the chance? Coward's choices. They brought my own anger into focus and I saw it clearly for what it was. Self-pity. Fear. I might not like where my mother had placed me, but I couldn't walk away from this fight. Not now.

"There's no choice," I said. "The Sertorians must be stopped. That's the bottom line." I felt some energy run through my muscles. My body was mobilizing; the memory of Accala the fighter was returning. "What do we have to do? The queen is in the place you showed me? The ruins near Lupus Civitas?"

Beyond the ruined city, girded by a crescent-shaped valley, lies this world's tallest mountain: Nova Olympus. At the foot of the mountain is a temple built in Minerva's honor. The queen lives within this mountain.

I could see it as he spoke to my mind. See it in a new way, not as I did in my dreams or in the holovids on my information nodes. I saw the crescent, the mountains, and the city as the Hyperboreans saw it. One whole. One body. I had a vision of it not as it had been, not the perfect crystal flower filled with ichor, but how it was now—sections of the walls pulsed with dark channels, an illuminated slick black film clung to the crystal stalactites that dripped from the roof of the cavern, and the walls cracked and split as the dark ambrosia slowly found its way through them. The queen's body was like a bird trapped in an oil slick, its wings heavy with sticky tar, unable to pull free, slowly drowning in pollution.

It was here that I was reborn, Lumen said. *The pollution prevents her from creating more children. I am the last.*

It reminded me of the Sertorians' mining site where I fought Licinus. Black poison eating white light, slowly, inevitably.

You just have to get me to Nova Olympus. The ichor I bring will give her the power to free herself, to clear the pollution from her body. That is my role. Then she can take my people far from here. I know you can do it, Accala. Please, help us.

It would mean heading east. Whatever had transpired while I'd been down there, in order to help Lumen, I'd still have to traverse the tournament course to Lupus Civitas. No escape. If the gods had a sense of humor, it was a dark one.

"What resources do we have at hand?"

This way, he said, taking a sharp right turn, moving the tunnel in a new direction.

The Hyperborean child who claimed to have my brother inside him had no facial expression, but I sensed a smile, I could feel it like sunlight falling into a dusty room. An image of me, a stray thought, was intermingled with the light— me fighting in the school athletics competition, mobilizing my team, leading them to victory. That's right, Aulus was there that day, cheering me on. The old Accala. I hardly recognized that girl.

"These tunnels of yours—how long can you keep generating them?" I asked.

Not for much longer, and I only do so now to keep us out of the way of the arachnoraptors, he said. *I can't spare any more ichor. So much was lost when the city fell and more again when you attacked me. When I leave this mountain my powers wil be severely limited. I must preserve every ounce if I'm to complete our mission.*

When the city fell. When I struck him. I was not without fault. He was letting me know that I had a responsibility to him, to these aliens, to undo the damage I'd done. And now that he'd mentioned it, I could feel the energy running from him, the cost involved in his keeping the tunnel open. He could move this whole mountain if he wanted, but he permitted himself only the smallest drips of power. Like a castaway who must ration a flask of water, he dared not drink it all. He must save it, use it sparingly in order to free the queen and liberate his people. I wasn't wrong to think of him as a little Spartacus.

"So if we must go aboveground, then how many Hyperboreans can you bring to the field?" I asked.

To fight? None but Concretus, he replied.

"None? But there were hundreds of warriors," I protested. "I saw them in the hives."

They have rejoined with me to conserve energy. As I journey back to my mother, I'm not only collecting ichor from the hives, I'm drawing the individual workers, singers, and warriors into me. I'm absorbing them as well as their ichor.

Again, the voice in my mind was different when he spoke of his people. It lost my brother's tone, the sense of his youth, and took on a distant, sonorous quality.

"Inside you? How many?"

Right now? I contain about forty thousand, give or take.

Gods. An ocean of ichor ready to be plucked up, poisoned, and turned into an endless supply of ambrosia. That was Aquilinus' dark dream. Right now Lumen was priceless—the most valuable commodity in the empire.

The queen bee gives birth. The hive is born of her. I'm the opposite. I collect and recombine. As we travel, more Hyperboreans will come to join with me, like adding notes to a song.

"That sounds like it will slow us down," I said.

It can't be avoided. When we lose Hyperboreans, it's like a symphony with missing notes. The song is an expression of the power of the ichor. If we lose too much ichor, then the song fails. We will be unable to leave this world, unable to carry our cargo home. Our death and the loss of the ichor will be tragic, but only a small tragedy compared to what will follow. Without the ichor to fuel them, the gods will not be able to uphold the ongoing song of creation. The galaxy will begin to turn in on itself and die much sooner than planned.

"How soon?"

Soon enough. A thousand years, maybe less. Countess lives will be lost, but the real tragedy will be cosmic in scale—the premature end of this aspect of creation, before it has time to know itself, before it can complete its song. The galaxy is a mirror of the gods. It is how they come to know themselves. The song must come to a natural conclusion and then return to its source. Then a new song, a new galaxy, is born. For the song to be perverted by human desire, twisted and warped by its power, is the greatest sacrilege, the worst outcome for any age of creation.

"So no pressure then," I said. I didn't want to seem flippant, but I had to keep things simple, practical. Focus on the next step. No thoughts of gods or universal consequences.

"The good news is that the Sertorians are desperate, and we're in a position to deal them a fatal blow. The entire empire is relying on them to deliver what they promised. The bad news is that the Sertorians are desperate—they'll be throwing everything they've got into finding you. The arachnoraptors are just the tip of the iceberg," I said. "When you said you'd show me resources, I meant weapons, soldiers."

We cannot tolerate weapons in this place, but there is a cavern, high above, near the surface, a place where the Hyperboreans confiscated weapons from Ro-

man expeditions over the centuries. *The weapons from the last conflict in my city were also placed there.*

"An arms stockpile?"

Yes, your discus is there. I had Concretus recover it—I know how important it is to you.

"Orbis is there? And armor?"

Yes.

"I can work with that. Let's get moving."

There was no use having weapons without soldiers to wield them, but right now anything was better than nothing, and holding Orbis in my hand would give me some much-needed strength.

I have one more thing to show you first. You mentioned soldiers. I knew we would need help to complete the mission, so I had Concretus take two of your allies as the city was collapsing.

"What allies? I have no allies."

This wasn't good. In the distance I saw a lit cell, similar to the one I was kept in but larger. There were two figures within it. They were naked, just like me. One was sitting; the other paced back and forth along the far wall.

We approached rapidly. I stepped into the cell and Concretus came after me just in time before the tunnel collapsed shut. They both turned to look at me.

"Gods, what have you done?" I whispered.

Julia Silana paused her pacing and stared at me, gobsmacked. The figure beside her, sitting on the icy ground, his knees pulled up to his chest, rocked back and forth, staring into space. His skin was an anemic white, his body so weak and skeletal that I barely recognized him, but the eyes left no doubt that this was the man who tried to brainwash me, to break me, to own me—Gaius Sertorius Crassus.

XXXVI

IT TOOK ME A moment to realize there was something else different about Crassus—he looked normal, no longer godlike. The glamour of the ambrosia had left him. If I expected some dramatic response, I got nothing. He seemed vacant, sitting quietly at the far end of the cell. I wasn't sure he even knew I was there. His body shivered, freezing to death, but he seemed detached from everything. He was drained, broken.

Julia, by contrast, stared at me, her eyes wide, one hand covering her mouth.

"I'm no underworld shade," I said. "It's me."

She took a hesitant step forward and craned her neck to get a better look at mine. "The ambrosia?" she asked.

"Yes. The Hyperboreans put me back together."

"There's not even a mark," she said in amazement.

Now I saw that she wasn't the same as the person I last saw, either. Her severed hand had been replaced. Not reattached like my head, but replaced entirely. But by what?

"The Hyperborean kid did it," she said, holding it up. "It's all solid ichor."

Words weren't enough to convey the thanks I owed Lumen for giving Julia back her hand, but he could see my heart—he knew how I felt. Lumen told me that he didn't have ichor to spare, and yet he did this. My own life meant nothing, but this . . . this gesture was beyond value to me. It went a small way to repairing the damage I'd caused when I was half mad with rage.

"It's a strange sensation," Julia continued. "I can feel with it just as I did before." She touched the tips of her ice hand with her left hand. "It's not even cold." Her crystal fingers moved quickly back and forth. Intrigued, I reached out and she let me touch it. The surface was translucent and contained the same swirling light present in Hyperborean bodies, but at the same time it felt like it was made of skin, muscle, and bone. It really was just like her hand had been before. There were even lines on the palm and fingernails. It was a perfect replica in ichor.

"What do you think?" she asked.

Before I could answer, Julia stepped forward and delivered a right cross to my chin with her icy fist that sent me reeling back. The pain was explosive, no ambrosia to muffle its impact.

"You're right," she said. "The barbarians put you back together good. Now I'm going to take you apart again."

Concretus stepped in suddenly and grabbed Julia's arm, holding her in place.

"I guess I deserved that," I said. I could taste blood in my mouth and my lip began to swell.

"And more," Julia said angrily before kicking uselessly at Concretus' leg. "Let go of me, you overgrown icicle!"

"Please, let her go," I said to the giant. He looked to Lumen and then his grip loosened, allowing Julia to pull her hand free.

For the first time I felt like I could sense something resembling a personality in the ice monster Lumen had named Concretus. He had a song that was almost tangible. It was uniquely his, but it also connected him to the greater song. He listened only to Lumen, and only because his queen had given him the role of guardian. He didn't like humans, or much of anything else, for that matter. He was driven to complete the Hyperborean goal of reunion with the source from which they came. Nothing else was of any concern. If Lumen was their Spartacus, this being was the Hyperborean Hercules, or Theseus. Focused, aloof, proud.

"I get the sense that you're not a prisoner here," Julia said.

"None of us are. The Hyperboreans are allies. They're on our side."

"You've opened up a dialogue with them? You can communicate?"

"I can, with Lumen here," I said. "We share . . . a bond."

I looked at Crassus quickly. Not a word, not a flutter from him as I pulled Julia aside and quietly filled her in on my mother's message so Crassus couldn't hear. She listened carefully, nodding from time to time. I found I couldn't bring myself to tell her about the Hyperboreans being messengers of the gods, and I couldn't talk about Aulus. It was a simple idea to grasp when you were connected to a being's heart and mind, but somehow trying to explain it in words, especially when I wasn't sure how I felt about the situation, seemed too hard. So I told the short version of the truth—that the Hyperboreans were using Lumen to gather up all the ichor, that my mother was helping them, that they needed our help to leave, and that the tunnels around us were being scoured by arachnoraptors. I even told her about Aquilinus' ability to possess the Blood Hawks from a distance.

"Gods, that's a lot to take in," Julia said when I finished. "When you're involved, Accala, everything's like some insane opera. Nothing's simple, and yet I feel sorry for these beings. I saw the city. It was the most perfect thing I've ever seen. It was hard for me to see it fall."

"That's why I must help them," I said. "To make up for that, but also because the Hyperborean mission and ours are virtually the same."

"If we can get this little walking ambrosia mine off this world, off the table altogether, then we can still foil the Sertorians," Julia agreed.

"Lumen. His name is Lumen," I said. "And it's not ambrosia, it's ichor. He's filled with the blood of the gods."

"Lumen." She turned to him. "Is that how you're called?"

Lumen stared back at her. Without the mind-to-mind bond I shared with him, he couldn't communicate. Most Romans would consider him a dumb animal, but Julia could sense his intelligence.

"What about your bodyguard?" Julia asked Lumen. "If we have to risk our lives to save you, will he step up and fight for us?"

Ah. Concretus will, more than likely, Lumen said.

"Yes, he will," I translated.

"Did the ice monster say anything at all, or was it the midget?" Julia asked. "I can't understand them, but I can see who you're looking at. I'm not stupid. Tell me what they really say, Accala, you owe me that much."

And more, I thought.

"Lumen says it's more than likely that he will."

"What do you mean more than likely?"

He is a servant of the gods, one of the most senior of his people, a guard to the queen. He considers humans . . .

I translated and then waited for Lumen to finish the rest.

"What?" Julia demanded.

Treacherous, deceitful, untrustworthy, two-faced. I'm not sure how many more synonyms I can think of to capture the feeling he's transmitting.

I hesitated but translated, and Julia simply shrugged.

"At least he's honest, and he's not too far wrong. What matters is that we have him. Lumen here is the thing Aquilinus needs. Fate has dealt us that card, put him right in our lap. From what you've told me, you don't have any idea what's going on up there. A lot has changed in the last two days."

"Tell me," I said.

"Accala?" Crassus looked at me from the far side of the cell like he was waking up from a long sleep. His eyes suddenly went as wide as saucers, and he jumped up and rushed toward me. "Accala! Darling! Thank the gods!" he yelled at the top of his voice.

Before I could think, I punched him in the face, sending him sailing across the cell and into the wall behind him. A solid punch to a frail body. He slid down the crystal surface right back into the spot where he sat before. I was glad to see that I was getting some of my coordination back.

"Accala . . ." he called in a pathetic tone. He looked wounded, like a child who just had his favorite toy smashed.

"And he deserved that," Julia said to me. And then to Crassus: "You'll shut up and keep the volume down, or I'll kill you myself. I tried, you know, to kill him, but they stopped me. I tried to explain to them that it was in everyone's best interests that he die, but they don't understand."

Perhaps he was mad, perhaps he was faking it. Either way, Gaius Sertorius Crassus was always dangerous.

I didn't know why Lumen rescued Crassus, but looking at him, barely able to stand, I couldn't think what use he would serve, except to slow us down or turn on us when our guard was dropped.

He will be of use, Lumen said, once again in an older and wiser voice than Aulus'. *Mother asked that he be saved.*

"The queen?"

Yes.

"What's wrong with him?" I asked Julia.

"Crassus the mighty beast master tried to take on the Hyperborean chieftain over there when he dragged us away. The chieftain broke his arms and legs and put him into the ice. They tortured him. I didn't think I could ever feel sorry for Crassus, but after what he went through . . ."

"Ice needles?" I asked.

"Ice needles," she replied. "When he came out, his arms and legs were healed, but he looked like this."

"They did the same thing to me," I said. "Believe it or not, they were trying to help. They flushed the polluted ambrosia out of his system."

"I worked that out just fine," she said, "but it drove Crassus mad. He's not just a cracked egg, he's been thrown in a bowl and scrambled."

"Don't listen to her," Crassus said quickly. "I'm no threat to you. I've never seen things more clearly. At first I thought it was impossible, but he showed me." He pointed at Lumen. "He showed me!"

"Showed you what?" I asked.

He was talking excitedly, his eyes were wide like a child opening presents at Saturnalia.

"They serve the gods," he whispered loudly.

"You can understand Lumen?" I asked Crassus. "You hear him speak?" I wondered how he managed that trick without my pin.

All three of you have the smallest amounts of my energy in you. Julia to heal her hand, and you and Crassus so that you could survive your wounds and be purged of the ambrosia. He has received the least, but he has a natural sensitivity and is able to sense some fragments of our song now, Lumen transmitted to me.

That was great, the last bloody thing we needed. It was bad enough that Crassus lived, but now this?

"Lumen," Crassus said slowly, pronouncing the name like he was swilling a fine wine between his teeth. "No, they do not speak to me with words, but I can catch glimpses of images and feelings. It's breaking me up to try and understand it; it's too much for me to see all at once. But the higher I climb, the farther away they seem. We are so very small, Accala. Our wings were borrowed. Like Icarus, we've flown too close to the sun. We are not . . ." He paused, as if trying to swallow something that had caught in his throat. "We are not the best and greatest form of life in the universe. These beings are greater than us."

"Speak for yourself," Julia said to Crassus. "He's been ranting like that for days," she said to me. "It's been driving me crazy."

Crassus knew the truth, but it unhinged him. He'd swung from being a total believer of Aquilinus to becoming obsessed with the Hyperboreans. There was no room in Crassus' universe for individual responsibility; he'd always looked for a bigger power to permit him an avenue for his own excesses. He glanced quickly at Lumen, his eyes filled with adoration like the small alien was Hermes himself come down from the clouds, and then he rushed forward again, coming low this time, throwing himself at my feet. I tried to step back, but the Sertorian gripped my left leg and held on for dear life like I was a ballast in a shipwreck. He looked up at me with manic, desperate eyes.

"You know what this means?" he demanded. "We were wrong. There *are* gods! And they're not like us. It's all blown to pieces, everything we believed. The proconsul's entire plan needs to be rewritten!"

"Let go of me," I said, kicking him. "What's happening on the surface?" I asked Julia. "And how do you know about it?"

She pointed to something in the corner that I'd missed when I'd entered. It was Julia's armilla and a small tool kit.

"The Hyperboreans threw some of my equipment in here after they fixed my hand," Julia said. "I wasn't going to look a gift horse in the mouth. I've been able to pick up small bursts of coverage."

"Coverage? You mean the tournament's still running? The last I saw was *Incitatus* firing on the stadium."

I had hoped that the emperor would bring things under control. Discipline Aquilinus and the Sertorians for overstepping the mark.

"Listen for yourself. I've been picking up bits and pieces. I've put together a compilation of the important information," Julia said, crouching down and passing me the armilla. She'd rigged up a small booster pack, and a long aerial protruded from its side. "Lean in close. I'll keep the power output and volume down so we don't attract the arachnoraptors."

I could hear the voice of Julius Gemminus excitedly running off at the mouth with the commentary. The signal was fuzzy, interspersed with static. I listened for a name, for a familiar audible string that would help give me context.

"Behold the mighty Viridians! Savage wolves. Be honest, haven't you, as I have, grown weary of their moral posturing?"

It was Aquilinus' voice.

"Their tiresome and arrogant lectures on virtue? Only a few years ago, at the height of their influence, it seemed that barely a day went past without some prominent Viridian strutting about the floor of the Forum like a peacock, making a nauseating Catonian speech that we all had to endure. Placing themselves above the rest of us. Now look where arrogance and pride gets you."

It sounded like the Wolves had survived, at least some of them, but what was Aquilinus up to? How was it that he had any say over the games?

Julius Gemminus' voice came in over the top as Aquilinus' speech came to an end. "All hail Emperor Aquilinus. Glory and honor to the divine House Sertorian."

"Emperor Aquilinus?" I dropped the armilla like a red-hot coal.

"Hey, be careful with that," Julia said, scooping it back up.

"Emperor Aquilinus? Why didn't you tell me at once?"

"Well there's not much you can do about it right now, is there? Besides, I'm not exactly well disposed toward you."

"*Emperor* Aquilinus?"

"Emperor Aquilinus," Julia confirmed. "He's revealed his seventh precept and expects everyone to worship him as a god now."

"I can't believe it."

"It's true," Julia said. She picked up the armilla, tapped at it, and Aquilinus' voice started up again.

". . . they've witnessed the proofs of my divine power, yet still these Viridians and their allied houses refuse to bow, to accept the inevitable supremacy of House Sertorian, and I know that out there many of their countrymen feel the same way. I'm going to educate these men. I'm going to teach them the lessons I've learned and see if I can discover any potential within them. Now that I've achieved the celestial realm, I'm going to look down on them from on high and burn them from heaven to earth, starting with their gods and priests, then their houses, then their families, and finally themselves. As to the consequences of continued resistance . . . well, that will be a surprise. We're going to hold a philosophical argument expressed in action. I'll leave it up to you to tell me if they have the right stuff, or if they pale in comparison against Sertorian power, the power we offer freely to those with the sense to seize it."

"How could this come to pass?" I asked.

"Aquilinus was already poised to strike after the secret of the ambrosia was revealed. It wasn't just the barbarian city you brought down; after that, the whole side of the mountain collapsed and opened up. Aquilinus' hand was forced. He couldn't allow the emperor to get his hands on the ichor or your little friend here."

"A coup. He staged a coup," I said. This was a nightmare.

"You know how many dignitaries were on that station?" Julia asked. "The rich, famous, and powerful paid a small fortune for their seats, and now Aquilinus has them all in one place, to take all the wealthy and powerful men in the empire hostage in one fell swoop, including your uncle and Emperor Numerius."

"But he can't just take over the Rota Fortuna and proclaim himself emperor of the galaxy." And then it hit me. "It's the same as when he took this world. He launched simultaneous attacks on key Viridian bases throughout our province."

"Yes, attacks on important capitals all over the empire. Regional magistrates and consuls have been imprisoned or had their homes bombed. And they can't do a damn thing about it. In Rome, the emperor left his idiot cousin Bucco in charge as regent."

Bucco—that fool Marcus and I had laughed at in the Colosseum when he was thrashed by the Sauromatae.

"It turns out Aquilinus had already bought him with a dose of ambrosia," Julia finished.

"But the Senate."

"All the non-Sertorian senators who weren't swayed by Aquilinus' false promises were executed. He announced that since Caligula turned the imperial palace into a whorehouse and gambling den to raise funds for the treasury, it was the least he could do to offer the Senate house for the same purpose. He's had the senators' wives sold to the highest bidders from the Talonite houses and made the Senate floor the center of gambling on the outcome of these new games of his."

"What of my father?"

"No word of him. I assume he's a hostage with the other spectators aboard the Rota Fortuna. They think you're dead, Accala."

"I suppose that's something. They won't be looking for me."

"And they won't be expecting you to ferry Lumen away from here."

"You're right."

"The way I see it, we've still got a mission to complete," Julia said.

"Tell me more about the games. How many survive?"

"I can't tell yet. At least a half dozen Caninines. I only know for certain that Cato and Strabo Flavius were killed by the Ovidians in fighting on the surface before the coup, but I'm not sure if any Viridians made it out of the tunnels alive."

"They were good men," I said. That meant Marcus might still be alive. I prayed that Minerva had spared him. "If he's made a successful coup, then why continue with the games? Why not just wipe out the Caninines altogether?"

"I'm not sure," Julia said. "Perhaps we'll find out when we get out of these tunnels."

"Can you get me the current broadcast?" I asked. "I need to know what's happening right now."

"Okay, but now we know the enemy is out there scouting, let's keep it short."

I leaned in to hear the coverage of the games. Julius Gemminus' commentary was just audible.

"Brocchus Ovidius throws the ball to Marcus Calpurnius Regulus, who fumbles it. It's touched the ground. What ball is it? Wait. Yes, the Temple of Saturn ball, has shattered. That's going to cause some major rape and pillage back in Rome."

Marcus was alive, thank the gods. But what the hell was going on?

"I don't follow," I said to Julia. "It doesn't sound like gladiator games. It's like ..."

"It's like a game show contest. He's got them carrying out ridiculous frivolities for his amusement. Right now the Caninines are playing against the Talonites in a trigon tournament. I was able to pick up a little of the match earlier on."

Trigon. I hadn't played it since the Academy. Players took up position at the points of a triangle and hurled the ball at the next player in the chain with all their might, right at him. If the thrower cast too wide and not at the catcher's body, then he lost a point. The catcher had to either catch the ball and then throw to the next player in the triangle with the other hand, or hit and rebound the ball back at the thrower. The catcher who dropped the ball or allowed it to strike the body lost a point. The best players used expensive, decorative glass balls because it raised the stakes and they had the skills not to drop them.

"But none of us are trigon players. We're gladiators," I said. "What's he thinking?"

"It's to humiliate them. All the Talonite players have been given ambrosia, so they never miss the ball, but none of the gladiators actually seem to be getting killed. It's all about dragging things out so that the Caninines have more time to make mistakes and drop the ball. Each ball has the image of a temple within it. If they drop the ball, Aquilinus has the real temple destroyed, the priests and priestesses raped, tortured, and killed."

"That sounds familiar," I said, remembering Crassus' tutorials on *Incitatus*. "The slaughter of priests and priestesses where Aquilinus spurned the gods to avenge his slain father."

"Right," Julia responded. "From what I can tell, Aquilinus has instituted a series of historical reenactments that depict his rise to power through the ranks of House Sertorian. This morning the Caninines dropped the first ball, and Aquilinus ordered the destruction of the Temple of Mercury in Londinium, along with twenty thousand clergy. By the time I was able to tune in again, it was midday, and hundreds of temples throughout the empire had fallen. Each time the ball is dropped, Aquilinus dares the gods to strike him down and boasts to the audience they have nothing to fear, that they should embrace the Sertorian future."

"So just then, the ball Marcus dropped—"

"They'll be destroying the Temple of Saturn in the Roman Forum as we speak," Julia said.

Gods, what a loss. So many lives, and the buildings—ancient, irreplaceable, almost alive in their own way.

"How has he marshaled the forces to cause such havoc? I can't believe the citizens of the empire stand by and allow such atrocities to take place."

"It's the citizens who are bringing them about. That's Aquilinus' bargain. He's using the games to leverage support. Those who wish to receive ambrosia, wherever they are in the empire, have to play their part by participating in the death and destruction. Average citizens are tearing the temples apart, brick by brick, joining in the pillaging and rape. Not all of them, mind you, but enough. Led, of course, by the Sertorians."

"Aquilinus is forcing them to squeeze the trigger on the gun he's got pointed at the empire," I said. "Then he can say the blood isn't on his hands alone. He's using the games to let everyone know that he's running the show. But high-stakes trigon? It's a farce. The audience won't go for that in place of real blood sport."

"And not just that. He temporarily paralyzed the Caninine Alliance players and had them stripped and dressed in armor that depicted them as their respective gods. The Viridians have had to dress in women's armor to emulate Minerva, the Calpurnians' armor has onions and turnips attached to depict Saturn's agricultural powers, and the Flavian armor has little wings sticking out the back to symbolize Mercury."

"Wait. The Viridians dressed in women's armor? And they did it?"

"It was that or be killed."

Aquilinus was trying to break the surviving Caninines as he tried to break me—transform them, warp them with punishment so they accepted his precepts. Or perhaps he knew they never would bow and whatever nightmarish punishments inflicted on them were purely for the benefit of the audience—a demonstration of what would happen if they didn't comply with Aquilinus' demands.

"Still. That's not like them," I said. Hell, it'd be funny if it wasn't such a damned nightmare. Viridian men in women's breastplates. How Carbo must have fumed at that. I'd have thought he'd have let himself be struck down rather than be feminized by Aquilinus. It was hard not to feel a sense of bitter irony. It was my own house that fought hardest against my doing anything martial with my life, and now its strongest competitors wore the garb of female gladiators, styled like modern-day Minervas. Aquilinus had a twisted sense of humor. But I could not underestimate him, mad as he was. He was playing for big stakes again—gambling that his strength and the prize he offered by way of the ambrosia would permit him to insult the gods without a single finger of reprisal being lifted by the citizens of the empire. And this was the ultimate insult, the ultimate bait. He knew that if the mob didn't rise up to challenge him over this, then they never would, that the people would accept his rule.

"And the Blood Hawks? Any mention of them?"

"Not a peep. From what I can tell, they're out. Dead from the fall when the mountain was destroyed."

Good. Whatever was going on up there, I felt certain I could deal with it as long as Licinus and the others had taken a one-way ride to Hades' dark halls.

"I need to get up and outside," I said. "I have to see what Aquilinus has done with the tournament. I can't formulate a proper strategy without more intelligence."

"You're going to get us out of this?" Julia asked. "You got us into this. I'll admit not everything that's happened is entirely your fault—the ambrosia and the brainwashing were a lot to bear, and things took a strange turn with these aliens—but you went crazy, Accala, and now you owe your house and your uncle for what went down. You owe me," she said, holding up her ice hand. "You have a debt of honor, Accala, and I'm gonna make sure that you pay it out in full. From now on, you'll do as I command. I was meant to take over if you went off the rails, and gods, did you go off the rails."

"You're right."

"You're agreeing with me? Well, that's a start at least." She pulled me close to her and whispered, "I don't trust these Hyperboreans. Their city was impressive, but they don't speak, they don't have proper faces. I can't tell what they're thinking."

"Well, I can, and I promise you, it's nothing diabolical. They just want to get away from here and take the ichor with them."

"As long as they'll follow you, that's all that matters. Now show me you can follow orders. Kill Crassus now. While you can."

I looked over at Crassus, coughing and shivering. He hardly looked formidable, and Lumen said there was a reason to spare him. But the Hyperboreans had been wrong before about the cruel nature of Romans, and I couldn't see what use he could possibly be to us in the state he was in.

"He's a serpent coiled and ready to strike, Accala. From what you told me, Aquilinus could take possession of him anytime he likes and endanger our mission. Do it now, then we can move on."

"No! You'll need me." Crassus came scuttling across the floor on hands and knees like a cowed dog. How did he hear us? "I do not beg for my life but for this chance to redeem myself before the gods. To serve them. I want to learn. I want to know more. I've made some terrible mistakes, done some terrible things, but it was the proconsul controlling me all along, and my addiction to ambrosia. When they used their needles, it took out all the darkness. There's not much of me left, but it's enough, because for the first time I'm free, just like you. Please, Accala, I want to serve them as you do. I don't want the poisoned ambrosia we've been sipping. I don't want wax wings. I've fallen back to earth, but this time I'll climb toward the gods the right way. I am not worthy to serve them, I am not worthy to serve their servants, these beings of light, and so I will serve you. I'll do whatever you say. Please trust me, there's no more Aquilinus. He's gone."

"You can't fight," I said to Crassus. "You're weak."

He tried to stand up as best he could. His legs were like matchsticks compared to what they were.

"I can."

"You can't," I said. "So what use are you to me?"

"I can help you win the audience."

"I can do that without you. You kept on telling me how good I was at shaping their opinions."

"I can tell you secrets. Your uncle, he was feeding Aquilinus information all along. Anything you'd tell her," he said, pointing to Julia, "would be passed on to my proconsul."

"I'm no traitor!" the redhead said, stepping forward to strike him.

Crassus threw up his hands to protect himself. "I didn't say you were. It was the uncle."

"I should kill you just for that," I said. He was still trying to warp and control my perceptions.

"It's true. He wanted the ichor as badly as Aquilinus did. Each wanted to be in control of the raw ingredient for ambrosia. They worked together to keep you moving so you'd find the storehouse the barbarians were hiding."

"It doesn't add up," I said. "They're enemies. They've always been enemies."

"Yes. They were going to fight over the ichor, but without you there was nothing to fight over, they couldn't find the ichor. So the proconsuls were wise, prepared to compromise and work together to get to the point where the ichor was uncovered."

"I don't believe you," I said. "You'll have to do better than that."

"I know how to beat Aquilinus," Crassus said quickly. "I know where he's weak."

"Tell me now."

"It's not as simple as that," he pleaded. "I need to see what the situation is aboveground. You know that."

"What if I demand your life?" I asked. "How loyal will you be then?"

He got up on his knees and beat his chest. "My life is yours."

"You betrayed me from the beginning," I said.

"Aquilinus tampered with my mind. When I spoke to you, my feelings were real, what I felt was real, but there were blocks, things I couldn't say, or think or remember. And now? I'm whole again, and my feelings haven't changed. More, my eyes are opened. The Hyperboreans have chosen you as their handmaiden because you see what is best for all of us. If you need my blood, then take it. Take it now."

Handmaiden. I didn't like that at all. It made me sound like some delirious white-robed Vestal Virgin throwing spring flowers into the air. Crassus' broken, skeletal body hardly looked ready for a fight. How much of him had been sustained by ambrosia that the absence of it had left this wreck? He was a pig and an enemy, but he was a great warrior, a masterful gladiator. And then to see him like that. So much for the overman. Strangely, though, I didn't feel hatred for Crassus. Only pity. I didn't buy that every bad thing he did was driven by Aquilinus. He was still a Sertorian, but my time in the Hyperborean cell and my connection with Lumen had opened something inside of me. Lumen's request that Crassus live wasn't just based on some future prognostication. Lumen truly believed that if I killed Crassus now, then it would send me down the wrong path and my goal to help both the Hyperboreans and the empire would never be realized.

"I'll take you both on if that's what it takes," Julia said, sensing my hesitation. "I'll play this game out by myself."

Gods. This wasn't happening. I wouldn't let things fall apart again. I couldn't go against Julia again. Her pragmatism was my touchstone. She stopped me wandering off track. She'd always been there for me, as my mission compass, my conscience. I owed her, but I'd sworn to serve the Hyperboreans as well. I needed to manage those allegiances. Crassus was the odd one out. Killing him was logical and just. It made no sense to bring him along, and if that was the price of getting Julia on board, of earning her trust, then it was worth it. Whatever insight Lumen had, he didn't understand Crassus; any use he may be would come at too great a cost. I formed a fist. A sharp blow to the throat, collapse his trachea, break the epiglottis, and the throat would swell. He'd choke to death in minutes.

Crassus was desperately calling out my name, begging incoherently. Julia yelled at him to quit his whining and urged me louder and louder to prove my loyalty. "What are you waiting for, Accala?" And Lumen? Lumen's body was still, but there was a noise, not the Hyperborean song, but a hum so loud that I could barely think straight.

I had made myself a sacrifice at Crassus' behest. Now it was only fair that he sacrifice his life in exchange. That would cancel things out, create a balance. The thought of him dead at my feet, struggling to breathe on dry land, just like drowning, sent a raw, thrilling spark through my body.

Then, in an instant, the far wall of the cell, the one Crassus had been propped up against, blew out, and giant black insects swarmed into the room wielding long scanner weapons. Arachnoraptors. They'd found us.

XXXVII

THERE WAS NO TIME to argue. We fell into a wedge formation. I was at the fore, Crassus and Julia flanked me on either side. We were naked and unarmed, but we were Roman. We were trained fighters, and now all conflicts were put aside. Now there was only survival.

There were a dozen arachnoraptors armed with transmission staffs, long antennae with power spheres at the rear and a small dish at the front end. The dishes boosted the creatures' scanning power but were also laced with razor-sharp edges and small ion blasters. A pike extended from the center of each dish, enabling the weapon to be used to shock or spear an opponent in combat.

They didn't rush us, though. They clustered together, climbing each other's backs, forming a pyramid shape. Black and shiny like beetles, stacked into a heaped pile, long spidery legs intertwining.

"They're forming a transmission cluster," Julia yelled. "They need to pool their power to transmit their message through the rock to the surface. Keep them apart, or Aquilinus will have us within the hour!"

We charged, and a half dozen of them moved from the rear of the cluster to bar our way. They leveled their staff weapons and opened fire. Needle-thin ion blasts peppered the space before us. As the blasts struck one another in midair, they broke out into star-shaped formations, clustering together to form an energy net that sought to ensnare and trap us. Arachnoraptors and their webs.

I rolled under the energy net and came up a few feet from the defensive line. The black alien shell that protected their lower extremities from damage didn't extend to their human upper bodies, which were less well protected by leather and steel armor.

I kicked the hooded head of the one nearest me, nearly breaking my foot in the process as it impacted with a metal plate inside the mask, and then shot past, heading for the organic pyramid.

"There!" Julia yelled, pointing at the largest of the human hybrids. It was climbing up to the top of the pyramid, and a beacon behind the dish on its transmission staff was pulsing a bright orange. "That's their broadcaster. Take him out and they'll be dead in the water."

Julia had reappropriated her armilla and was using it to generate a shield that Crassus was cowering behind. They were held down by incoming fire. It was up to me, but how could I do anything? More of them were breaking away from the pyramid. I couldn't take them all on my own.

Concretus brushed me aside as he came barreling past. He blasted through the guards, opening the way to the pyramid, before moving to kill those who were trying to kill us. I followed fast on his heels and jumped up onto the side of the formation, planning on climbing up until I got to the broadcaster. Instead, I was struck by a massive shock from one of the creatures' weapons. I hit the ground, my calves painfully locked, the muscles in my back in agonizing spasms. More arachnoraptors streamed in from the tunnel, joining the pyramid, reaching out their weapons toward the central broadcaster's staff to boost its power. Others threw themselves at Concretus as he pulled creatures off the pyramid, slicing at them with his ice-pick arms.

There were too many arachnoraptors. The broadcaster's beacon was glowing with power. I couldn't reach it in time. I forced myself up, ignoring the pain. Julia's shield was down, and she was being overrun by them. Crassus would fall after her. We were finished.

Then suddenly Crassus was charging at the pyramid. He had his hands on a transmission staff. He didn't jump on the side of the cluster of arachnoraptors like I did. He dove under, in between the dozens of spindly legs.

He wasn't going for the broadcaster; he targeted the pyramid from below. Crassus was lit by electrical sparks as the first shock hit him, but it didn't stop him. I lost sight of him in the cluster. And then nothing. I got my legs under me. There was no sign of change. The beacon was glowing like never before, and then without warning, the pyramid was breaking apart, toppling. He had levered it from underneath with the staff! The broadcaster fell down hard on its side and the beacon on its staff went out. Crassus was on it in an instant, his teeth buried in the creature's throat, tearing at it until it stopped moving.

The other arachnoraptors desperately tried to re-form the pyramid, but Concretus was relentless, his massive fists and ice-blade arms pummeling and cutting simultaneously. Their voice boxes removed, their death screams were silent. They scattered, heading back to the tunnels.

"Didn't you know they were coming?" I asked Lumen.

Yes, but it seemed that you needed to join together, and my memory of old stories you and Father used to read was that adversity creates bonds like none other. You faced the adversity and survived.

"Don't do that again. This isn't a child's story, this is real. The arachnoraptors are getting away, and if they manage to reach Aquilinus he'll send an army here to find you. Then it's all finished."

He nodded and raised his arms. There was a sudden fluctuation in the song, like an orchestra's crescendo, and then the rear cell wall glowed and rippled, becoming transparent, revealing the fleeing enemy. The arachnoraptors stopped in their tracks as a solid wall appeared before them, blocking the way. Then the walls to either side liquefied and rushed over the hybrids, flooding the tunnel with liquid crystal before solidifying, leaving the creatures trapped like flies in amber.

I know this is no game, Lumen said, *but if I had not brought you together then you could have killed Crassus.*

"And we need him?" I asked.

Yes.

"He can do that?" Julia asked.

I can, Lumen said, *but it costs me. That's the last time I can offer help of this kind.*

"If he does it too often, then they won't have the power they need to leave," Crassus added weakly. "We must do all we can to prevent Lumen from expending power. Every drop is sacred; the loss could be critical."

It worried me how much Crassus seemed to know. He was burned, his skin red and peeling. He was coughing up blood, not a pretty sight.

"Arachnoraptors," he coughed. "The legs are weak if you can tip them past a forty-degree angle."

And then he fell forward, hitting the icy floor face-first. I ran to his side and turned him over. There was a hole in his abdomen, beneath the right ribs—caused by the sharp pike on the end of the arachnoraptor's transmission staff.

"They did get a transmission out, but I don't think it was strong enough to reach the surface," Julia said, checking the readout on her armilla. "And if anything did get through, it'll take hours, days maybe to reach Aquilinus. I think we're okay for now."

Quickly, Lumen said. *This way. I left a small passage for our escape.*

I crouched down and struggled to help Crassus to his feet.

"Accala . . ." Julia started, but I gave her a sharp glance. He'd earned the right to live, at least for now.

"You don't have to understand or agree, and I'm sorry I'm not taking orders. But I've changed, got better, and I'm not leaving him behind, so you can either leave or help me," I said.

She cursed and helped me hoist him up, putting his right arm around her shoulders so we could walk him along. Before we could take three steps, Lumen signaled Concretus, who took Crassus from us and threw him over his shoulder like a sack of potatoes. Julia retrieved the broadcaster's transmission staff; we needed all the weapons we could get.

Lumen led us through a narrow passage back to the main tunnel network. *We have to move quickly. More of these will come.*

The shining tunnels of the Hyperboreans were unwelcomingly familiar. I couldn't wait to get out of there, back up to the surface for some fresh air.

I can't spare the power to make new tunnels. You'll have to follow me through existing tunnels, and we can't risk any more arachnoraptors finding us. His light faded, leaving us in pure darkness. *I'll lead you back up to the surface via the weapon store my people have accumulated. Listen to the song and you'll be fine. Don't wander from the path I trace out.*

I explained to the others what was happening.

"Song? What song?" Julia asked.

"I can hear it," Crassus whispered hoarsely. "Like a distant whisper."

"I can't hear anything," Julia said.

"Keep hold of my hand," I said. She took my hand with her one of ice. It wasn't cold. It was warm, like Lumen's hand.

"Don't let go," I said to her. I needed her with me now more than ever.

We walked for hours, an uphill course that burned my calves. Crassus tried his best to stifle his hacking cough. Julia was right. I didn't know why I was bringing him along. He deserved to die, by any fair measure, but I couldn't work out how to kill him without picking up the hot ember of revenge and madness that had burned me and led me down the path of destruction. I couldn't shake Lumen's words, that the Sertorian and I were linked. I'd fallen and been given a second chance. I'd asked Lumen and Julia for the opportunity to earn forgiveness for my sins. I wasn't sure I could deny Crassus the same opportunity without damning myself. For better or worse, the three of them—Lumen, Julia, and Crassus—were my touchstones with reality, they helped me focus on the path ahead toward redemption instead of the destruction behind me.

Lumen's song was like a road that I could follow despite the darkness. I could see him even with my eyes closed as a kind of ghost image. Suddenly that image vanished; the song was silent and I froze in place. I heard the sound of Crassus being dumped on the ground by Concretus. I was leading Julia, and suddenly I couldn't feel Lumen, couldn't hear his song.

The arachnoraptors were back. They were close. I could hear them talking in their skittery whispers, and it sent chills up my skin.

I reached out for Lumen in the dark but found nothing. He was gone. Fear crept over me like a suffocating blanket. Self-doubt needled at me. Was it his song that had faltered? Or was it my belief? I pulled the pin out and gripped it tightly, but there was no heat, no directional pull that would indicate a right path to follow.

"What's wrong?" Julia whispered.

"The enemy is near," I said as quietly as I could.

"Then lead us away from them," she said.

"I can't. I can't hear the song anymore. I can't find Lumen."

"We're lost?" Julia spat. "You're joking. What happened to our ironclad barbarian allies?"

"I don't know. I think it might be my fault."

"Really?" Julia asked. "I'd never have guessed. We've got to find him. If what you've said is true, he can't be allowed to fall into Aquilinus' hands."

Exhaustion. Tiredness. Suddenly any strength animating my newly re-bound body failed, and I nearly collapsed. Julia fumbled and managed to grab me before I fell. I needed to stay driven, the worst thing to do in a crisis was panic, but I was drained. My limbs felt like limp spaghetti. I didn't know how I could move forward. In a matter of minutes, everything had changed again, just when I felt like we were on the right track.

"We're at a crossroads," Crassus said.

"You think?" Julia snapped.

"No, an actual crossroads," Crassus said. "And you're about to take the wrong path. We have to head right."

"How do you know?" I snapped at the Sertorian.

"I can hear the song. Can't you?"

"This is where it starts," Julia hissed. "His lies and the treachery that follows. He's probably done something to sever us from the Hyperboreans. This is the moment. We're stumbling around in the dark, and now we've lost our best bet of getting out of here. We need to move fast to try to pick up Lumen's trail. We can't be carrying deadweight."

She squeezed my arm so hard that I nearly cried out in pain. My body was still so sensitive. It seemed to have lost all the years of conditioning I'd put into it.

"Now, Accala!" Julia whispered hoarsely. "Now is the time; there are no barbarians to stop us."

She wanted him dead, and without Lumen there to counsel me otherwise, suddenly all the wrongs I'd suffered at his hands sprang to mind. It would be so easy, and the gods knew Crassus deserved it. The tunnels of this mountain as his tomb, his body pored over by the arachnoraptors when they found him, dragging his corpse back to his old master. I wanted to straddle Crassus and choke the life from him, to watch the light fade from his eyes as his soul fell down into the depths of the underworld—to Tartarus, the darkest level of the house of Hades where Jupiter imprisoned his enemies. I could taste it. I thought that Lumen's clear light had banished my dark desires, but I felt them stirring up again a red rage inside of me.

But why didn't Julia kill him herself? Perhaps she looked to me for leadership, testing whether my resolve to spare Crassus' life would waver. But Crassus may actually have told the truth. What if he could hear the song?

"I can't," I said.

"Kill him now, or I will," Julia said. "I won't come unless he's dead. We're alone now, no Hyperboreans to protect us if Crassus turns on us."

I couldn't see Crassus, but I could hear his ragged breath. He said nothing, made no plea for his life.

"We're working with the Hyperboreans," I said, "and they saved Crassus, and you, for a reason. I'm certain of it."

"Tell me you don't believe all this crap about the gods?"

"I don't know what I believe right now except that when I followed the same feelings that are coursing through me right now, I destroyed a city, betrayed you and my house, and nearly ended my own life. This new Accala has to make different choices."

"You're as deranged as Crassus," she muttered to herself, but the fight was gone from her voice.

I found Crassus' hand in the dark and pulled him to his feet, surprised to find that a small portion of my strength had returned.

"You said you can hear the song?" I asked Crassus, ignoring Julia. "So tell us. Which way?"

"You'd better know what you're doing," Julia said, and I wasn't sure, in the darkness, whether she was talking to Crassus or me.

His hand closed about mine, and I suffered the contact while he pulled ahead. It seemed that he too had found some new strength. He led us through the darkness for what felt like hours, taking twists and turns, occasionally pausing to listen, and then a light appeared in the distance, dull and gray.

"The surface," Crassus said.

"It's dusk," Julia confirmed. "Night is about to fall."

The surface. I couldn't believe it was this near. So close, and I had nearly lost it. I would have run us right into the arms of the enemy.

"It would be suicide to wander out there in the dark, especially with Aquilinus in the orbital stadium watching over the course," Julia said.

"I'm not sure what choice we have if Lumen is out there," I said. "If the arachnoraptors have him, we must get him back before they can get him to Aquilinus."

"Here," Crassus said, pointing down a tunnel running off to the right. "The song is coming from this direction."

He was right. I could suddenly hear it again. So faint that until he mentioned it I wasn't even aware of it.

I took the lead now, pulling Crassus and Julia along behind me, taking turn after turn following the song, which grew louder and louder until we passed through a high arch leading into a vast cavern.

There I saw Lumen, faintly glowing, Concretus behind him.

"What happened!" I hissed as we approached. "We thought we'd lost you."

The raptors surprised me, Lumen said. *Concretus pulled me in here to protect me. We hoped you would follow the song.* I translated Lumen's words to the others.

"You," Julia said to the large Hyperborean warrior, poking at his chest with her index finger. "You're not going to do that again. We're a team. If you want us to look after you, you stay and look after us."

We will, Lumen said. *Concretus understands now. We both understand, but it was not I who left you.*

Lumen was not telling the truth. I could sense that much, though I didn't want to press him with Julia here. I translated Lumen's words for her.

"He's right," I said. "I was nervous, I lost track of his song."

This alliance was too fragile to dig any deeper than that, and I was exhausted, we all were. Lumen assured us that we were in a safe place and that the arachnoraptors were moving far away to the west of the mountain, and by the time they worked out that they'd gone the wrong way and headed back, we'd have at least a day's lead. Time enough to sleep before venturing out into the tournament field and encountering whatever games Aquilinus had orchestrated.

Lumen had already laid out some old robes and legion cots—steel base with a thermal mattress that generated its own heat. The cots and the robes smelled of mold, but Julia confirmed that the power cells in the cots were functional and able to warm us through the night. We set Crassus' cot away from us, near the edge of Lumen's glow, where Concretus stood guard.

"Before. In the tunnels," Julia said to me when we were alone. "You don't owe Crassus anything except a horrible and violent death. If you wanted to be merciful, you should have just walked away in place of beating him to death with your bare hands. That's more mercy than he ever showed you. I was there. I saw what you went through."

"It's not that."

"Then what?"

"I went off the plan. I disobeyed my orders. I betrayed you because I needed revenge. I tried to kill my enemies, and all that came of it was death and destruction. I was supposed to die, and I didn't. The very same beings that I abused gave me life back. They gave me another chance."

"But what you did and what Crassus did are two different situations. You were half mad with addiction."

"How do I know he wasn't? You saw how he was controlled, conditioned. Besides, I'm done making excuses. Whatever drove me to act as I did, I own it, I'm the only one responsible. Crassus needs to be spared, or my salvation isn't worth a damn, and I need it to be. I need to know I can really come back from the place I was in, or there's no hope for me. I know it seems crazy that I'm fighting to keep Crassus alive, but if you can't accept my reasoning, then at least accept my intuition."

Julia snorted in frustration and turned to make the best bed she could with the little we had. It was dark and we were tired. We fell into our cots.

I closed my eyes, and my head swam with all that had happened since I was reborn at the heart of this mountain. Since the great city-hive fell. When I was sure the others were asleep, I slowly rose from my cot. Lumen was still faintly glowing, sitting patiently, waiting for me. There was no sign of Concretus.

"The giant?" I asked.

He's standing guard outside the cavern. He doesn't need sleep, none of us does.

"Back there, with Crassus. That was a test, wasn't it?" I asked. "You left me on purpose to see what I would do."

In a sense, although it was you that turned from me. When you thought of killing Crassus, you turned away from the song and our shared connection. It was then that Concretus reacted. The song shows the right way. I followed it when I saved Crassus. He is an important part of what will follow.

"You're telling me you can see the future now? What will follow then?"

I can only see ripples, glimpses of the song, Mother sees more clearly than I can, but I can barely hear her now. All her energies are devoted to keeping the poisoning of the ichor at bay. But I do know that you will need both of your allies to get through the challenges ahead.

"Listen. The gods don't care about what I do or don't do. I'm just a person, one of many trillions spread throughout the galaxy. I make my own choices."

The path the gods have laid out for you, for all of us, is not about overpowering your will or forcing you to do something you don't want to do. It is the ideal path of your life. It's laid out for everyone. After that, we have the will to mess it up. We are the ones who turn off it and get lost and end up in shadow versions of the lives we were meant to live. The path of the gods is about life, it's about choosing the right action, in the right direction, at the right time.

"That's not easy," I said, "not by a long shot."

It's not easy to walk and it's easy to get lost, but if you want to see real justice carried out, if you want to be the best Accala you can be, then you have to get back on it. For you it is the path of justice, of duty. The stakes are high, and nothing less than your best will do. You can't afford to indulge in self-pity. The answer is not revenge, not to steal lives in exchange for those lives that were taken. You have to give up your anger and need for revenge. It must not fuel your actions. You have to embrace your duty if you want to redeem yourself and find who you are meant to be.

"Then what? What will drive me? What will put the fire back into my bones, make the blood course through my veins? My anger has always given me my drive. Right now I feel like a ghost! Worse, soggy pasta," I said, frustrated.

Justice. You know her.

"Minerva."

She was always your goddess, I remember.

"We've had some disagreements of late, she and I," I said.

I understand, but you should have faith, trust in the path. The gods test those destined for high office. You say you want to save the galaxy, so they drop a mountain of responsibility on your shoulders to see if you can stand the strain, to see if you're up for the task. He reached out; a sharp crystalline hand touched mine. *And I know you are, Sister.*

I didn't pull away. I kept the contact until I couldn't bear it anymore. The conflict I still felt, the part of me that wanted to accept him as my brother, was matched by another that found the notion impossible, repulsive.

"And Father?" I asked. "He's dead?"

No, he lives but is far from the song. He's lost, confused. When you fight, you do not fight for him, or your mother, or me. Not even for your house.

"The empire?"

No. Fight for yourself. Save yourself, find your path, and the rest will follow.

I nodded and returned to my cot.

I didn't know whom to trust and I was so tired, but I felt sure of one thing—that in choosing to spare Crassus, things had turned within me.

I had never truly served Minerva. I saw that now. You couldn't serve two masters. Since the war began I had been a slave to the chthonic Furies.

Lumen's song was growing stronger inside me now. The gods only knew that I wanted to kill Crassus, but I didn't follow the dark fire, I didn't pursue revenge. I must follow my duty, not my personal feelings, and now I could feel my inner fire returning. It wasn't the heat from the cot beneath me; it was something on the inside wanting to come out. A small flame burned—a blessing from the divine lady of wisdom—and, although weak, it did not flicker but burned with true spirit. I clung to that, wrapping myself in its small heat as I fell into a dark sleep.

* * *

WHEN I DREAMED, IT was of Rome. Of my father. We were standing in an old shop that my family used to visit. A used armory and provisions supplier in the agora. I dreamed the store was being closed down. I saw Crassus and Marcus there. I was trying to talk to them, but they were distant, always moving away to look at the weapons and armor. As I left the store I passed people in all the different house robes fighting over the last few items on sale. Whatever was so precious to them bore no interest to me. I closed the heavy door behind me. As I walked onto the street I realized I'd left Father behind, back in the shop, but when I went back to get him, I couldn't find the place again.

When I awoke, there were tears streaming down my cheeks. I reached up to touch them and found that while I still didn't feel the cold, my tears did. They'd been transformed into tiny crystals. My father was a prisoner and my brother was little more than a ghost in a shell, a walking crystal mausoleum.

I picked the tiny crystals out of my eyes and wiped them from my cheeks. A small glittering cluster of tears shone in the palm of my hand. I'd woken up enough to realize that it was light. I was surrounded by light and I could hear the sound of a sputtering whine—an engine! I was up on my feet in an instant, fearing that we'd been discovered.

"Settle. All's well." Julia's voice.

Julia was up on a rusted old transport tray, similar to the one that carried us to the contestants' quarters in Avis Accipitridae. The access panel to the engine was raised and Julia was crouched over it, tinkering with its guts, drawing from it the sound that had alarmed me.

We were in a vast cavern lined with rock, and an array of large stalagmites and stalactites jutted out from the ground and ceiling. The sun was rising. Its first light entered the cavern from small shafts high above, concentrating in the crystalline protrusions in the ceiling, from where it was refracted about the chamber again and again until the space was filled with soft light. The good news was we were not exposed. There was no way for anyone outside the mountain to see us.

"Where did that come from?" I asked Julia as I approached her transport.

She pointed behind me, and I turned to see in the far corner of the cavern what the darkness had concealed last night—a vast stockpile of rusty, rotting equipment. It looked like it had been there forever, and now I could smell the source of the mold I detected on the cots.

"Saturnalia came early," Julia said, and she sounded genuinely pleased, as if all this junk were the finest equipment money could buy. "I don't know if this old engine will even go, it's in such bad shape, but I'm working on it."

I must have displayed my doubts, because she continued, "It's this hand! It's not only much more sensitive than my other hand, I'm working easily with very fine wiring with very poor equipment, but it also generates its own energy. It's like working with a portable power pack." She gave a nod of recognition to Lumen. "He's been standing over me, putting things in front of me to experiment on. The hand will take whatever the base function of a tool is and enhance its power and capabilities." She hefted the arachnoraptor's transmission staff. "With something like this, the sky's the limit. The hand can power it to jam signals, boost signals, maybe even seize command of small ships and vehicles."

I have put as much power as I could spare into her hand. It is an extension of the power in your pin. The power I used to heal you and Crassus, to repair Julia's hand, it was all drawn from the energy stored in your pin, Accala. It too is a limited resource. You may use it to heal yourself in an emergency, but only once. Most of its power will need to be reclaimed, a backup if we fall short of energy. For now these are all the resources I can provide. I hope it's of some use, Lumen said with a flourish toward the pile. It was the kind of move my brother would have made, and it made my heart ache.

"Don't look so despondent," Julia said. "There are advanced weapons." She paraded around the pile like a game show hostess, indicating what she'd uncovered. "Ion pistols and rifles. Bombs. Missiles. Swords, armillae, skirmisher parts. There's electronics, fine tools. I removed the blocks on all the armillae, and I can do a whole lot more. And you can do a lot with that," she said, pointing to the bottom of the pile. I saw him at once. Orbis.

"I went to pick it up for you, but it started spinning as my hand drew near and nearly took my fingers off."

I rushed to her side at once. Orbis retracted his edge to accommodate my hand, and then I was whole again.

Julia reached down and picked up my most recent suit of armor and pushed it toward me, but I backed away.

"I can't wear those colors again," I said. "The mock hawk is dead."

"Some armor, even this armor, is better than no armor. Besides, it might buy us time out there. They might mistake us for Sertorians."

"No. I won't wear it."

I was about to ask after Crassus when I spied him a little farther around the corner, with Concretus watching over him.

Crassus was wearing the breastplate of his old suit of armor, black and red, but not the greaves or arm guards. He hovered at the edge of the pile, near the rest of the suit, like a blowfly, dancing from foot to foot.

"I didn't want to put it on," he said. "But I was so cold. Look, I carved out the red. I've undone the initiation of the precepts."

He had, too. All of the crimson grooves had been roughly scoured clean. There was blood dripping from his fingers and I saw in his hand a rusty knife that he'd used to do the work. As soon as he saw my eyes upon it he dropped the knife to the cavern floor.

"You need armor," I said, "and I don't see anything halfway decent here so wear it, but only as long as you remember exactly whom you're loyal to."

"Yes, of course, of course," he mumbled, and then burst out loud with excitement. "The gods will transform these weapons into mighty chariots and swords and spears that no one can stand against."

Lumen just looked at Crassus, and he clapped his mouth shut. He was in awe of the small alien, like a timid schoolboy terrified of saying the wrong thing in class lest his knowledge be found wanting.

"Or not," he said quietly.

"The gods! Pah!" Julia spat. "Whichever dog barks the loudest, eh, Crassus?"

Crassus avoided eye contact with her, but I could feel the tension between them.

"This is it, Crassus," I said. "Be lucky you get any armor at all, because you don't get a weapon."

"But how will I fight for the gods?"

"With your brain, I hope," I said. "You said you could help us anticipate Aquilinus, and that's what I expect you to do."

"Yes. Of course."

I got down on my knees and dug toward the bottom of the pile, looking for some bits and pieces of armor I could cobble together into a suit. What were we going to do with all this junk? Try to find a working ion blaster and give it to Concretus? Even fully kitted out with this rusty gear, we'd hardly be a match for Aquilinus and his newly acquired orbital station.

And then, in among cracked and splintered breastplates and greaves, I found a full suit of battered armor. It was made for a man, but apart from that it was good. It was antique, from the time of the seventh republic, the same period Orbis was forged. Gods only knew how it came to be there. Perhaps it was carried over by some early settler family as an heirloom or souvenir of a past campaign. Instead of being constructed from the hybrid metallic alloys of modern armor, this one had a ceramic base with grooves of lapis negra woven through it in imitation of the bones of a rib cage. I'd never seen anything like it. It had its fair share of dents, but it was solid and useful and bone white in color. It may have been Viridian once upon a time, but any semblance of house colors had long faded away. I strapped it on at once and, aside from the uncomfortable pressure on my breasts against the flat chestplate, it fit well. It didn't take long to find a tattered cloak and worn belt, then ratty gloves and boots to match. The latter being time-worn and slightly moldy but still functional. Julia followed my example and found an old suit of armor that belonged to a legionary from House Atilian, an ancient, lesser house that still had its yellow and black colors. My armilla was there, and I forced Crassus to pass his to Julia—who set up a block on all functions except the shield and a limited-range radio while we watched—and he did so eagerly and without complaint, looking at me for approval like a dog after a treat.

When I went to clip Orbis to the side of my belt, I found my discus pulling up and away from me, toward the lapis bands in the breastplate. The attraction was strong, as if he were magnetized, and I ended up using two hands to resist the pull. I didn't know what was happening, but I didn't like it. I couldn't have my primary weapon disabled going into battle, and so I instinctively cast Orbis away, a long throw with no return vector, until I could work out what was going on.

Instantly, a black tentacle shot out from my torso and snatched Orbis out of the air, swung him about like a sling, and threw him back out on the same trajectory with so much force that Orbis sailed across the cavern and embedded himself into the solid rock. The unexpected motion of the suit almost knocked me over. Before I knew it, the long tentacle arm had withdrawn to the breastplate as if nothing had happened.

"What was that?" Julia asked, eyes wide.

I stared down at the armor and wondered how I was going to recover Orbis. This thing was alive. Just like Orbis. I had to get it off of me before it could do more harm.

"No! Leave it on," Crassus yelled out, as I pulled at it. "They're discus arms. I've read of them but have never seen one in action. They are even rarer than your weapon. They work with your mind, not your conscious mind but your deep mind, to retrieve your weapon but also to help you cast it farther."

Armor designed specifically for a discus wielder. Now, this was an enhancement. This might not win any wars, but it made me feel much more capable. If I could get the thing to work. I ran my hands over the smooth surface of the suit.

"You see," he said. "The work of the gods."

"A lucky find," Julia said.

"When the gods are on your side, there is no luck," Crassus pontificated.

I wouldn't get drawn into the debate on either side, wouldn't buy into it, not Lumen's talk or Crassus' madness. I'd made that mistake when I bought into my uncle's flattery. If there were gods, then they could get on with their business. I'd focus on walking the right path, and if that meant they would help us, then so be it, and if not, then I'd do this without them.

"I'm not sure I'll keep it," I said. "I can't have an untested quantity in live combat. It took me years to master the basics of my discus; I don't have years to learn this. It might get me killed in the field."

You should take the armor. It is the same as your discus, Lumen said. *I can hear it. It follows the same song as your weapon. You'll learn to make them work quickly, I know it.*

All the same, I needed a backup. I picked up the nearest weapon to hand—a gladius, the weapon for which the gladiator was named. It was old, plain, simple, and utterly reliable—a black blade with conductive strips that traveled the length of its spine on both sides, transmitting an electric shock that was generated in the hilt. It was pockmarked with rust that looked like the pattern of the Ursa Major constellation, but the rust was only cosmetic, no more than wear to the blade's surface.

Julia and I worked together, but we still couldn't free Orbis—he'd lodged in the ice so deeply.

"You have to use the armor," Crassus said.

He's right, Lumen added. *Think of it back at your side, on your belt.*

I tried it, and straightaway a black arm, from the other side this time, reached out, pulled Orbis from the wall in a single jerk, and with lightning speed returned him to my side. This time I was ready for the action, and it didn't affect my balance at all.

"One side for casting, one for retrieving," I said. "You're right. I think I'll keep this after all."

Discus armor that synchronized perfectly with my discus. What could I have done in the arena back in Rome with a suit like this? Maybe it was a gift from the gods, maybe not. I wasn't going to think about the odds of finding such a thing, just think about the work ahead. One step at a time. All the same, it was hard to keep a slight smile from my face.

XXXVIII

WE MARCHED OUT OF the illuminated cavern and back into the darkness of the tunnels.

Julia came behind me, slowly riding the transport tray, which she had coaxed into shuddering motion. She was carrying a backpack, and over her armor she wore utility belts, with her own tools and the best tools she could find in the cavern. In her hands she carried the transmission staff.

"Ready?" I asked her.

"Ready," she replied, and then, "Just don't dig any new holes for us to climb out of. We're in enough of a pickle as it is."

I wished I could promise her exactly that, but the only happy outcome I could imagine was that somehow Julia lived and Lumen reached his queen and fled to safety. My life was already offered up on the altar to Minerva. I'd already let go of it to set things right. I only prayed it was enough.

Walking beside Crassus was strange. Aboard *Incitatus* he'd been more than handsome and powerful. He'd been regal, he'd had a noble bearing that was at least half the attraction. But now that was all gone. He was a simpleton, a madman, and yet somehow, strangely, there was an appeal in that too. It was the lack of responsibility, the lack of any burden weighing him down. I couldn't believe that I actually envied Crassus his madness.

After a short uphill march, the exit loomed ahead of us, a narrow crease in the rock face, through which streamed ever-brightening light. That light should have filled me with boldness, but I felt only hesitancy. There was a security in darkness. It would have been so easy to stay there, out of sight, unencumbered by the challenges ahead. One foot in front of the other, that was the only way. I kept my mind on my feet until we emerged into open space and found ourselves high up on the side of the mountain. Despite a strong wind, the air was a blessing. Cold but clean and sharpening of the mind. We'd left the underworld, survived one hell.

Julia had loaded anything that might be useful and that she could repair in time onto the transport tray. Most of the advanced weapons were drained of power and useless, and she had managed to salvage only some land mines. The rest she stripped for power and parts. Most important, we had armor and communications. The radios in our helmets worked well and integrated with our armillae.

The tray had a rail running round it and controls up front. It was a third as slow as a war chariot when unloaded and much slower than that with equipment and armored people riding it, but it was still faster than us running at full speed, and so was essential to our survival. I asked Lumen and Concretus to stay out of sight in the cave mouth with the transport tray while we scanned the area. Ahead of us the level ground terminated, becoming a steep slope that ran down the side of the mountain to the valley below.

"With that slope as a runway ramp, we'd get the sled up to a decent speed," I said to Julia.

The weather was blisteringly cold. I didn't feel it, but I could see it in the heaviness of the air, which had a blue tinge. The stratospheric stadium was high in the sky, and part of it was still smoking from the assault, but already there was repair scaffolding in place. No one up there would be looking our way— we'd be partly camouflaged by the mild snowstorm whipping a flurry of flakes about the sky. All attention would be focused on whatever torments Aquilinus had dreamed up.

"I thought the stadium was supposed to help regulate the weather," I said. "It seems to be heavy conditions for tournament viewing."

"You're right," Julia said. "Perhaps the atmospheric stabilizers on the stadium were hit when *Incitatus* opened fire."

It's the planet itself, Lumen said. *The ichor that formed this world held it together. Without it, it's falling apart.*

"How long do we have?" Julia asked after I'd conveyed Lumen's words.

Weeks, months, he replied. *I can't say for certain. The weather will become increasingly unstable.*

"As if things weren't bad enough," Julia groaned.

There was something going on in the valley, but it was hard to make out at first. We lay on our bellies and slowly moved close to the cliff edge.

Julia scanned the ground below and then passed me binoculars she'd fished out of the mountain stockpile.

"It's not good," is all she said.

I peered through the binoculars. After a minute or so, a wind came rushing through and whipped aside enough snow that I finally had a clear window. Gods. What mad circus was this?

The arena we faced only two short days ago—the raw environment of this world, bound by energy shields and electric advertisements, enclosed by an empyrean dome to demarcate a sacred gladiatorial testing ground—had been transformed into something else altogether. The clear sky of Olympus Decimus, obscured only by the static of snowfall or the darkness of storms, was now filled with clouds. Not real, actual clouds, but some idyllic simulacrum. Perfect cumulus clusters were ringed by halos of clear white light that projected beams of light onto the arena below. Projections from the station, they didn't move position, no wind affected them—they simply hung in place like ornaments in an overlit stage play.

Below, in a wide valley enclosed by impassable mountains, holographic projections of row after row of vast Grecian columns rose up and vanished into those clouds. It was supposed to be Olympus, the home of the gods. It looked plastic, cheap.

In the valley were three Talonite chariots—Ovidian, Arrian, and Tullian—fully armed with a complete crew complement, twenty-four contestants in all. While the chariot load of Tullians watched on from the sidelines, the Ovidians and two of the Arrian desultore skirmishers harried what was left of the Caninine Alliance, a ragtag crew of ten in two beat-up chariots—five Viridians; three Calpurnians, one of whom rode a desultore skirmisher; and two Flavians. They were alone, all their support teams dead or gone.

The Caninines raced desperately across what appeared to be a giant gameboard of clear, flat ice cut into sixty-four equal-size squares. They were heading for the only exit from the valley—a narrow path that led east between two hills. Beyond the valley, the path ran into a vast forest of crystalline trees that stretched on for miles before the Olympian ranges some three hundred miles away thrust up to touch the clouds: a perfect place to hide if only they could escape the valley and reach it. The exit was marked by a massive dolmen arch that spanned the two central squares on the eastern edge of the board. It was made of three giant pillars, not holograms but solid to my eye, each about two hundred feet in length. Two upright and one running horizontally to cap them.

Above the action, Julius Gemminus buzzed about, his voice projected by the floating spherae, carried and amplified by the valley.

"Here we are on day two in Emperor Aquilinus' celestial testing ground. Who will prove their worth? Will the Caninines come to their senses and bow to the new gods? The ancients had a saying: As above, so below. The choices the Caninines make here in our celestial arena are costing them heavily in the greater empire. Countless lives stand to be lost."

"Can these obstinate contestants pull themselves forward toward the divine as Emperor Aquilinus once did," Julius Gemminus continued, "or will they fall to the grave, plowed into the earth with their countrymen, no better than animals and slaves?"

"They're not armed," I said to Julia, as I looked on with the binoculars. The Caninines had been stripped of their weapons. Only the Talonites were armed, but I couldn't quite tell with what from where I sat. They looked like large staffs with bright yellow padded tops.

Around the edge of the field, the billboards were now filled with images of Sertorian propaganda—the very same sequences of Sertorian grandeur that Crassus forced me to watch during my time on *Incitatus*—interspersed with advertisements for ambrosia. No longer did we see Crassus and myself. Now there were shining forms of the deceased Mania, Barbata, Licinus, and Castor and Pollux, and the caption in huge letters: THE ASCENDED MARTYRS, HAWKS NO LONGER, NOW DIVINE EAGLES.

"What game are they playing?" Julia asked.

"It's petteia," I replied. "A board game nobles play. Except he's re-created it on a giant stage. Normally you move your pebbles to enclose the other player's pebbles. You win by blocking your opponent in or take a piece by surrounding it on two sides."

The petteia board was eight by eight squares. The squares in the giant board below us were demarcated with energy shields that soared up to fifteen feet high and changed at intervals. Aquilinus had forced the Caninines to play unarmed against the Talonites, and the shield walls were being manipulated into a labyrinth to force them to move as you would on a petteia board.

Based on their ability to move around without effort, the Talonites knew the pattern of the ever-changing shield walls, but the Caninines didn't have a clue. The Caninines seemed to be trying to reach the end of the course and exit through the archway, but they were obstructed by the ever-changing shield walls, and the enemy, who outnumbered them and outfinessed them with the speed that only ambrosia could impart.

"What's Aquilinus doing, splashing ambrosia about like that?" Julia said. "It was on scarce supply just a few days ago, and now I'd wager there's not a Talonite player down there that's not dosed up to the eyeballs."

"He's cutting into his own personal reserves," Crassus said. "He has to keep the empire convinced that he's in control of the ambrosia, even as his own supplies are dwindling."

"He's buying time until he can get his hands on Lumen," I said.

The Ovidians and Arrians worked together to flank a Caninine vehicle on either side, then aimed their weapons at it to take it out like a petteia piece. The movement of the shield labyrinth seemed designed to isolate Caninine players and aid the Talonites. The targeted Viridians, Calpurnians, and Flavians didn't stand a chance as the Talonites closed in on both sides and struck again and again.

The colorful staves caused no wounds, though, no contestant deaths; the chariots were too far apart for that. The hits were symbolic. After each successful hit, a flash filled the sky and a projection appeared upon the ice, revealing a horrific tableau. Thousands of faces, magnified so that their expressions were clearly visible to the viewers, appeared beneath the surface of the giant board. Their images were projected from Rota Fortuna and designed to make it seem as if their faces were trapped beneath the clear, flat squares. Men, women, children, all from Caninine houses, their names presented beneath their faces on digital placards. As each strike of the yellow staves hit the Caninine players, the faces registered their varying expressions of death as they were simultaneously executed. Those faces fell away to be replaced an instant later by more, the next in line waiting to die.

"Do you recognize any of the faces?" I asked Julia.

"None."

"They're a random selection," Crassus said. "He's demonstrating that the protection a house provides is irrelevant. He can pick anyone."

The Viridians were cut off from the Calpurnians and the Flavians by a sudden change in the shield formation. They drove forward toward the exit, and yet the

Talonite players on the sidelines remained motionless. I thought perhaps they were going to let them pass, but the moment the Viridians moved under the dolmen, the enemy rushed forward, forcing them to retreat back to the game-board. But why?

I scanned the pillars with maximum magnification. Gods, they weren't pillars. They had large metallic points attached to their pinnacles. "They're giant spears," I said. "He's making them pass under the yoke."

There was no greater shame for a Roman than to be forced by an enemy to pass under the yoke, no greater humiliation.

"It's just like the game of trigon," Julia said. "Aquilinus doesn't want them to exit too quickly. He wants the deaths of the hostages and the dishonor of the Viridians and their allies to be drawn out for the benefit of the audience."

"The Caninines don't understand," I said. I'd sat through all those sessions being tutored in Aquilinus' past. His decisions and precepts, his philosophy. "They think they have to get through the yoke and humble themselves in order to spare the lives of the hostages Aquilinus has rounded up. But you have to understand that's not how Aquilinus thinks. After he destroyed the temples and priests, he was arrested. His own countrymen wished to humble him and make him pass under the yoke. They tortured his allies when he refused, hoping that would motivate him, but he stood strong and let them all die, demonstrating his strength of will. They became martyrs to his ascension. The answer here is not to pass under the yoke. He'll kill them all anyway. They're expected to hold back and emulate Aquilinus."

"But that makes no sense. You're saying that if they win everyone dies, and if they lose everyone dies," Julia said.

"It doesn't have to make sense. The ambrosia's the carrot that you dangle in front of the donkey, but you also need a stick to hit the donkey so it knows the carrot is a good option. He's trying to convince the audience that he has the ultimate power to burn the empire and anyone who stands against him."

"Is that right?" Julia asked Crassus. "That he'll kill his prisoners no matter what?"

"Accala understands us," he said. "Aquilinus is demonstrating that the Caninines lack the strength to hold to their convictions and watch their country-men burn."

"And you love it," Julia said to him.

"To the contrary, I despise it. There's no competition here, no room for excel-lence. Only slaughter for amusement. The arena has been denigrated, trans-formed into a meat grinder. The Caninines have no chance at all."

"Unless we can give them one," I said. "We've got to get down there and stop this. At least give the Caninines a chance to escape."

"Quick! Take cover!" Julia said.

Take cover from what? No one could see us up here. Just the same, Crassus and I followed her lead and we threw ourselves down behind an outcropping of slate-gray rocks. I looked around the see what had alarmed her and then gave her a questioning look. She pointed out over the ledge into the air above the valley. Gods. He was so big and so close to us that I didn't see him at all at first. I thought he was just a visual distortion caused by the flurry of crystalline snow, but then he was impossible to miss. Aquilinus, the new, self-proclaimed Roman emperor, was at least six hundred feet tall. No, not a giant, but rather a giant projection. Three black projection spherae were totally dedicated to creating the massive form.

He wore flowing white robes, the imperial garland about his head, and in his hand he held a great crackling bolt of lightning. Above his head radiated two titles in shining gold letters: NEOS HELIOS, the New Sun, and NEOS JOVIS, the New Jupiter.

Gods. Aquilinus' ego, fed by the ambrosia, knew no limits. He was playing at being Jove himself. All this talk about the New Gods, enlightenment, and liberation for humanity, and the first chance he had, he was there playing at being the god of gods, and badly at that. This was hubris even beyond ancient Caligula, who sought to be declared a living god but only in Alexandria, never within the bounds of Rome herself, where only a dead emperor could be named a god.

"This was never the idea," Crassus said. "We were to dispel the myths, enlighten humanity. Not replace the gods and stand over the empire."

"You must be the stupidest Sertorian in existence," Julia said to Crassus. "The rest of your kind are in it for the power and the money. How has it taken you this long to work that out?"

The Calpurnian chariot came up to protect the Viridian rear, buying the Wolves time to shoot for the exit. Anticipating the game, as the enemy rushed in for the kill, the Viridian chariot, instead of retreating, turned right into the nearest chariot—the Tullian craft—and forced them to veer off to avoid a catastrophic collision. They'd created a gap, and the desultore skirmisher drove through at breakneck speed, the two Caninine chariots following hot on its tail. It was Marcus! He was driving the skirmisher, I was sure of it. This was the same strategy he taught me in the arena when confronting superior opponents—drive right at them, take them by surprise, and throw them off balance. And it was going to work. They were going to make it! Then the sky filled with thunder and lightning, and Aquilinus scowled with displeasure and threw a lightning bolt at them like a fisherman throwing a spear. Aquilinus' form was perfect, his whole body a flowing wave of movement; the bolt followed a clean and unhesitating line to its target.

Marcus! I had to bite my lip from crying out his name and signaling the enemy to our presence. The lightning flash hit the ground, and the skirmisher along with the Calpurnian chariot was blasted sideways, flying through the air. The area where it sped but a moment ago was now scorched black, the air around it filled with exploding ice and steam. But how? The lightning bolt was a projection, the same as Aquilinus himself. It was the stadium's ion cannon! A glowing tip beneath the stadium revealed that it had just fired. As he threw, the cannon shot along the line of the projected bolt, creating the illusion that the bolt was real.

Where the Calpurnian chariot had come to a rest there was some movement, and a moment later the survivors, two Flavians, struggled to their feet and set about righting their craft. Two bodies lay below, team leader Cossus and charioteer Trio Trigeminus, crushed by their own craft's weight, stone dead.

Now the unstable environment responded to Aquilinus' ion cannon strike. The very earth began to rumble and the ice shelf broke apart—great chunks of rock and crystal plummeted down, creating a wide crevasse. When the steam cleared, all that was left of a square mile of ground, the land between the eastern side of the yoke and the exit path between the two hills, was a single spine of solid ice. The ground to either side of the spine had fallen away to the depths below, leaving something resembling a makeshift bridge. That bridge must have been the strongest part of the ice shelf, a solid ridge that ran all the way down to the bottom of the dark crevasse below, and now the Caninines would have to pass over it if they sought to escape Aquilinus' torments.

Undeterred, Aquilinus fired another bolt, this one at the Ovidian chariot. They suffered a similar fate to the Calpurnians, an upturned chariot for displeasing their newly appointed master, but no dead.

And then, as the mist from the melting ice cleared, I saw a figure running toward the yoke. Marcus! He had jumped clear of the blast in time and now, while all eyes were on Aquilinus, he ran, heading for cover. He took shelter behind the great dolmen arch itself, concealing himself out of the sight of the enemy behind the pillar closest to the ice shelf, farthest from us. He made it! Not until this very moment, my mind and heart clear, looking down at him as he braved all for his house, did I realize the depth of feeling I had for him. He had always been there for me and, attuned as I was to Lumen and the song, I saw that his feelings for me were more than those of a mentor, but I was never able to accept it, too caught up with my need for revenge, and now that I was aware of it, I felt a reciprocity, a sense of tenderness, an overwhelming fear for his continued well-being.

Julius Gemminus appeared in the sky above the contestants.

"Magnificent! A magnificent display, Imperator!"

Julius Gemminus announced it with a loud, triumphal trumpet blast. A holographic arrow pointed to a shuttle on slow descent to the planet's surface from the Rota Fortuna.

"Here come the executioners from on high—the emperor's chosen to cull a member of the herd. Which dog lover will fall beneath their blades?" A bright spotlight fell on Marcus. They were targeting him. Soldiers from the station would gun him down without a fair chance to defend himself.

"I heard something about this on my armilla. Aquilinus toys with them and periodically sends down an execution squad to eliminate a gladiator from the competition who displeases him," Julia said.

"That can't go down well with the mob," I said. "Can you pick up the vox populi now?"

"Yes," Julia said. "I'm scanning it now. There's a lot of activity."

The air about Aquilinus was suddenly filled with hundreds of downturned thumbs, each one representing a billion voices that disapproved of Marcus' slated execution.

Aquilinus swept his holographic arm in a mighty arc, scattering the thumbs and obliterating them from sight, and then cast a bolt right into the face of Julius Gemminus and through the projection orb behind it, demonstrating his displeasure at the crowd's response.

Julia quickly tuned in to her armilla and flicked through the various feeds on the vox populi.

"What are you picking up?" I asked.

"The answer to why Aquilinus is continuing with the games," she said. "I'm reading between the lines here because none of them will come right out and say it, but from what I'm picking up from the various commentators, the mob is still sitting on the fence about Aquilinus' self-promotion to the throne. One half fear the Sertorians have committed hubris and that the gods in turn will seek vengeance, or they just plain hate the Sertorians, or they're pissed off the tournament isn't as competitive as it should be. The other half are desperate for ambrosia, or fear the Sertorians, or are allied with them."

"It's one thing to seize power," Crassus said, "but if you want to hold the empire, then you have to give the people what they want. There's a lot of Romans who won't buy into Aquilinus' idea until he can successfully conclude the games to their satisfaction."

"Gods, it would be a different matter entirely if women were included in the vote," I said. "They wouldn't tolerate this idiot at all."

"Perhaps," Julia said. "At any rate, the Arrians sense Aquilinus' vulnerability and are holding back lending Aquilinus military support until he's demonstrated he has more of the mob on side."

"Vultures," Crassus interjected. "They're waiting to see if Aquilinus falls so they can rush in and snatch up the ichor and the throne in one fell swoop."

"The people's voice cannot be drowned out, and that's where our chance lies," Julia said.

"Yes," Crassus concurred. "Aquilinus will be less likely to kill the Caninines if it's going to cause an empirewide riot. He can't risk losing the throne so soon. That's why he's restarted the games and that's why he's going to have to return to the rules of the tournament."

"Whoa, hold your horses. I'm all for winning the public opinion but I don't think the Ludi Romani audience is going to riot and challenge Aquilinus directly," Julia stated. "That doesn't seem likely."

"You are not a gladiator," Crassus said. "You don't know how passionate the citizens of our empire are about what takes place in the games. Right now trillions of Romans are watching every moment that transpires on this world. They are asking themselves a question: Dare we follow Aquilinus? It's not just a matter of accepting the precepts and taking the ambrosia; they must turn their backs on Jupiter during his sacred games. The reason the games are continuing is that Aquilinus has yet to prove to them that he's worthy to lead the empire."

"Aquilinus is overconfident. He's made a strategic error. With the odds so unfairly stacked against the Caninines, the thrill has gone out of the game. There's nothing but predictable outcomes in store for the audience. Let's fix that. You said they're scared of me? That means I'm in a position to spice things up a little. The mob will back anyone that can alleviate boredom and shake up predictable outcomes."

"You're thinking of jumping into the fight, I can tell," Julia said. "And I'm telling you right now that's a bad idea."

"We've got to do something. I can't leave them to die down there."

"That's exactly what you should do," Julia countered. "The Caninines are all but dead. The games Aquilinus plays with them will buy us some small time. We've got to go stealthily, just slip by. Get Lumen as far away from the Sertorians as we can. Then the sacrifice they make now will have counted for something. If Lumen is captured, none of it matters. Keep Lumen safe, don't ride him right in there. You'd be handing Aquilinus victory."

I looked down into the valley, at the Caninines being tormented while Aquilinus watched over them. The shuttle bearing Marcus' execution squad was halfway on its journey to the ground. "No. No other sacrifices," I said. "There's no use skulking around, not with the Rota Fortuna hanging over us. We'll never get all the way to Nova Olympus without being seen."

"The mob, the mob is the key. We have to get them on side," Crassus insisted.

"Don't listen to him, Accala," Julia protested. "They don't like Aquilinus, but from what I've heard, they don't like you much either. The mob didn't think well of you at the end, and Aquilinus has proclaimed you a traitor and a coward. Before the coup, they still had a camera or two hiding out in the tunnels—they saw what you did to the Sertorians. They're frightened of you. Winning over the mob is not an option."

"Julia, if you can pick up the vox populi then you can post to it too, right? I want you to set up a poll in my name and ask them if they'll follow me. Say, 'I'm alive and I'm fighting for the gods and justice. Aquilinus will be duly punished for his hubris. Do you choose a false emperor and lies, or the gods of our people and freedom?' Don't worry about it going down well now. I'm planning ahead," I said.

"This is only going to alert Aquilinus to our presence," Julia said. "It's all bad, Accala."

"Do it or I will," I said. "I'm asking you because I trust you, because that's your area of expertise. I know something about making the arena work to get the right outcome. Trust me."

"I should never have let you bunk with me. Any other bunkmate would have been fine," she mumbled. "I should have sent you on to the legionaries' quarters. They'd have used you for a punching bag and you'd never have made it off *Incitatus*. My mission would have been called off and I could have quietly slipped away from the Hawks and sat out the tournament at a warm bar in Avis Accipitridae," Julia complained, as she set up the post.

"I'm not asking the audience to riot, not yet. I just want to pique their interest, see if they'll back us to reenter the tournament."

"But how on earth do you think you're going to accomplish that?"

"Let's find out. I'm going to make it up as I go."

I headed back to the cave where Lumen and Concretus awaited.

"Julia, you said before you could hack into a transmission signal. Do you have everything you need for that at hand? To hijack a broadcast?" I asked.

"At hand? Is that supposed to be a pun?" she grumbled. "It's not funny, but it's not far off the mark either. With the power in this new hand of mine and the transmission staff, I can give it a good shot. How long I can make it work before they isolate my signal and shut me down is another matter altogether. What did you have in mind?"

"Everyone climb aboard," I said, ignoring Julia's questions as I took the controls of the flat craft and started it slowly forward.

"What? This isn't a good idea," Julia protested, as Crassus and the Hyperboreans boarded. "We're not equipped to defeat those chariots!"

"We've got one more thing in our arsenal that will give us the edge," I said.

"What's that?" Julia asked, still hesitating, still unwilling to climb on.

"The element of surprise," I replied as I reached out, snatched her right wrist, and pulled her aboard.

Before she could consider jumping back off, I grabbed the controls and drove us forward. In seconds we were hurtling over the edge of the cliff, plummeting down the steep slope toward the fight.

"No! Wait!" Julia called, but I was not stopping. I had to take the fight to Aquilinus. I didn't dare stop to think or I'd lose my nerve. I focused on my breath. I was alive, back from the dead. And while I breathed, I could act, and while I could act, there was hope.

ACT VI

WAR GAMES

Even as when oft in a throng of people strife hath risen,
and the base multitude rage in their minds, and now brands and
    stones are flying;
madness lends arms;
then if perchance they catch sight of one reverend for goodness and
    service,
they are silent and stand by with attentive ear;
he with speech sways their temper and soothes their breasts.

                    —Virgil, *Aeneid*

XXXIX

"ARE YOU COMPLETELY FUCKING crazy?" Julia screamed as we sped down the side of the mountain, gathering speed as we went, heading straight for the valley and the heart of the fight.

"More than likely," I yelled back. I passed Crassus his javelin from the weapons pile. "Weapons at the ready. Wait for my order and strike to kill."

The gladiators below might have been fresh and well armed, but they were not the best of the best. There couldn't have been more than a half dozen of the original Talonites left. The rest were subs, replacements. We could do this. My discus, Crassus' javelin, Julia and her staff—we could do this.

The smooth surface of the ice allowed us to gather great speed. As we descended at an angle to the gameboard, the faces of the tormented grew large and misshapen, transforming into a warped, hellish display before we were too close to make out distinct features at all.

We hit a bump and were launched into the air. My feet went out from under me, and it was only my grip on the sled controls that stopped me from flying right out of the vehicle altogether. I did a quick head check and saw the others were still all there. At this rate we'd have enough speed to hurtle us right through the cluster of enemy chariots. I needed to buy the Caninines time to clear that ice bridge— Minerva, I whispered in prayer, if you can grant Marcus the time to reach us before the execution squad reaches him, then make it so.

There might be a problem, Lumen said.

Concretus grabbed Lumen around the waist, held the rails of the sled with his other arms, and then stepped right off. The claws of his crystalline foot dug into the ice and rock. We were losing speed.

He doesn't want to do anything that will endanger me.

"Tell him to get back in right now or I'll come at him," I yelled. "He's not saving you, he's putting us all in danger."

He doesn't respond well to threats, Lumen said.

"Please," I begged Lumen. "Tell him to trust me. We'd never be able to make it all the way to Olympus without being spotted from the stadium. I'm a gladiator. This is the game I know how to play. It's the game I know how to win."

I had a sense of Concretus' indignation as he dug his feet into the ice to slow the sled enough to allow him to jump back on. He saw us, all Romans, as small, irritating insects—lesser beings that he must suffer in order to carry out his duty. Then we were picking up speed again, heading right into the heart of the conflict, but would we have enough momentum to drive through?

"Into position," I ordered. "I'm going to put the sled on autopilot the moment we arrive."

"Arrive where?" Julia yelled.

In the valley ahead of us, the Flavians had climbed aboard the Viridians' chariot, but it was too late for them to get through the yoke to the ice bridge. The shuttle from the station came in low, a ramp descending from its belly. Out of it came a new enemy chariot, shining gold and purple, Aquilinus' imperial killers in gold-and-purple armor stationed aboard it. They hit the ice three hundred yards out from Marcus' position, a landing that also cut off the Caninine chariot from the only path of escape.

Three hundred feet to go. The Talonites were all nicely clustered together. Once we made contact with the Ovidian, Arrian, and Tullian chariots we'd lose speed. We needed just enough momentum to cut through them. The moment they worked out what was going on and turned to counter our assault, we ran the risk of being caught dead in the space between the Caninines and the enemy—exposed on the ice for the Talonites to pick us off, or Aquilinus to steal our lives with his mock lightning, if he wasn't quick to recognize Lumen. Our best chance of saving the Caninines and imposing my own agenda on the games was a surprise attack—to even the odds. We'd clear a path for the Caninines to escape across the ice bridge and in the process take as many enemy lives as possible. We were almost on them and we had good speed, at least eighty miles per hour. I just hoped it was enough to break through.

"We're going to crash!" Julia yelled as we headed straight for the Talonite chariots. The Amber Boars were the closest and the lightest with both skirmishers out, the bulky Tullian chariot was fully manned, and the White Rams had only one skirmisher free.

"Like a ball hitting skittles," I said. "Wait for my order to attack."

I cast Orbis on a narrow trajectory first without activating my armor's arms, an ellipse with the shortest return arc, just as our sled smashed into the right rear of the black-and-amber Ovidian craft, the runt of the litter, tipping them right over as we barreled past. The Ovidians slid sideways as they went, colliding with the Tullians.

"Now!" I ordered, and we burst into action, attacking the enemy from behind.

Crassus stabbed with his javelin, and Julia struck with her arachnoraptor staff. As we sailed past, a pig-faced, pike-wielding Ovidian called Quadratus on a desultore skirmisher turned and looked at me, puzzled, unable to make out what I was doing there, what house I belonged to. As it dawned on him, he thrust his pike just as Orbis returned to me, passing through the back of the man's neck, killing him at once.

The dead body fell to the ground, and suddenly Crassus jumped off the transport and appropriated the Ovidian's skirmisher. He shot off on the vehicle in a wide arc behind us.

"Stop! Come back here!" I barked, but he wasn't listening. Was Julia right? Had he betrayed us already?

The Arrian chariot and its desultore skirmisher were closest now, the Tullians knocked twenty feet away by the last collision. I needed to give us a chance, to keep the Tullians out of this melee. I cast Orbis again, this time on a short and fast orbit. As he left my hand, the telescoping arm from the lapis armor reached out with a long, hooked curve and caught my discus, borrowing his momentum to swing him about like a great sling, throwing him fast and wide.

I drew my black-bladed gladius just as a lancer aboard the Arrian chariot, one of Aquilinus' replacement team members, used the reach of his weapon to attack me. As we clashed, lance against blade, I spied Julia at starboard keeping the Arrian skirmisher at bay. Concretus wasn't fighting. He was standing over Lumen in the center of the tray, shielding him from potential harm. Damn! With Crassus gone, I needed him to engage if we were going to make this work. His strength would mean the difference between survival and defeat.

As the Tullian chariot tried to move in, its driver took a cut to the neck, and his teammates discovered the perimeter I'd created with my discus. Anyone trying to flee or pull away, or anyone trying to get inside the circling discus' path, would be wounded. Orbis had three orbits in him before he lost speed and I had to recall him, but for now he was keeping the strong Tullians at bay and the weaker competitors close where I wanted them.

"Body count," I yelled as I slipped the Arrian's guard and cut off his lead hand.

"I've taken two," Julia replied.

Four to us, and from the sound of it at least two to Orbis. We were making progress, thinning the herd as we passed, but we were also running out of time. Orbis returned as the tray slowed. We were nearing the yoke. Hah! The Arrians were turning tail; they fled from us. Aquilinus on high was casting bolts at them to drive them back toward me, furious at their cowardice. We'd laid low at least six out of twenty-four with our surprise attack.

The transport tray came to a full stop right under the giant spears of the yoke.

Not in front, not behind, but right below the crossbeam. This was where we would make our stand.

The Caninines were still hanging back, reluctant to drive forward from their cover. I was close enough now that I could make them all out. My eyes flashed back to one man who didn't belong in the arena—my uncle Proconsul Quintus Viridius Severus. Aquilinus must have thrown him down here for his amusement. He was an expert strategist, able to analyze any situation. So come on. Work out what was happening. Get moving. Marcus had worked it out. The emperor's death squad had driven him out from his cover, and he was sprinting toward the Caninines.

Aquilinus was bellowing now. Lightning flashed, registering his displeasure. But none struck us. It was all show, at least for the moment.

Now the Viridians broke from their cover and headed for the bridge. Yes! That's it. Only they hadn't seen Marcus. They were off, and Marcus didn't have a hope of catching them. He was caught out in the open, five hundred yards from our position. I waved to him, indicating that he should head to us, but he retreated toward cover. The chariot with Aquilinus' death squad was heading toward him from the southeast, so he could make cover in time and give himself a chance at survival. He was smart. He was betting that Aquilinus would order them to come to the aid of the Talonites once he realized that I was in the field. And he was right. The gleaming purple-and-gold chariot diverted course, heading right at us. We had to get clear and across that bridge, but not before the Caninines made it.

Four Ovidians, the ones who managed to get out from under their upturned chariot, came at us on foot. The first to reach me was an Ovidian hoplite, Brocchus. He thrust at me with his spear, and I blocked while drawing backward and then cast Orbis along the shaft of his spear and into his jugular. Orbis returned just as the Caninines crossed the bridge in the Viridian chariot. They made it! They were safe for now. At least one part of my plan had worked.

"I need your giant in this fight. Now!"

But Concretus just stood there defiantly. He was not abandoning Lumen for one second.

Betrayed by Crassus, unable to get the barbarian on side, now it was down to just Julia and me.

The Talonite gladiators suddenly pulled back. Why? Had Aquilinus seen Lumen? The death squad was almost upon us. We were three hundred yards to the bridge and then another quarter mile to cross it. We'd never make it in time, not with these on our tail. The rest of my plan to rejoin the Caninines and let every Roman in the empire know I was back in the tournament was not working. I would have to take on these assassins first. Perhaps they were not that good. After all, I took down the Blood Hawks. Just maybe Aquilinus had bitten off more than they could chew.

I cast Orbis right at the chariot, and a steel whip snaked out to knock him off course. My new armor responded at once, a black arm shooting out to recover the discus. If I didn't have the armor, I'd have lost him for certain. Who could block Orbis like that? Knock him clean out of the air with supernatural accuracy? Now that they were close enough, I could make out their faces through the gaps in their helmets. The man with the steel whip snapped it in the air above him. He looked right at me, gave me a feral grin. It was Licinus. And driving the chariot, the Dioscurii. All of them. They were all there. Back from the dead. The static-filled transmission squawked in my helmet's speaker.

"Salve, Mock Hawk. So glad to see you're alive. Did you miss me?"

XL

"The New Gods," Aquilinus boomed above us. "No longer Blood Hawks, they are now Blood Eagles, the proof of my imperial power, descending from on high to punish those who oppose the natural ascendancy of the Roman people."

How could this be? Pale, strong little Mania stood beside the dark Barbata—a vision of lethal beauty, preparing to cast her trident. No wounds, no injuries. They were fresh and well armed, ready to kill.

"I buried them," I said to myself as much as to Julia. "They were dead."

"It doesn't matter," Julia said. "They're here now and we've got to deal with them. Keep it together, Accala."

How could they have survived? Did the arachnoraptors dig them out?

They fell into the waters below the city-hive, Lumen said to me. *All the ambrosia cast off in the process of gathering the ichor pooled there. Their bodies were saturated with it. It has given them a new lease on life.*

"They're stronger than before," I said. I could see it. They were radiant with ambrosia, and although I was cured of my addiction, thanks to Lumen, I was also weak, not as strong as these, not by a long shot.

Now what should I do? I had thought I was past this, that my fear of them died in Lumen's city-hive, that I was focused on the greater mission, but the sight of them sapped my strength and set my body to trembling. My knees felt weak, and I sank to the transport's floor.

"Get up, Accala," Julia hissed. "You wanted to take the lead, now get up and fight."

"Look at you," Barbata called out to me in a disappointed tone. "You're all plain again. Come over here. Give us the little barbarian, and I'll make you beautiful again. We'll be sisters," she said seductively.

I was still weak at the knees as Julia hauled me to my feet. "You can do this," she said to me.

Even with the new armor, we were overmatched. The three Talonite chariots I set out against, I could handle. Hades, I could handle any other gladiators in the empire, but not these. I had to think of something, or it was all going to end right here. We couldn't match them head-to-head.

"Julia, get this tub moving." We needed to get as close to the bridge as possible and the abyss on either side. The Sertorians could not be permitted to take Lumen.

"The engine's stalled," Julia yelled. "I need a push start to fire the dynamo."

"I need Concretus' strength," I said to Lumen. "Without him now, all is lost."

He nodded and turned to the giant, who despite his expressionless face seemed extremely irritated to have to leave Lumen's side, but he leaped down behind the transport and started pushing it toward the ice bridge. He pushed us like an old mine cart, and we were moving, gathering speed, only a hundred yards away, but now the Sertorians were closing. Twenty feet. I could hear the engine sputtering, but we didn't have any forward power yet. We couldn't escape, even if Julia got the engine running. Mania's darts flew about the air around us. Ten feet now. I couldn't take the Sertorians, but maybe I could buy us more time. Saving Lumen was the key, and if Concretus was as dangerous as I remembered from the caves, I needed him in this fight now, not playing workhorse or hovering over Lumen like an overanxious nanny.

"Faster!" Julia yelled as she desperately worked on the engine. "We need more speed!"

I went to lift Lumen up, but he seemed to be immovable, like a little mountain.

"Trust me," I said to him. All of a sudden he was light as a feather and I could pick him up easily. As Licinus' chariot pulled up alongside, Mania and Licinus ready to strike, I threw Lumen right onto their chariot. The side of his crystal body collided with Mania, sending her sprawling backward ungracefully onto the deck. Licinus looked surprised that I had just handed over the prize without a fight.

"Are you begging for mercy?" he sneered. "You've just given away your only bargaining chip."

"He's just on loan," I replied. "He'll be coming back in a minute."

One mighty leap, and Concretus was flying through the air, crashing onto the deck of the Sertorian chariot. The resulting impact sent Barbata stumbling backward as Concretus attacked Licinus, fighting his way to Lumen.

"The engine?" I yelled at Julia.

"I'm trying!"

Concretus had reached Lumen, but Licinus managed to bind the crystal giant's arms to his side, encircling the icy body with his steel whip. I threw Orbis at Licinus' chain and, with a power assist from the arms, hit it square in the middle. The impact ripped the end of the chain from the Sertorian leader's hands, creating just enough slack for Concretus to push the links of the whip up and over his head. Barbata and Mania had gotten to their feet, but I had one more trick. They were not used to the lapis arms of my new armor. As soon as Orbis returned, I cast him straight up, and then, as he came back down, the armored lapis band of my breastplate snaked out, caught up the discus, and swung him around before bringing him down like a hammer onto the starboard side deck of the Blood Eagles' chariot. The chariot tilted violently, sending

Concretus and Lumen over the edge and onto the ice. Concretus jumped back aboard our sled, Lumen in his arms. The Hyperborean giant shoved me aside with one of his arms as he moved past to the front of the transport, clearly unimpressed.

I needed Julia to get us moving, but she was standing beside me, weapon in hand.

"The transport's dead. Nothing can get it started," she said quickly. "And I just want to say one more thing for the record before we die—I told you so. I told you this was madness, and if there's any justice you'll spend the rest of eternity as a hell-bound shade with my words ringing in your ears!"

"Back to back!" I ordered, and we stood in the center of the tray with Lumen and Concretus in the middle. I could just make the Caninines out in the distance as they vanished into the hills. It was no consolation that we'd saved them, not if the Sertorians took Lumen now. Lumen's loss equated to the loss of the empire. Please, Minerva. If you do watch over us, then come now. Save us.

Barbata was about to board the tray, trident at the ready. Licinus was grinning from ear to ear. I heard a piercing war cry, and then a chariot collided with the Sertorian craft at high speed, sending it flying across the smooth ice toward the dark abyss alongside the ice bridge. An amber-and-black chariot—Ovidian colors—pulled about alongside us. Crassus! He was yelling, gesturing. "Climb aboard!" He hadn't abandoned us. He'd salvaged the chariot we'd overturned and brought it back into play, even docking onto it the desultore skirmisher he'd stolen from the dead Ovidian. We climbed on and were away.

"No!" The voice boomed like thunder. Aquilinus was raging overhead, driving the Talonites who had been holding back into the fray again and after us.

We were close to the bridge when I saw Marcus. Running right at us. He knew we were his last chance to get clear of the valley. I ordered Crassus to pull up. The Blood Eagles were stuck on the precipice, emergency grapples deployed to stop them falling into the abyss. Even if they came at us on foot, they wouldn't reach us in time. The other Talonites might, but it was a risk I was more than prepared to take for Marcus. As he ran, I could see the ridiculous vegetables attached to my lanista's breastplate. More sick humor from Aquilinus, mocking Saturn, the patron god of the Calpurnians who oversaw the growing of crops.

"Accala!" Marcus called as he leaped aboard, but then he saw Crassus at the helm and drew his sword.

"Go!" I yelled at Crassus. "He's with us, Marcus. You mustn't harm him, as least not now. Will you stand with us?" I asked Marcus, as we rocketed forward to the bridge.

Marcus nodded grimly and took up position on the starboard side. I ordered Julia to take the helm, and Crassus came to stand beside Marcus and me as the Tullian chariot drew alongside, trying to cut in front of us and drive us off target. They had to give us only a solid hit on the side, and at this speed we'd miss the bridge and go careening over the edge of the abyss, but Aquilinus must have ordered them to stop us, not kill us—he couldn't risk Lumen dying—and that gave us an advantage. Marcus and Crassus eyed each other for a split second and then turned and met the incoming assault.

I clashed with an Ovidian swordsman who'd climbed to the rear of the Tullian chariot. He was shaking, fear in his eyes, though he was no novice. He was terrified of me. I deflected his blade and took his sword hand with Orbis' edge. A Tullian halberdier, Arvinus, fell to Marcus; Crassus speared Culleo, a hoplite, through the eyehole of his arch-shaped face guard.

I never thought I'd see such a thing—Crassus and Marcus fighting side by side. And by the gods, did they work well together. Crassus was spearing anyone at mid to long range, and anyone who got past the tip of his javelin he deflected and redirected to Marcus with a short movement. Bulbous fell, quickly followed by two more substitute contestants.

Within seconds, most of the Tullian crew, including all of the substitutions, were dead. The remaining competitors hung back, their faces filled with fear. It was me. They had watched what I did to the Sertorians in the Hyperborean tunnels and thought I was some kind of demon. I was their worst nightmare come back to haunt them, and it gave us a slight advantage. They were not giving it their all. They were in awe of me, more scared of Orbis than they were of Aquilinus' thunderbolts. I wondered if the empirewide audience thought the same.

Our chariot rocketed forward, and we mounted the narrow span of the ice bridge with our pursuers forced into a row behind us. Once we were over the bridge, we could try to lose them in the vast forest of crystal trees. Aquilinus wouldn't be able to spot us from above. It was our best bet.

As Julia drove us forward, we took up position, protecting her from above with our shields from any missile assault. The enormous projection of Aquilinus Jove strode forward, filling up the sky, each step covering a hundred yards. He was livid, scowling. A lightning bolt formed in his vast hand. He was going to do it. He was going to kill us all, even Lumen. A quarter mile and we'd be clear of the bridge. Ten seconds and we could maneuver, thirty seconds and we'd have cover behind the hills, and a minute and we'd be into the trees. Right then, though, we were sitting ducks. Fifty feet. Forty feet.

A blast of ionic energy came streaking in. It sounded like an attack fighter with engines on full burn pulling a fireworks display behind it. Static microcharges, formed in the dry, icy atmosphere, glowed and sizzled in its wake. Prickling sparks covered my exposed skin. The pursuing Tullians had slowed, keeping clear of the blast, but instead of hitting us, the energy beam passed overhead, the heat singeing my hair. We were not the target at all; it struck the ice bridge ahead. The blast threw up a cloud of steam and filled the air with fist-size chunks of ice. I got my shield up in time, but Julia wasn't so lucky. She fell backward, and the rough brick of ice that struck her chest scuttled across the deck to my feet. The chariot started to swerve, and I sprang forward and seized the controls from her, swerving back on course, missing the abyss by inches. We passed through the steam cloud to be met with thirty feet of yawning blackness between the sudden end of the ice bridge and the safety of the opposite side.

"Full stop!" Julia yelled. "Stop or we're done for!"

But there was no stopping, no way back. The only way was forward.

I threw the switches that released the battering tusks, desultore skirmisher, and rear storage modules—survival equipment, food, emergency fuel that we desperately needed. I let it all fly into the abyss behind us. We couldn't carry any extra weight.

"We'll never bridge that gap, not even at full speed," Marcus yelled.

I jammed the thrust controls forward and opened the throttle, driving the chariot to its limit. Grasping the reins, I pulled them tight and straight, leaning my shoulders into the icy wind that threatened to tear me off the chariot.

"Hang on to something," I yelled behind me. And then the ground fell away beneath us.

My insides lurched like a rowboat in a sea storm. Time slowed as we sailed out over the dark abyss. The strong wind rushed down the canyon, whipping up snow. It was beautiful. The glittering crystals on the wind-sculpted hills ahead were like an armada of ancient ship sails. Only another ten feet of forward momentum before the chariot descended on an arc that would carry us straight into the cliff wall ahead. We were going to fall short. Remember your training at the Academy, I told myself. The tools of survival were at hand—my mind, my body, and the surrounding environment.

"Accala!" Julia yelled.

"I've got this!"

"Stop!" Aquilinus Jupiter boomed, terrified of losing his prize.

Wait. Wait. At the exact moment the chariot lost its forward thrust and gravity staked its claim, I threw Orbis with all my might, aiming him at the cluster of rocky outcroppings that lay to either side of the path ahead. My discus screeched through the air, embedding himself deeply into one of the boulders. Eyes closed, mind sharp, I held tight to a crystal-clear image: my armor's lapis arms, one finding Orbis and binding to the ring, and of the other arm gripping the chariot's mast. The arms snaked out; I could feel them like an extension of my own body. The right side wrapped around the mast like a leather strap and clung firm. The lapis negra was flexible and strong, the function of the arms was to send out and bring back. I was gambling everything on the armor's potential. Asking it to do something it was probably never designed for, trusting in the same craftsmanship that forged Orbis.

The thick prow of the Ovidian chariot collided with the cliff wall with a jolt and we fell.

I opened my eyes just as the lapis bands pulled tight. We were suspended in the darkness, hanging, the chariot tilted on its side. Thank the gods, Orbis was holding fast to the boulder above us. The hurtling winds found the side of the chariot, and we started to swing like a pendulum, back and forth. Everyone managed to stay in the chariot and secured themselves except for Julia, who was hanging over the edge, one hand gripping the railing.

"Accala!" she protested.

"Hang on a second."

"That's not funny!" she yelled.

We were nine feet over the edge. We had to get up before Aquilinus could consider throwing another bolt. I visualized the arms drawing together, returning to their original position but without letting go of their anchor points. The chariot shuddered but didn't move. It was too heavy.

Julia's hand can lend you power, Lumen said.

"Your hand," I said to Julia. "Reach out and touch my armor."

She stretched up her ichor hand and I grasped her wrist. She let go of the rail, and I had to use all my strength to pull her ichor hand toward me.

"Power." That was all I needed to say.

Julia touched the lapis band nearest her. The arms went to work. The chariot groaned in response as it was pulled up the side of the precipice, toward the edge above us.

I held tight to Julia as we were drawn up over the edge of the abyss and back onto solid ground. The chariot came up on its side, depositing us on the ice. We'd made it. As I got to my feet I saw a strange, flickering light covering us. The blast that destroyed the ice bridge had also set the crystalline rocks on either side of the path on fire. Swirling ichor mists ignited to produce hot green and blue flames.

Releasing one arm from the mast, I used the other to pull Orbis from the solid rock where he'd anchored.

"Quickly," I ordered, "right the chariot. Everyone aboard, make sure you stay close to Lumen, he's our protective talisman."

The pollution from the explosion had subsided, giving us a clear view of our enemies who had returned to the other side of the abyss. Giant Aquilinus stood behind the Talonites, another lightning bolt held tightly in his holographic hand.

"He's going to fire on us again," Marcus warned.

"No, he won't risk harming Lumen," I said.

"We must hurry to cover," Marcus insisted. "They'll head back to their shuttle and fly after us."

"Hold a moment. We have work to do here," I said.

Aquilinus chased after us, moved right through his fighters like a giant ghost. Three projection spherae trailed behind, generating his form. He had no need to worry about falling.

"Quickly, Crassus, check how my post on the vox populi is tracking. Julia, can you take control of the spherae that generate Aquilinus' body? I want to repurpose them to make a broadcast."

"Maybe, maybe. It's not impossible, as long as you don't get us killed in the next few minutes." She set to work at once, flipping open the access hatch on the transmission staff and searching through her utility belt for tools and parts.

"Crassus?"

"The poll's quiet. A hesitant billion or so votes in your favor, backing the gods and freedom. Ten billion for Aquilinus, but the upside is that the number of people viewing the poll is rising astronomically. They're not voting but there's an ever-increasing number watching, waiting to see what you're going to do next."

"Accala, he's almost halfway across," Marcus warned, his eyes firmly fixed on Aquilinus, who was walking on air over the abyss.

"I see him," I said. I quickly tapped at the chariot's controls, linking the vehicle's speakers to my armilla. "I'm ready. Julia?"

"Not enough time. I can try for one sphera. That's it."

"The middle one then," I said. "Fix it in place."

She stood up and leveled the transmission staff at Aquilinus.

"I'll do my best," she said.

The staff glowed and hummed, the point lighting up. "This is ridiculous," she said. "Even with this hand of mine boosting the signal it won't be enough to . . ." She stopped midsentence. "It tingles. I can feel it across the surface of my palm, on my fingertips—it's like little vibrating pinpricks. They're points of connection. Some of them relate to the movement of the spherae, some to the incoming and outgoing signals."

Julia swung her staff and the middle sphera leaped to her command, pulling off its current course to follow the directions she indicated. In response Aquilinus' torso suddenly warped and wobbled uncertainly.

"Hold it over the middle of the canyon," I ordered, "and set it up to broadcast to the vox populi. I want everyone to see this."

"You can't be serious," she said. "Just because I can move it around doesn't mean I've reprogrammed it. I'll need another minute to input the broadcast codes from the staff and set up a direct feed."

"Hurry then."

Aquilinus took another step, but Julia locked the middle sphera into position and his torso stayed anchored in place while the other two spherae moved ahead, creating a weird distortion—a giant head and legs warping like melting wax running back to the fixed torso.

Aquilinus paused, and surprise registered on his face, followed by outrage. "You go too far!" he boomed, the sound so loud that the planet itself seemed to respond, ice shelves cracking, wind whipping about. But then he took a step backward so his body regained its proper proportions. The so-called new emperor's whole performance hinged on the claim that he could replace the gods. He couldn't permit the audience to see me manipulate his image at will, so he stopped dead in his tracks, above the dark abyss, just where I wanted him.

"Accala, we're losing time. If we want to have a chance we need to get moving," Marcus insisted.

"Aquilinus can take us anytime he wants," I said. "We have to set up some ground rules here and now or we're finished. We need to get the audience to back us."

"How are you planning to do that?" Marcus asked.

"How else? I'm going to pick a fight."

XLI

"You're good to go," Julia said, "but you'd better hurry. They'll be working to override me."

I walked to the edge of the abyss, lit by the green and blue fires that sprang from the rocks to either side. In the distance, an avalanche of ice sheets came roaring down Lumen's mountain. The bad weather was intensifying.

"Aquilinus Sertorius Macula!" My voice boomed out, echoing between the surrounding hills. "Little Spot! Can you hear me?"

As they called Gaius Caesar Germanicus by his nickname Caligula, meaning *little boots,* so I made a play on Aquilinus' family name—Macula being a spot or blemish.

"You've got their attention," Crassus said. "Almost a hundred billion have weighed in on your side. Half a trillion, though, for Aquilinus. The people who were watching before are now voting, billions more are finding the poll with every passing minute. You're on the right track but we need more drama," he declared, like an engineer trying to spark a ship engine to life. "Big gestures, strong language. Call him out before the whole empire!"

"I will call you Little Spot, because that's what you are," I cried out. "A temporary stain on the empire that the gods will soon wipe away."

He had to debate me. Aquilinus couldn't fire on us while I had Lumen and he couldn't go anywhere while Julia had his projection fixed in place. If he didn't respond, he'd look weak and confused before the audience.

"Accala the traitor," he shouted. "Apostate of Roman advancement. You have abandoned belief in the self-made god for children's stories. And you, Gaius Crassus, I see you there behind her. You will be punished most severely of all, for having come so close to the light and then turning away from it."

"I'm no traitor, and the gods are real, Little Spot. The old temple to Minerva, built by the Viridian settlers, sits behind the ruins of Lupus Civitas, at the base of this world's tallest peak. That temple and this world are sacred to the gods, and they are displeased."

"Do you take the people of Rome for fools? Spare me your talk of the gods. We are the New Gods. The power we hold here and now is all that matters."

The projection of Aquilinus' face disappeared briefly and I looked to Julia.

"He's physically turning about up there in the stadium," she said. "He's talking to his people. They'll be trying to shut us down, we don't have long."

I had to play this carefully. Formally challenging a standing emperor, even a false emperor, would cost me votes. My line had to be just right—provoking yet still dutiful. At the same time I couldn't give away too many of Aquilinus' secrets, couldn't reveal his plans for the ambrosia or the significance of Lumen, because it might actually give him cause to destroy us. "Aquilinus! Why not give the surviving Caninines a fighting chance? Jupiter's sacred games are scheduled to run until the fifteenth of this month. Four more days remain. Allow my team here to enter the tournament. Even the odds and turn this farce into a real contest again."

"Your team? You've gone mad," he said, turning back to me. "Everyone saw your psychotic fit, and now we have the indisputable proof. You think you have a team? Three reject gladiators of different houses, an auxiliary, and two barbarians."

"We don't fight for a house, we fight for the empire, for Rome itself. It's what the people want, and if we're no real threat, if the gods don't exist, then why worry? You said this was to be a philosophical argument realized through action. Well, what good is that without two parties to enter into the debate? Use us to prove your case. Accept my challenge. Banish this poor excuse for a slaughterhouse and bring back the real games. Either that, or strike us down here and now."

Instead of giving me an answer, Aquilinus' body flickered and vanished. Two of the sphera plummeted from the sky in the darkness below.

"They've killed power to those two and are trying to take back the one we're using to broadcast," Julia said.

"You've got trillions of followers on the vox populi," Crassus said, "about thirty percent of the empire's viewing audience, but they're mostly on Caninine Alliance worlds. We need to get over half the audience to support you, that will rattle Aquilinus. Get more than fifty percent and he'll have to accept your challenge."

"That means winning the support of the Arrians," Marcus added. "They've always been weak, they always back the most likely winner. Get them on board, and we're home."

"You have much impertinence." Aquilinus' voice filled the sky now. Eyes, each one the size of a carrier ship, appeared from the clouds, beaming light. He was back but staying up out of harm's way, not game to take on a bodily form again. "I will consider your petition to my throne, but first you'll have to be removed from the field, reshaped into a proper team that will sufficiently amuse us."

"Accala! The Rota Fortuna," Julia said.

A Sertorian trireme was heading toward us from the orbital stadium. Legionaries were coming, armed with force projectors to trap us and stun grenades to halt us in our tracks. Vulcaneum auxiliaries with disruptors to seize up our chariot's engine. All the best advanced weapons. Beside the trireme flew the smaller shuttle that had dropped the Sertorians into the field earlier. Once it scooped them up, they'd be across this abyss and be on us in no time. Aquilinus had upped the stakes. We'd either have to go willingly, or they'd take us by force. But we couldn't leave the field.

"I can't hold it for much longer," Julia said. "I'm already starting to lose control."

"Get as tight a shot as you can of Accala," Crassus said to Julia, and then to me, "This is your last chance to win them over. A direct address is what's needed. Make it good."

"I'm no speechmaker," I said. "That's more my father's forte. I lack the talent."

"Just say what's in your heart, make your case for why they should follow you," Marcus said. "You're a gladiator in the arena. Tell the audience what they need to hear."

I'm here with you, Lumen said.

I looked up to the green light of the sphera, pulling myself up to full height. From the heart. Here we go. Deep breath.

"Romans. Countrymen. The people and the Senate of Rome below and the gods above—that is what makes the empire. That's what I represent here in this arena, this is what I stake my life to fight for. We have served and honored our gods, and they have always served and honored us in return, bringing us to high station. Look at our empire! Vast! Without compare. It is the greatest civilization the galaxy has ever known." I wanted my voice to be clear and powerful, but it was wavering, tinged with emotion that was hard to repress. "When we have seen strife and conflict it was because we had turned away from the gods. When we sought to deify our own greed instead of fighting for something bigger than ourselves. We become small on our own, we lose perspective, we lose the ability to keep the vastness of the empire bound together. The gods are the greater love and creativity, the greater communication and justice that bind us together, but our collective hubris is causing the empire to come apart at the seams. Whatever power Aquilinus offers is weak in comparison. And make no mistake: The gods are watching us right now."

"The poll is the top ranking item on the vox populi now and you're close to forty percent approval," Crassus said. "Keep going."

The trireme and shuttle were close now. Only thirty seconds to go before they'd land on the ice and we'd be lost.

"My cognomen is Camilla—the one who makes the offering at the temple, the handmaiden of the gods," I said. Out of the corner of my eye I could see Crassus grinning as I put to some good use the ridiculous title he gave me. "When the ships land and take us away, then the tournament is over. Now is the time to send a message. Vote for justice and the gods, and Aquilinus will hear you. He'll restore the games to their proper format, the way it has always been since the ancient days. Those contestants who were not here at the start of the games cannot now be introduced. All substitute players must be removed. Advanced weapons must not be used."

"It's not enough," Crassus said. The ships were right over us, access hatches opening. The shuttle had lowered its scoop base and was preparing to pick up the Blood Eagles. It was a matter of seconds now until we were either killed or taken. "You're at forty-five percent, but it's not enough to put us over the edge," Crassus continued. "We need two percent of the Tullians or Ovidians sitting on the fence to back you. Something big."

Something big. I took a deep breath and stepped forward. Everything rested on this. It was all about performance, about holding the spotlight long enough to tilt the odds in our favor.

"Aquilinus! I hear you're a gambler, so let's make a wager." My uncle told me that high-stakes gambling was the Sertorian leader's weakness. How could he resist a bet when the odds were stacked in his favor? "If you win, then it is a clear sign the gods play no part in the affairs of men. But if you lose, if my team wins the tournament with your best standing against us, then you must yield the imperial throne and accept the judgment of Rome's gods."

I stretched out my right hand. The fire that burned on the ichor-filled rocks was so hot. Every fiber of my being wanted to pull away, but I kept my palm outstretched, fingers inching toward the cloud of green and blue heat.

"Accala?" Julia called out. "What are you doing?"

"Remember I told you the story of Mucius Scaevola?"

Turning to look at Julia, my eyes conveyed an apology for her hand, for my betrayal. Lumen would not have the power to spare to make another. No thinking. I couldn't think. Only act. I plunged my hand into the flame.

"No!" Julia cried out.

There was no pain at first, just a strange heat. Then a wall of searing agony hit me. My skin burned raw as the flesh was charred, but I held firm and kept the pain from my face.

Crassus stepped up beside me. "This is what a true Roman is made of," he proclaimed. "This is why I left my house. She is mortal, she suffers, but she has no fear. The gods stand with her."

I was glad he spoke, because I could not. Sweat poured from my body. I could feel the cold again. Whatever protection I'd been given by the healing process I went through with Lumen, it was gone now, worn out by the harm I'd inflicted upon myself.

I raised my hand from the fire. It was still burning, flames eating away at fat and muscle.

"People of Rome! I sacrificed this hand in the hope that you will lend me yours! Give me your support!"

The light on the sphera cut out and the black sphere fell into the darkness below. We were out of time. The Sertorian trireme was touching down on the ice. I turned, dropped to my knees, and plunged my burning hand into the snow, extinguishing the flame. The pain was slightly diminished but the burn continued, penetrating deep into the tissue. For the first time I wondered if it was possible for a burn to penetrate so deeply that it would burn the bone itself, liquefy the marrow. The snow around my hand began melting from the heat. I dared not look at the hand itself.

"You've done it," Crassus said. "Fifty-five percent. Your support base is too large now for the emperor to ignore. He'll have to come to terms. Just wait and see."

The engines of the trireme fired and it was up in the air again, rocketing away with the shuttle. We had done it. Aquilinus couldn't afford to ignore us now.

Marcus and Crassus rushed forward to help me. "If I doubted you before, I do not now," Marcus said.

"You won't think I'm so desirable now," I mumbled, lifting my hand briefly out of the snow. I couldn't believe I had said that. I didn't even know which of the men I meant to address. I was delirious, in shock.

Aquilinus' giant eyes flashed in the clouds. Thunder boomed.

"You claim to speak for the gods," Aquilinus said. "I say you are a fool, a scared child seeking to frighten others into rejecting a glorious future. Before you go any further, allow me to offer you the chance to yield now. If you do, every Viridian prisoner held by my house will be released, including your father. On the other hand, I will permit you to persist with this folly of yours, but then members of your house will die, ten thousand at a time, for each hour you stay in the field. This is the price of challenging the emperor's power. Tell the people of Rome, do you still wish to join these games?"

Aquilinus was trying to make it sound like he was the one calling the shots, but I'd achieved exactly what I'd set out to accomplish. The Caninines had escaped and I could choose to have the games restarted with no advanced weapons, and no faux god in the field hurling thunderbolts like a toddler with a temper tantrum. We had a small chance, a fighting chance to save the empire, and I couldn't give that up, even for my own father and the lives of the Viridian prisoners. There was no choice. I just hoped my countrymen understood that.

A media sphera returned to hear and transmit my answer to the audience. I drew my hand from out of the snow and reclaimed my feet.

"I do," I replied loudly. "My team wishes to compete in the tournament of Jupiter. And in turn do you accept my wager? Will you return the contest to its proper form, and concede the throne if we win?"

"Very well. I accept. You can join with the Viridians in what's left of their Caninine Alliance, assuming they will take you back. I'll even pull out the new Talonite players I inserted into the mix. But I have additional conditions, as is the emperor's prerogative. I will continue to dictate my own format upon the games, though the editor shall ensure the contests are more evenly weighted."

"I live to serve," the winged head of Julius Gemminus said, appearing above us.

"The rules will be the same as before: elimination of players, with a gladiatorial finale in the ruins of Lupus Civitas."

"I agree to those terms."

"Not so fast. I have one more condition. The old emperor liked the Greek stories, so let us have a tragic Greek ending for you if you lose. When Caligula proved that the Cretan bull could have impregnated Pasiphaë to create the Minotaur, he re-created the scene in the Colosseum with a Germanic slave strapped to a wooden frame. I'd very much like to see you suffer that fate before the entire empire. The fate of a whore and an apostate. The bull chief of the Hyperboreans shall play the part of the Cretan bull. He's got plenty of spines, we'll make it work somehow, and when it's all over, I shall keep the small barbarian child as a trophy."

Aquilinus couldn't honestly think that there was a single bone left in my body that feared pain or disgrace. This was for the mob's benefit. He knew I wouldn't back down, no matter the cost. He was exercising dominance, reminding the mob that everything that happened in the arena was on his terms, for his amusement. And ensuring that the real prize, Lumen, would be his.

"Well?" Aquilinus asked.

"I accept. Let's get on with it."

"Then let the games resume!"

Aquilinus' presence in the sky vanished as the empyrean erupted with golden upturned thumbs. Massive approval, the elated cheers of trillions across the empire as the tournament stakes were set back on track. Fireworks were launched. Julius Gemminus' head came hovering toward us.

"Congratulations! Your application to play in the tournament has been accepted," the editor announced. "As you don't represent a house anymore, you'll be known as team Sub-Lupa of the Caninine Alliance."

Beneath the she-wolf. Aquilinus wanted to remind all of them that this was about me, that if he was guilty of hubris, then this woman who dared to stand up against him was equally guilty, maybe more so.

The sky was filled with the scene of the Caninines in the course ahead of us. A carrier drone came flying in from on high and dropped their weapons into a big pile in the snow before them. They quickly scrabbled to recover them and then they were off, heading toward the southeastern border of the forest.

"Get us out of here now before he changes his mind," Marcus said.

Marcus had been there before, playing games for mad dictators, triumphing under the constant threat of death. He was a blessing, the very man I needed beside me. Then Crassus took the reins and Marcus was pulling me into the chariot and we were rocketing away between the cover of the hills, heading for the forest. I fell back to the deck and pushed myself up against the chariot's central pole. The pain radiating from my burning hand blotted out everything else. It consumed all my attention and it was all I could do to remain conscious. Marcus gently laid me on the chariot floor while Julia treated my hand with some poultices she had stored in the compartments in her utility belts. I still couldn't bring myself to look at it.

"Gods. Go gently," I yelped.

"Well, what were you thinking?" she demanded as she deftly dressed my hand.

"I was thinking I'd do whatever it took to keep us alive and on track."

"It doesn't make what you did any less stupid. There," she said, injecting me and applying a poultice. "You won't be able to use that hand, but it shouldn't hurt so much for a few hours, then you'll need another shot. You're lucky there was a full medical kit stored under the deck, and some emergency supplies."

Lumen sat beside me, taking my burned hand in his.

Immediately I felt a soothing glow penetrate the flesh, cooling the heat, stopping its destructive advance.

I cannot spare any of my own energy, so I've used some of the power stored in your pin to stop the burning fire from penetrating further. Even so, the power left to you must be used sparingly. It too will be needed to complete the journey to Mother.

The word-image mother came as a rapid overlapping of forms—a queen bee at the heart of a hive, the tallest mountain of this world, a crown, brilliant light shining over a still lake—and had the echo of the image of my own mother. It reminded me of this being's innate alienness. Lumen was not born of a human womb, not my mother's womb.

"I thank you," I said.

Your hand will function as before, without restraint, but I was able to preserve its function only, not its form.

"I understand," I said. "I don't care how it looks, it's enough of a blessing that it works at all."

Just the same, I was relieved Julia had bandaged it up. The sight of a blackened palm, of twisted, charred fingers, would have been more than I could bear.

You must try to rest now, he said. *Your body has taken quite a shock.*

"No, not yet," I said. "Not until we have a plan."

As we traveled, the sky was filled with a mass projection from the stadium: the execution of the first hundred Viridians. I closed my eyes. I couldn't watch.

"It's not your fault," Julia said. "You were right. This is the only way."

"He wouldn't do it unless the mob approved," I whispered. "Whatever they think of the gods or Aquilinus, their overwhelming desire is for conflict, blood, and entertainment."

Mourning would come later, when we had triumphed. Now that I'd chosen this path, victory was the only option. I couldn't afford to stumble or die. Like Galactic Atlas, the weight of an empire was resting upon my shoulders.

XLII

"WE NEED TO MOVE quickly to dominate the games," Marcus said. "Aquilinus has agreed to this only because he needs to buy time to keep the mob at bay while he establishes power."

"And because he can't afford to see harm come to Lumen," Julia said.

As we went, Julia filled Marcus in on all that he'd missed, and he told us of the fall of the Rota Fortuna to Aquilinus' forces and the establishment of the yoke.

"He staged his coup when the mountainside was blown open. He canceled the games and had *Incitatus* sprayed with pure gold. The main promenade in Avis Accipitridae was prepared for a triumph, lined with rows of torture devices on either side, a unique torment for each audience member aboard the Rota Fortuna who wasn't of a house allied to the Sertorians. As he passed, lauded by their screams, he wanted to ascend in a shuttle to *Incitatus,* which would become his throne. Well, he ended up in his ship, but the coronation was postponed. Even the temptation of the ambrosia wasn't sufficient to allow the new self-proclaimed emperor to bring Jupiter's sacred games to an early conclusion. There were uprisings in pockets all over the empire; Sertorian buildings were burned and bombed. The mob demanded the games be played out, and he had to agree or face an empirewide rebellion.

"Until now he's kept the Sertorian team out of the field of play. They're supposed to be ascended gods like him now, and he brings them in only if he wants to punish us or deliver a coup de grâce to a struggling player, or pass judgment on his own players who displease him."

"And you got the yoke," I said. "Aquilinus reliving his greatest moments."

"The yoke, the temples, it's all a sick joke to Aquilinus," Marcus said. "You must understand, though, that the torment of our families and loved ones, as terrible as that was, was not what drove us through the yoke. We know our duty and we have our pride. Survival was our goal. Aquilinus isn't in the Rota Fortuna, he's in *Incitatus*. When he sends down his projection, he refers to it as riding *Incitatus*, as if it were an actual horse. He's clearly insane, no better than the ancient emperors he idolizes."

"He always was mad," I said. "Only now he has no compunction about expressing it."

"We thought he'd execute us all after we went through the yoke, but we persevered. The chance to still defeat Aquilinus was our only thought, and now you've done it, Accala," he said to me. "Lumen can mean the difference between life and death to the empire."

"And my father?" I asked Marcus. "Have you seen him?"

He shook his head. "I haven't but he could still be alive. Don't give up hope."

I lay back on the floor of the chariot and listened to the others talk. Julia's sedative must have gone to my head, because I could have sworn that when I looked back at Marcus, the vegetables I'd noticed hanging from his armor seemed to have a layer of skin on them and to be attached to his actual body through holes in his breastplate. When I asked him about it, he confirmed that the vegetables were in fact growing out of his body, and out of the bodies of all the members of the Calpurnian team, genetically sealed to the skin.

"It's to make us look like dullards. No more flute-playing bear and horn-playing chicken—we've become the new halftime show. After the coup, Aquilinus sent down his new Praetorian legionaries to capture us from above using tranquilizers. He took us to the Rota Fortuna. We were returned to the arena world, but we'd been genetically altered. It's a joke, you see. Our patron Saturn sows the seeds and so this is the fruit of the earth. Onions and potatoes. The vegetables can't be removed without opening mortal wounds in our bodies. He had a Calpurnian spectator altered as well. The administrator of Perfectus Salvare, the empire's largest salvage station. The Blood Eagles, as they call themselves now, were in attendance, and Licinus himself ripped a potato from the man's chest. It brought his heart out with it. The man bled to death at my feet. The surviving Flavians have little wings surgically attached to their backs—useless cupids. The wings flap back and forth as they move but can't do more than that."

"And they made the Viridians wear women's armor," I remembered.

"Gods! Not just women's armor," Marcus said. "They're actually growing breasts. Aquilinus has injected them with hormones—they're undergoing gene therapy—a complete sex-change treatment."

Crassus burst out laughing at the news. He couldn't help himself, drawing a dark look from Marcus.

I couldn't believe what I was hearing. A Gemini procedure, a sex change, had always been illegal under the ruling of the all-male Senate.

"The Viridians aren't taking it well. Aquilinus is stealing their virtus, emasculating them," Marcus continued. "As if the humiliation of the yoke wasn't bad enough."

"Gods, that's tragic," Julia said, trying to sympathize with Marcus.

"Tragically hilarious," Crassus said.

"Let's see you laugh tomorrow when we face whatever Aquilinus has to throw at us," Marcus said bitterly. "He doesn't seem well disposed toward you, Gaius Crassus. I'm certain that when he comes for us, he'll have concocted something extra special for you."

Marcus' comment ended the conversation on a dark note.

I turned my attention to the swirling snowflakes above. They were so beautiful, so many shining flakes whipped about by the winds. After days of no sky in the stifling tunnels, this was a welcome change, but I kept in mind that the increased weather activity meant one thing—danger. The more ichor Lumen took out of that world, the more chaotic the weather would become. We had to take care an avalanching ice shelf or an unexpected crevasse didn't finish us off and do Aquilinus' work for him.

Snowflakes were soon replaced by a canopy of crystal trees as we entered the forest. Fine, sentient tendrils on the branches caught the snowflakes and joined them together to form dense layers of leaves. That canopy seemed to provide us some protection from the cold; the intensity of the winds and the bite of the air seemed to have been blunted.

It is because this forest is alive with ichor. These are the lungs of this world. The trees heat the liquid ichor as it passes through, causing it to congeal, condensing its power. This is how I was able to absorb so much energy into this small frame.

"It's the strangest thing," Marcus said. "The branches are bending aside for us, forming pathways. All Crassus has to do is follow them."

The forest will let us pass through and then conceal the way behind us. It will shield us for now, but soon I must withdraw the last of the ichor contained within it, and then it will start to break apart.

I explained that it was Lumen's doing and that the forest would show us the best path to the ruins of Lupus Civitas.

As we took turn after turn through narrow pathways, branches bent up like trumpeters greeting a triumphant general and then slowly fell back into position the moment we passed. It'd be hard for the Talonites to follow, as the branches would not yield for them as they did for Lumen, and with luck we'd catch up the Viridians and our other allies in no time at all.

They have taken a route around the edge of the forest. They may intersect with us tomorrow.

We rode for hours until the light began to fail, but the forest continued to protect us from the harsh conditions that raged outside.

Julia treated my hand again and as the bandage was removed I forced myself to look at what it had become.

"It's improved," she said. "Vastly so."

The skin was discolored and had a new texture, like tanned leather, the pores melted into a smooth surface. There were splotches and streaks of dead white skin marbled across the back of the hand. It naturally took up the posture of a claw—perhaps the tendons had shortened with the injury—but as I flexed it and experimented I found it quite functional, as Lumen had promised, and that was all that mattered. Beauty be damned. I informed Julia that Lumen had a part to play in my hand's recovery and that I wouldn't be needing any more medicine for it.

Closing my eyes for a short rest, I must have dozed off because the next thing I knew Julia was shaking me awake.

"Lumen's guided us to a clearing to camp for the night," she told me quietly as we came to a stop. "I think we're going to be safe here, at least from the Talonites, but Marcus and Crassus are eyeing one another warily, and the bull chief is extending and retracting the sharp icicles along his arm anytime one of us comes too close to Lumen. If we all team up against Crassus—"

I cut her off. "Crassus stays for now. I told you that, and my decision stands."

Julia helped prop me up in the chariot. The clearing was small, ringed by thickly clustered crystal trees. There was a feeling of anticipation, as if the trees were waiting for something, like children rushing to the door to welcome a parent.

"You've sent Aquilinus back a step," Marcus said to me. "His coup looked like a done deal, but now he's on the back foot, trying to keep all the edges of the empire together before it starts splitting apart at the seams. You've proved yourself to me, and I'll vouch for you when we catch up with the Carbo and the others."

"But will you vouch for me?" Crassus asked him.

"Your actions will speak for you," Marcus said bluntly.

"Perhaps I should let them speak for me now," Crassus said in a threatening tone.

A shadow passed over Crassus' face. Confronting Aquilinus back at the precipice had shaken him. He'd sworn service to me, but he still saw Marcus and the other Caninines as a potential threat, and Marcus was a natural leader. He felt intuitively that he should be in command. To him I was still the old Accala. He didn't see that I was no longer a girl, not even a woman. I was the leader now. There was a tension in the air, each man waiting to see if the other would make a move. Crassus raised his spear, and Marcus turned to face him, sword at the ready. Behind them Concretus moved to stand before Lumen, ready to kill either of them if they threatened his safety. I couldn't have this. Not now.

"No fighting," I said as loudly as I could manage. "Kill each other and doom this whole mission. The Caninines are traveling along the forest's edge, we won't run into them tonight."

"It won't be your team if we catch up with the Viridian proconsul and Tribune Carbo. They'll be running the show," Crassus warned me.

"Be that as it may, right now this is my team and we'll pull in the direction I say. I need both of you. I'll vouch for you, Crassus, and my word will be enough. Swear peace now. Make a pax between you, at least until the tournament is over."

They hesitated, their eyes locked, not daring to even blink.

"Swear it now or both of you are out," I said. "And I will do this on my own if I have to, you'd better believe it."

Slowly they lowered their weapons. Crassus was the first to offer his arm. Marcus paused, looked at me, and then clasped the Sertorian's forearm. Now he began to sense my resolve.

There were two dome-shaped emergency shelters aboard the Ovidian chariot that we set up near the tree line. We agreed that Marcus and Crassus would take one, mindful of their promise not to fight, and Julia and I the other.

They will come soon. When they do, I ask that you do not interfere with them until the process is complete.

"Who will come?" I asked.

The last of my people bringing me the final deposits of ichor.

"I thought there would be more," I said.

They have died. The world cannot sustain them; the poison from the collapse of the city has been spreading throughout the world, and those belowground have been falling prey to its pollution. They do not have my mother's strength.

Darkness soon descended, and as the last of the light vanished, the forest provided a dull light of its own. Lumen walked into the center clearing. The ground beneath him paid honor to his step. Glowing, sparkling tendrils from the roots of the trees sprang up and tapped into his feet, the top of which opened, a hundred tiny pores like docking ports in a console, accepting the thin, shining roots. The trees began to dim, their energy and heat waning as they poured into him. The ground beneath us began to crack, like a monsoon plain in dry season. And then they appeared, all at once, as if they stepped out of the trunks of the trees themselves. The last of his people, hundreds of glowing Hyperborean workers, emerged from rocks and trees, from the dense foliage of the night forest. Lumen began to glow, and the first one came, twice his height, slender of frame. I could see the ichor flowing through the channels of his crystal body. We all watched in astonishment as the tall worker stepped into Lumen. It was like some conjurer's trick. He seemed to shrink in size like fruit drying in the sun, burning up in the smaller alien's light, shrinking and dissolving as he continued walking into him. I could barely look at it, the light was so intense. After a time, the flow of Hyperboreans came to an end and the glow subsided.

"That was one of the strangest things I've ever seen," Marcus said.

"They are the servants of the gods," Crassus said.

"I thought you didn't believe in the gods," Marcus said gruffly.

"Only a fool does not acknowledge the light when it's shining right before him," Crassus said.

As we started to set up the shelters, Marcus approached me.

"Accala, a word?" he asked.

"Of course."

He drew me aside to the edge of the camp.

"This is all happening quickly, as these things are wont to do."

"I can do this," I said. "I feel sharp, focused."

"I don't doubt it. This is your path, and we are following along in your wake, I saw it at once. I don't even question your choice about Crassus, though it will no doubt bring problems later on. The gods favor you, and I made the mistake of misjudging your motives once. I won't do it again. Tribune Carbo has explained the situation to me. I know your heart, your determination, and that's good enough for me."

"Then what? If you don't doubt my leadership . . ."

"It's not that. I thought, back in the mountain, I thought that I'd killed you. I just wanted a moment, this moment, before things get bad, to tell you I'm sorry and let you know that it pleases me that you are alive. That I'm happy to see you again."

He looked away, his face pained. I wasn't wrong, then—Marcus had feelings for me. I knew the legend of Marcus and Amphiara. He never got to say goodbye to her before she was killed, never got to tell her how he felt.

"I'm right here," I said.

"As am I," he said. "But when the arrow is loosed, it thinks only of the target." He reached out to touch my face. "I apologize for misjudging you, and I rejoice to see you alive." His fingers fell away, but in a reluctant, lingering way. "But you must stay focused. To survive and triumph—those must be our watchwords."

"Survive and triumph," I echoed. I had the sense it wasn't the first time he had spoken those words to someone he loved.

I took his hand in my good one. I wanted to feel human contact, to drive away the feeling of sickness that crept over me. His hand was warm, despite the plummeting temperature. I could feel his pulse. His heart was pounding.

"There is something I wanted to ask you," I said. "Before. Back in Rome. You talked about Crassus with admiration because he was a skilled gladiator. I had the sense that you meant that I was not."

He laughed at that. "Out here, perhaps on the last night before we die, with the whole empire at stake, and you're worried about some comment I made back in the training hall in Rome?"

"I value your opinion," I said, "and right now I need to know what you truly think of my abilities."

"I think that you're not a gladiator at all," he said. "You have the skills and the heart, but you're not made for the arena. It's not your path. I knew it from the first."

Not a gladiator? It was the only way I'd thought of myself those last two years. If not an arena fighter, then what?

"I'm a warrior," I said. "A soldier like my father."

"Not even that," he said. "It's too late for me. I was a soldier and then a gladiator and then a trainer of gladiators. I don't know how to be anything else. If the gods meant for that to change, then I wouldn't be here now. This is where I'm meant to be, the role I am meant to play in the great game of the gods. But you're something else. When I chose to become a gladiator, I did it as a way of turning my back upon the world. I rejected life and love and followed the path of death. I saw that in you—that's why I took you as a student—but there was a spark as well, something inside you that burned to live despite the anger and darkness that had veiled you. Death doesn't own you like it does me, or Crassus, for that matter. You're like a flame in the dark to men like us. This arena is a harsh testing ground, but the gods have a destiny marked out for you, Accala, mark my words. You have it within you to be something Rome hasn't seen for a long time."

I was at a loss; I didn't know what he meant. If I wasn't a gladiator or a soldier, then what was I?

"A hero," Marcus said. "You can be a hero."

We stood there silently for a few minutes, hand in hand, watching the wind howling through the trees, breaking off branches as it went. Lumen had drained the surrounding environment of its ichor and it was dying. Limbs smashed to the ground, creating a forest floor of shards and clouds of glittering dust. Marcus moved to leave and as we parted our fingers clung together like vines, reluctant to be separated, but then we were apart and heading to our separate shelters. Lumen and Concretus didn't feel the elements or need to sleep and so kept watch over the chariot, allowing us some welcome rest. As soon as dawn rose, we needed to find the Caninines. There was strength in numbers, and we needed all the strength we could get if we were going to go up against Licinus and his Blood Eagles.

I fell asleep thinking of the last thing I should have been thinking of at a time like that—Marcus' warm hand, his beating pulse, and his unexpected belief in me. But there was no room for anything between us. He could see it, and was wise to remind me of the way of the arrow. The games of a mad emperor cost him his heart once, and it would cost him again. There was no thought of life for me after this. To carry out my duty, I must shed all the different parts of myself—daughter, lover, woman, slave, fighter, gladiator. I must be the arrow. Nothing else.

*   *   *

THE FIRST RAYS of light revealed a forest in decay. The beauty of the evening before gave way to broken crystal limbs and brittle trees. All through the night, as the forest dried up and fell apart like an old woman's body, we'd heard crashing crystals tinkling and clanging as they struck the icy ground. No longer did the branches part for us. Now we had to shield the chariot and drive through, making an awful mess as we went. It reminded me of the destruction of Lumen's city—as one tree fell it took others nearby with it.

We emerged onto a wide, cyan green road that ran along the base of the hills—the ancient highway to Lupus Civitas that had been used by heavy transport vehicles—but before we could even come about and straighten up, our chariot was hit from the side, sending us flying sideways back into the trees, filling the air with showers of crystal shards.

"Ambush!" I yelled, drawing Orbis.

"Hold!" Marcus called. "Proconsul Severus, stay your hand. We're with you."

"Hold your fire." It was my uncle's voice. We'd found them—or, rather, they'd found us. One chariot and a desultore skirmisher. My family, our allies.

We dismounted. Pavo's crossbow was aimed at my head, Carbo's pike leveled at Crassus.

Nervo moved to take Lumen, but Concretus stepped between them and held out his arms in warning, spikes of crystal flashing in the morning light. Behind Nervo was the Flavian spearman Titus Flavius Cursor, small white wings fluttering from his back. Gods, but that looked bizarre.

"Lumen. They'll help us. Truly. Have Concretus stand down," I shouted urgently.

Lumen reached out and the great warrior slowly lowered his fists, but he stood his ground, barring any way to his charge.

"Hold!" Marcus called out again. "Accala's with us!"

"She is!" Julia insisted.

Next to Carbo, his official robes worn and bloodied, was my uncle Quintus. He looked as he ever did, though much older. The rest of the Viridians, though—their jaws had softened, their eyelashes grown. Still muscular and powerful, their bodies were changing. There was no doubt that although they were in some transitory stage, they were as much women now as they ever were men.

"Don't gawk," Carbo grumbled, his voice a higher register than before.

"Are you with us?" Quintus asked me. "After your recent performance in the Hyperborean tunnels, I'm not so sure. Or are you with these barbarians? Answer truly now, dear niece, and before the words leave your lips, remember how efficient I am at detecting the truth."

"I have allied myself with these aliens," I said. "But I am loyal to House Viridian. To the empire. As I have ever been. I swear it, Uncle."

"I don't trust her," Carbo snapped. "Not after she went crazy like that in the mines."

"And this Sertorian?" Quintus asked of Crassus.

"I have sworn loyalty to serve Accala and the Hyperboreans," Crassus said.

"It's true," I said. "He's risked his life for us several times over."

My uncle and Carbo took Marcus aside, and he quickly filled them in. When they were done, Uncle Quintus looked me up and down, his gaze lingering upon my deformed hand.

"Dear niece, you've earned us our weapons back and more. You've brought us a great prize, and that earns you the right to be heard and to have your petition considered," my uncle said. "Marcus and Carbo, execute the Sertorian, and then let's find cover so we can calculate our next move."

"No!" I barred the way to Crassus.

Now we had come to the test. I had to convince my uncle that we must rejoin him, that I was loyal and obedient, but at the same time keep things focused in the right direction and establish some authority to ensure the mission was carried out successfully. Crassus was important, not just to my own sense of self but also to this quest and its outcome. I was certain of it. I trusted Lumen and the queen's advice to keep Crassus.

"I take full responsibility for his conduct. I'm convinced he will be a useful asset."

"We all saw what transpired with Aquilinus. That was very brave," Quintus said, looking at my charred hand. "And you've created space, kept the enemy's teeth from our throat. We have time to mount a response now. But as for Crassus Sertorius . . ." he said, looking at the black-armored warrior.

Just then, Nervo signaled the alarm. Enemy war chariots were on approach, three miles behind us on the road.

"They must have pushed on through the night to deny us a lead," Carbo said.

"Maybe the bad weather cost them some men," I speculated.

Nervo used the telescopic lenses in his helmet to survey the teams. "The Talonites are reduced to six team members riding two chariots—the remnants of the non-Sertorian teams before all hell broke loose beneath the mountain," the charioteer said. "They're fresh as daisies. I'd bet they slept in comfortable tents and then turned the cameras off while they were ferried to the road by shuttle."

"Aquilinus can't help but cheat," Marcus said.

"The good news is the Blood Eagles look to have exited the field again," Nervo continued. "Aquilinus isn't using them, at least for now."

Thank the gods for that.

"We lost too much time waiting for Accala," Carbo said.

"No use crying over spilt milk," Uncle Quintus barked. "Accala's with us now. My Trojan horse has come home, haven't you?"

"Yes," I said.

"Then that's that, at least for now," my uncle said. "And you, Sertorian. You follow Accala's lead. Right now I'm not certain it's a bad thing having you close at hand. Perhaps Aquilinus will give something up to have you back, but if I see you take one step out of turn, you're gone. And by gone I mean I'll slit your throat myself. Understand?"

"I would expect nothing less," Crassus replied.

"Good. Let's move out. We'll resolve the matter of the Sertorian later. Remember, this isn't a game anymore. Make no mistake, this is the final battle of the war for possession of the empire. Aquilinus will be throwing everything he's got at us and more, but while we are in possession of this little gem," he said, pointing to Lumen, "we have a fighting chance. So stick together, guard the barbarian, and stay alive!"

And we were away again.

"I told you your uncle betrayed you, and I did not lie," Crassus said to me in a low whisper.

"If you want to repay me for saving your life, I suggest you shut your trap," I hissed. I didn't intend to make the mistake of trusting this poison-mouthed Sertorian. He clearly couldn't help himself from spreading lies and mischief, and I didn't intend to let him get away with even that much. Just the same, I didn't like the way my uncle talked about Lumen, the little gem he was in possession of, but Uncle Quintus didn't know Lumen, how else should he treat him?

Now we were a part of a team of eleven. Now we really did have a fighting chance. Marcus was beside me in his black armor, and Carbo headed up our team. My uncle and Nervo followed in the second chariot. I couldn't get used to seeing the Viridians in female breastplates, but they were still my countrymen, and the issue of their sex mattered to them, not me. All that mattered was that once more I served beneath the banner of the golden wolf, its head howling at the moon as it flickered in the wind. Just like that, I was a Viridian again, competing in the arena. Just like that, I was home. Fighting with the green and gold flying overhead, I could accomplish anything.

XLIII

As we headed toward the shining clouds ahead that marked our first challenge of the new tournament, I couldn't help sneaking glances at the strange modifications that the Viridian team had undergone.

"It's gene therapy," my uncle said when he noticed my curiosity. "They've been given slow-release estrogen capsules that lodge in the lining of the stomach. The amount gradually increases until the transformation is complete. They're losing muscle mass, getting weaker by the day"—he sighed—"but I must work with the tools before me."

"You might be surprised," Marcus said. "I've learned that women can be unexpectedly resourceful."

"It's an unfortunate turn of events," my uncle said quietly, "but one that we shall remedy when we emerge victorious from Aquilinus' circus."

It didn't even occur to him that he was insulting all women with his comments. In his mind, women were second-class citizens and always would be.

This was the first day of Aquilinus' new games, and we were all anxious to see whether he'd keep his word and make the games an even contest or simply continue to torture the contestants for entertainment.

"Work together and we survive," my uncle ordered. "We'll resolve any differences if we live out the day."

As we approached, the course's holographic decorations were projected from the Rota Fortuna above—the Grecian columns, the static clouds. Energy shields appeared on either side of the highway, directing our path. A cargo carrier descended, engines roaring as it dropped, hovering over the road ahead.

"On guard," Carbo said in a husky, feminine voice as the bay doors opened.

The carrier dropped a dozen large oblong orbs with pointed protuberances at either end onto the road. They hit and started spinning on a horizontal axis. Tops. They were giant spinning tops. They careened back and forth and when they struck the energy shields to either side of the highway sparks flew and the tops were sent shooting back onto the road at unpredictable angles, creating a dangerous obstacle course that we would have to navigate in order to escape to the road beyond.

"Slow on approach," Carbo ordered, "but don't dally. Remember the enemy is closing on our rear and I wager they won't have to suffer these obstacles."

Twenty yards out we were able to discern bodies strapped to the spinning orbs, one on each sphere, their arms and legs outstretched. They were naked—young and old, male and female.

Their identities were unknown, not because of the fast movement of the tops, but because each victim wore a hood over his or her face. Each spinning orb projected into the air above it a static holographic projection of a face with a plaque beneath it bearing a name.

"My sister. That's my sister's face," Tiberius Flavius Ambustus said.

"Yes it is." It was Julius Gemminus that spoke, his head flitting above us.

"She's in Galatia Smaragdus, safe with her mother," Tiberius said.

"I'm afraid to say that your mother has been raped and killed, and that your sister is most certainly a captive of Emperor Aquilinus' agents. These piteous souls strapped to the tops are mere props, Caninine audience members randomly selected from Avis Accipitridae and the Rota Fortuna—noble senators, prominent traders, the wealthy and powerful who were unable to accept the new emperor's ascension. They serve a valuable purpose today, though; they're stand-ins for your loved ones. Right now, live across the empire, those most dear to your little hearts have been seized. They stand by, their lives on the line if you choose to continue."

Titus Flavius Cursor proclaimed that they had his father; Carbo, his uncle; Nervo, his sister. My uncle spotted his wife, the prominent socialite Livia Viridius Publia. The rest remained silent, but I could see in their faces that Aquilinus knew their weak spots, had selected the people they would most hate to lose. I quickly scanned every projected face, terrified that I might find my father among them. But his face was absent along with any other I cared for. Each player had a top assigned to him except for Julia, Crassus, and me.

"Marcus?" I asked. "Do you recognize . . ."

"My nephew. My sister's boy," he said darkly.

This is what the empire could look forward to if Aquilinus won here. Endless suffering.

Julius Gemminus looked grim. "Do you bow now, or will you proceed and condemn those you love to die the most horrible of deaths?" he asked.

In answer, my uncle ordered the charge forward. Aquilinus' voice came booming from the clouds. "Was it Cicero who said that no man ever changed unless he be whipped to it? Well now, let's find out what it takes to make these Caninines see the light!"

Poetry filled the sky in fiery letters:

> When in this vain essay of words she sees Latinus fixed against her, and the serpent's maddening poison is sunk deep in her vitals and runs through and through her, then indeed, stung by infinite horrors, hapless and frenzied, she rages wildly through the endless city. As whilom a top flying under the twisted whipcord, which boys busy at their play drive circling wide round an empty hall, runs before the lash and spins in wide gyrations; the witless ungrown band hang wondering over it and admire the whirling boxwood; the strokes lend it life: with pace no slacker is she borne midway through towns and valiant nations.

It was from Virgil's *Aeneid*. A quote from *Aeneid* was the first thing I had thought of when I saw Aquilinus. It was all that programming aboard *Incitatus*. He fancied himself the new Aeneas, the founder of a new Rome, and wanted everyone else to think so too.

As we drove through the course, the two Talonite chariots reached us, but they seemed to be avoiding a direct attack. Instead they butted our chariot into the careening orbs. We struck against them again and again, and each time a face faded from the projection above, a life stolen by Aquilinus' game.

"My daughter!" I heard Tiberius Flavius Ambustus cry out. His sister's face was gone, replaced by a curly-haired girl.

"He's trying to break us," Carbo called out when we were midway through. "Expect no mercy, for he will grant none. Hold firm."

But the Flavian threw himself to his knees and begged for mercy, calling out that he would submit to Aquilinus' rule if he spared his daughter. Carbo's lasso whipped about the man, pulling him forward like a trussed-up boar. Before anyone could speak, the Viridian team leader's curved sword swung like a pendulum and took Tiberius' head off at the neck. "There's no mercy from Aquilinus!" he called out. "I'll kill any man or woman who is stupid enough to think otherwise! No one must break!"

When we finally reached the exit, I challenged Aquilinus, screaming at the sky for dramatic effect, knowing he was watching me along with trillions of my fellow citizens.

"You said you'd reinstate the tournament. These are only more of your game show contests, cheap deaths meant to break us, not real challenges. Where is the threat to the Talonites? What are their stakes? Where is the blood sport the arena demands?"

A lightning bolt shot down from the sky at the ground, forcing us to turn and move on. We sped along the road, still constrained by purple-tinged energy shields, the Talonites racing behind us.

"The audience isn't buying it," Julia announced. She was studying her armilla, observing trends on the vox populi. "Aquilinus' approval rating is falling as ours grows."

"We're paying a great price," my uncle spoke as we raced along, "but we're making progress. Aquilinus has made a tactical error. He has assumed that greed and fear are enough to steer the empire, but he's forgotten the citizens. He's shooting himself in the foot and can't even see it!"

"And more," Julia said. "Every few minutes, the vox populi is flickering out of existence. Aquilinus is trying to take it down."

"Can he?" I asked.

"No way. The second Aquilinus' people destroy the network, millions of anonymous Vulcaneum engineers are restoring backed-up versions."

"Like the ancient Hydra," I said. "Chop off one head and another reappears."

"Exactly," Julia said.

It was a dark day but a short one. The temper of every Caninine was frayed. I felt guilty. None of my loved ones had been killed. Had Aquilinus arranged it that way on purpose? To turn my new teammates against me?

We followed the road to the campsite Julius Gemminus had demarcated. My uncle called out for guarantees of safety once night fell but the cherubic face would provide none.

"My role is to give the emperor's divine imagination form. I cannot guarantee where his vision will lead, I can only act."

We set up camp in sight of this world's highest peak, Nova Olympus, the crown of the crescent mountains that encircled the ruins of Lupus Civitas, which lay out of sight. The peak pierced a ring of thin white clouds about three-quarters of the way up its height before terminating in the upper atmosphere.

There, Lumen said. *My mother.* Again his words conveyed a sense of overlapping images—my own mother, the goddess Minerva, the mountain ahead, a great jewel shining with ichor. There was no single word that could convey the meaning it had to him.

It looked so near, as if I could reach out and touch it, but the mountain was massive, dwarfing everything about it, and Carbo estimated that it would still be another two, maybe even three hundred miles before we would be able to catch a glimpse of whatever remained of the spires and towers of the old city's ruins.

"The other mountains fan out about the peak like low wings, forming a wide crescent," my uncle said. "A mile or two before that lie the ruins of Lupus Civitas."

"We don't have to climb that, do we?" Julia asked me.

I asked Lumen, and he assured me we only had to reach the base of the mountain to send him to safety.

Without the collegia's support craft, we had only the emergency survival shelters in the chariots. Carbo, in true Viridian style, insisted that we make our own tatty microcosm of a proper Roman camp with the resources we had at hand. My uncle occupied the command tent with Carbo, and the rest of us shared the remaining three tents, with Crassus stripped of his weapons and put into one of the men's tents with a survival blanket but denied his armor and its life-preserving heating element so that he could not flee in the night without fatal exposure to the cold. Crassus seemed all too happy to comply, not offering the least resistance, which made things easy but left me feeling a little uneasy. A serpent, coiled and waiting to strike, that's what Julia said, and that night, now that I was officially a Viridian again, I had difficulty getting that thought out of my mind.

My uncle ordered me to put Lumen and Concretus in the center of the camp. They didn't need shelter as we did, and Nervo was ordered to take first watch. I tried to convince my uncle and Carbo that they didn't need a guard, that they wouldn't go anywhere, but Uncle insisted the guard was for their protection, not to constrain them.

The sight of her helps, Lumen said. *She sings to both of us, can you hear her?*

Not only could I not hear the song, but Lumen's voice in my mind seemed to be weakening, but when I mentioned it to Lumen, he didn't reply. He seemed very inwardly drawn, mesmerized by the mountain on the horizon.

Concretus didn't seem to mind as long as he was by Lumen, and Lumen was fine as long as we were moving toward the mountain. But I minded. None of the Caninines actually tried to talk to Lumen. They just passed on instructions to me to pass on to him and Concretus, as if they were animals and I were the trainer. It seemed perfectly natural to Carbo and my uncle that they should risk their lives for us. We'd fought them earlier in the games and now they were prisoners, slaves who must come to heel and obey their Roman masters. A lifetime of habit, my countrymen would never see it any differently, I knew that. The old Accala couldn't have seen the injustice of it either, but now it stuck out like a sore thumb.

While we set up camp and prepared for the nexy day, I talked with Titus Flavius. I liked him. He was friendly, despite our dire circumstances, and he injected a light note into the serious Viridian atmosphere.

"The empire has teeth," he said. "It always has had and always will, I suppose."

"And a good thing too. A lion without teeth, an eagle without claws, what good would they be?" Carbo snapped.

"A sheep is still useful without killing parts," I said.

"Useful for eating," Carbo said. "Who wants to be eaten? You want to be a sheep, be a sheep. I'm no sheep."

"We all play our part," my uncle added. "We're all lambs to the slaughter, trust me. The only trick is: Can you be a wise sheep and move to the back of the flock when the farmer comes with his sharp knife?"

"What you did back there was a brave thing," Titus Flavius said to me, pointing to my hand. "I resented you before, but when I saw that, I knew you couldn't be with them."

"It is the will of the gods," Crassus said.

"You believe that?" Titus asked me. "That you're the champion of the gods?"

"No. At least not in the way you just meant it."

"Good. We Flavians are practical people. We tell it like we see it."

"They killed your father," I said. "I'm sorry."

"He was a good man. A pain in the ass, but a good man. I'll miss him. Could be we'll be reunited in Hades in the near future."

"Then tell us. Will we live these games out? What does your Flavian all-seeing wisdom have to say about that?" asked Pavo.

"To be honest, I don't know. I'm sick of the cold. It's all dry where we come from. All this ice sends fear into my bones, and I can't seem to shake it."

"That's a coward's talk," Pavo interjected.

"No, it's honest talk."

"The gods will judge who shall live or die," Crassus intoned.

"Shut the fuck up you piece of hawk shit," Pavo growled at Crassus. "What's all this talk of the gods. I thought your kind didn't believe in them." He turned to Titus. "What about you Flavians? You believe someone's looking out for us? The gods?"

"About the gods, I can't say for sure," Titus replied. "But I know a real Roman when I see one. Been so long I almost forgot what one looked like." He winked at me and smiled.

"She's no real Roman," Carbo sniped. "She's just a woman."

"So are you for the meantime," Marcus said. Carbo stared him down, but he seemed so ridiculous posturing and puffing himself up, trying to display how manly he was, that we couldn't help bursting out laughing.

Carbo had sent Caninus out on a skirmisher to scout out the Talonite position before we settled for the night, and he returned just as the sun began to set. Although the wind was low, it was still bone-numbingly cold.

"They've camped about four miles to the north, between two hills," Caninus said. "We're in no position to threaten them. They have a full camp—sentries, boundary markers, weather shield, sensors, command tent, you name it—but they're not close enough that they can cover the ground once the night weather sets in."

Nervo and Caninus made no attempt to hide their dislike of me. They were still put out about my killing of Mercurius and blamed me for Darius' death as well.

"Better not say too much," Nervo said as I approached. "Tomorrow she might decide she's a Hawk again and kill us."

"It was at Proconsul Severus' request," I stated.

"That you kill your own kind?" Nervo asked. "Your own blood?"

"In order to infiltrate the enemy, yes. I gave Darius the chance to let off, but he pressed the attack and so I had to defend myself and my mission."

"Shame he missed," Nervo said.

"Was it your mission to bring down the emperor?" Caninus asked. "It seems to us that if you hadn't gone berserk in the tunnels and exposed Aquilinus' mining operation, then he wouldn't have been forced to make his move on the stadium."

I had been wrong. I wasn't home. Not yet. Even now that they understood why I did what I did, they would never see me as one of them. Merely a woman, a traitor, a double agent.

"Don't mind them," Marcus said as he passed by. "It's a hard time for everyone."

"I'm sorry about Darius," I said to Nervo. He scoffed and bumped me as he walked away. Marcus' hand lashed out and slapped him on the side of the head.

"Apologize," he said simply.

Nervo was about to talk back, but when he saw the fire in Marcus' eyes, he swallowed hard and bowed his head. "I'm sorry," he mumbled. Marcus had reminded him of his duty but also shamed him.

But Caninus was not as easily convinced. "You won't get anything from me except a sharp blade," he said, his hand drifting to the knife at his side.

Marcus stepped in quickly, his hand gripping Caninus' wrist, stopping him from drawing his weapon.

"You'd think your own plight would give you some sympathy for others who face a difficult path," Marcus said. "Darius disobeyed a direct order when he attacked Accala. Mercurius failed in his duty. He chose to be an amateur, and it's as simple as that."

"Difficult path?" Nervo growled. "Accala-of-no-house lost no one today. Nor did her allies, the Sertorian and the Vulcaneum immune."

"Aquilinus did that on purpose and you know it," Marcus said. "He wants to split us, to get us arguing within the ranks. Tell me you're not so stupid that you can't see that?"

"Stop that," my uncle said, coming over. "Accala has made difficult choices under difficult circumstances. This is a challenging time—the empire is in flux, but there is also great opportunity. If we can hold together, we can come out of this stronger than ever, our great enemy felled and at our feet. Now stop squabbling and get on with your duties."

They bit their tongues but were none too happy about it. It seemed that they were looking for a scapegoat to make them feel better about the situation we were all in, and I was it. If I were a man, they would have looked at me differently. Still, now that my uncle had chastised them openly, perhaps a degree of common sense would stay them from seeking vengeance. We all needed each other now. Even Crassus. Every pair of hands could mean the difference between life and death.

"Come with me. Now that we have a moment, I need you to debrief me. Tell me your version of events," Quintus said to me. "Tell me everything you know about these Hyperboreans, and then we'll see what can be done."

What could be done for whom? I was not sure what he meant, but I suddenly felt uneasy, as I followed my uncle into the command tent.

Quintus had taken a seat in a simple chair behind a collapsible desk, his muddied and bloodstained robes spilling from his arms as he surveyed a holographic map of the terrain—the mountains and tundra that lay between our current position and the ruins of the old city. A red blip flashed, just before the last, vast tundra opened out on the way to the crescent mountains. My uncle quickly shut down the map with a wave of his hand. He looked at home, easily able to fit back into his old life as a military field commander, my father's comrade-in-arms.

I told him what he wanted to hear, the same thing I'd told Julia. Something told me not to talk about the connection between Lumen and Aulus. It was still too close, too personal.

"So these Hyperboreans, they believe that when they reach the mountain beyond the ruins of Lupus Civitas, they'll be free?"

"Yes. Their queen lies in wait," I explained. "She can transport them."

"A ship? They have a ship?"

"Of sorts," I said. "Lumen explained it to me. They'll transform into energy and travel far from here. Back to their home."

"With the gods?"

"I don't know," I said. "That's what Mother said. As long as it's far away from here, and no one can possess the ambrosia, what does it matter? Mother was right: For the good of the empire, the ichor must go."

My uncle hung his head when he heard me talk of my mother and her efforts to aid the Hyperboreans. "She had her heart in the right place," he said, "but your mother was always so headstrong, too willing to commit to her research without thinking of consequences."

"She tried to warn you," I said.

"Yes, yes, but this talk of the gods and this nonsense treaty with the aliens. It's all tales designed to get an impressionable young mind to carry out her plan, but things have changed. She knew only the Accala of two years ago. How much have you matured since then? How much have you grown through your ordeals? You don't need to hear children's stories, nor should you feel obliged to honor any hasty treaties your mother struck."

"What do you mean?" I asked. "We must transport the Hyperboreans to safety. They saved my life. I've sworn to aid them. It's the decent thing to do."

"That's part of the problem," my uncle said. "We seemed to have an understanding based on mutual need. Even you going off plan, I understood. That Accala was angry, filled with rage, she wanted her revenge, and in a drug-addled state she became a wolf that tore out her enemy's throat, her I understood. But you've changed. This new Accala, I wonder at her loyalty. You bring a Sertorian into our midst, treat him like one of us, you give commands without thinking of your superiors, and now you're making treaties with alien powers and insisting that I honor them. You've been out on your own for too long. You have much to prove if you wish to reclaim your place within the family fold."

I swallowed hard. It was not easy coming back to rein after my recent adventure, but I'd been raised a Viridian, and if I wished to be one of them again, then I had to learn to like the bridle of military discipline. Pushing back wouldn't get me anywhere. I had to give him the space to make the right decision. I knew he would.

"I understand, Uncle, and I am rightfully admonished," I said, bowing my head.

"Do you not wish to resolve this before they execute your father? Aquilinus is saving him to use as leverage, to bend you to his will. Can't you see that? Don't you want to do what's right by him? You don't want to go against me and bring more dishonor to your house, do you?"

"Of course not."

"You did swear loyalty to me and to your team, didn't you? That was a heartfelt oath, wasn't it?"

"Of course," I said at once. "You're right that I veered off the path once, for revenge, but I wasn't myself. Aside from that, my every action has been driven by loyalty to my house, as is my request that you honor my mother's wishes and help transport Lumen to safety."

"That's more like it. Good girl. Remember, no man, or woman, for that matter, can serve two masters. Remember where your home is, who your family are. Now go. Let me sleep on it. I'll give your words due consideration, you know I will."

He signaled to someone behind me. It was Carbo.

"I seek your leave to execute the Sertorian," Carbo said to my uncle. "He's without weapons or armor. We can do it quickly, and in the morning we'll set up a makeshift crucifix to hang him on as a warning to the other Sertorians."

"He has proved his worth so far, and we're going to need every hand we can get," I said quickly to my uncle. "He still has some role to play in this. I can feel it. He will aid us. You must spare him."

"Don't risk it," Carbo said. "Now is the time, while he's weak. Don't be misled by foolish sentiment."

"Now, now, Carbo. We need not be so fierce," my uncle said. "We must all work together to triumph. Accala has pledged her loyalty to us, let us show some leniency in return. Let us ensure that unity is the watchword. Yes?"

"Of course, Proconsul," Carbo snapped. He was a military animal. There was an unquestioning chain of command. Unfortunately, I was below him on the chain, so I couldn't expect to have as much influence as I'd like, now or in the future, but as long as I could keep my uncle on side, I could manage Carbo.

"Thank you, Uncle," I said. "When this is all over, I will kiss your feet."

"When this is all over, we will all be heroes, assuming we can survive each other. Carbo, you're dismissed." The tribune turned sharply, his cheeks red, barely containing his anger.

"Accala, you must give him some latitude," my uncle said. "The changes he's undergoing. He can be prone to hysteria. I'm sure you understand how it is."

"'Hysteria' is the word men use to describe women when they get angry for having all their choices stripped away from them unjustly."

"What choice do any of us have? We must play our roles to their conclusion. Now go and play yours. Remember what I have said."

As I left, I passed Julia. "I'm next," she said as she entered the tent.

As I was wondering what my uncle would ask her, I was suddenly struck from behind. Looking up, I saw Carbo standing over me, fists clenched.

"You've gone over to the barbarians, I know it, and the second you act in their interests over ours, I'll be there to steal your life. And next time you speak against me to Proconsul Severus, I'll rip your tongue out of your mouth and see you flogged. Your uncle commands me, but I command you. This is no longer a game, it's a military operation. You know what's at stake. We can no longer afford your chaotic antics. The crooked nail is either ripped out or hammered down. Remember that."

I picked myself up and brushed the snow from my armor. Carbo did not scare me. Sometimes you must suffer fools in order to reach a goal in everyone's best interests. I could make this work, play my part as a loyal Viridian as well as carry out my mother's mission. The Hyperboreans must leave this world with their ichor. I felt like an ancient charioteer trying to rein in a team of horses, to get them to all pull in the same direction at the same time. I could make this work. I had to.

It was dark, and everyone who was not on duty was getting whatever rest they could. I passed by Lumen and tried to talk with him, but he did not respond and I couldn't find the song; it had reverted to an unintelligible buzzing. When I tried to come close, Concretus loomed menacingly. I left them and crawled into the shelter. I lay back into the insulated sleeping bag and turned about trying to find a modicum of comfort. Just Julia and me to share the tent, and until she finished with my uncle, I was alone.

Surrounded by the sound of the whipping wind, I felt a stirring I thought had been eradicated from my system once and for all—a hunger for ambrosia. My burned hand tingled and ached, and I longed for the relief and healing ambrosia would bring. To be free from fear and doubt, to be powerful and certain. The craving built as I lay there, becoming stronger and stronger. Was the process I underwent at the hands of the Hyperboreans impermanent? Did Crassus feel this hunger too? I had to try to get through to Lumen in the morning, reestablish our connection. It shouldn't be difficult, he was right there. I had to do something to stave off the maddening craving. I wandered out of my tent and stumbled right into Marcus. He was dressed in robes, carrying a lantern.

"Can I speak to you a moment? In my tent," I said.

"Yes, I was just coming to speak to you."

We stepped inside the shelter and sat down on the hard ground.

"What did you want to talk about?" I asked.

"I'm not going to ask what went on between you and your uncle, but I saw Carbo strike you."

"You wanted to see if I was all right? It was nothing."

"I know you're strong. I just wanted to give you some advice. That's all."

"One more lesson?" I asked.

"In a sense. I've played a hand in changing the shape of the empire once before, when I had to take a stand against the emperor. When you find yourself in that situation, it's important to remember that you're not acting for your family, or even yourself. You're in a new arena; you're acting on behalf of the empire and the gods. Sometimes, in order to play the part that Fate demands of you, it is necessary to cut away other ties."

"You're saying I should not honor my family?"

"Of course not. You are Viridian and now you are back among your own people—that must be a great relief. But remember, it was you who called out Aquilinus and challenged him when the rest of us were scuttling about trying to survive. The gods gave you the insight to act at the right time in the right way. As you started this, so it must be you that finishes it. That is Fate. What I'm saying is that no one should deny you the right to see things through to the end. The justice of the gods must be carried out and can't be hijacked by mortal demands. You'll know what I'm talking about when the time comes, and when it does, don't be distracted by the idea of pleasing others or holding on to an idea of who you think you should be. Remember—nothing must stop the arrow from striking home, nothing must divert its path."

"I thank you. For that and for all you have given me." I took his hand in mine. "You're trembling," I said. "That's not like you."

"I'm not afraid of dying. I'm a gladiator and I've been here before. In the arena. With someone I cared about very much."

"Amphiara," I whispered, but he shook his head. He was not talking about his long lost love, but himself and me.

"You know about her," he said. "I suppose everyone does, though I never speak of it. What happened then, I lost a part of myself. I didn't think anything could hurt me like that again. You're not like her at all—you look, move, speak differently, but you share her spirit. I saw what you could be, poured so much of myself into you during training so you'd never choose the easy way, never be weak. Seeing her spirit in you, it's what made me want to protect you back in the Colosseum, to not let you go. But then I asked myself, What would Amphiara be without her fire? What would Accala be? You might as well be dead. Sometimes pain and suffering is the only path worth taking if it forges us into the person we are meant to be."

"You put your heart into me," I said, squeezing his hand.

"I thought my heart was dead, but when I heard that you'd joined their team, when I saw you in the parade . . ."

"I'm so sorry. I'm the one who must beg forgiveness. Ungrateful, spoiled, a traitor to my house—I felt all those things. They did things to me on the voyage over, and the ambrosia. It . . ."

"There's no need to explain. You weren't yourself. You are now. Nothing more needs to be said. Now it's like I've been repaired, made whole again."

"I'm glad one of us has," I said, holding up my ugly claw of a right hand.

He took it in his hand, cradling it gently. "That doesn't matter," he said. "Beauty is not skin deep, it's the soul below that counts."

My heart was racing, my cheeks burning. He needed me, and the gods only knew that I needed someone with me that night, and not just to take away the pain of the ambrosia withdrawal. I needed his warmth. I needed to feel loved.

"When I was in the tunnels with the Hyperboreans, I had time to think. I saw so many things clearly for the first time. I saw why you never took a wife or consorted with the noble ladies who are always hanging around the arena."

He looked down at the floor, embarrassed.

"The only way for a gladiator, even a trainer, to be with a noblewoman is as a gigolo, a dalliance . . ."

"You're not my trainer anymore," I said, turning down the light on the lantern until it gave off nothing but a dull glow.

I put my hand on his scarred face, the scars I gave him in the arena in Rome, and he turned away.

"I'm too old," he said. "You need a younger man."

"A fool like Caninus?" I asked. I turned his face back to mine and gave him the gentlest of kisses, the wing of a wren fluttering past his cheek, asking if he would return my affection.

"I can't," Marcus said.

"Because of Amphiara?"

"No. Look at me, I'm a joke. Bloody potatoes growing from my chest."

"What was all that you said about appearances not being important?"

"It's not just that. I passed under the yoke. Everyone saw. I'm no longer fit to be called a man anymore."

"You believe that old wives' tale?" I asked him.

"They took my virtus, stole my manhood. How can you wish to lie with a man so disgraced?"

I reached down, into his robes.

"Your manhood feels perfectly intact to me."

I leaned in and kissed him, and his lips pressed hard against mine. His kiss was passionate, his embrace like iron.

"I thought I'd lost you," he said and kissed me again.

The heat of our love dispelled the cold. It was like a torrent, a blessing, washing away my night with Crassus. We took comfort in each other's bodies, an earthy connection, no electric passion like with Crassus but rather a bliss, a forgetting, an absolution.

After he fell asleep I lay beside Marcus, studying his body in the dim lantern light. My ambrosia hunger was gone. Lying with Marcus was a deep, profound experience. I struggled to define what it meant to me and in the end decided that it made me feel like an adult. Up until that night I'd felt, while not a child, that I'd been struggling to keep my head above water in an adult world. When I challenged Aquilinus, something changed. The others treated me with a newfound respect, they saw me as someone worthy of looking up to, but after a night with Marcus I felt like I'd grown up to fill out my own body. My feelings for Marcus made me larger, like the inside of a basilica, and that feeling had dispelled what lingered of the hunger for ambrosia, at least for the time being.

His body was lean and hard, covered with scars accumulated over a lifetime, and now bulging in places with vegetables, the inflictions of another mad emperor. I traced the white lines of old scars with my finger. Some of them were jagged, some thin and straight, some of them wavy like the line of a river drawn on a map. There was a smooth curve ending in a cluster like an ion blast wound, which I knew from study was the ball scythe of the old-style gladiators—a slicing cut followed by a powerful blunt-force impact. I loved these lines. Each one had forged him into the man he was today, each one had tested his body and mind, his willingness to never give in.

* * *

WHEN I WOKE IT was still dark. Marcus had gone back to his tent, and Julia was sleeping beside me. I gently woke her and asked how things had gone with my uncle.

"We have our disagreements," she said, "but nothing that can't be resolved."

"You trust him, don't you? To do the right thing and help the Hyperboreans?"

"I trust him to do the right things for the empire and I trust him to honor his deal with the collegia. Don't worry; he's under a lot of pressure, but he'll come through. Just wait and see, he'll make sure the ambrosia is taken off the table altogether. Now get some sleep."

"Yes, he's my uncle. I trust him too and I wanted to thank you for trusting in me," I said. "And to tell you something." I shared the truth about the Hyperboreans, about Aulus and Lumen. "What do you think?" I asked her when I was done.

"I think that I was right."

"About what?"

"That your brother *was* the ichor."

"I suppose you were," I said.

My brother. That was how I'd described Lumen to Julia and that was how I'd come to think of him. The more distant he became, the more it occurred to me that I might lose him, and the thought of my brother leaving me again was disquieting.

"See, never knock a lateral thinker. We mechanics have our own philosophy; we don't need any fancy academy education."

"I'll admit I thought you'd have a more substantial insight to contribute."

"Well, it's strange all right, but this mission has been strange from the get-go." She held up her crystal hand. "I lost a hand and the Hyperboreans gave me a new one. If it's a gift from the gods, then I'll take it. I can tell you one thing. From the minute we met I could see you were falling into some terrible nightmare. Since you met this little barbarian you're heading in a different direction. This new Accala is a woman whose company I can tolerate! This whole mission is madness, and we're probably all gonna die, but you know what? Since I saw you on the cliff edge, putting your hand in the fire, I see things changing. I thought you were mad at the time but it's definitely set something in motion. We're on the right track and there's a slim chance we'll make something great, just like building a prototype engine. It's a delicate thing and it'll probably fall apart before we can get it to run at all."

"Then why keep going?"

"Because sometimes, if you take the right risks at the right time, it all works out and you end up creating something new that no one's ever seen before. Is that substantial enough for you?"

"You're an optimist. I only just spotted it now," I said. "That's why you hang in there with me. A gods-be-damned optimist."

"Don't tell anyone else. Now shut up and let me get some sleep."

Dawn was hours away, and knowing Marcus and Julia were firm allies gave me some inner peace. Just when I was drifting off, a great commotion started up in the camp. My teammates were scrambling into position, arms in hand.

"We're under attack!" I heard Caninus yell.

My hand flew to Orbis. Lumen and Concretus came rushing over to my side as I leaped out of the tent.

"Quickly!" Carbo ordered. "Send the alien to cover on the rise behind us. We'll defend him on the low ground."

"That's a good idea, go quickly," I said to Lumen.

Concretus picked him up in one swoop and moved to the rear as the others fell into place, forming a defensive arc.

"False alarm," Caninus said. "Some Hyperborean workers were wandering about out there. They must have tripped the perimeter alarm."

I could sense that Lumen had something urgent to tell me, but I still couldn't hear his voice. I called him to me, trying to remember the knack of mind-to-mind communication. He started forward ahead of Concretus when suddenly the icy ground beneath the Hyperborean warrior fell away. Concretus plummeted into the darkness of a deep crevasse then I heard the sound of a body hitting running water. An underground river. Lumen tried to rush after him, but I quickly gripped his wrist and held him back.

"We have to rescue him," I said.

"We can't," Pavo explained. "We have to move forward to avoid the enemy. That river is running right back in their direction. He's gone."

"Just as well it wasn't one of us," Carbo added without the slightest note of sympathy.

A sonic mine. We were not under attack, there were no incoming chariots, but there was the telltale blast pattern on the ice shelf where it fell away. This was an ambush—Carbo's work.

I led Lumen away, back toward my shelter. He came willingly, without complaint.

"Can you sense Concretus? Is he alive?" I asked Lumen.

But there was no answer. For now, at least, it seemed I was Lumen's only protector. What could I say to Marcus? That I thought Carbo just ambushed Concretus? It'd split the group at once, splinter us when we most needed to be together for survival. And I couldn't be sure; maybe the crevasse formed naturally or maybe it was an ancient land mine, but it didn't seem likely. I'd talk to my uncle when I got the chance to speak to him alone. He would believe me, he'd take action to see that Carbo didn't endanger the mission. Family looked out for family.

XLIV

THE NEXT MORNING WE packed up camp and headed out on the highway. Aquilinus' next challenge was marked by a shining icon in the distance and shield walls prevented us from leaving the road. Once again, the Talonites appeared behind us, driving us forward. Still no sign of the Blood Eagles. I still couldn't be sure that what happened the night before wasn't an accident—the gods knew that Fate had stolen enough lives since this tournament began. I still needed to speak to my uncle alone as soon as the opportunity presented itself. I was even more concerned about my inability to communicate with Lumen. What had changed in me that now the song had reverted to a buzzing hum, no more mind-to-mind transmission? I tried to comfort him, to tell him that I was there for him, even without Concretus I'd allow no harm to come to him.

"Accala, you have the attention of the mob," my uncle said as we neared the challenge. "Your words and actions must keep them focused on the emperor's promise of reinstating the real tournament. They're impatient, demanding, and we must fan those flames until they start to burn Aquilinus."

Julius Gemminus directed us off the highway and onto a high plateau banked by steep ledges. He ordered that we split into separate groups designated by house. The Viridian chariot also held Lumen and Crassus, leaving Marcus to head up the remaining chariot and Titus Cursor to pilot a skirmisher. As soon as we'd complied the shield walls generated from above suddenly appeared and precisely cut the space between our vehicles, separating our party into three lots. These shield walls were nonlethal, no electric charge; they were just meant to herd us in the direction of Aquilinus' choosing. We were driven into three corridors that ran parallel. We traveled like that for a mile before we reached the game zone.

Spherae hovered around the field but Aquilinus had learned his lesson and none came near enough for Julia to seize control of them.

Ahead of each of the three pathways was a unique, oddly shaped course, also demarcated by the energy fields.

The Calpurnian course comprised staggered cubes, four in all, each one connected by a narrow passage. Titus Flavius Cursor's course was a large domed sphere.

And ours, the one intended for the Golden Wolves, was a long, narrow channel, only seven feet or so across.

All the paths resumed on the other side of each course, running out to the open air and the triumphal arch beyond marking the exit.

"Emperor Aquilinus is asking you a question." Julius Gemminus beamed. "He let go of the gods, cut away the weakness in his own house, did not let the death of his family and friends deter him from seeking the truth, and in the end, when he was beaten and tormented by his enemies, he endured. He understood that you must let go of all attachments if you seek to ascend to divinity. Today you will be tested to your limits. You've nothing left but yourselves. You are where Aquilinus the man himself once stood. How much punishment will you endure before you accept the wisdom he is trying to impart? There are no gods, no force that can hold back death while we travel the mortal realm. Death will claim you as it claimed your gods, your allies, your families. Now is the time to cast off mortality and join with Aquilinus."

He wasn't just asking us a question. He was asking a question of the whole empire: How far will you let me push before you push back? Can I just swoop in and take it all without a word being spoken?

As Julius Gemminus made his speech, in the sky above us, large black cargo carriers dropped in. They took up position above us.

"The fustuarium supplicium—the punishment of cudgeling—was originally a legion punishment for disobedience, cowardice, or the commission of a serious crime," Julius Gemminus announced. "The perpetrator would run through a course between two rows of men who would beat him with cudgels, and if he lived he was considered to have paid for his crime. From that the sport of the obstacle gauntlet arose."

The editor's voice grew excited as he continued, "Let's watch these dogs run for us. Let's whittle them down and see if there's any sense left in them, any iota of wisdom that will lead them to the logical conclusion—that they can't win, that they must join with us or be trammeled into the earth as we rush to ascend."

"Contest!" I called out. "Where is the contest we were promised? Where are the true games?"

Laughter boomed from the sky. "You want conflict? Then choose. Face your enemies and prove your worth, or face the mystery obstacles."

Now the Talonite teams appeared, dropped in behind us. The sounds of war horns and drums boomed out from the sphera in the air above us. The enemy charged forward, coming in for the kill. They had advanced weapons loaded up on the front of their vehicles—ion blasters that fired repeatedly, shattering the ground ahead of them.

"Minerva, he's mad as a March hare," my uncle said. "If we make a stand, we'll be dead in seconds." Carbo quickly ordered us forward, to face whatever awaited us in the course ahead.

The thin ion bolts caught us, a horizontal hailstorm of energy. It was like being pierced by dozens of hot needles, narrow holes punched right through our bodies. We were hit again and again, but no one fell. They were using advanced targeting systems; they hit arms, shoulders, legs only, no fatal wounds to the head or heart. One seared the back of my hand, another hit Julia again and again, targeting her hand, but the hand strangely seemed to absorb the energy. They were draining us, wearing us down for what lay ahead.

We rushed down the narrow corridors, the Talonites hot on our tails. Just as we were about to enter the oddly shaped zones, our pursuers backed off and new shields appeared, covering the way behind us, sealing us in. Carbo called a full stop, and we quickly looked back and forth at one another through the transparent shields that separated us, wondering what would come next. Now the carriers used force field beams to lower their cargo, large black shipping containers, into each of the three corridors behind us. They passed effortlessly through the shields before coming to rest.

I heard howling at first, and then new pursuers rushed into the narrow way behind us, taking the place of the Talonites. Wolves. Dozens and dozens of large gray wolves, each the size of a fully grown man, came rushing in. Maddened, starving, they howled, streaming toward us along the channel, hungry for our blood. There was no way to turn around, to bring the chariots' weapons to bear. Forward was the only way. "Charge!" Carbo ordered.

The chariot was fast, but the wolves seemed unnaturally fast and able to keep up.

As we raced, all about us on the transparent shield walls that contained our course were projected the fates of the other teams. Marcus Calpurnius faced a different enemy: Large ravens with shining yellow eyes streamed into each of the square segments he had to race through. The monstrous birds swarmed him, plucking not at his eyes and face but pulling at the vegetables that hung from his breastplate, ripping and tearing. Marcus couldn't stop every beak and claw, and with the wounds he already suffered, he would soon die of blood loss.

Titus Flavius Cursor suffered a different fate. Sparrows with razor-sharp silver beaks surged in, thousands of them, filling the dome, crashing into one another, fluttering in a chaotic pathway, slicing Titus' skin again and again. He was going to be overwhelmed in seconds, except suddenly he rose above the flock, his small implanted wings flapping desperately, carrying him just above the swarm for a few seconds before the feeble wings tired and he sank back down into the flurry of silvered beaks.

This would be death by a thousand cuts—slow murder at the hands of our house emblems. Ripped apart by wolves, eaten by ravens, shredded by sparrows.

"Look out!" I called. Ahead, as we approached the exit, the way narrowed, and there was no way for the chariot to pass on level ground. Nervo yelled for us to hang on and then he tilted the craft. We all went skittering across, bracing ourselves as we hit the bottleneck. The chariot jammed.

"I'm going to have to turn it on its side to get it through. Everyone up!"

We climbed for our lives, taking up position on the high ground as the wolves hit. Caninus, Carbo, and I held them back while the others helped free the chariot so Nervo could power us clear. Except the wolves were coming in thick and fast, fifty, maybe more of them, a fast-moving blitz of teeth and fur, yellow eyes crazed with whatever process Aquilinus had put them through before sending them on to us. We took bite after bite, sharp teeth rending flesh. Nervo finally got our craft moving, but we were about to be overwhelmed. We would die, crushed by the pressure of the canine bodies, if not their fangs.

A trumpet blared, and suddenly a field appeared between us and the wolves. The teeth clashed against an invisible wall, keeping them from our throats.

"Stop! Stop!" Julius Gemminus called out. "All of you! Listen!"

I looked around. Marcus was on the ground, defending the final gate of his course, close to the exit. But in the spherical run, Titus Flavius was on his knees. An energy field now separated him from the sparrows, who flew above his bleeding body. He was broken, haggard; his head hung.

"Say it again," Aquilinus' voice boomed from the sky. "Say it louder so they can all hear."

There was a pause and then, "Mercy," Titus mumbled, but now there was a sphera above him, amplifying his words, cleaning up the sound so that there was no doubt that we were hearing a capitulation of the worst kind. I couldn't believe my ears. The last of his team. The father had died yesterday at the hands of Aquilinus' spinning tops. Now the son had had enough; he had hit his limit and couldn't go on. I felt it. I wanted to give in too, but I couldn't. I'd given my life to a higher cause, for something bigger than myself. No matter what Aquilinus took, he couldn't take the light at the heart of me, the numinous spark that was left when everything was stripped away.

"Do you accept me as your emperor?" Aquilinus asked. "Speak clearly and you shall be spared, raised up above others, even. The child who repents, having learned his lesson, is loved by the father even more than those who saw the light without suffering."

"If you will stop this," Titus said weakly.

"Then I will spare not only you but also your house. Offer up your prayers to me, and I shall grant them. Worship me with a sincere heart, and you may share in my divinity."

Titus slowly straightened up, raising his head, and then shook it with as much strength as he could muster.

"I didn't say anything. I was just coughing up some feathers that were stuck in my throat," he said, "but if you like I'll say something now. One man may bow to another. There is no shame in the stronger man defeating the weaker, the faster beating the slower, but a man is still only a man. When the emperor leads a triumph through Rome, the one who holds the laurel wreath above his head whispers to him that he is mortal, that he will die. It's a good idea. Keeps rulers from going crazy. I bet you don't have a guy like that, whispering the truth to you."

"Speak again!" Aquilinus boomed. "Speak again and quickly, or my fleet will burn your homeworld to the ground. A whole world wreathed in nuclear fire. Speak words that will assure your good fortune, not spell the doom of your people."

"Do what you will. We Flavians are not religious. I'm not sure I even believe in the gods, but we call it how we see it. I will never call you or any other living emperor a god. No self-respecting Flavian would. Shit, and it's just not our way, it's positively un-Roman."

The sky was filled with upturned thumbs. The crowd wanted to spare him. They admired his courage. Aquilinus was learning that being emperor wasn't all about getting what you wanted, that the citizens of the empire were always more powerful than any ruler or coalition of houses when they spoke with a single voice.

The fields kept us trapped, helpless to do anything but watch as the sky was cleared of constellations of thumbs, the people's voice erased as the sparrows rushed in, the whole dome filling with them, but somehow the cameras managed to get in and capture the action as the small creatures tore at Titus' body. Still, the Flavian's voice came through, taunting Aquilinus. "I've been cold ever since I came to this world. I'll take these warm feathers with me to the underworld." Brave Titus Flavius Cursor! The sparrows swarmed and soon only bloody bones remained.

Aquilinus, so used to having his followers heap praise upon him, didn't know how to placate an audience, couldn't judge when to hold back punishment and when the crowd would approve to see it delivered. He'd been a tyrant for too long to change now.

"The whole empire's talking about Titus Cursor's bravery," Julia said. "About his choice of a noble death over tyranny."

"Titus pushed him too far," Pavo said warily, "and now Aquilinus has got nothing to lose. He's going to kill us all."

"No," Crassus said. "Your Flavian ally has bought you all your lives. Aquilinus' advisers will be counseling him as we speak. His popularity is plummeting. He could release the wolves and ravens and kill us all, but he won't. He can't if he wants to win the crowd back."

"And he won't risk harming the barbarian boy," my uncle said gruffly. He had a firm grip on Lumen's wrist.

Just as Crassus predicted, the force fields constraining the deadly animals remained in place, allowing us to exit the course. Once we were clear, the walls became electrified and closed on the animals, killing them all in an instant.

Suddenly Aquilinus' celestial hologram—clouds and pillars, giant disapproving eyes looking down on us—flickered and vanished. Only Julius Gemminus' lonely head remained, zipping about with a confused expression.

"Ah, just a moment friends, we'll be moving things along in a moment," he said nervously.

"Julia?" I asked.

She was already at her armilla, running a power line out to her hand, desperately coding, issuing instructions, patching digital fires. "The collegia are fighting him, he's had teams seeking out the location of our bases, taking out entire cities to try to stop them from protecting the integrity of the vox populi system."

"Can he do it?" my uncle asked.

"We've had a long time to prepare for an attack," Julia said, more than a hint of pride in her voice. "We've got the entire forum mirrored in each house's primary systems. Every single data station, every shipboard computer contains the vox populi seed files, and the big secret is that every armilla is a node that can help reseed those files. Aquilinus could burn the empire to the ground trying to shut it down, but the vox populi and all the data it contains will just keep on keeping on."

Aquilinus appeared suddenly, filling up the space between heaven and earth—giant Jupiter draped in imperial toga, crackling lightning bolt in hand.

"It seems the collegia have failed," my uncle said.

"Don't be so quick to judge," Julia retorted. "The vox populi is still running and my colleagues in the Vulcaneum are taking the fight to the Sertorian data shapers, destroying their systems while they attack ours. Trust me, that giant god form avatar is Aquilinus' last-ditch effort to try to appear relevant."

"It sounds like we're gaining support," I said. "Let's make sure we stay alive long enough to make use of it!"

"Now I shall give my verdict!" Aquilinus boomed. "These nine have proved to be both unrepentant and unworthy of my divine inheritance. According to the newly revised Twelve Tables of Roman Law, they are guilty of high treason for worshipping dead gods, leading others to indulge in this illusion, refusing to honor the image of the emperor by libations and incense, and refusing to worship Aquilinus in his divine form and participate in the newly established imperial cult of the Blood Eagles. Ever generous, I offer you this one last chance. Will any of you pray to me for mercy and recant your illusions? Before the appropriate punishments are meted out?"

We were beaten down, weak, but we were defiant to the last. Even Carbo, who saw me as an enemy, a rival—we were as one now. We stood there, bleeding and exhausted, our unyielding eyes locking—no give, no weakness. Aquilinus was a fool to even ask. These remaining nine were strong to the last.

Julius Gemminus appeared with a holographic scroll before him, laying out our fate.

"Tomorrow, the members of the so-called Caninine Alliance will be dragged into the ruins of the old arena of Lupus Civitas for the most spectacular damnatio ad bestias event in the history of the empire. They shall be blindfolded, as they are unworthy of the light, and then crucified at low height, wrapped in the skins or draped in the feathers of their house emblems, and then slowly devoured by beasts. A special noon event will be held for Accala Viridius. In light of the bull chief having died in the field, an alternate barbarian suitor will be found for her or perhaps even a human paramour appropriately attired as a mock Hyperborean"—Julius Gemminus stuttered, his showmanship was faltering— "to . . . to consummate the emperor's victory. . . ." Aquilinus had a knife at his throat; Gemminus didn't want to be reading this out. I didn't blame him. Caligula had had the editor of his gladiatorial shows and beast baitings beaten with chains in his presence for several successive days, and would not kill him until he was disgusted at the stench of the man's putrefied brain. That's what happened to people who went against mad emperors.

"Then, finally, the Blood Eagles will descend to the sacred field to steal the last breath of life from these dogs. Their divine judgment will ripple throughout the empire. Each death will signal the bombing of a Viridian, Calpurnian, and Flavian world—an empirewide fire to cauterize the wound these rebels have caused with their disobedience."

"You cannot crucify us!" Carbo cried out. "We are citizens of Rome!"

Aquilinus' eyes flashed lightning. "In my empire, citizenry is acquired through obedience. Those who do not obey are no longer citizens. They are no better than beasts, rabid dogs that cannot be controlled, and shall be treated as such."

"Now we find out," I said. "We see which side the people of the empire have backed. Will they stand for us, against him?"

The mob wanted catharsis, a real contest, not this ideological horror show. Aquilinus was going to have to shift into damage control to stop the popularity drain. He had to triumph on all fronts—the propaganda war with the people of Rome, this tournament, as well as the efforts behind the scenes to claim Lumen and the raw ingredient of ambrosia—if he was going to keep his throne at all. But the sky wasn't filled with downturned thumbs, no thumbs-up, either. There was nothing. This didn't bode well.

"Julia?" I asked.

"What do the people say?" Uncle Quintus demanded.

"Wait. There's a fresh attack on the vox populi. The Sertorians are trying to stop a news update from getting out. It's the people, they're rioting," Julia said, tapping at her armilla. "All over the empire, they're taking to the streets, they're bombing Sertorian buildings, burning Sertorian ships. They're fighting back! His attack on the vox populi, the way we've been treated—the people are rebelling, striking out at Aquilinus."

"He will bend, just wait and see," Crassus said. "He knows he has to appease the mob now if he wants to have a chance at keeping the throne. His advisers will be telling him he has to do now what he should have done before. Give us an even chance at winning the games. No punishments rigged in the Sertorians' favor."

"Right," Julia confirmed. "Just now he's posted an empirewide transmission, ordering them to tune back in to the games. He's promised them that he'll make an announcement that will satisfy them and bring peace to the empire."

Suddenly the vox populi respawned itself, and the sky was filled with upturned thumbs demanding our survival.

"Yes!" Julia exclaimed. "They're with us!"

Emperor Aquilinus' game show was over. So what now? Would he honor his wager to finish the games?

"There's been some misunderstanding," Aquilinus' voice boomed out. "Many have not understood the importance of the work taking place here, but we will ensure that they are satisfied with the final arena, won't we, Julius Gemminus?"

"Oh, yes, Imperator," the small head agreed. "They will be ecstatic."

"An arena spectacular to satisfy their desire for blood and sand?"

Julius Gemminus flitted about the sky, his forced grin wider than ever. "Oh, my emperor, I believe I can give you all that you ask for and more. A true blood-and-sand arena spectacular, an end to the games that will sate everyone's appetites—in the crumbling arena of the ruined Viridian city of Lupus Civitas, in the shadow of this world's tallest peak—Wolves and Ravens toe to toe against your righteous gladiators, Imperator. Only give me tonight, I beg you. I'll need time to sculpt my greatest work."

"You shall have it," the giant emperor said, feigning graciousness. He made a grand, sweeping gesture toward Nova Olympus in the distance. "Go, contestants, camp tonight and rest. You shall be free from harm between now and tomorrow's event. Come fresh to the final arena tomorrow. Then we shall play this out once and for all!"

"Move out," my uncle ordered. "Make as much ground as we can before we camp for the night and stay close. Don't trust Aquilinus' word for a second."

As we raced through the snow, the Talonites who had harried us appeared again—keeping their distance but making certain we moved in the right direction toward Julius Gemminus' masterwork. Darkness approached, the temperature dropped, and we camped. We worked together quietly, tending each other's wounds as best we could with the remaining medical supplies.

Lumen's silence was chilling; he simply stared at me. Without our mind-to-mind connection, communication was impossible, especially as he wouldn't engage in mime or any other form of symbolic exchange. I was glad I had Marcus. The intimacy Lumen and I had shared by way of our connection drifted away like a half-remembered dream. I couldn't quite put my finger on how to find it again. It was like holding a message from a bottle written in the language of a faraway land.

The ambrosia hunger returned once more as darkness fell. It wasn't debilitating, just a lingering ghost of the suffering I'd endured before. We were drawing close to the end, but how it would all play out was a mystery. That great unknown was a weight that increased with each passing day, as did my desire for ambrosia. My body tried to convince me that I needed it, that ambrosia was the key to survival and victory. At once I visited my uncle's tent and asked if I could speak to him about Concretus, but he told me I should get some sleep, and we could discuss it in the morning. Carbo organized the watch roster and warned us all to be on guard in case Aquilinus tried to attack and hamstring us before tomorrow's games. I was grateful that Marcus and I weren't scheduled to guard the camp until later in the night. I needed him, to take the edge off so I could get any rest at all. Our lovemaking was satisfying, though this time the sex wasn't enough to stop the ambrosia withdrawal, an itch I couldn't scratch.

I awoke alone to sounds of struggle. Certain that the Blood Hawks must be attacking, I burst out, my heart racing, ready to cast Orbis. In the center of the camp, bound, gagged, and tethered to a post, were Crassus and Julia, looking beaten and bruised, but there was no Sertorian attack, at least not as far as I could see. Caninus stood guard over them. Behind him sat Lumen, not bound but guarded on either side by Pavo and Nervo.

This was Carbo's doing. Had Crassus tried to betray us? Something had gone terribly wrong, and I had to find my uncle and fix it before it got even more out of hand.

"What's going on?" I demanded of Caninus. "Julia is loyal. Release her at once."

"Dear niece. Come and we'll talk."

I spun about. Uncle Quintus stood in the opening to his tent.

"Uncle? I need to know what's going on. Right now."

"Julia had orders and she has violated them," he said. "She forgot that she's sworn to my service until this is all over. She's not your lackey, nor the collegia's. Come. No harm will befall them or you. Come and hear me out. Tonight we will turn Aquilinus' game on its head and steal victory."

I looked back at Julia and Crassus, and then steeled myself and entered the command tent. Quintus sat down behind his small desk and pressed the tips of his fingers together before his lips, observing me over the top of them.

"There's no chance as long as we're playing by Aquilinus' rules," he said. "You've made some bold plays, dear niece, and come out on top. Now Aquilinus can't afford to risk any of us actually surviving tomorrow. He's engineering some kind of plan to isolate Lumen, and then he'll take us down once and for all. The time for games is over."

I saw it now, clear as day. Carbo never acted alone. It was my uncle who had ordered Concretus' death.

"Does that involve using mines to bury our allies alive?" I asked.

"That was a necessary ruse. We can't have barbarians dictating terms," he said.

"The only terms he dictated were that no one should harm Lumen."

"And we won't harm him, I swear it."

"As long as he cooperates," Carbo said as he entered the tent. He was holding an ion pistol in his hand. My uncle must have smuggled it in when he was thrown into the arena. "Unlike your collegia bitch. That's what happens when you send in a woman to do a man's job. It's the humors. I felt it the moment this curse was forced upon me. Every member of your sex is unhinged. I can't wait for this to be over, to be a whole man again."

I wouldn't take his bait. I couldn't afford to get angry. They were essential to the mission. To get Lumen to the mountain I needed to ride the wave of Carbo's paranoia, not push up against it.

"What is Julia accused of that she should be treated in such a way? The collegia are working in our interests. Without them, the entire vox populi forum would be usurped by Aquilinus and he could destroy us with impunity."

"Julia has a means of bypassing the game shields that keep us penned in and under Aquilinus' power," my uncle said. "Tonight is our last night on this world. I ordered her to give us the shield codes, but she refused, at least at first."

"She took some persuading," Carbo added.

"Julia intended to stay the course with you, to take the barbarian and all his ichor to the alien queen and expected us to do the same."

"Leave? But to what end?" I demanded. "How can we leave Olympus Decimus? Aquilinus is no god, but the Rota Fortuna is always looking down on us."

"You remember I told you that I had hidden resources on this world? Well, now is the time to bring them to bear. There is a concealed Viridian base on Olympus Decimus," my uncle said. "The base of the twenty-fourth legion Viridius, built back when we were rulers of this world. A hidden operations center buried far below the ice, built to shield it from any form of attack."

The red marker I had seen on the map the night before, before he quickly shut it down. That must have been it.

"It's nearby, not far beyond the shield wall. There are armaments and a stealth shuttle with shield-piercing capabilities that's fast enough to burn right past the orbital station and into the Janus Cardo. We'll travel to a command post at the edge of Viridian space and watch as Aquilinus' coup falls to pieces. Then we'll be ready."

"Ready for what?"

"To make use of your barbarian and his ichor. He's going to help us raise up a new empire. A Viridian empire."

Gods, how could I not have seen this coming? My own countrymen had been infected with the same disease that was choking the whole empire—greed. They didn't see this as a chance to defeat evil and restore stability. They wanted to make their own play for the throne, to kick the Sertorians' feet out from under them and then follow in their footsteps as fast as humanly possible.

"Unfortunately, the shuttle can carry only eight: Carbo, myself, Nervo, Pavo, Caninus, Marcus, and our diamond barbarian boy of course. That leaves one spot. It's yours if you can work out where your loyalties lie."

"And Julia?"

"She's made her choice."

"I've made worse choices," I said.

"I know, but you are my niece, and blood still counts for something. You get a second chance to make the right choice."

He sounded just like Aquilinus before he killed Titus Flavius Cursor.

"Please do not do this," I pleaded. "I beseech you, Uncle, do not do this. If we become monsters in order to defeat monsters, then what does it matter who wins?"

"If there's one thing you learn in the espionage business, Accala, it is that we're all monsters. Wars are fought by monsters, they're won by monsters. There's no good, no virtue, no honor. There's just victory. Us or them. And it's my job to make sure it's us."

"Is this the kind of empire you want House Viridian to rule over? An empire of addicts and slaves?"

"What do you think they are now? Why do you think they watch these games with such interest? They are slaves to bread and circuses. That's why they're willing to jump like fish for the ambrosia. The house that wields it will reign supreme for millennia."

"But you saw them today. They're making a stand. They're fighting for us, they're fighting for the gods and for Rome."

He stood up and walked around his table, putting his hands on my shoulders.

"You're young. You see what you want to see. You know why the mob is raging? They're fighting for their entertainments and pressing Aquilinus to give them the ambrosia without having to pay too high a price. You can't have your cake and eat it, but they don't know that. You've spooked them about abandoning the gods, but as long as Aquilinus doesn't press the issue of his divinity too hard, they'll swing back in line with him. Idealism isn't tangible. The man who has the ichor and makes the ambrosia will command the empire." The ambrosia hunger was strong. My muscles ached, my head throbbed. It was hard to think straight, but I had to keep it together, had to get Quintus to see sense.

"Uncle, let the Hyperboreans go. The ambrosia will only bring suffering. This is the moment where we could go wrong, but it's not too late to choose another path. It's enough to see the Sertorians lose; we don't have to take more than our share. Let us do our duty, let me carry out my promise, my mother's promise, your sister's promise."

He backhanded me, sending me sprawling to the floor. Before I could move, Carbo had his weapon leveled at me, ready to fire the moment I tried to defend myself.

"Our duty is to our house!" my uncle shouted. "You think we are as you? That we don't know how to manage ourselves? We are men! We are soldiers. We have discipline, honor. You suggest I let these ignorant beasts walk away with the most powerful asset in the empire? You will remember your place if you wish to live. Are you a Viridian? Do you love your family? Or will you turn traitor and serve alien beings? You know nothing of the empire, of what it really takes to keep power. Virtue! The Gods! Pah! They aren't going to fix anything. The Sertorians aren't wrong. Survival of the strongest, the power to keep hold of what you have—that's the key. The ichor can secure our position, make sure no one ever threatens us again."

"There is no permanence in life, no absolute, everything changes. The experience I've had has taught me that," I said. "It's something we knew once, but we've forgotten it. The empire's become fixed, locked in outdated ideas, and we can't think of ourselves as anything other than houses fighting over a throne and crown. We have to break the mold and recast ourselves in a new form. There's a chance to remake the empire right here and now as something better than it was. But we can't choose the same path as the enemy."

"Your mother used to talk the same nonsense. You're her daughter, all right. The truth is that you are naïve and don't understand how the world works. You played your part well. Your idealism was necessary to accomplish the task at hand, but now it will only endanger us if you're allowed to wield power a moment longer. I'm sorry, dear niece."

Gods, Crassus had been right about my uncle all along. I put my hand to Orbis, but the blast from Carbo's ion pistol hit me square in the back, and then I was falling.

XLV

"Shall I finish her?" Carbo asked. All I could see of him was his boots as they stopped in front of my face. He must have used the stun setting. My whole body was frozen.

"No," Uncle said. "She's certainly done her part to add to our victory."

My uncle crouched down beside me, hovering over me like a spider that had caught an insect in its web. I used every ounce of willpower, trying to get up, but the bolt had locked up all my muscles in a kind of static seizure.

"You betrayed me. You betrayed House Viridian by colluding with Aquilinus. You have no honor."

My accusation didn't seem to faze my uncle, or Carbo, for that matter.

"Dear niece, the ambrosia is a powerful weapon, an empire-shaping weapon. So what if I formed a temporary alliance with my enemy? We needed one another. I handed them you, relayed information to them that you passed on to Julia. We formed an alliance of convenience that would last only until the ambrosia was discovered."

"If you can't see why, then we don't have much to discuss," I said.

"We'll discuss anything that pleases me," he said.

"Julia was in on it too?" I asked. I had to know.

"No. No, she knew nothing of my plans other than that she was to support you and keep an eye on your more rebellious tendencies. Aquilinus and I did nothing more than what the leaders of houses do—work with the assets at hand, use the pieces on the board to make the best moves we can in the game of empire. I needed the pin your mother spoke of and Aquilinus needed you to make it work. As for betraying you, I think that's unreasonable. I used you, certainly, but you made yourself available to be used from the beginning."

"You never expected me to survive the Blood Hawks," I said. "All that talk of sending me back to the Viridian team, of redeeming my name. All lies. You wanted me to lead the way to the ichor. After that I was expendable."

"I admit it. My guess was that you would find the ichor, Aquilinus was always going to make sure of that. In the process I was certain he would break you. My best scenario was that you would go mad and kill some of the Sertorians before you yourself died, but you've impressed me, Accala. You've delivered above and beyond expectations and that's why you will be permitted to live and see your hard work come to fruition. Maybe, when House Viridian rules the empire, you'll see me in a different light."

"You seek the throne for yourself. Our house's interests are a distant concern."

"You can say what you wish, it makes no difference now. I don't expect your father to survive Aquilinus' tender mercies—he's probably dead already—but you saw his face when you arrived on this world, all dressed up in leather, a pet Sertorian whore, the centerpiece of Aquilinus' propaganda campaign. The shame. I've never seen anything like it. So, after the Hyperborean child is doing what's required of him, I'm going to ship you to an outer colony and see you married to some feudal lord who'll tame your wild spirit."

I felt some feeling returning to my arms and tried to push myself up, before Carbo forced me back down with a boot on my neck.

"And the others? The redheaded plebeian and the Sertorian?" Carbo asked.

"It's better to put them out of their misery than leave them here for Aquilinus," Quintus said. "Do it quickly and quietly."

"What's going on?"

It was Marcus. I couldn't see him, but it was him. My voice box wouldn't work to call for help, but he must have heard some of what just transpired.

"Back to your post, Marcus. This doesn't concern you," Carbo barked.

"I'd say that assaulting our teammates concerns me greatly."

"I'm the leader of this alliance, and if I have to ask again, you'll be up on charges of insubordination, and in a time of war, that means crucifixion."

"We'll all be crucified tomorrow anyway if Aquilinus has his way."

Carbo moved toward him, but Marcus ignored him and sought my uncle's confirmation. "Proconsul?"

"You heard the commander. Start packing. We're moving out beyond the shield walls in fifteen minutes."

"You're right, sir. I beg your pardon," he said as he went. Just like that. No defiance, just acceptance. It wasn't like Marcus, not at all.

"Right, go on, Carbo. Leave the pistol."

Carbo handed the weapon to my uncle, who leveled it at me.

"Stay right where you are," my uncle said to me. "This will all be over in a moment."

Outside I could hear Carbo ordering Nervo and Pavo to pack up the camp. While they were busy, he and Caninus would carry out the executions.

There was a sudden commotion, and Carbo, Nervo, and Pavo came rushing back into the tent.

"Sir! The barbarian child and the Sertorian, they're gone," Pavo said.

Crassus! Had he betrayed me or, seeing things falling apart here, was he trying to help?

"What do you mean gone?" Quintus yelled, leaping up, his fist smashing down on the flimsy table, sending it flying.

"Caninus took a blow to the head, he was out cold. Crassus must have overpowered him. He stole Caninus' knife and the skirmisher."

Uncle Quintus crouched beside me again and grabbed my ponytail, pulling me up until we were face-to-face.

"Where is the diamond boy? Where has Crassus gone?" my uncle yelled. He was manic, his eyes filled with greed and anger. I couldn't answer that question, but I knew my uncle. Any second now he would come to the conclusion that Crassus was taking Lumen back to Aquilinus, that he was about to lose everything.

"The pin," was all I could manage to say. It was enough. I'd used it to find Lumen before. I could use it to find him again. Uncle Quintus needed me.

"Damn it! Hold off on killing the redhead. My niece appears to have some strategic sense after all. Mount up and get that barbarian brat back before Crassus can take him to his master. Make sure you bring Accala, she'll be useful."

Marcus rode on my uncle's chariot, while Julia and I were loaded onto Carbo's and bound to the rails by calcedonius bonds, the same kind the Sertorians had used to chain me aboard *Incitatus*.

"He said you refused to give them the shield codes. Thank you," I said quietly to Julia.

"Yeah? Well they got them out of me in the end."

"I've got us thrown in the deep end again. You're a hostage again. I'm sorry."

"No, you were right. We just keep putting one foot in front of the other. They were going to kill me, now they're not. We've got to work with what's right in front of us if we're going to survive." She looked over at Marcus on the other chariot and winked. I caught sight of something in Marcus' hand—the outline of a slim object, the length of an index finger, lit by the acid cyan lights of the chariot—the key to our bonds!

Then we rushed headlong into the night. Now all the elements seemed to rail against us—a snowstorm, biting winds that made my teeth ache.

"Which way?" Carbo barked. When he saw me hesitate, he raised a hand and instantly Caninus cut Julia with a long knife, a gash to the arm.

Gods, what would happen when it turned out I couldn't lead them to Lumen at all? But then the song started up. For the first time since I'd rejoined the Caninines, I could hear it clearly. No buzzing static, but a clear tone, filled with meaning and a strong directional pull. Lumen and I were connected once more. It couldn't be coincidence, he'd reopened communication so that I could find him. If Crassus really was taking him to Aquilinus, then finding Lumen was a top priority. My uncle making use of Lumen was definitely the lesser of two evils.

Let them come.

Aulus' voice, Lumen's voice, unfolded in my mind like a ray of sunshine. He was alive and I could hear him once more. Even though I was betrayed and at a disadvantage, some blockage between us had broken and been carried away.

I'm in trouble. My uncle has betrayed me. I tried to transmit the thought clearly as far as I could.

I need you, Accala. Come.

"Lumen's northwest of here," I said.

"There's forest that way," Caninus said. "Once they get into it, it'll be all but impossible to track them at speed."

"Full speed," my uncle ordered. "Risk everything. We must catch them up!"

I pointed, guiding the chariots, and prayed Lumen knew what he was doing.

We traveled at breakneck speed, heedless of the risk. Half a mile later we caught sight of the first sign of fresh tracks that hadn't been covered by snowfall. Carbo ordered a wide configuration, a two-pronged advance with a half mile between each chariot, motion sensors and antennas extended to catch any quarry that fell between us. The chariots began to draw apart.

"Accala!"

Marcus! He tossed the release key to the manacles into the air and threw our weapons from the locker on his chariot out onto the icy ground, before my uncle thrust at him with his dagger. My bound hands grabbed uselessly at the key. It fell onto the chariot floor. I used my boot to lodge it against the starboard wall and then started to slide it up with the blade of my foot. Pulling back on the manacles to stabilize myself, I forced the black security key up higher until it was just in reach of Julia's outstretched fingers. She touched the key to my manacles. I pulled my hands free and returned the favor.

We jumped from the chariot before Caninus could stop us, and I snatched Orbis up from the ground while Julia recovered her staff. Marcus rushed to our side, gladius ready, tower shield projected.

"The dense trees will hamper the chariots' efforts to follow us," he said. "Run."

We fled into the shiny forest. I was back in the tunnel again, following my instinct, listening for Lumen's song. Faith. I had to have faith. Mind clear, no fear, or we'd be lost out here in the cold and die at the hands of the weather before our enemies even had to raise a hand.

Got to keep running. My feet were numb. I struggled not to slip on the icy ground. Marcus explained that it was he who knocked out Caninus in an effort to free Julia, but that in the process Crassus had broken free, stolen a gladius from Caninus, and fled with Lumen before anyone could stop him.

I strained to hear the song over my ragged breath and the blood pumping in my ears. It was getting stronger as we drew closer, but there was a second, fainter song, which seemed to come from a different direction, and now I wasn't certain which one belonged to Lumen. We continued on and kept together for perhaps an hour, managing to keep our distance from the Caninine chariots and avoid any major injuries, and then I heard Julia swear. Marcus risked turning on the light on his armilla briefly, and we saw that we'd run right into the skirmisher Crassus had stolen. It was abandoned, jammed in between two crystal trunks to prevent anyone easily taking it.

In the darkness ahead came a manic chattering. It was Crassus, talking to himself.

"I can't. The gods. You can't go against the gods. Infinite power means an infinite potential for punishment."

We followed the sound and found two faint lights. One radiated from Lumen, and the other . . . it was Aquilinus. No god form this time. It was the proconsul I remembered from the podium when we first arrived on this world, and he was talking quietly to Crassus. It was a projection, a body of light cast from the black orb that was barely visible in the air behind him.

Crassus was like some ghost from the underworld. His body twisted, his fingers interlinked and turned inside out and behind him. His shoulders looked like they'd been dislocated by some invisible giant, but there was no one there with him, only the projection. He was crazed, his skin red from exposure, his eyes wide, staring at Aquilinus. In his hand was the gladius that he stole from Caninus. It was not his weapon of choice, but only Marcus could surpass him in its use. He was standing in front of what looked like termite mounds, tall icy protrusions like a forest of giant fingers in the middle of a flat clearing. Five rows deep in the mounds stood Lumen. He was holding on to one of the pillars with a small claw hand, looking like he was about to fall over. He was weak, but I couldn't see that Crassus had used any means to restrain him. Was he a prisoner?

"Gaius, you know my vision," I heard Aquilinus say as we drew near. "You know what's at stake. This small creature is no god, not even a servant of the gods. He's just an animal looking to protect his own. Don't allow him to trick you, to disenfranchise you from the true Elysium that I will bring into being. Can you turn your back on the pleasure and pain that I can offer, having tasted of it? You know the pain makes the pleasure even sweeter."

Crassus looked at Lumen, his eyes desperate, filled with doubt.

"I've made my choice," Crassus screamed. "Leave me!"

"It was never your choice to make, Gaius," Aquilinus said. "Let me back in. You can't hold me off forever."

Julia's hand closed on my arm. "Take him now, while he's distracted," she whispered.

"Wait," I said. "I want to see how this plays out."

There was a part of me that had to know if Crassus could be redeemed. If he could fight his own darkness and addiction, then so could I.

"You know where you belong, Gaius. Bring the prize to me and I will raise you up to my right hand. No more Licinus. Together we will rule the galaxy."

"Let me be, I beg you," Gaius Crassus moaned. "I serve her now. I serve the gods."

"She will not honor her word to you, and what of the others? They despise you. They will not show mercy. Only I give you a way toward triumph. How can you not choose the path to victory? What kind of a gladiator are you?"

"I will not," Crassus spat, each word an effort; his body looked like it was about to break, to snap into pieces with involuntary contortions. "I am a Roman. It's not just about will and power. There's more to life than that."

"You shall be punished, Gaius, most severely of all. I will make you deliver the slow torments that end Accala Viridius' life."

"Julia. Take out that orb," I whispered.

She reached out with her hand, and suddenly Aquilinus turned to look at us. The projection cut out, and the orb sped away before Julia could gain control of it. Aquilinus wasn't taking any chances; he wanted to make sure he was controlling the imperial conversation. No more free airplay for me.

"Crassus," I said as I lit up the scene with my armilla's light.

He jerked around violently as if my words were like a hot stove he'd accidentally brushed with his hand. He stared at us, right into the light of the skirmisher without blinking.

"Stay away," he warned, taking a step back toward Lumen.

"Don't let him get to you," I warned Crassus. "I heard it all. I know you're on our side."

"I'm trying my best, Accala. I'm trying so hard, but it's not enough."

"I know. I feel the ambrosia hunger too."

"How can you bear to live with it?"

"With what?"

"Doubt. Fear. Emptiness."

"You can't spend all your life worrying about whether the ground beneath your feet will hold you up. You just have to walk."

"I've never done that," he said. "I've always been supported by the truth. What I thought was the truth. Then Lumen let me see Olympus, and all the things I thought were true before were turned upside down. Now, though, Olympus is like a distant constellation and my old, fixed stars are calling to me. Lumen won't show me again. He won't show me, and I can't keep going without it. When you stand in Aquilinus' power, you feel it like a torrent, like you're standing before the sun. Your mind is filled with heroic images, classical quotes, but afterward there's a down period. Like your whole mind is filled with poison and darkness. You feel possessed, your mouth spews pollution. Things I never would have thought of on my own, strange passions and base desires consume me. There's nothing but emptiness, and my body knows that if I give it ambrosia, I'll feel full." Crassus' voice cracked, and he was hit by a wheezing cough. "When I saw the Hyperborean's light, I saw only clarity. But the pull of Aquilinus is too strong. He is a flame I can't resist. I see that now. I'm better off taking myself out of the equation."

I searched for the right words. "You made your choice, Crassus. You've chosen the right path. Now you do what the rest of us do. Move forward and live with it. I don't know what that alien child is to me, but I know that I have a duty to protect him."

"It's not enough," Crassus said. "I've been here before. I'm weak. I'll stumble and betray you. I don't want to be Aquilinus' pawn anymore. He knows my weak spots, just where to apply pressure. I know I'll fold again like I have before. I told him. About the Hyperboreans and their plan to escape. He knows he can't let you reach Nova Olympus. And now your Wolves have already turned on you. How can we win? It seemed to me that every man for himself was the only way forward."

"I don't like this," Marcus said. "Let me kill him, Accala. I'll do it quickly."

You will need him. We will need him, Lumen said.

I waved Marcus away and moved slowly toward Crassus. I needed to talk him down; he was wild, unpredictable, and Lumen looked so frail. One thrust of the gladius in Crassus' hand and his life would be over.

Crassus suddenly realized that I'd almost reached him, and he flipped the sword around so the point faced his throat.

"Stay back. It's better this way."

I don't know why I stopped him. I moved forward like lightning, pushing the center of the blade away before he could drive the point home into his neck. He fell forward awkwardly.

I went to catch him, and when he looked up at me I saw a different face. A face engorged with blood, a smile twisted with hate.

"Stupid bitch."

The gladius shot out. There was not a fighter in the world who could dodge Crassus at this range. But it was not Crassus, so I turned. Orbis swept across my body, and my discus caught the tip of the sword, sending it aside so that the blade only pierced my side instead of my heart. A rush of pain seared through my body. Marcus was upon the possessed Crassus in an instant, punching him in the face, forcing him away from me. I staggered back, fell to my knees, hand pressed into my side, trying to stanch the bleeding.

"We can never escape who we are," Crassus babbled mournfully, suddenly himself again and submitting placidly as Marcus pulled him to his knees, the point of his own gladius pressing into the place between Crassus' neck and collarbone. Marcus looked to me. The Sertorian would be dead the moment I gave the signal. "There's a spider weaving its web, and there's really no choice at all except to decide whether you want to be the spider or the prey caught up in the web."

He had spoken of this before. His nightmares of spiders and needles inside his body, of an external force controlling him. He grabbed his head suddenly as if hit by a wave of pain, throwing himself forward on the snow.

"The needles," he mumbled, "the needles."

"It's in your mind," I said. "There are no needles."

"They're sharp. The talons of the hawk. So sharp. They rake the back of my neck, claw the inside of my skull."

"Fight it, Crassus," I said, as I struggled to my feet. My hand closed around his fallen gladius. "It doesn't have to be like this." I was fighting for his soul, and at the same time I was fighting for mine, because there was nothing I wanted more right then than to pierce his heart with the blade.

"Listen, Accala," he whispered, "Aquilinus can use his bombers to re-create the attack that started the war, bomb your little god from the air if he's left no other choice. Aquilinus thinks it might turn all their ichor in Lumen's body into ambrosia, but he's not one hundred percent certain and he won't take the risk if he can help it."

Without warning, an ion bolt seared past my face and hit Crassus in the head. He fell hard, black blood flying from his head.

The Caninine chariots had found us. The scene was lit by their search lamps. Carbo stood at the front of his chariot, ion pistol in hand.

"Come. It's over. Give the child up," my uncle commanded.

Marcus threw his gladius like a large knife. It spun through the air and I heard Nervo yell out in pain, and then the lights were pulling away as the chariot driver inadvertently tugged the reins, forcing the craft around.

As they turned, Carbo fired again, hitting Marcus in the shoulder and sending him spinning down to the icy ground. I couldn't look after him. We were all wounded. I had to focus on Lumen's survival.

"I think that's enough of that," Quintus said. "Now bring the prize to me."

In the distance, the hunting horns of the Talonites sounded ominously. Aquilinus had sent in his men after all.

"Come and get him," I said to Quintus, backing into the cover of the forest of pillars. Julia followed, then Marcus got to his feet and moved beside me to form a barrier to Lumen.

Carbo, who had taken over the reins of his chariot from Nervo, signaled Pavo and Caninus to flank us, taking their chariots to the sides of the pillars. They could stop us from fleeing past them, but they could not come into the pillars without dismounting. They were forced to come in on foot.

"You can't win," Carbo growled.

"I don't have to win. I just have to stop you from taking him until the Talonites arrive. You don't want that, so back off now and we all get to walk away."

"You're bluffing," my uncle said. "You wouldn't let them have him."

We stood in a row, a pillar between each of us. Pavo and Caninus were pacing back and forth in the chariots like caged animals, desperate to come at us.

"Oh, enough of this nonsense," my uncle said, signaling the advance.

"Take them!" Carbo ordered, but before the Caninines could dismount, the horns sounded again and suddenly the Talonites were on us. Their two chariots approached from behind the Viridians and began firing their ion blasters. The Caninine chariots tried to turn to flee the onslaught, and Carbo fired his ion pistol. I grabbed Lumen and took shelter behind the pillars with Marcus and Julia, raising armilla shields as ions blasted about us.

Thirty seconds. That's how long I thought we could hold.

It will be enough.

There was a great crash, and charging through the forest like a tank, smashing pillars of ice aside as he came, was Concretus. Not dead. Now I understood the confused song signal I was getting in the dark when hunting for Crassus. Concretus was moving beneath us, through the deep tunnels and rivers of this world. Coming back to his master to fulfill his sacred duty.

The giant Hyperborean warrior rushed Carbo's chariot and hurled himself under it before rearing up and throwing his four mighty arms up into the air. The entire chariot flew up, and all five Viridians were cast sprawling into the snow. He was wounded too, cracked apart, plates of ice hanging off him, his body almost entirely coated with hoarfrost like barnacles covering a great whale. He was dying; I could hear his song line flicker and jump like a weak, irregular heartbeat. But Concretus was like a charging bull. Not letting up, he tore at the Caninines with his claws and fired spines of ice from his arms.

The Caninines raced for the safety of their other chariot. "Hurry, we're leaving!" Quintus called to me.

I didn't move.

"Accala, you're making a big mistake. Come back now and all will be forgiven," he screamed out, then signaled Carbo to flee the raging barbarian.

As my uncle and his men withdrew, Concretus targeted the Tullian chariot, seizing hold of it and flipping it up and into the Arrian craft. Balbus, Calida, and Cynisca screamed as the sharp blades on the side of the Tullian chariot ripped into them. Potitus Tullius and the Ovidians Costa and Spurius fell from the chariot. They tried to run, but Concretus was over them, tearing at them with his spiny fists, slicing limbs and throats.

Then the ion blasters on the Arrian chariot fired, sending burst after burst of blue-black light into the giant's body. Finally, the Hyperborean's spikes were firing uselessly into the ground as his mighty body fell, like the tall pine mast of a sailing ship struck by lightning. He lay unmoving, but I heard Concretus' voice in my mind for the first and last time.

Now you must protect him. Prove I'm wrong about your people. You couldn't hear the song because you left it, turned from it when you rejoined your people. The song is the true path of all beings but your people here do not yet know how to walk it. Don't wander from it again. Stay true.

Then his song line was gone.

We heard more triumphal horns, the sound of the Blood Eagles in the distance. Aquilinus had put them into the field, now that the rest of the Talonites were dead.

"Quick." Marcus mounted the abandoned Viridian chariot, dragged Crassus' unconscious body with him, and took the reins. I lifted Lumen into the chariot. "It's okay," I said. "I'm here now, Aulus, I'm here." I left my arms around him and pulled his small, cold body to me. I didn't care how much of Aulus he was or wasn't. He was all I had left, and I'd die before I let anyone harm him again.

We raced toward Lupus Civitas until the sound of the Blood Eagles died away, then we slowed to a stop.

"Are you okay?" I asked Marcus.

"Shoulder wound. I'll live. And you?"

"In one side and out the other," I said. "It hurts like hell, but it's clean. Didn't hit any organs."

"Accala, Crassus is still alive," Julia said, "but I don't think he's going to last long." Although the ion blast had not struck him dead on, a part of his skull was missing, and I could see bright red blood, the color of cough medicine, pumping out onto the chariot's floor. That was not a good sign.

"Can you hear me, Crassus?"

"Tell them," he said.

"Tell who what?" I asked.

"The gods. Tell them I served you. It was hard. I wanted to devour the boy, to take him away for myself, but I kept thinking of you. The words you spoke at the ice bridge. Mucius Scaevola."

"I said those things to the mob. To please them."

"No. It was the gods speaking through you. They hear you when you speak. So tell them that I tried to serve them. Maybe Saturn will show me mercy in the underworld."

"Nothing can be done, can it?" I said to Lumen. His body glittered like a great diamond in the dull light. I was surprised at the sadness in my voice. I never loved Crassus; mostly I hated him. But somehow his salvation was a reflection of my own path back to sanity.

There is something, Lumen said. *The power of your pin. Now it must be used to save you.*

"I'm fine. It's only a small wound."

An artery was struck. You're bleeding to death. You need to save yourself.

"How?"

I can be of little help. Even if I could spare the ichor, all of my energy is directed on absorbing and holding it. That is my energetic role between now and the end, should we reach it. If I start the ichor outflowing now, in this cycle, I will be unable to contain it. Look.

He held out his arm and I looked closely to see microfine cracks running the length of the crystal skin.

Even now I'm coming apart.

"What happens if you break apart before we get you to safety?"

I honestly don't know, but I don't think it will be good to find out. Too little ichor is causing this world to collapse about us. Too much . . . He shrugged. Another of Aulus' movements that broke my heart.

I reached up to my hair and pulled out Mother's pin.

My mother infused the pin with diamond ichor, the purest, densest concentration of energy. It's very powerful—even healing Crassus and repairing Julia's hand was only a small display of its potency—but like the ichor in me, it will be needed if we are to leave; not an ounce can be wasted. So she has placed a limit on the amount of power that can be drawn from it by me, or you, until we reach her in person.

"But the ichor can't be ingested by humans," I said. "That's why Aquilinus needs to turn it into ambrosia."

The ichor in your pin is different. My mother created it specially when I was created. It can be used by a human being, but only for a short time. Your bodies are not designed to contain such power.

"And I can use it to heal my wound?"

Yes. There's enough available power to close your wound and heal you completely. One dose of medicine, but only one. Until mother unlocks the pin's remaining power, there simply isn't any more to spare. I don't want you to die, Accala.

"I don't want to die either," I said.

There was no pain, but I felt light-headed all of a sudden. Blood was pouring out of the wound in an unstoppable stream.

"One dose . . ." I said.

Crassus, my enemy, lay dying.

"Accala, don't you even think about it," Julia said. "This was his choice. He wanted to take his own life. Let him die. For all our sakes. We can't risk Aquilinus possessing him again."

"All we've got is a chariot now," Marcus said. "Let the cold take him. He won't last long; it will be a quick death."

What I saw now when I looked at Crassus was not even a Roman or a human. I saw everything with a single eye. Good, bad, darkness, light—it was all keeping the galaxy turning, a pool of forces in contraposition, turning each other as they sought to resolve back into one.

I leaned over him, the point of the pin dangling over his injured head.

"Accala!" Julia and Marcus yelled as one.

"He's one of us now. He gets help, the same way you'll get help. We're all part of the same machine. If a part is broken you fix it," I said, quoting Julia.

"Or you throw it out and get a replacement part," she said.

"We don't have any replacements—you may have noticed that—so we have to repair what we have and hobble along. What do I do?" I asked Lumen.

Touch the pin to his body and imagine him in perfect health, with no illness or injury.

I put the pin to Crassus' tongue, and he pushed up to it like a baby seeking the nipple, so hard and fast that the pin pierced the flesh of his tongue and drew blood. I tried to pull away, but his hands clasped my wrist with a primal force and he sucked what he needed from its tip. Like a weak cub sucking from a mother's teat.

I could feel the strength, the life flowing back into him. Marcus seized my hand and moved it to my side, where my own wound burned.

"Your turn. Don't argue."

Crassus fell forward into a deep slumber.

Gods. It was agony and ecstasy all rolled into one. Being pulled back from death's door, my body waking as if from a great sleep and at the same time clawing at the remembrance of the nectar, my brain firing, endorphins rewarding me for satisfying its addictive demands.

The wound had closed over, but it was still bruised, black under the skin.

"You're still hurt, you have to take it easy," Julia said.

Crassus' eyes flicked open, wide with horror. "You should not have done that," he said.

The last ghost of ambrosia hunger has left you now, but Crassus' desire for it will return in time. It is embedded in his mind as much as in his body, but until then the power of the ichor will give him some time to think clearly.

Crassus looked up at me in my dirty white armor. I was not afraid of him, but there was an intensity, a focus that matched my own—a synchronous emotion that was frightening. We were driven by the same fuel, but was it for the same purpose?

Crassus scrambled to his feet. "I have to go. I can't stay near you. The craving will return again, and with it, my weaknesses. I can't be too close to him," he said, pointing to Lumen. "Don't you feel it too? The need for it?"

"Yes."

"It's like swimming in a freshwater lake as you die of thirst. I can't stand it. I've tried, but it's too hard. I will serve from a distance. I know things about the arena ahead. I know Aquilinus and what he will ask for. I can help."

He leaped from the chariot and skittered off into the night like a giant spider. Looking at the speed with which Crassus fled, it occurred to me that I might have given him too much of the pin's power and not kept enough for myself.

"Quintus won't leave without Lumen," I said. "Which means they won't give up on us. They'll be waiting ahead for us, and we've got to move now before the Sertorians catch up."

"And Crassus?" Marcus asked.

"With him, it's in the lap of the gods," I said.

Suddenly, a skirmisher pulled up beside us, piloted by Pavo.

"Pax!" he yelled. "I've come to join you. I've deserted Quintus Severus."

Marcus rounded with his weapon, but I placed a restraining hand on his shoulder.

"Hold. Speak quickly," I said to him. "I have no time and little patience for tricks."

"No trick," Pavo said urgently. "Things are changing. I felt a shadow over us. I heard your speech at the ice bridge. I don't care about the consequences. Let them come, let them kill us, only let me follow you."

"Quintus has sent him," Julia said.

Listen to him, as you did with Crassus, Lumen said. *Each person has their own song. He is following his.*

I reached out to Pavo. His thoughts were rough and fast, like an animal rushing through a wood, chasing its prey. But there was an honesty, a nobility. The hunt was a means of completing a circle of life and death, not for sport or cruelty.

"You can come," I said to Pavo. "Be quick about it." I was buying life in minutes, and if Pavo bought us more vital time, then he was welcome.

I sat beside Lumen as we raced out of the crystalline forests, holding his hand in mine as they faded behind us. He was weak; there were more cracks than ever in his shell. I tried to talk to him, but there were no more words. Not because I had turned away but because I sensed his every effort was required to keep the power contained within him. Metamorphosis. He was either changing or dying or both, and he needed to keep this form together until he could return to the queen. And what would happen then? What would happen to Aulus?

"Don't you leave me again," I told him. "I won't lose you."

One more leg to go and we were home free. As we traveled, Marcus sighted a faint form in the distance. Crassus, infused with ichor, keeping pace with our speedy chariot on foot. But there was no sign of the Viridians.

As we came up over a low rise, we caught sight of an archway, part of a long, crumbling wall that marked the entrance to the ruined city of Lupus Civitas. How many nights had I dreamed of this place? The site of the bombing of Olympus Decimus. Above the gate were large holographic projections of heroic Sertorian motifs. Their generals, their battles, historical revisionism at its worst, created histories to lend credibility to a people who had nothing but greed as their driving force.

As we approached, the archway transformed. All the motifs changed from reflecting Sertorian greatness to the low points of Viridian failure, and then the entire structure burst into holographic flame. Above the archway in a row of curved letters, a sign read

ABANDON HOPE ALL WHO ENTER.

It was a traditional warning above the gates of the underworld.

Julius Gemminus' winged head appeared beside the sign. I would have loved to wipe that plastic grin off of his face.

"Accala of No House! Abandoned by your own Wolves—outcast again!"

We slowed down. No use charging into whatever lay ahead until we heard what he had to say.

"Outcast, but you've managed to cobble together your own ragtag team, and you are the only competitors to reach this gate, so the games will continue."

The media spherae were out again. Now that Aquilinus had failed to recover Lumen, he'd decided it was in his interests to start up the live coverage once more.

"We have seen the old emperor oversee the chariot races and bestiarii rounds, and the new emperor has instituted his re-creations, and now only the final round remains—gladiatorial combat. Two sides fighting, whittling down until only one remains alive. But it can all stop now. If you lay down your weapons, bow and swear loyalty to the emperor, then you will all be taken from here and returned to Rome without any harm befalling you. Accala, you will be permitted to carry out your sacred duty as a daughter, serving your father until his death."

The space within the arch was filled with a projection of my father. On either side of him were Aquilinus' new Praetorians, the Crimson Inquisitors. The same torturers Crassus threatened to turn on Aulus back on *Incitatus* if I failed to obey him. Father was naked, chained between two posts, his scar-covered body exposed. They touched his chest with their shock sticks, holding them in place until he screamed out in pain.

"His pain can stop now," Julius Gemminus said. "If you agree to stop this, to surrender and exit the tournament."

I was in a bind. I was damned if I let my father die; a portion of the mob would turn against me for not fulfilling my duty as a daughter. And I was damned if I saw him spared and abandoned my teammates and my duty there in the field. This was about cutting away sections of my supporters in the audience.

"His eyes," Marcus said. "Look to his eyes."

My father's good eye was hard, unblinking. Stubborn, angry, unbreakable steel. He had the same eyes as mine, green and gray. They could pull the screams from his body, but they couldn't break him.

"Don't you want to stop all this? Your father won't die now. His death will take months. Come, remember your place. End this and live out your days by your father's side. You have no house to fight for. This is the end of the road for you."

"I have no house to fight for, but I'm still a citizen of the empire," I said.

I took the reins and drove the chariot toward the gate, Lumen by my side. Tears streamed down my face as I tried to shut out the sounds of my father's screams. Marcus, Julia, and Pavo sat in silence. This was my choice, not theirs.

"Come. Turn back," Julius Gemminus said. "A daughter has even more of a duty to her father than a son. She must tend to him, make sure he is looked after in old age."

I didn't need to ask Marcus or Julia how the mob felt. They didn't blame Aquilinus for this. He was the emperor, he could do what he liked. It was all on me: the unfaithful daughter. He had cast me in the role of the one undermining the most fundamental traditions of familial loyalty. I wondered if the chart even had scope to handle how low my approval would plummet. I had to break the mold of their expectations. I could no longer afford to be a daughter, the empire could not afford me to be a daughter.

I stopped before the arch. A red line across the path was projected onto the ground before me.

"If you cross that line, you're committing your own father to death," Gemminus said.

But there was only one choice. No matter the odds and obstacles that stood against me, I had to move forward. An iron ball was turning inside my stomach, driving me onward unceasingly. If my enemies got in my way, I would crush them. The ball didn't care for the size of the enemy; it didn't care about threats or fear; it cared only about moving toward the end. I made its turning my chant, my prayer, my every thought, letting it crush doubt and hesitation, letting it destroy the little Accala they sought to bait and chain and torment like a slave, like a piece on the board. But I was past being moved and manipulated. I made my own choices, had to create my own game where I fashioned the rules. Father, I'm so sorry. I can't do this. I must do this.

I crossed the line, and passed through the arched gate, into the ruins of Lupus Civitas. The only light in the predawn darkness lay in the distance— Julius Gemminus' reinvigorated Colosseum. The fire-blackened ruins rose up about me, dark broken shades of once great buildings looming like dead birds strung up on a line. My father's screaming suddenly stopped. I resisted the urge to look back, to see him hanging dead by his bound limbs.

I was filled with a righteous white fire like a clean-burning fuel. I was a weapon, and nothing would stop me from hitting home.

ACT VII

ARENA

Learn by this warning to do justly and not to slight the gods.
This man sold his country for gold, and laid her under a tyrant's
    sway;
he set up and pulled down laws at a price;
this other forced his daughter's bridal chamber and a forbidden
    marriage;
all dared some monstrous wickedness, and had success in what
    they dared.
Not had I a hundred tongues, a hundred mouths, and a voice of
    iron, could I sum up all the shapes of crime or name over all
    their punishments.

—Virgil, *Aeneid*

XLVI

WE PASSED THROUGH THE ruins swiftly and approached the Colosseum. It
was lit up like a cheap festival attraction. Now, instead of faux clouds and holographic pillars, Aquilinus had opted for a theme of damnation and fire. Beyond
the entrance, a long stone tunnel led to the bright lights of the arena. Julius Gemminus' winged head appeared above us again.

"Welcome, welcome to the final round! Our arena spectacular! Emperor
Aquilinus is proud to present the Arena of the Old and New Gods!"

Those very words lit up the sky above the arena in letters of fire. I snatched
up a spear from the chariot's arms locker and climbed down to the ground; the
vehicle was too wide to fit through the tunnel. Lumen, Marcus, Julian, and Pavo
followed my lead. Above us towered large statues of the Blood Eagles, ringing
the Colosseum, replacing the statues of the old gods that lay, broken and crumbling, beside them—great faces smashed, arms knocked away, bodies cracked
with the heat of the bombs dropped on the city.

The ion cannon of the orbital stadium could still destroy us at any time. There
was no choice but to move through the tunnel, toward the arena. Suddenly, the
way behind us was sealed, not by a door but by a large fan. It began to spin, faster
and faster, and before we could run the length of the tunnel, the air pressure sent
us hurtling forward, barely able to keep our feet. The arena floor ahead of us was

spinning too, fast like a children's carnival ride, so that as each of us was propelled into the circular arena, we were immediately flung and held against the outer shield wall by the centrifugal force. The wheel was turning so fast it was all I could do to grab Lumen by the hand and make certain we were not separated. I looked around as best as I could with my head pinned back. We were trapped around a spinning ring, separated from each other by energy shield walls that divided the ring into four equal wedge-shaped chambers. The walls were a transparent green—nonlethal energy fields. A thin layer of sand covered the arena floor. It must have been imported just for this. Its presence, not covered by snow, meant that the ceiling of the arena was sealed from the elements. In the middle of the arena there was another ring, also divided into four chambers, but motionless, like the hub of a wheel that stands still. Through the transparent walls of the energy shield that separated the inner from the outer ring, I could see our opponents for the final round adopting threatening poses as the editor introduced them each in turn.

Aquilinus appeared above the arena as Jupiter, and here were the rest of the New Gods: a half court, only six of the twelve Olympians. And they were more than straight copies of the old gods—these were underworld variations. Licinus was dressed as Mars in a horned helmet and blood-red armor with a black stripe running down his chest—the hellish River Styx. His armor gleamed new, spikes protruded from it, and his helmet was arched over the eyes with one long spine running down to protect his nose. War chain in hand, a spear driven into the sand beside him, Licinus was radiant; his armor was specially designed to emit a numinous glow, an artificial aura. Aquilinus was continuing with his bait and switch, giving the empirewide audience the chance to swap invisible gods for ones they could see. I had to convince them otherwise. Beside Licinus was Barbata in some cruel manifestation of Venus, with a mess of dark hair that writhed in snakelike tendrils as if it were alive—barely concealing her near nudity, partly snapping and grasping at the air around her, a Venusian Medusa. Mania, slender and young, was dressed in the gear of the huntress Diana: black armor, long knife at her side, and carrying a war bow with arrows that, Julius Gemminus announced, always found their way to their target. Castor and Pollux, the Dioscurii, stood ready to fight as one, two arms, one fighter, in black armor with red wings on their boots and helmets, depicting Mercury's speed and swiftness. In the place of their falx, the charioteers wielded a long knife with a triangular blade in the hand of one, and a shield on the arm of the other that had rotating energy blades spinning around its edge, ready to cut. By comparison, we looked old, dirty, wounded—suitable representatives of the ruined statues of the gods surrounding the arena—but which of the old gods our ragtag team was meant to represent, Aquilinus made no effort to explain.

Surrounding us, an audience looked on in judgment. It had been generated by the vox populi—each ghostly avatar representing billions, the flickering forms segregated into house sections and a section for what appeared to be the robes of the various collegia.

"Behold the New Gods!" Julius Gemminus proclaimed.

The wheel stopped abruptly and we hit the deck.

I regained my balance and surveyed the scene as quickly as I could. It was the Wheel of Fortuna, the device the orbital station above us was named for.

"You wanted a battle of the old and new gods," Aquilinus said, addressing me directly. "And so that is what I have created. The gladiatorial combats originated as funerary games, the gladiators were called funeral men. The fight was a ritual framed by the lawful rites of sacrifice. So in like mind, this last arena shall be the underworld funeral of the old gods, represented by Accala and her team. This is a landscape to test your argument. As the Olympians overthrew their parents, the Titans, and cast them into Tartarus, where the wicked are punished, my New Gods will overthrow you! Let us see if your gods are real and will stand by you now.

"This final match will see the conclusion of the bargain I struck with Accala Viridius before you all." Aquilinus now spoke to the audience at large. "If my team loses, I will give up my throne. If she loses, she will see her house fall forever. Every Viridian will be declared an enemy of the state and subject to execution on sight."

The audience of ghostly avatars cheered, going wild. They liked this. The mob had bought into Aquilinus' bargain. This was going to happen. The arena had become a little bit of Sertorius Primus, a morsel served up to the empire. A sign of what was to come.

Julius Gemminus continued. "You see before you three concentric rings," he announced to the audience. "On the outer are four long chambers enclosing Accala and her menagerie. In the middle are four similar chambers for the mighty Blood Eagles." The editor paused as the crowd cheered. "The third ring has at its center the winner's pedestal. This innermost ring is sealed off by an energy shield. One team must fall in its entirety for the field to be lifted. Then the victor— either the last person standing, or the senior team member, if more than one survive—will ascend the stairs. It is upon this pedestal that the victor will stand. The losers will be immortalized, fossilized into the ruined stadium as statues."

Surviving the wheel and ascending the pedestal was traditional in the Sertorian arenas, the ultimate proof of worthiness to lead, the supreme sign of might and righteousness. This was a great gaming wheel whose spin would decide the fate of the empire. Aquilinus had no intention that I, or any in my team, should survive to ascend those steps. This game would be rigged. I couldn't allow Marcus, Julia, or Pavo to fall. We were going to get through this together as a team. Then, as Julius Gemminus talked away, I saw it. The sunken eyes, the yellow pallor. The Blood Eagles were all dressed up to conceal a weakness—ambrosia withdrawal. They were finally running short on ambrosia.

"They're weak!" I yelled. "They're out of ambrosia!" Separated as we were, I couldn't tell if my words carried to the other side of the shields. I had no more time to communicate my vital insight as, with a flourish, Aquilinus' projection reached down from above and set our outer wheel spinning.

"Round and round and round we go!" Julius Gemminus proclaimed. "And where she stops, nobody knows! Who will fight whom first? The moment the wheel stops, the shields that separate the inner and outer rings will drop, and the first round of matches will begin!"

The wheel started fast, but soon it began to slow, taking on an ungainly pace—an internal rotor was controlling the speed of deceleration. Aquilinus knew exactly what kind of a matchup he wanted.

As the wheel came to a stop, the outer and inner wedges lined up, matching opponent to opponent in the first round. Mania the Huntress was waiting opposite me, eyes shining. Pavo was facing off against Barbata in her Venus getup. Marcus against Licinus, Julia versus the Dioscurii. A trumpet sounded and the shield walls that stood immediately between the opponents disappeared, but the remaining shields separating each pair from the rest of the players flashed for an instant and changed from green to red—they'd been electrified. I tapped one of them with my spear tip, and it let off a mighty spark big enough for my teammates to see. The walls were now weapons in their own rights.

"Lumen, stay behind me, out of harm's way. No one here wants to see you hurt."

He didn't answer. He was shining, more cracks than ever. Time was running out for him, and that meant no one could allow these games to run for too long. There were going to be lots of quick kills, rivers of blood on the sand.

Mania nocked an arrow and fired. Then another, and then a third. Fast! I swung Orbis out in sweeping arcs, catching the arrows in different places in their paths, redirecting them away before they reached me. Move forward, close the gap. Mania just stood there, a slim smile on her sweet little face. Why wasn't she following up? Then the first arrow struck me in the back, just below the right shoulder blade. As the arrow point penetrated, I fell forward and spun, lashing out with Orbis. Orbis caught the other two arrows and splintered one, destroying it, and sending the other away. I cast my discus in pursuit, and he followed the arrow on its course and cut it in half just as it was arcing around to come back for another strike. Trick arrows to match Orbis' return arc. The stories said that Diana's arrows never missed their mark. This must be one of Aquilinus' little jokes. What additional powers had been given to the other Sertorians?

I awkwardly ripped the arrow from my shoulder, then switched my spear to my left hand and threw it at her. A split second later Orbis returned and I cast him at once. Mania dodged the spear neatly, but it caused her to step right into Orbis' path, cutting her left shoulder. She screamed and swore, giving me a second to quickly survey how the others were holding up.

To my right, Licinus slipped past one of Marcus' gladius thrusts and punched him, sending him flying across the cell so fast and hard that I thought he was going to hit the electrified wall, but Marcus managed to roll and disperse some of the force of the Sertorian's blow, coming to a stop just inches away from certain death. Licinus was the new Mars in more than just appearance. He had superhuman strength. But how? Not from the ambrosia. He didn't have that kind of strength before, even when he was dosed up to the eyeballs.

"The armor," I shouted to Marcus. "His strength comes from the armor!"

Forbidden machinarii enhancements. It was anything goes in Aquilinus' arena, as long as it suited his team. Marcus nodded in acknowledgment as he recovered his feet, and then I was on again with Mania. Another volley of her seeker arrows. I used the arms from my breastplate, swinging Orbis in a pattern. The arrows flew off the shield of arcs it formed, clattering away, only it put me on the back foot. I couldn't attack. I lowered my guard, and then, as the arrows came, I snatched one with my arms, spun, and sent it back. Then another two. If I could throw a discus with them, then why not an arrow, just like Pavo's crossbow or a spear throw? Mania diverted one with her bow, one missed, but the third struck home, hitting her in the left hip bone. She shrieked, her white hair flailing about her, as she fell and then quickly pulled the arrow from her side, grimacing in pain.

To my left I caught sight of Pavo, his muscles straining as he tried to disentangle himself from Barbata's net. He was too late, though—her trident speared him in the upper chest. It was on his right side and it missed his heart, but it probably punctured a lung. He'd live, but for how long? It was a strange encounter to witness. Pavo was a strong competitor. How had Barbata delivered such a crippling wound so quickly? He didn't seem to be struggling or fighting at all.

I looked past Mania as she stood up. Beyond her, in the cell opposite, was Julia versus the Dioscurii. No match at all. The charioteers were moving apart, rejoining with lightning speed, one moment working together as one, then separating into two one-armed charioteers attacking from opposite angles. Their power was super speed, and they were using it to play a game of cat and mouse as they cut her to pieces. Their weapons flashed as they passed, paper-thin cuts to make her bleed. They were playing to the crowd's bloodlust. Julia was sensible, hovering near the rear curved wall of the cell, using the danger of electrocution to minimize their opportunity to come at her from both sides.

Mania closed in on me, long knife in her left hand. No traditional one-on-one, she ducked and rolled under my first swing and came up under my guard, stabbing me in the side as she passed. She was fast, but not as fast as the Dioscurii. I cast backward as she passed and heard a yelp of surprise. Spinning about, I saw she was missing some fingers. A lucky strike on my part. Good luck pulling the string on her bowstaff now.

Marcus and Licinus faced off. The whip lashed out, and Marcus threw up his arm, biting back the pain as the electrified surface wrapped around his forearm. But it was planned. He ran at Licinus, faster than the Sertorian could retract the whip. Licinus had only two options: focus on the whip and use the other hand to speed up, retracting it to gain control over Marcus' body, or let him come and focus on the spear to attack. He chose the spear, and it snaked out, right through Marcus' body. But Marcus angled himself at the last moment, and it took him through the shoulder. He drove down the spear's length, his hands closing around Licinus' throat. He was squeezing with all his might, but a flash of light revealed an armored membrane protecting the Sertorian's neck, hampering Marcus' assault. Then Licinus used his trick of transmitting electricity through his weapon, shocking his opponent. Marcus had gambled that he'd be able to squeeze the life out of Licinus before the electricity claimed him, and he'd guessed wrong. Marcus went limp, and I looked through the shield helplessly as Licinus lowered his spear, letting his opponent slide to the ground.

Suddenly, Licinus sank to one knee with a shout. Marcus had feigned his collapse and then attacked Licinus' legs, taking the Sertorian off guard. Throughout the fight, Marcus had been cutting the Sertorian's armor away, and plates of black and red littered the arena floor. Now Marcus pulled aside, staying out of the way of Licinus' fists, and was actually about to drive his gladius into the space between Licinus' neck and right trapezius.

I turned on Mania, who was edging away from me, protecting her wounded hand. With no bow and only one good hand, I'd make short work of her. In moments two of our enemies would lie dead on the arena floor.

"My interest in this combination is waning. Let's shake things up a little," Aquilinus' booming voice said from on high.

The Blood Eagles broke off combat at once and sped to their chambers in the middle ring. Force shields were reactivated as Aquilinus reached down and pretended to spin the arena wheel, triggering the motors to turn the platforms below. We were spinning again, thrown back to the rear walls of the cells by the sudden centripetal force. I braced for the electric shock, but it had been disabled. Cheating bastard. But, though Aquilinus had prevented Marcus and me from killing our opponents, the upside was that it saved Julia's life. Wounded by the Dioscurii's daggers, she had at least three puncture wounds she was trying to stem the blood from. She was going to die, but not yet. Aquilinus was happy to let things run while Julia was being cut up. Marcus was yelling something at me, but I couldn't make out what he was saying. He was desperately trying to pry himself free from the field that held him to the wall, trying to pull his sword arm up, but to swing at what?

The wheels slowed and I fell from the wall. Opposite me now were the Dioscurii, with their cold, expressionless faces, weapons gleaming in the bright light. They separated as they moved toward me, closing in on either side. The wall crackled behind me. Round two had begun.

Marcus faced Barbata now, but he had no weapon in his hand. Pavo had managed to untangle himself from Barbata's net, but he was struggling to stand. Out of breath, running on one lung, he was facing Licinus. And Julia was up against an angry Mania. Mania was done with arrows; she had to play up close. No distance weapon and fighting with her off hand. It might buy Julia a few extra seconds because the Sertorian was not going to make the Dioscurii's mistake and play games.

The Dioscurii were a sudden blur and then they were on me, weapons flashing. I was going to use the arms of my breastplate to keep them at bay, but they were too quick. I blocked the cut to my jugular but didn't catch the one to my thigh. I lashed out, but they were gone again. Damn fast.

I risked a glance back in Lumen's direction. He was shining. The air was heavy with ichor. He was drawing it into his small body, but from where?

Then then Dioscurii began to slow. Black fluid was seeping from their eyes and ears. A powerful light source behind me lit the arena and I risked a look back and saw Lumen. However much ambrosia was left in the Blood Eagles, Lumen was reclaiming it, emitting power as he'd done at the heart of the mountain, driving the impurities right out of their bodies.

Looking around I saw Licinus' eyes widen in shock. They were dying, vulnerable, and completely reliant on their armor enhancements and trick weapons. Lumen had given us our best chance at survival.

The Dioscurii were still moving faster than I could react. If I struck out where they stood, they'd already be gone, but the art of the discus was the art of anticipation. The strategy was to attack not where they were now but where they were going to be. But I'd get only one chance. I needed to entice them to rejoin. I threw in arcs, a scythe action that made it too hard to come at me from either side. Wait for it. Now. They rejoined in a blur and then slipped through my defense to start their attack. I was swinging like I was still holding Orbis. They went to counter but realized there was no weapon in my hand at the same time as Orbis came back to me, right through both their necks, severing their heads from their shoulders. For the first time, I saw emotion on the Dioscurii's faces. And all thanks to Lumen's intervention. Shock, surprise, they didn't see that coming. The headless bodies fell at my feet, and the sky was filled with golden thumbs. I was a hit. And then I realized they were not just cheering me. Pavo was dead at Licinus' feet, the steel chain wrapped around his throat. And Julia? I was shocked to see Mania lying dead on the sand. But how? Julia was no gladiator. The answer came when I recognized Marcus' gladius in Mania's back. Marcus must have found a way to bypass the energy shields. It was the spin. The shields must weaken as they spun, allowing a weapon to pass through. He had delivered a fatal wound to Mania. He had thrown away his weapon to save Julia's life.

I turned to see how Marcus was faring against Barbata in time to witness tragedy. He was just standing there. Barbata stood before him, brandishing her trident. There was no mistaking the swirl of red and purple light that surrounded them; Barbata had a hypnogogic machine. Some portable version of the machine they used on me aboard *Incitatus*. I studied her armor carefully. The effect seemed to come from a panel on her upper chest and was directed by her trident. Like the arachnoraptors' staffs, the trident was a transmitter that could focus the machine's effect into a beam for use in combat. But that information was no good to Marcus. His weapon was lowered; he was pleading with Barbata, "Don't do this. I love you!" and holding something out to her, maybe a ribbon, but I couldn't say for certain. I'd seen my father in Crassus' hypnogogic machine, but I knew who Marcus saw—his great love, Amphiara.

I screamed his name, trying to get him to snap out of it, but it was too late. The trident took him in the throat, and he fell to his knees and then to the floor.

As we were stuck in our segments, a new figure appeared in the arena: shrouded in black, a scythe in his hands, a long helmet covering his face. I didn't even see him enter; it was as if he just materialized. This was the man playing Hades, and he'd come to take the unworthy to hell. His pick hit the bodies in their center of mass before dragging them away, one by one; he took his time, like an elderly gardener raking leaves. The Dioscurii, Pavo, and Mania. He took Marcus last. My mentor, my lover. I weakened him, my need was what caused him—he who should never have fallen—to fall. The blood trailed after his body, making a red track on the sand as he was dragged off. Even the Sertorians were left in the same pile. No honor was given by Aquilinus to those who failed him.

XLVII

THE ENERGY SHIELDS rearranged to accommodate the number of remaining players, leaving one great wheel split into four equal parts. At the center, the shielded podium and the gold laurel crown awaited the victor. Julia was in the segment directly below me, Barbata to my right.

"And now that the weak and unworthy have fallen, and those with righteous skill and power as well as those who have survived by pure chance make up the final four!" Julius Gemminus boomed. "The wheel spins around and around, who will live and who will fly, fly away to death's door?"

The wheel turned slowly. I tested the shield but it held firm, no way for a weapon to pierce it. Speed was the key. That was the secret that Marcus had discovered before his life was stolen away. We had to have speed if I was going to be of any help to Julia. As we came to a stop, I was certain he'd give Barbata to Julia and have Licinus and me pair off, but the lineup was Julia facing Licinus. The snake-headed Venus and her hypnotic armor were mine.

I got it. Aquilinus thought Julia would be dead whomever she faced. He wanted to appease the mob by making a grudge match between Barbata and me. I had to have the chance to strike back at Marcus' killer to keep the audience happy. And if I survived, he wanted to build anticipation for a final round between Licinus and me—the ultimate test. That meant I had to finish Barbata quickly and then do what I could to keep Julia alive.

"Run!" I yelled at Julia. "Keep clear of the whip! I'll come as soon as I can."

She nodded and backed as far away from Licinus as the space would allow.

"That's a bit presumptuous, don't you think, my little vixen?" Barbata asked, pouting her full lips. "You're hardly a wolf anymore, are you, Accala-of-no-house? More a wily fox bitch who's playing out of her league. It's very disappointing. Will you fall to your knees before me and beg as your teacher Marcus did?"

I didn't take the bait and kept moving in, circling toward her while she talked, expecting Barbata to go right on the assault, but she just stood there babbling insults. I'd close the gap and finish her quickly. But as I started forward, she was suddenly gone, and standing in her place was Bulla.

It was not a projection; it really was her. There was even the smell of matted fur, the sour smell of Taurii blood that ran from the wound in the neck I gave her aboard *Incitatus*.

"You killed me," she said. "You led me to my death. You knew your father would do this, and you didn't care. I'm just chattel to you."

But it couldn't be Bulla. This was the effect of Barbata's portable hypnogogic machine, and I must defend myself and more.

I drove forward and struck, but Bulla was holding her ancestral weapon, a war hammer. She used it to block my weapon and then hit me with a back sweep, the hammerhead impacting my side. I flew across the sand and landed on my back. How could this be? An illusion didn't change physics. Barbata had a trident, no blunt-force weapon. Looking down, I saw no wound but it was painful to take a deep breath, and I was short on oxygen.

Lumen. Where was he? Huddled up in the corner of the wedge. Shining brightly, light seeping through the cracks of his body. I glanced down at my body again quickly and now I saw blood. No dent in my armor from a hammer blow but instead puncture wounds. It was all in my mind. Whatever Barbata was doing, it affected my perceptions. I quickly struggled to my feet as Bulla charged again, desperately circling out of the corner before she caught me with the sharp tips of her broad curved horns.

I cast Orbis and went to use the lapis arms in my suit, but they seemed to have vanished as a result of Barbata's illusion. I wore my old armor from the arena back in Rome—the outfit of Lupa She-Wolf. Bulla blocked my discus easily and knocked him aside, on an angle that sent him hurtling into the energy field, where he sparked and fell to the sand below. I was without arms.

Bulla took up position between me and the fallen discus, her damp nostrils flaring and steaming in the cold, preventing me from recovering my weapon. As I backed away from Bulla and closer to Lumen, I noticed a change. The Taurii's form began to dissolve, revealing Barbata. Lumen was the key. His light affected me, fought off the effect Barbata's ray had on my mind, and revealed the truth. Barbata hesitated, but only for a second, before slowly advancing. Lumen's radiance was powerful. If he couldn't keep it together, I wondered if we all would die here, everyone on and around this world, incinerated in a cataclysmic explosion. Now the illusion fell away, Lumen's light did the trick, and here was Barbata coming at me. But she didn't know I could see her as she truly was—her long hair writhing and hissing, her dark eyes scornful, and one shapely arm raised holding her weapon. I couldn't give myself away, so I carefully kept my eyes aimed toward where I expected to see Bulla. There was Barbata's trident with the hypnogogic device in it. The trident came lancing in, and I sidestepped it and grasped the shaft, pushing it aside and head-butting Barbata right between the eyes. That'd teach her to wear armor that was more for form than function. Trusting that she'd leave Lumen be, I kept moving past her, rolling at the last moment to recover Orbis, feeling the wind rush past as her trident missed me by a hair's breadth.

Barbata was on to me now, knew I could see through her tricks. I turned to throw, and my opponent was right there. She'd closed the gap to keep me boxed in.

The Sertorian thrust at me with her trident, and I stepped backward, avoiding certain death, then screamed and jumped forward as the field shocked and burned me from behind.

"I'm going to cook you alive," she said, thrusting again. I couldn't go back. My arms were numb, I could smell the foul stench of my burned hair, and I had only a few seconds before the pain from any nerve damage hit home. There was only one way available. I stepped into the thrust, angling myself to take it on the side. I gasped in pain but managed to lash out with Orbis, cutting her exposed thigh. She retreated. I'd slowed her down, and speed and maneuverability were everything in the arena.

Barbata couldn't get the grin off her face. She thought it was going to end there for me. I was surprised. She was not attacking. There was a flash and she was going to try her trick again. Now it was Marcus, smiling at me, admiration in his eyes, that made my chest tighten. Marcus, whom she just slaughtered. And then he warped and Crassus stood before me, in his prime once more, oozing charm. Depending on what angle I was looking at her, she appeared as Crassus one moment, Marcus the next.

And then the feelings hit me, as Barbata brought out the full strength of her secret weapon. The powerful feelings I had for Crassus, as manipulated as they were, and then the love for Marcus—they hit me like a truck. I couldn't find my fighting spirit; I felt only a tide of emotion. It made me want to drop to my knees and cry. I felt elated, excited, my heart palpitating, my hands shaking. But all those weeks in Crassus' hypnogogic machine had prepared me for this, and my mind responded automatically, by holding on to one fixed truth: Lumen.

I ducked underneath Barbata's thrust, came up on her right side, under her arm, and used both my arms to push her backward. The Sertorian screamed even before she hit the electrified wall. Before she could escape I rammed her with my shoulder, locking her up against the deadly field. Within seconds she caught on fire and I quickly stepped aside, leaving her staggering about before me, dead on her feet. Burning Venus. Another half-a-dozen steps with her snake headdress writhing wildly about, and then she fell to the floor, her body twitching, still on fire.

Hot tears streamed down my cheeks, stinging my eyes. My own blood was now visible, flowing from the wound Barbata had delivered to my side with her trident.

It was all I could do not to sink Orbis into Barbata's body, to cut her face up in revenge as I had before. But I held myself still. I had made an oath to myself as much as to any higher power. This was for the empire. This was for justice. It couldn't be personal. Not like before. This had to be different, or I'd be a lost soul, regardless of whether I won or lost, and maybe, with the entire empire watching my every move, they would too. I had to be the nobility of an empire that had thrown its own dignity aside like an old washcloth, sold it cheap for bread and circuses and the promise of a poisoned chalice of immortality.

Gods! What of Julia? I turned at once, the second my fingers closed about Orbis. Licinus was choking her slowly. Waiting for me to watch. Grinning maliciously when he saw me looking. How could I get to her? I remembered that spinning weakened the field. Marcus had paid with his life to send me that knowledge. The generator for the field was atop the pillar. It was the pivot point that made the fields turn. Would spinning it take the charge off the walls too? I ran to the far end of the cell and threw Orbis as hard as I could, using the arms of the breastplate to help accelerate him on his journey. Orbis hit the far wall, which erupted in a massive shower of sparks and then rebounded, back to my hand. I threw again, and again. Slowly it started to move.

Gradual turning, nothing major. Like a swing, I had to gather momentum, but although I had got it started, I couldn't build up enough momentum all on my own.

"Julia! The central field generator, it's got an engine. Make it turn. Help me!"

I threw again, and all the while Licinus was laughing as he extinguished Julia's life. Her hand was raised, though. She was giving me every last ounce of focus that she could muster. That magic hand that could control machines. Was this what Lumen meant? Was this how she would save the day? And then we were spinning, picking up speed, faster and faster. There was a color shift in the field. Licinus was scowling, and then I threw myself at the wall. It burned and for a moment I thought I was going to be stuck, dead like Barbata, but then I was through, falling to the sand on the other side.

Licinus freed Julia at once, sending her spinning off onto the sand, her face purple and sweating, her hands at her throat as she struggled to breathe in great gulps.

All of the shield barriers faded like morning mist carried away by a breeze, including the one barring entry to the podium.

"Well! The rules say that if it's down to two viable fighters, then the third and final round has commenced," Julius Gemminus announced. "The first to ascend the pillar of champions is the winner of the arena! Go to!"

But what of Julia? The Sertorians weren't big on odd numbers in their final fights. There. The black-robed figure appeared, moving toward Julia's writhing body with his scythe in hand. Death was coming to finish her off and even things up.

I had two fights on my hands now. I didn't want to engage the black-robed figure if I didn't have to, but he could not be allowed to take my friend.

Julia had more problems than her breathing. The knife wounds the Dioscurii had given her were still open, blood pumping out of the triangular punctures, an aberration of hope and nature, giving the body no chance to heal and close.

I cast Orbis at the reaper, and he vanished suddenly. Gone. No time to worry about where, or if he'd reappear. For the moment Julia was out of harm's way, and I had to focus all my efforts on surviving Licinus. I had underestimated him in the Hyperborean cavern, but I would be more careful this time.

His whip cracked sharply. Face red, his black-and-red armor shredded by Marcus' gladius, he was frightening to behold. Fast, strong, as good an impersonator of Mars as you could hope to find. The spikes that protruded from his armor gleamed in the floodlights.

The whip snaked out fast, aiming for my wounded side. I knocked it away with Orbis, but as we made contact, the whip folded and licked my shoulder, delivering a lancing pain. He grinned maliciously in anticipation of victory. I had nothing left but adrenaline. I cast Orbis, and Licinus knocked him aside quickly with his spear, but on an orbit that returned to me. He was fast, but not like the Dioscurii. The whip lashed out again, the length extending past me. As my weapon returned to my hand, Licinus' whip snaked back, wrapping around my waist. It was an unexpected move. Slowly now, like a boa constrictor, the coils of the whip squeezed me, and with each squeeze, they crushed and pulled, drawing me toward Licinus. He planned to entangle me, draw me in, and then skewer me with his spear. My enemy hadn't factored my armor into the equation, though. I had managed to activate the black bands moments before the whip could close tight, leaving me just enough wiggle room. I let him reel me in. He was playing it up for the crowd, raising his spear in victory, savoring the moment. His eyes locked with mine as the weapon's point came flashing down. Instantly my armor's lapis arms stretched open the whip's coils and pushed them up over my head, blocking the thrust. For that split second, until he could pull his spear back to either attack again or block, he was exposed. I cut at his throat, but he managed to pull away. Changing angle, I succeeded in scoring a long cut up the side of his face, knocking his helmet from his head. He was blinded for an instant, and before he could strike back, I attacked again, a diagonal cut across his right eye. Licinus staggered back, blood weeping from his wounds. One more shot to the throat and he'd be done.

A thundering boom echoed through the arena. Aquilinus had cast an ion bolt! The ground exploded behind me, the force of the impact sending me flying forward and onto Licinus. We both fell to the ground. He rolled me off and tried to mount me. I bucked and threw him over, rolling off to the side and springing up, at the ready.

But he was not fighting. He was already running to the exit. He was fleeing.

"Come back here! Fight, you bastard!" I screamed. "You coward!"

He fled to the sound of the crowd's boos and hisses, and I was left standing in the arena alone. I couldn't believe it, and I couldn't pursue him; I needed to look after Julia.

Kneeling by her side, I could see she was dying. Her breaths were short and ragged, her skin pale but sweaty. She looked up at me with resignation in her eyes. There was some first aid powder in pods on her utility belt. I broke them open and poured the contents over her wounds. She had taken a lot of damage, but the powder did its work and stopped the hemorrhaging.

A shadow fell over her body. The black-robed figure was shuffling toward us.

"You will stand away or I will kill you," I said to it. "She lives. You'll not take her."

He hesitated and then moved away. It seemed his orders were to claim only the dead. I took Julia in my arms. We had to keep moving, beyond the bounds of this arena, into the mountains beyond.

"No. The podium," Julia whispered. "Seize the golden wreath and win it properly, or the people won't follow. It must be done properly."

I laid her gently back down.

As I walked toward it, Aquilinus' holographic hand stretched above us. Another bolt struck the ground, sending me flying back from the force of impact. No direct hit, but he was making it clear what would happen if I tried to take the victory crown from the podium.

"You have no right to interfere!" I yelled at him.

The arena floor beneath Julia's cell suddenly fell away, forming a ramp that she tumbled down, rolling into whatever lay in the darkness below. It locked into place before I could get back to her. I had saved Julia, but for what? Once again they had her.

I moved toward the center ring, but the shield around the podium, the last shield remaining, had been reactivated. He was denying me victory, like a spoiled child who'd lost at a game and insisted the other children announce him the winner. He wouldn't let me ascend the champion's podium. In response, the ghostly audience were screaming their outrage, the voice of the empire ringing out in chaotic gongs of disapproval.

"Is this how the god-emperor Aquilinus plays?" I yelled to the crowd and the cameras above me. Now that Julia was out of the arena, they could bring their recording toys in close again without fear of them being hijacked. "I'm the only one left! I'm the winner. Your champion has fled the field like the coward he is. I demand you acknowledge me the victor and be done with it."

He had to acknowledge me, or that empirewide riot he'd been trying to quell would spin out of control.

Either way, now I'd won. He'd either let me win and honor our bet, or he'd deny me, and the citizens of the empire would riot to destroy House Sertorian.

"No, no. That's not how this is going to end," he boomed down at me like a disapproving schoolmaster. "Not by a long shot. I am a Sertorian emperor and this is still my game. So you will finish this the Sertorian way. No Sertorian champion is declared winner of a ludus until he or she has overcome the final challenge, a final test of ruthlessness."

In games in the Sertorian arena circuit, there was always a gladiator, often the most celebrated champion, who stood as the final obstacle before a victor could be crowned. In keeping with the theme of the New Gods, the last obstacle would be Hades himself.

"You are in the arena of the dead," he continued, "so if you wish to mount the podium and claim the prize, you must overcome death itself. Only then will you prove your thesis and win our wager. If you can do that, then I will gladly admit you are the winner with all it entails."

The ratings were against Aquilinus, but some of the audience were cheering now. They felt the injustice of this, but they couldn't resist the lure of a final bloody showdown, especially after being cheated of a conclusive result to my fight with Licinus. I considered fleeing the arena as Licinus had done, but I'd lose the crowd in an instant and they were the only thing standing between me and an ion bolt from the orbital cannon.

"Give me your best shot!" I yelled at him. "It doesn't matter what you throw at me. I won't stop until I've brought you down."

"Then behold Hades," Aquilinus announced, "the killer of all things, even gods, and certainly of a mangy wolf who doesn't know her place."

His black form appeared out of thin air between me and the podium steps. Slightly stooped, robed in black from head to toe, a long, shining steel skull mask. Damn. This was why I didn't see him enter the arena before. He had some cloaking technology. It must be a chameleon device, I'd read about them—they used projections of the environment around the device to render the wearer invisible. Still, this coughing, hobbling excuse for an underworld god couldn't be Aquilinus' champion and I was certain it wasn't the same person who'd played the role of Hades earlier in the games. Here was no ambrosia-laden Olympian. He was slow, limping. I wouldn't have a problem taking him, invisibility trick or not.

I strode toward him, Orbis in my left hand, at the ready. He was holding his ground, letting me close the gap. I dropped into my stance and started to wind up for the throw, but before I could cast, he vanished. I dropped low, extending my senses, listening for a clue, watching for some sign of his presence.

In the old stories it was Hades' helmet that gave him the power of invisibility. I cast wide in short arcs, back and forth, cutting the space up into a grid to pinpoint his location.

The sand gave me no clues. He must have antigravity discs on the soles of his boots. That meant he was not only going to leave no tracks but he'd also be able to slide around the arena like quicksilver. That limp wasn't going to slow him down much.

Pain and a pool of blood blossomed on the robes of my unarmored left shoulder. I saw the point of the scythe only as it was passing away from my body. I lashed out with Orbis, but he was gone.

Hades must have been anticipating my plan and moved ahead of the grid I was marking out. Damn smart and I didn't sense him at all. Another hit to my arm, in exactly the same place. I managed to hold in the scream the first time, but the repetitive aggravation of my exposed nerves was more than I could stand, and a cry of pain tumbled out of my mouth.

I swung again. Another miss. I had only my right hand now, my burned hand, which lacked the finesse of my left. Minerva. I couldn't stand here like a training dummy waiting to get hit. I needed to even up the odds. I blinked, clearing my vision, as snowflakes hit my eyes. The snowflakes! That was it! The shields were down now. Aquilinus didn't need to keep us penned in, and the snowflakes were filling the air, falling on the sand, covering up the blood. The snow was the key. I watched the flakes fall. There. A distortion in the air where they stopped suddenly, their path to the ground disrupted by an obstacle—that's my man. I cast, strong and true. There was a loud clang as Orbis struck the helmet, sending it flying from Hades' head. The black-robed man stumbled back, falling to one knee just five feet from me, his head bowed. An old man with a bald spot and white hair. When he looked up, I froze in my tracks. Two eyes—one human, one red and mechanical—stared back at me. Gods, no. It was Father.

XLVIII

"Father?"

I was so sure he'd been killed when Aquilinus tortured him. He didn't answer. Had they drugged him? Brainwashed him?

"Father?"

"Accala," he said, just loud enough so I could hear, "you have to understand. I was never going to kill you. Just stop you. I made a deal."

His speech sounded clear, his eyes were focused, not disoriented. He knew what he was doing. The scythe he'd been holding before was gone, replaced by long, sharp pike.

"A deal? I don't understand."

"To do what you cannot. To save you, to preserve the remnants of the empire so that House Viridian will have some hope of surviving this . . . folly of yours."

I stepped back, looking down at him, barely able to believe what he'd just said.

"What have you done?"

"I've given Aquilinus what he wants: I promised you to him in marriage. You will fall today in the arena, but you will not die, you will live. Your marriage will protect our house from destruction."

"As a slave. Worse, as a whore to the warlord who usurped the empire."

"Don't you dare lecture me," he spat. "I followed you here because I knew someone would have to clean up your trail of destruction. You blunder into everything without thought of the outcome. You don't know what you're doing."

"I know exactly what I'm doing."

"You can fool yourself, but I'm your father, I know you."

I wouldn't let him get to me. I couldn't do this father-daughter nonsense. Not now. Aquilinus put him in here to throw me. This was Aquilinus' final card, the one thing he thought would make me buckle. But I couldn't stop now.

"You still don't see it," I said to him. "You don't see me, but it doesn't matter. I'm fighting for the empire."

"*I* don't see it? I might have only one eye, but you're the one who's blind. You're drowning and pulling the entire empire down with you."

The spherae hovered low. No Julia to stop them now. They wanted to capture every juicy detail. Father versus daughter in a final arena challenge. The ghost audience was up on their feet, cheering. Our pairing was a masterstroke. Aquilinus' downward trend was over. He'd played his hand well. Aquilinus had ridden the wave of the audience's displeasure, knowing that when this turn of events was revealed, his popularity would skyrocket. They wanted it. Every single one of these death-loving bastards in our galactic audience wanted to see this play out.

Somehow I had to convince my father to yield and at the same time win the crowd back to my side, but they were not going to settle for any outcome that didn't end with blood on the sand.

"This all hinges on whether you believe that I can triumph," I said to Father. "Forget my disobedience to you. If I fail, I will have committed the greatest evil, and hubris and the empire will pay the price, you're right. But if I triumph, then it's the greatest good, the empire saved, our enemy dashed and ruined, everything reestablished. It's the highest stakes hanging by a thread, I admit it, but I bet on myself and that the gods are with me. I will not break or yield. I stand for hope, and you are standing against hope. You're bargaining for scraps from Aquilinus' table as if we've already lost, when the last battle is still to be fought and we're in sight of victory."

The sky was filled with light and choruses of trumpets.

"You won't change my mind," he said.

"I know."

A drumroll began to sound above us.

"If you wish to serve, then do it this way, Accala—the only hope is of survival, not victory. Serve your house, serve me and yield," he demanded as he rose to his feet, pike at the ready.

"I cannot," I said. "No more than you can."

His pike drove forward, and I parried with Orbis and swung at him. Even though he was limping, his arms were good and he could bring both of them to bear against my one. His pike was custom-made, short and thin so he could maneuver it quickly.

Now I saw firsthand why he was regarded as one of the last great heroes of the empire. Turning his pike this way and that, he weaved in and out of the defensive pattern I was making with Orbis and my arms. He was skilled, not as fast as he would have been in his youth, but he compensated, using small angles to attack and redirect my discus. He had kept up his training at his private gymnasium; he still had it. With all that experience and know-how, he was through my defenses like water through an aqueduct, slipping this way and that.

"Stop this. It doesn't have to be this way," I said.

"You always talk too much. Like your mother. If I stop, then he will kill all of the prisoners aboard the stadium," he said. We traded blows, like running an exercise. Testing each other, trying to find a way through each other's defenses. This was like the game we played when I was a child, when he trained us at home. Except now the odds were much higher, and no quarter was given. He was pushing me to my limits. "How did you think it would be otherwise? Your mother and I taught you to assess the odds, to think logically. You're surrounded. Aquilinus looks down over us. This is his game, he holds all the cards. It's the empire at stake here, Accala. They all came to the games, the most powerful senators, the leaders of the noble houses, the artists and celebrities. It's the empire in microcosm, all its best and brightest. Do you understand? These are our stars, our constellation. If they die, then the empire is truly lost forever. Now yield."

"And if I don't?"

"You will," he insisted.

Father's pike shot for my eye, I blocked and it had already circled around, sweeping at my thigh. I sidestepped and threw an elbow into his face that caught him unawares, forcing him a step back to recover his guard.

He held a finger up, touching the blood that ran from his broken nose.

"That was impressive," he grunted. And then the pike came again.

"Aquilinus has bought you," I said, trying to keep the anger from my voice. "And cheaply."

They hadn't brainwashed him; they'd just given him an ultimatum: the death of everything he held dear—the empire he'd spent his entire life upholding, creating, forging in the Senate—or rein in his daughter. I understood even if I didn't approve. In his eyes, filled with sorrow and rage, I could see that if I didn't yield, he was going to kill me. In his mind he was choosing the empire, putting it first; only he was wrong. He thought I couldn't do it. That was the real reason he was here. Otherwise he'd have told Aquilinus to go to hell. He was here because deep down he didn't think his little girl had it in her to come through, to overcome the enemy, to be victorious in battle.

I couldn't believe it had come to this. A family row in this godsforsaken arena, in this place of all places, with so much at stake. This was not what I wanted. I couldn't do it. For all the grief he'd caused me, for all the suffering, he was still my father. He'd been kind to me, loved me. Before the bombing, he was there for me. If I killed him, that father would die as well, along with any chance that he could recover his life, refind who he was before it all went bad.

"I won't yield, but I won't kill you either," I said.

The crowd roared their disapproval. The voices of the mob fill the air about us. "Kill! Kill! Quick!"

"Daughter, I have taken the poison given to criminals and the damned, the same that Seneca took to end his life. It was part of the deal. I'm already dead. Any honor I achieved in this life is already washed away. You cannot spare me here. Do not force me to keep going. Make it so that only I die in the arena today. Yield."

I couldn't stop the tears from flowing, from the cry in my heart. Dead already. I couldn't allow myself to waver, even for him.

"You're wrong to trust Aquilinus. He will never honor his word," I said. "There might still be a way to save you, but only if you stop this and lay down your arms."

"He has written an executive order and signed it," Father said. "All the prisoners will be permitted to live. Set free beyond the Barbaricum Wall. There will be hope of raising a resistance there."

"He will never do that."

"He will if it means getting his hands on the alien child. I've been watching from above. That's what he wants. That is his ticket to power. That's why he sent me."

"To talk sense into your hysterical daughter?"

He slid in under my guard again, and I took a cut to the shoulder.

"To stop you from crushing what is our only remaining hope," he said. "You have crushed everything else; not one decision you have made has borne fruit. You have taken an event that should have resolved a civil war and turned it into a deadly coup d'état that has destabilized the empire and nearly destroyed our house. All to satisfy your own need for revenge."

"You're right. But I'm on the right path now. I've died to that idea, and now I fight for the empire. It is our own proconsul's decisions that have doomed us. He has played a game for glory and power instead of the common good. I was a pawn in that game, but no more. Nothing can come by following the path of appeasement."

"It is the only alternative, the only hope of recovering power."

"Power is a nightmare. That's the game we've been playing all this time, and it's a cosmic joke. Look at us. This is what comes of power for the sake of power. It's self-inflicted torture, not something to be desired. The only reason to wield power is to serve. It's a weight the gods put upon you, and you endure it for the benefit of others for as long as you can bear it."

"Words are only words," he said. "Action speaks louder."

He was set in his ways. I was set in stone. He was dead already, thanks to the poison. I couldn't allow him to take me with him.

Like rams locking horns, we clashed. Pike against discus. I was faster, but I was worn out, and judging from his speed and strength, they'd fed Father ambrosia. The moment our weapons touched, mine became suddenly heavy. He had tricks, skills; he could transfer his body weight into the weapon just enough that it made mine hard to wield and manipulate, but not so much that he was off balance and I could use his weight against him. Suddenly I was moving through mud, and he was sticking to my every move, waiting for the opening that would allow him to slide the point of his pike through my guard. He was good. Better than good: He was great. I was faster, but he was sneaky. A lifetime of tricks and strategy. I had the advantage of youth, but he had experience, and that was a powerful ally. He was holding back, though. The pace picked up. The torture must have taken its toll because his guard was starting to drop. I had a clean shot at his neck and let it go, and he grunted in disgust. I guess I was holding back too.

I stepped away, disengaging, and lowered Orbis.

"What are you doing?"

"I won't stop, but I won't harm you. You'll have to kill me. We'll die together and join Mother in the underworld. Do it."

"If you were really fighting for the empire, you wouldn't stop for anything," he criticized.

"And if I don't yield to you, then I'm an obstinate daughter who thinks only of herself. There's no victory. The emperor was right, you were right. I'm a gladiator, but I'm also a daughter, your daughter. Strike me down. Wash away your disgrace if you believe it's best for the empire. I won't marry Aquilinus, but I'm tired of fighting with you. I can't do this anymore."

His eye shone, and he looked at me strangely. An expression I couldn't recall seeing before.

"You were a pigheaded little girl," he said. "You never accepted my authority before, not even when you were a knee-high toddler. My brother said I should have beaten you, but I knew he was wrong. Some spirits don't bend, they break."

"I broke, and they put me back together. I learned how to bend, to to live my life for something other than myself."

"Raise your weapon," he said.

"No."

"Raise it and fight. You want to pass me? You want to prove yourself to Rome? They're all watching. Show them. No quarter."

"I won't kill you."

"I'm already dead, but I see you, Accala. Probably for the first time. I see that those qualities I objected to in you, the determination and bullheadedness, are my own. They're qualities that have allowed me to persevere and triumph in times of difficulty. I can't believe I didn't see that before now."

His expression. It was pride. He was proud of me.

"I've never surrendered in my life," he said. "Not once. I never learned how to yield even a little, and perhaps I'm a worse man for it. And you, you are a gladiator and possessed of some skill. You know how to swing that discus better than I ever could. Strike quickly, warrior to warrior, and do not dishonor me."

"Please, Father."

"Show me!"

He swung, and Orbis flew up as if of his own accord. The cold air froze my tears before they could run. We fought. I showed him no quarter, nor he me. Back and forth like a dance.

"Yes. That's it! Good!"

There was a fire, an exchange of martial heat. The cold and snow forgotten. Only the dance. My skill matched his. He warded off a swing, and I pressed down on the shaft and slid up to his throat, grabbing the weapon's tip with my free hand, locking it in place. It was a fatal blow, and he didn't try to stop the discus but rather turned his neck slightly and seized my wrist with his right hand, stopping the final, lethal movement from finishing him.

His hand locked over mine. I couldn't move Orbis; it was trapped between his pike and hand. He controlled me now, but he couldn't move either. My body was wound up, ready to deliver all its energy into the strike. The second he let go, the stored momentum would drive Orbis through to the conclusion of his path.

"Don't do this," I said. "You know I love you. I don't want to lose you. Not like I lost them."

He smiled weakly at me, his eye sparkling.

"The gods stand with you. I'm sorry it took me so long to see it. My daughter. A hero."

"No!"

He let go and reached out to touch the side of my face, a tender, fleeting touch before the discus slipped forward, cutting through one half of his neck, severing his jugular and brain stem in one stroke.

I dropped Orbis as his hands went slack. He fell to the ground, lifeless. I cradled his body, my hand closing over the artery that pumped his lifeblood out, his heart still beating, forcing the blood out between my fingers in great red pulses.

I didn't know how long I knelt there, but when I rose, my hands were covered with his blood, my white armor splattered and streaked with it—a clear handprint in the center of my chest, his handprint, his parting gesture.

Accala!

The voice sounded loudly in my head. Lumen. He was failing. I laid my father's body down and rushed to gather up the small Hyperborean. Mourning would come later. Always later. I picked him up like a child, holding him across my arms, ignoring the pain from the wounds I carried. I had to keep moving forward.

"The crown!" the crowd chanted. "Seize the crown!"

"You still think this is a game?" I cried out to them. "This is no game, this is a sin against the gods, and you are complicit. You get the leaders you deserve. You have welcomed evil, and so you must endure it. You don't get to sit on the fence anymore. You've made your choice."

The boos and heckles of the virtual crowd followed me as I carried Lumen past the podium, Orbis in hand. I'd won, only it wasn't official until I seized the crown and held it aloft. Those were the ancient rules. The gladiator with crown in hand is Jupiter's chosen champion. I walked past the podium. Let the crown rot, let them all rot if they thought I'd dance to their tune after their complicity in my father's death. Since my time in the caves with Lumen, winning the games had been important to me only as a means to an end. I had to help the Hyperboreans by getting Lumen to the mountain. That was the only path to redemption. Lumen and I approached the exit gate to the Colosseum, where a green energy field barred the way.

The crowd suddenly roared with excitement as Crassus shot out into the air, emerging from one of the ramps that led into the arena from below. He was riding the chariot we'd abandoned at the entrance. There was someone aboard. It was Julia! He'd rescued her. He was heading for the arena's northern exit, but as he passed by the central podium, he pulled up. The crown was there, right in front of him.

"Crassus! Don't you dare! Don't even think about it," I yelled.

I instantly regretted not seizing the crown when I'd had the chance. I'd spurned the mob and the very idea of the contest, to try to teach them a lesson, to show them what was important, but it hadn't occurred to me that I'd left it open for another to claim victory. I started to head back toward him, but he'd already leaped from the chariot and plucked the crown from its pedestal. The ghost audience screamed its approval, howling with delight. Before remounting the chariot, Crassus stooped and picked something up off the ground—a gladius with a shining raven emblem on its butt—Marcus' weapon.

And then Crassus was off, hurtling back out of the arena before Aquilinus could stop him, laurel crown tucked under his arm, Julia in hand. If I saw him again, I was going to kill him. I'd had enough of Crassus. Julia was right. I should have taken his life long before now.

Please. Keep moving forward. To my mother. I can't contain the power much longer, but I can put what spills out to some use. The force field won't stop you.

I passed through the energy field that barred the exit without harm. No resistance, no electrical charge. Behind the arena, the ruins of the city spread out before me. Aquilinus had no defenses in place, no hidden surprises. He hadn't expected me to get this far. I started to run toward the mountains, cradling Lumen in my arms. Perhaps two miles away, maybe three. A few miles of ruin-scattered tundra was all that lay between us and real victory. Lumen was emitting so much energy that I could barely see in front of me for the intensity of the glow. Every step came with the expectation of destruction, that Aquilinus would rain down a cascade of ion bolts from the station and end my life. That's what the mob, like some jilted lover, would have him do, it's what would grant him universal support. They hated me now more than ever. I'd spurned them, lectured them, held up a mirror to their own darkness, but I was holding Lumen, and even now Aquilinus wouldn't risk destroying him. The sun was high over the mountains. The others had sacrificed themselves so that I could be there. By the time the golden sun set, this would all be over, one way or another.

ACT VIII

LADY JUSTICE

Tell the stars in their arising:
be thy charge, O Roman, to rule the nations in thine empire;
this shall be thine art, to lay down the law of peace,
to be merciful to the conquered and beat the haughty down.
—Virgil, *Aeneid*

XLIX

QUICK. HAD TO BE quick. Get out of Lupus Civitas and to my goal. Get Lumen to the mountain. Only my legs wouldn't work right, and Aquilinus was coming. The Blood Hawks were finished, but Aquilinus was far from done. He'd send everything left in his arsenal to stop us. He couldn't allow us to reach the mountain. I saw the orbs hovering, greedy red eyes still blinking, still filming. The whole empire was watching to see what happened next.

We traveled to the city limits without any threat or obstruction. There was no sign of danger. No Praetorians, no ion cannon. No Crassus. The mountain stretched up into the clouds ahead, unexpectedly steep and sharp, like a spear tip, piercing the heart of the clouds that gathered around its heights. I understood now why the first colonists to this world dedicated it to Minerva, why they built a temple into the mountain's base. Somehow, despite its spearlike quality, there was something embracing about the mountain, something feminine. The mountain was encircled by a crescent-shaped canyon. The colonists saw Minerva when they looked at it and hoped and prayed that she would protect them.

Just a few more miles and we'd have made it. But now we would be exposed, crossing open tundra without the cover of the city ruins. The canyon could be entered only through a narrow mouth. Once we were in there, we'd have all the cover we needed. Then Lumen would be home.

Images flickered across the screen of my mind as I walked. Our mother, the goddess Minerva, a bird flying free from a cage, a ship sailing over the horizon. Freedom. Home. Mother. All those things.

Minerva. Her ruined temple awaited. Just three more miles.

A coughing fit wracked my body, and I nearly dropped Lumen. He was heavy in my arms, so heavy. Come on, legs. Stop burning, get moving.

We had barely made it fifty feet when Lumen began to writhe in my arms, twisting in pain.

"Are you going to make it?" I asked.

A flurry of images replied. Moths, cocoons, goblets overfilling with water, dams busting, insects dragging crackling transparent husks of their old bodies behind them. Things that were too small to contain what was within them. Change. Containment failure. Metamorphosis.

Keep moving. I no longer cared if the Hyperboreans were servants of the gods or just desperate aliens who needed to escape this world. I owed them and I needed them. Needed to serve something bigger than my fellow Romans tearing apart the empire from the inside out. Needed to believe in light and beauty, that in the mountain ahead there might be something as perfect as the alien city I'd helped destroy.

A great rumbling sound filled the air, like a thunderstorm rolling over us. Coming in high over churning ocean waters—*Incitatus'* black-and-ruby triremes—a hundred ships, each carrying a dozen talon fighters. They cleared the waters and circled above us like a flock of vultures, casting an ominous shadow out across the shining plain. The sight of them filled me with dread. I'd dreamed of them hundreds of times, but none of that prepared me for the fear I felt at the sight of them now, at the sight of the command ship, a large black-gray trireme with a white underside and red double-bar markings. It was Licinus. Now I knew where he'd run off to. He was reprising his most famous role, at the helm of his Black Peregrine command bomber. It was from the belly of that craft that nuclear fire was dropped on this world. He was here as a threat. Either I stopped and gave up Lumen, or this world would burn again and no one would have its precious ichor. Aquilinus was through bargaining and playing games. The opinion of the mob was irrelevant to him, as was any attempt to present himself as a beneficent and enlightened ruler. For him it was all or nothing now. The will and power to achieve victory at any cost.

But triremes never make noise—they are silent killers. So where was the rumbling sound coming from? The answer came from the hills of the north. A platoon of golden thunder tanks with metallic green markings came rolling out from the foothills. Despite their antigravity plates, they were made of such heavy, dense armor that they needed noisy rocket engines to drive them forward. The green sensor eyes slid back and forth along the front shield screens of the tanks as they advanced. My uncle had made it to his hidden base and was coming with what remained of his Caninine alliance to claim his prize, armed to the teeth with the weapons of the old twenty-fourth legion Viridius that once guarded this world—the Thunder Wolves. There were four command tanks, and the surviving Viridian team members—Carbo, Caninus, Nervo, along with my uncle—each controlled their own tank, plus an additional dozen that trailed just behind. Fifty-two in total. The slave tanks were programmed to mimic the attacks of the four commanders. Each one was armed with ion cannons and surface-to-air missiles. Enough to give the triremes a run for their money.

The two great houses of the empire, Houses Sertorian and Viridian, had just put advanced war machines into the field and made it official: The Tournament of Jupiter was done. Right here, right now, on the surface of Olympus Decimus, the war for possession of the empire was going to be fought out to the end.

The tanks came to a stop and held position a mile to our left, and the triremes circled around the same distance out to our right. We were trapped in between with at least two miles of ground left to cross before we'd reach the cover of the crescent valley.

They were not firing. This was a showdown. They were waiting for Lumen and me to make our move. They didn't want to risk killing him, but they wouldn't allow the other side to have him either. My mother's voice, quoting Marcus Aurelius, came to me.

If you are doing what is right, never mind whether you are freezing with cold or beside a good fire; heavy-eyed, or fresh from a sound sleep; reviled or applauded; in the act of dying, or about some other business.

"We keep going," I said to Lumen, and started moving forward again. We would be safe in the crescent canyon. The height of the mountains made it near impassable from the rear, even by air, and the narrow entrance made it impossible to lay siege to from either side by land. The only way in was the narrow entrance. I could manage only a half run. It wouldn't be enough, but what choice was there? Either we stood and let them dictate our future, or I moved and kept on moving. There was hope in movement.

The Sertorians responded first. The launch bays of the triremes opened, and talon fighters swarmed out to fill the sky. The escalation had begun. In response, the thunder tanks began to slide out, rockets driving their massive weight forward, turrets crackling and burning with ionic energy.

The talons opened fire, but they were targeting not Lumen and me but rather the icy ground that was ahead of us. The chains of ion blasts swept the ice, matched only by the thunderous rounds of the tanks. They were working together to stop us, laying waste to the ground between us and our goal. Great sheets of frozen rock reared up, and the air was suddenly filled with clouds of icy pollution.

I was half pulling, half dragging Lumen behind me now. He was glowing, throwing light on every particle of dust and ice in the air, making it impossible to see the right way through. I struggled around the crater before me. Running water. The blasts had revealed a river beneath the ice. Just when I'd circumnavigated the crater, we found ourselves at the edge of another vast hole. And then a new blast hit. It shook the ground beneath us, and I toppled forward. Lumen was thrown out of my grasp and into the darkness below. There was a splash as he hit the rushing water.

Accala!

Suddenly the bombardment stopped. I was rooted at the edge of that hole, holding my breath, scanning the dark waters for any sign of him. I imagined in that moment that the Sertorians in their fighter planes, the Viridians in their tanks, the false and true emperors, the billions in the audience—all watched with bated breath. Lumen, the prize, was lost. And then I saw a small light in the darkness below as it was whisked away under the ice. I couldn't lose him. He was everything. I clipped Orbis to my belt, and taking a deep breath, I dove into the darkness.

L

I WAS FALLING. TOO long. I hit the water hard before it yielded and drew me under its surface. The powerful current carried me along. The image of me hiding behind my mother's robes, pulling at the green cloth, wrapped up in it, came to me. Being enveloped. The difference was that this kind of envelopment would kill me. I was facing backward, away from Lumen, and couldn't make out his light. Using all my strength, I moved my arms and legs to turn around. There. I started kicking in the direction of the light ahead of me, letting the current throw me after him.

Accala.

I'm coming.

If I didn't run out of breath first. The impact had knocked most of the breath out of me—my lungs were on fire. But he was only a few feet away. Straining and kicking, I stretched, and my fingers touched his foot. I willed myself another few inches forward until I could grasp an ankle. And then I pulled against the current, my hands moving up his body until I had him in an embrace. But to what end? The river must run for miles, and even if it carried us right under the mountain, we still wouldn't arrive alive. I was out of breath and Lumen was coming apart beneath me. No longer cracks in the skin, now ravines, now arms moving apart from his body, torso coming apart at the seams like an old doll. The light was blinding, filling the water. The heat he was releasing was burning my skin, driving away the freezing cold. Was it radiation, or was it a cold that was so intense that my body felt it as heat? Survival was out of the question.

Hold on, he said.

Hold on to what? I couldn't keep hold of him. I was struggling to gather him up as he came apart, and the last of my breath was sneaking out of my mouth in small handfuls like disobedient children fleeing their teacher's whip.

Then Lumen was gone and something else was in his place. A large peglike shape, which I grasped awkwardly with my arms and legs. It was tapered at the top, sharp—a spike, perhaps? And then we were moving upward, against the rushing water. I didn't know how. The force of the underground river was prodigious, but somehow Lumen was moving against it. Suddenly there was a great cracking sound as we erupted through the surface of the ice above us. Cold air hit my wet face, and I drew deep shuddering breaths as I continued to rise, hanging on for dear life. Momentarily blinded by the glare of daylight, when my eyes focused, the first thing I saw was a talon fighter flash by. Was he flying low or . . . ? No, I was high. Very high up.

Gods. I was atop something. A creature. Like Concretus except massive in form, a two-hundred-foot monster, a colossus like something in the ancient stories, only this one was made of shining crystal. Beneath each of the great facets I could see movement. It was bodies—interlinked bodies of Hyperboreans, thousands and thousands of them, pressed together like a puzzle, flexing and tightening, each body like a separate muscle.

Accala.

The voice that sounded in my head was Lumen's, but it was deeper, as if amplified by a great bass drum.

"Lumen?"

I've changed. They were all compressed, but since I couldn't keep it together, I've become a larger container, to keep them all inside. This new form is a kind of defense mechanism. Like the bee sting. I am a weapon, but if I hold on to this form for long, it truly will kill me.

A footfall sent vibrations up from the ground, and I nearly fell to my death.

"Lumen!"

I've got you.

The spine I was holding changed shape, his body re-forming beneath me into a makeshift saddle, a lip where I could ride, and it was moving up, carrying me from his shoulder until I was perched on his head. The crescent canyon was still a few miles away, and the fighters were still wheeling around us, but they hadn't opened fire yet.

"A weapon, you said?" I asked.

This form will break apart too, much more quickly than the first one. I need to reach Mother before that happens. But yes, in the meantime I am strong.

I could feel him, feel the entire gargantuan body crushing the ice, impacting it with each step. I could feel the thousands, tens of thousands, of bodies that were part of him. We were connected. It was almost as if I could control his movement.

You can. We are as one.

"Then run. As fast as you can."

Yes.

And we were away, eating up tundra in a blur as we went. The footfalls of the colossus shook the ground beneath us, creating a thunderous staccato rhythm. They felt as if they were my own legs running, as if I were the giant. We'd be within the safe confines of the canyon in a minute, maybe less at this breakneck speed. I could see the temple ruins from up here.

We were completely exposed, but neither side seemed to know quite what to do in light of this development—an ice monster charging across the tundra.

There was a rumbling again, but it was not from the tanks. It was the earth itself.

My mother is impatient.

Ahead, the queen began to shed her garments. Great sheaths of granite and ice tumbled down her sides into the crescent valley below. The sudden noise was deafening. When the rumbling ceased, the mountain was gone. Beneath her stony exterior, her true form was revealed—a giant, perfect equilateral diamond with a sea of shining life swimming within it. No Roman building, no temple, no palace ever shone as brightly or reflected such brilliance.

Her body is pure diamond ichor, the same substance as your pin, condensed over eons.

The great storehouse of energy to which Lumen would provide the spark. She shone, the sun revealing her majesty—a treasure beyond price, a mountain of ichor that humans could consume and utilize. The power of the gods, without any addictive side effects.

"They can't have her," I said.

A talon fighter got a bright idea and brought his ship in alongside for a closer look. Before I could think, I reached out for him as if I were casting Orbis. Except I was moving Lumen's body. In place of a discus, a large spiked protrusion rose up from his arm and loosed like a spear fired by a catapult. The talon was split down the middle and burst into flame. The spear kept on traveling, hitting the craft behind it too, taking both down to the ground in a ball of fire.

Another talon moved into position before us and opened fire. Then the tanks started shooting, and in an instant we were caught in the crossfire of green and red ion blasts.

They were not going all out, though. There were rows of tanks hanging back, entire wings of talon fighters. They were trying to cripple us, stop us in our tracks. But still we were moving forward, our momentum undeterred.

I ran a zigzag course, but Lumen was hit, again and again, and every time an ion blast struck home, he shed Hyperborean bodies. They fell from him like flakes of dead skin, dozens at a time, and when they hit the ground their light faded and died. Their losses were like physical injuries to me, and they fueled Lumen's desperation. The loss of comrades, of energy. Each death subtracted from the ichor pool, took away from the power they would need to flee this world.

The wind was our only ally. The whipping gusts, as the planet's weather system broke down, were picking up some talons and careening them into one another. But even with that help, we were an easy target.

A Sertorian talon slipped in on an attack vector to my left, heading straight at us. The pilot had seen me, and he'd positioned himself well. In three seconds, he'd have a clean shot. Except he didn't know that he was just inside the range of Orbis' arc.

Gripping the horn of my saddle, I unclipped my discus from my belt and, as Lumen drove forward, cast Orbis out behind me in a wide arc. Two seconds. Three. The Sertorian had the perfect shot, but just before he could take it, Orbis cut right through his talon's cockpit. I didn't know if the man died then and there, but the desired result was the same—his talon dove and shot like an arrow into the front line of Viridian tanks to my right. Two golden tanks went up in an explosion of green hellfire. Like clockwork, Orbis returned.

I waited to see if they took the bait and fired on each other, but no such luck. One more mile.

As we closed in on the mountain, the level of incoming fire picked up. We were about to pass right in front of the tank position—easy targets. Ion blasts from tanks hit our left side, stinger missiles from the talons hit our right, and a hundred bodies flew off, littering the way behind us, the impact breaking apart their conjoined forms—sending Hyperborean body parts scattering across the ice like shards of a shattered glass bowl. We were getting too close for their liking. There was no thought of sparing us now, only of elimination. If neither side could have us, then both meant to wipe us off the face of this world. I needed to refocus them.

I made a sharp turn toward the tanks, momentarily ignoring the canyon.

Accala?

"Don't worry. Remember when I threw you to the Sertorians to get Concretus in the fight? Sometimes you have to take the long way around to get the result you want."

The tanks suddenly stopped their barrage. Uncle Quintus was wondering why I was coming at him.

Accala.

"Just another second."

We were a half mile off the tanks when I raised Lumen's great colossus hands and stood my ground. There. Would Quintus understand in time? That I was surrendering?

There was a lull of a few seconds while new orders came through, and then, as sweet as a gift from the gods themselves, the Viridian surface-to-air missiles flew upward and started targeting the talons. Desire made it easy to lead the greedy. And now the talons were firing back, Aquilinus desperate that my uncle not take possession of Lumen.

"Now! Run for the canyon, Lumen!"

Now that they were shooting at each other, fewer were targeting us. We'd still take additional hits, but not as many as if we'd kept rushing through the crossfire.

The way ahead was clear, but for how long?

"Charge! Give it our all!" I cried to Lumen.

Every Hyperborean entity in his body knew what was at stake, they threw all their energy into this last push. A hundred yards out from the mouth of the valley, a new chain of missiles struck us from the rear. A large chunk of Lumen's back fell away like a great mountain avalanche.

"Keep it together! Keep running! We're going to make it," I said.

Fifty yards out from the mouth of the crescent valley, almost clear of the killing zone. Out the corner of my eye I saw a chariot come sailing at high speed along the edge of the canyon wall above us: Crassus and Julia, signaling us. What were they doing? Something was wrong.

"Stop! Pull up!" I screamed to Lumen, but he couldn't stop now. He had put all his momentum into clearing the canyon entrance.

A blast hit us square in the back. Close range. But that was impossible, we were all clear. I turned in time to see the last of the holographic cloak fade from a Viridian command tank. One of the four command tanks I'd seen earlier must have been a drone as well. My cunning uncle had used misdirection and the same technology that had camouflaged my father in the arena to position himself for the killing shot if all else failed. We were still moving forward, but Lumen had a gaping hole in his midriff from the tank bolt. He was shedding bodies (some of them dripping like melted wax down his front and back) at a great rate. We moved into the canyon, the tank pursuing us, and then the chariot was there. Crassus had sent it right over the edge of the cliff. It was falling, nose-first, like a large javelin. He had timed it so that it would hit the armored vehicle just as it passed into the canyon. The chariot struck the tank and the sharp prow of Crassus' chariot pierced the armor at its weakest point, the entry hatch on top, but not before the turret released another ion charge at Lumen at close range. I saw the chariot split the tank open like a tin can before bursting into flame. Black smoke billowed up from the wreck.

And then I was falling through space. It was so high up. The hard ground rushed up to meet us. There was sudden pain, and then I was a crumpled mess, struggling to keep the darkness at bay.

There was no more Lumen; his mind had crumbled apart as his mind had collapsed. I sensed it dispersing like motes of dust in a windstorm. A light scorched the side of my face. It was coming from the temple ruin at the base of the diamond mountain. We'd made it! Safe for the moment inside the canyon. Rays burst out from Minerva's temple, and long tendrils of light, like curling fingers, gathered up the scattered Hyperborean forms, leading them into the mountain.

The mass of the Hyperborean colossus, the part that had Lumen at its heart—the head, part of the chest, and one arm—began to pull itself forward toward the temple arch. As it crawled, thousands of other bodies, some whole, others in parts, dragged themselves forward as well. On the ground, over each other, over the large mass of the colossus like stampeding horses in slow motion, part solid, part liquid, overlapping waves slowly returning to shore. There were thousands of them and their light was fading. They were so very slow. It would take them more time than we had. It was like a procession of quicksand, fading points of light trying to find their way back to a distant sun. I had to buy them time. The enemy were still outside busily killing one another, but it wouldn't be long before they remembered why they were fighting in the first place and turned their attention back to us. I struggled to my feet and limped toward the wreck of the Viridian tank. Maybe there was a weapon inside, something I could use to guard the mouth of the canyon.

A figure emerged from the black smoke of the tank wreck. Covered in sweat and soot. My uncle, Quintus Viridius Severus, his ion pistol leveled at me.

"Tell the Hyperboreans to stop. Tell them to stop now," he commanded.

"I won't," I said.

He shot, but not at me. An ion charge hit the solid ichor rock of the mountain behind the temple arches and, although it wasn't a direct shot into the light, the gateway reacted with a quivering waver that let me know it was part of the queen, and that any harm at this point could jeopardize the mission, perhaps even kill her.

"Let them go," I yelled.

"Make them stop!" he said. "That ichor is mine!"

He was a seasoned killer. I would never be able to make a cast before he pulled the trigger. But perhaps I could put enough power into it that it would kill him after the fact. We both would die, but the Hyperboreans would have more time. An acceptable outcome.

"I won't tell them to stop and I won't surrender," I said.

"We don't need you to surrender," my uncle said.

We? Carbo! Before I could locate him, the strangest sensation hit me, cool and sharp. I looked down to see the shaft of a javelin embedded in my chest, right through my heart. No feeling of hot ambrosial ants this time, just shock and pain. Carbo emerged from the shadows to the northwest, a look of grim satisfaction on his face. They had both been in the command tank. I went to fall back, but the javelin point had traveled clean through my breast to the rocks behind me and they were holding me up, stopping me from keeling over.

Things started moving in slow motion. It was the adrenaline. I was processing information at an increased rate, or maybe this was just what happened when you were dying.

A spear took Carbo, right through the side of the neck. The Viridian leader fell to his side, and my uncle was shooting up into the rocks above. I spied Crassus darting back out of range—it was he who had killed Carbo.

Then a familiar weapon speared my uncle in the midriff, sending him stumbling backward. The sharp points of the arachnoraptor transmission staff. Julia's weapon. She emerged from her hiding place on the rocky ledge above. She'd taken her due, paid my uncle for betraying her, for betraying us. Except he was not falling. He was stubborn, and now, even as he died, he was leveling his pistol at Julia.

Crassus dropped down on my uncle from on high like a giant spider. He was wielding a gladius. I knew that weapon. Even from this distance it had an ethereal sheen: Marcus' gladius.

My uncle turned reflexively and fired at Crassus. The gladius flashed, and the Sertorian actually blocked the ion bolt with his sword in midflight, deflecting it. I'd never seen a move like that. So fast, so precise. It must have been the ichor from my pin. Then he was moving past my uncle, the gladius flashing as it stole his life. Quintus fell at Crassus' feet, his hands clawing at the Sertorian's legs as he died.

Julia was yelling my name as she climbed down.

Was this how it would end? What would Crassus do now? Would he help or hinder my mission? His addiction and his loyalties were tearing him apart. Would he stand with me and Julia? Or would he try to seize the day for himself? I slid backward down the javelin until I hit rocky ground. My limbs had stopped moving. The hit to the solar plexus had short-circuited my nervous system. I was like a heavy rag doll.

Then the same light that moved to envelop the Hyperboreans reached out for me. Long tendrils, rays like rosy fingers wrapped around my body, enfolding me in pure light.

I was walking. Effortlessly, free from pain. My body was all light. Beside me walked the other aliens, into the shining light at the heart of the mountain. I was inside the temple, and then through it, inside the mountain itself.

The radiant brightness increased to the point where I lost a sense of where the walls and ceiling were, if there were any at all. A sea of light. Was this it? Was I dead? Was this truly Olympus? Mortals were not meant to behold the gods. The gods had to appear in disguise. They were too bright, too powerful for us to behold them in their true form. Unless we were dead. I felt a moment of panic. I needed to go back. To help Crassus and Julia.

At the center of the sea of light was a shimmering pool, even brighter than the light around us. That was where the procession was leading. Or was it a burning jewel like I saw in the great city beneath the ice? Reality wasn't clear-cut here. As the crystalline aliens ahead of me merged themselves in the pool, they melted, dissolving, mixing with the light, vanishing into it. Caretakers no longer, the Hyperboreans returned their essence, their energy, to the source from which they came.

This is Mother.

"Where are you?"

Here. Outside. In many places. We need time to complete our work.

"Then let me go back," I said.

I was drawn along with the procession; my body of light couldn't resist the call of the pool. And I could feel the queen. She was sentient, powerful, she was the light-filled pool and her power was intense, exposing my every thought and feeling, unpacking me until, like Lumen, I was spread out in the light, in many places at once. Was this what it was like to stand before a god?

Brilliant, ecstatic, unendurable, humbling. I felt more myself than I'd ever been at the same time as I was fading apart into something bigger, like droplets of blood being diluted in an ocean. It was like waking up and dying, coming home and departing all at once.

Her light was so bright. I tried to look into it but had to turn away. When I turned from her, it was into darkness, like falling under the dark waters below the ice. Her illumination was suddenly gone, and I was drowning in fear and confusion and relief. Yes—the darkness was comforting and also enveloped me. It took me in like a weary stranger and stripped away pain and memory until I was blissfully confused and could barely remember why I was here at all. And then the radiance shone again. As if on a turntable, I was spinning. I couldn't tell whether it was fast or slow, only that I couldn't bear the brightness. It was too much, and yet turning from it was pain and darkness. How could I bear to exist like this?

As you have done your entire life. It is not the darkness we fear. It is the light. We are comforted by death and the promise of silence, the quiet of the underworld. We turn from the light because we cannot bear our own divinity. You want to know if you're going to die? Tell me, can you bear the light of life?

The voice was so familiar, so comforting.

"I can't look at you," I said. "But I can't die. My people have done terrible things to your people. I have committed acts of which I am ashamed. I must be allowed to go back. I have to set things right. I have to fix things. I need just a little more time."

It's all right. You can look at me.

"I can't."

The light dimmed. It became less raw, less intense, so that I could look into it. She was taking on a form, just like in the old stories. She was clothing herself in human form so that I could stand to look upon her. Like blurry eyes wiped clean, I began to make out a body. Her helmet shone bright like the sun, her spear glinted in the light. The first Romans who came to this world built a great temple to Minerva in this place, and here she was. My goddess. And she looked so familiar, not like the goddess depicted in the statues.

Accala. Come closer, darling.

It was her voice. The voice of my dead mother, Alexandria Viridius Camilla.

LI

COME, ACCALA. COME, IT's all right. You've grown so much. Let me look at you.

She gestured to me and I moved to stand before her. The same green eyes flecked with hazel, the same face and body that I remembered, not the haggard and anxious face I last saw in the recording Lumen showed me.

She wrapped me up in her arms, drawing me close. And then Aulus was there, no more body of diamond and ice. We were back together again. A family. Heat, warmth, love rushed over me. But it was not right. It was not them. Those beings were more than my mother and brother, and therefore less.

Not less, she said.

"You're not my mother," I said. "Lumen's not my brother. They were put into the ichor, their life and memories absorbed into the Hyperborean sum total. That's what you do, isn't it? Absorb and reflect."

He is and he isn't, my mother said. *I am but I am not. Who are you? Are you Accala your father's daughter? Accala your mother's daughter? Accala the gladiator, Accala who grows fruit trees on her balcony? The Accala before the fires that rocked this world, or the one after?*

"I'm all of those things."

All of those experiences are inside the container that is Accala. A prism that captures experience, sensation, feeling, thought, all bundled up into one. A shining droplet of water. Now imagine all the other droplets, every separated being in the galaxy, and then every separated thing in existence, see all those droplets coming together to form a vast sea. An infinite number of prisms, all together. This is the sense in which I am your mother, your brother, your goddess. We are all one.

"The droplet has no sense of itself as part of the sea," I said. "While we are droplets, we must behave as droplets. Some parts of my mother might be within you, but that does not make you her. Or the goddess Minerva."

I am simply more droplets, a bigger container. If you call that a goddess, then it is a goddess. I am like a wave, a tide. I have brothers and sisters. We do not interfere with the world as a child plays with a toy, but I am in the manifest universe. I am a force that has movement on the outside and inside people's hearts.

"But now you are trapped here."

Even the tide is beholden to the forces of giants. Much power has been put elsewhere; cause and effect shape us also, only on a bigger scale. There is a greater force beyond us, a container that holds us that we are gradually dissolving into as you are dissolving into us.

Her words shook me. The sense they carried frightened me, threw me into a state of trembling and awe. Her words were like swift birds flying to somewhere I couldn't follow.

Your deep soul knows I speak the truth, though, doesn't it? It remembers the greater nation of which it is a citizen. It pines to return there, knowing that it is not annihilation but addition, not forgetting but the ultimate remembrance of all that we are. The rainbow is not less for its interrunning rays of color, nor the sea for its waters. It is the individual united as one thing that brings beauty and power, the greatest expression of creation.

The words fell away as I beheld the vision of creation of which she spoke. A cascade of images and feelings. Images of my mother. My childhood. Our time together. Like the flickering images of my cameo back in Rome but with feeling, presence, as if I were there, completely there in each image so that each second of change felt like hours, days. My memories were stretched out before me like an unraveling bandage, like a series of cameo slides. There was a nostalgia, as if I were viewing my past from a great distance away, like an old woman at the end of her life. Things seemed faded and bright at the same time. Certain memories shone more brightly than others. As the stream of images drew closer toward the bomb blast that shook this world, the light became intense, blotting out all images before and after it. She reached out and took the tape of images and folded it into a loop, like an infinity strip.

You see, she said, pointing to the scene of me holding the notification of my mother and brother's deaths in my hand, staring blankly at the legionary delivering the news.

At this moment, you were dead. Your heart had stopped beating, it was quiet in your chest, heavy and useless like a broken clock.

The color resumed after the caves, after I was beheaded and put back together.

Lumen brought you back to life in more ways than one. Your heart was a stone, and he squeezed it until it began to beat again.

I looked down at my breast, and for the first time since entering the mountain I remembered that I was wounded. Mortally wounded. The area around the wound was stained red. Blood was pumping from the hole in my chest, the hole in my heart.

But the aspects of your soul that you require for mortal survival still cling to you. Your body is still close.

Her fingers of light stretched out, cradling my heart as it beat weakly like an exhausted bird, desperately flapping against the wind.

This heart is worn out, she said. *It's had to come too far too fast. A long journey in such a short space of time.*

"Am I going to die now?" I asked.

Life or death is not about whether your heart continues to beat, she replied. *There is an essence that exists before, that remains after.*

"Droplets in the sea."

Yes. Life is forever present. It is something we turn away from and must turn back to. This choice transcends the flesh. It is about how we live each moment. This is the gift of the gods to our children. Now look again.

The band turned in space, running like a belt on an old engine, and I saw that on the flip side of the strip that held all of the scenes of my life there was another sequence. Ancient Rome. The rise of the Romanii. The battle with the Etruscans. The conquering of the tribes of Italy, the conquest of Europa, Phrygia, the galaxy. It was the history of the empire.

There were broken faded scenes along its length too. The death of Julius Caesar, the battle for the republic, the mad emperor Neo Heliogabalus. And in between them were moments of heroism. Mucius Scaevola, Horatius on the bridge, Scipio Africanus defeating the Carthaginians.

You see. There have been moments when the empire's heart has stopped too. Moments where it could have died and has been revived by heroes. By those who chose to live. It takes only one man or woman, the right word, the right action at the right time, to restart the heart of a civilization, to reignite the creative fire of hope and inspiration. The empire is like a person, a civilization a little like a god. A vast container of ideas, of hopes and dreams and energies.

"But you are bound by the material now. The world of things weighs you down."

Yes, we have been pulled too close to the material, and its gravity has earthed us, held us down. We have to return, to travel back to where we came from. To a place where we can help balance the creative forces that govern the universe. Your mother longed for a golden age. While the creative seeds of the universe are earthbound in this place, that can never come to pass.

"Then let me fix it. Let me help you. Let me stop the empire's heart from freezing. I'll die if I can keep it beating, keep it turned toward life."

The strip moved around my heart. My heart and that of the empire overlapped.

I will keep your heart here for now and give you another, she said.

She reached out and past the side of my face, like Lumen performing one of his magic tricks. My hair tumbled down over my shoulders.

She held her closed fist out before me and slowly opened it, light leaking out between her fingers. There was my pin, the pin she sent me.

We saw you from far away. Saw that your path led here. We sent you this pin to carry you to us like a cast spear. To aid us in our hour of need.

The brilliant golden pin shone in her palm, and then my mother's form withdrew into the light, and something else came out. The pin grew into a spear of light that flew as if from a great distance, gathering light as it flew, and hit me in the heart, right where I'd been wounded. It entered me like a needle, like an arrow hitting a flying bird, fast and sharp, and took my breath away. Pain wasn't the right word. It was like the point of orgasm, the point of dying, the point of being born. How could she stand to hold so much power in place? This single splinter was splitting me apart. Then suddenly things aligned, like overlapping circles all lining up into one form. I felt new, consumed by a numinous light.

I was not Accala anymore. I was the archetype of Accala, the perfect, realized Accala. A crystal lit by a small sun.

Go and close the loop, she said. *You wish to save the empire? Your people? Then act without fear or desire. Be the unwavering arrow and strike the target true. If you weaken, the power will destroy you. If you can act as a judge for a higher court than the human heart, your empire will survive.*

And then, without any sense of movement, I was standing outside the mountain again, surrounded by biting winds and the fires of war. I was back in the real world, and yet nothing was the same as when I'd left it. I could sense the streams of ichor in the ice all around me, running back into the mountain. Eddies and currents that conveyed a malleability that I was oblivious of before. Where I had seen only solid rock and ice, now I saw liquid potential, substances that could be shaped with thought, word, and motion. My body was free from pain, my thoughts like mercury, quick and sharp and penetrating.

Crassus and Julia had turned the turret of the partially ruined Wolf tank toward the canyon mouth and were firing into the gap. There was a burning pile of tanks nearby. They'd held the tanks at bay so that the Sertorians could pick them off from above. I moved past them without a word. I was in a dream. My feet barely touched the ground.

The canyon was shining like a brilliant mirror. Something was lighting it up, driving away the shadow of the mountain. It was me. I was glowing like a small sun, brighter than the light of the portal, more radiant than the strobing flashes of energy and fire around me as the battle of houses continued to play out.

"Are you glowing?" Julia called out as I passed. "Or have I just taken a hit to the head?"

"Yes."

"So what do we do now?" she yelled. Fear was in her voice. She could sense I was different, that something had changed, that the fight was far from over. I could see so many things with this small splinter of the queen's power. I knew that back in the hall, the Hyperboreans were still milling through the portal, rejoining the mountain. I saw now that the mountain would soon become a spear of pure energy, and Lumen was the lens, both ignition and focal point that would direct the energy into the pool. The accumulated ichor of this world would leave this place in an instant and reappear somewhere else, far from here.

"Julia? I'm going to need to split my concentration, and it's going to weaken me. I need you now more than ever. Use your hand. Seize the ships' navigation systems. Keep them from laying down so much fire."

Julia reached out. In a moment she would begin careening talon fighters into one another. Crassus used the immobile tank to shoot through the canyon mouth—together they could hold their position and protect the Hyperboreans as long as someone was taking the brunt of the attack on the field outside.

Now there were no more distractions, nothing to disturb the conversation I intended to have with Tribune Licinus and his fleet. Everything was so clear; so much confusion was caused by a lack of perspective.

I stepped out of the canyon on the open tundra. The howling snow and wind settled as I passed through the burning ruins of the thunder tanks. The firefight had reduced the ruins that peppered the snowfield to smoldering heaps of stone and steel. They looked like funeral pyres. I walked until I reached a clearing, a clear white canvas upon which to paint my picture. Above me, the Sertorian attack fleet hung in the sky, waiting. I stood alone before them, one tiny speck amid the burning tundra, a bright and shining target to every talon fighter, trireme, and bomber up there. The ships had reoriented themselves so that they now faced me head-on, ready to commence their bombing raid, and at the lead was Tribune Licinus. Nuclear payload hung beneath his ship, ready to inflict nuclear fire upon the surface of Olympus Decimus once again.

Behind them was Emperor Aquilinus, the holographic god, so large only his torso was visible, sky-embracing arms encircling his bomber fleet, his massive projection generated by *Incitatus*. Aquilinus' real body was aboard *Incitatus*, his flagship at the rear of his fleet, high above the surface, hovering in the empyrean, the borderline of sky and space. He thought he had the upper hand, literally. This was his greatest re-creation, the bombing of Olympus Decimus. The same number of ships, the same fleet, the same leader, the same bomb. But this time it was going to be different. This time I was here.

LII

THE BOWL OF THE sky had become the new arena from which the stadium audience looked down on us. I could feel them, hear their thoughts. They were watching me. They'd seen me die twice now. They were wondering if anything could save them from the wrath of the gods. Even the Numerian emperor was apprehensive—but admirably not for his own skin but for the fate of the empire in his care. He truly feared what would become of his subjects under the rule of the Sertorians.

The conversation began. Talons came first, testing me. I held my ground as missiles and charges impacted upon me, around me. The icy ground was scorched. When the clouds of steam evaporated, I stood in a crater of black and melted ice, unharmed. My armor had been blasted away. I was naked, clothed only by my radiance, my black hair blowing in the wind.

A buzz started up among the viewing audience. Even some of the bomber pilots thought it. Their assault should have killed me. I was not human. The title given by the audience back in Rome's Colosseum sprang to their lips—Minerva's daughter, the handmaiden of justice. They were fearful, excited. Terror and wonder at the same time. They thought I'd come to judge them, that they'd committed hubris by throwing in with Aquilinus. They were right.

Aquilinus had styled his Ludi Romani team as an extension of his body, and the fleet seemed to be positioned with a similar logic. Licinus' bombers were the body, the triremes and talons were the wings, and *Incitatus* was the head. One great coordinated Sertorian form assembled to strike down a single woman. I had to gather my courage, hold to this state between life and death. That was the only way to beat such a being.

It was my turn to respond. I began the dissection of the talons using Orbis as my scalpel. The lapis negra mineral he was forged from was capable of absorbing large amounts of energy and was nearly indestructible—the perfect instrument. I infused my discus with energy and sent him out. He flew up, trailing an arc of light and heat. His arc passed through a row of neatly positioned talons, destroying each one in turn. Orbis returned to me having transformed six Sertorian ships into shooting stars. They tumbled from the sky, adding to the piles of burning wreckage. Back in the canyon, I could sense Julia and Crassus, working together to hold other talons at bay, shooting down any that came near their post. Julia had gotten the hang of her job. She was doing better than I ever imagined, redirecting ships into one another, or angling them so that Crassus could finish them off with the cannon.

We were making an impression, letting Aquilinus know we were serious. I sent Orbis out on another killing arc while the enemy responded with more missiles and energy fire. While I awaited his return, I sought out Licinus' mind.

I found it easily. It stood out, geometrically neat lines of anger and action. Here was a mind that was trained to rage and destroy all that it didn't understand in the most efficient manner, and right now I was at the top of his list. He knew I had power, though. He was frightened by what I intended to do, confused by the inability of his talons to kill me. But he was consoled by his bomb and eager to release its fire again, to scorch the earth and his enemies.

Licinus sensed me, which was a surprise. His finger was hovering over the button to drop the bomb, but he immediately switched to a different panel and fired two stinger missiles at me. I returned my concentration to my body as they came screaming down. These had more power than the weapons the talon fighters used, and I didn't know how much damage this body could take. I didn't want to waste the queen's power. Lumen had taught me that every ounce must be treasured for when it was truly needed.

I raised Orbis like a conductor's baton and made a sweeping movement. The ground before me broke, and a great shelf of ice reared up like a shield. The missiles struck it in place of me, blasting it to pieces. I walked through the debris unharmed. I reached out and directed a powerful geyser, which broke through the ice beneath Licinus' ship and shot upward, striking its black-and-red underside, and then moved around it. As I closed my fist, it solidified, forming a large version of my own hand, holding Licinus' frozen bomber in place. His thrusters burned, trying to drive up, to break the grip of my ice hand, but it took only a little of my power to hold him and his bomb in place. As he recognized his help-lessness, Licinus' thoughts became erratic. If he fired, it would be a suicide mis-sion now. He'd die in the resulting explosion.

Surprisingly, for all his evil, Licinus was a warrior, and I saw that his greatest fear was to die an ignoble death, struck down from a distance instead of in the heat of battle with a sword in his hand. And there was more. Like the conflict I saw raging within Crassus, there was confusion, a foreign presence that he struggled with for control over his own fate.

As I stared into Licinus' mind, that other presence—Proconsul Aquilinus—stared right back at me, challenging my right to be there.

Licinus was just another piece on the board. My true opponent was, and always had been, Proconsul Aquilinus. He was there in Licinus' mind, sitting in the back of his head like a spider in a web, directing the tribune's action, pulling strings of fear and desire to achieve his desired outcomes. The puppet master.

"You can't trust anyone, you know," he said to me. "You have to do everything yourself if you want to run an empire."

His words drew me. He was summoning me to meet with him, to parlay. "A temporary pax. I have one final offer to make you."

I reached back with my mind to the temple arch. There were still thousands of Hyperboreans in the process of merging with the queen. More time. He was offering an asset I was short on, and I couldn't see the downside right now.

"Stop firing on the canyon, stop trying to take the mountain, and I'll come," I said.

The order went out, and the remaining ships held their fire and began circling back into formation around Licinus' trapped command bomber. In my body, I was standing alone on a vast plane of burning ice once more.

Aquilinus drew my mind toward him again, and suddenly, just as with the queen, I found myself elsewhere, away. Now I was standing in a vast chamber that I recognized at once—the emperor's palace back in Rome—and opposite me, sitting upon the imperial throne, was Aquilinus Sertorius Macula.

We were not in Licinus' mind but somewhere else, the center of the web, a place between the many minds the proconsul had spread himself out over. I could see him opposite me now, clear as day. The little man with the shining eyes. He wore a purple toga, the emperor's colors. Rich tapestries hung from the walls, the gentle breeze blew white silk curtains, and outside I could see Rome, but not as it was now—as it once was in the ancient days. It was gleaming, cov-ered in white marble. So beautiful that it made my heart ache.

"Not many people get invited to my inner sanctum. You should feel privileged," he said, sipping from a glass of wine in his hand. "Come, you've proved yourself. I'll meet your demands. Let us talk as equals and make a civilized covenant."

The contrast between my last two weeks of icy hell versus the opulence of this chamber threw me. It commanded all my attention with its sensuality, its comfort and ease. It might be an illusion, but it was a good one. My mind and body sighed to stand within it. Fruit trees, warm breeze, and real yellow sunlight, not what passed for light and warmth on Olympus Decimus.

"This is how things are back on Mother Earth," he said, motioning to the vast chamber. "I sit upon the throne already by way of my proxy, Bucco Numerius. As you have come to see, I am many people in many places. He is the regent, but I am in him. I pull his strings."

"You are a little man pretending to be bigger than he is," I said. "A petty puppeteer."

"You know that's not true," he said. "You can sense my greatness. As it stands, you have uncovered one of my secrets, found your way to this place. The aliens have given you some impressive power, more than I possess, I admit it, but you cannot hold it for long. Your newfound power will be short-lived, and it has earned you the right to negotiate with me directly, nothing more."

"We have nothing to negotiate over," I said.

"The way I see it, we have reached an impasse. You stand in my way, but I have a nuclear weapon. You can't imagine that I won't revisit its fire upon this world."

"You'll only end in destroying Lumen. He's close to death already. If you burn this world there won't be anything left. No Lumen, no ambrosia."

"Perhaps, but know that if I can't have the ichor, then no one will, not even the Hyperboreans."

"Without the ichor, you'll lose the throne. You were premature in launching your coup."

"In no small part thanks to you. You have inconvenienced me, but my web extends to many fronts. I've been playing the game of houses for a lifetime, and you are still a child. I play the game on multiple levels while you see only what's directly in front of you. Why do you think your father agreed to my terms?"

"Because you threatened to destroy everything he had fought for during his life."

"That is simply not true. Look around you."

The room was suddenly filled with people: senators, merchants, citizens, all bedecked in fine robes, all followed by barbarian slaves carrying treasure behind them. The robes depicted the eight houses, even House Viridian.

"You know that this is what I want for the empire," he said, motioning to the luxurious chamber. "You think they're coming to my side just for the promise of ambrosia? I already had most of them on side. I promise wealth and prosperity for each and every citizen. A new economic golden age. I've made no bones about that."

"Empty words. You promise an iron fist wrapped in a velvet glove. A galaxy subjugated to your will, crushed of the hope of freedom."

"What freedom?" he sneered. "There's never been freedom in the empire. Not even in the days of the republic. Even then the equestrian class would vote on behalf of the citizens they ruled. There is no such thing as freedom, nor as justice. These are pipe dreams that an empire encourages to maintain order. A dictatorship is no different; it just achieves the same outcome by different methods, only with one major advantage—efficiency. What I say will come to pass without discussion or obstacles. I promise a future without gods, without houses. The pax I promise will be permanent because I am asking the people to sacrifice their dearly held pipe dreams in exchange for tangible realities—money, comfort, more slaves, and now I offer them godhood. Who are you to stand in the way?"

His words were not words. I saw them as black and red barbs, spider bites appearing on my body. He was not a bird of prey; there was no nobility there. He was a spider disguised as a hawk, a dark and bulbous creature hiding in the shadows. Poisonous barbs, sticking web. But his web couldn't catch me. As the queen shed her clothing, I must keep shedding my mortality. The power I'd been given was easily lost, and Aquilinus knew it. I must keep even, balanced, celestial.

"You offer to satisfy their urges, but an empire is held together by shared ideals. You give them things they don't need, that they only think they want, in exchange for intangible principles that are priceless, beyond value. It's like the shiny bead trick we used to perform on barbarians with no concept of individual ownership when we'd occupy their worlds. Empire must be a common goal, a shared dream of greatness. Anything less is slavery, no matter what's been offered in exchange. You seek to become not Jupiter but Hades, ruling over an empire of lost and tormented souls. A land of the dead where everyone's choices are formed for them, their lives beholden to whatever whim you dictate. Life is there all the time; the power of the gods is there for any to wield and utilize to improve themselves and the empire, but you're working to help them forget that they ever held that power. Not godhood—you offer them slavery."

"And what do you offer them?"

"I offer them peace."

"A peace cannot be sustained without the fear of war. The emperor whom you fight for used planet-killing battleships to maintain his peace."

"I have seen inside his heart. I know of his love of the people. I have seen inside yours."

"What matters the intention of the giver if the gift is good?"

"It's everything, because there's no such thing as a free gift. A gift comes with obligations, expectations. The spirit with which it is given is everything. The reason we go to war, the reason we grant power, the reason we give gifts—these things shape the empire and decide its continued survival. There is nothing else. Intention is everything, and yours is bad."

"I admire you. I desire you, Accala," he said. "You know that, you've felt it. I've felt you reciprocate. The attraction Crassus felt for you was mine. That was my passion, my interest. I find you remarkable, fascinating. You alone have stood against me. You are splendid, a rare bird. Even more, you could still stand with me as the empire falls to its knees in submission. An empress."

He waved his hand, and suddenly I was standing there resplendent in imperial robes. Empress Accala. The rainbow colors of the other houses interweaved around the central stripe of imperial purple. And part of me wanted it. There was a chord he was strumming somewhere at the back of my brain that made everything he was saying make perfect sense. Like all the weight of the world would vanish in an instant if I just gave in.

"I've felt you by way of your proxies," I said. "You're little more than a rapist."

"I am an emperor, and I offer you the best deal of all, the greatest trade in exchange for one small sacrifice. Your family and your house restored to their former glory. That would be my wedding present to you. House Viridian absolved of its sins against me, your family honor and fortune restored. You can return to your estates. You will have the platform of the empress, and I will not constrain your powers. You may talk about what you will, lobby for what you will."

He was not lying. I could sense his conviction.

"Why? Why would you do that?"

"I respect you. You are a shining star that should not be put to waste, a delicacy that should not be hastily devoured. I do not fear you, because I know the empire and its people. Uncertainty is what they fear. They would endure any level of tyranny in order to maintain the status quo. I promise them stability.

"I can offer you much. All that you wanted. You know the Sertorians don't place limitations on their women. You could shine. You could shape the empire as you wish, the only constraint would be on overthrowing me. You would have to swear loyalty, be subject to me, your master, your husband, but in all other respects, you would be free. I've seen into your heart aboard *Incitatus*. Through all my limbs I saw your heart, your desires, your passion. I know that you are more like us than you care to admit."

Then I saw the trick. It was my power that was lending this illusion its believability, my mind that was adding richness, texture, sensuality to this fantasy. He was just making the container with his words and then letting me fill it with my mortal desires. He had altered my mind and body, and now he was banking on those seeds he had planted to bring home a harvest. That was how his game was played. But he didn't know what had happened to me in the tunnels. He was only beginning to understand that I was not his creature anymore. That I was not Accala Viridius nor Accala the Mock Wolf. I was something else. All those things and much more.

"You had my pin once. Do you remember the design?" I asked.

"An arrow with three gold apples."

"It's the seal of my female ancestors, passed down from mother to daughter. My mother once told me that the apples were meant to represent the story of Atalanta, who swore that she could only marry a man who was fast enough to catch her. In exchange for promising to make a sacrifice to her the goddess gave Melanion three golden apples to slow Atalanta down as she couldn't resist stopping to pick them up."

"It's one more children's story to be eradicated when the New Gods come to power."

"The old stories have meaning. The pair wed, but Melanion was so distracted he forgot to make his sacrifice, and the goddess transformed them into beasts. My mother told me that the arrow represents independent thought and that a woman in our family should never marry a man who would try to drop shiny baubles and steal away our ability to reason and exercise the intellect. I'm afraid all you've got to offer is rotten fruit."

"If you will not serve, then you will be my slave," he said. He waved his hands, and shackles appeared around my wrists and ankles, a heavy chain around my waist. Orbis, my weapon, was gone.

"You see? This is my place of power. You are weak here."

I saw much. That he was not just a play god. He possessed power and more. There was a greater power behind him, something that he wasn't fully aware of, a dark womb from which he grew and fed. As the queen was Minerva but not Minerva, my mother but not my mother, so Aquilinus was Hades but not Hades. It was the energy of darkness, of the underworld. As Minerva shone, Hades drew darkness to himself and from that darkness fed those who followed him. Aquilinus had been feeding off of evil for so long that it had eroded his humanity and left something terrible in its place.

"I'm not here for me. I don't hate you, nor do I fear you. I am here in service to Rome. I am Minerva's spear delivering justice. You are the cancer that threatens to smother the heart I seek to save."

"You are a woman, weak on your own. The powers that be, the people, will never accept you as more than that."

"They already do. Don't you sense it?"

I could hear them chanting my name across the empire. Daughter of Minerva. Lady Justice, Lady Liberty.

"Can't you hear it?" I asked. "They're already turning on you. No more half-truths and false words. There's nothing you can tempt me with, no threat that holds water. I see through the illusions you cast."

The chains vanished at my merest thought. Orbis reappeared in my hand. I reached out with my mind, and I could see his web stretching out from his throne. Seven lines. Six to the teammates, one to Bucco Numerius.

"You said you were many people in many places, but that was a lie. There are seven. That's the extent of your power," I said. I waved my hand and the illusion of the galactic capital vanished, replaced by a large metallic hold. *Incitatus*. This was Aquilinus' private chambers. His body was floating in a tube of ambrosia in the center of the hold, surrounded by hundreds of machines. Wires that ran from his body led out to a series of boxes that had names stamped upon them: Crassus, Licinus, the Corvinus brothers, Barbata, Mania, Bucco—seven victims. Only two boxes—the ones with the names Licinus and Crassus—were lit up. The others were now dead, including the emperor's nephew, who I saw now had been assassinated on the Senate floor.

This was a vision of the real world, and he couldn't bear for me to see him like this—weak, vulnerable. My dispelling his illusion struck a chord of fear. He knew my words rang with truth, and if there was one thing that terrified Aquilinus, it was the very thing he accused the citizens of the empire of fearing the most: uncertainty, confusion, lack of control.

A new projection appeared in front of the tube. A hologram of the emperor, a projection to hide his encapsulated body.

I reached out to touch Licinus' control box. There was a memory there—of the first attack on Olympus Decimus, the one that killed my mother and brother. As Aquilinus reached out through Crassus to rape me, so too did he reach out through Licinus to throw the switch. It was his pleasure, his impulse, that decimated this world the first time, and right now he was ready to relive the event.

"Seven is the total number of lines you can hold at any one time," I said. "That's why Lurco was on the team; the other line was redirected to control the emperor's nephew," I said.

Laid out before his tube was a great holographic strategy board depicting the surface of the planet below. There they all were, shining digital markers. There was me on the field, surrounded by shining triangles representing his ships. All this time I'd been a piece on the board, in his private war game; that was how he saw us. But now I could be a player of the game, an opponent with perspective who saw the board objectively, with clarity and detachment, his pieces against mine.

"You like to talk, don't you?" I asked. "I like to act."

"Don't try to bluff me," he said. "I know what you are capable of. I've had much time to study you."

"My whole life, people have told me what they think I'm capable of. You're about to be the latest in a long line of disappointed fools," I countered. I was all bravado. It took all my effort to keep things where I wanted them, but I'd had plenty of practice at this, thanks to Crassus' machine—keeping parts of myself hidden and strong while letting others seem weak. While I kept my focus on the battle for control over Licinus firm, I let my guard slip a little so the proconsul could see more of my mind than I might otherwise allow. He was swearing at me, his mouth dripping curses.

"You bitch. You little slut. You are the one who's nothing. I will crush you and turn you into a pet for my amusement. You will crawl. You will never be empress, you will be my pet wolf. As you were before, so will you be again. A toy for my entertainment. The pleasure and pain centers of your brain wired to my satisfaction. There is nothing you will not do to amuse me and the senators of my court. You will be the laughingstock of the empire. I will imprison your family for the sole purpose of watching you suffer."

This was the true form of this so-called emperor-god. The red face, the spewing invectives like a child throwing a temper tantrum when he didn't get his way.

"Caligula wished that the empire had a single neck so that he could cut through it. I will surpass him in vision and realization. I will unite Rome under House Sertorian, one neck ready for the leash."

I let him rant and chased the line of consciousness that ran to Licinus. He sensed what I was up to and raced after me, throwing more energy down the line he used to control his puppet.

He drove Licinus to push the button, commanded him to release the bomb, but I was already there, freezing the muscles of his hand in place as I froze his ship, locking the tendons that controlled his fingers.

Aquilinus applied his pressure to Licinus' mind, and we fought over control of the tribune like a pair of wrestlers, testing each other for the slightest weakness that would cost the match.

"You can't win," Aquilinus said. "I've been with Licinus so long, he is mine."

The proconsul was right. I couldn't win this particular battle because it was two against one. Licinus wanted to kill himself. Aquilinus had pushed some buttons, pulled some wires in his brain. He was an adrenaline-pumping suicide bomber. All fear gone, he was desperate to blow himself up for the glory of House Sertorian and the proconsul.

"You're growing weaker," he said. "You can't fight me and keep your mind closed at the same time. The Hyperboreans are preparing to leave. They think that they can escape me. You think I haven't anticipated that? I won't allow it." I felt him reach out to my mind. "As you see into me, so I see into you," he said. "They're not as strong as they pretend, and neither are you. Their power is already burning you up. You can't hold on much longer."

He was right. The power was burning me up, threatening to destroy my body. I couldn't allow him to bait me, to lead me down a path that would see the energies turn back on me. It was such a subtle balance, justice. I could not indulge even for an instant, or the power would set me on fire, burn me from the inside out. Desire, fear—they were the same thing. Different ends of the same stick. One burns, the other freezes, both would kill my goal and end my life.

"I don't need to hold on," I said.

I let my control over Licinus slip and rushed back to my body. Things were as I'd left them—the entire mind-to-mind encounter with Aquilinus had only taken a matter of seconds.

I felt the surge in Aquilinus as he thought he'd achieved victory. *Incitatus* drew closer. He'd positioned himself to fire on the mountain in case the bomb wasn't enough to stop the Hyperboreans.

I could still hear him too. His voice was like a distant echo, making the *tch-tch* sound of a disapproving schoolmaster. "You are a disappointment, Accala Viridius. I was right to reject you."

Licinus was like an archer who had held a bow pulled and at the ready for too long. The moment I released my mental grip, he fully embraced his master's command and slammed his hand down on the button.

But Aquilinus had missed a move. He was spread out, distracted, too smart for his own good. He'd put all his focus into a heavy-handed push for control over Licinus' body and whether the button would be pressed or not.

When I'd first trapped Licinus' ship in my ice hand, he'd activated his thrusters to drive him up in an effort to escape. They'd been running this whole time, and Aquilinus never noticed, never realized their significance. I'd lured him into position, made him doubt and act out of fear. Like Aulus' magic trick, I'd kept Aquilinus' attention focused on one hand—Licinus'—while the other hand—my fist of ice—had been working its magic, slowly letting go, slowly opening. So much focus on who was in control of Licinus, neither of them noticed that I'd let go, neither noticed the bomber's ascent. Up, up into the sky it flew. Aquilinus realized my final move in the same instant that he became aware that Licinus was no longer on the ice world but above it, beneath *Incitatus*.

He had time for one final word—"magnificent"—and then the bomb's atmospheric detonation claimed *Incitatus* and his entire fleet in a matter of seconds, incinerating them in the blast wave as rings of expanding light and nuclear fire once more brought fire to a world of ice.

LIII

THE SKY WAS RAINING metal, hot iron hail. Like shooting stars, the flaming ruins of *Incitatus* fell to the earth, a meteor shower of sculpted metal. This time the explosion had taken place in the upper atmosphere, and the surface of the planet was spared the worst of the bomb's destruction. The Rota Fortuna had been hit. The emperor, all the empire's best and brightest. Had they perished or been spared? The station hung, burning, above the planet. I was burning too. The queen's power was more than my mortal frame could bear. I looked back to the mountain, to the canyon entrance. I fell to my knees and then to my side on the icy ground. I looked on as the last of the Hyperboreans entered the mountain, which glowed like a burning spear tip. And then they were all gone, rejoined, and now the only question was whether all of this had been worth it. Had enough ichor got through for them to leave?

Now that the other distractions had been removed, I could hear the Hyperboreans' song again, the collective harmony of millions of minds. The same power that was burning me was also connecting me to them. The mountain was a vehicle of light and sound—architecture, design, power source, passengers all bound up in a perfectly proportioned collective thought. Their song was loud, vast, and beautiful. The sound of a songbird, stretched out across eons, spread out on a course that took them away from here, to another realm. No longer broken-winged birds, this droplet of the gods was stretching its healed limbs and preparing to soar to a place where the human mind could not follow.

But it was not enough. I could sense that. There was something missing. I felt panic creep over me.

Accala?

Aulus stood before me as I knew him, bright and shining. Dressed in his toga. Freckles and ruffled hair blown by the wind.

"Aulus? You must go."

Now my mother stood beside him. Beautiful, resplendent in her robes.

One last thing remains, she said. *We must take back that which we have given you.*

Of course. They needed to take the pin back, the last spark of power. It was the difference between success and failure.

I was not thinking straight. I tried to reach into my chest, to pull it out and give it to her like an apple I had in my pocket, but I couldn't move my arms.

I could sense scout ships, reinforcements, Praetorian Guards heading out from their deceres-class supercarriers now that the shield enclosing Rota Fortuna had been destroyed by the bomb blast. They were coming for the imprisoned emperor Caesar Numerius Valentinius, and when they freed him, everything would change.

"You must go," I said. "Now."

Mother stepped forward and tenderly touched my face. So warm. And then her hand was reaching into me, plunging into my breast, to my heart. I gasped as I felt it come out of me, and my eyes rolled back into my head. I felt my heart open like a flower releasing pollen. The burning was fading away, but I ached for the loss of that power. And then I was sinking, falling. I thought I was in my body, but I wasn't. I was above it, below it, in a hundred places in proximity to it. Now I was hurtling back from that point of divine perspective, back into my mortal body and all its emotions, weaknesses, wounds, and limitations. It came out like a splinter and I found myself suddenly reanimated. I was on all fours, covered in sweat despite the cold, my stomach empty but retching. Merely human, I felt the tide of emotions threatening to overwhelm me. If I hadn't been through a similar process of recombination with Lumen back in the caves, I think the shock might have been enough to kill me. I sat up on the ice, reaching out to Mother and Aulus as they began to move away. I still didn't know what these beings were to me, but so much had taken place, so much, and now this final good-bye. I couldn't bear to see them go.

Aulus took my hand. *It'll be just like the old stories, Accala. Mother and I will travel to the home of the gods. We'll be set in the stars like the old heroes.*

"And I'll be left here, in the dark, again. I'll be alone."

No. We'll always be with you. I can already sense it. It's a realm not limited by time or space as ours is. Every time you think of us, we'll be there.

I felt a sudden pang, a sense of loss and wishing that things could go back to how they were before any of this happened.

Nothing is forever, my brother said. He released my hand and walked toward my mother's outstretched arms.

He stepped into her, and her light enveloped him like a mother bird closing its wings around a chick.

"Stay with me," I pleaded.

We are always with you, they said.

The light of the mountain beyond grew strong and encompassed their bodies, dissolving them. And then they were gone.

I had the sense of a door being closed, of a ship sailing out from a port.

I looked for as long as I could stand the radiance—I wanted to see them go, wanted to make sure the job was done—and then I had to turn away before the light consumed me. It was too much. There was a streak. I looked up to see the sky ablaze, and then the mountain of light was gone, a flash already fading into the distant sky, joining with the stars. I was left in this world that was crumbling, cracking, falling to pieces. The still burning Rota Fortuna threw cyan-phosphorus light onto the landscape.

I'd done it, completed my mission. The Hyperboreans were gone and the mountain of ichor with them. All that remained were its foundations, a twenty-foot-high mesa in the center of the crescent valley.

I just lay there. Weak, limp, willing my eyes to remain open. Victory. I'd completed what I'd set out to do, overcome the odds, set things right. But I didn't feel triumphant. No radiant glory. A vacuum of feeling, a black hole of nothingness. Aulus was wrong. It was not like the old stories. All I felt was dry-throated exhaustion.

This world didn't have long now that the Hyperboreans had taken their power from it. I had to find Crassus and Julia and flee its surface.

The cold bit into my body. Back to reality—survival first. I was naked, exposed to the elements. There was no shortage of armor in the mouth of the crescent valley. I didn't know how long it would be until the emperor's administrators arrived, but I didn't want to die of exposure. There was a reasonably intact suit of armor on the body of a dead Viridian nearby. It was my uncle. After checking that its internal power cell was still functioning, I tore the battered armor off his body and dressed myself in it. A merciful heat covered me.

Holding the queen's power had healed many of my wounds, and I couldn't feel the ambrosia addiction anymore, but I was weak, like a newborn calf. Barely able to stand, I staggered over the icy ground, back to the canyon. Crassus and Julia. We could work together to escape this world, but they were nowhere to be seen. The command tank was burning faintly, ruined and useless. I stumbled and fell to my side. Lying there in the cold of the weckage-strewn battlefield, I slipped in and out of consciousness. Some time must have passed, because when I opened my eyes next, it was dark.

Sparks of light were descending from the Rota Fortuna. The emperor's men! There were survivors on the orbital stadium and they were coming. They'd take us from Olympus Decimus.

When they looked for someone to blame—and there would have to be a scapegoat—there was no doubt in my mind that it would be to me that the fingers of the senators would point. Would they chain me and drag me back to Rome? A traitor to be cast off the Tarpein Rock as an example to others? Here was the she-wolf who had defiled the games, they would say. The woman who betrayed her house, who murdered her father. The woman who stirred the pot and threw the empire into chaos.

Dark thoughts swirled like a black tide, and a sobbing moan welled up and freed itself from my mouth. Must get up. Be upright and coherent, try to explain myself to them, at least try to bargain for some kind of pardon for Julia. Come on. Move! My limbs were slow to respond. I managed to raise myself to one knee. They were coming. What now? Would anyone care about the outcome of the tournament? I crumpled to the ground again, and wept uncontrollably. The internal tides of emotion were so powerful. The snow fell around me, and with it came the combined recollection of all that had happened on the voyage to this world, my dark transformation, the massacre, my family and then resurrection as light, the death of Marcus, the defeat of my enemies, my loss of identity. My mind was stretched to its limits just to survive this. How could I possibly face what came next?

"Accala? Accala?" It was Julia.

"Call her name, bitch. Call it out!"

"Accala?"

In the darkness I could make out a figure moving toward me. I willed myself to sit up, my fingers closing around Orbis.

It was Crassus. And Julia. She was ahead of him on all fours, a cord wrapped around her neck like a makeshift leash. His javelin was prodding the soft side of her throat with its razor-sharp point. Then he spotted me.

"You've been a bad girl, Accala. So naughty."

This wasn't Crassus. It was Aquilinus. Gods, I was so sure I'd killed him, but he must have still had a line connecting him to Crassus. In that final moment he must have transferred everything into the one nearby host available to him. No more hanging around the fringes subtly controlling and manipulating his subjects. He'd taken Crassus over entirely, body and soul.

"You didn't think you'd get rid of me so easily, did you?"

"What do you want?" I asked as I stood shakily, trying to keep myself steady. I needed to buy time, to pull myself together.

"What else? I'm here to make a deal. You think you've won, but this is my game, my empire, and you're going to compensate me for the loss I've suffered here."

"I've got nothing," I said. "The ichor's all gone."

"You're the most valuable asset on this world now, and I plan to make you mine. I have men, hidden and waiting to transport me away. They will come soon. For both of us."

Empire's most valuable asset? What did he mean by that? I was a liability, a heavy stone about the neck.

"Your weapon," he snapped. "Throw it away."

I held it out to drop it to the ground, but he was quick to stop me.

"No! Throw it away. Far enough that you won't be able to recover it. You won't be needing weapons where I'll be taking you."

I hesitated, but he pressed the javelin tip into Julia's throat, drawing blood, making her wince in pain.

"Now," he said. He stuck the javelin in her already wounded shoulder, drawing a pained scream.

A calmness settled over me, and the image of how the crescent canyon looked from the top down flashed into my mind—a semicircle of rock with the mesa at its center, like a great eye looking up to the gods. It reminded me of a rough-hewn Colosseum. It was big, though, a long circuit, longer than I'd ever thrown, longer than anyone had ever thrown, if I wanted my discus to return to my hand. And no lapis negra breastplate to help. Just flesh and bone, tendon and muscle. Marcus. My mentor. He said I'd never have it in me to match Julius Ovidius' record cast. Now it was time to find out. I was filled with a newfound energy. One last burst of fire, and I used it to spin. Three times, gathering momentum, speed, and then I loosed Orbis behind me. I had gotten so much momentum that I nearly fell flat on my face as he left my hand. Back into the shadows of the canyon. Gone.

"Now, on your knees," Aquilinus spat. He threw a length of rope on the ground. "Tie it around your neck, just like your friend here. Do it and I'll free her." He pulled Julia up to his side. Her face was bulging with lack of oxygen, and she was clawing at the rope, trying to release some of the pressure as it bit into her skin. I picked it up and started to loop it around my throat. He grinned with delight.

"Now you know your place. You'll be spending a lot of time on your knees. You don't realize your own value. No normal person could contain the power they put into you. I will breed little godlings from you." I thought back to his cursing when I found his hidden chamber aboard *Incitatus*. All his dark delusions. "There are still places where I can survive. Still places beyond the reach of the empire where I have power. You'll be a pretty prize, most useful."

Orbis always sought to return to me along the shortest possible path the casting arc would allow. I'd put spin on my throw so that he would hug the canyon wall, gathering speed, traveling full circle. But would he make the distance? Orbis only had to strike a boulder or nick the canyon wall, and he'd lose ground and fall short. Even now, he could be spinning uselessly on the canyon floor, his journey at an end. And then I heard a faint hum, a familiar drone of the air being cut.

"Julia," I called out. "Remember on the ship? The advice you gave me when we first met in the cabin?"

Her eyes widened in acknowledgment and she threw herself flat on the ground. Aquilinus' grip on the rope loosened for just an instant, and he pulled forward. He knew something was up. He threw his body aside as Orbis came soaring past. His neck was clear of the discus' razor edge, but he instinctively threw his left arm up in the air to shield himself. Orbis returned to my grasp in the same instant that his hand hit the ground, fingers still wrapped around his javelin.

The Sertorian surged forward, faster than I could react, roaring like an animal. He closed quickly before I could bring Orbis to bear, spitting at me, clawing at my face. I had nothing left, no fight in me, the cast had taken everything, and Aquilinus was like a rabid dog, wild and insane, every part the barbarian. His remaining hand clawed at my exposed skin, raking flesh. He hugged me close and bit my ear so hard it bled. I was trying to break free, to get him off me, but his grip was driven by mania.

"Mine. Mine," he whispered in my ear again and again.

My reply was a scream accompanied by a sharp head butt straight to his nose. It broke and he reeled back in pain, his eyes watering, blood flowing. I cut at him with Orbis. He knocked the flat of the discus aside with his stump, opening him for me to deliver a cross to his jaw. As he fell back, I sat up and pushed forward, coming up on top of him, straddling his chest. In that moment he managed to trap my weapon hand between his upper arm and body. I howled with rage, my inner beast responding in kind, my right fist raining blows upon his face in a hammering action, crashing his skull into the hard ground. If I couldn't cut him, I was going to beat his brains out.

I caught a glimpse of a bronze raven's head on the butt of the gladius sheathed on his belt. The sword he was struggling to reach now. Marcus' sword.

The moment of distraction allowed Aquilinus to get a hand to the weapon, and he swung up at me, forcing me to roll off of him to avoid a severed jugular. We came to our feet at the same time and stood at the ready—gladius versus discus. Aquilinus was pressing his stump into his stomach to try to stanch the bleeding. It was Crassus' body, but it was the only one Aquilinus had got right now and he had to make it last. Was this it, then? If I killed him this time, would he stay dead?

Our weapons clashed as if with their own life, desperately cutting and hacking to and fro, back and forth. I blocked a thrust and then hooked Orbis' inner ring about the hilt, catching the weapon in place, stopping him from drawing it back to thrust again. I knew the gladius, I knew *this* gladius. I had its greatest exponent to model my technique from, and even at his best, neither Crassus nor Aquilinus was a match for Marcus. Before Aquilinus could recover, I used one of Marcus' moves, a follow-up cut to the face with a kick that drove him backward. I spun again and delivered a cut to his other hand, disarming him literally. His right hand flew away with the sword. Before the blade could hit the ground, I plucked it from the air.

"You don't deserve to hold his blade," I said as I advanced on him, discus in one hand, gladius in the other.

His face was filled with fear. Only bloody stumps left to defend himself with.

I used Orbis and Marcus' sword to cut into the shell of his armor in a diagonal arc from top right to bottom left, and then spun, following up with a sword cut to his face along the opposite backhand arc from right temple to left jaw. I stepped in and knocked his head back with my elbow, opening the side of his neck for the killing thrust. This was it.

And then I was flying sideways into the snow. I looked up to see an armored figure standing over me. A shock staff crackled with purple electricity in the night—a Praetorian Guard, the lion's head of House Numerian on his breastplate. More Praetorians arrived, purple-and-black armored suits on hover platforms, racing across the ice. I was barely conscious. I tried to get back to my feet. I had to finish this. Aquilinus had to die. I wouldn't get another chance. A shock staff hit me again and I was down. On my back, my muscles in spasms.

From above, lights flooded the scene, sirens sounded. Scout ships, reinforcements, rescue vehicles arrived. Armed soldiers in purple armor flooded the canyon from all directions. One stood over Aquilinus, shock stick leveled at his body, preventing him from rising as well.

"Let her up," a voice said, and the Praetorian who hit me couldn't act too quickly to pull me up, but only to my knees.

"Stay there," he whispered. "The emperor is here."

He emerged from the darkness, robes billowing.

Aquilinus suddenly started yelling. "It is I, Gaius Crassus! She tried to kill me. I am the rightful winner of the tournament. Protect me, Imperator!"

"We've have had quite enough from you today," the emperor said, pointing at Aquilinus. A Praetorian stepped in and hit him over the back of the head with his staff, sending him falling forward, face-first into the snow, unconscious.

A Praetorian Guard tribune rushed forward to the emperor.

"Sire! Are you safe?"

"I'm fine, Brutus."

Gods. It was Brutus Numerius Africanus, the commander of all of Rome's legions.

Next came flying cameras. The media and officials had gotten themselves together and caught up with us.

"Wait!" I called out. "Crassus! He's not . . ." I started to rise, desperate. I had to let him know it was Aquilinus in there, that he had to kill him now, but the Praetorian stepped forward, and the end of his staff cracked on my skull. I hit the ice.

"Leave her," I heard the emperor order.

He came to stand over me.

"It's all right, you've done your part, Accala Viridius Camilla. Your part and more!"

I lay there, barely sensible, as a fat man, a tournament official, came up and bowed before the emperor, talking to him in an animated fashion. It was Julius Gemminus—pleading for his miserable life.

"Yes, yes, you're right," I heard the emperor say.

A holographic seal was projected into the air above the emperor—an eagle encircled by golden laurels. The emperor raised his hand and shouted out, "I declare the Tournament of Jupiter ended!"

"But the winner, sire?" Julius Gemminus pleaded. "You must announce a winner."

"First I'll decide who is going to live and die. Then we'll settle the matter of the games."

Was it the Tarpein Rock, then? Let them kill me, as long as Aquilinus shared my fate. As long as the threat to Rome was removed. There was so much noise and activity, I couldn't make any sense of what was going on. My head slumped to the side, and I saw my own blood forming a pool around me. Aquilinus must have wounded me.

"Thank you, Bright Lady," I whispered to swift-winged Minerva. She came to my aid not when I asked for it but when I needed it. An offering. I owed her an offering, and all I had left was my life.

I heard Julia calling my name, and then there was only darkness.

EPILOGUE

And Camillus returning with the standards. Yonder souls likewise, whom thou discernest gleaming in equal arms, at one now, while shut in Night, ah me! what mutual war, what battle-lines and bloodshed shall they arouse, so they attain the light of the living! father-in-law descending from the Alpine barriers and the fortress of the Dweller Alone, son-in-law facing him with the embattled East. Nay, O my children, harden not your hearts to such warfare, neither turn upon her own heart the mastering might of your country; and thou, be thou first to forgive, who drawest thy descent from heaven; cast down the weapons from thy hand, O blood of mine. . . . He shall drive his conquering chariot to the Capitoline height triumphant over Corinth, glorious in Achaean slaughter.

—Virgil, *Aeneid*

Rome, Mother Earth. Four weeks later.

ROME SHONE. ETERNALLY BRILLIANT, oblivious of the ebbs and tides of the game of houses. She went on as she always did. Gleaming crystalline towers and domes, grand temples.

The people lined the streets, thousands of them, silently staring at me as I passed them by at the head of my father's funeral procession. No jeering and abuse, none of the hatred I had seen in their eyes when I left Rome. Today they looked upon me with respect, awe even. The bells tolled as we neared the temple. My father was a hero of the empire, a famous tribune. It was normal for people to respond to the priest's call by spontaneously joining the procession, crying out their feelings, expressing their grief, rushing to pay their respects. But they were all too busy watching me, wondering if I'd suddenly bring down the gods from on high. What happened on Olympus Decimus was nothing short of a miracle, but already they'd blown the story out of proportion—Athena coming down from the clouds, touching me with her spear, the gods watching from above as I carried out their will. They whispered to one another, barely able to contain their excitement as I passed. They'd been a plague since I returned, a veritable human pestilence, gathering outside the Wolf's Den, throwing flowers in my path when I tried to walk the streets to clear my head. They still called me daughter of Minerva, Lady Justice. I tried to stay clear of them now, remained locked away in the safety of the Wolf's Den while their numbers outside, chanting my name, increased day by day. I chanted my own prayers in the family temple. I made offerings to Minerva; I prayed for my mother, my brother, my father, Marcus, and Bulla.

* * *

I COULDN'T BRING MYSELF to watch any footage of the games, but I reviewed the journalists, politicians, and social commentators who wrote about it and came upon one woman of the Scribaneum, a collegium dedicated to recording history for the imperial archive. Out of all the requests I received, I accepted hers alone on the condition that she never speak a word or share my record with anyone while I was alive, and she agreed. We'd been meeting each day to discuss, as best I could recount, my experience of what happened to me. I thought it would be helpful, a way of walking away from a life that I no longer wished to participate in. Once it was done, I'd find a new life, a simpler, healthier way of being.

* * *

I HELD THE PIN in my hand as the procession made its way through the city streets. Just a useless piece of metal once more. I clutched it like a talisman, hoping for some communication from the Hyperboreans, some dream that my mother and brother continued or a signal that they'd reached the distant home they set out for, but there was nothing. At night I didn't sleep. I took medication to trick my body into a sleeplike state. I couldn't face my dreams—they were heavy, dark, and when I awoke, their content slipped away, leaving me with feelings of dread and fear. So I stayed away from the machine that was Rome. But not today. Today was my father's funeral and I had to go out among the gleaming marble, the triumphal arches. I had to pass through the mob.

The Praetorians kept the crowds contained to the sides of the streets with their shock staves. I was dressed in black lugubria, the robes of mourning. On either side of me were Viridian senators and other members of my extended family. The sound of lowing horns and a morose requiem accompanied us as we slowly shuffled along the road toward the temple where the cremation would take place.

"Make way!" the crier priest at the procession head called out. "Here is the body of Lucius Viridius Camillus! Join us and offer your prayers to a hero of the empire!"

Heralds repeated the message, musicians blew their horns, torchbearers lit the way, and porters nudged the street traffic to the side as we progressed. My father traveled ahead of us on his bier, ready to be set alight, for his soul to travel to the afterlife.

Things had been unbearable back on Olympus Decimus, but they were simple—live or die, fight and win. Here the immediate danger was gone, but everything was in a kind of gray limbo. The mechanisms of empire continued: politicking, imperial shuffling for position. My aunts and uncles had come and petitioned me to get involved in the realignment of power, to speak for House Viridian, but I couldn't give a fig. For me everything was gray, not life but a play of life that I was watching, like a dream I couldn't manage to wake up from. I felt useless, like a mechanic without tools, a soldier without a sword. Perhaps things would make sense after the funeral.

* * *

WHEN I AWOKE AFTER the fight on Olympus Decimus, I was naked, floating in a shallow pool of warm bright blue liquid. As I tried to sit up, a hand appeared, a slender blue hand, and gently pushed me back down. A face appeared above mine—a young blue-skinned girl. At least, I thought she was female. An alien that looked androgynous; I couldn't tell what sex it was. Trailing across its body, beneath its skin, were slow-moving white spirals. She—I decided it must be a she—looked like a river nymph, a beautiful, slender ripple traveling across the surface of a pond. Three others joined the first, surrounding me. I didn't feel anxious; I was perfectly relaxed, almost sleepy like I was dreaming. Except I was sure I was awake. There was no pain, my lungs didn't hurt anymore, no more stinging of the wind on open cuts. The remembrance of what had happened came to me as if from a distance. Marcus. Mother. Aulus. Father. And Aquilinus, living on in Crassus' body. The spike of anxiety forced me to try to move again. The hand touched me again, and the worry was gone, just like chalk wiped from a blackboard. Celtoi. The word seemed to rise up in my mind as if from a great depth. I'd heard of these aliens who lived beyond the borders of the empire. They were water beings with healing powers who communicated through dreams, directly to the depths of the mind. These were the emperor's personal attendants—the only four Celtoi within the empire.

They were sent as tribute to Rome in exchange for leaving their worlds in peace. Four unique members of their species—a healer, a musician, a courtesan, and a poet. They all looked the same to me; I couldn't tell which was which. I could feel their thoughts swapping back and forth, below the surface of my mind, just out of my reach like whispers from a distant room. Then images arose from deep within my mind. A sailboat on a still lake—they were telling me to be calm. A feeling of relaxation washed over me. Their method of communication was similar to the Hyperboreans, and simple for me to comprehend after my recent ordeal. But how long had I been asleep? The image of a sun passing from east to west filled my mind. It turned again and again. Ten times in total—ten days, almost as long as I was in the Ludi Romani.

I looked past the faces to the space above them. This was no ordinary place. I was surrounded by a field of slow-spiraling blue energy; it reminded me of a tent. But I was still alive. I could see through the porthole set into the far wall. Dark space. I was aboard a ship, then.

I had to get out and back into the real world. Was the emperor having me healed so I could survive the trip back to face trial and execution? I had to make sure Julia was safe.

I sat up and the Celtoi seemed concerned, their thoughts flittering back and forth. They were surprised that I could resist them. Perhaps some of the Hyperboreans' power lingered within me. Or maybe it was just that after all that had happened I was more stubborn than the average person and not willing to be subdued.

They let me rise from the pool. Their hands gently pulled me out and helped me stand. The emperor's alien attendants had done their job well—aside from being as weak as a newborn kitten, I was healed; all my breaks, bruises, and cuts seemed to have completely vanished.

Eight hands dressed me in clean, warm clothes, a thermal robe—plain white without house colors, which made me slightly anxious. It reminded me that I was still an outcast. I had walked away from the game of houses. I was alone in a galaxy in which belonging is a necessary ingredient for survival.

The spiraling energy tent subsided and faded, and I found myself in a luxurious cabin. Not Sertorian, no desperate attempt to impress, this chamber had been arrayed with fine bronze and gold fittings, simple but elegant linear designs. There was a golden lion emblazoned upon the domed ceiling. House Numerian. These were the emperor's personal chambers.

As I exited through large steel doors, I was faced with Julia hobbling toward me down the corridor, walking with the aid of a cane.

"Accala!"

"Julia! What's going on?"

"We're going home," she said.

"Home?"

"Rome! We're going back to Rome."

"What about Olympus Decimus?"

"Gone. Or in the process of going. We evacuated the planet just as it was turning in on itself. The ichor was keeping it all together. It won't be long before it's nothing but asteroids and dust."

It was like receiving the letter informing me that Mother and Aulus had died. Notification of a life-changing event that I felt I should have witnessed directly.

"Now tell me, how are you? Are you okay?" she asked.

"I'm fine," I said impatiently. "Tell me what's going on. Where's Crassus?"

"Ah, that," she said. "Don't worry about him right now. I'll tell you everything, but a lot's happened. Come with me and I'll fill you in."

"But Crassus—"

"I know, just hold your horses and let me talk."

"Why?" I asked suspiciously.

"To reassure you. To tell you how things have played out. To tell you that you're a hero."

I looked at her like a simpleton. What was she saying? I understood the words, but I couldn't quite connect how they could be relevant to me.

"It's true," she said. "House Sertorian has been stricken from the Council of Eight, all its members banished or executed."

"And the emperor? Where is he?"

"Back in Rome already. He's been cleaning house. He's re-forming the Senate as we speak."

"And the Viridians?"

"Hailed as saviors of the empire, their status intact, elevated, even. Thanks to you."

"Gods. I can't believe it."

"All because of what we did here. Because of what you did."

"Wait. If the emperor's back on Mother Earth, then what am I doing in his chambers? Aboard his ship?"

She gave me a wide smile that ran from ear to ear.

"Because it's not his ship."

"I don't understand. Are we prisoners?"

"Well, Brutus Numerius Africanus is captaining it for now, but that's only until you're fit to take command. This is your ship. A gift from the emperor."

I took a step back, my face screwed up as I struggled to process what she was saying.

"I know," she said. "It's pretty fantastic, isn't it? You should see the engines on this thing. I've been down there for days tinkering with them. It's been very recuperative for me."

"But . . ."

"You've been promoted. The emperor has issued an empirewide statement praising your courage. They've been ordered to erect statues in your honor in all eight provinces. And you've been given a rank."

"As what?"

"A centurion. And not just any centurion. You're appointed to the quaestor-ship. You'll be a military judge, a centurion with the power to administer the imperial law instantaneously—judge, jury, and executioner all in one."

"Only men can be in the military," I stated.

"Not anymore. The emperor reopened the Quaestorium just for you. You're the first woman officer in . . . well, in the empire's history, I think. There are a hundred men aboard this ship waiting to take your orders. The ship's been renamed too. *Minerva's Spear*. In your honor."

"Tell the emperor he can give the job to someone else."

"You can't really turn down the emperor."

"I just did."

Julia held out her hand, offering a white leather strip, battered and cracked, caked in blood.

"They found it in Marcus' hand when they recovered his body. We're bringing him home for a state funeral. The committee thought that he'd pulled it from his own costume, that he meant it as a gift for you."

The sixth tassel. The mark of primus paulus—the highest rank of gladiator. I took the strip and held it tightly. It wasn't Amphiara that he saw in his last moments. His desperate declaration of love was for me. This was what he was holding out, an offering, a gift to show his love and respect. Marcus loved me. I was the thing he was most terrified to lose. Damn the emperor, that tassel from Marcus was a promotion I was able to bear. Sweet Marcus. He deserved a better death than at Barbata's hands. How I wish I could have held him as he passed after all that he sacrificed for me. In the entire empire, where could another man like him be found?

"Now tell me, what of Crassus?" I asked.

"Ah. Come and get settled. Eat something, and then I'll tell you about Crassus."

I grabbed her by the shoulders and fixed her with a fierce glare.

"Tell me now," I insisted. "Right now."

And she did, and then I turned around and walked back toward the chambers. I felt like I was made of rubber.

"It's okay," she called out after me. "Really, Accala, it's all going to be okay."

Minerva's Spear was everything I could have hoped for in a ship. She was fast, sleek, and deadly—the finest trireme in the galaxy—an honor I could never have imagined would be bestowed upon me, and I cared for it not at all.

I left Brutus to manage the crew on the journey back and kept to my cabin. I banished the Celtoi and spent my days staring out the window into space, running away from every responsibility, refusing every audience, even with Julia. My mother once read to me a classical description of a conversation between Socrates and Plato. The man witnessing said that listening to it was like falling into a labyrinth. *We thought we were at the finish, but our way bent round and we found ourselves as it were back at the beginning, and just as far from that which we were seeking at first.* That was how I felt. Like I'd set out to work out my problems and the empire's problems, only to find myself right back at the beginning. No progress. Great sacrifice all for nothing.

*   *   *

WHAT DID HONORS HEAPED upon me matter when the emperor allowed Crassus to walk free, and worse, allowed the people of Rome to treat him like a hero, a tournament champion?

Julia told me that his final assault upon my person wasn't televised, that the nuclear explosion temporarily disabled the media spherae, and Julia's report, the word of a collegia plebeian, was not taken into account. They saw Crassus on my side in the field and they saw me walk past the podium and leave the crown. They thought I left it for him, that it was my will that he be crowned champion, that I didn't want the crown for myself. Commentators and pundits remarked on my choice, but none dared to question it too loudly for fear of bringing down upon themselves the wrath of my rapidly growing following.

And I couldn't say a thing.

Julia transmitted the emperor's command—that I remain silent about Aquilinus and Crassus if I wished to see House Viridian's fortunes continue to improve. When would the dust from this whirlwind I'd stirred up ever settle?

The old veterans who fought beside my father had turned out for the funeral. They carried his bier upon their shoulders, each one a highly decorated member of House Viridian, their armor clanking on the cobblestones of the ancient road that led through the center of the old city. Old salts, their bodies a collection of bionic limbs and spare parts, they carried him with a silent, solemn respect. None of them gave me the time of day before taking up the bier. There was nothing about me they liked, and I didn't blame them. They understood that this funeral should be about my father, about his life and his sacrifices, about his fight to preserve the empire. Instead it was about me. I, who ended his life. Should I even be there? In the position of honor? As a centurion, I was the highest-ranking direct descendant, an honor intended for a male.

The rest of them, cousins, uncles, and aunts, marched behind me. I couldn't face them. I'd shrivel and die beneath the collective gaze of anger and disappointment.

Behind me and to my right marched Appius Viridius Murena. The name *Murena* was derived from the word "eel." A second cousin, my father's cousin, and head of the emperor's secret police, Rome's curiosi. It was he who took over the role after my uncle Quintus was promoted from there to the proconsulship of our house. I had always liked him more than Quintus. He had a natural charm in place of my uncle's direness, but not much more. Beside him walked Julia, here representing the emperor. I was not the only one who'd had a promotion.

*　*　*

THE DAY BEFORE THE funeral, they'd come to me in my chambers where I lay on my bed, staring at the cameo of Aulus and my mother.

"My condolences," Appius Murena said. Beside him stood Julia. I'd avoided her until that moment, but you couldn't lock the door when the emperor sent his representatives to see you.

Julia was wearing imperial sigils of the curiosi on the shoulder straps of her dress toga—the emperor's man now—the first of the collegia to be granted a noble title and lands.

"You're a spy now?" I asked her.

"I was a spy before."

"Now you're the emperor's man."

"Can you guess who I'm supposed to spy on?"

"Me?"

"Good guess," she said.

"He wants to keep me under observation."

"Of course he does. You're the hero of the hour, but you're amassing a following. He wants to make sure you keep your feet on the ground."

"Know my place, you mean?"

"Not as a woman. He doesn't want you to marry, to follow your husband's orders. He wants you to act as a quaestor. Know your place in the empire. You have one, a position of honor and power. Isn't it better this way?"

"There will be no 'way.' The hero of the hour is Aquilinus dressed up as Gaius Sertorius Crassus. I'm the curiosity of the hour, the imperial freak show. Don't you see? The emperor knows it's Aquilinus. He's keeping him around. He's behind all this."

"Yes."

"That's the best you've got to say?"

"You can't mourn forever," Murena said. "I saw the footage of your final fight with your father. The entire empire did. He sacrificed himself so that you could keep fighting in his stead. You honored him. He gloried in your strength. Why do you think that not a single citizen has dared label the accusation of patricide upon you? They know, Accala. They see what you do not."

"Forget this moping about the house," Julia added. "You're not suited to life here, you never were. It's time to fly, Accala. To reap the rewards of all that you've fought for, all that you've sacrificed. You wanted to remake the empire, now's your chance. Let's show them."

"Are you both finished?" I asked, standing up from the bed. "Listen carefully. I don't care about this. I want to know about you," I said to Julia. "What happened to the cloud city? You know I sent letters to the emperor on your behalf?"

"I know and I thank you for that. My sister is receiving top treatment—she's been flown here to Rome. And he offered me that position as an engineer on the cloud world—he did, I swear it—and I turned it down."

"But that was your dream," I said.

"I had a dream, things happened, now I'm a different person with different dreams."

She held up her right hand and pulled off the glove she wore. Had I been so distracted that I forgot about her hand? The one crafted for her by Lumen was gone; no ichor remained now that the Hyperboreans were gone. It seemed that Julia had been fitted out with a machinarii replacement.

"I'm sorry," I said.

"I accept what I am, what's become of me," Julia said as she slipped the glove back on. "I have another dream now, one you stirred within my breast. From within the curiosi, having the emperor's ear—I can do more for the collegia and for my sister and others like her than I ever could before. You should find a new dream too, Accala."

"I have only nightmares now," I said.

"That's because you're not doing what you're meant to be doing. You're heading down the wrong path. You need to come. With me. Everyone thinks you're being solemn, communing with the gods, but I know better. You're moping."

"Leave me."

"Julia told me you were talking about Plato and Socrates on the voyage home," Murena said. "You know life's not like the pointless labyrinthine words of philosophers. Life's more like a spiral. You experience the same lessons, but each time on a different plane. You're learning, improving all the time. You're back at the beginning, but now you possess hard-won experiences, and from them is born a wisdom the empire could well use."

"Leave me be. Now."

Julia held out a small message disc with the imperial seal.

"He asked me to give this to you. It will explain everything."

"It's my father's funeral tomorrow. This is hardly the time to . . ."

"We'll leave you," Julia said, "but please, activate the disc when we're gone. Hear what he's got to say."

As they departed, I heard Appius Murena say, "I didn't realize Aquilinus had beaten her down so badly. Her father's fire is gone, she's broken."

"She's no coward," Julia replied. "She was filled with the power of the gods and then emptied. She's been put up on the high mountain and shown how everything fits together and then been thrown back down into a mortal body. She's disillusioned. Imagine if you were suddenly turned into an ant with the memory of having been immortal. I'd rather be crucified."

Julia understood. Perhaps it was her hand that gave her that insight. Not that that changed a thing. Not a single thing.

I stared at the disc for an hour or two and then placed it on my bedside table, beside my cameo, and tapped its central ring. I expected a holographic recording, but instead the form of a man appeared, sitting behind a marble desk, scrolling through items on a tablet. There was a chime and he looked up, right at me. It was the emperor and the connection was live. This was a personal audience, albeit at a distance.

"Imperator," I said, rising from the bed to kneel.

"No, no, sit. Come, let us talk informally. We have some shared history between us, you and I."

I'd been taught to venerate the emperor my entire life. Even after what I'd been through, it was difficult to sit still and relax, even in a transmitted presence.

"You'll have to excuse me for not coming in person, but the current climate is delicate. Those followers of yours who crowd the Aventine in the hope of catching a glimpse of you, well, it wouldn't do to have the emperor coming to you in that kind of environment, would it?"

"I hate it," I said.

"The people's adoration?"

"I hate it, every minute of it. I wish they'd just go away."

"I know you do. You've proved yourself loyal to me, to the empire and the Pax Romana. You could have aided your traitorous uncle, but you didn't."

"He was no less greedy than any other proconsul desperate to seize glory for his house, as you once were for yours."

"I suppose I was, though it's not polite to bring such things up," the emperor said.

"You did say we could speak informally."

"I suppose I did. It wasn't your uncle's greed that I objected to, it was his foolishness. He thought only of his house and not of the empire's well-being. The ichor would have been too much power for any one house to wield. Sometimes, wisdom is in leaving a thing be, even something of great power and value."

"That's why I couldn't stand with him."

"You sided with Lady Minerva instead, and what a powerful ally she turned out to be. She was within you, her power filling a chosen hero, just like the ancient stories."

"It wasn't like that."

"Then what was it like?"

"It's hard to explain. Like I was two people at once: a fragile, straw Accala and one who could touch the sky."

As I spoke, I realized that I was providing a description that fitted the emperor's first impression perfectly, but when I searched for the right words to say it in a way that sounded logical and self-effacing, I found myself at a loss.

"It's a performance I can't replicate," the emperor said. "We've got to take steps, or the cult of Accala will rise up. They'll become unstoppable. They love you."

"They don't love me. They don't know me."

"They adore you, you should see what they've been writing on the vox populi. The curia, the curiosi, the frumentarii, my Praetorians—they can't stop sending me reports. You've got their hackles up. They're worried."

"There's nothing to worry about. I want to go to the Amalfi Coast. I'm going to retire completely from public life like Scipio Africanus."

"That sounds nice. So no more public profile, then?"

"I wanted to step out into the empire and show them a woman could seize justice, could shake Atlas' pillars, and I did it. Now I want to retire. I want peace and quiet, to tend the orchards at our ancestral villa."

"Now you see, it's talk like that has me concerned. Scipio Africanus went and worked his farm, but the moment they called him back to war, he fulfilled his duty and trounced the enemy."

"There is no duty left for me to perform. Only a daughter's duty."

"But you'd always be there, you see? Waiting for history to poke you into action again. That's far too concerning for my advisers."

"You're going to have me killed, then?"

"I wish it were that simple. A martyred Accala would be more dangerous than a living one. You, I can reason with. A mob with leaders and zealots, there's no reasoning with them. They'll twist everything you've done, interpret your life to suit their own desires. No, I'm not going to kill you. I'm going to offer you a job."

"You already did, I turned it down."

"You don't get to turn down the emperor's offer. It doesn't work that way. You say, 'Thank you, Imperator, it is an honor to serve.'"

"No."

"No?"

"Why have you not executed Gaius Crassus? You know full well that Aquilinus possesses him. The greatest enemy to the Pax Romana strolls around Rome as a hero."

"The answer to that question is a state secret and lies on the other side of my offer. Accept and I will tell you. Until I know you work with me, I can say nothing."

"I refuse to be manipulated."

"This is Rome, fitting square pegs into square holes is what we do. The nail that sticks up gets hammered down."

"And if I don't accept?"

"Then you'll be elevated to the throne in a matter of months. All my prognosticators and analysts say so. My house will fall, yours will rise, and you'll have my job. Then, when the empire needs you elsewhere, you will be tied down to the throne, desperately trying to work out how to run an empire. How's that for a threat? I think I've read you well enough to know that you don't want my job."

"No."

"So?"

"Let me think about it."

"Your father told me you were stubborn. Now I'm beginning to understand. You have two days. After that . . . well, let's not get into that now."

The image faded out and the power cell in the disc died. There would be no return call; I'd had my audience.

* * *

DRESSED IN HIS SENATORIAL robes, my father was laid on a simple bier constructed from dried branches of wicker and sage. I would be the one to light it when we reached the temple, sending his spirit up with the smoke, up to paradise—to the Elysian Fields. That's where I hoped he would go, what I'd prayed for. I never understood what Lumen said about death being a remembering and never got the chance to ask him. Now it was too late.

Above the bier shone a large holographic portrait. My father appeared as a younger man, smiling with both eyes intact, eyes that were lit with hope—a man I never knew. The image slowly morphed, shifting through the stages of his life until it came to rest upon his final portrait, an image captured in the Senate in the days before I joined the Sertorian team.

"It is a dark day for Rome, Accala," Murena said as he walked beside me in his black dress armor. "She has lost a great hero."

I couldn't hold back the tears now. The last of my mother's Stoicism had been leached out of me. They streamed down over my cheeks, hot and shameful tears that I had no right to let flow.

"Let me mourn in silence," I said. "I have disappointed him. I can barely stand for the weight of the shame I feel."

Murena scowled. "This is a difficult day for you, but remember that you are a Viridian. Stand strong. I may not be your favorite uncle, but I know you well enough," he said, "and I've never known you to indulge in self-pity. Hold back your tears until you are out of public view."

I turned on him, anger suddenly burning inside of me, evaporating the tears.

"What do you know of strength? Slinking about in shadows like an eel? You accuse me of cowardice?"

I turned from him to see the audience crowded behind the banners, watching me, the lines four deep. And I hated them, hated their being here, gawking at me. They'd transformed my father's funeral into an arena event. They were here to watch me perform, to see firsthand, here in the streets of the capital, the end of the conflict that they'd been watching from a distance.

"Go!" I yelled at them. "Leave me alone or I swear to the gods I will burn you!"

There was fear in their eyes, a worried murmur, and then they were falling away. Some of them couldn't get out of there quickly enough at the thought that what happened to the Sertorians on Olympus Decimus might be visited on them now. Suddenly they were too close to the action for comfort.

"That was not wise," Murena said beneath his breath.

The procession recommenced. I was glad that my father traveled ahead; I couldn't bear to be close to him, not until I gave him the final kiss, because once he was close, I'd be unable to stop the tears. I was not some weak schoolgirl. I wouldn't disgrace his memory anymore. His last days had been filled with worry and dishonor because of me. The last weeks of the voyage home had opened my eyes to many things. The hollowness that I was left with on the surface of

Olympus Decimus had not departed; if anything, it'd grown worse. I was already looking for a way to remove myself from the emperor's service. I wouldn't be a centurion or quaestor or any other thing while he supported Crassus' freedom and banned me from speaking out. And I couldn't speak out. I couldn't throw the empire into any more turmoil right now. It needed time to heal itself, time to pull together and solidify, but it was time that Aquilinus would use to strengthen his position. I knew it, the emperor knew it. I didn't know what game he was playing, but I wanted no part of it. I was going to rest, to remove myself from the game of houses. My first taste was enough for a lifetime. I wanted to go away, somewhere where it was quiet. Perhaps I'd take my father's advice. Find a good man and marry. Anything but more of what I'd just been through.

Too late, I realized that something was wrong. I didn't see who bumped into me. Whoever it was, there were more than one of them and they were coming right through the middle of the funeral procession. Gods, we were in a crossroads. There was another procession running right across ours. What idiot scheduled this? I turned, trying to stop the man who bumped me before he disrupted the funeral. I was surprised to see it was a soldier, a Praetorian.

"Make way! Stand clear!" he called out, his voice projected out above the lowing horns by the vocal amplifier in his armor. The soldiers moved to separate our processions, giving the other one prominence.

"What? Who dares do this?" I called out. I was more than a little irritated. My father deserved more than this, more respect from the society he served his whole life, and I meant to see that he got it.

I was shoved aside as another Praetorian strode past me, and then they were streaming out from the side streets, polluting our procession with their presence, hundreds of citizens. There were too many to stop. The veterans holding the bier were swearing, but they couldn't drop their cargo to challenge the sudden onslaught. These people were not attacking, they didn't have weapons, none of us did—citizens were forbidden from carrying them within the walls of the city. Their mass pushed my father's bier aside, disrupting the veterans who held him up. I rushed to his side, shielding his body, stopping it from falling to the ground.

"Into the side street!" I called out, directing our procession into an alley and out of the crossroads as the mass of cheering people filled the street like a flash flood.

I was furious. What in the name of the gods was happening?

I was just about to punch the nearest reveler out of frustration when I realized they were part of a parade—a triumphal procession. They were en route to the Capitoline Hill, and we had to yield the way. That was the law. It was the custom. In Rome, winning always came first. Even my father's funeral must yield for a state-sponsored celebration of a great victory. But who was the hero? What victory? I felt a sinking feeling in the pit of my stomach.

"What's happening?" I demanded of Murena. He should have known about this. He knew everything.

"Make way for the champion of Jupiter! Make way for the victor of the tournament!" a herald announced.

Crassus. Aquilinus. I hadn't been paying attention to what had been happening in Rome. I'd been so distracted, concentrating on the funeral arrangements. I had no idea that the procession for the victor of the Ludi Romani was taking place that very day.

Thousands came now, cheering, carousing. Romans dressed in the togas belonging to the seven remaining houses ran alongside the procession, streaming past us.

I'd done this. I sent them away, drove the audience away, right into Aquilinus' arms. They'd ignored the triumph, came to me to pay their respects, and I drove them from me and into this.

I pushed aside the Praetorians who had lined up to clear the street, struggling to see over the heads of the cheering crowd.

"There! Up on the float! It's him!" someone in the crowd said.

A gap appeared and I got a clear view. A large hovering aer chariot came cruising down the street, surrounded by cheering citizens, clamoring to touch the robe of the honored hero who sat upon it. Crassus was dressed in fine white armor, shining like the marble that graced the buildings of the capital; he'd relinquished his former allegiance to the disgraced House Sertorian. He looked around, resplendent and smug, like a snake that's stuffed itself with mice. A golden laurel crown rested upon his head, artificial machinarii hands in place of the ones I severed when we fought. He couldn't see me; I was thrust to the back by his adoring fans. No, not fans, worshippers. Crassus the God! Crassus Apollo! They adorned him with divine titles, screamed with adulation as he passed.

I started pushing against the crowd, trying to get through to him. In the crush of the mob, they didn't know who I was, they couldn't see me, couldn't hear my voice. I would have hit them if I could have, cleared a way with my knees and elbows, but the crowd was too densely packed. It might as well have been a brick wall for all the progress I made.

"Quickly," I said to Murena. "A weapon! You must have a weapon of some kind concealed on your person. I can't bear to see him up there."

"Accala, listen to me now. You must not touch him or harm him in any way," Murena said. "The emperor has forbidden it. The mob sees both of you as divine champions."

"Both of us?"

"They call him your heavenly consort." Gods, each day things only got worse.

The throng was moving past, driving me back into the alleyway with the rest of my family. They'd moved away from me. They could see how distraught I was, how agitated.

"Do you see?" Murena said. "This is an omen. You can't turn power away when it's offered to you. You must wield it or be trampled underfoot. Rome will wait for no man—or woman—even one touched by the gods. You scorn your followers, but Crassus lavishes his with attention. You wish to honor your family and the gods, then you must take what they have given you and serve. You think you've been through all this for nothing? You are a hero, you have a destiny, and now you must play the hero's part or disaster and chaos will befall the empire. They're all looking to you. Step up. Gather your courage and shine, Accala."

"You don't understand!" I protested. As the words flew from my mouth, I realized what I was saying and whom I was saying it to. He was the head of the curiosi. He knew everything.

I pointed an accusing finger at him. "You chose the route the funeral procession would take," I spat. "You orchestrated events so that I would see this."

"Because a true Viridian is strengthened by pain, sharpened by suffering, not dulled by it, not weighed down by shame." He held me with his gaze, fixing me in place. In that instant he reminded me of my father. Viridian strength was there in his eyes, surrounding me, covering me. He was my father's cousin, and the words he spoke were the same ones I would have heard from my father's mouth if he were alive. "I can talk all day, but I wanted you to see the truth of the empire. I wanted you to see what will overrun it if you do not pick up arms and carry on your father's legacy. Accept the emperor's offer. As a quaestor you would have the power to right wrongs. To take justice into your own hands."

The crossroads was empty now. I could see clear through to the giant statue of Minerva, the Palladium, in the distance, her mighty spear held above her.

I contained my anger, let the ember burn inside. Now was not the time.

Julia was right about my experience. About divine perspective. The world seemed gray by comparison, but only because I'd been fearful of embracing my humanity again. I'd kept my emotions bottled up, worried about what might happen next, not trusting myself. But now I saw that there were no guarantees. The fragility of mortal life was balanced by the sweetness, the powerful currents, the counterbalance of thought and emotion. I couldn't be a god, couldn't see things that way. I was down here again, in the mud of existence, and I needed to embrace my humanity and pray that what I'd been through would be enough to keep me grounded.

Crassus' triumph tapered off, and our procession started up again. I didn't have time to think as the crowd of Viridians started shuffling forward. The horns sounded again, the chief priest started calling for the people, none of whom were actually left in the streets, to come and join in the hero's funeral and pay their respects. The veterans grumbled and cursed, but everyone else carried on as if nothing had happened. We marched on to the temple. My boots echoed on the ancient road, matching my heart that pounded within my chest, full of dire intent.

We reached the temple, and I stepped up to stand beside him. Lucius Viridius Camillus. My father. He looked pale and old. I barely recognized him. They'd removed the wounds and scars I'd opened in his body. I leaned over and kissed him gently on the lips with reverence and respect. If the action freed his spirit as it was meant to, I didn't feel anything, but I did whisper a promise to him before I straightened up.

"You will serve?" Murena asked.

I stepped back and lowered the torch. The fire burned brightly, like the righteous anger in my breast. I held my ground before the burning flames until they were so strong that I lost sight of my father's body and was forced to step back. I stood there for a long time, until he was nothing but smoke and ash. Murena stood beside me patiently, waiting. Finally, I gave him my answer.

"I will serve."